LYLE

OFFICIAL

ANTIQUES
REVIEW 1998

LYLE

OFFICIAL

ANTIQUES

REVIEW 1998

A PERIGEE BOOK

A Perigee Book
Published by The Berkley Publishing Group
A member of Penguin Putnam Inc.
200 Madison Avenue
New York, NY 10016

First edition: December 1997
ISBN: 0-399-52352-9
ISSN: 1089-1544

Published simultaneously in Canada.

The Putnam Berkley World Wide Web site address is
http://www.berkley.com

Printed in the United States of America

10 9 8 7 6 5 4 3 2 1

INTRODUCTION

This year over 100,000 Antique Dealers and Collectors will make full and profitable use of their Lyle Antiques Price Guide. They know that only in this one volume will they find the widest possible variety of goods – illustrated, described and given a current market value to assist them to BUY RIGHT AND SELL RIGHT throughout the year of issue.

They know, too, that by building a collection of these immensely valuable volumes year by year, they will equip themselves with an unparalleled reference library of facts, figures and illustrations which, properly used, cannot fail to help them keep one step ahead of the market.

In its twenty eight years of publication, Lyle has gone from strength to strength and has become without doubt the pre-eminent book of reference for the antique trade throughout the world. Each of its fact filled pages is packed with precisely the kind of profitable information the professional Dealer needs – including descriptions, illustrations and values of thousands and thousands of individual items carefully selected to give a representative picture of the current market in antiques and collectables – and remember all values are prices actually paid, based on accurate sales records in the twelve months prior to publication from the best established and most highly respected auction houses and retail outlets in Europe and America.

This is THE book for the Professional Antiques Dealer. 'The Lyle Book' – we've even heard it called 'The Dealer's Bible'.

Compiled and published afresh each year, the Lyle Antiques Price Guide is the most comprehensive up-to-date antiques price guide available. THIS COULD BE YOUR WISEST INVESTMENT OF THE YEAR!

Anthony Curtis

The publishers wish to express their sincere thanks to the following for their involvement and assistance in the production of this volume.

ANTHONY CURTIS (Editor)

EELIN McIVOR (Sub Editor)

ANNETTE CURTIS (Editorial)

CATRIONA DAY (Art Production)

ANGIE DEMARCO (Art Production)

NICKY FAIRBURN (Art Production)

DONNA RUTHERFORD

MALCOLM GLASS

CONTENTS

7

ANTIQUES REVIEW

ANTIQUES REVIEW

ACKNOWLEDGEMENTS

AB Stockholms Auktionsverk, Box 16256, 103 25 Stockholm, Sweden
Abbotts Auction Rooms, The Auction Rooms, Campsea Ash, Woodbridge, Suffolk
Academy Auctioneers, Northcote House, Northcote Avenue, Ealing, London W5 3UR
James Adam, 26 St Stephens Green, Dublin 2
Jean Claude Anaf, Lyon Brotteaux, 13 bis place Jules Ferry, 69456, Lyon, France
Anderson & Garland, Marlborough House, Marlborough Crescent, Newcastle upon Tyne NE1 4EE
Antique Collectors Club & Co. Ltd, 5 Church Street, Woodbridge, Suffolk IP12 1DS
The Auction Galleries, Mount Rd., Tweedmouth, Berwick on Tweed
Auction Team Köln, Postfach 50 11 68, D-5000 Köln 50 Germany
Auktionshaus Arnold, Bleichstr. 42, 6000 Frankfurt a/M, Germany
Barber's Auctions, Woking, Surrey
Bearnes, Rainbow, Avenue Road, Torquay TQ2 5TG
Biddle & Webb, Ladywood Middleway, Birmingham B16 0PP
Bigwood, The Old School, Tiddington, Stratford upon Avon
Black Horse Agencies, Locke & England, 18 Guy Street, Leamington Spa
Boardman Fine Art Auctioneers, Station Road Corner, Haverhill, Suffolk CB9 0EY
Bonhams, Montpelier Street, Knightsbridge, London SW7 1HH
Bonhams Chelsea, 65–69 Lots Road, London SW10 0RN
Bonhams West Country, Dowell Street, Honiton, Devon
Bosleys, 42 West Street, Marlow, Bucks SL7 1NB
Michael J. Bowman, 6 Haccombe House, Near Netherton, Newton Abbot, Devon
Bristol Auction Rooms, St John Place, Apsley Road, Clifton, Bristol BS8 2ST
British Antique Exporters, School Close, Queen Elizabeth Avenue, Burgess Hill, Sussex
Butterfield & Butterfield, 220 San Bruno Avenue, San Francisco CA 94103, USA
Butterfield & Butterfield, 7601 Sunset Boulevard, Los Angeles CA 90046, USA
Canterbury Auction Galleries, 40 Station Road West, Canterbury CT2 8AN
Central Motor Auctions, Barfield House, Britannia Road, Morley, Leeds, LS27 0HN
H.C. Chapman & Son, The Auction Mart, North Street, Scarborough.
Chapman Moore & Mugford, 8 High Street, Shaftesbury SP7 8JB
Cheffins Grain & Comins, 2 Clifton Road, Cambridge
Christie's (International) SA, 8 place de la Taconnerie, 1204 Genève, Switzerland
Christie's Monaco, S.A.M, Park Palace 98000 Monte Carlo, Monaco
Christie's Scotland, 164–166 Bath Street Glasgow G2 4TG
Christie's South Kensington Ltd., 85 Old Brompton Road, London SW7 3LD
Christie's, 8 King Street, London SW1Y 6QT
Christie's East, 219 East 67th Street, New York, NY 10021, USA
Christie's, 502 Park Avenue, New York, NY 10022, USA
Christie's, Cornelis Schuytstraat 57, 1071 JG Amsterdam, Netherlands
Christie's SA Roma, 114 Piazza Navona, 00186 Rome, Italy
Christie's Swire, 2804–6 Alexandra House, 16–20 Chater Road, Hong Kong
Christie's Australia Pty Ltd., 1 Darling Street, South Yarra, Victoria 3141, Australia
A J Cobern, The Grosvenor Sales Rooms, 93b Eastbank Street, Southport PR8 1DG
Cooper Hirst Auctions, The Granary Saleroom, Victoria Road, Chelmsford, Essex CM2 6LH
The Crested China Co., Station House, Driffield, E. Yorks YO25 7PY
Cundalls, The Cattle Market, 17 Market Square, Malton, N. Yorks
Clifford Dann, 20/21 High Street, Lewes, Sussex
Julian Dawson, Lewes Auction Rooms, 56 High Street, Lewes BN7 1XE
Dee & Atkinson & Harrison, The Exchange Saleroom, Driffield, Nth Humberside YO25 7LJ
Garth Denham & Assocs. Horsham Auction Galleries, Warnsham, Nr. Horsham, Sussex
Diamond Mills & Co., 117 Hamilton Road, Felixstowe, Suffolk
David Dockree Fine Art, The Redwood Suite, Clemence House, Mellor Road, Cheadle Hulme, Cheshire
William Doyle Galleries, 175 East 87th Street, New York, NY 10128, USA
Downer Ross, Charter House, 42 Avebury Boulevard, Central Milton Keynes MK9 2HS
Dreweatt Neate, Holloways, 49 Parsons Street, Banbury
Hy. Duke & Son, 40 South Street, Dorchester, Dorset
Du Mouchelles Art Galleries Co., 409 E. Jefferson Avenue, Detroit, Michigan 48226, USA

ANTIQUES REVIEW

Duncan Vincent, 1 Station Road, Pangbourne, Berks RG8 7AY
Sala de Artes y Subastas Durán, Serrano 12, 28001 Madrid, Spain
Eldred's, Box 796, E. Dennis, MA 02641, USA
R H Ellis & Sons, 44/46 High St., Worthing, BN11 1LL
Ewbanks, Burnt Common Auction Rooms, London Road, Send, Woking GU23 7LN
Fellows & Son, Augusta House, 19 Augusta Street, Hockley, Birmingham
Fidler Taylor & Co., Crown Square, Matlock, Derbyshire DE4 3AT
Finarte, 20121 Milano, Piazzetta Bossi 4, Italy
John D Fleming & Co., The North Devon Auction Rooms, The Savory, South Molton, Devon
Peter Francis, 19 King Street, Carmarthen, Dyfed
Fraser Pinney's, 8290 Devonshire, Montreal, Quebec, Canada H4P 2PZ
Galerie Koller, Rämistr. 8, CH 8024 Zürich, Switzerland
Galerie Moderne, 3 rue du Parnasse, 1040 Bruxelles, Belgium
Geering & Colyer (Black Horse Agencies) Highgate, Hawkhurst, Kent
The Goss and Crested China Co., 62 Murray Road, Horndean, Hants PO8 9JL
Graves Son & Pilcher, 71 Church Road, Hove, East Sussex, BN3 2GL
Greenslade Hunt, Magdalene House, Church Square, Taunton, Somerset, TA1 1SB
The Gurney Collection
Halifax Property Services, 53 High Street, Tenterden, Kent
Hampton's Fine Art, 93 High Street, Godalming, Surrey
Hanseatisches Auktionshaus für Historica, Neuer Wall 57, 2000 Hamburg 36, Germany
William Hardie Ltd., 141 West Regent Street, Glasgow G2 2SG
Andrew Hartley Fine Arts, Victoria Hall, Little Lane, Ilkely
Hauswedell & Nolte, D-2000 Hamburg 13, Pöseldorfer Weg 1, Germany
Giles Haywood, The Auction House, St John's Road, Stourbridge, West Midlands, DY8 1EW
Muir Hewitt, Halifax Antiques Centre, Queens Road/Gibbet Street, Halifax HX1 4LR
Hobbs & Chambers, 'At the Sign of the Bell', Market Place, Cirencester, Glos
Hobbs Parker, Romney House, Ashford Market, Ashford, Kent
Holloways, 49 Parsons Street, Banbury OX16 8PF
Hotel de Ventes Horta, 390 Chaussée de Waterloo (Ma Campagne), 1060 Bruxelles, Belgium
Jacobs & Hunt, Lavant Street, Petersfield, Hants. GU33 3EF
P Herholdt Jensens Auktioner, Rundforbivej 188, 2850 Nerum, Denmark
Kennedy & Wolfenden, 218 Lisburn Rd, Belfast BT9 6GD
G A Key, Aylsham Saleroom, Palmers Lane, Aylsham, Norfolk, NR11 6EH
George Kidner, The Old School, The Square, Pennington, Lymington, Hants SO41 8GN
Kunsthaus am Museum, Drususgasse 1–5, 5000 Köln 1, Germany
Kunsthaus Lempertz, Neumarkt 3, 5000 Köln 1, Germany
Lambert & Foster (County Group), The Auction Sales Room, 102 High Street, Tenterden, Kent
W.H. Lane & Son, 64 Morrab Road, Penzance, Cornwall, TR18 2QT
Langlois Ltd., Westway Rooms, Don Street, St Helier, Channel Islands
Lawrence Butler Fine Art Salerooms, Marine Walk, Hythe, Kent, CT21 5AJ
Lawrence Fine Art, South Street, Crewkerne, Somerset TA18 8AB
Lawrence's Fine Art Auctioneers, Norfolk House, 80 High Street, Bletchingley, Surrey
David Lay, The Penzance Auction House, Alverton, Penzance, Cornwall TA18 4KE
Gordon Litherland, 26 Stapenhill Road, Burton on Trent
Lloyd International Auctions, 118 Putney Bridge Road, London SW15 2NQ
Brian Loomes, Calf Haugh Farm, Pateley Bridge, North Yorks
Lots Road Chelsea Auction Galleries, 71 Lots Road, Chelsea, London SW10 0RN
R K Lucas & Son, Tithe Exchange, 9 Victoria Place, Haverfordwest, SA61 2JX
Duncan McAlpine, Stateside Comics plc, 125 East Barnet Road, London EN4 8RF
McCartneys, Portcullis Salerooms, Ludlow, Shropshire
Christopher Matthews, 23 Mount Street, Harrogate HG2 8DG
John Maxwell, 133a Woodford Road, Wilmslow, Cheshire
May & Son, 18 Bridge Street, Andover, Hants
Morphets, 4–6 Albert Street, Harrogate, North Yorks HG1 1JL
Neales, The Nottingham Saleroom, 192 Mansfield Road, Nottingham NG1 3HU
D M Nesbit & Co, 7 Clarendon Road, Southsea, Hants PO5 2ED
John Nicholson, 1 Crossways Court, Fernhurst, Haslemere, Surrey GU27 3EP

Onslow's, Metrostore, Townmead Road, London SW6 2RZ
Outhwaite & Litherland, Kingsley Galleries, Fontenoy Street, Liverpool, Merseyside L3 2BE
Phillips Manchester, Trinity House, 114 Northenden Road, Sale, Manchester M33 3HD
Phillips Son & Neale SA, 10 rue des Chaudronniers, 1204 Genève, Switzerland
Phillips West Two, 10 Salem Road, London W2 4BL
Phillips, 11 Bayle Parade, Folkestone, Kent CT20 1SQ
Phillips, 49 London Road, Sevenoaks, Kent TN13 1UU
Phillips, 65 George Street, Edinburgh EH2 2JL
Phillips, Blenstock House, 7 Blenheim Street, New Bond Street, London W1Y 0AS
Phillips Marylebone, Hayes Place, Lisson Grove, London NW1 6UA
Phillips, New House, 150 Christleton Road, Chester CH3 5TD
Andrew Pickford, 42 St Andrew Street, Hertford SG14 1JA
Pieces of Time, 1–7 Davies Mews, Unit 17–19, London W17 1AR
Pooley & Rogers, Regent Auction Rooms, Abbey Street, Penzance
Pretty & Ellis, Amersham Auction Rooms, Station Road, Amersham, Bucks
Harry Ray & Co, Lloyds Bank Chambers, Welshpool, Montgomery SY21 7RR
Peter M Raw, Thornfield, Hurdle Way, Compton Down, Winchester, Hants SC21 2AN
Rennie's, 1 Agincourt Street, Monmouth
Riddetts, 26 Richmond Hill, Bournemouth
Ritchie's, 429 Richmond Street East, Toronto, Canada M5A 1R1
Derek Roberts Antiques, 24–25 Shipbourne Road, Tonbridge, Kent TN10 3DN
Rogers de Rin, 79 Royal Hospital Road, London SW3 4HN
Russell, Baldwin & Bright, The Fine Art Saleroom, Ryelands Road, Leominster HR6 8JG
Schrager Auction Galleries, 2915 N Sherman Boulevard, PO Box 10390, Milwaukee WI 53210, USA
Selkirk's, 4166 Olive Street, St Louis, Missouri 63108, USA
Skinner Inc., Bolton Gallery, Route 117, Bolton MA, USA
Soccer Nostalgia, Albion Chambers, Birchington, Kent CT7 9DN
Sotheby's, 34–35 New Bond Street, London W1A 2AA
Sotheby's, 1334 York Avenue, New York NY 10021
Sotheby's, 112 George Street, Edinburgh EH2 2LH
Sotheby's, Summers Place, Billinghurst, West Sussex RH14 9AD
Sotheby's Monaco, BP 45, 98001 Monte Carlo
Southgate Auction Rooms, 55 High St, Southgate, London'N14 6LD
Spink & Son Ltd, 5-7 King St., St James's, London SW1Y 6QS
Michael Stainer Ltd., St Andrews Auction Rooms, Wolverton Rd, Boscombe, Bournemouth BH7 6HT
Mike Stanton, 7 Rowood Drive, Solihull, West Midlands B92 9LT
Street Jewellery, 5 Runnymede Road, Ponteland, Northumbria NE20 9HE
Stride & Son, Southdown House, St John's St., Chichester, Sussex
G E Sworder & Son, 14 Cambridge Road, Stansted Mountfitche, Essex CM24 8BZ
Taviner's of Bristol, Prewett Street, Redcliffe, Bristol BS1 6PB
Tennants, Harmby Road, Leyburn, Yorkshire
Thomson Roddick & Laurie, 24 Lowther Street, Carlisle
Thomson Roddick & Laurie, 60 Whitesands, Dumfries
Timbleby & Shorland, 31 Gt Knollys St, Reading RG1 7HU
Tool Shop Auctions, 78 High Street, Needham Market, Suffolk IP6 8AW
Truro Auction Centre, Calenick Street, Truro TR1 2SG
Venator & Hanstein, Cäcilienstr. 48, 5000 Köln 1, Germany
T Vennett Smith, 11 Nottingham Road, Gotham, Nottingham NG11 0HE
Duncan Vincent, 92 London Street, Reading RG1 4SJ
Wallis & Wallis, West Street Auction Galleries, West Street, Lewes, E. Sussex BN7 2NJ
Walter's, 1 Mint Lane, Lincoln LN1 1UD
Wells Cundall Nationwide Anglia, Staffordshire House, 27 Flowergate, Whitby YO21 3AX
Woltons, 6 Whiting Street, Bury St Edmunds, Suffolk IP33 1PB
Peter Wilson, Victoria Gallery, Market Street, Nantwich, Cheshire CW5 5DG
Wintertons Ltd., Lichfield Auction Centre, Fradley Park, Lichfield, Staffs WS13 8NF
Woltons, 6 Whiting Street, Bury St Edmunds, Suffolk IP33 1PB
Woolley & Wallis, The Castle Auction Mart, Salisbury, Wilts SP1 3SU
Worthing Auction Galleries, 31 Chatsworth Road, Worthing, W. Sussex BN11 1LY

ANTIQUES REVIEW 1998

T HE Lyle Antiques Price Guide is compiled and published with completely fresh information annually, enabling you to begin each new year with an up-to-date knowledge of the current trends, together with the verified values of antiques of all descriptions.

We have endeavored to obtain a balance between the more expensive collector's items and those which, although not in their true sense antiques, are handled daily by the antiques trade.

The illustrations and prices in the following sections have been arranged to make it easy for the reader to assess the period and value of all items with speed.

You will find illustrations for almost every category of antique and curio, together with a corresponding price collated during the last twelve months, from the auction rooms and retail outlets of the major trading countries.

When dealing with the more popular trade pieces, in some instances, a calculation of an average price has been estimated from the varying accounts researched.

As regards prices, when 'one of a pair' is given in the description the price quoted is for a pair and so that we can make maximum use of the available space it is generally considered that one illustration is sufficient.

It will be noted that in some descriptions taken directly from sales catalogues originating from many different countries, terms such as bureau, secretary and davenport are used in a broader sense than is customary, but in all cases the term used is self explanatory.

A Brunsviga Nova 13Z German cylinder calculator with 10-, 8-, and 13-place working, 1932. (Auction Team Köln) $116

A Madas calculator, with seven sliding indices with digital displays, operating handle and *Gilbert Wood, London and Manchester* retailer's label, in black-painted metal case, 19¼in. (Christie's) $733

A Russian Original Odhner cylinder calculator, , circa 1900. (Auction Team Köln) $311

A rare export version of the 7 row manual Exact (Addi-7) rapid reckoner, 1933. (Auction Team Köln) $120

An Adder adding machine, in copper-plated case of cash register form, the base stamped with 1902 patent number. (Christie's) $419

A Belgian Master, battery-powered, rack adding machine, in the 'Crocodile' style, with red and green lights. (Auction Team Köln) $94

A National Model 4225 cash register with two row keyboard with pop-up price numbers, American, 1936. (Auction Team Köln) $145

A famous Multaddiv calculator, by The Shires Multaddiv Machine Co., with six sliders and digital indices, in mahogany case, 18½in. wide, American, circa 1910. (Christie's) $5,235

Coinometer Model B, a four-row American coin changer with eight coin chutes and change tray, 1923. (Auction Team Köln) $186

A four-function Alpina adding machine with base, original leather case and connector, 1961.
(Auction Team Köln)
$1,400

An Archimedes Model B German stage platen machine with 9, 10 or 16-place reckoning facility, 1906.
(Auction Team Köln)
$1,400

A Hamann Automat Model V fully automatic electric adding machine, 1931, German.
(Auction Team Köln) $140

The Millionaire, an export version of the famous Swiss adding machine by Otto Steiger, St. Gallen, 1895.
(Auction Team Köln)
$1,790

A black Curta Type II four function miniature drum calculator by Kurt Herzstark of Liechtenstein/Vienna, with tin box, 1948.
(Auction Team Köln)
$467

An Adix three place adding machine with latch drive and 9 keys, by Pallweber & Bordt, Mannheim, 1903.
(Auction Team Köln)
$660

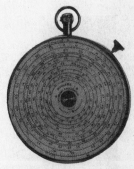

The Little Giant Adding Machine cash register by the Kel-San Mfg. Co., Ohio, with written till receipt roll, with lockable drawer, 1928.
(Auction Team Köln) $93

A British calculator, by T. J. Marshall & Co., with three sliding indices and four-place digital display, 5¼in. diam.
(Christie's) $314

Fowler's Universal Calculator, a large logarithmic calculating dial, by Fowler of Manchester, 85mm. diameter.
(Auction Team Köln) $100

Plains quilled and beaded tipi bag, the soft hide rectangular container with box beading on the flap, 24$\frac{1}{2}$in. long. (Butterfield & Butterfield)
$2,070

Hopi kachina doll, representing Butterfly Maiden kachina, wearing white manta and painted jewelry, 15in. high. (Butterfield & Butterfield)
$3,450

Cheyenne beaded possible bag, decorated with contrasting colored bands of polychrome beading, 9$\frac{1}{2}$in. long. (Butterfield & Butterfield)
$1,610

Wasco sally bag, the softly woven cylindrical container drawn with vertical rows of repeated butterflies, fish, and quadrupeds, 4$\frac{1}{2}$in. diameter. (Butterfield & Butterfield)
$977

Large Navajo rug, with enormous stepped diamond medallion containing hooked cross center, 8ft., 10in. x 9ft. 10in. (Butterfield & Butterfield)
$6,900

Tlingit polychrome rattletop basket, the straight sides false-embroidered with a pair of horizontal bands, 4$\frac{1}{4}$in. diameter. (Butterfield & Butterfield)
$1,092

Navajo pictorial rug, depicting a cornstalk Yei running up the center, 7ft. 1in. x 3ft. 11in. (Butterfield & Butterfield)
$4,025

Zia polychrome pottery jar, attributed to Trinidad Medina, with high shoulder and in-tapering neck, 9in. high. (Butterfield & Butterfield)
$1,610

Navajo Germantown rug, the borderless weaving divided into four even rectangular sections, 6ft. 6in. x 4ft. 3in. (Butterfield & Butterfield)
$4,025

Apache pictorial olla, worked in a grid of outlined vertical diamond chains, 13½in. diameter.
(Butterfield & Butterfield)
$3,737

Hopi tableta, painted on masonite, with kiva step in-cut sides and crenellated top, 17in. high.
(Butterfield & Butterfield)
$1,380

Zuni polychrome pottery jar, painted in three horizontal bands of arabesques and birds, 9¼in. diameter.
(Butterfield & Butterfield)
$1,840

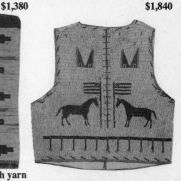

Sioux beaded dress, with heavily beaded bodice, aligning concentric triangular devices across the open pale-blue field, 52in. long.
(Butterfield & Butterfield)
$6,900

Plateau cornhusk bag, with yarn decorations of a central sawtoothed diamond surrounded by mirror-image depictions of stylized floriforms, 15in. wide.
(Butterfield & Butterfield)
$920

Sioux beaded pictorial vest, fully beaded on hide, with cloth lining, showing four concentric box motifs on the front, 18in. long.
(Butterfield & Butterfield)
$2,185

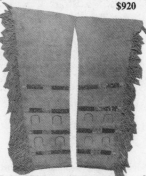

Apache pictorial olla, with expansive sides, tapering shoulder and flaring neck, 11½in. diameter.
(Butterfield & Butterfield)
$4,312

Pair of Plains quilled man's leggings, heavily fringed along the open side seams, quilled on both sides, 28in. long.
(Butterfield & Butterfield)
$2,070

Navajo pictorial rug, depicting a standing Yei figure, holding prayer feathers and ceremonial regalia, 4ft. 1in. x 2ft. 6in.
(Butterfield & Butterfield)
$3,162

Apache pictorial tray, the shallow bowl with four-petaled rosette on the base, 2³/₄in. high. (Butterfield & Butterfield)
$690

Pair of Cheyenne beaded moccasins, with fully-beaded toe and ankle, the tapered cut cuffs with yellow pigment, 9¹/₂in. long. (Butterfield & Butterfield)
$920

Flathead beaded war shirt, the soft hide garment with open side seams, strung over the shoulder and down the sleeves with beaded panels, 31in. long. (Butterfield & Butterfield)
$40,250

A Plains woman's beaded and fringed hide dress, circa 1900, the top colorfully decorated in pink, green and blue beads with a scrolling rose vine, 50in. long. (Sotheby's)
$805

Sioux beaded saddle blanket, of characteristic H-form, with canvas center surrounded by panels of beadwork, 55in. long. (Butterfield & Butterfield)
$2,300

Plateau beaded knife sheath, with fully-beaded front depicting a pair of spade motifs over a section of diagonal outlined stripes, 9¹/₄in. long. (Butterfield & Butterfield)
$3,450

Sioux beaded child's vest, with fully beaded front and back on hide, with two pair of elaborate geometric configurations, 13¹/₂in. long. (Butterfield & Butterfield)
$1,610

Pair of Sioux beaded and quilled moccasins, worked on soft hide, with a perimeter beaded band showing tipi motifs and linear devices, 10¹/₄in. long. (Butterfield & Butterfield)
$977

Northeast California basket, the straight flaring sides fully decorated with diagonal bands of repeated linear stepped pattern, 5¹/₂in. high. (Butterfield & Butterfield)
$805

Panamint pictorial basket, of
flattened hemispherical form,
aligning two rows of human
figures, those at the base
wearing wide-brimmed hats,
4½in. high.
(Butterfield & Butterfield)
$3,450

Cheyenne beaded moccasins,
fully beaded on the toe with
alternating green and white
panels, 10½in. long.
(Butterfield & Butterfield)
$1,150

Two Navajo rugs, circa 1920,
each worked in tones of brown,
black, red and white with
geometric designs, 76 x 54in.
(Sotheby's) $1,265

An Eastern Sioux pictorial
quilled hide vest, circa 1890,
colorfully decorated all over
with American flags, buffalo, a
butterfly and stylized blossoms,
21in. high.
(Sotheby's)
$6,900

Two Plateau cornhusk bags,
each with yarn decoration, one
showing a blossoming plant
surrounded by small birds, 11in.
(Butterfield & Butterfield)
$747

A Sioux quilled and fringed hide
ceremonial pouch, circa 1900,
the circular pouch solidly
decorated on the front in dyed
porcupine quills on a pink
ground, 10¾in. high.
(Sotheby's) $3,450

Plains beaded war shirt, of one-
piece construction, multiple hide
thongs fastening the open side
seams and along the sleeves,
39in. long.
(Butterfield & Butterfield)
$10,925

Maidu polychrome basketry
bowl, the slightly rounded sides
decorated with two
complementary zigzag bands,
5in. diameter.
(Butterfield & Butterfield)
$1,380

Apache beaded strike-a-light,
the body of the soft square hide
pouch fully beaded in
alternating red and black zigzag
lines, 6in. long.
(Butterfield & Butterfield)
$1,725

A French Dynamomètre coin-operated test-your-strength machine, in working order, 1935.
(Auction Team Köln)
$235

Elephant postcard dispenser by Sächsischen Cartonnagen Maschinen AG, Dresden, gives a bar of chocolate with every tenth packet bought, when elephant trumpets. (Auction Team Köln)
$15,570

Roulette Iris, by Jentzsch & Meertz, Leipzig, for the Swedish market, bell rings on winning, circa 1931.
(Auction Team Köln)
$1,478

French Roulette Bussoz game machine, for one-penny coins, circa 1925.
(Auction Team Köln)
$855

A British made Plentywin amusement machine, for one penny coins, circa 1955.
(Auction Team Köln)
$650

Bajazzo pinball-type gaming machine by Jentzsch & Meertz of Leipzig, circa 1930.
(Auction Team Köln)
$740

Bryan's Clock Tower, an English wooden cased games machine, circa 1952.
(Auction Team Köln)
$855

The Little Stockbroker, an Art Deco style gaming machine by Granville Bradshaw, England, in red and gold painted aluminium case, 1929.
(Auction Team Köln)
$545

Looping the Loop, a pinball type games machine, possibly Swedish.
(Auction Team Köln)
$700

An Egyptian hollow bronze head of a cat with deep set eyes, Late Period, after 500 B.C., 2¾in.
(Bonhams) $2,893

An Egyptian Old Kingdom unfinished polychrome painted limestone fragment, showing a procession of offering bearers heading into a tomb, Late 6th Dynasty, circa 2200 B.C., 24in. long.
(Bonhams) $24,360

A South Arabian alabaster bearded male head of stylized form, the eyes inlaid, circa 1st century B.C./A.D.., 8½in. high.
(Bonhams) $2,284

A limestone head of a female with thick wavy hair, wearing a head-dress and earrings, Palmyra, circa 3rd century A.D., 11½in.
(Bonhams) $4,110

An Apulian Red-Figure dish on a low ring base, the interior decorated with a winged hare, Greek South Italy, 4th century B.C., 9½in. diameter.
(Bonhams) $1,142

A hollow-backed terracotta male protome, the thick hair centrally parted, pierced at the top, Greek South Italy, circa 5th century B.C., 7¼in.
(Bonhams) $289

An Egyptian wooden kneeling figure of a male from a funerary setting, with engraved details, late 18th Dynasty, 14th century B.C., 3¼in. high.
(Bonhams) $3,654

A Roman marble relief fragment showing the head of a boy in profile, 1st-2nd century A.D., 5in.
(Bonhams) $2,588

An Apulian black-glazed calyx krater with upturned handles, the out-turned rim with ovolo decoration, Greek South Italy, late 4th century B.C., 19in. high.
(Bonhams) $3,958

A Tarentine terracotta appliqué in the form of a flat backed openwork gazelle, late 4th century B.C., 6.6cm. (Bonhams) $2,740

A Roman deep blue glass bottle with broad pear-shaped body, some silvery iridescence, early 1st century A.D., 7.2cm. high. (Bonhams) $1,675

A Palaeolithic schist slab, schematically engraved with elephants, Western Sahara, circa 8000-7000 B.C., 13¼ x 9in. (Bonhams) $10,657

An Attic Black-Figure pelike decorated with added crimson and white, with incisions to show on one side Herakles wielding his club, late 6th century B.C., 11¾in. high. (Bonhams) $1,827

A quartzite finely modeled Shabti head of Akhenaten wearing the Khat and Uraeus, El-Amarna, New Kingdom, Amarna Period, 1379-1362 B.C., 2in. (Bonhams) $21,315

An Egyptian bronze head of a cat with finely engraved whiskers and ears, much of their original gold inlay remaining, Third Intermediate Period, 1069-656 B.C., 2¾in. high. (Bonhams) $7,004

A well detailed Roman bronze lamp in the form of a Legionnaire's sandaled foot, circa 4th-5th century A.D., 4in. long. (Bonhams) $3,958

A Romano-Egyptian limestone fragmentary relief showing the facing wreathed head of a youth set within a shell niche, circa 4th century A.D., 9¾ x 10¼in. (Bonhams) $731

A Roman fluted bronze handle with central ridged band, the terminals styled as satyr's heads, circa 2nd century A.D., 9½in. long. (Bonhams) $913

A Roman bronze tintinabulum in the form of a winged phallus with the hind legs of a lion, circa 1st century A.D., 5¼in. high.
(Bonhams) $5,481

A Boeotian stylized terracotta horse with black painted linear decoration, mid-6th century B.C., 4¾in. high.
(Bonhams) $1,142

An Etruscan terracotta antefix showing the facing head of a youth with long wavy hair, circa 2nd century B.C., 6½in.
(Bonhams) $639

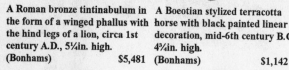

A Cypriot bichrome ware sizeable barrel flask, the body curving to pronounced nipples, the decoration on a buff background, Cypro-Archaic, circa 7th-6th century B.C., 14in. high,
(Bonhams) $1,675

A large Amlash bronze halberd axeblade, of lunate form, cut away from the shaft to form two 'D's on either side of the central join, circa 19th-17th centuries B.C., 14.9cm. high.
(Bonhams) $639

An Egyptian bronze mirror surmounting a steatite and alabaster handle in the form of a papyrus column, Middle Kingdom, circa 2000 B.C., 11in. high.
(Bonhams) $22,838

An Attic Red-Figure kylix on a pedestal foot, decorated around the exterior on one side with a standing draped female, 8.6cm. high.
(Bonhams) $2,750

A fragment of a Roman marble fluted sarcophagus, the central circular panel showing a male figure holding a rotulus, later 3rd century A.D., 15in. high,
(Bonhams) $989

A sizeable gesso painted wood and bronze ibis, sacred to the god Thoth, the eyes inlaid, Late Period, circa 7th-3rd centuries B.C., 10in. high.
(Bonhams) $15,225

ARMOR

A full suit of articulated armor, closed helmet with pierced visor, two-piece breastplate, holding a hand and half sword, 70 in. high. (Wallis & Wallis) $1,628

An Indian mail and lamellar shirt, 17th century, possibly Deccani, a pair of convex rectangular plates at the front closed by laces and cut with Islamic inscriptions. (Sotheby's) $856

A late Victorian copy of a full suit of armor, on its dummy holding a late 19th century Mahdist cruciform hilted sword, figure 6 ft. overall. (Wallis & Wallis) $1,938

A rare papier mâché full armor, 19th century, probably French, close-helmet with high roped comb, pivoted two-part visor and gorget-plates at front and rear. (Christie's) $4,637

A Turco-Persian 18th century armor, comprising khula khud, breastplate, armguard and round iron shield with gilt decoration of hunting scenes. (Auktionsverket) $7,130

Good reproduction suit of 16th century style armor, 19th century, comprising globose breastplate, gorget and arm defences, circular shield and sword, 6ft. 3in. high. (Butterfield & Butterfield) $4,950

ARMOR

A full armor, in 16th century style, helmet of great-bascinet type with trellis visor, cuirass with rounded breast-plate. (Christie's) $4,637

A 19th century Persian chiseled steel matching helmet, shield and arm guard; khula khud with one piece bowl and twin plume sockets.
(Wallis & Wallis) $1,472

A composite cuirassier armor, comprehensively early 17th century, of bright steel, studded with iron-rivets and with plain turns along the edges. (Christie's) $7,728

A German black and white composite half-armor, circa 1560, burgonet with two-piece skull made in one with the pointed neck-guard and fall, breast-plate with prominent central projection. (Christie's) $8,114

A rare Italian breastplate of anime construction, circa 1540-50, formed of eight lames with medial ridge and cusped upper edge. (Sotheby's) $6,774

A composite English cuirassier armor of blackened steel, circa 1640, complete with a pair of leather high boots in the 17th century style. (Sotheby's) $17,825

ARMOR

A 17th century backplate, line engraved borders, the neck deeply struck with James II ordnance view mark.
(Wallis & Wallis)　　$465

A 17th century secret of unusual form, brim band pierced to sew into hat, broad bands intersect at circular pate plate.
(Wallis & Wallis)　　$620

An English Civil War period cavalry trooper's breastplate, of typical form with musket ball proof, opposite side chiseled with similar sized disk in bas-relief.
(Wallis & Wallis)　　$620

A late gothic breastplate, Italian or Flemish, circa 1490-1500, of rounded form with a very low medial ridge, 14in. high.
(Sotheby's)　　$2,070

A pair of German black and white mitten gauntlets, circa 1540, each with short tubular cuff embossed for the ulna, decorated thoughout with raised broad panels, 12½in.
(Sotheby's)　　$3,162

A French Second Empire brass faced breast and backplates, the heavy breastplate with plain brass studded decoration, retaining original leather backed brass shoulder chains and clasps.
(Wallis & Wallis)　　$152

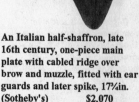

A half-shaffron, Flemish or Italian, third quarter, 16th century, one-piece main plate, the edges cusped and tapering below ocular fringes, 21½in.
(Sotheby's)　　$4,600

A good 17th century Indian mail and lamellar shirt, long sleeves and skirt, square collar, with Devanagri and Arabic inscriptions.
(Wallis & Wallis)　　$1,046

An Italian half-shaffron, late 16th century, one-piece main plate with cabled ridge over brow and muzzle, fitted with ear guards and later spike, 17¾in.
(Sotheby's)　　$2,070

26

ARMOR

Life Guards officer's cuirass, both plates of nickel silver ornamented with brass studs, bound with ¼in. black leather and dark blue velvet edging.
(Bosley's) $1,419

A rare elbow-gauntlet for an officer of harquebusiers, English, circa 1630–40, possibly Greenwich, with long open cuff of shot-proof weight unusually drawn-up to a standing flange, 16¾in.
(Sotheby's) $3,450

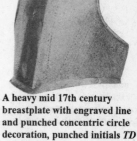

A heavy mid 17th century breastplate with engraved line and punched concentric circle decoration, punched initials *TD* at neck.
(Wallis & Wallis) $542

A breast-plate, and a gauntlet for the left hand, the first circa 1570, probably German, the second late 16th century, probably Italian, the first of peasecod form, 12½in. and 8½in.
(Christie's) $2,125

A pair of Italian fingered gauntlets, early 17th century, each comprising a pointed bell-shaped cuff with turned roped edge, five articulated metacarpal plates and a knuckle-plate, fingers of overlapping scales.
(Christie's) $4,250

An Italian breast-plate of 'Pisan' type, late 16th century, of peasecod form with characteristic etched decoration arranged in bands with, at the top, with single narrow skirt plate, 18½in. high.
(Christie's) $3,284

A German shot-proof breastplate, early 17th century, of flattened form with medial ridge, narrow flanged base, 13¾in. high.
(Sotheby's) $1,200

An extremely rare early parrying manifer, an exchange-piece for the German Foot Tournament, circa 1500–30, made in one piece for carrying over the left forearm, 24in.
(Sotheby's) $17,250

A breast-plate, early 16th century, probably German, of globular form with prominent inward turn at the neck, flange at the bottom for the skirt, 13¼in. high.
(Christie's) $1,159

27

BAYONETS

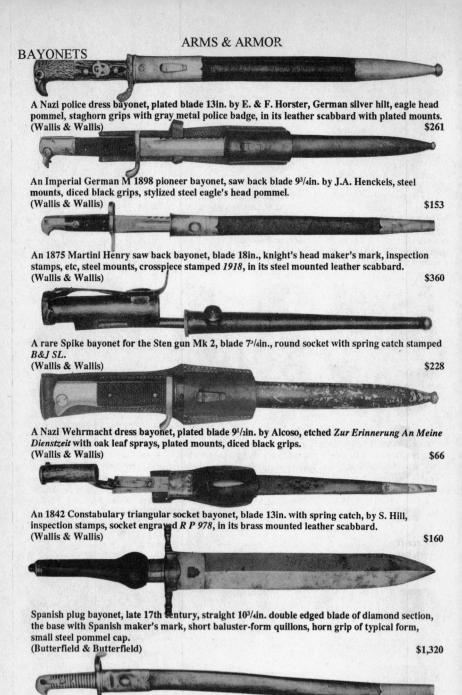

A Nazi police dress bayonet, plated blade 13in. by E. & F. Horster, German silver hilt, eagle head pommel, staghorn grips with gray metal police badge, in its leather scabbard with plated mounts.
(Wallis & Wallis) $261

An Imperial German M 1898 pioneer bayonet, saw back blade 9³/₄in. by J.A. Henckels, steel mounts, diced black grips, stylized steel eagle's head pommel.
(Wallis & Wallis) $153

An 1875 Martini Henry saw back bayonet, blade 18in., knight's head maker's mark, inspection stamps, etc, steel mounts, crosspiece stamped *1918*, in its steel mounted leather scabbard.
(Wallis & Wallis) $360

A rare Spike bayonet for the Sten gun Mk 2, blade 7⁵/₄in., round socket with spring catch stamped *B&J SL.*
(Wallis & Wallis) $228

A Nazi Wehrmacht dress bayonet, plated blade 9¹/₂in. by Alcoso, etched *Zur Erinnerung An Meine Dienstzeit* with oak leaf sprays, plated mounts, diced black grips.
(Wallis & Wallis) $66

An 1842 Constabulary triangular socket bayonet, blade 13in. with spring catch, by S. Hill, inspection stamps, socket engraved *R P 978*, in its brass mounted leather scabbard.
(Wallis & Wallis) $160

Spanish plug bayonet, late 17th century, straight 10³/₄in. double edged blade of diamond section, the base with Spanish maker's mark, short baluster-form quillons, horn grip of typical form, small steel pommel cap.
(Butterfield & Butterfield) $1,320

A scarce brass hilted 1853 artillery carbine bayonet, recurving blade 22¹/₂in., reversed steel crosspiece, in its brass mounted leather scabbard.
(Wallis & Wallis) $547

BAYONETS

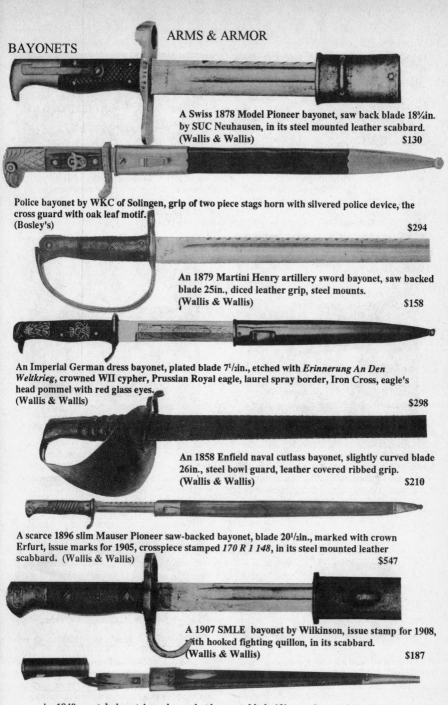

A Swiss 1878 Model Pioneer bayonet, saw back blade 18¾in.
by SUC Neuhausen, in its steel mounted leather scabbard.
(Wallis & Wallis) $130

Police bayonet by WKC of Solingen, grip of two piece stags horn with silvered police device, the
cross guard with oak leaf motif.
(Bosley's) $294

An 1879 Martini Henry artillery sword bayonet, saw backed
blade 25in., diced leather grip, steel mounts.
(Wallis & Wallis) $158

An Imperial German dress bayonet, plated blade 7½in., etched with *Erinnerung An Den
Weltkrieg*, crowned WII cypher, Prussian Royal eagle, laurel spray border, Iron Cross, eagle's
head pommel with red glass eyes.
(Wallis & Wallis) $298

An 1858 Enfield naval cutlass bayonet, slightly curved blade
26in., steel bowl guard, leather covered ribbed grip.
(Wallis & Wallis) $210

A scarce 1896 slim Mauser Pioneer saw-backed bayonet, blade 20½in., marked with crown
Erfurt, issue marks for 1905, crosspiece stamped *170 R 1 148*, in its steel mounted leather
scabbard. (Wallis & Wallis) $547

A 1907 SMLE bayonet by Wilkinson, issue stamp for 1908,
with hooked fighting quillon, in its scabbard.
(Wallis & Wallis) $187

An 1840 constabulary triangular socket bayonet, blade 13in., spring catch, in its brass
mounted leather scabbard.
(Wallis & Wallis) $91

CASED SETS

Cased Colt Model 1851 navy revolver, serial No. 53129, .36 caliber, 7½in. barrel with single line New York address, blued finish, varnished walnut grips, in original burgundy velvet-lined walnut case with Colt's patent powder flask by Dixon & Sons.
(Butterfield & Butterfield)   **$5,225**

A 16-bore over-and-under percussion Howdah pistol, by Thomas Elsworth Mortimer, 97 George Street, Edinburgh, circa 1840–1850, with rebrowned polygroove rifled twist octagonal barrels, checkered figured walnut butt, London proof marks, 38.3cm.
(Christie's)   **$3,478**

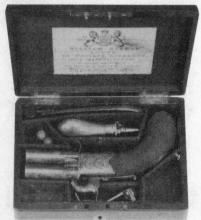

A cased 80-bore turn-over percussion pocket pistol, by Westley Richards, London, circa 1840, with case-hardened turn-off barrels numbered *3* and *4*, signed scroll engraved case-hardened box-lock action, finely checkered figured walnut butt, Birmingham proof marks, 14.6cm.
(Christie's)   **$2,318**

A rare cased 80-bore Bentley Patent five-shot percussion revolver, inscribed *W. Coffin, Bristol*, mid-19th century, with blued octagonal sighted barrel, case-hardened cylinder with chambers numbered from 1 to 5, Birmingham proof marks, 9³/₈in.
(Christie's)   **$1,546**

A fine cased 54-bore Tranter Patent five-shot double-action percussion revolver, No. 12277. T., circa 1865, with blued scroll engraved octagonal sighted barrel, scroll engraved case-hardened cylinder, checkered walnut butt, Birmingham proof marks, 13in.
(Christie's)   **$5,410**

A cased pair of 54-bore Belgian percussion target pistols, inscribed *Johan* (sic) *Manton, London*, circa 1850, with sighted twist multigroove rifled octagonal barrels each inscribed *London* on the top flat, figured walnut half-stocks, 17¹/₂in.
(Christie's)   **$4,250**

CASED SETS

A cased Colt .36 1862 Model Police percussion revolver, No. 13791 for 1862, with blued 5½in. barrel stamped with New York address, blued fluted cylinder, case-hardened frame, silvered trigger-guard and grip-strap, varnished walnut grips, London proof marks, 10¾in.
(Christie's) $5,796

A cased 54-bore Tranter Patent Second Model double-trigger self-cocking five-shot percussion revolver, No. 3,702. T, circa 1855, with blued octagonal sighted barrel, case-hardened cylinder, bright patent rammer, checkered walnut butt, London proof marks, 29.6cm.
(Christie's) $2,898

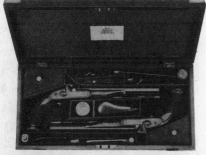

A cased pair of 20-bore percussion dueling pistols, signed *D. Egg, 4 Pall Mall, London*, circa 1830, with rebrowned signed twist octagonal sighted barrels, checkered butts, in original lined and fitted brass-bound mahogany case, London proof marks, 39.1cm.
(Christie's) $6,182

A good 6 shot .450in. center fire Tranters Patent double action revolver, 10½in. overall, barrel 5¼in. with B'ham proofs and engraved *Jas Beattie & Son, Regent St, London*, number 30144, hinged ejector rod beneath barrel, loading gate on right.
(Wallis & Wallis) $935

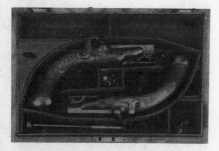

A cased pair of 60-bore Irish back-action percussion revolvers, by Trulock & Son, Dublin, circa 1840, with short etched twist octagonal barrels, silver fore-sights, case-hardened patent breeches, figured walnut three-quarter stocks, 7in.
(Christie's) $1,641

An unusual cased pair of 80-bore French saw-handled percussion pistols, by Devisme, Paris, No. 1235, circa 1860, with blued octagonal sighted barrels each inlaid with three silver lines at the muzzle and breech and signed in silver letters on the top flat, 6in.
(Christie's) $2,512

ARMS & ARMOR

CASED SETS

Cased Colt London Model 1849 pocket percussion revolver, serial No. 6651, .31 caliber, 4in. barrel with two-line London address, British proofs and domed screwheads.
(Butterfield & Butterfield) $3,575

A good cased .31 Colt 'Root' Model 1855 sidehammer pocket pistol, numbered 6657 with 3¹/₂in. barrel, five shot fluted cylinder, spur trigger, and wrap round plain wood grip.
(Bosley's) $2,250

A 5 shot 54 bore Tranters Patent double action percussion revolver No. 14099T, 12in., barrel 6in. London proved, top strap engraved *John Blissett, 322 High Holborn, London*, hinged cylinder locking catch, spring catch retains cylinder pin, checkered walnut grip.
(Wallis & Wallis) $2,300

Boxed Harrington & Richardson New Automatic double action revolver, serial No. 2218, .38, 3¼in. barrel, nickel plated finish, checkered hard rubber grips.
(Butterfield & Butterfield) $357

Boxed Colt officer's Model 32 heavy barrel revolver, serial No. 656853, .32 Police, 6in. heavy barrel, target sights, checkered walnut grips with Colt medallions, maroon box with target.
(Butterfield & Butterfield) $605

A pair of 16 bore flintlock dueling pistols by Tomlinson, 14in., rebrowned octagonal barrels 9in. London proved, fullstocked, roller bearing frizzen springs, engraved brass furniture, flattened checkered grips.
(Wallis & Wallis) $2,800

32

CROSSBOWS

German sporting crossbow, mid 17th century, robust steel bow retained by cords and fitted with plaited string, ebonized wooden stock, 21in.
(Sotheby's) $3,795

A small crossbow, Spanish or English, late 16th-early 17th century, perhaps for a child, of recurved form struck twice with maker's mark, slender walnut tiller swelling at the gaffle pivot, 20¾in.
(Sotheby's) $1,283

A fine Saxon sporting crossbow with etched steel bow, circa 1730-40, probably Dresden, struck with a cockerel mark and retained by gold-plated cords with four original woollen pompoms, 24¾in.
(Sotheby's) $12,400

A German slurbow, circa 1720-1730, fruitwood stock fitted with foresight and leaf backsight and carved with cherub mask, 20¾in.
(Sotheby's) $2,875

A German sporting crossbow for a child, 17th century, with slender recurved blackened steel bow retained by its original cirds and fitted with a small iron stirrup, with original string, the bow 16½in.
(Sotheby's) $1,035

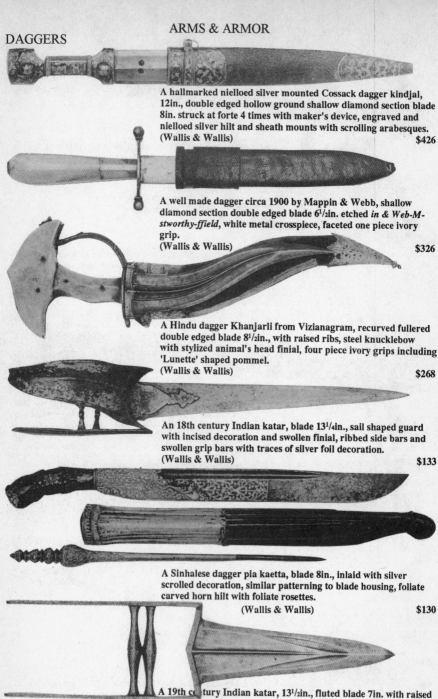

A hallmarked nielloed silver mounted Cossack dagger kindjal,
12in., double edged hollow ground shallow diamond section blade
8in. struck at forte 4 times with maker's device, engraved and
nielloed silver hilt and sheath mounts with scrolling arabesques.
(Wallis & Wallis)   **$426**

A well made dagger circa 1900 by Mappin & Webb, shallow
diamond section double edged blade 6½in. etched *in & Web-M-
stworthy-ffield*, white metal crosspiece, faceted one piece ivory
grip.
(Wallis & Wallis)   **$326**

A Hindu dagger Khanjarli from Vizianagram, recurved fullered
double edged blade 8½in., with raised ribs, steel knucklebow
with stylized animal's head finial, four piece ivory grips including
'Lunette' shaped pommel.
(Wallis & Wallis)   **$268**

An 18th century Indian katar, blade 13¼in., sail shaped guard
with incised decoration and swollen finial, ribbed side bars and
swollen grip bars with traces of silver foil decoration.
(Wallis & Wallis)   **$133**

A Sinhalese dagger pia kaetta, blade 8in., inlaid with silver
scrolled decoration, similar patterning to blade housing, foliate
carved horn hilt with foliate rosettes.
    (Wallis & Wallis)   **$130**

A 19th century Indian katar, 13½in., fluted blade 7in. with raised
central rib, hilt gold damascened with flowers, foliage and
geometric borders.
(Wallis & Wallis)   **$173**

34

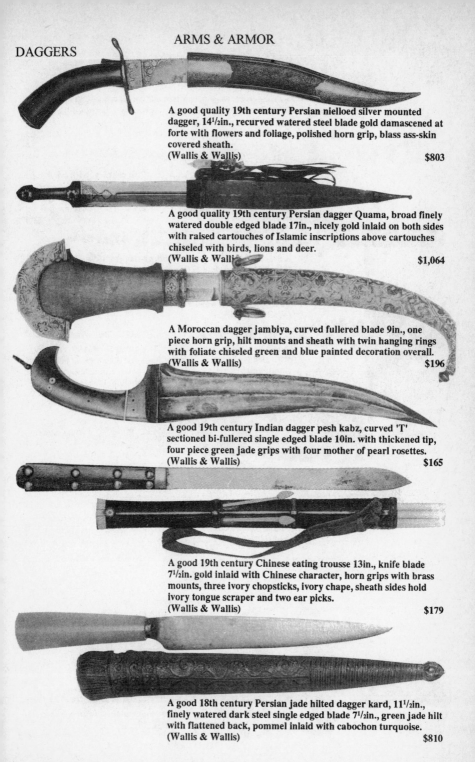

A good quality 19th century Persian nielloed silver mounted
dagger, 14½in., recurved watered steel blade gold damascened at
forte with flowers and foliage, polished horn grip, blass ass-skin
covered sheath.
(Wallis & Wallis) $803

A good quality 19th century Persian dagger Quama, broad finely
watered double edged blade 17in., nicely gold inlaid on both sides
with raised cartouches of Islamic inscriptions above cartouches
chiseled with birds, lions and deer.
(Wallis & Wallis) $1,064

A Moroccan dagger jambiya, curved fullered blade 9in., one
piece horn grip, hilt mounts and sheath with twin hanging rings
with foliate chiseled green and blue painted decoration overall.
(Wallis & Wallis) $196

A good 19th century Indian dagger pesh kabz, curved 'T'
sectioned bi-fullered single edged blade 10in. with thickened tip,
four piece green jade grips with four mother of pearl rosettes.
(Wallis & Wallis) $165

A good 19th century Chinese eating trousse 13in., knife blade
7½in. gold inlaid with Chinese character, horn grips with brass
mounts, three ivory chopsticks, ivory chape, sheath sides hold
ivory tongue scraper and two ear picks.
(Wallis & Wallis) $179

A good 18th century Persian jade hilted dagger kard, 11½in.,
finely watered dark steel single edged blade 7½in., green jade hilt
with flattened back, pommel inlaid with cabochon turquoise.
(Wallis & Wallis) $810

A German Weimar period officer's dress dagger, blade 13½in.,
etched with military trophies and foliage, gilt hilt mounts,
straight crosspiece with fluted domed finials.
(Wallis & Wallis) $398

An Italian left-hand dagger, early 17th century, with tapering
double-edged blade of hollow diamond section with flattened
section for the thumb on one face, iron hilt comprising double
arched 'crab-claw' quillons and oval side-ring, 49.2cm.
(Christie's) $3,670

A scarce early 17th century ballock dagger, 16¼in., deeply
fullered tapered double edged blade 10¾in., stamped in the
fullers *Iohanni*, wooden hilt with swollen bilobate guard,
flattened grip sides, swollen pommel with pierced brass
quatrefoil button washer.
(Wallis & Wallis) $1,702

A left-hand dagger in Italian 17th century style, 19th century,
with slender tapering blade of flattened diamond section at the
point, notched ricasso pierced with two circular holes for sword-
breaking, spirally fluted quillons with globular terminals,
60.3cm.
(Christie's) $2,512

A rare 19th century Indian rock crystal dagger kard, finely dark
watered steel single edged blade, 7¾in., thickly gold
damascened at forte with flowers and foliage, one piece rock
crystal hilt. (Wallis & Wallis) $2,325

A late 19th   century all steel Syrian dagger Haladie, 20½in.,
recurved   fullered blades 8in. with punching blade on
knucklebow   ribbed steel grips.
            (Wallis & Wallis) $332

An early Bali kris, wavy etched pamor blade 14½in., wooden hilt
wound with short tufts of bristles, filigree copper cup.
(Wallis & Wallis) $98

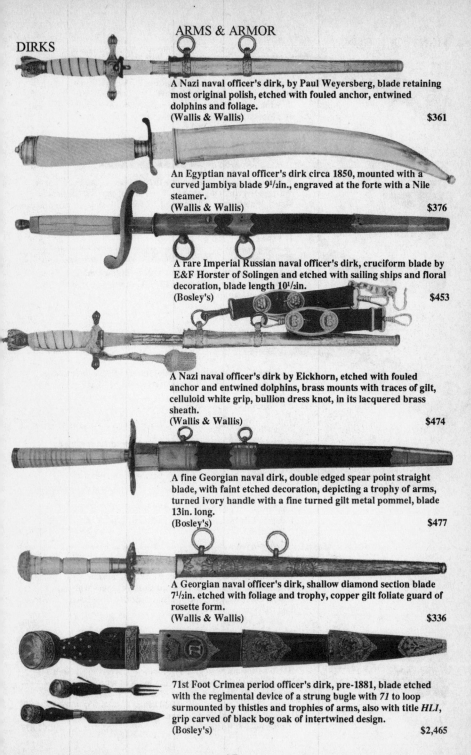

A Nazi naval officer's dirk, by Paul Weyersberg, blade retaining
most original polish, etched with fouled anchor, entwined
dolphins and foliage.
(Wallis & Wallis) $361

An Egyptian naval officer's dirk circa 1850, mounted with a
curved jambiya blade 9¹/₂in., engraved at the forte with a Nile
steamer.
(Wallis & Wallis) $376

A rare Imperial Russian naval officer's dirk, cruciform blade by
E&F Horster of Solingen and etched with sailing ships and floral
decoration, blade length 10¹/₂in.
(Bosley's) $453

A Nazi naval officer's dirk by Eickhorn, etched with fouled
anchor and entwined dolphins, brass mounts with traces of gilt,
celluloid white grip, bullion dress knot, in its lacquered brass
sheath.
(Wallis & Wallis) $474

A fine Georgian naval dirk, double edged spear point straight
blade, with faint etched decoration, depicting a trophy of arms,
turned ivory handle with a fine turned gilt metal pommel, blade
13in. long.
(Bosley's) $477

A Georgian naval officer's dirk, shallow diamond section blade
7¹/₂in. etched with foliage and trophy, copper gilt foliate guard of
rosette form.
(Wallis & Wallis) $336

71st Foot Crimea period officer's dirk, pre-1881, blade etched
with the regimental device of a strung bugle with 71 to loop
surmounted by thistles and trophies of arms, also with title HLI,
grip carved of black bog oak of intertwined design.
(Bosley's) $2,465

ARMS & ARMOR

Rare U.S. Ellis-Jennings repeating flintlock rifle, with 36in. .54 caliber barrel marked at the breech *US/JM/P*, sliding lock with four touch holes built on the Jennings Patent and equipped with an automatic priming magazine.
(Butterfield & Butterfield)   **$11,000**

A dog-lock blunderbuss, circa 1670, with massive brass barrel with reinforcing ring at the shaped belled muzzle, the breech struck with barrelsmith's mark *IF* and with stepped ramp at the rear, plain iron tang, walnut full stock with raised apron at the barrel tang, London proof marks, 43in.
(Christie's)   **$3,478**

A 10 bore Indian pattern Brown Bess flintlock musket, 55in., barrel 39in. London proofs with EIC stamp and *RTM 145*, fullstocked, regulation lock with Tower and crowned GR, regulation brass mounts.
(Wallis & Wallis)   **$1,033**

A 22-bore Balkan miquelet-lock gun, late 18th century, with sighted etched twist octagonal barrel swamped at the muzzle, inlaid in silver with dots and interlaced scrollwork, the tang overlaid with embossed silver, the butt divided by silver bands, 45in. barrel.
(Christie's)   **$3,671**

A 140-bore Silesian wheel-lock tschinke, second quarter 17th century, with swamped octagonal sighted barrel cut with eight grooves and with three panels of punched decoration retaining faint traces of gilding, the pierced cock engraved with a hare, foliage and a monster's head, 33$\frac{1}{2}$in. barrel.
(Christie's)   **$10,046**

A late 18th century Indian matchlock gun torador, 69in., polished barrel 50in., fullstocked, polished steel lock sides with match holders, steel trigger, stock polychrome decorated overall with floral designs.
(Wallis & Wallis)   **$300**

English flintlock wall gun by Mortimer, circa 1800, round 34in. barrel with one inch bore, breech marked with Birmingham proof and *EI*, flat lock engraved at the tail *Mortimer/Great Queen/Street/London*, and ahead of the lock with the Tower of London, engraved brass trigger guard, sideplate and buttplate.
(Butterfield & Butterfield)   **$4,675**

FLINTLOCK GUNS

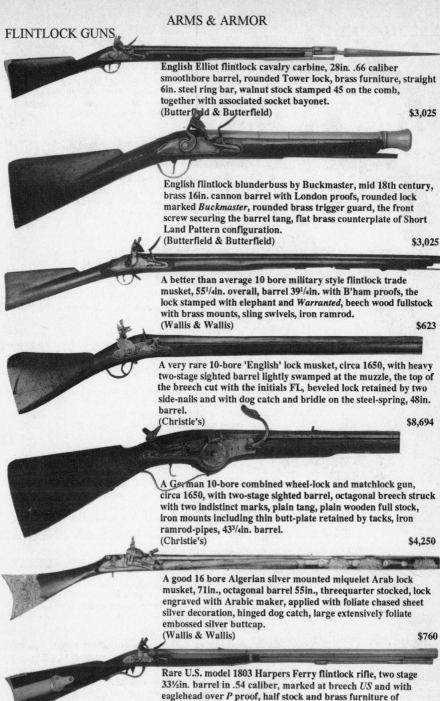

English Elliot flintlock cavalry carbine, 28in. .66 caliber
smoothbore barrel, rounded Tower lock, brass furniture, straight
6in. steel ring bar, walnut stock stamped 45 on the comb,
together with associated socket bayonet.
(Butterfield & Butterfield) $3,025

English flintlock blunderbuss by Buckmaster, mid 18th century,
brass 16in. cannon barrel with London proofs, rounded lock
marked *Buckmaster*, rounded brass trigger guard, the front
screw securing the barrel tang, flat brass counterplate of Short
Land Pattern configuration.
(Butterfield & Butterfield) $3,025

A better than average 10 bore military style flintlock trade
musket, 55¼in. overall, barrel 39¼in. with B'ham proofs, the
lock stamped with elephant and *Warranted*, beech wood fullstock
with brass mounts, sling swivels, iron ramrod.
(Wallis & Wallis) $623

A very rare 10-bore 'English' lock musket, circa 1650, with heavy
two-stage sighted barrel lightly swamped at the muzzle, the top of
the breech cut with the initials FL, beveled lock retained by two
side-nails and with dog catch and bridle on the steel-spring, 48in.
barrel.
(Christie's) $8,694

A German 10-bore combined wheel-lock and matchlock gun,
circa 1650, with two-stage sighted barrel, octagonal breech struck
with two indistinct marks, plain tang, plain wooden full stock,
iron mounts including thin butt-plate retained by tacks, iron
ramrod-pipes, 43¾in. barrel.
(Christie's) $4,250

A good 16 bore Algerian silver mounted miquelet Arab lock
musket, 71in., octagonal barrel 55in., threequarter stocked, lock
engraved with Arabic maker, applied with foliate chased sheet
silver decoration, hinged dog catch, large extensively foliate
embossed silver buttcap.
(Wallis & Wallis) $760

Rare U.S. model 1803 Harpers Ferry flintlock rifle, two stage
33½in. barrel in .54 caliber, marked at breech *US* and with
eaglehead over *P* proof, half stock and brass furniture of
standard pattern.
(Butterfield & Butterfield) $2,750

A 26 bore Caucasian ball butted miquelet flintlock holster pistol, 18¹/₂in., barrel 13³/₄in. inlaid with silver scrolls, fullstocked with black leather covered wood, ball butt inlaid with white metal wire work and triangular mother of pearl sections.
(Wallis & Wallis) $628

A 32 bore flintlock dueling pistol, by Durs Egg, London, circa 1790, with slightly swamped rebrowned twist octagonal sighted barrel signed at the breech and with gold-lined vent, figured walnut full stock, London proof marks, 15¹/₄in.
(Christie's) $2,898

A 16 bore Light Dragoon flintlock pistol, 15in., barrel 9in., Tower proved, fullstocked, lock engraved *Tower* and crowned *GR*, regulation brass mounts.
(Wallis & Wallis) $747

A silver mounted Turkish flintlock holster pistol, 19in., barrel 12¹/₄in. chiseled with foliage at breech and with indistinct maker's stamps, fullstocked, Italian export lock engraved *F Moretti*, roller bearing frizzen spring, Eastern silver furniture.
(Wallis & Wallis) $900

A 20-bore Turkish silver-mounted flintlock holster pistol, late 18th century, with gold-damascened barrel retained by a silver filigree muzzle band, the top of the breech with a gold-damascened inscription, gold-damascened beveled lock, wooden full stock entirely covered with silver filigree, beadwork, 19¹/₂in.
(Christie's) $2,125

Caucasian flintlock pistol, round 11⁷/₈in. barrel with narrow top rib and slightly flared muzzle, decorated overall with gold florals and bands, lock of typical form and decorated en suite to barrel, ball trigger, black leather covered stock.
(Butterfield & Butterfield) $3,025

A 20 bore Turkish miquelet flintlock all metal holster pistol, 21¹/₂in., barrel 14¹/₂in. with a little silver inlay at breech, white metal fullstock chiseled overall with scrolling foliage in relief.
(Wallis & Wallis) $1,200

FLINTLOCK PISTOLS

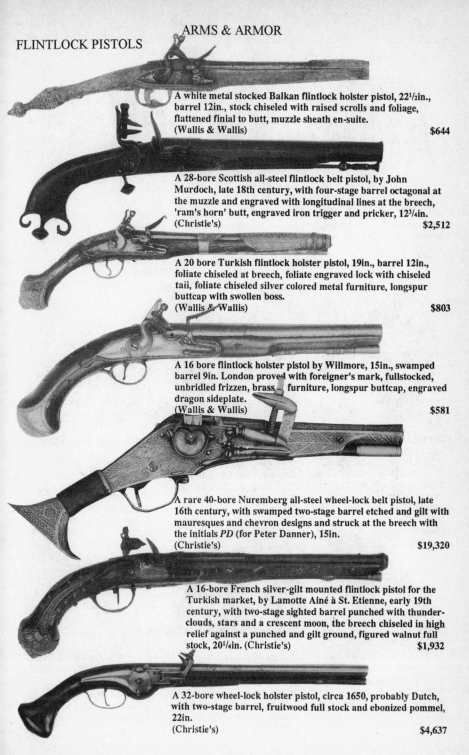

A white metal stocked Balkan flintlock holster pistol, 22½in., barrel 12in., stock chiseled with raised scrolls and foliage, flattened finial to butt, muzzle sheath en-suite. (Wallis & Wallis) **$644**

A 28-bore Scottish all-steel flintlock belt pistol, by John Murdoch, late 18th century, with four-stage barrel octagonal at the muzzle and engraved with longitudinal lines at the breech, 'ram's horn' butt, engraved iron trigger and pricker, 12¾in. (Christie's) **$2,512**

A 20 bore Turkish flintlock holster pistol, 19in., barrel 12in., foliate chiseled at breech, foliate engraved lock with chiseled taii, foliate chiseled silver colored metal furniture, longspur buttcap with swollen boss. (Wallis & Wallis) **$803**

A 16 bore flintlock holster pistol by Willmore, 15in., swamped barrel 9in. London proved with foreigner's mark, fullstocked, unbridled frizzen, brass furniture, longspur buttcap, engraved dragon sideplate. (Wallis & Wallis) **$581**

A rare 40-bore Nuremberg all-steel wheel-lock belt pistol, late 16th century, with swamped two-stage barrel etched and gilt with mauresques and chevron designs and struck at the breech with the initials *PD* (for Peter Danner), 15in. (Christie's) **$19,320**

A 16-bore French silver-gilt mounted flintlock pistol for the Turkish market, by Lamotte Ainé à St. Etienne, early 19th century, with two-stage sighted barrel punched with thunder-clouds, stars and a crescent moon, the breech chiseled in high relief against a punched and gilt ground, figured walnut full stock, 20¼in. (Christie's) **$1,932**

A 32-bore wheel-lock holster pistol, circa 1650, probably Dutch, with two-stage barrel, fruitwood full stock and ebonized pommel, 22in. (Christie's) **$4,637**

HELMETS

A scarce SS 1935 Model steel parade helmet, original decals and black paint finish.
(Wallis & Wallis) $408

French Napoleonic period Cuirassier's helmet, polished steel skull with manufacturer's date stamp of 1812.
(Bosley's) $2,472

9th Foot (Norfolk) officer's forage cap, mid 19th century Kepi-style example with flat peak, to front gold bullion '9' with Britannia seated above.
(Bosley's) $498

A 17th century Indian mail and plate helmet from the Bikaneer Arsenal, shaped radial plates linked to crown disk and vertical brim plates, with lamellar section to neck.
(Wallis & Wallis) $684

Grenadier Guards officer's foreign service helmet, to the front a superb fire gilded Grenadier Guards officer's pagri badge with red and blue translucent enamel backing.
(Bosley's) $1,988

1st Huntingdonshire Mounted Rifle Volunteers helmet, the boiled leather skull with silvered metal regimental helmet plate with title *1ST OR DUKE OF MANCHESTER'S*.
(Bosley's) $755

9th Queen's Royal Lancers officer's foul weather cap, 19th century, black oil cloth with gilt metal trim to the peak.
(Bosley's) $1,132

A well-made copy of an Innsbruck late 15th century sallet, 19th century, with one-piece skull with low central ridge pierced with a small circular hole, 9in. high.
(Christie's) $3,477

City of London Yeomanry Bandsman lance cap, lance plate to front with battle honors of South Africa 1900–1902.
(Bosley's) $954

HELMETS

An 1818–34 Roman pattern Heavy Dragoon officer's helmet, black glazed metal edged with gilt metal turned edge.
(Bosley's) $7,550

A close helmet, probably French, and of the latter half of the sixteenth century, the visor and bevor bearing traces of gilding.
(David Lay) $8,786

French 19th century Cuirassier's officer's helmet, front with a Medusa's head, below this a flaming grenade.
(Bosley's) $1,545

A German black and white comb morion, circa 1600, with two-piece skull and high comb, embossed on each side with a stylized fleur-de-lys within a circle of tongue ornament, 10¾in. high.
(Christie's) $1,739

Coldstream Guards officer's bearskin, black fur of good shape terminating with tail to the rear, internal wicker frame.
(Bosley's) $1,738

A good dark green Kilmarnock bonnet of the Queen's Bodyguard for Scotland, Royal Company of Archers, gilt badge upon green silk rosette with white silk backing.
(Wallis & Wallis) $299

Diplomatic Service foreign service helmet, with a post 1902 Royal Arms badge, complete with gilt metal spike and alternative white cloth covered zinc button.
(Bosley's) $355

A good officer's 1855 (French) pattern shako of the 50th (Queen's Own) Regiment, black beaver with patent leather peaks.
(Wallis & Wallis) $1,123

A fine Panzer officer's peaked forage cap, with bright pink piping and silver bullion insignia, complete with cap cords.
(Bosley's) $392

HELMETS

An ERII troopers white metal helmet of the Life Guards, brass mounts, plume spike, leather backed graduated link chinchain and ear rosettes.
(Wallis & Wallis) $836

A cabasset circa 1600, formed in one piece, pear stalk finial to crown, brass rosettes around base, beaked brim tip.
(Wallis & Wallis) $426

A good fireman's brass helmet, pointed front peak and broad back peak, comb ornamented with dragons, helmet plate bearing torch and crossed axes.
(Wallis & Wallis) $489

A post 1902 other rank's lance cap of the 9th (Queen's Royal) Lancers, black patent leather skull and top, black cloth sides, brass ornamentation, plate, simulated cord rosette and button.
(Wallis & Wallis) $785

A well made 19th century copy of a late 16th century close helmet of 'Maximilian' type, fluted skull with roped comb, pierced sights and radial breaths.
(Wallis & Wallis) $996

An officer's gilt metal of the 3rd (Prince of Wales's) Dragoon Guards, silver plated helmet plate with blue and red enameled gilt center, gilt ear rosettes and chinchain with velvet backing.
(Wallis & Wallis) $1,110

A Victorian officer's black japanned Albert pattern helmet of the Queen's Own Royal Yeomanry (Staffordshire), silver plated acanthus ornamentation and mounts.
(Wallis & Wallis) $1,334

A good NCO's bearskin of a Vol Bn The Royal Welsh Fusiliers, white metal grenade badge with applied Prince of Wales's feathers on the ball.
(Wallis & Wallis) $304

An Imperial Bavarian ersatz (pressed felt) Infantryman's Pickelhaube, brass helmet plate and mounts, leather lining and chinstrap, both cockades.
(Wallis & Wallis) $398

HELMETS

An Imperial Bavarian other rank's Pickelhaube of a railway battalion, German silver helmet plate, spike and mounts, leather lining and chinstrap.
(Wallis & Wallis) $474

An English Civil War period pikemans pot, made in two halves with low comb, base of skull embossed with horizontal line and ornamented rivet heads.
(Wallis & Wallis) $1,368

An Imperial Prussian artilleryman's Pickelhaube, brass helmet plate, ball top and mounts, leather backed brass chinscales.
(Wallis & Wallis) $413

An officer's gilt helmet of The 4th Royal Irish Dragoon Guards, silver plated helmet plate, with green, red and light blue enameled center, white hair plume with rosette, leather lining.
(Wallis & Wallis) $623

A WWI Brodies pattern steel helmet, contained in its rare officer's leather trimmed haversack with fitted compartment for helmet marked *G E Briddon* and address.
(Wallis & Wallis) $212

An other rank's 1844 (Albert) pattern white metal helmet of the 1st (Royal) Dragoons, brass acanthus ornaments, mounts, leather backed chinchain and ear rosettes, helmet plate, black hair plume.
(Wallis & Wallis) $805

A well made copy of a late 15th century helmet sallet, forged in one piece with raised medial ridge, pierced sight, turned over borders.
(Wallis & Wallis) $2,800

An other rank's white metal helmet of the Life Guards, brass peak binding and leather backed chinchain with ear rosettes, white hair plume with plain brass rosette, leather lining.
(Wallis & Wallis) $608

An Imperial Prussian artillery officer's Pickelhaube, helmet plate, chinscales and mounts with traces of gilt finish, leather and silk lining.
(Wallis & Wallis) $505

1st (or King's) Dragoon Guards trooper's helmet, 1871 example, silvered skull decorated with brass laurel leaves.
(Bosley's) **$1,120**

A cabasset circa 1600, formed in one piece, 'pear stalk' finial to crown, studs around base.
(Wallis & Wallis) **$289**

Scottish Rifles 2nd VB officer's Home Service green cloth helmet, worn by the regiment from 1881–1892.
(Bosley's) **$1,117**

Russian Imperial Horse Guard Regiment helmet, 1846 pattern trooper's helmet, tombak skull surmounted by a silvered metal ornate Imperial double headed eagle.
(Bosley's) **$9,060**

An Italian close-helmet, comprehensively circa 1570, with one-piece skull with prominent roped comb between a pair of narrow raised ribs, pointed visor with central division, 12in. high.
(Christie's) **$4,637**

17th Regiment of (Light Dragoon) Lancers, Crimea Period Troop Sergeant's lance cap, believed to be one of only two know examples of the other rank's issue.
(Bosley's) **$9,579**

City of London Imperial Yeomanry officer's lance cap, post 1902, skull of black patent leather with the upper portion of pale blue melton cloth.
(Bosley's) **$5,890**

Civil Defence WWII steel helmet, black painted shell with transfer to the front, *S.P.B.C.* above a town crest, with initials *ARP* below.
(Bosley's) **$68**

A cuirassier helmet, circa 1630, probably German, with two-piece skull rising to a low comb, visor and bevor pivoting at the same points, 12¹/₂in. high.
(Christie's) **$2,318**

HELMETS

The Honourable Corps of Gentleman-at-Arms helmet, the fire gilded skull with scrolling foliate overlaid decoration to the peak.
(Bosley's) $7,750

Royal Tank Regiment Foreign Service helmet, 10th Armored Motor Battery officer's Wolseley pattern foreign service helmet, nine fold khaki pagri.
(Bosley's) $906

The Royal Dragoons trooper's 1847 (Albert) pattern helmet, gilt brass helmet plate overlaid with cut star bearing strap inscribed *The Royal Dragoons*.
(Bosley's) $1,132

A post 1902 officer's blue cloth ball topped helmet of The Royal Artillery, gilt mounts, helmet plate, velvet backed chinchain and ear rosettes, in its tin case with nameplate.
(Wallis & Wallis) $518

A lobster-tailed pot, second quarter 17th century, with ribbed hemispherical one-piece skull with separate ring-shaped finial, pointed fixed fall with turned edge pierced for the adjustable nasal bar, 11in. high.
(Christie's) $1,352

12th Prince of Wales Royal Lancers lance cap, pre 1901 other rank's lance cap, patent leather body, peak and crown with ornate gilt metal fleur bosses to each corner.
(Bosley's) $1,208

5th Royal Irish Lancers trooper's lance cap, Edwardian, regimental lance plate to front with battle honors up to South Africa 1899–1902.
(Bosley's) $1,284

A rare Italian 'casquetel', circa 1510, with rounded skull rising to a low keel and embossed with fan-shaped fluting on each side, large movable peak, 9³/₄in. high.
(Christie's) $3,284

Lancashire Fusiliers post 1908 Territorial Bn. officer's fur cap, gilt metal flaming grenade to front with silver mounted sphinx.
(Bosley's) $1,132

ARMS & ARMOR

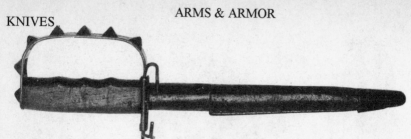

A US WWI Model 1917 trench knife, knuckleduster dagger, triangular blade 9in., base of guard stamped *US LF & C 1917*, shaped wood grip, in its steel mounted leather covered sheath. (Wallis & Wallis)
$153

A scarce Nazi Luftwaffe knife, clipped back blade 8in. by Waffen Loesche Berlin, small oval steel guard, staghorn grip secured by 3 screw bolts, in its black painted metal sheath. (Wallis & Wallis)
$550

A Nkundo prestige knife 'Mf'imo' from the Mongo area of Central Zaire, early 20th century, broad tapered blade 12¼in., wooden hilt and sheath extensively decorated with brass nail head. (Wallis & Wallis)
$345

A Bowie type knife, curious spatulate blade 8in. by *Underwood, 55 Haymarket*, also stamped crown, *ER*, German silver crosspiece, staghorn grips, in its leather sheath. (Wallis & Wallis)
$304

A scarce Far East Fairbairn-Sykes fighting knife, double edged spear point blade, with straight oval cross guard. (Bosley's)
$100

An unusual Mediterranean knife, Italian or Sardinian, late 17th/first half 18th century, with a single-edged blade, the lower half of robust section and inlaid with the name *Bermudes* in alternate gold and silver letters on the back-edge, 10¼in. (Sotheby's)
$1,840

KNIVES

A Nazi Hitler Youth knife, diced black grips with enamel emblem, plated mounts, in its black painted metal sheath.
(Wallis & Wallis) $116

A Third Reich SS silver gilt desk paper knife presented by Himmler to SS General Werner Lorenz, blade inscribed and with Runic patterns on handle with SS Runes, all with black enamel background. (Wallis & Wallis) $3,022

A Central Mongo bridal knife Bosaka from Equatorial Province of Zaire circa 1920, as used for dowry, swollen 'Concorde' shaped blade 15½in., copper wound wooden hilt.
(Wallis & Wallis) $50

An Ngombe chief knife Bosal from the Ubangi region of NW Zaire, early 20th century, blade 15in. pierced at forte, copper wound and covered hilt with later leather covered pommel.
(Wallis & Wallis) $50

A very rare 1st pattern Fairbairn Sykes fighting knife, nickel plated with checkered design, double edged spear point blade, the ricasso with etched panel.
(Bosley's) $734

A Lokele bridal knife Simi from NE Zaire circa 1900, used as dowry, 17¾in., finely incised blade 12¾in., massive iron pommel, rattan wound wooden grip.
(Wallis & Wallis) $50

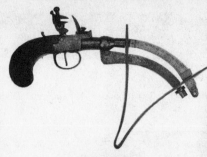

A J. Erskine mahogany cartridge magazine, for 100 rounds.
(Bonhams) $226

A rare Liège flintlock box-lock V-spring powder-tester, circa 1800, with plain action, thumbpiece safety-catch, and flat-sided checkered butt, 10³/₄in.
(Christie's) $1,159

Scots Guards Colonel's color, pre 1901, scarlet silk flag, to the center, the Scottish Lion, flanked by Battle Honors.
(Bosley's) $1,132

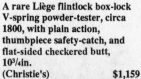

A good painted metal side drum of the 2nd Bn The Leicestershire Regt circa 1935, by *Henry Potter & Co*, bearing well painted regimental Tiger over *Hindoostan* scroll and 22 battle honors.
(Wallis & Wallis) $638

Wells Fargo & Co. wooden strongbox, of wood and wrought iron construction, painted manufacturer's label inside reads: *Manufactured by/J.Y. AYER/3470 SEVENTEETH ST./ S.F. CAL.*
(Butterfield & Butterfield)
                                             $7,150

A signed black and white presentation 6 x 8in. photograph of Adolf Hitler, showing Hitler three-quarter length in uniform, in hallmarked silver frame.
(Wallis & Wallis)
                                            $13,175

Scarce Dahlgren 12 PDR boat howitzer, circa 1869, serial No. 107, 4¹/₂in. bore, 55in. bronze barrel marked with fouled anchor *12 Pdr Boat Howitzer 1869.*
(Butterfield & Butterfield)
                                            $14,300

A good 19th century Indian gold and silver damascened steel shield dhal, 14in., raised central bosses and reinforced border all with shaped edges, gold damascened overall.
(Wallis & Wallis) $497

6th (Inniskilling) Dragoons shabraque, pre 1901 example from an officer's charger, black melton cloth edged in a single wide line of regimental pattern gold bullion lace.
(Bosley's) $1,019

MILITARIA

South Lancashire Regiment presentation silver bugle, hallmarked with presentation inscription, mounted with a silver regimental band pattern badge with last Battle Honor South Africa 1899–1902.
(Bosley's) $632

Royal Canadian Dragoons Boer War leather chest, polished brown leather farrier's or saddler's chest bearing various issue stamps for 1900 and 1901.
(Bosley's) $795

A good officer's full dress shoulder belt and silver mounted pouch of the 2nd Dragoons (Royal Scots Greys), gilt regimented lace with blue edging on red morocco.
(Wallis & Wallis) $1,255

An embroidered trumpet banner of The Queen's (R W Surrey) Regt, blue grosgrain with red/green/red central band, embroidered on both sides with cypher, Sphinx, naval crown, Paschal Lamb, 1661 and title scroll.
(Wallis & Wallis) $99

A French etched circular iron parade shield in late 16th century style, of shallow convex form, the outer face etched with a Mannerist segmented pattern of scrolls, flowers and foliage, 20¹/₄in. diameter.
(Sotheby's) $2,300

A good George VI painted brass side drum of The Black Watch (R Highland Regt), bearing regimental title, badge and 39 battle honors *Guadeloupe 1759* to *Kut al Amara 1917*.
(Wallis & Wallis) $502

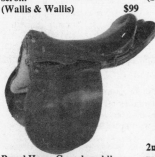

Royal Horse Guards saddle, post 1902 example, high brass cantle with padded panels and brass D rings to attach equipment.
(Bosley's) $211

2nd Grenadier guards regimental Victorian side drum, pre 1901 example, emblazoned with the Royal Arms and regimental device of the flaming grenade.
(Bosley's) $954

Scots Guards 3rd Company color, pre 1901, the Union flag, to the center the Scottish Lion surmounted by a Victorian Crown, flanked by Battle Honors.
(Bosley's) $1,963

A .30–30 Marlin Safety Model 1893 take down underlever half tube magazine rifle, 42$\frac{1}{4}$in. overall, octagonal barrel 24$\frac{1}{4}$in., number 431431, ratchet rearsight, locking lever releases barrel for easy removal, the frame topped for saddle ring.
(Wallis & Wallis) $712

Winchester Model 1895 saddle ring carbine, serial No. 387844, .30-06 caliber, 22in. barrel, blued finish, standard wood configuration with sling mounts and shotgun butt.
(Butterfield & Butterfield) $1,320

U.S. New Model 1863 Sharps percussion carbine, serial No. 83322, .52 caliber, 22in. barrel with model designated, standard carbine configuration with steel patchbox.
(Butterfield & Butterfield) $935

Winchester Third Model 1873 musket, serial No. 570470B, .44–40, 30in. barrel, standard configuration, walnut stock and fore-end.
(Butterfield & Butterfield) $1,760

A .44/77in. Remington falling block sporting rifle No. 64, 45$\frac{1}{2}$in., half octagonal barrel 30in. stamped *E Remington & Sons, Ilion NY*, halfstocked, frame stamped *Hepburns Pat Oct 7th 1879*, side lever lowers breech.
(Wallis & Wallis) $600

Rare U.S. model 1847 sappers percussion carbine, round 26in. .69 caliber barrel dated *1855* on the tang, front barrel band with bayonet mounting, lock dated *1854*, walnut stock, complete with rare brass hilted sword bayonet by Ames.
(Butterfield & Butterfield) $8,250

A 16 bore boxlock percussion underhammer Charlesworths Patent walkingstick gun, 35$\frac{1}{2}$in., turn off twist barrel 28$\frac{1}{2}$in., Birmingham proved, engraved *Charlesworth Patent No 48*, turned baluster ebony handle with brass ferrule, walnut handle.
(Wallis & Wallis) $450

Henry Model 1860 lever action rifle, serial No. 4585, .44 caliber, 24in. barrel, standard model with varnished walnut stock retaining sling swivel.
(Butterfield & Butterfield) $9,350

52

A 16 bore German percussion sporting rifle made up from
military parts, 46³/₄in., barrel 30¹/₂in. stamped *43* at breech parts,
unusual ramped rearsight to 550 (metres?), halfstocked, lock
stamped *SP.SR & ST SUHL*.
(Wallis & Wallis) $456

A .303in. long Lee Enfield Mark I bolt action military pattern
rifle, 49¹/₂in. overall, barrel 30in., number *M127* at breech and
3391 on frame, the barrel engraved *J Stansby & Co, Manchester*.
(Wallis & Wallis) $330

Spencer Civil War repeating carbine, serial No. 38915, .52
caliber, 22in. barrel, frame marked *Spencer Repeating/Rifle Co.
Boston, Mass./Pat'd. March 6, 1860*.
(Butterfield & Butterfield) $990

A .303 BSA Lee Enfield bolt action box magazine sporting rifle,
44¹/₂in. overall, barrel 25in., number *182125*, two folding leaf
rearsights to 300 yards, and ladder rearsight to 1000 yards.
(Wallis & Wallis) $330

Spencer Civil War New Model repeating rifle, serial No. 101091,
.52 caliber, 30in. barrel marked *NM* at breech, buttstock painted
on right side with longhorn steer head and *Texas* with Texas flag,
obverse painted *C.S.A./1861* with Confederate flag.
(Butterfield & Butterfield) $2,750

Rare U.S. Sharps Model 1855 Navy rifle, serial No. 20278, .52
caliber, 28in. barrel equipped with saber bayonet stud on
underside, walnut stock with brass fore-end band, patchbox and
buttplate, together with brass hilted saber bayonet.
(Butterfield & Butterfield) $6,050

A double barreled 12 bore percussion sporting gun by Marison
of Norwich, 44¹/₂in., twist barrels 28in. engraved *Norwich* with
gold line at breech, halfstocked, locks foliate engraved with
pheasants.
(Wallis & Wallis) $550

Scarce U.S. Model 1841 Jenks percussion navy rifle, the 30in. .54
caliber barrel marked at the breech *W. Jenks/U.S.N./RP/P/1844*,
lockplate marked *N.P Ames/Springfield/Mass*.
(Butterfield & Butterfield) $3,850

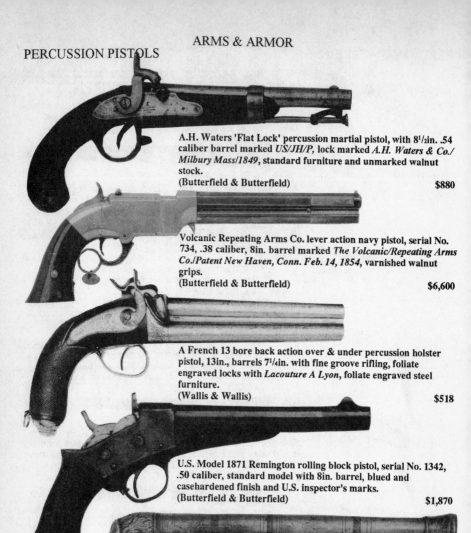

A.H. Waters 'Flat Lock' percussion martial pistol, with 8¹/₂in. .54 caliber barrel marked *US/JH/P*, lock marked *A.H. Waters & Co./ Milbury Mass/1849*, standard furniture and unmarked walnut stock.
(Butterfield & Butterfield)
$880

Volcanic Repeating Arms Co. lever action navy pistol, serial No. 734, .38 caliber, 8in. barrel marked *The Volcanic/Repeating Arms Co./Patent New Haven, Conn. Feb. 14, 1854*, varnished walnut grips.
(Butterfield & Butterfield)
$6,600

A French 13 bore back action over & under percussion holster pistol, 13in., barrels 7¹/₄in. with fine groove rifling, foliate engraved locks with *Lacouture A Lyon*, foliate engraved steel furniture.
(Wallis & Wallis)
$518

U.S. Model 1871 Remington rolling block pistol, serial No. 1342, .50 caliber, standard model with 8in. barrel, blued and casehardened finish and U.S. inspector's marks.
(Butterfield & Butterfield)
$1,870

A Day's Patent combined truncheon and percussion pistol, circa 1823, with brass turn-off cannon barrel decorated with bands of ornamental turning and stamped with initials *JR*, brass action decorated en suite, flush-fitting trigger, Birmingham proof marks, 15³/₄in.
(Christie's)
$2,898

A boxlock percussion traveling pistol fitted with spring bayonet converted from flintlock, 8in., turn off barrel 2¹/₂in., fitted with spring bayonet released by sliding trigger guard, frame engraved *H Nock London*.
(Wallis & Wallis)
$473

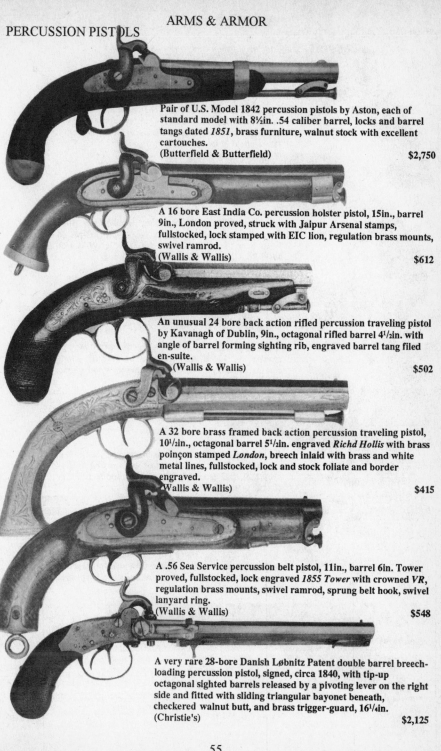

Pair of U.S. Model 1842 percussion pistols by Aston, each of standard model with 8½in. .54 caliber barrel, locks and barrel tangs dated *1851*, brass furniture, walnut stock with excellent cartouches.
(Butterfield & Butterfield) $2,750

A 16 bore East India Co. percussion holster pistol, 15in., barrel 9in., London proved, struck with Jaipur Arsenal stamps, fullstocked, lock stamped with EIC lion, regulation brass mounts, swivel ramrod.
(Wallis & Wallis) $612

An unusual 24 bore back action rifled percussion traveling pistol by Kavanagh of Dublin, 9in., octagonal rifled barrel 4¹/₂in. with angle of barrel forming sighting rib, engraved barrel tang filed en-suite.
     (Wallis & Wallis) $502

A 32 bore brass framed back action percussion traveling pistol, 10¹/₂in., octagonal barrel 5¹/₂in. engraved *Richd Hollis* with brass poinçon stamped *London*, breech inlaid with brass and white metal lines, fullstocked, lock and stock foliate and border engraved.
(Wallis & Wallis) $415

A .56 Sea Service percussion belt pistol, 11in., barrel 6in. Tower proved, fullstocked, lock engraved *1855 Tower* with crowned *VR*, regulation brass mounts, swivel ramrod, sprung belt hook, swivel lanyard ring.
(Wallis & Wallis) $548

A very rare 28-bore Danish Løbnitz Patent double barrel breech-loading percussion pistol, signed, circa 1840, with tip-up octagonal sighted barrels released by a pivoting lever on the right side and fitted with sliding triangular bayonet beneath, checkered walnut butt, and brass trigger-guard, 16¹/₄in.
(Christie's) $2,125

PERCUSSION REVOLVERS

U.S. Starr Arms Co. Model 1863 single action percussion revolver, serial No. 38347, .44 caliber, 8in. barrel, blue finish, walnut grips with government inspector's cartouches. (Butterfield & Butterfield) $1,540

A Holland & Holland '.45 caliber' Webley New Model Army Express double action revolver, No. 834, nickel-plated overall, 5¹/₂in. barrel engraved on top strap *HOLLAND & HOLLAND/98 NEW BOND STREET, LONDON,* **walnut grips. (Bonhams)** $729

A 5 shot .31in. Colt Rootes single action percussion pocket revolver No. 12458, 8in., octagonal barrel 3¹/₂in., underlever rammer, sheathed trigger, side hammer, wooden grip. (Wallis & Wallis) $474

Colt Model 1851 Navy percussion revolver, serial No. 128321 I, .36 caliber, 7½in. barrel marked *Address Col. Sam'l Colt New York U.S. America,* **blue finish, checkered ivory grips. (Butterfield & Butterfield)** $9,900

Elaborate engraved gold inlaid Colt Model 1895 Bisley revolver, serial No. 272278, .38–40 W.C.F., 7¹/₂in. barrel, engraved entirely with fine scrolls and decorated with gold inlaid scrolls and borders, hand checkered ejector and cylinder pin release. (Butterfield & Butterfield) $4,125

U.S. Colt single action army revolver, serial No. 96239, .45 caliber, 7½in. barrel, D.F.C. Inspector's marks, walnut grips. (Butterfield & Butterfield) $3,850

PERCUSSION REVOLVERS

U.S. Rogers & Spencer percussion army revolver, serial No. 3902, .44 caliber, blue finish, standard martially marked model.
(Butterfield & Butterfield) $1,430

A scarce 6 shot .455in. 'Webley Fosberry' semi automatic revolver, 11³/₄in. overall, barrel 7¹/₂in., number 3590, retailed by Wilkinson, Pall Mall, London, the frame stamped with winged bullet and .455 Cordite, 2 piece checkered walnut grips.
(Wallis & Wallis) $1,500

A 6 shot .36 Colt Navy single action percussion revolver No. 57811, 12¹/₂in., barrel 7¹/₂in. stamped *Address Saml Colt New York City*, underlever rammer, wooden grip.
(Wallis & Wallis) $1,660

A .44 Colt third Model Dragoon revolver, with six shot cylinder, 7¹/₂in. barrel, brass trigger guard and brass back strap.
(Bosley's) $2,869

A Leopold Gasser 11.4mm. 'Montenegrin' revolver, No. 170380, 9¹/₂in. round barrel with integral foresight and blade rearsight insert on reinforce, stamped with patent details and *GUSS STAHL*, rod ejector to right with brass head, retained by a spring-loaded locking screw.
(Bonhams) $226

Colt single action army revolver, serial No. 345565, .32 caliber 7¹/₂in. barrel, blued finish, custom carved ivory grips.
(Butterfield & Butterfield) $2,200

PERCUSSION REVOLVERS

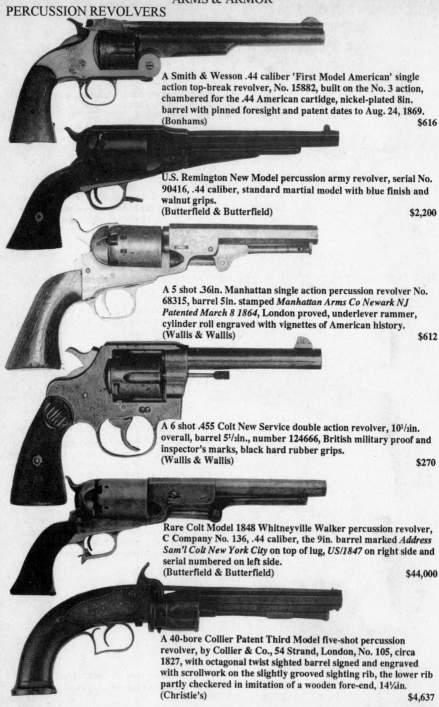

A Smith & Wesson .44 caliber 'First Model American' single action top-break revolver, No. 15882, built on the No. 3 action, chambered for the .44 American cartidge, nickel-plated 8in. barrel with pinned foresight and patent dates to Aug. 24, 1869.
(Bonhams) $616

U.S. Remington New Model percussion army revolver, serial No. 90416, .44 caliber, standard martial model with blue finish and walnut grips.
(Butterfield & Butterfield) $2,200

A 5 shot .36in. Manhattan single action percussion revolver No. 68315, barrel 5in. stamped *Manhattan Arms Co Newark NJ Patented March 8 1864*, London proved, underlever rammer, cylinder roll engraved with vignettes of American history.
(Wallis & Wallis) $612

A 6 shot .455 Colt New Service double action revolver, 10¹/₂in. overall, barrel 5¹/₂in., number 124666, British military proof and inspector's marks, black hard rubber grips.
(Wallis & Wallis) $270

Rare Colt Model 1848 Whitneyville Walker percussion revolver, C Company No. 136, .44 caliber, the 9in. barrel marked *Address Sam'l Colt New York City* on top of lug, *US/1847* on right side and serial numbered on left side.
(Butterfield & Butterfield) $44,000

A 40-bore Collier Patent Third Model five-shot percussion revolver, by Collier & Co., 54 Strand, London, No. 105, circa 1827, with octagonal twist sighted barrel signed and engraved with scrollwork on the slightly grooved sighting rib, the lower rib partly checkered in imitation of a wooden fore-end, 14¹/₄in.
(Christie's) $4,637

PERCUSSION REVOLVERS

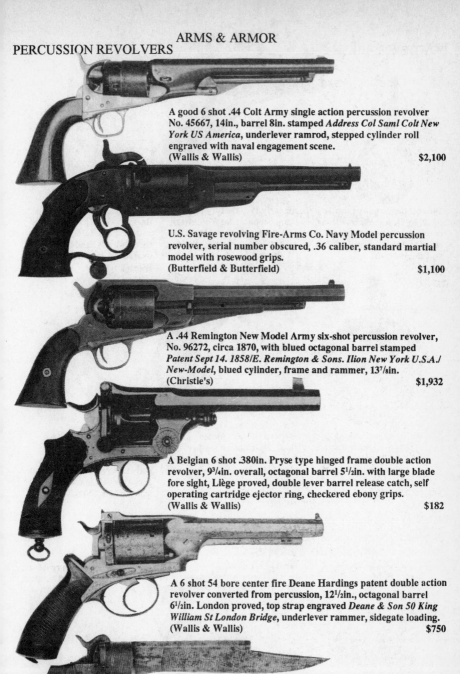

A good 6 shot .44 Colt Army single action percussion revolver No. 45667, 14in., barrel 8in. stamped *Address Col Saml Colt New York US America*, underlever ramrod, stepped cylinder roll engraved with naval engagement scene.
(Wallis & Wallis) $2,100

U.S. Savage revolving Fire-Arms Co. Navy Model percussion revolver, serial number obscured, .36 caliber, standard martial model with rosewood grips.
(Butterfield & Butterfield) $1,100

A .44 Remington New Model Army six-shot percussion revolver, No. 96272, circa 1870, with blued octagonal barrel stamped *Patent Sept 14. 1858/E. Remington & Sons. Ilion New York U.S.A./ New-Model*, blued cylinder, frame and rammer, $13^7/\mathrm{8}$in.
(Christie's) $1,932

A Belgian 6 shot .380in. Pryse type hinged frame double action revolver, $9^3/\mathrm{4}$in. overall, octagonal barrel $5^1/\mathrm{2}$in. with large blade fore sight, Liège proved, double lever barrel release catch, self operating cartridge ejector ring, checkered ebony grips.
(Wallis & Wallis) $182

A 6 shot 54 bore center fire Deane Hardings patent double action revolver converted from percussion, $12^1/\mathrm{2}$in., octagonal barrel $6^1/\mathrm{2}$in. London proved, top strap engraved *Deane & Son 50 King William St London Bridge*, underlever rammer, sidegate loading.
(Wallis & Wallis) $750

A 120-bore Dumonthier Patent six-shot combined pin-fire revolver and dagger, circa 1870, the blade etched on each side with a trophy of arms, the cylinder engraved with scrollwork and grotesque masks, scroll engraved butt-cap and trigger-guard, $14^1/\mathrm{2}$in.
(Christie's) $1,835

POWDER FLASKS

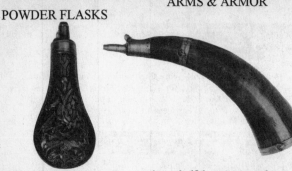

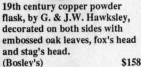

19th century copper powder flask, by G. & J.W. Hawksley, decorated on both sides with embossed oak leaves, fox's head and stag's head.
(Bosley's) $158

An early 19th century powder horn, probably for Volunteers, 13¹/₂in. overall, turned brass mounts with 2 hanging rings.
(Wallis & Wallis) $198

19th century copper powder flask, by G. & J.W. Hawksley, with embossed decoration of three horse's heads, within an oval floral decorated frame.
(Bosley's) $237

A German inlaid priming flask, circa 1580–1600, with wooden body of hemispherical section, the inner face inlaid with a circular pattern of engraved horn foliage, 11.1cm.
(Sotheby's) $3,450

An early 19th century Cossack nielloed silver mounted powder flask, 7³/₄in., black leather covered ivory end cap, foliate chiseled nielloed silver mounts, brass charger lever and suspension loops.
(Wallis & Wallis) $520

A Saxon 'Musketeer's' priming-flask, late 16th century, of triangular form, the wooden body covered with black leather and with well-made blackened iron mounts, 5¹/₂in. high.
(Christie's) $1,835

A Tyrolean large engraved bone powder-flask, 19th century, with wooden body applied with large triangular bone sides, bone top with turned nozzle, 20¹/₂in.
(Sotheby's) $2,875

A French carved ivory powder-flask, Dieppe School, mid-19th century, with slightly curved body carved in relief with a large and continuous design of mythological and exotic beasts, 10in.
(Sotheby's) $1,150

A fine and rare German ivory priming-flask incorporating a compass and sun-dial, late 17th century, with plain flat-sided circular body, 9.8cm.
(Sotheby's) $4,887

POWDER FLASKS

A good quality gun size powder flask, 8in. overall, the patent German silver top by James Dixon, charger from 2¼ to 3 drams, the body covered with woven basketwork.
(Wallis & Wallis) $145

A Black Forest staghorn powder-flask, and a Black Forest staghorn box, each mid-19th century, the first with natural horn body finely carved in cameo on the outer face, 7½in. and 5½in.
(Christie's) $3,671

A fine Italian carved boxwood priming-flask, mid-17th century, probably Tusco-Emilian, with circular body formed with recessed flat sides carved in low relief, 4³/8in.
(Sotheby's) $2,300

An important Spanish gold-damascened iron priming-flask made for the Farnese family, Dukes of Parma and Piacenza, late 16th century, originally blued and now oxidized to russet, 3³/8in.
(Sotheby's) $20,700

A German carved ivory priming-flask, late 17th/early 18th century, formed from a short tusk, with curved body decorated over its full surface with an interlaced pattern of scrolling foliage terminating in a monster's head, 6½in.
(Sotheby's) $1,495

A good quality gun size powder flask, overall 8½in., German silver charger unit marked *Extra Quality Sykes Patent*, graduation from 4–5 drams, the body covered with woven basketwork.
(Wallis & Wallis) $266

A French carved ivory powder-flask, Dieppe School, mid-19th century, finely carved in high relief, both sides decorated with a woodland vignette, 20cm.
(Sotheby's) $2,070

A gunner's cowhorn powder horn, 13³/4in. overall, brass nozzle with sprung lever charger, 2 brass hanging rings, wooden base plug with screw in stopper.
(Wallis & Wallis) $144

An East European inlaid wooden powder-flask, circa 1720–30, probably Bohemian or Polish, with large flat-sided circular rootwood body, 6³/4in.
(Sotheby's) $1,955

SWORDS

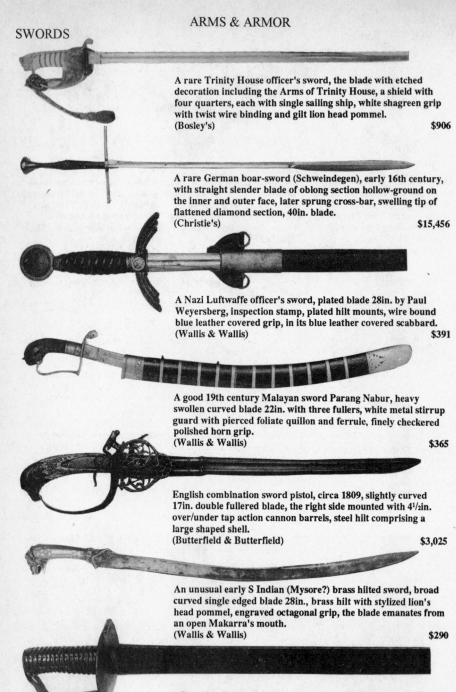

A rare Trinity House officer's sword, the blade with etched decoration including the Arms of Trinity House, a shield with four quarters, each with single sailing ship, white shagreen grip with twist wire binding and gilt lion head pommel.
(Bosley's) **$906**

A rare German boar-sword (Schweindegen), early 16th century, with straight slender blade of oblong section hollow-ground on the inner and outer face, later sprung cross-bar, swelling tip of flattened diamond section, 40in. blade.
(Christie's) **$15,456**

A Nazi Luftwaffe officer's sword, plated blade 28in. by Paul Weyersberg, inspection stamp, plated hilt mounts, wire bound blue leather covered grip, in its blue leather covered scabbard.
(Wallis & Wallis) **$391**

A good 19th century Malayan sword Parang Nabur, heavy swollen curved blade 22in. with three fullers, white metal stirrup guard with pierced foliate quillon and ferrule, finely checkered polished horn grip.
(Wallis & Wallis) **$365**

English combination sword pistol, circa 1809, slightly curved 17in. double fullered blade, the right side mounted with 4¹/₂in. over/under tap action cannon barrels, steel hilt comprising a large shaped shell.
(Butterfield & Butterfield) **$3,025**

An unusual early S Indian (Mysore?) brass hilted sword, broad curved single edged blade 28in., brass hilt with stylized lion's head pommel, engraved octagonal grip, the blade emanates from an open Makarra's mouth.
(Wallis & Wallis) **$290**

A Georgian figure of eight naval cutlass, blade 29¹/₂in. stamped crown *GR*, sheet iron guard, black painted ribbed iron grip.
(Wallis & Wallis) **$286**

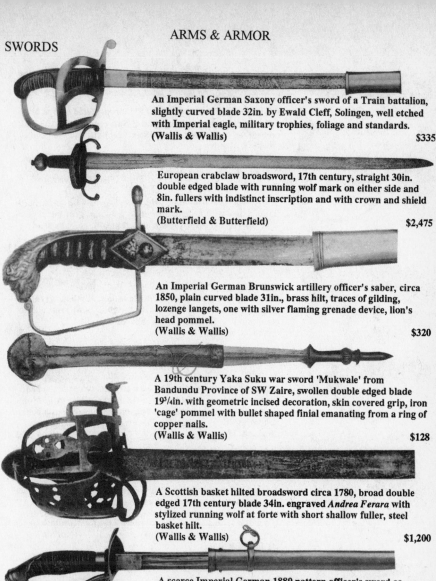

An Imperial German Saxony officer's sword of a Train battalion, slightly curved blade 32in. by Ewald Cleff, Solingen, well etched with Imperial eagle, military trophies, foliage and standards.
(Wallis & Wallis) $335

European crabclaw broadsword, 17th century, straight 30in. double edged blade with running wolf mark on either side and 8in. fullers with indistinct inscription and with crown and shield mark.
(Butterfield & Butterfield) $2,475

An Imperial German Brunswick artillery officer's saber, circa 1850, plain curved blade 31in., brass hilt, traces of gilding, lozenge langets, one with silver flaming grenade device, lion's head pommel.
(Wallis & Wallis) $320

A 19th century Yaka Suku war sword 'Mukwale' from Bandundu Province of SW Zaire, swollen double edged blade 19³/₄in. with geometric incised decoration, skin covered grip, iron 'cage' pommel with bullet shaped finial emanating from a ring of copper nails.
(Wallis & Wallis) $128

A Scottish basket hilted broadsword circa 1780, broad double edged 17th century blade 34in. engraved *Andrea Ferara* with stylized running wolf at forte with short shallow fuller, steel basket hilt.
(Wallis & Wallis) $1,200

A scarce Imperial German 1889 pattern officer's sword as carried by Colonial troops, double fullered plain blade 34in., stamped at forte with crown Erfurt by P.D. Luneschloss, gilt hilt with crowned Hohenzollern eagle in guard, stamped beneath guard *I O J R 8 1*.
(Wallis & Wallis) $701

A George V RAF sword of an officer of Air Rank, blade 31¹/₂in., some original polish, etched with Royal Arms, RAF eagle, blank scrolls, and foliage, brass hilt, eagle head pommel, wire bound white fishskin covered grip.
(Wallis & Wallis) $550

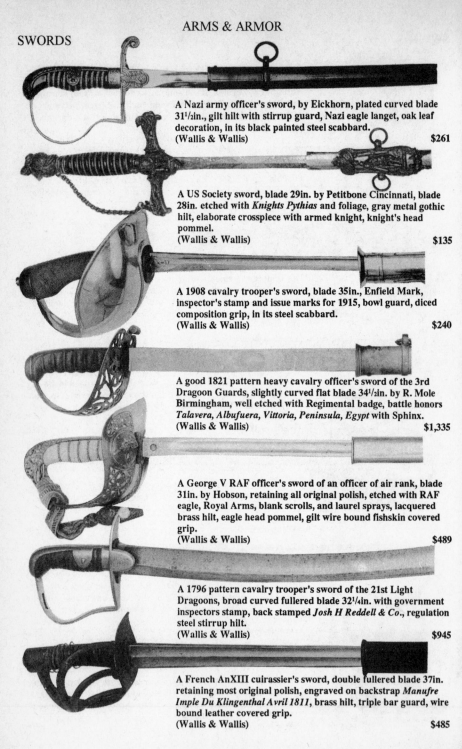

A Nazi army officer's sword, by Eickhorn, plated curved blade 31¹/₂in., gilt hilt with stirrup guard, Nazi eagle langet, oak leaf decoration, in its black painted steel scabbard.
(Wallis & Wallis) $261

A US Society sword, blade 29in. by Petitbone Cincinnati, blade 28in. etched with *Knights Pythias* and foliage, gray metal gothic hilt, elaborate crosspiece with armed knight, knight's head pommel.
(Wallis & Wallis) $135

A 1908 cavalry trooper's sword, blade 35in., Enfield Mark, inspector's stamp and issue marks for 1915, bowl guard, diced composition grip, in its steel scabbard.
(Wallis & Wallis) $240

A good 1821 pattern heavy cavalry officer's sword of the 3rd Dragoon Guards, slightly curved flat blade 34¹/₂in. by R. Mole Birmingham, well etched with Regimental badge, battle honors *Talavera, Albufuera, Vittoria, Peninsula, Egypt* with Sphinx.
(Wallis & Wallis) $1,335

A George V RAF officer's sword of an officer of air rank, blade 31in. by Hobson, retaining all original polish, etched with RAF eagle, Royal Arms, blank scrolls, and laurel sprays, lacquered brass hilt, eagle head pommel, gilt wire bound fishskin covered grip.
(Wallis & Wallis) $489

A 1796 pattern cavalry trooper's sword of the 21st Light Dragoons, broad curved fullered blade 32¹/₄in. with government inspectors stamp, back stamped *Josh H Reddell & Co.*, regulation steel stirrup hilt.
(Wallis & Wallis) $945

A French AnXIII cuirassier's sword, double fullered blade 37in. retaining most original polish, engraved on backstrap *Manufre Imple Du Klingenthal Avril 1811*, brass hilt, triple bar guard, wire bound leather covered grip.
(Wallis & Wallis) $485

A WWII Italian naval flag officer's sword, slim blade 33in. by 'Dani Ivorno', etched with arms of Savoy, fouled anchor, Italian eagle, military trophies and foliage, brass hilt with crown. (Wallis & Wallis) $214

A French Model 1854 cuirassier sword, double fullered blade 38in., spear point, backstrap engraved *Mre Imple De Chat Mai 1859*, brass hilt with triple bar guard, wire bound leather covered grip.
(Wallis & Wallis) $398

An 1889 Prussian infantry officer's sword, plain, straight double fullered blade 32in., gilt brass hilt, wire bound fish skin covered grip with crowned WR II cypher in its chromed scabbard. (Wallis & Wallis) $212

A French 1822 heavy cavalry trooper's sabre, plain, slightly curved blade 38in., retaining all original polish, engraved on backstrap *Manufre Role de Klingenthal Juin 1827*, brass hilt, triple bar guard, ribbed leather covered grip. (Wallis & Wallis) $180

A scarce Imperial German 1889 pattern cavalry trooper's sword, (as carried by German cavalry stationed in China), pipe back clipped backed blade 32in., trace of maker (E&F Horster), and sharpened for service use, steel basket guard with Chinese dragon to cartouche. (Wallis & Wallis) $290

A rare English 'Mortuary' smallsword circa 1650–60, slender diamond section blade 31½in. deeply struck in the fullers *Sahagum*, underside of shellguards deeply chiselled with two stylised human bust portraits amidst foliage. (Wallis & Wallis) $1,060

A scarce 1912 pattern George V cavalry officer's sword of the type carried by the 10th Hussars, blade 35in., by Henry Wilkinson, Pall Mall (no. 53981), etched with *X Royal Hussars* Regimental badges, Royal Arms and cypher, foliage and initials *HPC*. (Wallis & Wallis) $520

ARMS & ARMOR

TSUBAS

Kinai School iron shin no maru-gata tsuba, with sukashi leaf and flower design, 17th/18th century, 2½in. diameter.
(Eldred's) $132

A shakudo iroe zogan tsuba, signed *Edo ju Shozui*, 19th century, the irregular plate formed as a sack of Hotei carved in takabori, 6.9cm.
(Christie's) $2,475

Iron mokko form tsuba, with relief depiction of a dragon with gleaming golden eyes, 3¼in. long.
(Eldred's) $275

A silver Inabanosuke tsuba, signed *Yoshioka Inabanosuke*, 18th century, the silver nanako plate of irregular oak leaf shape, carved and pierced to resemble a butterfly, 6.5cm.
(Christie's) $11,385

A large iron tsuba, signed *Togakushi Ishiguro Koretsune sen*, 19th century, carved in relief and decorated with a galloping tiger, 9.8cm.
(Christie's) $5,300

A circular iron nanako tsuba with cloisonné decoration, signed *Yoshitoshi* and *Kao*, 19th century, the thick plate decorated with shells and fish in shippo inlay and gold wire, 8cm.
(Christie's) $2,850

A circular iron yoshiro style tsuba, 18th/19th century, pierced in cloud patterns and decorated with a snowflake design, 8.7cm.
(Christie's) $1,155

A large oval copper tsuba, signed *Kitokuan Kogetsu*, late 19th century, carved in relief with Benzaiten trying to read a document, 9.4cm.
(Christie's) $2,275

A large iron tsuba with Omori style decoration, 19th century, the thick iron plate boldly decorated with a peony and a karashishi, Mito school, 8.1cm.
(Christie's) $1,140

TSUBAS

A 19th century Japanese tsuba with flower head decoration with gilt highlighting, to the center a five character signature.
(Bosley's) $205

A shakudo nanako Ishiguro Masatsune tsuba, 19th century, the oval plate decorated with a rusu moyo of Fukujin with iroe takazogan of crane, 7.3cm.
(Christie's) $2,475

An oval Shakudo tsuba by Muneyoshi, 19th century, decorated with ho-o sennin, the reverse with a waterfall, 6.5cm.
(Christie's) $2,850

A large rounded-square copper tsuba, signed *Hamano Noriyuki,* late 19th century, the mottled plate decorated with Emma-o and oni, 9.7cm.
(Christie's) $3,300

A rounded square iron jakushi tsuba, late 18th century, carved in relief and decorated with gold and silver nunome zogan with sages in a mountain, 8.5cm.
(Christie's) $1,000

An octagonal iron Momotaro tsuba, signed *Kazuhiro Saku,* 19th century, the front plate decorated with Momotaro and his attendants, 9.5cm.
(Christie's) $4,125

An iron mokkogata tsuba by Morikazu, 19th century, signed, carved and decorated in iron takazogan with geese and clouds, 8.4cm.
(Christie's) $1,330

A circular iron Heianjo zogan monsukashi tsuba, 17th century, the plate pierced and decorated in brass Heianjo zogan with mon, 8.3cm.
(Christie's) $4,950

A large iron tsuba with shibuichi takazogan, signed *Toshiyoshi,* 19th century, decorated with Wasobei, frowning at a figure in his hand, 8.8cm.
(Christie's) $1,900

ARMS & ARMOR

Lancashire Hussar officer's uniform, of the pattern worn by an officer of the regiment circa 1860, the jacket of dark blue cloth.
(Bosley's) $1,510

Irish Guards officer's scarlet tunic, post 1902 example, with dark blue facings to the cuff and collar, to each epaulette, three Order of St. Patrick rank stars.
(Bosley's) $393

A General's full dress scarlet tunic, blue facings, gilt lace trim, shoulder cords with crown/star/crossed baton and star, good gilt buttons.
(Wallis & Wallis) $136

QAIMNS, a rare nurse's uniform, epaulettes with metal rank stars denoting Lt., medal ribbons 1939/45 Star, Africa Star, Italy Star, Defence Medal and War Medal.
(Bosley's) $181

9th (Queen's Royal Light Dragoons) officer's tunic, mid 19th century 1856 pattern tunic, dark blue melton cloth, with regimental scarlet facings to the cuffs and collar.
(Bosley's) $636

17th Lancer's scarce trooper's uniform, Edwardian other rank's lance cap, tunic of dark blue woollen cloth with white plastron front, overalls plus breeches of regimental pattern.
(Bosley's) $1,854

A good ERII officer's full dress scarlet tunic of the Welsh Guards, blue facings, heavy gilt embroidered trim to collar, cuffs and skirts, embroidered leek collar badges.
(Wallis & Wallis) $456

Civil War uniform jacket of Elisha Hunt Rhodes, navy blue wool with quilt lining and brass buttons with tag inscribed.
(Skinner) $14,950

A post 1902 Major's full dress scarlet doublet of The King's Own Scottish Borderers, blue facings, gilt lace and braid trim including 3 loops and buttons to cuffs.
(Wallis & Wallis) $350

A late Victorian Major's full dress blue tunic of the Yorkshire Dragoons, white facings, silver lace and braid trim including heavy cuff and collar ornaments.
(Wallis & Wallis) $760

4th (Royal Irish) Dragoon Guards frock coat, post 1902 officer's example of dark blue melton cloth, double breasted, breast medal ribbons of 1911 Coronation, Queen's and King's South Africa medals.
(Bosley's) $264

A good Captain's full dress blue tunic of The Royal Marines band, scarlet collar with embroidered collar badges, solid centres, incorporating a small lyre at the top of the wreath.
(Wallis & Wallis) $220

ARMS & ARMOR

29th Indian Lancers (Deccan Horse) officer's tunic, post 1902 pattern tunic, dark blue melton cloth with white facings to the cuffs, collar and plastron front. (Bosley's) $1,661

A Nazi cavalry officer's full dress tunic, yellow backing to collar patches, epaulettes and cuff bars, dark green collar and Brandenburg cuffs. (Wallis & Wallis) $76

7th Dragoon Guards officer's mess jacket, scarlet melton cloth of stable jacket form, dark blue velvet facings to the cuff and collar. (Bosley's) $604

A Wachtmeister's parade tunic, of the 126 Pioneer unit, with black piping to the collar, cuffs and epaulettes, to the right cuff arm badge of Schirrmeister (motor transport NCO). (Bosley's) $408

A rare Nazi Kriegsmarine U Boat officer's ¾ length gray double breasted leather jacket, complete with grey buttons with anchor devices together with companion matching gray leather overalls. (Wallis & Wallis) $785

Royal Artillery post 1902 officer's dress uniform, full Colonel's example, the tunic of dark blue melton cloth with field rank gold bullion decoration to the cuffs. (Bosley's) $509

UNIFORMS

11th PAO Hussars officer's Astrakhan, last pattern of patrol jacket of dark blue melton cloth, to each cuff dark blue mohair lace and astrakhan wool.
(Bosley's) $2,114

A scarce Major's full dress scarlet tunic, circa 1902, of the Lothians and Berwick Imperial Yeomanry, blue facings, gilt lace and braid trim, pair associated overalls.
(Wallis & Wallis) $282

Life Guards officer's uniform, scarlet tunic, with blue velvet facings to the cuff and collar, each with gold bullion embroidery.
(Bosley's) $716

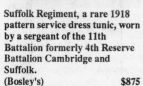

Suffolk Regiment, a rare 1918 pattern service dress tunic, worn by a sergeant of the 11th Battalion formerly 4th Reserve Battalion Cambridge and Suffolk.
(Bosley's) $875

German General Staff Hauptmann's tunic, four pocket example of army green cloth with provision for medal bar and awards to the left breast and pocket.
(Bosley's) $365

A good ERII bandsman's full dress scarlet tunic of the Coldstream Guards, blue facings, embroidered shoulder strap badges, blue fleur de lys white lace trim.
(Wallis & Wallis) $261

ARMS & ARMOR

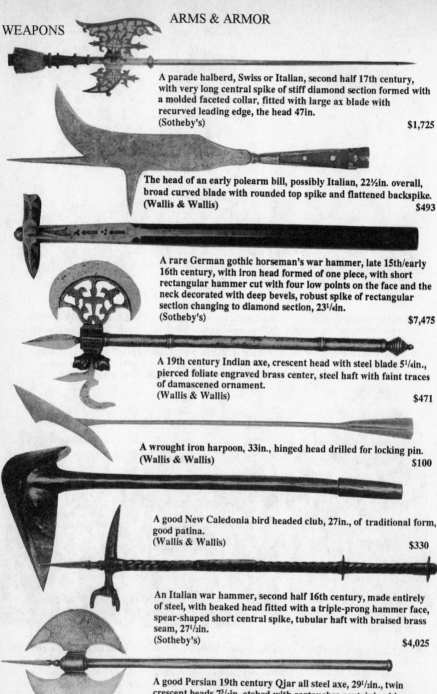

A parade halberd, Swiss or Italian, second half 17th century, with very long central spike of stiff diamond section formed with a molded faceted collar, fitted with large ax blade with recurved leading edge, the head 47in.
(Sotheby's) $1,725

The head of an early polearm bill, possibly Italian, 22½in. overall, broad curved blade with rounded top spike and flattened backspike.
(Wallis & Wallis) $493

A rare German gothic horseman's war hammer, late 15th/early 16th century, with iron head formed of one piece, with short rectangular hammer cut with four low points on the face and the neck decorated with deep bevels, robust spike of rectangular section changing to diamond section, 23¼in.
(Sotheby's) $7,475

A 19th century Indian axe, crescent head with steel blade 5¼in., pierced foliate engraved brass center, steel haft with faint traces of damascened ornament.
(Wallis & Wallis) $471

A wrought iron harpoon, 33in., hinged head drilled for locking pin.
(Wallis & Wallis) $100

A good New Caledonia bird headed club, 27in., of traditional form, good patina.
(Wallis & Wallis) $330

An Italian war hammer, second half 16th century, made entirely of steel, with beaked head fitted with a triple-prong hammer face, spear-shaped short central spike, tubular haft with braised brass seam, 27½in.
(Sotheby's) $4,025

A good Persian 19th century Qjar all steel axe, 29½in., twin crescent heads 7¾in. etched with cartouches containing kings, flowers and foliage, the rest silver damascened with arabesques.
(Wallis & Wallis) $518

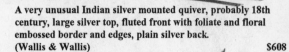

A very unusual Indian silver mounted quiver, probably 18th century, large silver top, fluted front with foliate and floral embossed border and edges, plain silver back.
(Wallis & Wallis) $608

A Saxon miner's Guild ax, dated *1681*, with iron head of characteristic type pierced with small circles and a slipped-circle, and with the point rising to a brass acorn finial, 35in.
(Sotheby's) $2,415

An Italian military forked spear, circa 1530–50, with long tapering blade and a pair of curved basal prongs each of flattened diamond section, on a later octagonal wooden haft, the head 29¼in.
(Sotheby's) $1,495

An early Malayan sword Parang Ginah, 24½in., elongated sickle shaped blade 17in., turned hardwood hilt, rounded forte, baluster flared pommel with turned button and silk tassel.
(Wallis & Wallis) $282

An unusual triple bladed polearm Chauves-Souris, head 20½in. with central rib and scrolled edges, integral socket, side straps retained by wrought rings.
(Wallis & Wallis)   £1,245

A Turkish horseman's early 19th century war hammer, 24¾in., thick square section steel head with chamfered corners, on its wooden haft with octagonal ferrule and grip.
(Wallis & Wallis) $188

A Zande war sword Konda from the Uelle region of NE Zaire circa 1900, curved ribbed blade 27in., copper wound wooden hilt.
(Wallis & Wallis) $66

A very rare Turkish or Polish war-hammer, 17th century, the iron head comprising a hammer-head of rectangular section balanced by a long fluted downcurved beak-shaped fluke, decorated overall with narrow engraved bands of wrigglework and circles of radiating lines, 27⅝in. (Christie's) $4,250

Josef Goebbels, signed sepia postcard, Hoffman No. 74.
(T. Vennett-Smith) $992

Maria Callas, signed card, 4 x 3.5, 1973.
(T. Vennett-Smith) $275

Al Jolson, signed and inscribed, 4½ x 6in., head and shoulders.
(T. Vennett-Smith) $115

Eva Peron, a scarce signed and inscribed sepia 7 x 9in., showing her head and shoulders in profile in hat.
(T. Vennett-Smith) $1,680

Harry Houdini, a scarce hardback edition of Index of Quotations, edition by J.C. Grocott, signed to title page in pencil by Houdini, with personal *ex libris Houdini* bookplate.
(T. Vennett-Smith) $1,200

Enrico Caruso, signed postcard three quarter length in bowler hat, also with facsimile signature, hand-addressed by Caruso.
(T. Vennett-Smith) $368

Yitzhak Rabin, signed color 5 x 7in., head and shoulders, with map in background.
(T. Vennett-Smith) $160

Charles and Diana Christmas greetings card, with colored 4 x 5½in. photo showing them sitting with the two Princes.
(T. Vennett-Smith) $992

Florenz Ziegfeld, a rare signed 8 x 10in., showing him three quarter length seated at desk.
(T. Vennett-Smith) $656

Irving Berlin, signed 4 x 6in., in military uniform.
(T. Vennett-Smith) $336

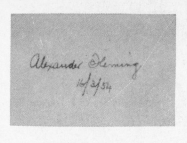

Alexander Fleming, signed card, 3.5 x 2.5, 16th March 1954.
(T. Vennett-Smith) $153

Mountbatten of Burma, signed 6½ x 8½in., head and shoulders.
(T. Vennett-Smith) $224

Harry Houdini, autograph signed note, *'March 28-04 house breaking and jailbreaking once travelled together I have chosen the latter and am doing well thank you Harry Houdini'*.
(T. Vennett-Smith) $1,216

Haile Selassie, Emperor of Ethiopia, signed 8 x 10in., head and shoulders in ceremonial uniform.
(T. Vennett-Smith) $304

Ronald Reagan, typed, signed letter as President, one page, 11th December 1984, to Samuel L. Devine, thanking him for his letter of congratulations.
(T. Vennett-Smith) $416

Glen Miller, signed and inscribed 5 x 7in., half-length playing trombone.
(T. Vennett-Smith) $288

Winston S. Churchill, typed, signed letter, one page, 14th June 1955, to Christina Foyle, declining an invitation to a luncheon for Manny Shinwell.
(T. Vennett-Smith) $640

Jerome Kern, signed and inscribed art style, head and shoulders, Beverly Hills, 1944.
(T. Vennett-Smith) $336

Theodore Roosevelt, signed postcard, published 1912.
(Vennett Smith) $350

Grace Kelly, signed card as Princess, 5.5 x 3.5.
(T. Vennett-Smith) $74

Yitzhak Rabin, signed color photograph, 7x9in.
(Vennett Smith) $63

W. Somerset Maugham, signed 6½x4½in. reproduction of painting, with autograph signed letter of Ingrid Bergman.
(Vennett Smith) $210

Arthur Conan Doyle, autograph, signed letter, one page, no date, requesting seating arrangements, with pencil sketch by Ollier at head.
(T. Vennett-Smith) $432

Adolf Hitler, sepia postcard, signed in pencil, written on verso in another hand *Garmisch Partenkirchen Olympiade 1936.*
(Vennett Smith) $1,600

Louis Armstrong, signed theater program page, also signed by Velma Middleton, 8½x12.
(Vennett Smith) $103

Franklin D. Roosevelt, signed envelope August 1931, with photocopy of original letter to Mr A.B. Rams.
(T. Vennett-Smith) $99

Marie Curie, small signed piece, 2.5x.75, overmounted in brown beneath photograph.
(Vennett Smith) $638

Virginia Woolf, signed piece, 2½x1, overmounted beneath reproduction photograph. (Vennett Smith) $212

Pablo Picasso, autograph signed note on postcard in French sending greetings, 1917. (T. Vennett-Smith) $726

General Franco, signed postcard, 25 September 1958, head and shoulders, in uniform. (Vennett Smith) $197

Winston S. Churchill, signed letter, two pages, 12th January 1904, to A. Wilkinson, declining an invitation to be President of the Young Britons Society. (T. Vennett-Smith) $1.320

John F. Kennedy, a good signed inscribed 11x14 photograph, apparently signed during Kennedy's visit to Germany. (Vennett Smith) $2,000

Charles Dickens, autograph signed letter, one page, 20 July 1859, asking to give the bearer a copy of Carlyle's *French Revolution*. (Vennett Smith) $577

Muhammed Ali, signed color 8x10 photograph, three quarter length in ring. (Vennett Smith) $130

A signed colour 11 x 8½ by Richard Nixon, Gerald Ford, Jummy Carter, George Bush and Ronald Reagan individually. (Vennett Smith) $1,350

Jacqueline Kennedy, signed and inscribed 8x10, head and shoulders, looking to one side. (Vennett Smith) $410

Ian Fleming, paperback edition of Dr. No, 7th printing by Pan 1962, signed to title page. (T. Vennett-Smith) $800

Leo Tolstoy, signed color postcard to reverse, with address and annotations in another hand. (T. Vennett-Smith) $643

Cole Porter, a rare signed and inscribed 5 x 7in. photo by Phyfe, head and shoulders. (T. Vennett-Smith) $544

Prince Charles and Princess Diana, a rare signed color 8 x 11in. to mount, 1983, showing the Prince and Princess with baby Prince William, previously given to a New Zealand politician. (T. Vennett-Smith) $1,952

Abraham Lincoln, a fine signed document, appointing William Cuddy of Missouri, to be Surveyor General for Illinois and Missouri, dated 17th July 1861 and signed by both. (T. Vennett-Smith) $3,680

Jacqueline Kennedy, a hardback First Edition of the Burden and the Glory, by John F. Kennedy, signed and inscribed by Jacqueline Kennedy '*For Prime Minister Wilson with respect and good wishes*', dated January 1967. (T. Vennett-Smith) $1,331

Rocky Marciano, signed clipped piece, 3 x 1¼in. with his address, laid down to album page, beneath magazine photo. (T. Vennett-Smith) $80

Charles De Gaulle, autograph note signed on personal card, 3.5 x 2.75. (T. Vennett-Smith) $275

Muhammed Ali, signed front cover to Sports Illustrated, October 1977, address tag to cover. (Vennett Smith) $145

Mikhail Gorbachev, hardback edition of Memoirs, signed by both him and Raisa to title page.
(T. Vennett-Smith) $272

Pablo Picasso, signed reverse of a 6 x 4 postcard, featuring illustration of *'The Old Jew'*, dated by Picasso 18.11.64.
(T. Vennett-Smith) $1,350

Robert Graves, signed 7 x 10in., half-length wearing hat in old age.
(T. Vennett-Smith) $184

Ernest Shackleton, signed sepia photograph showing him on board the Nimrod, together with two unsigned snapshots on board.
(T. Vennett-Smith) $352

Colour 10x7 photograph signed by Margaret Thatcher, Jimmy and Rosalynn Carter, half-length standing at presidential podium.
(Vennett Smith) $197

Marty Feldman, signed and inscribed album page, with two doodles, 5 x 3in., double mounted in brown and mottled cream beneath sepia photo, 13 x 21.(T. Vennett-Smith) $93

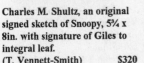

Charles M. Shultz, an original signed sketch of Snoopy, 5¾ x 8in. with signature of Giles to integral leaf.
(T. Vennett-Smith) $320

Duke and Duchess of Windsor, signed 5.5 x 3.5, monogrammed card, by both Edward and Wallis, op, 1976.
(T. Vennett-Smith) $166

Josephine Baker, early 8 x 10in., full-length kneeling in satin evening dress with tiger's head, unsigned.
(T. Vennett-Smith) $72

Amy Johnson, signed sepia postcard, head and shoulders in flying goggles.
(T. Vennett-Smith) $122

Gustav Mahler, signed document in German, filled in with pen, 28th April 1899.
(T. Vennett-Smith) $979

Josephine Baker, signed postcard, full-length in satin evening dress, 1933.
(T. Vennett-Smith) $291

Juan Peron, typed signed letter, one page, Buenos Aires, 3rd November 1950, to the ambassador of France, Hector Madero, on official stationery.
(T. Vennett-Smith) $99

Albert Schweitzer, signed and inscribed hardback edition, 'The World of Albert Schweitzer', to half title page, signed beneath full portrait.
(T. Vennett-Smith) $214

Mahatma K. Gandhi, signed album page, 6 x 7, 2nd November 1931, also signed by two other people, dated in another hand.
(T. Vennett-Smith) $421

Field Marshal Montgomery, signed 6 x 8 'Montgomery of Alamein' three-quarter length standing by a car in later years.
(T. Vennett-Smith) $99

W. F. Cody, autograph signed letter, 30th May 1908, on Buffalo Bill's Wild West headed notepaper.
(T. Vennett-Smith) $765

David Hockney, signed color 5 x 7, head and shoulders with hand on chin, with painting in background.
(T. Vennett-Smith) $69

Winston S. Churchill, 3 x 3.5, signed to mount, laid down to card, 4 x 6 overall. (T. Vennett-Smith) $1,023

Mark Twain, signed piece, 4.5 x 3.5, 14th July 1896, laid down to slightly larger album page. (T. Vennett-Smith) $490

Yasser Arafat, signed color 5 x 7, together with letter from secretary. (T. Vennett-Smith) $132

Alfred, Lord Tennyson, autograph signed letter, one page, 26th May n.y. (1872), on personal stationery, routine content. (T. Vennett-Smith) $182

Edward VIII, signed 4.5 x 6.5 to mount, as Prince, 1920, head and shoulders in navy uniform, photo by Dan Dyk, 7.5 x 10.5 overall. (T. Vennett-Smith) $280

Walt Disney Studios, two album pages, 7 x 4, with original sketches of Mickey Mouse and Donald Duck, both by Jesse Loynes. (T. Vennett-Smith) $260

Mother Teresa, signed 7 x 10, half-length, praying at Congress Philadelphia 1976, reproduction signed in recent years. (T. Vennett-Smith) $190

Harry Houdini, signed piece, *'Harry Handcuff Houdini'*, 20th May 1911, Finsbury Empire, 3.5 x 4. (T. Vennett-Smith) $1,010

Mikhail Gorbachev, signed colored 8 x 10, head and shoulders, speaking into microphone. (T. Vennett-Smith) $264

A Gustave Vichy 'Le cuisinier' musical automaton, French, circa 1885, the standing figure with papier-mâché head, brown glass eyes, brown real hair wig and beard, 29in.
(Sotheby's) $9,994

A Vichy/Triboulet musical automaton of a pair of clown musicians, French, circa 1910, each with papier-mâché face, one happy, one sad, 26in. high.
(Sotheby's) $54,510

A Gustave Vichy musical automaton of a negro fruit seller, French, circa 1870, the head turning and nodding towards a tray containing three papier-mâché fruits, 26in.
(Sotheby's) $23,621

A Leopold Lambert musical automaton of Pierrot serenading the moon, French, circa 1890, the papier-mâché headed figure with articulated protruding tongue, fixed brown glass eyes, 21½in. high.
(Sotheby's) $17,262

A musical carousel automaton with turned ebonized angle columns, coin mechanism, musical movement playing six airs, carousel with static horses and riders, two dancing dolls and an automated organ-grinder in the center, 25½in.
(Christie's) $24, 633

A Roullet et Decamps automaton of a man pulling a lady in a pram, French, circa 1875, the seated bisque headed lady with closed mouth, fixed blue glass eyes and blonde mohair wig over cork pate, 34cm.
(Sotheby's) $2,907

A Roullet et Decamps musical automaton of a Mexican strummer, French, circa 1880, in the original elaborate puce, cream and green satin outfit, 27in.
(Sotheby's) $12,719

A Gustave Vichy musical automaton of a lady at her toilette, French, circa 1880, the bisque forearms holding handglass in the left, puff in the right, 25in.
(Sotheby's) $7,631

A Roullet et Decamps musical automaton of the mask seller, French, circa 1910, the papier-mâché clown face with open mouth and articulated nose, upper jaw and lids, 90cm.
(Sotheby's) $193,550

An Henri Phalibois automaton whistler, French, circa 1900, the papier-mâché headed figure with open mouth, glass eyes winking alternately, fair hair wig, 38in.
(Sotheby's) $36,340

A Gustave Vichy musical automaton of a waltzing couple, French, circa 1880, each in sky-blue and cream silk-satin, 13½in.
(Sotheby's) $6,905

A Gustave Vichy musical automaton of a 'domino piano player', French, circa 1870, the papier-mâché figure seated on a stool at an upright piano, 75cm. high.
(Sotheby's) $19,987

A rare Gustave Vichy musical automaton of a nurse and baby, French, circa 1885, the François Gaultier head impressed 5, with closed mouth, fixed blue glass eyes pierced ears and blonde real hair wig, 17in.
(Sotheby's) $7,631

An Henri Phalibois musical automaton of a wedding couple, French, circa 1880, the bride with bisque head, the groom with papier-mâché head, 26¾in. without dome.
(Sotheby's) $9,994

A Roullet et Decamps musical automaton of a lady harpist, French, circa 1880, the head turning from side to side and lowering as her bisque hands move, 25in.
(Sotheby's) $11,811

A Roullet et Decamps clockwork dromedary and rider, French, circa 1880, the seated figure with bisque head, the kid covered dromedary with brown glass eyes, 18in.
(Sotheby's) $11,811

A Gustave Vichy musical automaton 'Fillette Piano', French, circa 1890, the metal hands moving across the bone and ebony keyboard, her head nodding and turning, 13½in.
(Sotheby's) $8,177

A fine and rare Roullet et Decamps musical automaton of a snake charmer, French, circa 1900, standing holding a serpent in left hand, a trumpet in her right, 90cm.
(Sotheby's) $245,690

A musical automaton of a fiddler, French, circa 1910, probably by Renou, cross legged playing a fiddle in blue and pink satin outfit, 24½in.
(Sotheby's) $4,754

German silver singing bird automaton, 20th century, shaped rectangular form box, with chased figural landscape scenes.
(Skinner) $2,415

A Roullet et Decamps musical automaton of a negro lyre player, French, circa 1890, turning and nodding her head as she plays the lyre, 28in.
(Sotheby's) $9,994

A Phillip Vielmetter tinplate mechanical clown artist, German, circa 1910, the lithographed toy drawing sketches of well known historical figures, 4¾in. wide.
(Sotheby's) $1,280

A Roullet et Decamps musical automaton of a butterfly catcher, French, circa 1875, the Jumeau head with closed mouth, fixed blue glass paperweight eyes, pierced ears and blonde mohair wig, 23½in.
(Sotheby's) $14,536

A Michel Bertrand Vichy-style pierrot writer automaton, 20th century, the seated figure of Pierrot writes a letter, falls asleep, wakes up and stretches, 25in.
(Sotheby's) $19,199

A Leopold Lambert automaton, French, late 19th century, the internal mechanism causes her to turn her head, raise her basket of flowers and sniff her bouquet, 18½in.
(Sotheby's) $2,925

A Roullet & Decamps girl with cart automaton, French, circa 1910, with *Simon & Halbig 1079* mold bisque head, bisque hands, keywind to one side, 13in.
(Sotheby's) $950

An unusual banjo playing automaton, probably Renou, late 19th century, the papier mâché headed figure in original purple, green and crimson brocade and satin outfit, 19¼in.
(Sotheby's) $9,143

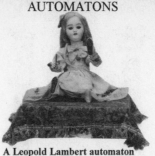

A good Vichy/Triboulet 'Paysan & Nourisson' automaton, French, circa 1910, the figure seated on a chair back feeds his pet piglet a biscuit, 31in. overall. (Sotheby's) **$21,942**

A Leopold Lambert automaton of a girl putting on her shoes, French, circa 1900, figure moves both hands as if to put on her shoe, 13in. wide. (Sotheby's) **$4,571**

A Roullet et Decamps automaton of a drinking lady, French, circa 1880, the three-wheeled metal platform containing the keywind mechanism, 11in. (Sotheby's) **$1,599**

A Roullet et Decamps musical automaton of a magician, French, circa 1880, head stamped in red *Deposé Tête Jumeau* with closed smiling mouth, brown glass paperweight eyes. (Sotheby's) **$89,270**

A good Renou pull along balancing clowns automaton, French, late 19th century, the wheeled platform with lithographed paper covering applied with gilded wooden see-saw, 13½in. long. (Sotheby's) **$2,377**

A very rare and original Gustave Vichy bird trainer automaton, French, circa 1895, the male figure stands holding a feathered bird in his left hand, he brings a flute to his mouth, the figure 43in. high. (Sotheby's) **$140,280**

A pull along Punchinelle on stubborn horse automaton, French, circa 1910, the figure jumps up and down and waves his stick and squeaks, 10¼in. (Sotheby's) **$2,194**

An A. Tharin automaton picture, French, circa 1845, comprising a lithographed and hand colored figure of a mother teaching her son the piano, 13½ x 12in. (Sotheby's) **$1,097**

A Leopold Lambert musical automaton of a magician, French, circa 1890, the black papier mâché head with articulated lower jaw and upper lids, 27in. high. (Sotheby's) **$7,314**

A rosewood marine stick barometer, L. Casella, circa 1850, 37in. (Bonhams) $1,449

Mahogany large boxwood strung banjo barometer, by Linnell of London, 19th century, 43in. (G. A. Key) $458

A mahogany stick barometer, C. Tagliabue, circa 1810, 38¹/₂in. (Bonhams) $1,208

Mahogany cased banjo barometer, by G. Rossi of Norwich, 19th century, 38¹/₂in. (G. A. Key) $519

Banjo barometer, arched pediment, vernier dial below, inlaid throughout with panels of floral marquetry, late 19th century, 31in. (G. A. Key) $491

A Regency satinwood and mahogany stick barometer, J. Field, London, first quarter 19th century, 37¹/₄in. high. (Christie's) $14,950

A 19th century mahogany, boxwood strung and inlaid wheel barometer, signed *F. Molten St. Lawrence Steps, Norwich*, 3ft. 10in. (Phillips) $604

An early Victorian mahogany marine stick barometer, Cary, London, second quarter 19th century, 35¹/₄in. high. (Christie's) $6,900

BAROMETERS

A reproduction walnut stick barometer, J. Hallifax Barnsley, Inventor, 4ft. high. (Phillips)

$1,661

Large aneroid banjo barometer, the central thermometer flanked on either side by fluted Corinthian columns, late 19th century, 38in. high. (G. A. Key) $500

A Queen Anne walnut column barometer, Daniel Quare, London No. 24, circa 1710, 39¼in. high. (Christie's) $79,500

Mahogany satinwood strung banjo barometer, by A. Molinari, Halesworth, early 19th century, 37½in. (G. A. Key) $604

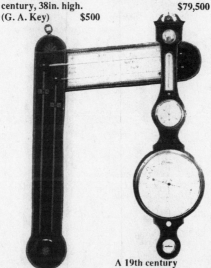

A Victorian boxwood and ebony-inlaid mahogany wheel barometer, Joseph Somalvico, Leather Lane, Holborn, No. 67, 36¼in. high. (Christie's)

$1,495

A Regency mahogany and satinwood inlaid twin-tube angle barometer, Samuel Lainton, Halifax, circa 1810, 37in. high. (Christie's) $12,650

A 19th century mahogany combination wheel barometer with timepiece, signed *Giobbio, Devizes & Trowbridge*, 3ft. 11in. high. (Phillips) $1,238

A Victorian ebonized and rosewood barometer, Joseph Somalvico, London, third quarter 19th century, 44in. high. (Christie's) $4,370

87

BAROMETERS

A George II walnut-cased wheel barometer, by John Hallifax, Barnsley, circa 1740, 44in. high. (Christie's) $57,250

An early Victorian rosewood and mother-of-pearl inlaid banjo clock barometer, inscribed *V. Silvani, Brighton,* 51in. high. (Christie's) $3,634

A George III stick barometer by T. Blunt, London, mahogany veneer. (David Lay) $4,415

Regency mahogany banjo barometer with boxwood stringing, circular silvered face by J. Boyall, Spilsby, early 19th century, 37in. high. (G. A. Key) $538

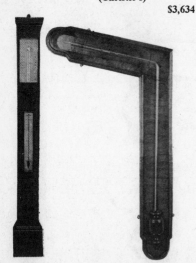

An early Victorian rosewood bow-front stick barometer, Adie & Son, Edinburgh, second quarter 19th century, 42¼in. high. (Christie's) $4,370

George III mahogany 'angle' barometer, third quarter 18th century, signed *John Berry, Manchester,* with etched brass plaque and ogee molded borders, 44in. high. (Skinner) $5,175

Dutch neoclassical gilt metal mounted mahogany barometer/thermometer, third quarter 18th century, T.A.M. Bekking Rotterdam, 41in. high. (Skinner) $1,495

Dutch neoclassical inlaid mahogany barometer/thermometer, circa 1800, by A. Peja, Amsterdam, 48in. high. (Skinner) $3,450

BASKETS

Nantucket basket, Nantucket Island, Massachusetts, 20th century, 11¹/₂in. diameter.
(Skinner) $1,150

A woven oak splint potato basket, Lehigh County, Pennsylvania, 19th century, the oval form with tightly woven ends fitted with a bentwood ash carrying handle, 12in. high.
(Sotheby's) $1,150

Nantucket lightship oval basket, labeled *Made on Board ... shoal lightship Isaac Hamblen*, 12¹/₂in. long.
(Skinner) $1,610

Nantucket work basket, Nantucket Island, Massachusetts, early 20th century, with pivoting cover, 5³/₄in. diameter.
(Skinner) $2,990

Nest of seven Nantucket baskets, 20th century, 5–11⁷/₈in. diameter.
(Skinner) $12,650

Nantucket basket, S.P. Boyer, Nantucket, Massachusetts, stamped on base *Boyer*, with hinged bail handle, 12¹/₄in. diameter.
(Skinner) $1,150

Nantucket basket, Nantucket, Massachusetts, 19th century, 7¹/₈in. diameter.
(Skinner) $805

Two twined open baskets, Attu, Aleutian Islands, circa 1900, each of cylindrical form, 5½in. high.
(Sotheby's) $1,265

Nantucket basket, Nantucket Island, Massachusetts, early 20th century, round with swing handle, 6¹/₂in. diameter.
(Skinner) $863

Nasturtium, 1908. $190

Gainsborough, 1902. $51

Italian, 1906. $260

Venice, 1910. $120

Stories, 1910. $433

Waterlilies, 1909. $243

Sentries (Belgium), 1914. $416

Village (Universal), 1893. $347

Bell, 1911. $138

Windmill, 1924. $1,562

Casket (Fame), 1906. $659

Holiday Haunts, 1926. $120

Bookstand, 1905. $486

Sevres (Christmas Casket), 1897. $780
(Christie's)

Syrian, 1903. $259

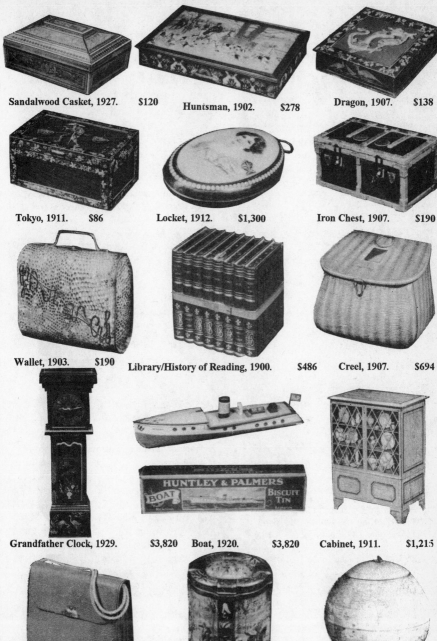

Sandalwood Casket, 1927. $120

Huntsman, 1902. $278

Dragon, 1907. $138

Tokyo, 1911. $86

Locket, 1912. $1,300

Iron Chest, 1907. $190

Wallet, 1903. $190

Library/History of Reading, 1900. $486

Creel, 1907. $694

Grandfather Clock, 1929. $3,820

Boat, 1920. $3,820

Cabinet, 1911. $1,215

Wallet (Brown), 1914. $259

Tournament, 1896. $104
(Christie's)

Globe on Ball Feet, 1906. $729

The New York and Harlem Rail Road Co.,
1871, 100 x $50 shares. (Phillips) $455

The Central Appalachian Co. Ltd, Kentucky,
dated *Brussels 1892,* FRs 500 bearer shares.
(Phillips) $155

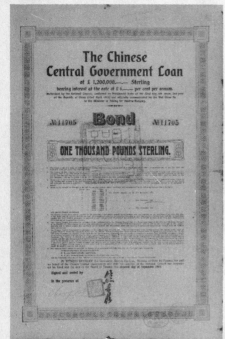

Poyais loan 1823, £100 bond, signed by Wm
Richardson the Chargé d'Affaires.
(Phillips) $225

Chinese Central Government loan of
£1,200,000 sterling, September 1913, bond
11705 for £1,000. (Phillips) $3,648

Italy, Soc. Italiana Segnalatore Automatico,
1911, one share. (Phillips) $190

Chinese Central Government loan of
£2,000,000 sterling, October 1913, bond no.
14299 for £500. (Phillips) $2,080

Royal Siamese Government 7% sterling loan 1922, £100 bond. (Phillips) $146

Canadian North Pacific Fisheries, 1911, $100 share certificate. (Phillips) $30

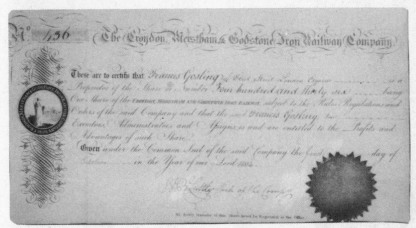

The Croydon, Merstham and Godstone Iron Railway Company, 1804, one share issued to Francis Gosling of Fleet Street, London.
(Phillips) $3,320

American Merchants Union Express Co. 1869, 100 x £100 shares, signed by Wm Fargo as President. (Phillips) $300

London And Brighton Railway Company 1847, bearer certificate no. 4 for £50. (Phillips) $660

Florida Central Railroad 1877, $1,000 bond, issue 590 bonds. (Phillips) $167

State of Florida, Tallahassee 1870, $1,000 bond, green embossed seal. (Phillips) $210

Chinese Central Government loan of £300,000 sterling, bond no. 264 for £1,000. (Phillips) $2,280

Cayuga and Susquehannah Rail Road Co., 1843, $15 shares. (Phillips) $140

Kingdom of Westphalia, 1808 loan, 100 franc bond, dated 1809. (Phillips) $455

Great Republic Gold and Silver Mining Co. of Virginia, 1867, £50 bond. (Phillips) $230

The Southern Inland Navigation and
Improvement Co., 1871, $1,000/£200 bond.
(Phillips) $68

Durham Junction Railway Co., Newcastle-
upon-Tyne, 1834, five x £100 shares.
(Phillips) $940

Russia, 1855 State credit note for 25 roubles,
violet. (Phillips) $1,800

Osaka City Harbor Construction Loan 6%
1933 1000 yen bearer bond.
(Phillips) $825

Theatre Royal, Drury Lane Company of
Proprietors, 1812, one share on thick paper.
(Phillips) $1,130

The United States Centennial International
Exhibition, 1776-1876, dated 27th November
1875 for a $10 share. (Phillips) $1,900

Austrian cold painted bronze
bear, painted in tones of brown
and white, 5¹/₂in. long.
(Skinner) $978

Chinese bronze large circular
jardinière, the border applied
with exotic bird mounts, 19th
century, 18in. high.
(G. A. Key) $319

French bronze setter with
pheasant, by Jules Moigniez
(1835–1894), black patination,
22¹/₂in. long.
(Skinner) $2,070

French bronze portrait plaque
of Louis XIV, by Bertinetti
(Italian, 17th century), the king
shown in right profile, 6in.
diameter.
(Skinner) $2,530

Continental bronze bust of a
Renaissance woman, circa 1880,
molded in relief with scrolling
foliage and stippling, 23¹/₂in.
high.
(Skinner) $2,300

French bronze figure of a
classical youth, late 19th
century, the seated male
wearing winged sandals, 21in.
high.
(Skinner) $1,840

French bronze bust of Napoleon
Bonaparte, signed *Chaudet*
(1763–1810), circa 1890 and
titled, with dark brown patina,
13¹/₄in. high without stand.
(Skinner) $1,150

Austrian cold painted bronze
peacock, early 20th century,
blue, orange and red tones, 8in.
high.
(Skinner) $575

A 1930s bronze figure after the
original by Lorenzl cast as a
naked dancer poised on one foot,
cast signature, marble base,
13in. high.
(David Lay) $1,098

Spanish bronze figural group of a monkey seated atop an elephant, late 19th century, signed *J. Campeny*, 23in. high. (Skinner)   **$2,300**

Austrian bronze figure of a harem girl with a leopard, circa 1920, by A. Chotka, on a carpet-form base, 6in. high. (Skinner)   **$805**

Bruno Zach (Austrian, active 1918–1935), Erotic nymph, dark brown patinated bronze, signed, 6³/₄in. high. (Skinner)   **$1,495**

Italian School, 20th century, Appealing to the Emperor, indistinctly signed and dated *1931*, bronze with dark to medium brown patination, 25in. high. (Skinner)   **$1,840**

Chinese gold splash bronze tripod censer, 18th century, Xuande six character mark on base, flared sides on three elephant head feet, 7¹/₂in. diameter. (Skinner)   **$11,500**

K. Himmelstoss (German, late 19th/early 20th century), The Pearl Gatherer, brown patinated bronze, signed and dated *1903*, 12¹/₂in. high. (Skinner)   **$748**

A Regency bronze tazza base, having circular top with three eagle supports, 11¹/₂in. high. (Russell, Baldwin & Bright)   **$918**

French bronze figural group of a lion and lioness, by Leon Bureau, on a rockwork base, 23¹/₂in. high. (Skinner)   **$2,300**

A cold-painted bronze and ivory figure, cast and carved from a model by Lorenzl, of a young woman poised on tiptoe with arms outspread, 37.5cm. high. (Christie's)   **$4,636**

A 19th century French inkstand in ormolu and champlevé enamel with central urn flanked by pair of cherubs and pierced gallery, 14in. wide.
(Russell, Baldwin & Bright) $1,530

J. Lavroff, stalking panther, 1930s, green patinated bronze cast as a lean panther, 11¼in.
(Sotheby's) $2,812

Continental bronze dog head inkwell, late 19th century, the shaggy head hinged to reveal inkwell, with circular dish, 9in. diameter.
(Skinner) $1,150

Hagenauer, pair of heads, 1930s, patinated bronze, modeled as a highly stylized male and female head with a long stylized tress, 15in. and 15½in.
(Sotheby's) $22,494

Louis Chalon, 'Orchidee', circa 1900, gilt and patinated bronze, cast as a naked nymph metamorphosing into a single orchid flower, 25¼in.
(Sotheby's) $8,248

Two bronze chariot wheel axle fittings, possibly Western Zhou, exterior with continual symmetrical scrolling design, 10in. high.
(Skinner) $805

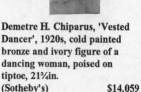

Tom. Campajola (Italian, 20th century), A Wild Ride, indistinctly signed, circa 1930, bronze with medium brown patination, 18in. high.
(Skinner) $2,760

Demetre H. Chiparus, 'Vested Dancer', 1920s, cold painted bronze and ivory figure of a dancing woman, poised on tiptoe, 21¾in.
(Sotheby's) $14,059

Lorenzl, 'Diana', 1920s, cold painted bronze figure of a naked female running with three eagerly bounding hunting dogs, 13in.
(Sotheby's) $3,936

Lorenzl, female bust, 1920s, cold painted bronze modeled as a stylized female head and shoulders, 14½in.
(Sotheby's) $6,561

Amadeo Gennarelli, 'The Chase', 1920s, modeled as a kneeling female nude, aiming her bow at a fleeing group of deer, 15⅜in.
(Sotheby's) $3,749

Demetre H. Chiparus, 'Yambo', 1920s, cold painted bronze and ivory figure of an exotic dancer with a long veil, 23¾in.
(Sotheby's) $56,235

A bronze figure of a running elephant, on oval rustic base, signed *Barye*, 5½in. high, 8in. wide.
(Andrew Hartley) $1,177

A pair of Charles X bronze tazze, the twin handled shallow gadrooned dishes on tall fluted and spreading socles with stepped rouge griotte marble plinths, 9¼in. high.
(Christie's) $782

A Napoleon III bronze figure of the soldier of Marathon, cast after a model by Jean Pierre Cortot, with foundry signature for *F. BARBEDIENNE*, 21¾in. wide.
(Christie's) $956

Demetre H. Chiparus, 'Les amis de Toujours', 1920s, modeled as a a standing woman flanked by two borzoi hounds, 10¾in.
(Sotheby's) $14,996

Louis Chalon, Sea maidens vase, circa 1900, patinated bronze, cast with swirling waters and three maidens with linked hands, 17¼in.
(Sotheby's) $5,061

Pozzi, woman and deer, 1920s, modeled as a partially clad kneeling female figure feeding two small deer, 16¾in.
(Sotheby's) $1,780

Claire Jeanne Roberte Colinet, 'Modern Venus', 1921, silvered and gilt bronze figure of a dancer in a flowing dress and close-fitting headdress sitting back on her heels, 18¹/₂in. high. (Sotheby's) **$5,279**

A large silvered bronze figure, cast from a model by Joe Descomps, of a naked young woman reclining on a naturalistic base on a rectangular black onyx base, 41cm. high. (Christie's) **$5,192**

J. Lormier, dancer, 1920s, patinated bronze and ivory, modeled as a young dancer in mid-step, on a stepped brown onyx and black marble base, 14³/₈in. high. (Sotheby's) **$2,815**

A patinated bronze figure, cast from a model by J. Starke, modeled as two seated grizzly bears, one sucking its paw, signed in the bronze, dated *1918*, 20.5cm. high. (Christie's) **$1,113**

'Huntress', a patinated bronze figure group, cast from a model by Lorenzl, of a naked woman running with three leaping hounds, 32cm. high. (Christie's) **$2,596**

'The Mask Dance', a gilded bronze figure group cast from a model by Aurore Onu, of two naked female nymphs, on a tapering green and black striated rectangular onyx base, 61cm. high. (Christie's) **$4,451**

Large gilt bronze seated Amitabha, Ming Dynasty, seated dhyanasana with his hands in dhayana mudra, 19¼in. high. (Butterfield & Butterfield) **$9,775**

Two American patinated spelter figures, one modeled as a sprinting runner, the other as a basketball player, 19.4cm. high. (Christie's) **$334**

Good cast bronze figure of Buddha, Thailand, Chen sen style, 15/16th century, his slender face framed by snail curls carved in high relief, 13¾in.(Butterfield & Butterfield) **$3,450**

A Regency brass-bound
mahogany bucket, with two
brass bands and a looped hinged
handle terminating in two
scrolls, 12in. high.
(Christie's) $1,076

A George III brass-banded
mahogany bucket, of tapering
circular shape with foliate
hinged handles and a lead-lined
interior, 12in. high.
(Christie's) $2,815

A George III brass-bound
mahogany bucket, the navette-
shaped body with three brass
bands and hinged loop handle,
13in. high.
(Christie's) $2,815

A George III brass bound
mahogany peat bucket with
ribbed slatted sides and later
tin liner, 14¾in. diam.
(Christie's) $2,145

A matched pair of George III
brass-bound mahogany buckets,
each with tapering body and
loop handles, 17½in. high.
(Christie's) $14,352

A George III brass-bound
mahogany bucket, the
cylindrical body with three
brass bands and surmounted by
a hinged loop handle, 14½in.
high.
(Christie's) $1,319

A George III mahogany and
brass bound bucket of pointed
ovoid form, with triple center
band, 36cm. wide.
(Phillips) $540

A red-painted chinoiserie-
decorated toleware pail and a
decorated toleware serving tray,
early 19th century, the pail
decorated with oriental figures
in gilt, 16in. long.
(Sotheby's) $3,162

An early 19th century
mahogany and brass bound
bucket of pointed ovoid form,
with brass carrying handles,
36cm. wide.
(Phillips) $675

18th century mahogany letter box of two compartments, each inset with brass plaques inscribed *Answer'd, Unanswer'd,* mid 18th century, 8¹/₂in. (G. A. Key) $573

Victorian bone inlaid ebony and quill box, mid 19th century, the interior with tray of lidded compartments, 11¹/₂in. wide. (Skinner) $345

George III parquetry inlaid sarcophagus-shaped tea caddy, with fitted interior of two wells and a cut glass mixing bowl, on disk feet, 7½in. high. (Skinner) $1,725

18th century tortoiseshell tea caddy, applied in the center with a plated ball finial, similarly escutcheon and name plate below inscribed *R*, on ball feet, 6¹/₂in. high. (G. A. Key) $750

Unusual Victorian painted papier mâché jewelry cabinet, mid 19th century, lift top with fitted interior, two doors enclosing small drawers, 10in. wide. (Skinner) $518

Victorian painted and découpage jewelry box, third quarter 19th century, with lifting top and pair of doors, decorated with Chinese scenes on a mustard yellow ground, 11¹/₂in. wide. (Skinner) $805

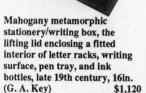

Chinese Export gilt decorated black lacquer humidor, mid-late 19th century, decorated with working men about a warehouse, pewter lined interior, 10³/₈in. wide. (Skinner) $748

Mahogany metamorphic stationery/writing box, the lifting lid enclosing a fitted interior of letter racks, writing surface, pen tray, and ink bottles, late 19th century, 16in. (G. A. Key) $1,120

Late Georgian satinwood and amboyna tea caddy, early 19th century, fan inlay and oval panels of amboyna, crossbanded throughout, 4¹/₂in. high. (Skinner) $316

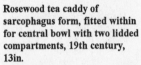

Rosewood tea caddy of sarcophagus form, fitted within for central bowl with two lidded compartments, 19th century, 13in.
(G.A. Key) $290

Early 19th century elm saddler's work box, fitted with a leather work tool, 17in. wide.
(G. A. Key) $29

Burr walnut tea caddy with ebonized rim, interior fitted for two domed compartments and with brass escutcheon, 19th century, 9¹/₂in.
(G. A. Key) $319

Victorian burl walnut brass mounted tea caddy, circa 1850, domed top opening to two lidded wells, each with tea name plaque, the exterior with openwork straps, 8³/₄in. wide.
(Skinner) $748

George III inlaid mahogany knifebox, late 18th/early 19th century, of serpentine outline, with checkered banding and a fitted interior, 9in. wide.
(Skinner) $374

Late Victorian flame mahogany stationery cabinet, the sloping front enclosing a fitted interior with perpetual calendar, letter racks etc, late 19th century, 12in.
(G. A. Key) $212

A late 19th century papier mache japanned tea caddy with oriental figures in town scenes, containing two lead canisters, 8in. wide.
(Dreweatt · Neate) $245

Coromandel jewel box, the cover inset with an initialed brass name plate with fitted interior, by John Bagshaw & Sons of Liverpool, 19th century, 12in. wide.
(G. A. Key) $375

George III boxwood and harewood inlaid tea caddy, late 18th century, with three foliate inlaid oval panels, 6³/₄in. wide.
(Skinner) $316

A William IV tortoiseshell veneered tea caddy, with a shaped front and flared apron, the interior fitted with two lidded canisters, 20cm. wide. (Phillips) **$1,350**

A carved walnut saltbox, Eastern Pennsylvania, early 19th century, the rectangular slanted and hinged lid opening to two wells, 10¾in. long. (Sotheby's) **$862**

A Georgian rectangular inlaid mahogany tea caddy, with brass handle to the lid, on bracket feet, 9½in. x 5¼in. (Anderson & Garland) **$125**

An ivory and silver inlaid tortoiseshell sewing box, early 19th century, the hinged lid opening to an interior lined in blue silk and fitted with various ivory and wood needlework tools, 9in. long.. (Sotheby's) **$2,300**

Pair of George III carved and inlaid mahogany knife urns, early 19th century, each with gadrooned finial and inlaid with swags of cornhusks, ribband and crossbanding, 24in. high. (Skinner) **$7,475**

A wallpaper-covered oval band box, 19th century, covered in glazed blue wallpaper with red and yellow stylized floral and foliate decoration, 19¾in. wide. (Sotheby's) **$460**

A Georgian squat octagonal-shaped burr-walnut tea caddy with boxwood stringing and ivory key-plate, 8in. x 5in. (Anderson & Garland) **$783**

A carved and painted poplar sewing box, Lehigh County, Pennsylvania, circa 1840, the rectangular hinged top fitted with an oblong pin cushion, 10¾in. long. (Sotheby's) **$1,035**

A late 18th century Anglo-Indian ivory veneered vizagapatam sewing box of sarcophagus form, with two silvered metal ring turned handles, 29cm. wide. (Phillips) **$1,500**

A painted bentwood bride's box, Continental, late 18th/early 19th century, the lid colorfully painted with a couple each in a formal costume, 18¾in. long. (Sotheby's) $1,610

A George III ormolu-mounted black and polychrome papier-mâché casket, decorated overall with Venetian capriccio scenes, trelliswork, C-scrolls, bunches of roses and other flowers, 10½in. wide. (Christie's) $48,438

A late 19th century French enameled and gilt metal casket, the lid and sides with Sèvres style 'jeweled' panels, 18.5cm. wide. (Bearne's) $1,147

A Regency tortoiseshell and plate mounted tea caddy, English, circa 1810, the sides and hinged cover with blonde tortoiseshell veneered panels, 6in. wide. (Christie's) $999

A pair of George III silver-mounted mahogany cutlery-boxes, the silver mounts probably by Joseph Wyatt, each with hinged sloping molded serpentine-fronted lid, 15in. high. (Christie's) $6,279

A George III mahogany and crossbanded knife box, the sloping lid with a broken outline, the interior fitted for stationery raised on ball feet, 38cm. high. (Phillips) $870

Red painted pine lidded wall box, America, late 18th/early 19th century, 12in. wide. (Skinner) $1,495

A George III rolled paperwork tea caddy of hexagonal form, the panels decorated in gilt, blue and green, 16cm. (Bearne's) $573

A George III mahogany, harewood, satinwood and tulipwood urn, the domed hinged top inlaid with oak leaves and acorns, 17in. high. (Christie's) $12,558

Russian malachite veneered metal rectangular box, 19th century, gilt wash interior, 4¹/₂in. wide.
(Skinner) $690

Shaker peg rack and divided oval carrier, 20th century, rack 69in. long, carrier 10¹/₂in. long.
(Skinner) $575

Painted decorated miniature chest, possibly Pennsylvania, circa 1820, polychrome shells and strawberries, 12³/₄in. wide.
(Skinner) $13,800

George III fruitwood apple-form tea caddy, circa 1790, golden yellow color, foil lined interior, 4¹/₂in. high.
(Skinner) $1,150

Painted and marquetry inlaid mahogany ladies' jewelry cabinet, America, dated *1905*, with spring loaded drawer, lower compartment with painted reserve of American shield, 18¹/₄in. wide.
(Skinner) $633

Regency tortoiseshell tea caddy, early 19th century, with pagoda shaped top and two interior lidded compartments, 6³/₄in. long.
(Skinner) $1,035

Painted pine and oak writing box, probably Massachusetts, early 18th century, the pine overhanging rectangular hinged slant lid, 18in. wide.
(Skinner) $10,350

Victorian oak miniature hall letterbox, circa 1880, with hexagonal-shaped top and glass inset door, all above a drawer on a circular foot, 17in. high.
(Skinner) $3,565

Amusing Victorian mahogany dog house, late 19th century, 16in. high.
(Skinner) $920

Gilt decorated box, 19th century, front inscribed *Tainter's Boston Express*, 9in. wide.
(Skinner) $575

Shaker horsehair sieve, 19th century, 8³/₈in. diameter.
(Skinner) $345

Wavy birch footed box, New England, early 19th century, with ivory escutcheon and shaped skirt, 14in. wide.
(Skinner) $546

Carved and stained wood display cabinet, America, 19th century, with geometric, animal and floral decoration, alligatored surface, 16¹/₂in. high.
(Skinner) $316

George III painted papier mâché tea caddy, circa 1790, stenciled with anthemion in the borders, mounted with oval painted and inset plaques, 4in. high.
(Skinner) $575

George III inlaid mahogany serpentine fronted letterbox, circa 1790, formerly a knife box, with stringing, shell inlay, 15¹/₂in. high.
(Skinner) $345

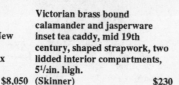

Large Shaker oval box, probably New Lebanon, New York, 19th century, with original pumpkin paint, six finger, 15in. long.
(Skinner) $8,050

Victorian brass bound calamander and jasperware inset tea caddy, mid 19th century, shaped strapwork, two lidded interior compartments, 5¹/₂in. high.
(Skinner) $230

George III marquetry inlaid fruitwood oval tea caddy, circa 1800, inlaid with foliage, 4¹/₂ x 5¹/₂in.
(Skinner) $403

Wonder Photo Cannon, Chicago Ferrotype Co., Chicago, bright-nickeled body, and base developing tank.
(Christie's) $1,504

Ticka camera, Houghton Ltd, London, with lens cap and instructions, in maker's box.
(Christie's) $384

Summa Report camera no. 0200, C. Tiranti, Rome, 6 x 9cm. plate or rollfilm, four-lens turret, in maker's fitted leather case.
(Christie's) $7,402

Field camera, half-plate, brass and mahogany, with black leather bellows and retailer's label *Harrod's Ltd. Brompton Road, S.W.,* a London Stereoscopic Co., Rapid Rectilinear 7 x 5 lens no. 17294.
(Christie's) $384

Peregrine III no. 4/25849, Kershaw, Leeds, 120-rollfilm, with a Taylor-Hobson Adotal 80mm. f/2.8 lens no. 344463 in a Talykron shutter, in maker's ever ready case.
(Christie's) $1,312

Gemflex I TLR no. 6783, Showa Optical Works Ltd., Japan, 14mm. rollfilm, the back plate marked *Made in Occupied Japan,* with a Gem viewing lens and a Gem f/3.5 25mm. taking lens.
(Christie's) $839

Nikon F3 no. 1324861 black, with a photomic head HP and an MD-4 Motordrive no. 123780, and a Nikon Speedlight SB-15 flash no. 1104829.
(Christie's) $558

Bertram Type BCI no. 1052, Bertram, Germany, 6 x 6/6 x 9cm., with a Schneider Xenar f/3.5 105mm. lens no. 3581912, and two others.
(Christie's) $881

A very rare Eastman Kodak No.5 Folding camera Improved Stereo, for 5 x7 in. roll film, in leather case, 1893.
(Auction Team Köln)
                                $8,700

Leica M4 no. 1181922 black-paint (? re-painted), with a Leitz black Summicron f/2 50mm. lens no. 1926544, in maker's ever ready case, in a Leitz box.
(Christie's) $6,168

Ladies patent watch camera, J. Lancaster & Son, Birmingham, 1 x 1¼in. metal-body, sprung six-section lens tube, single meniscus lens.
(Christie's) $31,723

Leica M3 no. 994208 chrome, with a Leica-Meter MR and a Leitz Summaron f/2.8 35mm. lens no. 1627208, in maker's ever ready case.
(Christie's) $1,062

Ermanox Reflex no. M. 99919, Ernemann, Germany, 4½ x 6cm., with an Ernemann Ernostar f/1.8 10.5cm. lens no. 917079 and three single metal plate holders.
(Christie's) $6,168

Collapsible camera no. 12592, H. Mackènstein, Paris 13 x 18cm., polished mahogany-body, removable viewfinder, red-leather bellows and a lens with built-in sprung shutter.
(Christie's) $458

Hasselblad Lunar Surface outfit, Hasselblad, Sweden, comprising an EL Data camera no. TEE14222, with battery pack, and a Carl Zeiss Planar f/2.8 80mm. lens no. 4867375.
(Christie's) $4,250

Tailboard camera, P. Zigliara & Co, Genova, 13 x 18cm., with a brass-bound Planastigmat lens and double darkslides, in a leather case.
(Christie's) $300

Leica M1 no. 1040074, chrome, with a Mikas-M 1/3 x microscope attachment and Leitz cable release, a Weston exposure meter.
(Christie's) $1,224

Ladies' camera, J. Lancaster & Son, Birmingham, 5 x 7in. the exterior covered in red grained and gilt-tooled leather, the camera of polished mahogany.
(Christie's) $1,504

Leica R4 Gold no. 1651992 commemorative no. 1007, with a Leitz gilt-barrel Summilux-R f/1.4 50mm. lens no. 3295233 and instructions.
(Christie's) $4,537

A Graflex Speed Graphic, Ektar 4,5/101mm. lens coupled to distance meter, with flash and cable, 1950.
(Auction Team Köln)
                             $295

Reflex stereo camera, French, 45 x 107mm., with focal-plane shutter and a pair of Carl Zeiss, Jena Tessar f/4.5 7.5cm. lenses no.s 136246 and 136244.
(Christie's) $846

Certotrop camera no. 58xx53, Certo, Germany, 6½ x 9cm., brown enamel and tan-leather body covering and bellows and a Voigtländer Heliar f/4.5 11.4cm. lens no. 529538.
(Christie's) $265

German matchbox camera, 18 x 10mm. brass-body, sports finder, focusing scale/?, 2, 1, 0.5, sliding stops marked 6.3, 11 and a Carl Zeiss, Jena Tessar f/2.7 2.5cm. lens no. 784950.
(Christie's) $7,866

A 120-rollfilm Hasselblad 500EL/M camera no. UUE34985 with a Carl Zeiss Planar f/2.8 80mm. lens no. 5263222, a prism viewfinder a battery charger, two boxed Opto fiber screens.
(Christie's) $926

Novelty camera, a boxform novelty in the shape of a camera, the pull-cord activating a nodding donkey which opens the camera front and internal whistle.
(Christie's) $384

Super Ikonta 533/16 no. N16874, Zeiss Ikon, Germany, the top plate engraved M.F. 993, with a Carl Zeiss, Jena Tessar f/2.8 8cm. lens no. 2574211 in a Compur Rapid shutter.
(Christie's) $962

Hasselblad SWC no. TIW5970 Hasselblad, Sweden, 120-rollfilm, with magazine back no. TE135644, a Carl Zeiss Biogon f/4.5 38mm. lens no. 3472060 and finder.
(Christie's) $1,915

Nikon F no. 6550894, chrome, photomic head, with a Nippon Kogaku Nikkor-S Auto f/1.4 50mm. lens no. 372020, in maker's ever ready case.
(Christie's) $531

Septon Pen Camera Works, Japan, a 16mm. Septon Penletto combined camera/pen with lens and instruction sheet, in maker's box.
(Christie's) $3,839

Leica CL Anniversary no. 1402858 commemorative no. 219-C, with a Leitz Summicron-C f/2 40mm. lens no. 2636979, in maker's case.
(Christie's) $1,152

Twin-lens Contaflex no. 75848 Zeiss Ikon, Germany, with a Carl Zeiss f/2.8 8cm. viewing lens no. 1781307 and a Carl Zeiss Sonnar f/2 5cm. taking lens no. 1549067.
(Christie's) $2,622

Stirn No. 1 Vest camera no. 7565, C.P. Stirn, Germany, 4cm. diameter exposures, with lens and exposed glass plate, in maker's box.
(Christie's) $2,820

Rolleiflex 3.5F no. 2278920 with meter, a Heidosmat f/2.8 75mm. viewing lens no. 3787225 and a Carl Zeiss Planar f/3.5 75mm. taking lens no. 3782500 in a Synchro-Compur shutter.
(Christie's) $567

Dressler & Heinemann, Munich, a 4 x 4cm. walnut-body boxform Minor camera with removable viewfinder, rubber-band shutter, metal plate holders.
(Christie's) $2,967

Sliding stereo camera Murray & Heath, London, the camera for 2¼ x 2¼in. plates, mahogany boxform body, removable focusing screen with brass retaining pin.
(Christie's) $5,313

E.C.O.M., Italy, a 120-rollfilm Stereo Minatur camera no. 00001 with a pair of Ecom Color lenses.
(Christie's) $6,981

Leica 250FF Reporter no. 352339, the camera with motor linkage and with a Leitz Summarit 5cm. f/1.5 lens no. 1420001.
(Christie's) $14,099

Lewis-pattern daguerreotype camera, 3¼ x 4¼in., wood-body, with removable focusing screen, hinged top, slide focusing, black leather bellows and a Darlot brass bound lens no. 90193, a spirit burner.
(Christie's) $7,084

Leitz OOFRC, plated lever wind, on Leica III No. 182135, Summar 2/50mm. No. 303424 lens.
(Auction Team Köln)
                               $4,350

A Carl Zeiss Hasselblad Objektiv Prototype CF24mm., 1:3,5/24mm., Fisheye for circular picture on 6x6.
(Auction Team Köln)
                    $7,120

An Eastman Kodak No. 1 camera for 100 pictures, Rapid rectilinear 1:9/57 lens, from 1889.
(Auction Team Köln)
                    $1,265

Photoret camera, Magic Introduction Co., New York, 2in. diameter film, nickel body.
(Christie's) $529

A Voigtländer Brilliant binocular mirror reflex camera with Voigtar 1:3,5/75 mm lens, post 1933.
(Auction Team Köln) $70

San Giorgio, Italy, a 16mm. Safo camera no. 200455 with built-in extinction meter and a San Giorgio Essegi 3.5cm. f/3.5 lens, maker's ever ready case.
(Christie's) $8,377

Heidoscope no. 3734, Franke and Heidecke, Germany, 6 x 13cm. with magazine back, a Carl Zeiss Triplet f/4.2 7.5cm. viewing lens no. 644021.
(Christie's) $1,137

A K100 Turret 16mm ciné camera for 16-64 b/sec, with two Ciné Ektar and one Elgeet 3,0/75mm lenses.
(Auction Team Köln)
$395

A 70mm Grandeur sound wide-process film camera, fitted with Mitchell-magazine No. 20, used by 20th Century Fox in 1929.
(Auction Team Köln)
$9,890

A Bell & Howell 70-DR 16mm ciné camera, gray green case, motor for 8-64 b/sec.
(Auction Team Köln)
$237

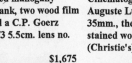

Kino Model E no. 732062, Ernemann, Germany, 35mm. with polished teak body, hand-crank, a Carl Zeiss, Jena Tessar f/3.5 5cm. lens no. 271174.
(Christie's)
$2,447

Cinematographic camera, Alfred Darling, Brighton, 35mm., polished mahogany-body, hand-crank, two wood film magazines and a C.P. Goerz Kino-Hypar f/3 5.5cm. lens no. 568621.
(Christie's)
$1,675

Cinematographic camera, Auguste Lumière, France, 35mm., the body of green-stained wood.
(Christie's)
$7,402

A Siemens Model B 16mm camera, with Busch Glaukar 2,8/2 cm lens.
(Auction Team Köln)
$205

A unique Prototype Tricolor (Version 2) 35mm film camera with Taylor Hobson Cooke Kinic 1:2/5cm. lens, circa 1930.
(Auction Team Köln)
$6,330

Sept camera no. 5305, André Debrie, Paris, 35mm., with a Roussel Stylor f/3.5 50mm. lens no. 38467.
(Christie's)
$670

CARVED BIRDS

A rare and important carved and painted wood miniature figure of a bird, the Deco-Tex carver, Pennsylvania, 20th century, 2¾in. high.
(Sotheby's) $1,092

A pair of broadbills, Steve and Lem Ward, Crisfield, Maryland, dated *1968* and *1966*, each carved in the round with head turned to one side.
(Sotheby's) $2,587

A carved pine guinea hen group, Pennsylvania, late 19th century, comprising three stylized guinea hens, perched on three branches, overall height 14¼in.
(Sotheby's) $1,725

A carved and painted wood figure of an eagle, signed *Stephen Polaha*, Reading, Pennsylvania, 20th century, the stylized eagle standing erect with head up, 15½in. high.
(Sotheby's) $632

A carved and painted pine figure of a fan-tailed rooster, Schoharie County, New York, the standing full-bodied figure with head up and tail fanned, 10in. high.
(Sotheby's) $1,380

A carved and painted pine articulated Gooney bird, Pennsylvania, early 20th century, the stylized bird with chip-carved wings, painted black, 6¾in. high.
(Sotheby's) $517

A carved and painted wood figure of a bird, 'Schtockschnitzler' Simmons, Pennsylvania, circa 1900, painted red with black wings and head, 7in. high.
(Sotheby's) $5,462

A carved and painted wood figure of a rooster and a figure of a hen, John Reber, Germansville, Pennsylvania, early 20th century, 5¾ and 6¾in. high.
(Sotheby's) $14,950

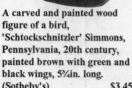

A carved and painted wood figure of a bird, 'Schtockschnitzler' Simmons, Pennsylvania, 20th century, painted brown with green and black wings, 5¾in. long.
(Sotheby's) $3,450

A pair of cut glass and gilt-bronze chandeliers, circa 1910, each with eight scroll branches, the central stem applied with drops and faceted finials, 79cm. high. (Sotheby's) $4,514

W.A.S. Benson, three light chandelier, 1880s, brass, the central circular band with six scrolls curling down to stylized foliate terminal, 49¼in. drop. (Sotheby's) $4,124

A cut glass and brass chandelier, circa 1900, the central baluster and finial within a framework of scrolls, applied with rosettes and moulded bands, 111cm. high. (Sotheby's) $3,611

A cut glass and gilt metal mounted chandelier, 19th century, the baluster column cut with leaf design and mounted with panels of ormolu foliage, 60in. high. (Christie's) $20,631

One of a pair of Continental blue and clear glass chandeliers, modern, each with eighteen solid hexagonal S-scrolled arms, 99cm. high approximately. (Sotheby's)

(Two) $30.693

One of a pair of gilt-bronze and glass ceiling lights, Paris, circa 1910, each with three molded glass panels in the form of shells, 62cm. high. (Sotheby's)

(Two) $12,638

A gilt-bronze and cut glass chandelier, French, circa 1890, the central stem beneath a crest cast with anthemion and scrolls, 125cm. high. (Sotheby's) $7,583

Degue Art Deco glass and wrought iron chandelier, elaborate press-molded frosted glass plafonnier light bowl with four matching shades, 15³/₄in. diameter. (Skinner) $2,530

Tiffany bronze and favrile glass chandelier, elaborate cast bronze foliate framework, enhanced by eight gold-blossomed lily lights, 48in. high. (Skinner) $26,450

An Italian carved white marble chimney-piece, in the 15th century style, the rectangular shelf with foliate and egg-and-dart carved underside, above the frieze carved to the center with a roundel depicting Hercules slaying an adversary, 84in. wide; 67½in. high.
(Christie's) $11,436

A Victorian rosewood fire surround and overmantel, the upper section with carved bird and floral surmount, 6ft. 3in. wide.
(Russell, Baldwin & Bright) $8,415

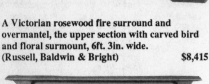

A French white marble chimney-piece, in the Empire Revival style, late 19th century, the rectangular shelf with a molded edge, above a plain frieze flanked to each side by a Bacchic lion-mask, 76in. wide; 53¾in. high.
(Christie's) $3,871

A carved walnut chimney-piece and overmantel, in the early 17th century Venetian manner, 19th century, the overmantel with architectural pediment, surmounted by a pair of reclining putti, above a shaped panel carved with a scene depicting Vulcan's forge, 81¼in. wide; 110in. high.
(Christie's) $25,512

A carved pine chimney-piece, second half 19th century, the frieze with foliate-carved edge above shaped lozenges, the projecting shaped jambs each headed by tied laurel swags and diamond rosettes, 94in. wide; 59^1/$_2$in. high.
(Christie's) $4,223

A grey-veined and statuary marble chimney-piece, the rectangular breakfront shelf with a molded edge, above a frieze centered with a tablet carved in high relief with a mask and hung with ribbon-tied drapery, 95in. wide; 64in. high.
(Christie's) $12,316

A George III carved pine chimney-piece, the rectangular breakfront shelf with stepped underside, above the frieze centered by a projecting tablet carved with a foliage-laden urn, 71^1/$_2$in. wide; 56in. high.
(Christie's) $1,319

A George III statuary marble chimney-piece, the rectangular breakfront shelf above the frieze, centered by a projecting bas-relief tablet carved with classical maidens and a man leading a lamb to be sacrificed, 68^1/$_2$in. wide; 55^3/$_4$in. high.
(Christie's) $22,873

A George III carved pine chimney-piece, the frieze carved in high relief with scrolling foliage, the shaped ingrounds carved with flowerheads, 57^1/$_8$in. wide; 56^1/$_4$in. high.
(Christie's) $2,287

A stone chimney-piece, in the Louis XV style, 19th century, the serpentine-shaped shelf above the paneled frieze centered by a shell motif, 45^1/$_2$in. wide; 40in. high.
(Christie's) $2,287

Fulper effigy bowl, three figures supporting a rolled edge bowl, vertical stamp mark, 7¹/₂in. high. (Skinner) $690

Five Rockwell Kent 'Salamina' ceramic plates, designed in 1939 for Vernon Kilns, Vernon and Los Angeles, brown stamp marks, 16¾ x 9½in. diameter. (Skinner) $546

Bennington Pottery Rockingham pitcher, ribbed pattern, 1849 mark, 8in. high. (Eldred's) $165

A flint enamel poodle, Lyman Fenton & Company, Bennington, Vermont, 1849-1858, with fruit basket in mouth, applied coleslaw mane and ears, 8¹/₄in. high. (Christie's) $2,070

Cobalt decorated three-gallon stoneware crock, J. Norton & Co., Bennington, Vermont, mid-19th century, decorated with a foraging game bird, 10⁵/₈in. high. (Skinner) $403

A rare glazed Kaolin Pottery figure of a ram, Pennsylvania, 19th century, the standing figure with molded horns, ears, collar and bell, 5¾in. high. (Sotheby's) $6,325

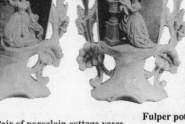

Roseville pottery covered jar, floral panels under a matte brown glaze, RV mark, 9¹/₂in. high. (Skinner) $403

Pair of porcelain cottage vases, attributed to Bennington, mid 19th century, 8¾in. high. (Skinner) $460

Fulper pottery vase, four buttresses under a butterscotch flambe glaze, vertical mark, 8¹/₄in. high. (Skinner) $230

BERLIN

K.P.M. painted porcelain plaque, circa 1900, depicting a maid in the bullrushes, 9³/₄ x 7³/₈in.
(Skinner) $3,105

Pair of K.P.M. (Berlin) painted porcelain covered vases, late 19th century, decorated with figural reserves and foliate sprays, 13¹/₂in. high.
(Skinner) $3,680

A Berlin porcelain oval plaque, finely painted with the Virgin of the Immaculate Conception after the original by Murillo, 17.5cm. high.
(Bearne's) $1,195

BESWICK

Beswick model of a large T'ang Horse, No. 2205, mainly decorated in bronze with green detail, 13in. high.
(G. A. Key) $362

Beswick model of a Cairn terrier with ball on left leg, decorated in beige with brown stripes and red ball, No. 1055A, 4in. long.
(G. A. Key) $51

Large Beswick Dalmatian dog, 14in.
(G. A. Key) $169

BOW

A Bow bocage porcelain figure of a man with plumed hat and cream and puce coat, 15.5cm. high.
(Bearne's) $423

A pair of Bow porcelain figures, one in the form of a traveler playing a flute, the other in the form of a woman with flowers in her apron, 19.5cm. high.
(Bearne's) $1,274

A Bow porcelain chamber stick group of two birds looking down on a nest of chicks, 18.3cm. high, late 18th century.
(Bearne's) $574

BRITISH

Fieldings Crown Devon covered cheese dish, the sloping cover elaborately decorated in the neo-classical manner, 10in.
(G. A. Key) $83

Fieldings Devonware drainer dish on stand, decorated with the 'Spring' pattern, 7¹/₂in. wide.
(G. A. Key) $84

A late 18th century pottery figure of a reclining doe with sponged ocher details on green oval base, 6in.
(Russell, Baldwin & Bright)
                              $490

T. & J. Carey toilet jug, decorated throughout in blue with floral borders, also with scene of the lady of the lake, early to mid 19th century, 12in. high.
(G. A. Key) $483

Pair of English painted ironstone footed sauce tureens, mid 19th century, each painted in the famille rose palette, depicting trelliswork, Chinese figures, and gilded foliage, 8in.
(Skinner) $431

A caneware jug, molded with a version of the Phillips & Bagster boar and stag hunting scenes, 21.5cm. high.
(Bearne's) $183

A Britannia pottery figure of 'Wee Macgregor', dressed as an Irish International player, his right foot resting on a football, 14in. high.
(Christie's) $843

Falcon Ware toilet set, printed in colors with English cottage scenes, printed and impressed marks.
(G. A. Key) $121

An Aller Vale Pottery model of a seated cat with an elongated neck and orange glass eyes, 29.3cm. high.
(Bearne's) $997

BRITISH

J. & R. Riley oval meat dish, printed in blue with the 'Dromedary' pattern, scene of camel and its handler, circa 1825, 16½in.
(G. A. Key) $240

Lladro figurine, 'Chit Chat', 05466, 8in.
(G. A. Key) $155

Paragon 'Playtime Series' decorative cup and saucer, printed with nursery rhyme scenes etc, printed marks.
(G. A. Key) $99

A W.H. Baron terracotta vase, covered in a cream slip carved with a design of a bird chasing an insect amongst foliage, 33.5cm. high, signed and dated 1893.
(Bearne's) $423

Losol Ware toilet set, decorated with the 'Athole' pattern, comprising: jug and bowl; tooth vase; soap dish and chamber pot.
(G. A. Key) $245

Decorative porcelain jug of octagonal baluster form, with foliate molded spout, 'English Rose' pattern, probably by J. & R. Godwin, 19th century, 7½in. high.
(G. A. Key) $153

Brownfields plate, printed in mauve with scene by Phiz, impressed and printed marks and registration diamond for 1862, 10in.
(G.A.Key) $40

Gien porcelain ink stand of oval form, applied with motif of a central shell and joined by two dolphin mounts, flanking two circular ink pots, 9in. wide.
(G. A. Key) $183

Elkin Knight two handled soup tureen stand, the center decorated with scene of 'Byland Abbey, Yorkshire', 12½in. wide.
(G. A. Key) $113

CANTON

A large Canton jar, the hexagonal body painted with alternate panels of figures in conversation and butterflies amongst foliage, 66.5cm. high.
(Bearne's) $975

Canton well and tree platter, China, 19th century, 18in. long.
(Skinner) $633

A 19th century Canton famille rose porcelain vase, of bulbous form with flared rim, gilt mask ring handles, reserves depicting figures and garden scenes, 12¾in. high.
(Andrew Hartley) $382

CARLTON WARE

Carltonware cheese dish, the sloping cover with crimped rim with gilt border and printed in colors, 'Chrysanthemum' pattern, 9in.
(G. A. Key) $63

Carlton Ware advertising ornament, modeled as a foaming tankard with a toucan handle, inscribed *My Goodness My Guinness*, printed mark, 7in. high.
(G. A. Key) $445

Carltonware Art Deco style conical baluster formed jug, gilt handle, decorated in green with 'Handcraft' pattern, printed mark and impressed No. 493, 6½in. high.
(G. A. Key) $153

CHELSEA

A rare Chelsea model of a hound, modeled seated on an oval grassy base, wearing black collar, 5cm., red anchor mark.
(Phillips) $2,580

A pair of Chelsea groups of gallants and companions emblematic of the Seasons, Winter and Spring, circa 1765, about 35.5cm. high.
(Christie's) $13,816

A Chelsea teaplant coffee-pot, with spirally-molded brightly colored teaplants, 1745-49, 13.5cm. high.
(Christie's) $8,200

CHINESE

Chinese Export blue and white platter, China, 19th century, with Fitzhugh border, 15¾in. long.
(Skinner) $460

Whimsical Chinese Export style porcelain elephant form inkwell, late 19th century, with hinged neck and brass collar, 5¼in. high.
(Skinner) $518

Chinese Export platter, China, 19th century, in the Imari palette, 13¾in. long.
(Skinner) $259

A German ormolu-mounted Chinese porcelain Yixing ewer, late 17th/early 18th century, molded in the shape of a tree trunk with branches forming the handle, 13¼in. high.
(Christie's) $26,910

A pair of Chinese Guangdong figures of mythical three-legged toads, modeled with wide open mouths, seated on pierced wave-form bases, 11½ in. high.
(Christie's) $5,980

A 19th century Chinese famille rose porcelain bottle vase with flared rim, the neck and body painted with scaly dragons chasing flaming pearls, 15½in.
(Andrew Hartley) $668

A Chinese famille rose shaped rectangular plate, boldly and brightly painted with a pseudo tobacco leaf pattern, 40.5cm. wide, Qianlong.
(Bearne's) $3,695

Pair of rose medallion and brass wall sconces, China, 19th century, originally fitted for gas, electrified, 8¼in. high.
(Skinner) $977

A 19th century Chinese porcelain blue and white charger, depicting a river scene with a floral border, 18in. wide.
(Andrew Hartley) $465

CLARICE CLIFF

A Clarice Cliff vase in the form
of a fish, tinged in light brown
on a bed of pink and green
weed, 23cm. high.
(Bearne's) $287

A Clarice Cliff Bizarre vase,
Carpet pattern in orange, gray
and black, 7³/₄in.
(Russell, Baldwin & Bright)
                              $4,590

Clarice Cliff Newport three slice
toast rack, decorated with the
'Secrets' pattern, of red roofed
cottages beside an estuary, 6in.
wide.
(G. A. Key) $267

Clarice Cliff Newport Bizarre
cylindrical vase with collar rim,
decorated with abstract pattern
of parallel orange, lemon, green
and blue bars, black rubber
stamp mark, 8in. high.
(G. A. Key) $926

A Clarice Cliff Bizarre
cylindrical pot, Autumn pattern,
trees with sinuous trunks and
blue leaves by purple bushes,
3in. high.
(H.C. Chapman) $281

Clarice Cliff Newport baluster
vase, molded and painted in
colors with motifs of parrot
perched on a branch, sepia
rubber stamp mark, shape No.
844, 8¹/₂in.
(G. A. Key) $145

Clarice Cliff Fantasque vase of
spreading baluster form,
decorated with the 'Melon'
pattern of stylized fruit in
colors, shape No. 365, 8in. high.
(G. A. Key) $534

Clarice Cliff Wilkinsons Bizarre
Biarritz plate, decorated with
the 'Tralee' pattern of sinuous
gray stemmed tree with shaded
green foliage, 10¹/₂in. high.
(G. A. Key) $314

A Clarice Cliff cylindrical
'Orange Roof Cottage' pattern
biscuit barrel and lid, with
original cane handle, 6¹/₄in.
high.
(David Lay) $930

COALPORT

Coalport ornate two handled urn formed goblet, painted with scene within a heart shaped foliate gilt cartouche, 'Pass of Killiecrankie', 5in.
(G. A. Key) $181

A pair of 19th century Coalport porcelain ice pails, in the form of campana urns with pineapple finials, gilt entwined loop handles, 15½in. high.
(Andrew Hartley) $3,322

Coalport miniature chamberstick and extinguisher, of circular form, applied with a ring handle and painted with geometric patterns, early 19th century, 2½in.
(G. A. Key) $255

COPELAND

Copeland Crystal Palace Art Union bust of Ophelia, by W.O. Marshall, R.A., incised marks and with inscription, 11in.
(G. A. Key) $137

Copeland late Spode bordalou, printed in blue with the 'Tower' pattern, mid 19th century, together with wicker carrying case, 9½in. and 11½in.
(G. A. Key) $832

An early Victorian Copeland Parian bust of Clytie, raised upon a waisted socle, impressed *C. Delpech*, 1855, 15in. high.
(Spencer's) $575

CREAMWARE

A late 18th century creamware teapot of globular form, painted chinoiserie design in iron-red, blue and gilt, 4in. high.
(Russell, Baldwin & Bright) $428

A Bovey Tracey creamware jug, covered in a green sparkle slip, painted with foliage in cream and brown, 16.4cm. high.
(Bearne's) $1,083

A rare George III creamware small bellied mug inscribed with black brushwork *Heath and Long Life to our Sovereign Lord the King*, 3⅞in. high.
(David Lay) $1,678

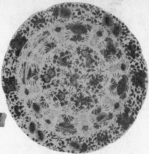

A delft plate, probably Bristol, the center painted with a head and shoulders portrait of Queen Anne, 22.5cm. diameter. (Bearne's) $10,511

English delft money box, modeled as a pig with a long snout and curly tail, incised decoration on three feet, 18th/19th century, 6½in. long. (G. A. Key) $318

Dutch delft circular plate with dished border, painted in blue with flowering foliage etc, 18th century, 10in. (G. A. Key) $183

Delft circular charger, the rim painted with stylized foliage and geometric panels, the center with motif of jardinière of flowers, early 18th century, 13½in. diameter. (G. A. Key) $542

Dutch delft tea canister and cover of rectangular form, decorated in blue with figure amidst foliage and exotic birds, 18th century, 5in. (G. A. Key) $683

A Dublin delft blue and white pierced circular basket, circa 1755, Henry Delamain's factory, the centre with a landscape vignette, 6⅜in. diameter. (Christie's) $10,338

An English delft shallow dish, painted in polychrome enamels, the center with a colorful bird and foliage, 20.2cm. diameter, circa 1750. (Bearne's) $503

Delft blue and white flower brick of rectangular form, the border painted with figure, exotic birds and foliage, 18th century, 6in. (G. A. Key) $531

An 18th century English delft charger painted with a parrot on flowering branch in polychrome, 14in. (Russell, Baldwin & Bright) $612

CHINA

Royal Crown Derby yellow ground ewer, England, circa 1891, twisted leaf handle, raised gilt foliate decoration, 11in. high.
(Skinner) $230

Crown Derby porcelain two-handled vase and cover, England, circa 1889, mask heads to handle terminals, 4¾in. high.
(Skinner) $690

Derby figure of William Shakespeare, naturalistic face and hands, his tunic and pantaloons with gilt detail, late 18th century, 11in. high.
(G. A. Key) $800

DOULTON

A pair of Royal Doulton stoneware ewers, by Hannah Barlow and Emily Stormer, each incised and painted with a group of ponies in a moorland setting, 31.4cm. high.
(Bearne's) $1,051

An Aesthetic Movement pair of Doulton stoneware oil lamp bases, each ogee body applied with circular panels, 31.5cm. high.
(Bearne's) $430

Pair of Royal Doulton decorative large baluster vases, spreading necks, on a central gray/beige washed ground, impressed marks by Bessie Newbery, late 19th century, 13½in. high.
(G. A. Key) $466

A Doulton pottery Jester face mask, in red, yellow and green glazes, 11½in. high.
(Andrew Hartley) $372

A pair of Royal Doulton 'Slaters Patent' stoneware vases, each baluster body slip trailed and painted by Emily Partington, 30.5cm. high.
(Bearne's) $319

A Royal Doulton figure, Charley's Aunt, HN1534, 8in. high.
(Russell, Baldwin & Bright) $367

DOULTON

A large Royal Doulton Flambé model of an elephant with trunk curving downwards, 33cm. high, signed for Fred Moore.
(Bearne's) $3,460

Pair of Doulton stoneware vases, England, late 19th century, set in four-prong wood bases, unmarked, 17½in. high overall.
(Skinner) $920

Royal Doulton character jug, 'The Trapper', D6609, (Canadian Centennial Series 1867–1967), 7in. high.
(G. A. Key) $96

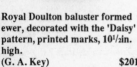

Doulton Lambeth Commemorative jug, treacle glazed neck inscribed *Victoria, Queen and Empress 1837/1897 Dei Gratia*, and inscribed *She Wrought Her People Lasting Good*, impressed marks, 6½in.
(G. A. Key) $96

Royal Doulton Dickens ware tea service, comprising: sucrier; four cups; six saucers; cream jug; rectangular sandwich plate; six tea plates and cream jug, all with printed marks.
(G. A. Key) $579

A Doulton stoneware jug, decorated by Florence Barlow and Emma Martin, decorated with groups of beaded roundels on a blue ground, 21cm. high, dated *1879*.
(Bearne's) $299

Royal Doulton baluster formed ewer, decorated with the 'Daisy' pattern, printed marks, 10½in. high.
(G. A. Key) $201

Pair of Royal Doulton vases of tapering baluster form with pale green rims, deep blue necks, impressed marks by Florrie Jones, probably circa 1930, 9½in. high.(G. A. Key) $192

A Doulton stoneware jug, by George Tinworth and Emma Martin, the baluster body incised and painted with panels of leaves, 23.2cm. high.
(Bearne's) $692

DOULTON

Royal Doulton character jug, 'The Poacher', D6429, 6¹/₂in. high.
(G. A. Key) $72

Pair of Royal Doulton Art Nouveau style ewers, trefoil necks and looped handles, by Frank Butler, impressed marks, 11¹/₂in. high.
(G. A. Key) $483

A large Royal Doulton character jug, entitled 'The Mikado', withdrawn 1969.
(Bearne's) $330

A Doulton 'Silicon' biscuit barrel with plated mount, the engraved cover with a sphinx knop, decorated by Eliza Simmance, 18.3cm. high.
(Bearne's) $393

Royal Doulton Art Deco period toilet set, the borders painted in green, also decorated with panels of stylized foliage in colors, printed marks and registration number for circa 1910/20.
(G. A. Key) $289

Doulton Lambeth faience charger, England, late 19th century, handpainted scene of classical females in a courtyard setting, artist signed *Linnie Watt*, 15³/₄in. diameter.
(Skinner) $518

A Doulton stoneware mug by Arthur Barlow, the tapering cylindrical body incised and painted in brown with three bands of scrolling foliage, 14.7cm. high.
(Bearne's) $409

Pair of Royal Doulton vases of conical baluster form, cream pellet molded spreading necks, by Ethel Beard, late 19th/early 20th century, 11in.
(G. A. Key) $380

A Royal Doulton stoneware three-handled brown glazed mug, inscribed *Royal Corinthian Yacht Club, Crew Prize*, 15.2cm. high, circa 1900.
(Bearne's) $149

DRESDEN

CHINA

Dresden porcelain figure of a nodder, Germany, circa 1900, enamel floral decorated, 10¼in. high.
(Skinner) $920

A pair of Dresden porcelain male and female figures, 'Blind Man's Buff', in lilac and floral costumes, raised on scrolled and encrusted bases, 9½in. high.
(Andrew Hartley) $1,782

Dresden porcelain model of a dog, Germany, circa 1900, black and gray painted for accents, 13½in. long.
(Skinner) $575

FRENCH

Camille faure enameled vase, black, yellow and cream colored geometric designs, signed *C. Faure, Limoges*, 8½in. high.
(Skinner) $1,380

Pair of Mosanic Gallé style models of seated cats with glass eyes, blue detail on a lemon ground, 8in.
(G. A. Key) $828

A Clement Massier earthenware jardinière, decorated by Lucien Lévy-Dhurmer, washed with an iridescent gray/gold and purple glaze, 7in.
(Sotheby's) $2,342

Tin glazed earthenware figure of a pedlar, probably France, 19th century, boy with lamb in a basket, 8½in. high.
(Skinner) $316

A pair of 19th century Samson porcelain famille rose jars, with artichoke finial on domed lid, the ovoid body depicting exotic birds and flowers, 21½in. high.
(Andrew Hartley) $6,644

Emile Gallé, Pug dog, 1880s, tin glazed earthenware, modeled as a pug in a pierrot diamond-checked coat and black mask, 12in.
(Sotheby's) $5,249

GERMAN

A Frankfurt majolica lobed dish, painted in manganese and underglaze blue with a Chinese figure in a garden, 32.3cm. diameter.
(Bearne's) $462

Pair of Volkstedt figures of a boy and girl each standing on a rocky base and holding a large basket, late 19th century, 7in.
(G. A. Key) $395

German painted porcelain plaque of The Wave, after Dupuis, the nude figure resting on the surf, impressed marks, 8^{1}/$_{2}$ x 5^{5}/$_{8}$in.
(Skinner) $1,955

A 17th century German stoneware flagon with tiger glaze, having silver mount with mask, bird and scroll decoration, 9^{1}/$_{2}$in. high.
(Russell, Baldwin & Bright)
                           $1,530

A pair of Hannoversch-Münden figures of mermaids, circa 1765, their hair and scales in manganese and with yellow cloaks, on blue wave bases, 6in. high.
(Christie's) $10,695

A Königliche Porzellan-manufaktur floral vase, 1914-18, porcelain, the gourd shaped body decorated with dense floral clusters entwined with leafy creepers, 10½in.
(Sotheby's) $3,562

Pair of Villeroy & Boch painted bisque figures, Germany, circa 1890, male and female subjects in Renaissance costume, 28^{1}/$_{2}$in. and 31in. high.
(Skinner) $2,070

Pair of German porcelain bocage figural groups, late 19th century, each depicting a musician in a flower-filled surround with an animal, 9^{3}/$_{4}$in. high.
(Skinner) $345

Pair of Sitzendorf decorative two handled porcelain urn formed vases on integral plinths, printed in colors with scenes after Kaufmann, 15^{1}/$_{2}$in. high.
(G. A. Key) $479

GOLDSCHEIDER

E. Tell for Goldscheider, Loïe Fuller, circa 1900, earthenware, modeled as the dancer Loïe Fuller with raised arms, 28in.
(Sotheby's)   **$4,874**

A pair of Goldscheider pottery bookends, in the style of Wiener Werkstätte, each modeled as a kneeling girl with head turned to the side, 8in. high.
(Christie's)   **$2,531**

A Goldscheider terracotta wallmask, modeled as a young woman with green coiled hair and orange features, 25cm. high.
(Christie's)   **$500**

HÖCHST

Höchst porcelain figural group of two dancing children, mid 19th century, painted factory marks, 5¹/₂in. high.
(Skinner)   **$374**

A Höchst group of a boy with pet animals, circa 1775, modeled by J.P. Melchior standing by his dog's kennel wearing contemporary dress of cap, jacket, waistcoat, breeches and hose, 6⁷/₈in. high.
(Christie's)   **$4,991**

A Höchst milking group, modeled by J.P. Melchior, she milking a brown marked cow drinking from a pail, her companion holding it by a tether, circa 1770, 18.5cm. wide.
(Christie's)   **$2,800**

HUMMEL

Hummel figure, 'Homeward Bound', No. 334.
(Bearne's)   **$231**

Hummel figure, 'Eventide', No. 99.
(Bearne's)   **$199**

Hummel figure, 'Little Bookkeeper', No. 306.
(Bearne's)   **$135**

CHINA

IMARI

18th century Japanese Imari circular plate, decorated in the typical manner in colors, 9in. (G. A. Key) $425

Pair of Japanese Imari large baluster vases, spreading necks, decorated in the traditional manner in typical colors, 19th century, 12in. high. (G. A. Key) $345

Imari circular saucer dish, geometric border and decorated in the center with motif of fence flowers etc, 18th/19th century, 9in. (G. A. Key) $61

LENCI

A Lenci female mask wall plaque wearing a brightly decorated head scarf, 12¼in. high. (David Lay) $455

Lenci, Woman with Muff, 1932, polychrome glazed earthenware modeled as a young woman in a red hat, 14½in. (Sotheby's) $7,872

A Lenci Art Deco ceramic figure with box and cover, molded as the head, shoulders and torso of a young woman, 21.4cm. high. (Phillips) $1,725

LIVERPOOL

Liverpool jug, England, early 19th century, oval medallion portrait of John Adams surrounded by Plenty, Justice and Cupid, 9¾in. high. (Skinner) $4,025

Christians Liverpool coffee cup, the outer body decorated with Chinese figures in colors, late 18th century, 2½in. (G. A. Key) $111

Liverpool jug, England, early 19th century, transfer printed creamware enhanced with polychrome enamels, *Proscribed Patriots* on one side, 10⅞in. high. (Skinner) $1,840

133

MAJOLICA

Italian majolica centerbowl, 19th century, lion mask relief with torsos terminating in paw feet supporting the bowl to a shaped triangular base, 14in. diameter.
(Skinner) $978

CHINA

European majolica ink well, winged griffin attendant, polychrome colored on an oval base, late 19th century, 4in.
(G. A. Key) $192

Unusual majolica style large teapot of baluster form, the spout and handle modeled as duck's head and the finial also modeled as a duck, 11in. high.
(G. A. Key) $88

MALING

Maling decorative circular dish with small handles and a white ground with colored rosettes, 7in. wide, 1930's.
(Lyle) $65

A Maling 'Model of the old castle, City of Newcastle on Tyne' made for the North East Coast Exhibition, May 1929, 5in. high.
(Anderson & Garland) $610

Maling Ringtons Tea commemorative octagonal covered container, the border decorated in blue with scenes of various monuments, printed mark, 6in. high.
(G. A. Key) $304

MARTINWARE

Martin Bros. bellarmine molded with heraldic pattern of shield, rampant lion and angels clutching swords, base incised *Martin Bros., London*, 19th century, 9in.
(G. A. Key) $736

A stoneware Martin Bros. grotesque double-face jug, dated 1903, 19cm. high.
$1,800

A Martin Brothers vase, the writhen globular body with four handles modeled as snakes biting the rim of the vase, 1899, 27.5cm. high.
(Christie's) $3,675

MASONS

A Masons Ironstone large mug with spreading base of octagonal form with serpent handle, in blue and red, 5½in. high, impressed mark.
(Russell, Baldwin & Bright)
$237

Mason's Ironstone extensive toilet set, comprising: jug and bowl; chamber pot; two covered soap dishes; vase and large drainer dish.
(G. A. Key)
$425

A Masons Ironstone large mug with fluted body and rim, serpent handle, in blue and red, 5in. high.
(Russell, Baldwin & Bright)
$490

A Masons Ironstone jug of octagonal baluster form with serpent handle, in blue and red, 9½in. high.
(Russell, Baldwin & Bright)
$490

A 19th century Mason's Patent Ironstone china dinner service with oriental floral design of fan and other reserves, fifty-nine pieces.
(Russell, Baldwin & Bright)
$16,524

Mason's toilet jug of octagonal form, applied with a snake handle, decorated in colors with the bright Imari pattern, circa 1840, 10in.
(G. A. Key)
$432

Pair of large Mason's ironstone vases of square baluster form, painted with the bright Imari pattern, printed marks, early 19th century, 11in.
(G. A. Key)
$597

A Masons Ironstone jardinière, twelve sided with two dragon mask handles, the spreading base with floral bands, 9½in. high.
(Russell, Baldwin & Bright)
$1,163

A pair of Masons porcelain pedestal vases with mask-head handles, each painted on one side with fruit, 19.4cm. high.
(Bearne's)
$982

MEISSEN

Meissen putto-form porcelain open salt, late 19th century, the figure seated with a seashell.
(Skinner) $489

Two Meissen porcelain putto figures, late 19th century, with mottos on base, 5in. and 5¹/₂in. high.
(Skinner) $1,035

A Meissen box and cover modeled as a partridge, circa 1745, naturalistically modeled and with brown and gray markings, 5¹/₄in. long.
(Christie's) $4,000

A pair of Louis XV ormolu-mounted Meissen figures, modeled by Johann Friedrich Eberlein, each of a lady wearing long robes falling in thick drapes, holding a bunch of flowers in one hand, 12¹/₂in.
(Christie's) $16,146

A Meissen garniture of three vases, circa 1755, moulded with foliage and scrolls, applied with flowering branches and painted with flower-sprays, the central vase 11in. high.
(Christie's) $21,033

A pair of Meissen rococo-scroll and foliage-molded candlesticks, circa 1750, on spreading scroll and foliage-molded lobed feet, entwined with flowering branches, 7in. high.
(Christie's) $6,238

A Meissen (K.P.M.) chinoiserie teapot and a cover, circa 1723, painted with an Oriental man and child before a steaming kettle and with similar figures before a bowl of flowers, 6¹/₂in. wide.
(Christie's) $7,130

A pair of Meissen figures, one in the form of a boy sitting on a chair reading a book, his companion wearing a lacy dress, 13cm. high.
(Bearne's) $1,672

A Meissen hexagonal baluster tea-caddy and a cylindrical cover, circa 1725, of inverted baluster form, painted by Johann Gregor Höroldt with chinoiserie scenes of figures at various pursuits, 3³/₄in. high.
(Christie's) $4,991

MEISSEN

A Meissen oil-pot and a cover, circa 1735, painted with vignettes of figures, fishing and in boats before buildings in landscapes, 5½in. high. (Christie's) $2,852

Pair of Meissen porcelain putto figures, late 19th century, each with inscribed base, *Te blesse et soulage*, 5¼in. high. (Skinner) $1,035

A Meissen arched rectangular tea-caddy and cover, circa 1745, painted with a continuous hunting scene with a man shooting a boar, 5¼in. high. (Christie's) $12,477

A Meissen model of a sparrow-hawk, circa 1740, modeled by J.J. Kändler with brown, black, gray and red plumage with yellow beak and claws, 11¼in. high. (Christie's) $5,500

Pair of Meissen figures of bull dogs, seated with a pup, having black and brown glazes, 7in. high. (Russell, Baldwin & Bright) $1,500

A Meissen two-handled pot-pourri vase and a cover, circa 1750, painted with gallants and companions in landscape vignettes after Watteau, 8½in. high overall. (Christie's) $3,030

METTLACH

Mettlach porcelain 'cameo' punchbowl and undertray, signed *Stahl #2602*, bands of figures and grapes, 13in. high. (Skinner) $632

Mettlach plaque of a castle, circa 1902, enameled incised decoration and gilt rim, 17in. diameter. (Skinner) $230

Mettlach etched porcelain two-liter moon-shaped Stein ewer, #1124, decorated in Renaissance manner with figural portraits on both sides, 15½in. high. (Skinner) $460

MINTON

Minton majolica Shakespeare commemorative jug, England, circa 1875, 9³/₄in. high.
(Skinner) $977

A graduated set of four Minton saltglaze pottery jugs, each finely molded with hunting scenes below a black glazed neck and shoulder, 21.2 cm. to 14.5cm.
(Bearne's) $398

Minton majolica cat pitcher, England, circa 1874, 9⁷/₈in. high.
(Skinner) $2,645

A Minton Secessionist ware pottery charger, painted with water lilies in shades of purple and blue, printed and impressed marks, 15in. wide.
(Andrew Hartley) $800

A pair of Minton 'Dresden-style' pot-pourri vases and covers, circa 1835, painted with panels of exotic birds perched in branches and bouquets of flowers, 18¹/₄in. high.
(Christie's) $3,208

A Minton parian figure group, 'The Lion in Love' after W. Geef, modeled as a scantily clad maiden clipping the claw of a roaring lion, marks for 1863, 40cm. high.
(Winterton's) $499

A pair of Minton Secessionists ware pottery blue ground vases, slip trailed banding in purple and lime green glazes over similar stylized leaves, 11½in.
(Andrew Hartley) $930

Pair of Minton figure group spill vases, the lady and gentleman with brightly painted costumes, 7in. high.
(Russell, Baldwin & Bright)
                           $857

A Minton majolica jardinière and stand, relief molded with strawberry plants on a pink ground, 9¹/₂in.
(Russell, Baldwin & Bright)
                         $1,346

MOORCROFT

A Moorcroft ginger jar and cover, Ophelia, on blue ground, 1993, 6in. high.
(Russell, Baldwin & Bright)
$321

A Moorcroft Macintyre biscuit barrel, the ovoid body tube lined with irises, in tones of yellow and blue, circa 1900, 14.5cm.
(Winterton's) $1,014

Large baluster vase, pomegranate pattern, circa 1920, signed *W. Moorcroft* in green and impressed, 8½in.
(G. A. Key) $796

William Moorcroft Art Deco period ewer, painted with the 'Peacock Feathers' pattern, in gray/green, on a washed ground, circa 1930, 9in. high.
(G. A. Key) $1,056

A fine pair of Moorcroft 10¼in. circular plaques with raised and painted blackcurrant and foliage decorated signed in blue.
(Anderson & Garland)
$845

A Moorcroft two-handled vase, Moonlight Blue, green trees on a blue ground, 5in. high, circa 1920, signed.
(Russell, Baldwin & Bright)
$795

Moorcroft baluster vase, orchid and spring flowers pattern, circa 1950, 4in.
(G. A. Key) $382

Circular covered bowl, spring flowers pattern, circa 1930, signed *W. Moorcroft*, 6in.
(G. A. Key) $669

A Moorcroft vase flambe, Ochre Poppy design on a blue/gray ground, circa 1920, 6½in. high.
(Russell, Baldwin & Bright)
$1,530

PEARLWARE

CHINA

English Pearlware circular ribbon dish, the pierced hipped rim applied to a basketweave molded border, early 19th century, 7¹/₂in.
(G. A. Key) $67

An early 19th century pearlware cylindrical tea caddy with domed detachable lid, painted and printed in blue and ocher floral banding, 5in. high.
(Andrew Hartley) $429

English Pearlware quatrefoil dish, scroll molded handle and the center printed in underglazed blue with scene of figures in an eastern garden, early 19th century, 8in.
(G. A. Key) $80

PLYMOUTH

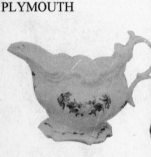

A Plymouth porcelain cream boat, the rococo molded body brightly painted with sprigs and sprays of flowers, 13.8cm. long.
(Bearne's) $1,242

A Plymouth group of two putti emblematic of Spring, 14.5cm. high, impressed letters S & D (flower festoon R). (Phillips) $640

A Plymouth porcelain teapot and cover, painted with insects, flowers and foliage in the kakiemon palette, 15.2cm. high.
(Bearne's) $440

POOLE POTTERY

Poole pottery circular large vase of conical baluster form, densely decorated with stylized flowers, 10in.
(G. A. Key) $547

A large Poole Pottery deep plate, decorated with 'The Ship of Harry Paye', drawn by Arthur Bradbury and painted by Ruth Pavely, dated 1948, 38.3cm. diameter.
(Bearne's) $634

Poole Carter Stabler & Adams two handled baluster vase, rim decorated in typical colors with flying birds, stylized clouds and foliage, decorator's initials P.N., dated 1929, molded mark, 7in.
(G. A. Key) $208

POTSCHAPPEL

Potschappel porcelain cabinet cup and saucer by Carl Thieme, with a pink ground with a landscape decoration. (G. A. Key)
$160

A pair of Potschappel pedestal jars with ram's head handles and pierced covers, brightly painted on either side with romantic scenes, 68cm. high. (Bearne's)
$2,946

A Carl Thieme Potschappel porcelain table centerpiece, the shaped base with an 18th century lady with two suitors, 55cm. high. (Phillips)
$1,600

PRATTWARE

Pratt Ware plate, the center decorated with scene of 'The Truant', within an acorn border, 9in. diameter. (G. A. Key)
$208

An early Prattware mug with fine leafage molding and painted in green, ocher and puce with blue rim, 5in. high. (Russell, Baldwin & Bright)
$428

Prattware polychromed earthenware plaque, England, late 18th century, depicting a bacchanalian scene, 10$\frac{1}{2}$in. high. (Skinner)
$748

QUIMPER

Quimper decorative baluster formed ewer, the body painted with scene of piper and maid carrying an umbrella in a landscape, 19th century, 7$\frac{1}{2}$in. (G. A. Key)
$263

Large Quimper jardinière, baluster form, decorated with scrolling foliage and geometric patterns etc, in faience colors, in the typical manner, 12in. (G. A. Key)
$199

Covered Quimper coffeepot with Breton female decoration, marked *Henriot Quimper France 744 ter.*, 10in. high. (Eldred's)
$209

REDWARE

A rare glazed Redware handled water jug, Pennsylvania, circa 1840, of barrel form, the ribbed upper section surmounted by a ribbed strap handle, 11¼in.
(Sotheby's) $1,092

A rare scroddle-glazed Redware bank, probably Philadelphia, dated *1833*, in the form of a miniature Empire chest of drawers, 6¼in. high.
(Sotheby's) $805

A rare cobalt and slip-decorated Redware chamberstick, Isaac Stahl, Powder Valley, Pennsylvania, 1938, with molded candlesocket on a flaring support, 5in. high.
(Sotheby's) $575

A manganese-decorated Redware cookie jar, Isaac Stahl, Powder Valley, Pennsylvania, dated *1941*, the domed line-incised cover with crimped edge, inscribed on the underside, 9in.
(Sotheby's) $805

A rare glazed Redware dog bank, attributed to George Wagner Pottery, Weissport, Carbon County, Pennsylvania, circa 1890, 6¼in. high.
(Sotheby's) $1,380

A fine and rare sgraffito-decorated Redware jug, probably commemorative, American, possibly Pennsylvania, late 19th century, 7in.
(Sotheby's) $4,025

A rare polychrome-decorated Redware hanging flower pot, George Wagner, Weissport, Pennsylvania, mid-19th century, with overhanging molded rim pierced for hanging, 10½in.
(Sotheby's) $920

A rare slip-decorated Redware plate, Pennsylvania, second quarter 19th century, of shallow bowl form with a stylized flower and flower-pot, on an orange field, 8¼in. diameter.
(Sotheby's) $805

A manganese-glazed Redware flowerpot and drip-plate, Isaac Stahl, Powder Valley, Pennsylvania, 1940, of tapering conical form with two ruffled rims, 7½in. high.
(Sotheby's) $460

CHINA

ROOKWOOD

Rookwood Pottery standard glaze vase, Cincinnati, Artus Van Briggle, 1891, two-handle form decorated with daisies, 5¾in. diameter.
(Skinner) $805

Rookwood Pottery standard glaze vase dated *1892*, initialed by Harriet Strafer, no. 612 W, 6in. high, 6in. wide.
(Skinner) $400

Rookwood Pottery vase, signed *Elizabeth Neave Lingenfelter Lincoln,* dated *1904*, having chocolate brown to moss green ground, 7in. high.
(Du Mouchelles) $300

ROYAL COPENHAGEN

A Royal Copenhagen group in the form of a dandy with a cane and top hat, strolling with his companion, 29.5cm. high.
(Bearne's) $377

An 18th century Copenhagen charger, painted pair of exotic birds perched on a tree, 14in.
(Russell, Baldwin & Bright) $673

A Royal Copenhagen vase, decorated in tones of blue and gray with a clipper at sea with headland in the distance, 36.5cm. high.
(Christie's) $556

ROYAL DUX

A Royal Dux centerpiece, in the form of a young woman in a sedan chair in conversation with her two attendants, 39cm. high.
(Bearne's) $2,150

A pair of Royal Dux figures of a lady and a gentleman, each standing holding a large wicker basket, circa 1900-20, 41cm. high.
(Winterton's) $1,716

A Royal Dux porcelain figure of a milk maid with a cow, in pink, green and ivory coloring, raised on shaped rustic base, 8½in. wide.
(Andrew Hartley) $800

143

SATSUMA

CHINA

Large Satsuma bowl, Meiji period, signed *Dai Nihon, Kyoto*, the interior decorated with overlapping chrysanthemums, 16in. diameter.
(Skinner)   **$17,250**

A combination Satsuma mask and bowl, the mask in the form of a chubby face, the jet black hair decorated with flowers, 22.3cm. high.
(Bearne's)   **$2,309**

A Satsuma tray with shaped rim, painted two circular reserves of warriors and travelers with floral ground, 14½in.
(Russell, Baldwin & Bright)
                    $99

A tripod flaring cylindrical koro painted and gilt with chrysanthemums issuing from behind wicker fences, 5½in. high.
(Christie's)   **$2,548**

Satsuma coffee service, with gilt rims, painted with bamboo trees in colors on an off white ground with gilt detail throughout, circa early 20th century.
(G. A. Key)   **$168**

A fine and well painted 19th century Satsuma 14½in. circular tapered vase richly painted male and female figures in a landscape setting.
(Anderson & Garland)
                    $3,287

A Satsuma pottery vase, by Ryozan, the reserve depicting figures in a garden, the reverse with birds and flowers, signed, 13in. high.
(Andrew Hartley)   **$3,100**

A pair of ovoid vases painted and gilt with panels of ladies and children at leisure in flower strewn gardens, 12½in. high, signed *Ryuun Fuzan*.
(Christie's)   **$1,213**

Satsuma vase, Japan, late 19th century, geometric banded borders with scene of an artist decorating scrolls and birds in a floral landscape, 12in. high.
(Skinner)   **$259**

SEVRES

Sèvres white biscuit bust of Comtesse du Barry, France, 19th century, inscribed on the reverse *Pajou Sculpteur*, 22¹/₂in. high.
(Skinner) $2,300

A Sèvres porcelain cabinet plate, the center painted with a couple strolling in a garden, 24.5cm. diameter.
(Bearne's) $478

A Sèvres library bust of Louis XIV with finely molded gilt details, with socle base in Pompadour pink, 10in.
(Russell, Baldwin & Bright)
                              $176

Pair of Sèvres style ormolu mounted painted porcelain urns, 19th century, each with a pink ground and with oval cartouches painted with bawdy peasant scenes, approximately 15in. high.
(Skinner) $3,335

A Sèvres biscuit group of 'La Curiosité' or 'La Lanterne Magique', third quarter 18th century, modeled as a youth operating a magic lantern, 6¹/₄in. high.
(Christie's) $2,852

Pair of Sèvres bisque and blue glazed porcelain figures of Cupid and youthful Psyche, after the model by Falconet, circa 1872, each with inscribed and shaped enamel bases, 12¹/₂in. high.
(Skinner) $1,380

SPODE

Early Spode circular plate, dished border, printed throughout in blue with the 'Lucano' pattern, early 19th century, 10in.
(G. A. Key) $129

A pair of Spode porcelain two-handled ice pails with liners and covers, each piece painted with fruit within gold and apple green bands, 30cm. high.
(Bearne's) $1,752

Spode Pearlware vase with scrolled handles, decorated with blue fleur de lys and colored flowers on a ground of fish roe pattern, circa 1800, 5in.
(G. A. Key) $383

STAFFORDSHIRE

Staffordshire model of the Duke of Wellington on horse back, wearing a black cocked hat and clutching a telescope in his right hand, 19th century, 12in. high. (G. A. Key) $288

Pair of Staffordshire seated spaniels, mainly decorated in iron red with naturalistic faces, late 19th/early 20th century, 7¹/₂in. high. (G. A. Key) $241

Staffordshire model of a seated portly Toper, painted in colors, 19th century, 6in. (G. A. Key) $80

Staffordshire cow creamer, applied with half length figure of a milk maid, mainly decorated in iron red and black with blue detail, early 19th century, 6in. high. (G. A. Key) $445

Pair of historic blue Staffordshire soup plates, impressed Stubbs, second quarter 19th century, 'Fair Mount near Philadelphia', 10in. diameter. (Skinner) $374

Staffordshire group of 'The Tithe Pig', Parson, wife carrying a child and husband carrying a pig in one arm and staff in the other, late 18th/early 19th century, 5in. (G. A. Key) $487

Staffordshire group of child and dog, child with naturalistic face and the dog with black body markings, 19th century, 4in. (G. A. Key) $198

Pair of Staffordshire pen stands, modeled as poodles carrying baskets in their mouths, on deep blue gilt lined bases, 19th century, 4in. high. (G. A. Key) $1,021

Staffordshire pottery figure group, 'The Tithe Pig', farmer's wife handing her child to the vicar, 19th century, 6in. (G. A. Key) $302

146

STAFFORDSHIRE

Historic blue Staffordshire tureen, Joseph Stubbs, second quarter 19th century, Philadelphia, Fair Mount, NR., 16¹/₂in. long.
(Skinner) $2,070

Pair of Staffordshire figures in the Ralph Salt manner of 'Shepherdiss' and 'Gardner', both painted in colors, 19th century, 5¹/₂in.
(G. A. Key) $364

Early Staffordshire study of naked man seated beside a barrel, painted in colors with gilt detail, early 19th century, 3¹/₂in. high.
(G. A. Key) $64

Staffordshire model of a gleaner, naturalistic face and wearing a green tunic, iron red, mauve and lemon tinted waist coat, possibly Wood, early 19th century, 9in. high.
(G. A. Key) $72

Pair of Staffordshire models of zebras, naturalistically painted, on green and yellow color washed bases, 19th century, 5in. high.
(G. A. Key) $204

Staffordshire porcelain study of a seated piper with a dog seated to his left, the dog with black detail, early 19th century, 6in. high.
(G. A. Key) $126

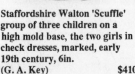

Staffordshire Walton 'Scuffle' group of three children on a high mold base, the two girls in check dresses, marked, early 19th century, 6in.
(G. A. Key) $410

Pair of Staffordshire seated spaniels, naturalistic faces, iron red body markings, gilt collars and leaves, black tipped feet, 19th century, 6¹/₂in. high.
(G. A. Key) $258

Staffordshire family group of a couple and their child, all wearing 19th century costume and painted in colors, 19th century, 8¹/₂in. high.
(G. A. Key) $63

STONEWARE

An incised cobalt-blue decorated salt-glazed stoneware pitcher, attributed to Zellers, D. P. Shenfelder Pottery, Reading, Pennsylvania, dated *1904*, 7⅞in. (Sotheby's) $402

A cobalt-blue decorated salt-glazed stoneware pitcher and three mugs, attributed to Richard Remmey, Philadelphia, dated *1902*, 10½in. high. (Sotheby's) $287

A cobalt-blue decorated salt-glazed stoneware crock, impressed *Connolly, New Brunswick, New Jersey,* 19th century, of cylindrical form with strap handles, 11in. high,. (Sotheby's) $7,475

SUNDERLAND LUSTER

Sunderland luster jug, printed en grisaille and overpainted in colors with scene of Sailor's Farewell, 19th century, 7½in. (G. A. Key) $319

Dixon Phillips & Co. Sunderland luster wall plaque of rectangular form, heavily moulded with scrolls and printed en grisaille in the center, 19th century, 8in. (G. A. Key) $129

Decorative Sunderland luster jug, the rim molded and decorated with vine and hop design with green detail and similarly decorated below with scene of hunters, 19th century, 6in. high. (G. A. Key) $137

SUSIE COOPER

A Susie Cooper pottery jug, carved either side with a goat charging with its head lowered, 21.5cm. high, signed. (Bearne's) $228

Susie Cooper twenty-one piece tea set, all decorated with pale blue comma design on a white ground, 20th century. (G. A. Key) $438

'Skier', a Crown Works Nursery Ware Kestrel cocoa pot and cover, gazelle *SCP* mark, 5in. high. (Christie's) $1,220

WALLEY

Exceptional Walley pottery vase, reticulated oviform with repeated leaf design under a light brown glaze with green highlights, 6in. diameter. (Skinner) **$1,725**

Walley pottery vase, bulbous-form under a frothy green speckled glaze with a brown rim, impressed marks, 7in. high. (Skinner) **$489**

Unusual Walley pottery tile, depicting the profile of a sitting dog in a white glaze on a green glazed ground, impressed marks, 8¹/₄in. diameter. (Skinner) **$316**

WEDGWOOD

A Wedgwood Fairyland lustre octagonal bowl decorated with 'Dana' pattern, the interior with fairies, rainbows and long-tailed birds, 18cm., Portland Vase mark and no. Z5125. (Phillips) **$1,827**

A Wedgwood Creamware oviform teapot and a cover, painted in the manner of David Rhodes in iron-red, green and black, circa 1768, 14.5cm. high overall. (Christie's) **$1,480**

A Wedgwood pearlware bough-pot and pierced cover of D-shape, molded, incised and washed in dark brown to simulate a barrel, impressed mark, circa 1790, 7¹/₂in. wide. (Christie's) **$538**

WEMYSS

Wemyss model of a pig, painted with sprays of clover, with pink tipped ears, nose and trotters, marked, circa 1900, 6¹/₂in. (G. A. Key) **$628**

Pair of Wemyss pottery pillar candlesticks with cherry design, square platform bases, 12in. high. (Russell, Baldwin & Bright) **$796**

Wemyss saucer dish, decorated with roses with green leaves, within blue green border, 19th century, 4¹/₂in. (G. A. Key) **$40**

WORCESTER

Worcester drainer dish of circular form, the center decorated in blue with the 'pine cone' pattern, crescent mark in underglazed blue, 18th century, 7¹/₂in.
(G. A. Key) $496

Worcester coffee cup, printed and overpainted with scene of mausoleum and figures etc in a landscape, 18th century, 2¹/₂in.
(G. A. Key) $199

Royal Worcester porcelain covered vase, England, circa 1888, running laurel relief to scrolled handles and footrim, 17¹/₂in. high.
(Skinner) $1,495

Pair of fine Royal Worcester porcelain figurines, classical maidens carrying vessels, painted in colors, late 19th century, 14in.
(G. A. Key) $294

A pair of Chamberlain Worcester porcelain armorial plates, the green and gilt banded border with crest and shaped gadrooned rim, 10½in. wide.
(Andrew Hartley) $578

Grainger Worcester white ground vases of ovium form, middle and bottom with hand painted detail of birds and foliage to the center, circa 1893, 8in.
(G. A. Key) $1,073

An English porcelain beaker, probably Chamberlains, Worcester, painted on one side, with a portrait of the 'White Backed Coly', 10cm. high.
(Bearne's) $535

Worcester teapot of globular form with a foliate molded finial, decorated with a blue geometric border, late 18th century, 8in.
(G. A. Key) $166

Royal Worcester pot pourri holder formed as a globe, decorated with sprigs of flowers in colors with gilt detail on a blush ground, date cipher for 1907, shape No. 991, 3in.
(G. A. Key) $113

WORCESTER

A fine Worcester fluted coffee cup and a saucer, each piece decorated with alternate panels of European flowers and deep blue sections, late 18th century. (Bearne's) **$680**

A Royal Worcester pot-pourri bowl with pierced cover, standing on three paw feet, 20.3cm. high, circa 1910. (Bearne's) **$377**

Worcester porcelain teapot and cover, bullet shaped with decorative sprigs and bouquets of flowers, bud flower finial, circa 1770. (G. A. Key) **$291**

A pair of Royal Worcester porcelain spill vases, painted with pink roses on ivory ground with gilt edging, one signed *E Spilsbury,* 9in. high. (Andrew Hartley) **$974**

A pair of Chamberlain's Worcester porcelain campana shaped vases with gilt lion mask loop handles, painted floral reserves with scrolled surrounds, 9½in. high. (Andrew Hartley) **$2,325**

A pair of Royal Worcester porcelain figures of woman representing Joy and Sorrow, each swathed in classical dress, 25cm. high. (Bearne's) **$725**

Flight Barr & Barr dessert plate of hexafoil form, the centre painted in colors with grapes and cabbage leaves, early 19th century, impressed mark, 8in. (G. A. Key) **$287**

A pair of Royal Worcester glazed parian figures of a Japanese lady and gentleman, each standing by an urn table, 40cm. high, dated *1875*. (Bearne's) **$1,510**

Royal Worcester painted porcelain dessert plate, signed *T. Lockyer*, date code for 1923, painted with fruit, gilded edge, 8½in. diameter. (Skinner) **$345**

BRACKET CLOCKS

A Regency mahogany striking bracket clock, Vulliamy, London, No. 674, the brass-lined break-arch case surmounted by a foliate cast handle, 15in. high.
(Christie's) $7,084

A 19th century ebonized bracket timepiece, engraved silvered dial signed *J.C. Jennens 25 Gt. Sutton St. Clerkenwell,* 9in. high.
(Phillips) $1,057

A George III mahogany musical bracket clock, *Jno. Anderton, London,* the brass-lined case with foliate brass handle to break-arch top, 18in. high.
(Christie's) $12,397

A Regency brass-inlaid rosewood striking bracket clock, Thomas Moss, London No. 315, circa 1825, the five pillar twin-gut fusée movement with anchor escapement and strike on bell, 27in. high.
(Christie's) $11,907

An early 18th century ebony and gilt brass mounted bracket clock, the square brass dial signed *J. Mondehare, Londini fecit,* with mock pendulum and date apertures, 37cm. high.
(Phillips) $6,342

A George III mahogany bracket timepiece with alarm, Robert Wood, London, fourth quarter 18th century, the break arch silvered dial engraved with a Roman and Arabic chapter ring, 16¼in. high.
(Christie's) $4,993

A George III ebonized striking bracket clock, *Thos. Hill. Fleet Street London,* first quarter 18th century, five pillar twin fusée (wire lines) movement, 15¾in. high.
(Christie's) $6,452

A William and Mary ebonized bracket timepiece with alarm, *William Cattell Londini Fecit,* with carrying handle to gilt-metal repoussé basket top, 13½in. high.
(Christie's) $7,590

A William & Mary small sized ebony bracket timepiece, Joseph Knibb, London, circa 1695, the plinth case with gilt carrying handle to cushion molded top, 11½in. high.
(Christie's) $18,975

BRACKET CLOCKS

An 18th century mahogany bracket clock, the 8in. circular silvered convex dial signed *Willm Addis, London*, 1ft. 7¹/₂in. high.
(Phillips) $5,436

A late 17th/early 18th century ebony and silver mounted bracket clock, the square brass dial signed at the base *Joseph Windmills Londini*, 39cm. high.
(Phillips) $33,220

A George III brass-lined ebony quarter-chiming bracket clock, Percival, London, fourth quarter 18th century, on brass bracket feet, 15¹/₂in. high.
(Christie's) $18,245

A Regency brass-lined and ebonized striking miniature bracket clock, Paul Barraud, London, first quarter 19th century, the arched cream-painted dial with Roman chapter ring, 8in. high.
(Christie's) $15,364

An early 19th century mahogany, ebony inlaid and brass mounted musical bracket clock, the case with Egyptian therm figures to the corners, dial signed *Robt Wood, Kent Road*, 1ft. 11in. high.
(Phillips) $7,248

A George III gilt-brass lined ebony striking bracket clock, Allam & Clements, London, circa 1770, the five pillar twin fusée movement with verge escapement and strike on bell, 17¹/₂in. high.
(Christie's) $15,748

A Queen Anne ebony striking bracket clock, Thomas Tompion and Edward Banger, No. 459, circa 1705, twin subsidiary rings for pendulum regulation and strike/silent.
(Christie's) $103,540

A William and Mary ebonized Dutch-striking bracket clock, Joseph Knibb, London, circa 1695, the gilt dial with silvered Roman and Arabic chapter ring, 12¹/₄in. high.
(Christie's) $48,012

A Charles II ebonized quarter repeating bracket timepiece, Thomas Tompion, London No. 42, circa 1685, single gut fusée movement, verge escapement, 12in. high.
(Christie's) $112,725

BRACKET CLOCKS

A George III florally-painted green and gilt lacquered quarter-chiming large bracket clock, John Monkhouse, London, third quarter 18th century, 27in. high.
(Christie's) $11,523

Regency period mahogany bracket clock, applied on either side with ring handles, early 19th century, 11in. high.
(G. A. Key) $1,834

A George III ormolu-mounted ebonized quarter chiming automaton bracket clock for the Chinese market, unsigned, first quarter 18th century, 28¼in. high.
(Christie's) $8,539

A late Victorian oak bracket clock, the musical movement with five hammers striking on five coiled gongs, with cushion pediment, on shaped molded base, 25in. high.
(Christie's) $1,857

Mahogany cased bracket clock with dome formed top and crossbanded case, raised on four brass ball feet, striking movement to a single bell, 19th century.
(G. A. Key) $1,073

A 19th century mahogany bracket clock, the case with chamfer top, surmounted by a finial, raised on four brass ball feet, the circular painted dial signed *Frodsham*, 18½in. high.
(Phillips) $1,530

A bracket clock by Thomas Gray, London with eight day fusee repeater movement, having arched silvered chapter dial in mahogany case, 20in. high.
(Andrew Hartley) $2,782

George III gilt bronze mounted mahogany quarter striking automaton bracket clock, Thomas Gardner, third quarter 18th century, with triple fusée, 20in. high.
(Skinner) $18,400

A carved gothic style oak bracket clock, German/English, circa 1880, in a case surmounted by five gothic finials, corner cluster columns, 25in.
(Bonhams) $966

BRACKET CLOCKS

A rosewood bracket clock, Thwaites & Reed, circa 1840, the twin fusée movement striking on a bell, 19½in. (Bonhams) **$2,737**

An oak chiming bracket clock with bracket, Jennens & Son, London, circa 1860, the arch with subsidiary for chime/silent, regulation and chime select, 29½in. (Bonhams) **$1,359**

A Regency mahogany cased bracket clock with white enamel circular dial, two train fusée movement, 17in. high. (Russell, Baldwin & Bright) **$1,989**

An 18th century bracket clock with arched dial, inscribed *Jn. Dwerrihouse, Berkley Square*, two train fusée movement, 17in. high. (Russell, Baldwin & Bright) **$6,120**

A 19th century oak bracket clock, with eight day quarter chiming movement on eight bells and a gong, dial inscribed *Wales and McCullock London*, 20½in. (Andrew Hartley) **$2,250**

A Queen Anne ebony grande sonnerie striking bracket clock, Thomas Tompion & Edward Banger, No. 443, circa 1705, the molded base on gadrooned bracket feet, 17½in. high. (Christie's) **$120,450**

A mahogany bracket clock, the arched case surmounted by a carrying handle on bracket feet, the circular enamel dial inscribed *Dutton, London*, 10in. high. (Phillips) **$1,359**

A early 19th century bracket clock by Hudson Otley with eight day movement having white enamel dial in mahogany case, 20½in. high. (Andrew Hartley) **$1,160**

A George II blue lacquer and gilt chinoiserie quarter-chiming large bracket clock, for the Turkish market, William Kipling, London, circa 1730, 23¼in. high. (Christie's) **$7,682**

CARRIAGE CLOCKS

A French gilt-brass striking carriage clock with alarm, No. 5599, third quarter 19th century, foliate engraved gorge case, 4½in. high.
(Christie's) $3,680

A gilt metal carriage timepiece, English, Dwerrihouse & Fletcher, circa 1845, the single fusée movement with a lever escapement, 5¼in.
(Bonhams) $1,359

A French gilt-brass grande sonnerie striking carriage clock with calendar and alarm, Richard, No. 455, third quarter 19th century.
(Christie's) $10,350

An early Victorian gilt-brass giant carriage timepiece, E. J. Dent, London, No. 10509, circa 1850, the four pillar chain fusée movement with Harrison's maintaining power, 7½in. high.
(Christie's) $3,073

A Charles X ormolu striking carriage clock, unsigned, circa 1830, the white enamel chapter disk with blue Roman chapters and blued steel trefoil hands, 5½in. high.
(Christie's) $7,590

A French silver mignonette carriage timepiece, J. Rossel & de Lacour, Paris, first quarter 20th century, the cariatid case with panels of pierced foliage to each side, 2¾in. high.
(Christie's) $2,070

An early French gilt-brass striking carriage clock, unsigned, movement No. 659, circa 1845, the twin barrel movement with gilt platform lever escapement, 6½in. high.
(Christie's) $3,226

A French porcelain-mounted gilt-brass striking carriage clock, Drocourt, circa 1870, the twin barrel movement with silvered platform lever escapement, 5¾in. high.
(Christie's) $7,970

A French gilt-brass quarter-striking carriage clock with alarm, Gve. Sandoz, Paris, last quarter 19th century, the cariatid case with stiff leaf and berry cast cornices, 5¼in. high.
(Christie's) $5,520

CARRIAGE CLOCKS

An engraved and porcelain paneled repeating carriage clock, French, circa 1880, in a gilt corniche style case engraved with foliage, 7in.
(Bonhams) $6,601

A silver and tortoiseshell carriage clock, French/English, 1910, the French gong striking movement with a lever escapement, 6½in.
(Bonhams) $1,932

A French gilt-brass and enamel striking carriage clock with alarm, No. 1959, last quarter 19th century, anglaise riche case, 6¼in. high.
(Christie's) $2,300

A French gilt-brass and cloisonné enamel quarter-striking carriage clock with alarm, last quarter 19th century, the case with panels of polychrome foliate enamel, 4½in. high.
(Christie's) $6,900

A mid 19th century English fusée timepiece carriage clock in an engraved gilt case, rectangular eight day brass keywind fusée movement, Harrison's maintaining power, circa 1837, 120 x 76 x 54mm.
(Pieces of Time) $2,437

An early Victorian nickel-plated brass quarter striking giant chronometer carriage clock, Dent, London, No. 14806, circa 1850, the substantial movement with five pillars and twin-chain fusées, 7¾in. high.
(Christie's) $145,791

A 19th century lacquered brass and porcelain paneled carriage clock, signed for *Manoah Rhodes & Sons Ltd, Paris* depicting an Eastern harbor scene, 7½in. high.
(Phillips) $1,057

An engraved gilt one-piece repeating carriage clock, French, circa 1840, enamel dial with Roman numerals, signed *Jules A Paris*, in an engraved one-piece case, 7in.
(Bonhams) $1,570

A French gilt-brass and cloisonné enamel grande sonnerie striking carriage clock with alarm, Drocourt, No. 17490, last quarter 19th century, 5¾in. high.
(Christie's) $4,370

CARRIAGE CLOCKS

A French silver small carriage timepiece with alarm, L. Leroy & Cie, circa 1890, the simple arched case with molded handle to top, 4in. high.
(Christie's) $1,898

A French gilt-metal and silver grande sonnerie giant carriage clock, the gilt case with hinged escapement viewing portal, 10in. high.
(Christie's) $5,313

A gilt brass repeating carriage clock, French, circa 1880, the gong striking and repeating movement in a case with corner columns, 8¹/₂in.
(Bonhams) $966

A Victorian gilt-metal striking giant carriage clock, Charles Frodsham, No. 2188, the massive twin chain fusée movement with five double-screwed pillars, 9in. high.
(Christie's) $26,565

Victorian brass and glass cased carriage clock with Grecian style handle, dial inscribed *Goldsmiths Co., 112 Regent Street, London, W*, Paris made, 4in. high, with original traveling case and key.
(G. A. Key) $243

A brass cased repeating carriage clock, French, circa 1890, silvered chapter ring with Arabic reserves and decorated center, set to a gilt mask, signed for *Mappin Brothers, 220 Regent St., London*, 8in.
(Bonhams) $830

A brass and paste set repeating and alarm carriage clock, French, circa 1880, gilt chapter ring with Arabic numerals, signed for *Jones, London*, alarm subsidiary below, 8in.
(Bonhams) $1,359

A French gilt-brass and porcelain-mounted grande sonnerie striking carriage clock, third quarter 19th century, 6in. high.
(Christie's) $12,075

An ornate cast ormolu repeating carriage clock, French, circa 1850, enamel dial with Roman numerals, signed *Bolviller A Paris*, in an ornate gilded case with mermaid handle, 8¹/₄in.
(Bonhams) $680

CARRIAGE CLOCKS

An elaborately decorated electrotype carriage clock with alarm, French, circa 1860, gilt dial signed *Le Roy et fils A Paris*, 6¼in.
(Bonhams) **$1,435**

Brass and glass cased carriage timepiece with bombé sided top and base, 5in. high, late 19th century.
(G. A. Key) **$160**

A French gilt-brass grande sonnerie striking carriage clock with calendar and alarm, second quarter 19th century, 6¼in. high.
(Christie's) **$5,520**

A Victorian gilt-brass four-train giant exhibition carriage clock with chronometer escapement, perpetual calendar and equation of time, M. F. Dent, Chronometer Maker to the Queen, circa 1862, 15½in. high.
(Christie's) **$131,095**

A French gilt-metal and enamel striking carriage clock, unsigned, last quarter 19th century, the cartouche dial on a silvered background and enameled in multi-colors, 6½in. high.
(Christie's) **$2,846**

A French gilt-brass and porcelain-mounted mignonnette carriage timepiece, No. 233, last quarter 19th century, the bambu case with porcelain panels to each side painted with chinoiserie figures, 3½in. high.
(Christie's) **$6,325**

A Victorian gilt-brass striking giant carriage clock, Payne & Co., London, foliate engraved gilt mask, similarly engraved glazed side panels, 8¼in. high.
(Christie's) **$8,855**

An early Victorian gilt-brass quarter-chiming giant exhibition carriage clock, Edward White, London, No. 756, second quarter 19th century, 14¾in. high.
(Christie's) **$87,007**

A 19th century French miniature gilt brass caryatid carriage timepiece, the movement with lever platform escapement, 3½in. high.
(Phillips) **$831**

CLOCK SETS

A siena marble clock garniture, French, circa 1900, flat top case with a bronze lion and ball, together with a pair of matching urn-shaped garnitures, 19¹/₂in.
(Bonhams)   **$1,888**

A white marble and ormolu clock garniture, French, circa 1900, the bell striking movement in a drum case surmounted by a cupid with bow and arrows, with a pair of gilt urn garniture, 11in. (Bonhams)   **$1,368**

A brass and champlevé enamel clock garniture, French, circa 1890, 3¹/₂in. gilt dial with Arabic numerals and enamel decorated center, the gong striking movement in a case with domed top and cone finial, together with a pair of matching urn garnitures, clock 13¹/₂in. (Bonhams)   **$1,359**

A black slate and bronze Egyptian Revival clock garniture, French, circa 1880, 4in. dial with gilt Roman numerals, signed *A. Bealle Horloger de la Mouni, Paris, 93 Palais Royal 94*, together with a pair of obelisk side garniture, 16in. and 20in.
(Bonhams)   **$2,576**

A gilt ormolu mounted clock with a pair of candlesticks, French, circa 1840, the bell striking movement with a silk suspension in a square case, together with a pair of circular based candlesticks with decorated stems, 17in.
(Bonhams)   **$3,864**

An ormolu and porcelain mounted clock garniture, French, circa 1880, in a case surmounted by two putti with a tortoise all sitting on an arched pediment, together with a pair of matching putto candelabra with wood bases, 14¹/₂in. (Bonhams)   **$3,864**

CLOCK SETS

French porcelain garniture of two handled central clock, circular Roman chapter ring, the center decorated with coastal scene, together with two matching two handled vases, late 19th century, clock 9in., vases 7in.
(G. A. Key) $636

An ormolu and white marble clock with matched garniture, French, circa 1880, 4in. enamel dial with Arabic numerals and floral swags, the center signed *Kinable, Paris*, together with a pair of side urn garnitures, 18in.
(Bonhams) $3,703

A 19th century French gilt and oxidized brass clock garniture, the clock case in the form of a temple, the 4½in. chapter ring with Chinese characters, the twin train movement stamped *Marti* striking on a bell, 1ft. 3in. high, together with the matching pair of candelabra.
(Phillips) $830

An ormolu and porcelain clock garniture, French, circa 1875, 3in. enamel dial with Roman numerals, signed *Deprez A Paris*, bell striking drum movement in a round case, together with a pair of matching garnitures and a single candelabra, 21in.
(Bonhams) $2,416

A black slate and bronzed Egyptian Revival clock garniture, French, circa 1880, 4in. dial with gilt Roman numerals signed *A. Bealle Horloger de la Marine, Paris 93 Palais Royal 94*, together with a pair of obelisk side garniture, 16in. (Bonhams) $4,983

A white bisque timepiece garniture, French, circa 1890, 2¾in. enamel dial with Arabic numerals, case modeled as a barrel flanked by two figures in period costume, together with a pair of matching two-light candelabra on round base, 11in. (Bonhams) $1,585

161

LONGCASE CLOCKS

A William and Mary walnut longcase clock, Esaye Fleureau Londini Fecit, circa 1700, 6ft. 8in. high. (Christie's)

$21,821

Grain painted tall case clock, Riley Whiting, Winchester, Connecticut, 1813–30, 91in. high. (Skinner)

$2,760

A Victorian ebonized longcase regulator, J. W. Benson, London, circa 1860, 73in. high. (Christie's)

$11,523

Cherry tall case clock, Asa Hopkins, Litchfield, Connecticut, 1820–30, 91¹/₂in. high. (Skinner)

$2,990

A William and Mary walnut and floral marquetry miniature longcase clock, Charles Goode, London, circa 1695, 68in. high. (Christie's)

$134,769

English Renaissance Revival carved oak tall case clock, circa 1880–1900, retailed by Tiffany & Co., 103in. high. (Skinner)

$13,800

A late Victorian mahogany quarter-chiming longcase clock, A. & H. Rowley, London, circa 1900, 98in. high. (Christie's)

$12,650

A rare Napoleon III mahogany early electric regulator, Constantin Louis Detouche, Paris, 7ft. 4in. high. (Christie's)

$78,540

LONGCASE CLOCKS

A Regency mahogany longcase regulator, James Condliff, Liverpool, 6ft. 7in. high. (Christie's)

$33,206

A walnut marquetry month going longcase clock, William Prevost, London, circa 1690, 7ft. 1in. (Bonhams)

$6,644

A Regency mahogany longcase regulator, Thomas Rigby, Pentonville, 6ft. 7¹/₂in. high. (Christie's)

$6,021

Painted pine tall case clock , Riley Whiting, Winchester, Connecticut, circa 1830, 83in. high. (Skinner)

$4,888

A Biedermeier boxwood-inlaid walnut year-going longcase regulator, Franz Lehrner, circa 1820, 84in. high. (Christie's)

$36,490

A Louis XV ormolu-mounted rosewood and tulipwood month-going regulator with year calendar and equation of time, Jean-André Lepaute, circa 1775, 82¹/₄in. high. (Christie's)

$38,410

A George III brass-lined ebony musical and astronomical large bracket clock, Thomas Cowley, London, fourth quarter 18th century, 61in. high. (Christie's)

$34,569

A Regency crossbanded and chequer-strung mahogany longcase domestic regulator, James Bowie, Kirkcaldy, 6ft. 6in. high. (Christie's)

$2,834

LONGCASE CLOCKS

Mid Georgian crossbanded walnut tall case clock, 18th century, works by Thomas Vernon, London, 87in. high. (Skinner)

$3,335

A black and gilt japanned longcase clock, Christopher Goddard, London, circa 1750, 7ft. 9in. (Bonhams)

$2,576

An 18th century, oak, eight day Cornish longcase clock by Richard Wallis, 78½in. high. (David Lay)

$2,418

A Georgian longcase clock, inscribed *Thackwell, Ross,* 7ft. 3in. high. (Russell, Baldwin & Bright)

$2,601

A Federal carved maple tallcase clock, dial signed *Abner Rogers, Berwick, Maine,*1800-1820, 99½in. high. (Christie's)

$8,050

A Chippendale grain-painted flat-top thirty-hour tall-case clock, Henry Hahn, Reading, Pennsylvania, dated 1784. (Sotheby's)

$23,000

A William and Mary oak early Provincial musical thirty-hour longcase clock, *James Delance, Froom, Fecit,* circa 1700, 92in. high. (Christie's)

$15,364

An 18th century longcase clock by George Clapham, Brigg, in chinoiserie black lacquered and gilded case, 97in. high. (Andrew Hartley)

$4,134

LONGCASE CLOCKS

Jones, London, an eight-date longcase clock, 229cm. high. (Bearne's)

$2,230

Federal cherry inlaid tall case clock, Nicholas Goddard, Rutland, Vermont, 89¼in. high. (Skinner)

$5,175

An early 19th century regulator longcase clock, *R.A. Parkin, Liverpool*, 7ft. 6in. high.(Russell, Baldwin & Bright)

$5,049

Federal cherry tall case clock, possibly Massachusetts, circa 1810, 85in. high. (Skinner)

$6,900

A Louis XV ormolu-mounted rosewood and tulipwood month-going regulator with year calendar and equation of time, Jean André Lepaute, circa 1760, 82¼in. high. (Christie's)

$37,950

A late 18th century mahogany longcase clock, brass dial signed *John Bell, Hexham*, 8 day movement, 82in. (Dreweatt Neate)

$2,119

A Federal transitional yellow and red grain-painted thirty-hour tall-case clock, Oley Township, Berks County, Pennsylvania, circa 1825.(Sotheby's)

$74,000

A Georgian mahogany longcase clock with white painted dial with Roman numerals, 87in. high. (Anderson & Garland)

$1,678

LONGCASE CLOCKS

A mahogany longcase clock, John Kent, Manchester, circa 1780, 7ft. 10in. (Bonhams)
$3,775

A mahogany longcase clock, David Smith Levens, early 19th century, 6ft. 11in. (Bonhams)
$3,220

An oak and mahogany longcase clock, unsigned, circa 1860, 85in. (Bonhams)
$1,127

A 30-hour oak longcase clock, John Brees, Llanvehangel, late 18th century, 6ft. 7in. (Bonhams)
$680

A substantial Edwardian mahogany quarter chiming longcase clock, signed for *Mappin & Webb, London*, 8ft. 1in. high. (Phillips)
$6,946

A mahogany longcase center seconds regulator, Thomas Schmidt, London, circa 1900, 6ft. 1in. (Bonhams)
$2,114

A chiming mahogany longcase clock, unsigned, 18th/19th century, in a case with swan-neck pediment, 7ft. 1in. (Bonhams)
$2,114

A pollard oak and yew veneered longcase clock, Joseph Fordham, Booking, second half 18th century, 84in. (Bonhams)
$3,703

LONGCASE CLOCKS

A 19th century mahogany longcase clock, signed *Michael Gottlob Schwarz, London*, 7ft. 1in. high. (Phillips)
$3,624

A good burr walnut longcase clock with inset barometer, Jno Cowell, London, circa 1750, 8ft. 6in. (Bonhams)
$16,100

Thomas Mudge and William Dutton, a George III mahogany month going regulator, 6ft. high. (Phillips)
$69,460

An olive wood veneered longcase clock, Stephen Rimbault, circa 1760, 7ft. 3in. (Bonhams)
$5,957

An early 18th century longcase clock with arched brass dial inscribed *Josh Allsop, East Smithfield*, 7ft. 6in. high. (Russell, Baldwin & Bright) **$3,749**

A small size mahogany cased weight driven longcase regulator, English, mid 19th century, 5ft. 11in. (Bonhams)
$4,991

An 18th century green lacquer and chinoiserie decorated longcase clock, *Joseph Oxley, Norwich*, 6ft. 9in. high. (Phillips)
$2,114

George III mahogany and walnut oyster veneer tall case clock, third quarter 18th century, Sam Cochran, London, 81in. high. (Skinner)
$2,300

MANTEL CLOCKS

A large carved beech cuckoo mantel clock, Black Forest, circa 1840, the twin fusée wood posted movement sounding on a single cuckoo and gong coil, 23³/₄in.
(Bonhams) $906

A gilt ormolu mantel clock, French, circa 1870, the bell striking movement in a drum, flanked by flowerhead candle holder, 14in.
(Bonhams) $885

A George III ebonized balloon clock, the enamel dial with molded bezel and signed *Leroux Charing-Cross*, 1ft. 9in. high.
(Phillips) $2,567

A chiming boulle and ormolu mounted mantel clock, English/ French, unsigned, circa 1880, 8in. silvered chapter ring with gothic style Roman numerals, 25in.
(Bonhams) $4,991

An ormolu and porcelain paneled mantel clock, French, circa 1880, 3¹/₂in. porcelain dial with Roman numeral reserves on a light pink ground, the center decorated with a putto, 12¹/₂in.
(Bonhams) $680

An ebonised chiming mantel clock, English, circa 1880, signed for *J. J. Peters & Co., Bristol*, the triple fusée movement chiming on eight bells and hourly gong, 26in.
(Bonhams) $2,898

A 19th century French tortoiseshell and gilt metal mounted mantel clock, the twin train movement stamped *A.D. Mougin 88198*, 55cm. high.
(Phillips) $695

An ormolu, bronzed and alabaster mantel clock, French, circa 1880, surmounted by reclining figure of a lady on a hammock, 15¹/₄in.
(Bonhams) $1,047

A 19th century French bronze mantel clock, the enamel dial signed *Brulfer a Paris*, the twin train movement with *Japy Freres* stamp, 1ft. 1in. high.
(Phillips) $3,322

MANTEL CLOCKS

A 19th century French gilt bronze mantel clock, the case depicting a classical philosopher seated in an ornate chair containing the clock, 2ft. high.
(Phillips) $906

A gilt ormolu mantel clock, French, circa 1880, 3¹/₂in. enamel dial with blue Roman numerals, signed for *Mahlen ..., 79 Theobald Rd., London*, 15in.
(Bonhams) $1,932

A bronze and gilt drum timepiece, English, circa 1820, the single fusée movement, signed for *F. Battens, 23 Gerrard St, London*, 7¹/₂in.
(Bonhams) $1,449

A gilt and porcelain mounted mantel clock, French, circa 1890, the gong striking movement in a six-sided case surmounted by an urn finial, 15in.
(Bonhams) $1,888

A black slate and red marble perpetual calendar combination clock, French, circa 1880, central visible Brocourt escapement, center seconds hand signed *Le Roy Paris*, 17¹/₂in.
(Bonhams) $2,114

A beech cuckoo mantel clock, Black Forest, circa 1840, the wooden posted twin fusée movement sounding on a cuckoo and wire gong at the hour, in a typical chalet style case, 17³/₄in.
(Bonhams) $634

A two-day marine chronometer mahogany mantel timepiece, BrockBanks & Atkins No. 814, early 19th century, circa 1815, 10¹/₂in.
(Bonhams) $2,898

A small gilt ormolu mantel clock, French, circa 1880, the bell striking movement in a cast case surmounted by doves of peace, 10¹/₄in.
(Bonhams) $612

A mahogany cased mantel clock, William Coxhead, circa 1840, the four pillar twin fusée and gut line movement striking on a bell, 19in.
(Bonhams) $1,932

MANTEL CLOCKS

A bronze and siena marble mantel clock, French, circa 1860, 3¹/₄in. silvered chapter ring with Roman numerals, signed *Honoré Pons A Paris*, 21¹/₂in.
(Bonhams)   **$1,610**

A Directoire ormolu-mounted porcelain and enamel quarter striking mantel clock, circa 1795, the central plaque signed *Manufacture de M. Le Duc, D'Angouleme à Paris*, 14in. high.
(Christie's)   **$16,100**

A Charles X ormolu month-going portico clock, circa 1825, signed *Ionoille à Paris*, the case with foliate and dentiled moldings to the stepped top, 24³/₄in. high.
(Christie's)   **$5,175**

A William IV ebony-inlaid satinwood small mantel timepiece, Widenham, London, circa 1835, the case with line and foliate ebony inlay to the arched top with flanking acroteria, 9¹/₄in. high.
(Christie's)   **$8,642**

A William IV rosewood four-glass striking mantel clock, Charles Frodsham, London, No. 864, circa 1835, original oak traveling case with baize-lined and padded interior, 11in. high.
(Christie's)   **$21,125**

A Revolutionary mahogany month-going masterpiece table regulator with remontoire, equation of time and year calendar, Cronier Jeune à Paris, 1800/Dubuisson a 1800, 20¹/₂in. high.
(Christie's)   **$158,650**

A Swiss ormolu grande sonnerie traveling clock, Robert & Courvoisier, No. 1571, late 18th century, foliate-cast case with arched scroll pediment, 8³/₄in. high.
(Christie's)   **$10,925**

A Restauration ormolu mantel clock, circa 1817, the case emblematic of chivalric love with shouldered clock case surmounted by an axe and shield, 15in. high.
(Christie's)   **$4,600**

An ivory-mounted silver and enamel travel timepiece, Wegelin Fils, Genève, first half 20th century, the silvered Arabic chapter disk with blued moon hands, 4in. high.
(Christie's)   **$6,325**

MANTEL CLOCKS

A marble and bronzed spelter mantel clock, French, circa 1890, the bell striking movement in a white marble arched top case surmounted by a putto, 13³/₄in.
(Bonhams) **$830**

A George III ebony-cased and silver-mounted mantel marine chronometer, Howells and Pennington for Thomas Mudge No. 3, circa 1795, 9in. high.
(Christie's) **$30,728**

A gilt spelter and porcelain mounted mantel clock, French, circa 1880, 3¹/₂in. porcelain dial with Roman reserves, decorated center on a pink ground with a scene of a couple below, 16in.
(Bonhams) **$574**

A Napoleon III ormolu and porcelain mounted perpetual calendar striking mantel clock, Delettrez, Paris, the case of oval outline surmounted by a garland of ribbon-tied oak leaves, 16³/₄in. high.
(Christie's) **$7,969**

A Regency brass-inlaid rosewood striking traveling clock, J. T. Bell, London, circa 1820, the gilt engine-turned dial with Roman chapter ring and blued steel trefoil hands, 7in. high.
(Christie's) **$14,404**

A Louis XVI ormolu striking Transitional mantel clock, Romilly, Paris, circa 1785, the convex Roman and Arabic enamel chapter disk with finely pierced and chased ormolu hands.
(Christie's) **$17,250**

An Augsburg gilt-metal and ebony automaton striking lion clock, Jeremias Pfaff, Augsburg, circa 1670, rampant lion with automaton glass eyes and jaw, 13³/₄in. high.
(Christie's) **$53,130**

A German hexagonal gilt-metal striking table clock with alarm, *Joh: Gottl: Freudenburg. Breslau*, the molded base on turned gilt-brass touple feet, 3¹/₄in. high; 4¹/₂in. dial diameter.
(Christie's) **$7,461**

A mahogany balloon cased electric mantel timepiece, Eureka Clock Co., circa 1910, 4¹/₂in. enamel chapter ring with Arabic numerals, visible movement in center, 14in.
(Bonhams) **$680**

MANTEL CLOCKS

French gilt bronze mantel clock, third quarter 19th century, depicting a seated woman on a shaped chair, 14¹/₂in. high. (Skinner) **$1,150**

French red boulle mantel clock, the border applied with gilt metal foliate scrolls, supported on four scrolled feet, early 20th century, 9in. (G. A. Key) **$205**

Victorian pink mottled marble and brass colonnade mantel clock with French drum case striking movement, 15in. high. (G. A. Key) **$291**

A Directoire ormolu-mounted black and white marble quarter-chiming mantle clock, late 18th century, the circular white enamel Arabic dial signed *Robert et Courvoisier*, 21³/₄in. high. (Christie's) **$3,450**

A Napoleon III Egyptian Revival black marble and gilt-bronze mounted striking mantel clock, *Japy Frères et Cie, Paris*, circa 1875, the tapering case with recumbent sphinx mount to the stepped top, 14¹/₄in. high. (Christie's) **$3,680**

A Directoire bronze and ormolu striking pendule l'Afrique, Deverberie, Paris, circa 1795, the drum-shaped case surmounted by the seated figure of a half-draped huntress, 17³/₄in. high. (Christie's) **$37,950**

English Edwardian brass and silvered metal windmill clock, circa 1895, retailed by Shreve, Crump & Low, with subsidiary barometer/thermometer, 17in. high. (Skinner) **$2,415**

Federal mahogany and mahogany veneer pillar and scroll shelf clock, Seth Thomas, Plymouth, Connecticut, circa 1818, with thirty-hour strap wood movement, 30¹/₄in. high. (Skinner) **$3,105**

Louis XVI gilt bronze and white marble figural mantel clock, circa 1790, Cronier, Paris, depicting Diana with a bird, with foliate mounts, clock 14¹/₂in. high. (Skinner) **$3,105**

MANTEL CLOCKS

French gilt and patinated bronze mantel clock, circa 1835–40, depicting the intrepid explorer Hudson, 24in. high. (Skinner) **$2,415**

French Egyptian Revival basalt, bronze and cloisonné mantel clock, late 19th century, with sphinxes, mask and ring handles and rocaille feet, 16¹/₂in. long. (Skinner) **$288**

Decorative brass cathedral mantel clock, with turret pediment, applied with a bud finial, eight day movement, 7in. (G. A. Key) **$1,115**

A Charles II olivewood tic-tac turntable clock with strike and alarm, *Thomas Tompion, Londini Fecit*, circa 1673, the case in the grande architectural style with oyster veneers, 24¹/₂in. high. (Christie's) **$401,775**

Fine Meissen porcelain cathedral clock, the central turret crested with foliage and scrolls, the movement by Howell & James, late 19th century, 13in. (G. A. Key) **$4,778**

Mahogany and mahogany veneer pillar and scroll shelf clock, Erastus Hodges, Torrington Hollow, Connecticut, circa 1830, with thirty-hour wooden weight driven movement, 29in. high. (Skinner) **$3,220**

Louis XVI style gilt bronze mounted white marble lyre-form mantel clock, late 19th century, the dial signed *LeRoy, Paris*, with foliate cast mounts, 16in. high. (Skinner) **$2,300**

Ornate Blanc-de-Chine timepiece, molded with scrolls etc. and on four foliate molded scrolled feet, circular Roman chapter ring with gilt bezel, 13in. high. (G. A. Key) **$722**

A Pfeilkreuz figural alarm clock, the brass case surmounted by a fireman holding a bell which he hits with a hammer as an alarm, circa 1900. (Auction Team Köln) **$1,867**

MANTEL CLOCKS

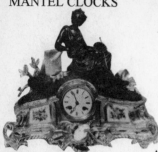

A 19th century French mantel clock with eight day movement having white enamel dial, in ormolu case, 14in. high.
(Andrew Hartley) $1,350

A 19th century French mantel clock, the eight day movement with white enamel dial painted with floral swags, in tortoiseshell and gilt metal case, 13¼in. high.
(Andrew Hartley) $3,180

A silvered bronze and ivory mantel clock, from a model by F. Preiss, the rectangular dial set within green onyx frame and flanked by two naked young female figures, 25cm. high.
(Christie's) $3,894

A French onyx and cloisonné mantel clock, Paris, circa 1880, with an ivory annular dial, the case of portico form, supported by columns, 55cm. high.
(Sotheby's) $5,087

A French gilt-bronze mantel clock, circa 1870, with a white enamel dial, surmounted by a cherub and flanked by further putti, the Japy Frères movement with outside countwheel, 47cm.
(Sotheby's) $5,451

A French perpetual calendar mantel clock, with eight day movement, with exposed Brocot escapement, 63¾in. high.
(Andrew Hartley) $1,550

A 19th century Meissen porcelain mantel clock, with eight day drum movement, on stepped oblong flower encrusted base, 18in. wide.
(Andrew Hartley) $3,100

A late Louis XV ormolu mantel clock, surmounted by a cockerel resting on rolled documents and flanked by a studious cherub seated on books, 13in. wide.
(Christie's) $17,940

A 19th century French mantel clock with eight day drum silk suspension movement, in ormolu case surmounted by a figure of a seated Greek philosopher, 21in.
(Andrew Hartley) $1,395

SKELETON CLOCKS

A brass skeleton timepiece, English, circa 1850, the single fusée movement with a half dead beat escapement and six spoke wheel, 11in.
(Bonhams) $708

Brass skeleton clock with circular silvered Roman chapter ring, single train striking on bell movement, within glass dome, by T. Evans, 15in.
(G. A. Key) $1,408

A George III ormolu and white marble astronomical miniature striking skeleton clock, in the Louis XVI style, Martinet, London, circa 1780.
(Christie's) $55,695

An Empire veined Siena marble, brass and ormolu month-going astronomical striking skeleton clock, attributed to Verneuil & Nicol, white enamel Roman and Arabic annular dial, 25¼in. high.
(Christie's) $35,420

A late Victorian brass skeleton timepiece, the single chain driven movement with pierced silvered chapter ring, in elaborately cast frame, 14¼in. high.
(Christie's) $1,325

An important Empire ormolu mounted and Spanish brocatelle marble month-going astronomical skeleton clock, *Verneuil Her. Mien.*, original velvet-lined base and glass dome, 32½in. high over dome.
(Christie's) $95,480

A Victorian brass Lichfield Cathedral skeleton clock, J. Smith and Sons, circa 1860, the Gothic-pierced silvered Roman chapter ring with blued steel hands, 21in. high.
(Christie's) $5,520

Brass skeleton clock, circular Roman chapter ring, single train striking on bell movement, on ebonized socle within a glass dome by Webster of London, late 19th century, 14in. high.
(G. A. Key) $1,250

A Victorian gilt-brass and white marble Lichfield Cathedral striking skeleton clock, unsigned, the pierced brass turreted frame with six double-screwed pillars, 15¾in. high.
(Christie's) $1,594

WALL CLOCKS

Mahogany cased marquetry inlaid circular drop dial clock, Roman chapter ring, 19th century, 17in.
(G. A. Key) $319

A small mahogany convex drop dial wall timepiece, English, circa 1840, the round plate single fusée movement in a case with a turned surround, 12in.
(Bonhams) $2,492

A George III mahogany striking hooded wall clock, Ellicott, London, fourth quarter 18th century, 32in. high.
(Christie's) $24,966

Unusual Edwardian wall clock/ barometer, the broken arch pediment crested with ball finials, Gustave Becker, German manufacture, early 20th century, 31in. high.
(G. A. Key) $480

Porcelain faced wall clock, with scrolled corners, gilt rim, decorated in colors with figures of lady and gentleman in 17th century costume, 10in.
(G. A. Key) $276

A Black Forest wall-mounted cuckoo clock, 19th century, the triple barrel chain-driven single fusee movement striking on a coiled gong, 38in. high.
(Christie's) $3,000

A Gustav Becker regulator, two part enamel dial with Roman numerals and brass bezel, black steel hands, circa 1880.
(Auction Team Köln)
                                 $390

A small oak cased railway drop dial timepiece, English, circa 1900, 8in. painted dial with Roman numerals, marked *BR (NE) 1874*, 13in.
(Bonhams) $982

A shitan wood weight driven pillar timepiece, Japanese, mid 19th century, brass movement with pierced and engraved front plate and flanked by turned corner columns, 13$\frac{1}{2}$in.
(Bonhams) $1,359

176

WALL CLOCKS

A Louis XV ormolu cartel clock with pull quarter-repeat and alarm, circa 1750, backplate with the engraved signature, *JEAN FOL A PARIS*, 13in. high. (Christie's) $25,300

Continental mahogany wall clock, mid 19th century, French works, the case probably Italian, the twelve-sided case enclosing a brass dial, 17in. diameter. (Skinner) $1,265

A William and Mary walnut and mahogany hooded wall clock with strike and alarm, *Thomas Tompion, Londini fecit*, circa 1695, 15¹/₂in. high. (Christie's) $15,180

Federal banjo mahogany timepiece, probably New Hampshire, circa 1820, eglomisé tablet inscribed *patent* and the pendulum tablet *'Constitution's Escape'*, 34in. high. (Skinner) $1,610

A large mahogany dial timepiece, English, early 19th century, 18in. silvered dial with Roman and Arabic numerals, signed *Dunlop, London*, 21¹/₂in. (Bonhams) $1,771

Mahogany and mahogany veneer wall timepiece, Aaron Willard, Boston, early 19th century, the molded wooden bezel enclosing a white painted dial, 30in. high. (Skinner) $2,990

A Charles X mahogany quarter-striking wall-regulator with detent escapement and ten second remontoire, Honoré Pons, Paris. A N. XII, circa 1825, 32¹/₂in. high. (Christie's) $64,963

An oak dial timepiece, Camerer Cuss & Co., circa 1910, the fusée single movement in a case with turned surround and pegged back. (Bonhams) $547

A rare Napoleon III early electric mahogany wall regulator, unsigned, rectangular case on detachable concave-molded wall bracket, 23in. high. (Christie's) $10,626

WATCHES

Longines, a stainless steel openface keyless split second chronograph pocketwatch, 1970s, the nickel plated bar movement jeweled to the center, 67mm. diameter.
(Christie's) $2,492

A silver cased Masonic watch, Swiss, circa 1920, mother of pearl dial with Masonic symbols and marked *Love your fellow man Lend him a helping hand*, 52 x 60mm.
(Bonhams) $2,093

An early 18th century French oignon with silver cock and decoration in a plain silver consular case, signed *De Lorme a Paris*, circa 1725, 54mm. diameter.
(Pieces of Time) $3,510

A mid 18th century French verge madè for the Turkish market with a fine gilt and enamel dial in a silver consular case, signed *Jn Leroy a Paris 9741*, circa 1780, 60mm. diameter.
(Pieces of Time) $4,602

An 18 carat gold openface pocket chronometer, signed Frans. Lancaster, Liverpool, No. 570, 1804, the frosted gilt full plate chain fusée movement with Earnshaw spring detent escapement, 59mm. diameter.
(Christie's) $4,744

A 19th century English fusée lever with the owner's name on the dial in a silver open face case, full plate gilt keywind fusée movement with dust cover, signed *Alex Purvis*, 51mm. diameter.
(Pieces of Time) $274

An 18th century gold pair cased verge watch, signed *Moses Fontaine & Danl. Torin London 1386*, with enamel dial, the inner case marked for *London 1740*, 48mm. diameter.
(Phillips) $1,888

A bi-color alarm strut timepiece, Baume & Mercier, recent, white dial with Roman and raised baton numerals, signed, with date aperture at 6 o'clock, 46mm.
(Bonhams) $378

A large chrome plated split seconds chronograph watch, Omega, 1960s, enamel dial with Arabic numerals, fly-back sweep seconds hand operated by the pendant, 64mm.
(Bonhams) $725

WATCHES

An unusual Swiss quarter repeating automaton verge in a silver open face case, full plate gilt fusée verge movement, plain cock with polished steel index, circa 1810, 58mm. diameter.
(Pieces of Time) $7,644

A silver and enamel sprung shutter sports watch, Tavannes, circa 1930, silvered dial with Arabic numerals, signed *Tavannes La Captive*, signed nickel movement, 46 x 33mm.
(Bonhams) $272

A late 18th century French verge in a silver open face case, dial with central polychrome enamel scene of a soldier sitting on a drum, signed *Lamy a Paris*, circa 1790, 50mm. diameter.
(Pieces of Time) $811

Gold Swiss captain's chronograph, a late 19th century Swiss lever with two time zone indications and center seconds chronograph, plain 18 carat full hunter case, 52mm. diameter.
(Pieces of Time) $3,994

Hamilton & Co., a gold Masonic keyless pocket chronometer, signed, 1894, in hunter case decorated overall with chased and engraved foliate and geometric patterns, 53mm. diameter.
(Christie's) $3,795

A rare late 17th century French oignon alarm with mock pendulum in a shagreen covered gilt metal case, deep full plate fire gilt movement with slender Egyptian pillars, signed *Pia a Paris*, 59mm. diameter.
(Pieces of Time) $7,268

An early 19th century gold enamel and pearl set watch, the movement with virgule escapement signed *Gray & Constable London*, 55mm. diameter.
(Phillips) $3,322

A gold and steel keyless dress watch, signed *Audemars Piguet*, model *Royal Oak, No. B56131*, circa 1985, the nickel plated bar movement jeweled to the center with 20 jewels, 45mm. diameter.
(Christie's) $1,771

An 18ct. gold open watch, Swiss, 1922, enamel dial with Roman numerals and subsidiary seconds, signed for *Tiffany & Co.*, Glasgow import mark for 1922.
(Bonhams) $393

WATCHES

A 19th century gilt brass pocket barometer, the 1³/₄in. silvered dial signed *Wood, late Abraham, Lord Street Liverpool,* in a fitted traveling case, 2½in. diameter.
(Phillips) $453

An 18ct. gold full hunter minute repeating watch, Swiss, circa 1920, signed for *Asprey Bond St London,* the outer covers engraved with a crest, 50mm.
(Bonhams) $2,093

A chrome plated split seconds stop watch, Omega, circa 1964, the gilt fast beat 15-jewel movement in a polished case with inner dust cover, 65mm.
(Bonhams) $451

An unusual English verge, formerly probably with pedometer, polychrome enamel dial in a gilt metal consular case, full plate fire gilt movement with signed and numbered dust cover, circa 1805, 56mm. diameter.
(Pieces of Time) $928

A fine and rare gold and enamel verge pocketwatch, signed *Williamson,* second half 18th century, the frosted gilt fusée movement with unusual glazed bridgecock and ruby endstone, 48mm. diameter.
(Christie's) $23,023

A gold and enamel open faced verge watch, Swiss, Dufalga, Geneve, circa 1780, enamel dial with Roman and Arabic numerals, the gilt square baluster pillar movement in a pierced bridge balance cock, signed, 47mm.
(Bonhams) $1,585

A 19th century Swiss independent seconds lever with dual time indications made for the Turkish market in a gold open face case, signed *Lattes Freres & Ci Geneve,* 51mm. diameter.
(Pieces of Time) $2,145

A 19th century Swiss cylinder in a silver gilt form watch set with turquoise and amethyst together with a matching key, keywind gilt bar movement with suspended going barrel, circa 1850, 60 x 35mm.
(Pieces of Time) $874

A large black finish split seconds chronograph watch, Omega, 1970s, black dial with Arabic numerals, signed *Omega Olympic,* subsidiaries for running seconds and 30-minute recording, 65mm.
(Bonhams) $830

WATCHES

A chrome cased novelty watch, the dial signed *Guinness Time* above a smiling full glass, with subsidiary seconds and rocking toucan, 50mm. diameter.
(Phillips) $378

A quarter repeating Swiss lever with a concealed erotic scene in a gold full hunter case, circa 1890, 52mm. diameter.
(Pieces of Time) $14,430

An 18ct. open faced verge watch, John B. Croft, London, 1830, gilt dust cover and in a case with an engine-turned back, 45mm.
(Bonhams) $604

A fine late 18th century Swiss verge gold and enamel pearl set watch in the form of a stag beetle, small full plate gilt fusée movement, finely pierced and engraved bridgecock with star shaped steel coqueret, circa 1790, 58 x 28mm.
(Pieces of Time) $9,360

A 20th century Swiss lever in a silver case in the form of a skull with matching silver chain, nickeled three quarter plate keywind movement with going barrel, circa 1930, 45 x 30 x 28mm.
(Pieces of Time) $1,182

A rare late 18th century English cylinder with visible balance in a gold and enamel form case, on the back a polychrome enamel scene of a couple in a garden, signed *Recordon London*, circa 1790, 46 x 85mm.
(Pieces of Time)
$19,508

A silver openface verge pocketwatch with painted dial and visible balance, signed *G. Mercier*, early 19th century, the frosted gilt chain fusée movement with verge escapement, 59mm. diameter.
(Christie's) $2,834

An 18ct. gold full hunter quarter repeating triple calendar and chronograph watch, Swiss, circa 1906, in a plain polished case with the repeating slide at 6 o'clock, London import mark for 1906, 52mm.
(Bonhams) $3,020

A rare Swiss lever watch of 8 days duration in an unusually large nickel open face case and morocco box, reversed three quarter plate gilt keyless movement, signed *Jacot*, circa 1890, 73mm. diameter.
(Pieces of Time) $1,033

WATCHES

A Guinness Time pocket watch, the dial with subsidiary seconds and automated toucan, the dial signed *Ingersol*.
(Bearne's) $423

A 9ct. gold half-hunter pocket watch, the white enamel dial with subsidiary seconds, signed *Thomas Russell & Sons*.
(Bearne's) $267

Dent, London, an 18ct. gold fob watch, the case with engraved decoration and enameled floral plaque.
(Bearne's) $472

A quarter repeating verge clockwatch in silver gilt, agate and paste outer case, inscribed *Crawford, London,* with a frosted gilt two train fusee verge movement, 50mm. diameter.
(Christie's) $5,693

An 18ct. gold dress watch, silvered dial, signed *Cartier*, damascened nickel keyless lever movement signed *European Watch and Clock Co., 1929*.
(Bonhams) $1,224

A gilt oignon verge pocket watch signed *Iean Martinot à Paris*, late 17th century, the frosted gilt chain fusee verge movement with pierced Egyptian pillars, 57mm diameter.
(Christie's) $1,898

Robert Parker, London, an 18th century gold repoussé pair cased pocket watch, the outer case decorated with figures amongst scrolls.
(Bearne's) $755

Robert Ward, London, an 18th century gold quarter repeating pair cased pocket watch, outer pierced repoussé case, 48cm. diameter
(Bearne's) $2,265

Io M. Brandel Ian**sp, a silver pair case alarm pocket watch, the case pierced and engraved with scrolling foliage, 42cm. diameter.
(Bearne's) $755

WRIST WATCHES

Rolex, a stainless steel Oyster Perpetual Datejust wristwatch, the silvered dial with raised baton markers and center second.
(Bearne's)   **$695**

A Swiss gold circular Rolex wristwatch, the signed white dial marked in ⅕th seconds, with Arabic numerals and red sweep seconds, 29mm. diameter.
(Phillips)   **$1,189**

A Swiss gold, single button chronograph wristwatch, retailed by Sabina, 1920s, 39mm. diameter.
(Christie's)   **$1,139**

An 18 ct. gold perpetual calendar self-winding wristwatch, signed *Audemars Piguet*, recent, with automatic movement, the white dial with raised gilt baton numerals.
(Christie's)   **$9,488**

Breguet, an 18 carat gold water-resistant and self-winding wristwatch, with automatic movement, the silver engine-turned dial with polished Roman chapter ring, date aperture, blued steel moon hands, 35mm.
(Christie's)   **$12,334**

Blancpain, a rare pink gold eight day tourbillon calendar wristwatch with power reserve indication, the matt silvered dial with raised Roman numerals, 34mm. diameter.
(Christie's)   **$30,360**

Patek Phillipe, a gentleman's gold rectangular wristwatch, the monometallic balance with micrometer regulation jeweled to the center with 18 jewels.
(Christie's)   **$8,539**

Blancpain, an 18 carat gold self-winding waterproof calendar wristwatch with bracelet, white dial with applied Roman and baton numerals, 38mm. diam.
(Christie's)   **$7,590**

Cartier, a stainless steel and gold-colored wristwatch, the square dial with Roman numerals, center seconds and date aperture.
(Bearne's)   **$1,258**

WRIST WATCHES

Cartier, a gold tortue wristwatch, signed *Cartier*, Paris, circa 1985, with nickel finished jeweled lever movement, 28mm. wide.
(Christie's)   **$2,846**

Rolex, a stainless steel self-winding water-resistant two time zone calendar wristwatch, signed, recent, 40mm. diameter.
(Christie's)   **$3,036**

Patek Philippe, a lady's 18 carat gold and diamond-set wristwatch with mother-of-pearl dial, recent, with quartz movement, 27mm. diameter.
(Christie's)   **$14,231**

Jaeger-LeCoultre, a fine and rare limited edition minute repeating reversible wristwatch, signed, recent, with manually wound jeweled movement, 42 x 26mm.
(Christie's)   **$45,540**

Audemars Piguet, a gentleman's steel self-winding calendar wristwatch, signed, model Royal Oak, No. 146D28147, recent, with automatic movement, 37mm. diameter.
(Christie's)   **$3,226**

Cartier, a gentleman's large gold self-winding rectangular wristwatch, 1980s, with nickel plated movement, the white dial with Roman numerals, 35 x 28mm.
(Christie's)   **$6,641**

An 18ct. gold water resistant wristwatch, Vacheron & Constantin, 1956, the fine damascened nickel movement with five adjustments, in a polished case, 34mm.
(Bonhams)   **$1,329**

A stainless steel triple calendar chronograph wristwatch, Universal 'Tri-Compax', circa 1940, the signed nickel movement in a polished case with a screw-on back, 35mm.
(Bonhams)   **$1,963**

Rolex, an 18 carat gold wristwatch, signed, model Cellini, recent, with quartz movement, cream dial with applied Roman numerals, 37mm. diameter.
(Christie's)   **$2,846**

WRIST WATCHES

Blancpain, an 18 carat gold self-winding waterproof calendar wristwatch, signed, recent, with jeweled lever movement, 38mm. diameter.
(Christie's) $3,036

An 18ct. gold automatic center seconds calendar bracelet watch, Rolex 'Daydate' ref. 1803, gilt dial with raised baton numerals.
(Bonhams) $4,669

A large stainless steel pilot's wristwatch, Longines, circa 1940, the large gilt movement jeweled to the center in a cushion shaped çase, 40mm.
(Bonhams) $580

A lady's yellow and white gold wristwatch, signed *Cartier, Paris, model Ceinture*, circa 1985, the yellow and white gold case with stepped bezel, 25mm. wide.
(Christie's) $2,125

An 18 carat gold electronic calendar wristwatch, signed *International Watch Co., Schaffhausen*, circa 1980, with electronic movement, 37mm. wide.
(Christie's) $885

Patek Philippe, an 18 carat gold minute repeating tourbillon wristwatch, signed *Patek Philippe*, ref. 3939HJ, movement No. 1903010, modern, 33mm. diameter.
(Christie's) $274,725

A stainless steel automatic center seconds calendar bracelet watch, Rolex Oyster 'Datejust' ref. 1603, circa 1970, silvered dial with baton numerals, 35mm.
(Bonhams) $725

Universal, a large steel chronograph wristwatch, 1940s, the frosted gilt three-quarter plate movement jeweled to the center with monometallic balance, 46mm. diameter.
(Christie's) $1,612

Audemars Piguet, a lady's gold steel calendar quartz wristwatch, signed, model Royal Oak, No. 494, recent, with quartz movement, 25mm. diameter.
(Christie's) $2,846

WRIST WATCHES

An 18ct. gold rectangular cased bracelet watch, Patek Philippe, modern, ref. 3599/1, brushed gold dial with raised baton numerals, signed, 28 x 190mm.
(Bonhams) $2,492

Breguet, a limited edition 18 carat yellow gold jump-hour self-winding wristwatch, recent, in circular case with ribbed band, 36mm. diameter.
(Christie's) $13,283

A lady's unusual 18 carat gold wristwatch, signed *Jaeger-LeCoultre, No. 35012*, 1937, gold half cylindrical case with curved glass and bar lugs, 23 x 15mm.
(Christie's) $1,417

An unusual early gold wristwatch with screwed back, signed *Rolex*, No. 759130, circa 1920, the spotted nickel plated movement jeweled to the third with bimetallic balance, 33mm. diameter.
(Christie's) $2,125

An 18ct. gold slim cased wristwatch on a 9ct. gold bracelet, Vacheron & Constantin, 1964, the fine damascened nickel 17-jewel movement adjusted to five positions and temperature, 33 x 170mm.
(Bonhams) $1,057

An unusual limited edition platinum mystery watch with the signs of the zodiac, signed *Jaeger-LeCoultre*, circa 1950, the nickel plated movement jeweled to the third with gold alloy balance, 32mm. diameter.
(Christie's) $7,438

Breitling, a steel chronograph wristwatch with adjustable calculating scale, signed, model Co-Pilot, No. 769, 1950s, 36mm. diameter.
(Christie's) $1,233

A 14ct. gold automatic center seconds bracelet watch, Rolex Oyster Perpetual, 1969, the signed nickel movement in a polished case, 34mm.
(Bonhams) $1,771

Breitling, a gold and steel water-resistant self-winding calendar chronograph wristwatch, signed *Breitling*, No. B13048 1 70324, recent, 40mm. diameter.
(Christie's) $1,328

WRIST WATCHES

A rare early 20th century quarter repeating gold Swiss lever wristwatch, keyless gilt bar movement with going barrel, circa 1920, 35mm. diameter.
(Pieces of Time) $9,576

Piaget, a lady's 18 carat gold wristwatch, signed *Piaget*, circa 1990, with quartz movement, ribbed gold dial, 20mm. wide.
(Christie's) $1,139

An 18ct. gold water resistant wristwatch, Patek Philippe, ref. 2545, circa 1960, silvered dial with raised baton numerals and subsidiary seconds, 32mm.
(Bonhams) $3,775

A mid-size stainless steel wristwatch, Rolex Oyster ref. 2574, circa 1940, the signed nickel movement adjusted to six positions, in a polished case, 28mm.
(Bonhams) $695

Breguet, a self-winding water resistant chronograph wristwatch, signed, model 3460BA, marine, recent, with automatic movement, silver engine-turned dial, 36mm. diameter.
(Christie's) $17,078

An 18ct. gold rectangular wristwatch, Vacheron & Constantin, 1937, the shaped damascened nickel movement jeweled to the barrel, 23 x 40mm.
(Bonhams) $2,114

A stainless steel chronograph wristwatch, signed *Breitling, No. 350245*, circa 1950, the nickel plated movement jeweled to the center with monometallic balance, 32mm. diameter.
(Christie's) $885

A large stainless steel aviator's chronograph wristwatch, Longines, circa 1940, black dial with Arabic numerals and subsidiary seconds, 48mm.
(Bonhams) $2,718

A large stainless steel single button chronograph wristwatch, signed *Hy. Moser & Co.*, circa 1920, the nickel plated movement jeweled to the center, 45mm. diameter.
(Christie's) $2,125

Japanese cloisonné enamel plate, decorated with quail and grasses, 12in. diam. (Eldred's) $165

A pair of 19th century cloisonné enamel vases in double gourd form with passion flower design on a blue ground, 10¾in. high. (Eldred's) $495

Japanese cloisonné enamel plate, decorated with geese landing on a pond, 12in. diam. (Eldred's) $176

Good cloisonné and gilt decorated bronze baluster vase, 19th century, the neck supporting two dragon handles, and the body inset with dragon panels, 18in. high. (Butterfield & Butterfield) $5,750

An Imperial cloisonné enamel barrel-shaped jar, incised Qianlong six-character mark and of the period, applied with two lion-head handles suspending loose and decorated around the body with a lotus meander, 3¾in. high. (Christie's) $10,500

Cloisonné and gilt decorated censer, Qianlong period, the body of fangding type, raised on four scrolling dragon heads, pierced cover with lion finial, 7in. high. (Butterfield & Butterfield) $1,495

Fine cloisonné enamel floor vase, Meiji period, signed *Tanaka,* ornately decorated with large reserves of birds and flowers, 23¾in. (Butterfield & Butterfield) $5,175

Pair of massive Chinese cloisonné enameled metal vases, each with gilt bronze handles cast as phoenix birds, 25¼in. high. (Butterfield & Butterfield) $5,175

Large cloisonné enamel and nephrite inlaid ding form censer and cover, 18th century, of rectangular form, walls and legs with nephrite plaques, 19¼in. high. (Butterfield & Butterfield) $5,750

CLOISONNÉ

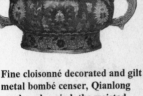

A cloisonné enamel archaistic two-handled bowl, Gui, impressed Jingtai four-character mark, 16th century, applied with two c-scroll handles issuing from gilt dragon-heads, 10¼in. wide. (Christie's) $4,582

Pair of turquoise ground cloisonné enameled metal and nephrite candlesticks, the upper sections with saucer-shaped drip pans, 14½in. high. (Butterfield & Butterfield) $2,300

Fine cloisonné decorated and gilt metal bombé censer, Qianlong mark and period, the waisted neck and tall foot banded with flowerheads, 13in. high (Butterfield & Butterfield) $48,875

Cloisonné enamel vase, Meiji period, with four shaped reserves showing writhing dragons and female immortals, 12in. (Butterfield & Butterfield) $1,500

Pair of cloisonné enamel vases of inverted pear shape with bird and flower cartouches on a black floral ground, Meiji Period, 12in. high. (Eldred's) $633

A late Ming cloisonné enamel square vase, Hu, 17th century, variously decorated on each side of the body with a pair of cranes, a pair of peacocks, a parrot in a pine tree above a dog, and a pair of deer, 15in. high. (Christie's) $3,818

A very rare early Ming turquoise-ground cloisonné enamel box and cover, 15th century, 4¾in. diam. (Christie's) $47,725

Pair of cloisonné enameled metal candle stands, each cast in multiple sections with balustraded hexagonal drip pan, 18th/19th century, 9in. high. (Butterfield & Butterfield) $4,887

A late Ming cloisonné enamel octagonal stand, 17th century, the top decorated with a gentleman at a desk playing a qin flanked by two attendants, 13in. diam. (Christie's) $3,818

Near pair of brass Queen Anne candlesticks, England, mid 18th century, 9³/₄in. high.
(Skinner) $1,840

Stickley Brothers copper plate, cleaned patina, 13¹/₂in. diameter.
(Skinner) $431

Pair of brass andirons, decorated with foliate design, 21¹/₂in.
(G. A. Key) $184

A brass and turned mahogany kettle on a stand, English, circa 1780, with goose neck spout and fitted lid raised on a perforated burner, raised on cabriole legs.
(Sotheby's) $1,955

Pair of Jugendstil copper vases, hammered surface, incised lines and raised floral sprays, impressed ostrich mark, 12in. high.
(Skinner) $1,035

A rare group of decorated wrought iron and brass cooking utensils and hanging rack, the utensils dated *1854*, Pennsylvania, five pieces.
(Sothebys) $10,350

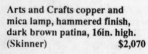

Arts and Crafts copper and mica lamp, hammered finish, dark brown patina, 16in. high.
(Skinner) $2,070

Brass footman, applied on either side with two hexagonal handles, raised on splayed front legs with hoof feet, 19th century, 18in. wide.
(G. A. Key) $239

An early 18th century Dutch brass warming pan, the domed lid with embossed coat of arms in a laurel surround, 46¹/₂in. long.
(Andrew Hartley) $496

A brass club fender with green-leather upholstered seat, above scrolling front centered with a shield, 72in. wide.
(Christie's) **$2,111**

A Dutch brass bowl, now adapted to a companion stand, on turned baluster stem and arched tripod support.
(Christie's) **$410**

A Georg Jensen copper and brass cigar box, on four short stepped feet, the hinged cover stamped in low relief, 19cm. diameter.
(Christie's) **$556**

A rare copper tea kettle, Benjamin and/or Joseph Harbeson, Philadelphia, circa 1800, with a hinged strap handle, 11in. high.
(Sotheby's) **$1,955**

A Dutch brass cylindrical jardinière, embossed with fleur-de-lys and figures of lions within cartouches, 19½in. high.
(Christie's) **$1,070**

A brass and mahogany hot water kettle on stand, pear shape with fitted lid and bail handle, the faceted spout terminating in an animal head.
(Sotheby's) **$1,250**

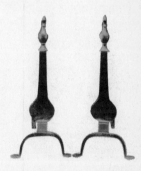

A pair of George III brass candlesticks, with knopped stems and shaped round bases, 7½in. high.
(Dreweatt · Neate) **$380**

A cast iron and brass mounted firegrate, with pierced and engraved frieze, 29in. wide.
(Dreweatt · Neate) **$1,450**

Pair of brass and wrought iron knife blade andirons, America, last quarter 18th century, 22½in. high.
(Skinner) **$1,840**

A John Pearson Arts and Crafts repoussé decorated copper bowl decorated at the center with a symmetrical vase of flowers, signed and dated *1893*, 14in. diameter.
(David Lay) $1,598

Large copper kettle on a brass stand, supported on three hoof feet and with ebonized ring turned handles, 14in.
(G. A. Key) $244

A brass and steel fire grate, with arched back plate, the railed basket above a pierced frieze with paterae, 27½in. wide.
(Andrew Hartley) $3,171

A William IV brass bushel-measure, by Bate, London, the cylindrical body with octagonal baluster handles stamped *Imperial Standard Bushel/County/of/Gloucester/1834/Bate, London*, 25in. wide.
(Christie's) $1,759

French brass firefighter's helmet, 19th century, with stylized gadrooned plume and flaming urn plaque, inscribed *Sapeurs Pompiers*, with leather chin strap, 9in. high.
(Skinner) $431

Paul Louis Mergier, Dinanderie vase from the Evolution series, circa 1925, polychrome patinated copper, decorated with two female figures and a deer amidst foliage, 10½in.
(Sotheby's) $3,749

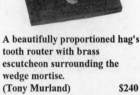

Copper jelly mold in the form of a turreted monument, incised *L & P* and *No. 395*, 4½in.
(G. A. Key) $137

A pair of brass andirons, 19th century, each formed as a sphere surmounted by a flaming urn finial, on confronting C-scroll and acanthus cast base, 28¾in. high.
(Christie's) $2,270

A beautifully proportioned hag's tooth router with brass escutcheon surrounding the wedge mortise.
(Tony Murland) $240

A nickel-plated brass 'King's Screw' corkscrew with applied brass royal arms, bone handle and iron side handle. (David Lay) $334

An Edwardian novelty corkscrew, the handle modeled as a salmon with red glass eyes, Birmingham, 1909. (Phillips) $699

A brass 'King's-Screw' corkscrew, the arms embossed with the word patent, bone handle, iron side handle. (David Lay) $425

A waiter corkscrew by Syroco Wood, Syracuse, NY, the figure parodying Senator Volstead, who introduced Prohibition, circa 1930. (Auction Team Köln) $295

An unusual late 19th century plated steel German figural corkscrew of a soldier in uniform and lady in undergarments embracing, 7cm. long. (Phillips) $750

A 'Gentleman' corkscrew by Syroco Wood, Syracuse, New York, circa 1930, in the form of Senator Volstead, who brought in Prohibition in 1919. (Auction Team Köln) $171

A Japanese Angler black and yellow painted cast metal corkscrew, with bottle opener on the angler's hat. (Auction Team Köln) $202

A Barman Opener corkscrew, aluminium, Italian patent, 27cm. long. (Auction Team Köln) $124

A George III corkscrew with tapering case having barrel-shaped mother-of-pearl handle with silver ribbed bands, Joseph Taylor of Birmingham, circa 1800, 9.8cm. long. (Phillips) $608

A wooden room setting filled with mainly bone filigree miniature furniture, the furniture mainly Indian, circa 1840, the stained pine room with two glazed windows, 13¾in.
(Sotheby's) $1,370

A large and impressive carved and painted dolls house, probably English, mid 19th century, the front and sides painted in red brick effect, the front in three sections, 76in. wide, 44in. high.
(Bonhams) $2,983

An open doll's house, circa 1930, painted white with blue detailing, red roof, one side with six glazed casement windows, a bathroom addition to the side, 34¼in. wide.
(Sotheby's) $2,925

A doll's house, English, circa 1910, the hinged front panel with bay windows, pierced balcony, hinged front door below pediment, 37in. high.
(Sotheby's) $1,645

An extremely large wooden doll's house/museum room display, French, modern, commissioned by the Au Nain Bleu shop Paris, suitable for displaying large dolls and furniture.
(Sotheby's) $914

A doll's house, in 18th century style, applied with the date *1768*, the steeply sloping roof inset with timepiece, 28⅜in. high.
(Sotheby's) $1,188

'Villa Livslyst' a carved wooden doll's villa, Danish, circa 1860, with deeply sloping detachable roof, large single room inside with original red floral wallpapers, 25in. wide.
(Sotheby's) $658

A doll's villa, French, late 19th century, with lithographed paper covered roof, cream painted facade with faux half timbering, 37in. high.
(Sotheby's) $2,926

A painted and carved doll's house 'St. Elmo', English, early 20th century, two side openings revealing four rooms, with original flooring and paper blinds, 25in. high.
(Sotheby's) $727

A large and unusual doll's house, late 19th century, with unusual scrolling Dutch-style gabled window, red mansard roof, and attic, 39in. high. (Sotheby's) $5,851

A painted grocery store 'Min Lille Butik', Danish, early 20th century, the back wall fitted shelves, arched pediment, four wooden drawers, painted tiled floor, 22½in. long. (Sotheby's) $1,005

A doll's house in the form of a suburban villa, circa 1885, with lithographed brick and stone papered facade, 29in. high. (Sotheby's) $10,239

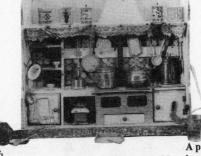

A miniature doll's house, German, late 19th century, the papered wood façade opening to reveal two rooms with original wall paper, 11½in. high. (Sotheby's) $690

A miniature kitchen, probably German, circa 1900, of pale green painted and tinplate cooking range, 20½in. long. (Sotheby's) $804

A painted and carved doll's house, English, circa 1900, the lower façade with papered brickwork, opening at the side to reveal four rooms, 30in. high. (Sotheby's) $272

A grocery store, French, circa 1890, the yellow, red and blue façade with two paper labels to the corner columns depicting two gentlemen drinking and a sailor and parrot, 15in. (Sotheby's) $1,907

A stained wood doll's house, English, circa 1840, centrally opening to reveal four rooms with fireplaces, 34½in. high x 41in. wide. (Sotheby's) $8,642

A miniature hat shop 'Maison Marianne', the shop modern, the contents mainly late 19th century, the wooden shop with large glazed window to one side, hinged roof flap for access, 19in. (Sotheby's) $1,645

A pressed bisque swivel-head doll, French, circa 1870, impressed *4*, with closed mouth, fixed blue glass eyes, pierced ears, brown real hair wig, 17in.
(Sotheby's) $1,272

A Jules Steiner bisque 'clown' doll, French, circa 1890, orange mohair wig and five-piece papier-mâché body, in green outfit with net trim, 11¾in.
(Sotheby's) $2,544

A shoulder papier-mâché doll, German, circa 1830, the cloth body with wooden arms in cream woollen boteh-embroidered dress, 14in.
(Sotheby's) $727

A Kämmer and Reinhardt bisque character 'Baby Kaiser', German, circa 1909, with molded blonde hair, five-piece composition body in white knitted jumper and white pinafore, 15in.
(Sotheby's) $960

An all bisque bathing baby with egg, German, circa 1920, the figure with painted features, blue intaglio eyes, moulded green swimmer cap and molded white shirt, possibly by Heubach, 7in. tall.
(Bonhams) $403

A Bru Jeune pressed bisque swivel-head doll, French, circa 1880, impressed *Bru Jne 7* on head and shoulders, kid body with bisque forearms and wooden lower legs, in cream silk and net tutu, 17in.
(Sotheby's) $10,902

A scarce M. Poulbert for S.F.B.J. bisque doll, French, circa 1910, the unusual face with closed pouty mouth, deep recessed fixed brown glass eyes, 13¾in.
(Christie's) $6,360

A fine large William and Mary swivel-head wooden doll and her baby, English, circa 1690, baby circa 1730, the face with rouged cheeks and red painted mouth over a thin layer of gesso.
(Sotheby's) $45,425

An exceptional Kämmer and Reinhardt molded bisque character doll, German, circa 1909, open/closed mouth with painted blue eyes in wistful expression, 21¾in.
(Christie's) $170,956

A shoulder papier-mâché doll, German, circa 1850, black painted center-parted hair and gusseted kid-leather body with separately stitched fingers, 13in. (Sotheby's) $1,635

A William and Mary wooden doll with glass eyes, English, circa 1695, the painted face with rouged cheeks and mouth, inserted rare glass eyes, 19¾in. (Sotheby's) $36,340

A François Gaultier pressed bisque swivel-head doll, French, circa 1870, with closed smiling mouth, blonde real hair wig over cork pate, 22in. (Sotheby's) $1,362

A Simon and Halbig bisque swivel-head doll, German, circa 1888, the domed head with closed mouth, blonde mohair wig, gusseted kid body with bisque lower arms, 15¾in. (Sotheby's) $1,920

An unusual pair of papier-mâché 'Town crier' containers, German, circa 1870, each with painted features and hooked chins and noses, blonde real hair wigs, the larger 15¾in. (Sotheby's) $3,997

A Shirley Temple composition doll with sleeping eyes and blonde curly wig, dressed in original blue and white spotted frock and badge, 17½in. high, in original cardboard box. (Christie's) $758

A papier-mâché headed doll with inset eyes, open mouth with teeth, painted hair with brown wig and kid body with individually stitched fingers, 16in. high. (Christie's) $758

A Kämmer and Reinhardt bisque character 'Gretchen' doll, German, circa 1909, ball jointed wood and composition body in cream knitted dress and matching bonnet, 10in. (Sotheby's) $2,544

A Jumeau pressed bisque swivel-head fashion doll, French, circa 1870, the gusseted kid-leather body with separately stitched fingers and toes in eau de Nil silk dress, 24in. (Sotheby's) $4,179

A Jumeau bisque doll, French, circa 1890, with fixed brown eyes, open mouth, brown wig, in original French costume, 20in.
(Sotheby's) $2,377

A large S.F.B.J./ Jumeau bisque doll, French, circa 1910, with weighted blue glass eyes, dark brown wig, 29in.
(Sotheby's) $1,645

A Bru bisque doll, French, circa 1890, in pink cotton gown, beige wool and plush edged coat with capelet, 17¾in.
(Sotheby's) $1,646

A J.D. Kestner googly eyed bisque doll, German, circa 1913, impressed *J.D.K. 221*, with round blue fixed eyes, watermelon smile, raised eyebrows, 11½in.
(Sotheby's) $2,560

A miniature bisque doll in original box with clothes, German, circa 1910, unmarked, with blue eyes, open mouth, composition body with molded footwear, 6¾in.
(Sotheby's) $1,097

A rare Albert Marque moulded bisque character doll, French, circa 1915, with closed pouty mouth, well defined nose, fixed blue glass paperweight eyes, 22in.
(Sotheby's) $113,602

A good shoulder bisque doll, possibly Simonne, French, late 1860's-early 1870's, with fixed blue glass eyes, blonde wig, 12½in.
(Sotheby's) $1,736

A Kämmer & Reinhardt bisque character boy, German, circa 1920, curved limb composition body in original blue cotton romper suit,
(Sotheby's) $1,553

A rare Bucherer articulated Charlie Chaplin figure, Swiss, late 1920's-early 1930's, with molded head, ball-jointed metal body, 7½in.
(Sotheby's) $695

German wooden doll with brown inset eyes, painted hair and jointed body, dressed as a boy, 22in.
(Christie's) $686

A J.D. Kestner all-bisque doll, German, circa 1887, impressed *153 9*, with open mouth, upper teeth and dimple in chin, 7½in.
(Sotheby's) $1,635

A large 'Pauline' papier-mâché headed doll, French, circa 1850, with open mouth and four bamboo teeth, kid body, 32in.
(Sotheby's) $1,817

A Unis 'Bluette' bisque doll with clothing and accessories, French, circa 1925-35, with extensive wardrobe of approx. 35 pieces of costume and a girl's magazine 'La Semaine de Suzette', December 1936.
(Sotheby's) $2,011

A Bru Jeune bisque doll, French, circa 1880, with fixed blue eyes, closed mouth on jointed wood and composition body, 11in.
(Sotheby's) $1,499

A Jumeau bisque head doll having brown mohair wig over cork pate, dressed in a whitework baby gown with original French shoes, 21in.
(Phillips) $2,625

A swivel-head fashion doll, French, circa 1875, in original green taffeta and black velvet trimmed gown, black leather shoes, 12in.
(Sotheby's) $1,280

A shoulder papier-mâché doll, French, circa 1850, the painted face with closed mouth, rouged cheeks, pierced nostrils, black pupil-less eyes, 16½in. high.
(Sotheby's) $1,544

A Jumeau molded bisque doll, French, circa 1880, brown real hair wig over cork pate and jointed wood and composition body, 13½in.
(Sotheby's) $5,814

A Bähr and Pröschild bisque doll, German, circa 1893, impressed *309 9*, with closed mouth, dimple in chin, weighted blue glass eyes, 18in.
(Sotheby's) $863

An early Jules Steiner pressed bisque doll, French, circa 1865, real hair wig and six ball jointed wood and papier-mâché body containing pull-string crying mechanism, 21in.
(Sotheby's) $3,816

A J.D. Kestner bisque character baby, German, circa 1920, in original lace trimmed muslin dress and elaborate lace trimmed bonnet and christening cape, circa 1900.
(Sotheby's) $951

A Kämmer and Reinhardt/Simon and Halbig bisque character 'Mein Liebling' doll, German, circa 1911, in cream and black checked dress trimmed with black velvet, 17in.
(Christie's) $5,088

A bisque head googley-eyed doll, Germany, circa 1920, with weighted side glancing blue eyes, painted watermelon mouth, possibly by Marseille, 7in. tall.
(Bonhams) $774

An Armand Marseilles mould 390 with blue lashed sleeping eyes, blonde mohair wig, green muslin frock, bonnet, bag and shoes, 24in. high.
(Christie's) $469

A Jules Steiner walking doll, with bisque socket head, shoulders and moving arms, blonde ringleted mohair wig, 14½in. high, circa 1880s.
(Phillips) $1,639

A Bru pressed bisque swivel-head Bébé, French, circa 1875, impressed *3/0*, with open/closed mouth, fixed pale blue glass eyes, 13in.
(Sotheby's) $11,265

A Bru crescent and dot pressed bisque swivel-head doll, French, circa 1875, the gusseted kid body with bisque forearms, in peach silk and lace dress, 12in.
(Sotheby's) $6,905

A Tête Jumeau molded bisque doll, French, circa 1885, with open/closed mouth, fixed blue glass paperweight eyes, pierced ears, brown real hair wig, 10in.
(Sotheby's) $3,089

A fine and rare pressed bisque doll, probably by Pannier, French, circa 1875, impressed *C. 8 P.*, fixed bulbous blue glass paperweight eyes, pierced ears, blonde real hair wig, 20in.
(Sotheby's) $57,986

An 'H' pressed bisque doll, probably by A. Halopeau, French, circa 1880, impressed *4 H*, with open/closed mouth and showing white between lips, 21½in.
(Sotheby's) $36,340

A Käthe Kruse painted cloth doll, German, circa 1920, numbered in red on the left foot and with original label, the head stitched in three sections with finely painted features, 15in.
(Sotheby's) $4,417

A Simon & Halbig mould 1349 with blue sleeping eyes, pierced ears, blonde mohair wig, jointed wood and composition body, 14in. high.
(Christie's) $1,083

A Grödnertal wooden pedlar doll, German, circa 1820, the peg-jointed wooden body with red painted slippers, in original red striped dress, 8¼in.
(Sotheby's) $2,362

A Jumeau swivel head bisque doll, French , circa 1875, blonde mohair wig over cork pate, kid body gusseted at elbows, hips and knees, 18½in.
(Sotheby's) $2,016

A Gebrüder Heubach bisque character boy, German, circa 1910, the domed head with painted light brown hair, blue intaglio eyes, closed mouth, 15in. (Sotheby's) $1,609

A pull along horse-drawn gig with bisque headed doll, German bisque headed doll with wired limbs, wooden hands and feet, 15¼in. long. (Sotheby's) $1,134

An S.F.B.J. bisque character doll, French, circa 1910, brown painted molded hair, jointed wood and composition body, 16½in. (Christie's) $1,999

A François Gaultier bisque swivel-head doll, French, circa 1870, impressed *3* on head and *FG* on shoulder, in blue and white striped skirt, blue silk shirt and overskirt, 17in. (Sotheby's) $4,361

A Renou pull along stubborn horse and bisque dolls automaton, French, circa 1900, German bisque headed girl rider, a boy with Limoges bisque head behind, 11in. (Sotheby's) $1,370

A poured wax shoulder head child doll, English, possibly by Meech, circa 1860, inserted blonde mohair wig, on a cloth body with poured wax lower limbs, 26in. (Bonhams) $968

A 1950's Kathe Kruse Little German Child doll with synthetic head, painted features, fair mohair wig and cloth body, 18in. high. (Christie's) $750

A Decamps walking doll and cart automaton, French, early 20th century, the doll with Limoges bisque head, fixed blue glass eyes, open mouth with moulded teeth, 14in. long. (Sotheby's) $731

A Dep Tête Jumeau bisque doll, circa 1900, jointed wood and composition body, inoperative pull-cord voice mechanism, 19½in. (Sotheby's) $2,194

A decorative cast iron stove with pierced cover plate, 54cm. high. (Auction Team Köln) $202

An Ever Handy American pencil sharpener by the Hunt Pen Co., Camden, NJ. (Auction Team Köln) $20

A Turntable 98 cast iron apple peeling machine by the Goodell Co, Antrim, USA, 1898. (Auction Team Köln) $116

A copper and wrought-iron cauldron on stand, Pennsylvania, late 18th century, of circular form with hinged bail handle and riveted tabs, 12in. diameter. (Sotheby's) $345

A Regal Shoe Company safe, by York Safe & Lock Co., Boston, with double combination doors, and steel inner chamber, black with gold decoration, both combinations known, circa 1915. (Auction Team Köln) $935

A good steel-mounted walnut slaw cutter, Pennsylvania, 19th century, pierced with a heart motif mounted with side rails below, 21½in. high. (Sotheby's) $575

A wooden coffee grinder, cast iron cover plate and mechanism, with serpentine handle, circa 1900. (Auction Team Köln) $155

A French hourglass-shaped, hand-forged coffee grinder, 18th century. (Auction Team Köln) $272

A single thread mystery chain stitch machine, with separate thread box and integral tension adjuster. (Auction Team Köln) $310

A Siemens W 250 T bakelite fan.
(Auction Team Köln) $100

An American chopping machine,
cast iron mechanism for blades,
in a rotating container, 41cm.
wide, circa 1880.
(Auction Team Köln) $101

A rare wooden butterchurn,
circa 1830, height circa 70cm.
(Auction Team Köln) $100

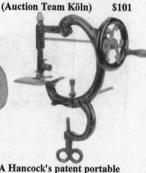

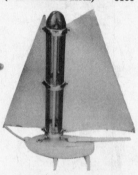

**Twenty-eight white, opaque light
bulbs with bayonet mounts, each
with a photographically printed
portrait of a member of the
Royal family or Army, 4¾in.
high each.**
(Christie's) $1,571

**A Hancock's patent portable
sewing machine with hooked
needle, horizontal rear-mounted
thread wheel and open table-
clamp, stamped *Pat. Aug 6.
1867*, 6¾in. wide.**
(Christie's) $2,094

**A Punning designer heating
lamp, electric heater in the form
of a yacht, the two chromed tin
sails serving as heat reflectors,
circa 1930.**
(Auction Team Köln)

$295

**A Universal E 9410 heart-
shaped, push-button toaster,
1929.**
(Auction Team Köln)

$700

**An early American cast iron
coffee grinder by the Enterprise
Mfg. Co., Philadelphia, circa
1875.**
(Auction Team Köln)

$350

**A must press with cast iron hand
wheel, frame and base, the
container of blue enameled tin,
circa 1900.**
(Auction Team Köln) $140

An AEG Type D detector.
(Auction Team Köln)
$638

A Wimshurst-type electrostatic generator, blade diameter 40cm., demonstration model.
(Auction Team Köln) $109

An Isaria G detector in original condition, 1925.
(Auction Team Köln)
$935

Large Wimshurst machine with two coaxial plates, 2 Leyden jars and two conductors with rubber handles, circa 1900.
(Auction Team Köln)
$622

A brass polarising machine labelled *Institut d'Optique du Dr J G Hofmann, Paris*, and laboratory thermometer 0-30°, circa 1900.
(Auction Team Köln)
$171

An early Clemançon dimmer from the Pathé Palace, Lyons, rheostat for cinema lighting, circa 1900, 51cm. high.
(Auction Team Köln)
$186

An early demonstration model electric motor, on mahogany base, total height 14.5cm.
(Auction Team Köln)
$506

A Ramsden-style electrification machine, by Phywe, one conductor on hard rubber isolator, 1930.
(Auction Team Köln)
$506

A large Ruhmkorff coil, by Klingelfuss, Basel, circa 1900, 19cm. diameter.
(Auction Team Köln)
$256

A south Staffordshire enamel writing-box, circa 1770, the hinged cover printed and painted with figures tending their flocks, 6⁷/₈in. wide. (Christie's) $5,693

An unusual south Staffordshire bodkin-case, circa 1765, the cover molded as the head of a man in blue and white uniform with red cloak, 5in. high. (Christie's) $1,897

A south Staffordshire enamel snuff-box, circa 1765, the maroon body embellished with raised white flowerheads and scrolls, 3¹/₈in. wide. (Christie's) $2,846

A jeweled gold-mounted enamel frame, marked *Fabergé*, St. Petersburg, 1899–1903, the aperture within a border of seed-pearls, 3¹/₈in. high. (Christie's) $63,000

A George II enamel and gold royal presentation snuff-box, by George Michael Moser, circa 1760, containing an enamel miniature of George, Prince of Wales, later King George III, the box 3¹/₈in. wide. (Christie's) $431,340

A silver-gilt guilloché enamel desk clock, by Fabergé, St. Petersburg, circa 1890, shaped as a star, the aperture with white enamel dial, 4³/₄in. high. (Christie's) $63,000

A south Staffordshire small enamel snuff-box, circa 1765, the cover painted with a scene from L'Après Diner, after an engraving by Larmessin, 2³/₈in. wide. (Christie's) $1,043

A south Staffordshire enamel étui, circa 1780, the pink ground painted with shepherd lovers and their flocks in country settings, 4in. long. (Christie's) $3,415

A Birmingham enamel snuff-box, circa 1765, the white ground cover printed and painted with Les Amours Pastorales, after Hancock, 3³/₈in. wide. (Christie's) $4,934

A Swiss gold and enamel snuff box, Francois Joanin, Geneva, circa 1810, hinged cover with painted enamel scene of figures in a landscape, 3⁷/₈in. long. (Christie's) $9,775

A south Staffordshire enamel étui, circa 1770, the white ground enamel body painted with raised posies of flowers against gold trelliswork, 4in. long. (Christie's) $4,175

A Birmingham or south Staffordshire tobacco-box, circa 1770, printed and painted on the cover with figures in a Dutch inn in the manner of Teniers, 4³/₄in. wide. (Christie's) $3,605

A Birmingham enamel snuff-box, circa 1765, the white ground body printed and painted with a gentleman and a lady holding a bird in a birdcage, 3³/₈in. (Christie's) $1,518

A south Staffordshire enamel tea-caddy, circa 1770, the pink ground sides printed and painted with four cartouches depicting seated lovers, 3¹/₄in. high. (Christie's) $3,036

A Birmingham enamel snuff-box, circa 1765, the white ground body printed and painted on the cover with a gallant leaning on a plinth, 3¹/₈in. wide. (Christie's) $1,898

An unusual south Staffordshire enamel snuff-box, circa 1770, the pink ground body printed and painted on the cover with ships in a harbor, 3in. wide. (Christie's) $3,036

A south Staffordshire enamel étui, circa 1780, the front, back and cover painted with figures and animals in architectural and landscape settings, 2³/₄in. high. (Christie's) $3,795

A south Staffordshire enamel snuff-box, circa 1770, the cover painted with Venus, Adonis and two putti with a hound, 3¹/₄in. wide. (Christie's) $3,795

Maja-Tee, Germany, circa 1900 sig. *Ludwig Kübler Göttingen*, convex, 124½ x 79½cm.
(Christie's) $2,387

Turmac Cigarettes, Philip Morris Turmac SA., Bruxelles, circa 1931 (T.P.B. 1931), flat, beaded edge, 60 x 80cm.
(Christie's) $4,433

Cigarettes John Thomass, Belgium, circa 1925, convex, 69½ x 49½cm.
(Christie's) $510

Seelig's Kandierter Korn-Kaffee, Emil Seelig AG, Heilbronn, Germany, circa 1905, convex, 71 x 48cm.
(Christie's) $1,773

Cameras Kodak Film, Kodak SA, Lausanne, circa 1955, flat, 48 x 63cm.
(Christie's) $169

Pez Peppermint, van Melle Deutschland GMBH, Detmold, circa 1950, flat, folded edge, 73 x 48cm.
(Christie's) $845

Weck, Weck GMBH & Co., Wehr-Oflingen, Germany, circa 1930, sig. *CRD* (C. Robert Dold), convex, 59 x 39½cm.
(Christie's) $1,159

La Vache Qui Rit, Bel SA, Bruxelles, circa 1934 (T.P.B. 1934), sig. *Benjamin Rabier*, convex, 49½cm. diameter.
(Christie's) $1,364

Gritzner Nähmaschinen, Maschinenfabrik Gritzner AG, Durlach, post 1900, flat, folded edge, 89 x 60½cm.
(Christie's) $1,364

Zuban Zigaretten, G. Zuban, München, circa 1920, convex, 60½ x 47cm.
(Christie's) $3,410

St. Michel, Gosset S.A., Bruxelles, circa 1936, (T.P.B. 1936), convex, 31cm. diam.
(Christie's) $845

Fivaz & Cie S.A., Payerne, post 1928, after a design by Eric de Coulon, convex, 47½ x 35cm.
(Christie's) $218

Caballero Cigarettes, sig. *Fabr. Laurens BV, Den Haag*, circa 1950, flat, folded edge, 58 x 37½cm.
(Christie's) $2,592

Produits Casino, Casino, St. Etienne, post 1935, after a design by A.M. Cassandre, flat, 73½ x 69cm.
(Christie's) $748

Chocolat Frigor Cailler, Cailler SA, Vevey, Swiss, circa 1929, sig. *Leonetto Cappiello*, convex, 49½ x 35cm.
(Christie's) $8,867

Sunlight/Savon, Seifenfabrik Helvetia, Olten, circa 1903, after a design by John White, convex, 55½ x 36½cm.
(Christie's) $6,804

His Masters Voice (verso), Columbia Records (recto), England, circa 1930, flat double-sided, 61cm diam.
(Christie's) $816

F-L. Cailler Chocolat au lait, Cailler SA Vevey, Switzerland, circa 1934, sig. *KB* (Karl Bickel), convex, 101 x 71cm.
(Christie's) $3,380

Velma Suchard, Chocolat
Suchard SA, Neuchâtel, circa
1910, convex, 66 x 33cm.
(Christie's) $2,592

Radio, L.L., Radio Lucien Levy,
Paris, circa 1930, after a design
by C. Favre, flat, 46cm. diam.
(Christie's) $481

Sunlight/Seife, Seifenfabrik
Helvetia, Olten, circa 1900, flat
in wooden frame, 192 x 114cm.
(Christie's) $4,422

CHOCOLAT
DELESPAUL-HAVEZ
EN VENTE ICI

MILKA
SUCHARD
CHOCOLAT AU LAIT PUR DES ALPES

Für Alle Wäsche Persil, Henkel
& Cie. AG, Düsseldorf, post
1922, after a design by Kurt
Heiligenstaedt, convex, 59 x
39½cm.
(Christie's) $2,041

Chocolat Delespaul-Havez SA,
Lille, circa 1925, after a design
by one of the Delespaul-Havez
factory workers, flat, folded
edge, 42½ x 60cm.
(Christie's) $1,705

Milka Suchard, Chocolat
Suchard SA, Neuchâtel,
Switzerland, post 1906, after a
design by Joseph Husson,
convex, 150½ x 99cm.
(Christie's) $44,337

Nur Mit Ozonil, Dr. Thompson's
Seifenp., Düsseldorf, circa 1930,
convex, 59 x 39½cm.
(Christie's) $1,224

Miss Blanche, The Netherlands,
circa 1950, flat, folded edge, 82½
x 116½cm.
(Christie's) $1,296

Aber Tantchen...Persil, Henkel
& Cie, AG, Düsseldorf, circa,
1927, convex, 59 x 39½cm.
(Christie's) $1,173

Chlorodont, Leo Werke,
Obertshausen, circa 1915,
convex, 59½ x 39½cm.
(Christie's) $6,805

Tungsram SA Belge, Bruxelles,
circa 1931 (T.P.B. 1931), flat, 30
x 50cm.
(Christie's) $338

Rossa Zigarettenfabrik,
Munchen, circa 1920, convex, 74
x 49cm.
(Christie's) $8,185

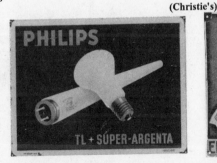

Bière D'Adelshoffen, Grande
Brasserie Alsacienne
D'Adelshoffen, Schiltigheim,
France, circa 1925, convex, 49½
x 33cm.
(Christie's) $1,296

Cigarettes Laurens Ed. Laurens
SA, Grange-Canal GE,
Switzerland, circa 1930, flat,
beaded edge, 60 x 80cm.
(Christie's) $1,296

Sandeman Port & Sherry,
Seagram Nederland BV,
Amsterdam, circa 1951 (T.P.B.
1951), after a design by Georges
Massiot, flat, folded edge, 86 x
52cm.
(Christie's) $7,502

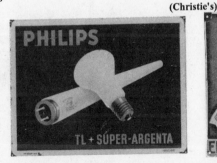

Tungsram Radio, Tungsram
AG, Zurich (CH) circa 1930,
flat, folded edge, 45 x 33cm.
(Christie's) $10,885

Philips TL Super-Arenta,
Philips, Eindhoven, circa 1950,
flat folded edge, 72½ x 97½cm.
(Christie's) $442

La Tribune, France, circa 1930,
sig. F. Martin 30, convex, 29½ x
19½cm.
(Christie's) $1,769

Haecht, Belgium, circa 1954
(T.P.B. 1954), flat, folded edge,
98 x 48cm.
(Christie's) $592

Martini Vermouth, Martini &
Rossi SA, Meyrin, Switzerland,
post 1940, flat, folded edge, 68 x
110½cm.
(Christie's) $591

Pasta Medicinal Couto, Belgium,
circa 1935, convex, 69½ x
198½cm.
(Christie's) $1,633

Schicht Radion Wäscht Allein!
Unilever-Apollo G.M.B.H.
Vienna, circa 1928, flat, folded
edge, 96 x 48cm.
(Christie's) $818

Fyffes, Germany, circa 1925,
convex, 33 x 50cm.
(Christie's) $186

Pastilles Valda, France, circa
1930, after a design by Falcucci,
flat, folded edge, 97 x 40cm.
(Christie's) $1,293

Mercedes, Manz AG, Bamberg,
circa 1930, convex, 70 x 43cm.
(Christie's) $1,908

Cinzano À Base de Vin, France,
circa 1955, sig. *Jean Colin*, flat
folded edge, raised letters, 48 x
97cm.
(Christie's) $550

Torck, Delamare et Cerf,
Bruxelles, circa 1925, flat,
folded edge, 102 x 52cm..
(Christie's) $1,293

ELECTRIC

A Trico vacuum car fan, with
screw V-ring.
(Auction Team Köln)
$155

The Crosley Temperator fan,
with gold-bronze craquelé cover,
110V, circa 1930.
(Auction Team Köln) $116

An Ozoniseur table fan on cast
iron base, French, circa 1910,
40cm. high.
(Auction Team Köln)
$390

An early General Electric table
fan, with decorative cast iron
cover and base, 110V, circa
1901.
(Auction Team Köln) $140

A Junior bakelite fan by Edla,
France, with aluminium back
and grille and drawer behind for
storing flex.
(Auction Team Köln) $109

A swivel table fan on cast iron
base, four blade brass fan and
basket, circa 1935.
(Auction Team Köln)
$506

General Electric chromium
swivel table fan, 110V,
American.
(Auction Team Köln)
$390

A Circulair horizontal fan by the
Electro Mfg. Co. of America.
(Auction Team Köln)
$233

A desk-top chrome fan, 220V,
circa 52cm. high.
(Auction Team Köln)
$170

A fan with pagoda sticks, the leaf painted with three shaped vignettes of lovers in landscapes against a trompe l'oeil of lace, circa 1760, 11in. (Christie's) $3,846

Brasserie Universelle, a chromolithographic advertising fan, with two cat portraits, with wooden sticks, circa 1910, 10in. (Christie's) $314

A fan, the leaf painted with figures in a landscape, the verso with birdcatchers, with carved, pierced and painted ivory sticks, French, circa 1770, 11in. (Christie's) $1,224

A fan signed *J. Donzel*, the leaf painted with two ladies watching putti setting up a net across a bridge, the mother of pearl sticks carved and pierced, circa 1885, 11in. (Christie's) $2,622

Dubonnet, signed *A.M. Cassandre*, a chromolithographic advertising fan, published by E. Chambrelent, with wooden sticks, 1932, 9in. (Christie's) $380

White Peacock, signed *A. Thomasse*, a fan, the shaped silk leaf painted, signed on verso *Duvelleroy*, the horn sticks carved and pierced to resemble peacock feathers, circa 1908, 10in. (Christie's) $629

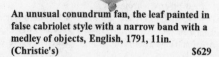

A rare 17th century fan, the kid leaf stained ocher and slotted with the tortoiseshell sticks, 12in. (Christie's) $2,447

An unusual conundrum fan, the leaf painted in false cabriolet style with a narrow band with a medley of objects, English, 1791, 11in. (Christie's) $629

A fan, the leaf painted with lovers in a landscape, the ivory sticks carved and painted with figures, circa 1870, 10in. (Christie's) $559

L'Oracle, a printed fan, the silk leaf printed in color and embroidered with sequins, circa 1890, 11in. (Christie's) $385

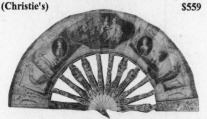

King David Playing the Harp before King Saul, a fan, the leaf painted with a trompe l'oeil of landscape paintings, the ivory sticks carved and pierced with figures and gilt, circa 1770, 10in. (Christie's) $839

A rare Court fan, the paper leaf painted with figures in Turkish dress, the gilt metal guardsticks set with colored paste birds and flowers, English, mid 18th century, 11in. (Christie's) $3,146

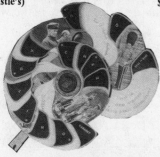

The Silver Jubilee of T.M. King George V and Queen Mary, and unusual expanding cockade fan with photographs of the reign and Gala Supper menu. (Christie's) $1,135

A mask fan, the black gauze mount with a black velvet mask, with wooden sticks, the upper guardstick as a lady dressed as a marotte, circa 1890, 14in. (Christie's) $436

Esther before Asahuerus, a painted fan, the verso with a lady in a landscape, tortoiseshell sticks carved, pierced and gilt, French, circa 1775, 10in. (Christie's) $1,049

Derby Day, a wooden brisé fan painted with comic scenes of the moral young man 'going' and 'returning', possibly by Col. Crealock, circa 1868, 9in. (Christie's) $489

FANS

Averhaln, signed *A. Thomasse*, a fan, the shaped silk leaf painted with game birds, signed *Duvelleroy, Paris,* mother of pearl sticks, circa 1910, 10in.
(Christie's) $2,272

A fine brisé fan, decorated in various golds with hiramakie and takamakie, and with Shibayama style birds and flowers, Japanese, late 19th century, 10in.
(Christie's) $13,980

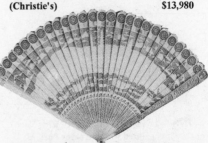

King Charles IV of Spain and his Queen, Maria Luisa of Parma, a printed fan with portraits after Goya, circa 1830, French, 7in.
(Christie's) $1,573

The Hongs of Canton, an ivory brisé fan carved and pierced with the hongs flying flags, a pagoda beyond, circa 1790, 10in.
(Christie's) $10,838

Calendrier pour 1898, a chromolithographic pressed carton brisé almanac fan commemorating the Fête Nationale Ottomane, 1898, 9in.
(Christie's) $436

Palettes, two chromolithographic advertising handscreens in the shape of palettes, American, 1880 and 1882, 11in. and 9in.
(Christie's) $157

L'Aiglon, signed *F. Creven*, by Alexandre, a fan, the silk leaf painted with five scenes from the play starring Sarah Bernhardt, with pierced horn sticks, circa 1900, boxed, 8in.
(Christie's) $1,224

Louis Martin's, signed *Geo. Desain*, a chromolithographic advertising fan with three figures in flying machines, with wooden sticks, circa 1915, 9in.
(Christie's) $734

A Canton gilt filigree brisé fan, with blue, green and red cloisonné enamel flowers, circa 1840, 9in.
(Christie's) $4,862

A tortoiseshell brisé fan lacquered recto and verso with an owl perched in a tree, the guardsticks decorated with Shibayama work birds and flowers, Japanese, late 19th century, 10in. (Christie's) $5,244

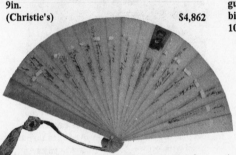

Johann Strauss II, a wooden brisé autograph fan, the sticks inscribed, dated and signed with musical quotations, 21 signatures, 1892-3, 11in.
(Christie's) $3,496

An ivory cockade brisé fan, carved and pierced with five vignettes of figures and pagodas, circa 1790, 8in. radius.
(Christie's) $6,992

A pair of lacquer handscreens, painted and lacquered with shipping scenes, with wooden handles, circa 1870, 15in.
(Christie's) $559

Conundrums, a printed fan, the leaf a hand colored etching with riddles and conundrums, with wooden sticks, 1800, 10in.
(Christie's) $664

A fan, the leaf painted with lovers in a rocky landscape, the ivory sticks carved and pierced with pairs of figures and gilt, Chinese, circa 1770, 13in.
(Christie's) $2,098

A racing fan, signed *T. Puging*, the canepin leaf painted with five racehorses at full gallop, with giltmetal pencil attached and clipped to long string, circa 1890, 9in.
(Christie's) $454

FASHION

A robe of black net, embroidered with gilt hammered wire stripes with coral bead at neck, 1920s. (Christie's)

$479

A gentleman's suit of rose pink satin, tamboured with floral ribbon borders, late 1770s. (Christie's)

$8,550

A gentleman's jacket of brown velvet with deep notched lapels, lined with brown linen, 1830-40. (Christie's)

$616

A mantle of lime green cannelé silk, woven with turquoise velvet poppy heads, circa 1910. (Christie's)

$375

A tea-gown of Paisley style silk with a Watteau back and red tasseled waist cord, circa 1885-90. (Christie's)

$352

A cocktail dress of black chiffon, embroidered with clear bugle beads, mid 1920s. (Christie's)

$909

A pair of rose pink harem trousers, silk bodice, the legs overlaid with pink chiffon, 1909-14. (Christie's)

$427

A robe of ivory satin brocaded with scarlet chenille buds, the skirts en polonaise, circa 1780. (Christie's)

$1,444

218

A gentleman's anaconda full length coat, belted, said to be by Christian Dior, circa 1974. (Christie's)

$1,231

A midnight blue cocktail dress, the skirts embroidered with peacock feathers and beads, mid 1920s. (Christie's)

$226

A waistcoat of ivory satin embroidered in gilt thread and tinsel, 19th century in 18th century style. (Christie's)

$222

A cocktail dress of black chiffon, with à jour panels looped with clear bugle beading, circa 1924. (Christie's)

$512

A gentleman's banyan of canary yellow silk damask, woven with shells and foliage, early 19th century. (Christie's)

$1,368

A dress of midnight blue chiffon emboidered with chinoiserie pink peonies, circa 1920. (Christie's)

$854

A dress of black lace woven with silver lamé flowers, in the manner of Raoul Dufy, circa 1920. (Christie's)

$939

A black wool coat, with fox fur high collar and cuffs, labeled *Paquin, Paris, 1929.* (Christie's)

$375

A divorce corset of white cotton, the sides and back corded, with lacing over hips, 1820s.
(Christie's) $734

Embroidered gentleman's waistcoat, America, circa 1800, print silk with linen lining.
(Skinner) $690

A child's tulle overdress, with lace insertions and trimming, 1830s.
(Christie's) $173

A shoulder mantle of black satin, brocaded with trompe l'oeil ribbon meander and apple blossom, labeled *Worth*, mid 1890s.
(Christie's) $1,368

A young girl's fancy dress constume representing badminton, with simulated net hanging from the waist, with associated racket and shuttlecocks, late 19th century.
(Christie's) $1,224

A sleeved waistcoat of pale blue silk damask, with puffed insertion at armholes, belonging to King George III, with letters of provenance.
(Christie's) $8,550

A 'hot pants' cat suit of brown and tan leather with patch pockets, zip fastening, labeled *Sir Mark of Oxford Street*.
(Christie's) $70

A French embroidered cap, 17th century, executed in white linen on a white linen/cotton twill ground with scrolling foliage, 10in. high.
(Sotheby's) $4,600

A blue denim gentleman's jacket with curved lapels and brass buttons, Vivienne Westwood, 1987.
(Christie's) $351

A gentleman's tie of ivory silk printed with newspaper clippings of Schiaparelli news items, Schiaparelli, 1930s.
(Christie's) $1,056

A baby's corset of wadded cotton, 18th century.
(Christie's) $952

A Paisley shawl, woven with a black center, the ends with two flame edged cypress tree motifs, 1840s, 64 x 144 in.
(Christie's) $489

A 'Pirate' shirt and sash of blue, pink and yellow striped Madras cotton, labeled *World's End Mclaren Westwood, Born in England.*
(Christie's) $352

A short jacket of chestnut brown silk, shirred horizontally with elasticated thread, with short sleeves, fastening with a large laminated hook, 1930s, labelled *Schiaparelli.*
(Christie's) $2,736

A needlework chasuble, finely worked in tent stitch in brightly colored silks, trimmed with siiver metal braid, early 18th century.
(Christie's) $2,052

A lady's rattan sun bonnet, bound and lined in yellow silk, embroidered with flowers and butterflies, possibly Manila, early 19th century.
(Christie's) $769

A coat of white wool printed with black 'op-art' chevrons, labeled *The French Room Harrods*, late 1960s.
(Christie's) $141

A cap of gold net with a band of ribbon work roses and other flowers in the manner of M. Panizon, 1910-12.
(Christie's) $222

A trouser suit of ivory chiffon printed in pinks and blues, probably Pucci, 1970s.
(Christie's) $122

A full length dress of green and mauve chiffon, labeled *Thea Porter Couture,* 1970s.
(Christie's) $122

A cocktail dress, the blue bodice worked with blue beads, black skirts, circa 1925.
(Christie's)
$786

An old rose linen-look maxi coat, double breasted, with wide lapels, labeled *BIBA.*
(Christie's)
$229

A bias cut evening dress of midnight blue chiffon, with spaghetti straps and a matching shoulder cape, mid 1930s.
(Christie's)
$210

A smock of ivory silk with a high waist, bodice, sleeves and cuffs embroidered in floss silks, early 20th century.
(Christie's)
$559

A cocktail dress of black silk jersey, with pleated draped bodice and pleated skirt, labeled *Holt Renfrew Canada,* circa 1950.
(Christie's)
$280

A black crêpe high necked top and flared trousers, with pink printed wool jersey maxi waistcoat, all labeled *BIBA,* 1970s.
(Christie's)
$668

A suit of black wool, straight skirt, jacket and sleeveless jerkin, mid 1950s. (Christie's) $375

A coat of psychedelic printed lurex, predominantly purple, labeled *Pierre Cardin*, 1967. (Christie's) $131

A young boy's coat of olive green changeable silk, lined with ivory silk, 1790s. (Christie's) $769

A cocktail dress of black chiffon worked with clear and yellow bugle beads, circa 1926. (Christie's) $839

A dress of ivory wool printed with a blue seaweed meander, trimmed with blue woollen braid, circa 1845. (Christie's) $512

A suit of powder blue ciselé velvet, embroidered with borders and pockets of ribbonwork flowers, late 1770s. (Christie's) $18,810

An evening dress of ivory checkered organza, with cap pleated sleeves, the hem trimmed with flowers, 1930s. (Christie's) $1,026

A sleeveless buff coat or jerkin, the fronts trimmed with plaited yellow and red silks, second quarter, 17th century. (Christie's) $1,538

Lana Turner, a circa 1960s liquor decanter set from the actress' Hollywood home, designed with a silver metal circular top and a square glass bottle.
(Christie's)   **$863**

Rocky, IV, a pair of boxing trunks from the third sequel starring Sylvester Stallone, and three color photographs from the film, 10 x 8in.
(Christie's)   **$4,025**

Die Hard, 1988, a police shield #881 and photo I.D. dated 3–15–80 used by Bruce Willis as 'Detective John McClane'.
(Christie's)   **$10,350**

The Prince and the Showgirl, 1957, an evening wrap worn by Marilyn Monroe as 'Elsie', pale gray and rose colored organza with pleated ruffle detail.
(Christie's)   **$16,100**

Aliens, 1986, an alien 'face-hugger' creature, constructed with a reptilian body, eight tentacles and long tail, 47in. long.
(Christie's)   **$4,600**

Baywatch, 1989–, a red bathing suit worn by Pamela Anderson Lee as 'C.J.', the one piece suit features the familiar patch Baywatch Lifeguard.
(Christie's)   **$1,380**

Beverly Hillbillies, 1994, a rocking chair used by actress Cloris Leechman as 'Granny', signed *Granny Claris Leechman 8/18/93*.
(Christie's)   **$6,325**

Sign of the Cross, 1932, a necklace worn by the actress Claudette Colbert as 'Poppaea' in Cecil B. deMille's saga, designed by Travis Banton.
(Christie's)   **$2,185**

Star Trek, 1966–69, an original hand communicator, with hinged metal cover over imitation dials and lights, 4¼in. long.
(Christie's)   **$7,475**

FILM MEMORABILIA

The Fugitive, 1963–1967, a wanted poster from the classic television series, accompanied by a color photograph of the actor from the series, poster, 16½ x 12½in., framed.
(Christie's) $3,220

Star Trek, The Next Generation, 1987–1994, a facial head and neck appliance worn by actor Michael Dorn as the Klingon, 'Lieutenant Worf', molded on a plaster base.
(Christie's) $920

To Please a Lady, 1950, a pair of trousers worn by Clark Gable as a ruthless midget-car racer, with two black and white photographs of Mr. Gable, 8 x 10in.
(Christie's) $575

A 'gold idol' made for 'Raiders of the Lost Ark', the gold-colored plaster figure with base impressed 2, with a copy of a letter of provenance, 8in. high.
(Sotheby's) $2,870

The Graduate, 1967, a jacket worn by Dustin Hoffman, lined in gray and cream silk, with video and a color publicity photograph, 8 x 10in.
(Christie's) $8,050

Clark Gable's personal script for The Misfits, 1961, co-starring Marilyn Monroe, Montgomery Clift and Eli Wallach.
(Christie's) $20,700

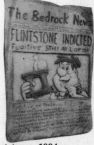

What Ever Happened to Baby Jane?, 1962, a dress worn by Joan Crawford, the deep pink dress is designed with a cut velvet floral pattern.
(Christie's) $5,175

Waterworld, 1995, a pair of boots worn by Kevin Costner, with side buckles, distressed and treated with algae and seaweed, with color photograph from the film, 8 x 10in.
(Christie's) $1,150

The Flintstones, 1994, a newspaper from the story of the modern stone age family, the painted styrofoam front page reads The Bedrock News Flintstone Indicted, 27 x 19in.
(Christie's) $2,760

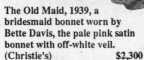

A pair of Marilyn Monroe's stiletto shoes, circa 1952, scarlet, with 3½in. heels, stylized belt and buckle, with a copy of a statement of authenticity. (Sotheby's) $2,512

The Old Maid, 1939, a bridesmaid bonnet worn by Bette Davis, the pale pink satin bonnet with off-white veil. (Christie's) $2,300

Clark Gable, a collection of Mr. Gable's favourite golfing equipment, with two tone leather and canvas golf bag with club socks and a matching ladies' bag. (Christie's) $8,050

An original miniature 'King Kong' figure created for the classic monster film starring Fay Wray, the head of the six inch ape figure carved of wood, the leg and arm joints of connected metal, the figure covered with a fur-like fabric. (Christie's) $8,050

Vivien Leigh/Gone with the Wind, a bodice of printed lilac cotton in a pattern of scrolling leaves and flowerheads, the lower half of the puffed sleeves and the front of the bodice trimmed with black buttons. (Christie's) $12,334

A tie of dark green silk by Nicole Miller decorated with a pattern of American footballs, in common mount with color still of Brad Pitt wearing identical tie in the 1995 film Seven, 24¾ x 16in. overall. (Christie's) $1,043

Oliver Hardy, the comedian's trademark black felt bowler hat, *O. Hardy* is typed on a Twentieth-Century Fox tag on the inside lining, with two signed photographs. (Christie's) $7,475

Teenage Mutant Ninja Turtles, 1993, a Ninja Turtle head used during the film, of green rubber, together with a clapboard used on the set, 13½in. (Christie's) $2,300

Chair used in the Warner Brothers classic Casablanca, 1942, brown cane with red painted wood, seat upholstered. (Christie's) $2,530

Clark Gable, a sterling silver cigarette box engraved *Clark Gable*, 6in. long.
(Christie's) $1,943

Clark Gable, a leather backgammon set belonging to the actor; the square camel colored leather case constructed with a front closing clasp.
(Christie's) $4,370

Staying Alive, 1983, a pair of white capezio dance shoes worn by John Travolta, signed and inscribed on both shoes in blue ink *John Travolta Staying Alive!*.
(Christie's) $1,725

Gone With the Wind, 1939, a pair of undergarment pantaloons worn by several actresses before and during the filming of Gone With The Wind, with four black and white photographs from the film, 8 x 10in.
(Christie's) $4,025

Independence Day, 1996, a uniform worn by Will Smith, including a brown Class A two piece uniform with jacket metals, matching trousers, hat, beige shirt, with a color photograph from the film, 8 x 10in.
(Christie's) $8,050

Clark Gable, a United States passport issued to Clark Gable, the 1948 proof of citzenship features a black and white photograph of Mr. Gable on the inside cover, signed in blue ink over the photograph, *Clark Gable*.
(Christie's) $11,500

Mae West, a handbag of black suede with perspex and gilt metal clasp, stamped inside *Koret*.
(Christie's) $180

Oliver Hardy, a circa 1930s passport belonging to the comedian, used during his United Kingdom tour with Stan Laurel, 6 x 3¾in.
(Christie's) $3,450

Star Trek, 1966–1969, an original Tricorder with 'spinning moray' from the series.
(Christie's) $12,650

Batman Forever, 1995, a black felt facial mask worn by actor Chris O'Donnel as 'Robin'.
(Christie's) $1,150

Four prop bullion bars from 'The Italian Job', 1969, the 'gold' pieces contained in a wire carrier with metal straps, each bar 10in. long.
(Sotheby's) $1,165

A pair of black kid leather high top boots worn by Audrey Hepburn as 'Eliza Dolittle' in the film My Fair Lady, 1964.
(Christie's) $1,610

Battle for the Planet of the Apes, 1973, a facial appliance used for an ape costume, the rubber mask mounted in a shadow box, accompanied by a letter of authenticity.
(Christie's) $1,840

Pulp Fiction, 1994, a pair of prop pistols used by John Travolta and Samuel L. Jackson, designed as chrome stunt guns painted with simulated pearl handles, with color photograph from the film, 5 x 7in.
(Christie's) $4,370

Clark Gable, It Happened One Night, 1934, the gold plated britannia statue with the engraved front plaque, *Academy of Motion Picture Arts and Sciences First Award 1934*, 12in. high.
(Christie's) $607,500

A shooting waistcoat of brown drill, with zip fastening, two side pockets and chest pocket, made for Roger Moore in the 1988 Eon film Octopussy.
(Christie's) $2,846

Wolf, 1994, a medallion worn by Jack Nicholson, designed with a raised image of a wolf, looped on a suede cord necklace.
(Christie's) $1,725

A silver fiberglass death mask, made for Marlon Brando in the 1978 Warner Bros. film Superman, 10½in. long.
(Christie's) $2,657

A Star is Born, 1953, a pair of pumps worn by Judy Garland, with black and white wardrobe still of Ms. Garland from the film, 8 x 10in.
(Christie's)   **$1,150**

A pair of Marilyn Monroe's sunglasses, 1950s, green-tinted lenses with pale tortoiseshell frames, with a copy of a statement of authenticity by Elaine Barry Barrymore.
(Sotheby's)   **$3,947**

Jaws, 1975, a painted gray foam latex shark designed with mechanical rods which pull and contort the fins, gills and mouth, 4ft. long.
(Christie's)   **$16,675**

Marlon Brando, a pair of knee breeches of cream cotton, labeled *MGM Studio*, and a black and white still from the 1962, M.G.M. film Mutiny On the Bounty.
(Christie's)   **$1,232**

The Munsters, 1964–1966, a head appliance worn by actor Fred Gwynne as 'Herman Munster', with color photograph of the actor as 'Herman', 8 x 10in.
(Christie's)   **$5,175**

Marilyn Monroe's evening dress, 1950s, in black silk, the full-length, strapless gown with beaded, floral decoration, together with a statement of authenticity.
(Sotheby's)   **$3,229**

Back to the Future II, 1989, a flying harness used by actor Michael J. Fox as 'Marty McFly', with many loops and straps used to fasten him to the overhead cables in hoverboard sequences.
(Christie's)   **$575**

A pair of orange satin high heels worn by Natalie Wood as 'Louise Hovig' in the 1962 film Gypsy, trimmed with dark orange beads, with black and white publicity photograph.
(Christie's)   **$1,495**

Basic Instinct, 1992, a bed used by Michael Douglas and Sharon Stone, designed in a modern style with curved head and foot boards, with two color photographs from the film, 8 x 10in.
(Christie's)   **$2,990**

Shirley Vance Martin, Jackie Coogan in My Own Play 'My Boy', 1921, album containing six gelatin prints of Jackie Coogan, each approx. 9¼x7¼in. (Butterfield & Butterfield)
$1,610

Metro-Goldwyn-Mayer, a sign from the legendary film studio, circa early 1970s; the brass tone logo design features the trademark roaring lion over an ornate scrolled ribbon banner, 7ft. long.
(Christie's) $4,830

Paul Newman, a black and white half-length portrait photograph by Terry O' Neil of subject in the 1975 film The Mackintosh Man, 29½ x 23in.
(Christie's) $603

The Pride of the Yankees, 1942, a New York Yankees home pinstriped flannel jersey worn by actor Gary Cooper, together with a black and white still, 8 x 10in.
(Christie's) $8,050

Bonnie and Clyde, 1967, an off-white linen summer dress, with black and white photograph of Faye Dunaway wearing the dress, 8 x 10in.
(Christie's) $4,600

Die Hard With a Vengeance, 1995, a white cotton studio-distressed tank top worn by actor Bruce Willis, the tank top has simulated dirt and blood stains.
(Christie's) $633

Hook, 1991, a brass and silver tone hook created for the film starring Dustin Hoffman, together with a section of black curled 'Captain Hook' hair, mounted with a color photograph, 18 x 24in.
(Christie's) $2,990

The Ten Commandments, a painted bronze set of scales from the 1956 Paramount film, the terminal modeled as Anubis, 36¾in. high.
(Christie's) $2,225

Psycho III, 1996, a model house used for a miniature perspective of certain scenes in the film, of board and features detailing of a horror house and window cut out, 49¼in. high.
(Christie's) $3,450

Sam Shaw; a photograph of Marilyn Monroe, 1950s, a vintage black and white print, image 8½ x 10¼in.
(Sotheby's) $493

Laurence Olivier, a pigskin wallet decorated with 9ct gold mounts and monogram *L O*, containing small photograph.
(Christie's) $307

Brigitte Bardot, a black and white head and shoulders portrait photograph, signed by photographer, 12 x 10in.
(Christie's) $493

Gypsy, 1962, a straw cloche worn by Rosalind Russell as 'Mama Rose' in the film, the burnt orange hat trimmed around crown with large silk and velvet flowers.
(Christie's) $690

A 17th century style panniered dress of apricot crêpe with laced stomacher, made for Raquel Welch in the 1973 Panama film The Three Musketeers.
(Christie's) $1,422

The Charge of the Light Brigade, 1936, a soldier's sword used by Errol Flynn, together with a matching metal sheath and two black and white photographs, 10 x 8in.
(Christie's) $7,475

Laurence Olivier, a white metal pin modeled as a roll of film engraved with presentation details ... *A Laurence Olivier per Henry V*, 2½x1½in.
(Christie's) $153

Citizen Kane, 1941, a wooden Rosebud sled from the film directed by and starring Orson Welles, 34¾ x 15½in.
(Christie's) $233,500

Dan Ackroyd/The Coneheads, a full mask of heavy flesh-painted latex, signed by Dan Ackroyd in black felt pen.
(Christie's) $820

The Birth of a Nation, 1915,
Epoch, United Artists, one-sheet,
41 x 27in.
(Christie's) $16,715

The African Queen, 1951,
Romulus, British quad, paper-
backed, 30x40in.
(Christie's) $7,340

Gloria Swanson, What a Widow,
1930, United Artists, one sheet,
41 x 27in.
(Christie's) $569

  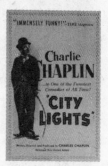

King of the Jungle/Djungelns
Konung, 1933, Paramount,
Swedish, one-sheet, 28 x 39in.,
linen-backed.
(Christie's) $334

The Hunchback of Notre Dame,
1939, R.K.O., British quad,
paper-backed, 30x40in.
(Christie's) $1,660

Charlie Chaplin, City Lights,
1950s re-release, United Artists,
U.S., one-sheet, 41 x 27in., linen-
backed.
(Christie's) $706

Go Ape, 1974, Twentieth
Century Fox, US one-sheet,
paper-backed, 41x27in.
(Christie's) $560

Titanic, Twentieth Century Fox,
British quad, paper-backed,
30x40in.
(Christie's) $1,135

La Dolce Vita, 1960, Cineriz,
Italian, four-folio, linen-backed,
79x55in.
(Christie's) $3,845

Mary of Scotland, 1936, R.K.O., US one-sheet, linen-backed, 41x27in.
(Christie's) $4,370

Louisiane/The Love Mart, 1927, Warner Bros., French, linen-backed, 63x94in.
(Christie's) $1,223

The Big Broadcast of 1938, 1937, Paramount, U.S. one-sheet, 41 x 27in., linen-backed.
(Christie's) $3,157

Marlene Dietrich, Morocco/Marruecos, 1931, Paramount, Spanish one-sheet, 39 x 27½in., linen-backed.
(Christie's) $5,572

Creature from the Black Lagoon, 1954, Universal International, British quad, paper-backed, 30x40in.
(Christie's) $3,845

Marlon Brando, On the Waterfront/Fronte del Porto, 1958 re-release, Columbia, Italian, linen backed, 55 x 39in.
(Christie's) $1,328

Alfred Hitchcock, Spellbound, 1945, United Artists, British double crown, 30 x 20in.
(Christie's) $721

Room at the Top, 1958, Remus, British quad, paper-backed, 30x40in.
(Christie's) $735

The Eagle of the Sea, 1926, Paramount, US one-sheet, 41x27in.
(Christie's) $190

Gone with the Wind, 1939/1940,
M.G.M., U.S., one-sheet, 41 x
27in., linen-backed.
(Christie's) $11,144

The Beatles, Help!, 1965, United
Artists, British quad, 30 x 40in.
(Christie's) $759

Charlie Chaplin, Modern Times,
1936, United Artists, U.S., one-
sheet, 41 x 27in., linen-backed.
(Christie's) $16,715

Paul Robeson, The Emperor
Jones, 1933, United Artists, U.S.,
one-sheet, 41 x 27in., linen-
backed.
(Christie's) $10,215

Once Upon a Time in the West,
1968, Paramount, U.S., half-
sheet, 22 x 28in.
(Christie's) $780

Gloria Swanson, Sadie
Thompson, 1928, United Artists,
U.S. one-sheet, 41 x 27in., linen-
backed.
(Christie's) $1,392

The Human Monster, 1939,
Monogram. U.S., one-sheet, 41 x
27in.
(Christie's) $557

The Fly, 1958, Twentieth
Century Fox, British quad,
paper-backed, 30x40in.
(Christie's) $1,135

Charlie Chaplin, The Kid, 1921,
First National, U.S., one-sheet,
41 x 27in., linen-backed.
(Christie's) $22,287

The Ghost Breakers, 1940, Paramount, U.S., one-sheet, 41 x 27in., linen-backed.
(Christie's) $649

Colleen, 1936, Warner Bros., U.S., half-sheet, 22 x 28in.
(Christie's) $278

Fatty Arbuckle, Out West, 1917, Paramount, U.S., one-sheet, 41 x 27in.
(Christie's) $2,972

Boris Karloff, Mr Wong Detective/Detektive/Mr Wong, 1938, Swedish one-sheet, 39½ x 27in.
(Christie's) $569

Italian Cinema, 8½, 1963, Cineriz Italian, British quad, 30 x 40in.
(Christie's) $607

Alan Ladd and Veronica Lake, The Blue Dahlia, 1946, Paramount, U.S., one-sheet, 41 x 27in., linen-backed.
(Christie's) $3,529

Black Cast, Stormy Weather, 1943, T.C.F., U.S., one-sheet, 41 x 27in., linen-backed.
(Christie's) $1,857

The Postman Always Rings Twice, 1946, M.G.M., U.S., half-sheet, 22 x 28in., style A.
(Christie's) $780

The Last Will of Dr Mabuse, circa 1940s re-release, U.S., one-sheet, 41 x 27in., linen-backed.
(Christie's) $464

Guys and Dolls, 1955, M.G.M., U.S., one-sheet, 41 x 27in. (Christie's) $409

Goldfinger, British, 1964, 30 x 40in. (Sotheby's) $663

Thirteen Women, 1932, R.K.O., U.S., one-sheet, 41 x 27in. (Christie's) $1,114

Citizen Kane/Citoyen Kane, 1941, R.K.O., Belgian, linen-backed, 16x14in. (Christie's) $1,335

The Cruel Sea, 1953, Ealing, British quad, paper-backed, 30x40in. (Christie's) $490

The Old Dark House, 1993 re-release, Universal, US one-sheet, 41x27in. (Christie's) $26,220

Mr Skeffington, 1944, Warner Bros. British double crown, linen-backed, 30x20in. (Christie's) $385

Darling, Anglo-Amalgamated, British quad, paper-backed, 30x40in. (Christie's) $385

Love Before Breakfast, 1936, Universal, US, one-sheet, paper-backed, 41x27in. (Christie's) $3,845

Frankenstein, 1931, Universal, French, 63 x 47in., linen-backed. (Christie's) $24,144

Black Narcissus, 1957, Rank, US title card, 11x14in. (Christie's) $560

Hollywood, 1923, Paramount, French, linen-backed, 63x47in. (Christie's $17,500

Gun Crazy, 1950, King Brothers Productions, US one-sheet, linen-backed, 41x27in. (Christie's) $1,750

The Man from Planet X, 1951, Universal Artists, British quad, paper-backed, 30x40in. (Christie's) $960

Heat/Calore, 1972, Warhol, Italian two-folio, linen-backed, 55x39in. (Christie's) $700

Salomé, 1953, Columbia, Italian, four-folio, linen-backed, 79x55in. (Christie's) $7,865

The Graduate, 1969, Embassy, US half-sheet, paper-backed, 22x28in., unfolded. (Christie's) $350

Gone with the Wind, 1939/1940, M.G.M., U.S., one-sheet, 41 x 27in., linen-backed. (Christie's) $7,058

Harrison Ford, signed color photograph, 8x10, half length as Indiana Jones.
(Vennett Smith) $90

Katharine Hepburn, signed postcard, full length seated on set.
(Vennett Smith) $260

W.C. Fields, a sepia toned photograph of the actor signed *W.C. Fields*, 10 x 8in.
(Christie's) $920

John Wayne, a black and white machine print photograph signed and inscribed in black felt pen, *Good Luck Myrna, John Wayne*, 9x7in.
(Christie's) $512

The Marx Brothers' autographs, circa 1946, a sepia film still from 'A Night In Casablanca' signed and dedicated in ink by Groucho, Harpo and Chico, 10 x 8in.
(Sotheby's) $1,898

James Dean, a circa early 1950s black and white photograph of the young actor sitting on a stool; signed and inscribed in black ink, *To Lance my best regards James Dean*, 10 x 8in., framed.
(Christie's) $8,050

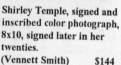

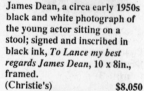

Shirley Temple, signed and inscribed color photograph, 8x10, signed later in her twenties.
(Vennett Smith) $144

Mae West, a personal check made out for $80,000 cash and signed in black ink together with a black and white photograph of the actress.
(Christie's) $805

Rock Hudson, signed and inscribed 8x10 photograph, head and shoulders with coat over shoulder.
(Vennett Smith) $88

Sal Mineo, signed and inscribed 5 x 7, head and shoulders. (Vennett Smith) **$120**

A signed publicity photograph of Humphrey Bogart, circa 1940, black and white, signed in black ink, 5¼ x 6¼in. (Sotheby's) **$1,802**

Orson Welles, signed 5 x 7in., head and shoulders. (T. Vennett-Smith) **$352**

Abbott & Costello, a circa 1940s black and white photograph signed in blue ink *To Bill one of the nicest person we know–All our Best Lou Costello, Bud Abbott*, 10 x 8in. (Christie's) **$920**

Lucille Ball, a circa 1950s photograph of the actress signed in blue ink *Best Wishes Lucille Ball*, together with a typewritten letter, 9¼ x 7in. (Christie's) **$2,990**

Barbara Streisand, a color photograph of Ms. Streisand, signed in blue ink on the lower half of the photograph *Barbara Streisand*, 15¼ x 12¼in., framed. (Christie's) **$575**

A signed publicity photograph of Marilyn Monroe, 1958, black and white, signed and dedicated *To Charles Grene* in black ink, 7½ x 9¼in. (Sotheby's) **$7,590**

A black and white photograph of Charlie Chaplin as 'The Tramp', signed by the star in 1972 at New York's Philharmonic Hall, 8¼ x 9¾in. (Christie's) **$863**

Boris Karloff, a piece of paper signed in black ink *To Johnathon Boris Karloff*, 2x 2¼, in common mount with a black and white publicity photograph. (Christie's) **$136**

Clark Gable, a good signed and inscribed 7 x 8in., head and shoulders.
(T. Vennett-Smith) $608

Rudolph Valentino, signed album page, 3.5 x 3, London, 2-8-23.
(T. Vennett-Smith) $577

Lucille Ball, signed 7 x 9½in., with scarcer full signature partially in dark portion, in red.
(T. Vennett-Smith) $176

Charles Chaplin, a fine signed sepia 6 x 8½in., head and shoulders seated in profile, 1935, contemporarily overmounted in ivory.
(T. Vennett-Smith) $672

Laurel and Hardy, a rare black and white full-length publicity photograph, circa 1932, inscribed *To 'A.C.' Our best wishes 'always', Stan Laurel, Oliver Hardy*, 10 x 7in.
(Christie's) $1,139

Harold Lloyd, signed and inscribed sepia 6 x 8.5, with first name only, 28th October 1937, also with facsimile signature.
(T. Vennett-Smith) $214

Robert De Niro, signed, color, 8 x 10in., head and shoulders from Cape Fear.
(T. Vennett-Smith) $96

Clark Gable, signed theatre program, in pencil, to cover, New Theatre Northampton, 19th April 1943, 'Warn That Man', 5 x 4.
(T. Vennett-Smith) $215

Jodie Foster, signed color 8 x 10in., half-length in basque and stockings, slightly weak colors.
(T. Vennett-Smith) $96

Joan Crawford, signed postcard, Milton Series 21B, Film Weekly (trimmed).
(T. Vennett-Smith) $63

Errol Flynn, signed piece, 5 x 3, laid down to album page.
(T. Vennett-Smith) $245

Hoot Gibson, signed and inscribed, 8 x 10in., head and shoulders in cowboy hat, rare.
(T. Vennett-Smith) $336

Mongomery Clift, small clipped signature, 3 x 1.75 laid down to color 4 x 6 with name annotated in another hand.
(T. Vennett-Smith) $140

Charlie Chaplin, a typescript letter, signed on Charlie Chaplin Music Publishing Co. paper, April 6th, 1916, to an English fan, 6¾ x 4¾in.
(Christie's) $1,043

Travolta and Newton John, signed 8 x 10in. by both John Travolta and Olivia Newton John, from Grease.
(T. Vennett-Smith) $157

Richard Burton, signed and inscribed 8 x 10in., full-length playing cricket during a break from one of his movies.
(T. Vennett-Smith) $144

Marilyn Monroe, signed and inscribed album page, to Fred Steimetz who traveled on the ship Arosa Kulm.
(T. Vennett-Smith) $1,392

Audrey Hepburn, a black and white portrait photograph of subject, signed and inscribed in blue ink *With love from Audrey*.
(Christie's) $663

Fred Astaire, signed sepia 5 x 7, head and shoulders.
(T. Vennett-Smith) $145

Sean Connery, signed color 8 x 20, half-length seated as Bond.
(T. Vennett-Smith) $161

Tala Birell, signed sepia 5 x 7, head and shoulders, 1937.
(T. Vennett-Smith) $83

Charles Chaplin, a fine signed and inscribed sepia 7.75 x 9.5, half-length seated in a chair, dated 1942.
(T. Vennett-Smith) $734

Laurel and Hardy, signed and inscribed sepia 8 x 10, head and shoulders with bowler hats, photo by Stax, annotated to reverse, 1932.
(T. Vennett-Smith) $858

Errol Flynn, signed and inscribed sepia 8 x 10, head and shoulders in cravat, 'N.N.' in slightly darker portion.
(T. Vennett-Smith) $396

John Wayne, a fine signed 8 x 20, three-quarter length in cowboy outfit.
(T. Vennett-Smith) $574

Marie McDonald, The Body, signed sepia 8 x 10, half-length seated, scarce.
(T. Vennett-Smith) $115

William Boyd, signed and inscribed 7.5 x 9.5, 'Hoppy', full-length on horse.
(T. Vennett-Smith) $107

Leslie Howard, signed sepia
5 x 7, head and shoulders.
(T. Vennett-Smith) $168

Spencer Tracy, signed sepia
5 x 7 , head and shoulders.
(T. Vennett-Smith) $153

Ward Bond, signed sepia 5 x 7,
head and shoulders.
(T. Vennett-Smith) $92

Edward G. Robinson, signed 8 x
10, head and shoulders with
pipe, collected in person at a
London hotel.
(T. Vennett-Smith) $107

Marx Brothers, early 8 x 10,
signed by all four, in a scene
from a movie, all with first
names, signatures faded to a
greater or lesser degree.
(T. Vennett-Smith) $643

Boris Karloff, signed and
inscribed sepia 8 x 10, head and
shoulders, annotated to reverse,
1933.
(T. Vennett-Smith) $347

Audrey Hepburn, signed and
inscribed postcard, head and
shoulders.
(T. Vennett-Smith) $116

Anita Ekberg, signed 8 x 10,
head and shoulders in earlier
years, signed recently.
(T. Vennett-Smith) $56

Peter Sellers, signed postcard,
head and shoulders, in very dark
portion.
(T. Vennett-Smith) $53

Shirley Temple, signed sepia 5 x 7, as a teenager, head and shoulders with hand on chin.
(T. Vennett-Smith) $132

Bing Crosby, signed inscribed sepia 8 x 10, head and shoulders, 1933.
(T. Vennett-Smith) $54

Veronica Lake, an excellent signed and inscribed sepia, 5 x 7, head and shoulders in costume.
(T. Vennett-Smith) $528

Rita Hayworth, signed and inscribed 11 x 14, full-length kneeling in satin nightdress on bed.
(T. Vennett-Smith) $352

Marx Brothers, signed album page, 4.5 x 4, by Groucho, Chico, Harpo and Zeppo, each with full name, 1930.
(T. Vennett-Smith) $1,102

Audie Murphy, signed and inscribed sepia 5 x 7, half-length with horse, to Richard and family.
(T. Vennett-Smith) $191

Claude Rains, signed, 5 x 7, head and shoulders, partially signed in darker portion.
(T. Vennett-Smith) $231

Betty Grable, signed and inscribed 6 x 8, head and shoulders.
(T. Vennett-Smith) $140

Laurence Olivier, signed 4 x 6, *'The Mahdi'*, unusual in this form.
(T. Vennett-Smith) $91

Boris Karloff, signed and inscribed sepia 5 x 7, head and shoulders.
(T. Vennett-Smith) $245

James Stewart, original ink sketch of Harvey, signed, 5 x 8.
(T. Vennett-Smith) $346

David Niven, signed sepia 5 x 7, head and shoulders, annotated to reverse, 1938.
(T. Vennett-Smith) $124

Laurel and Hardy, a good signed and inscribed sepia 8 x 10, by both Stan Laurel and Oliver Hardy, showing them full length in characteristic pose.
(T. Vennett-Smith) $825

Stan Laurel, signed and inscribed 7 x 9.5, head and shoulders holding bowler hat, together with a similar of Oliver Hardy with secretarial signature, 1931.
(T. Vennett-Smith) $252

John Carradine, signed 8 x 10, head and shoulders, modern reproduction signed in later years, scarce, slight corner crease.
(T. Vennett-Smith) $132

Douglas Fairbanks Snr., signed 6.5 x 8, three quarter length, 1934.
(T. Vennett-Smith) $99

Tom Mix, signed and inscribed 5.5 x 6.75, full-length on horse.
(T. Vennett-Smith)   £153

Harold Lloyd, signed and inscribed sepia 7.5 x 9.5, head and shoulders, 1935.
(T. Vennett-Smith) $124

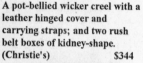
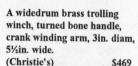

A pot-bellied wicker creel with a leather hinged cover and carrying straps; and two rush belt boxes of kidney-shape.
(Christie's) $344

A widedrum brass trolling winch, turned bone handle, crank winding arm, 3in. diam, 5½in. wide.
(Christie's) $469

A Bernard Woods, black japanned tin of 21 salmon flies, and a tin of May flies.
(Christie's) $260

A Continental fishing barrel casket/seat, 19th century, the hinged lid with applied fish motif, lion mask ring handles, 12in. high.
(Christie's) $1,714

Alfred Ronalds: The Fly-Fishers Entomology, Liverpool 1913, Edition de Luxe, 2 vols, 4to, illustrated, volume two with 48 mounted flies.
(Christie's) $1,714

An oak and brass banded bait box, 19th century, the oval part hinged top with chain carrying handle, clasp and tapered sides, 5½in. high.
(Christie's) $506

A framed and glazed display of hooks, swivels, spears etc. circa 1900, the display mounted on green velvet, 37 x 25¹/₂in.
(Sotheby's) $735

A Hardy Bros. black japanned fly box and contents, containing approximately circa 230 salmon flies with four lift-out trays, 9½in. wide.
(Christie's) $2,617

A framed and glazed display of lures and hooks circa 1900, comprising of a selection of hooks, lures and spoons, 37 x 25¹/₂in.
(Sotheby's) $3,125

A Hardy line winder, folding chrome with a wooden handle and two *"By Appointment"* logos.
(Christie's) $164

A fine Bambridge maker, Eton-On-Thames, oak, oblong fly-tying cabinet, the hinged lid with concealed compartment to the underside, enclosing lift-out compartmented tray, 17¼in.
(Christie's) $6,139

A solid brass salmon gaff with a mahogany handle.
(Tony Murland) $75

A.C. Farlow and Co., landing net, turned wooden handle with Farlow and Holdfast logos.
(Christie's) $181

A 'Hardy Zane Grey' sea spinning reel, 4¼in. in a fitted leather case with implements.
(Bearne's) $3,245

A treen pocket line winder and tackle container, the central cylindrical section with four compartments and six winding arms around, 6in. high.
(Christie's) $342

A C Farlow & Co., black japanned fly box, with six lift-out trays and containing 315 salmon and trout flies, approx. half gut-eyed.
(Christie's) $1128

A Malloch's japanned fly box, the hinged rectangular lid, enclosing twelve cream-painted trays containing over 480 gut-eyed flies, 19 x 14in.
(Christie's) $5,416

An interesting framed and glazed display of artificial baits by Guillame of Redditch circa 1900.
(Sotheby's) $3,125

CASED FISH

A Malloch cased Salmon, inscribed *"Tay N.B., Lower Stanley, Pitlochry Pool, Feb 7th 1911, weight 42lbs, length 51, girth 25½, killed by P.A. Scott."* (Christie's) $5,236

A half block plaster trophy of a tarpon, realistically painted, 6ft. long, some fin damage. (Sotheby's) $550

A stuffed and mounted brown trout by J. Cooper & Sons, displayed amongst reeds, bow fronted case, 13 x 27in. (Sotheby's) $1,100

A Bream, mounted in a bow-fronted case among reeds and inscribed, *"Bream, 12lb, Taken from Oxfordshire Gravel Pit, 1987"*. (Christie's) $270

A Roach, mounted in a bow-fronted case, damaged, in the Cooper style with label, *"Roach, caught by W. Bunce, in the Lea, Sept. 4th 1909, Weight 1lbs 9ozs."* 20in. wide (Christie's) $506

A perch mounted in a setting of reeds and grasses in a gilt lined bowfronted case, inscribed *Perch 11lb. 9ozs., Caught at Tottenham Reservoirs by G. Gillson 9 March 1925*, 18in. wide. (Bonhams) $770

A Perch, mounted in a bow-fronted and gilt-lined case amongst reeds, inscribed, *"Perch, 2lbs 11ozs, Taken by E. White at Bedfont, Oct 1925"*, 22in. wide. (Christie's) $795

A Tench, mounted in a bow-fronted and gilt-lined case amongst reeds, bears label, *"Tench, caught by Mr G. Bates, at Cheshunt, July 7th 1912, Wgt. 3lbs 8½ozs."* 23½in. wide. (Christie's) $686

CASED FISH

A Rainbow Trout, mounted in a bow-fronted case, inscribed, *"Rainbow Trout, 22lb, Died in Stewpond at Avington 1988."* 40in. wide.
(Christie's) $342

A Common Bream, mounted in a bow-fronted and gilt-lined case amongst reeds with a rocky base, bears illegible label, 27in. wide.
(Christie's) $542

A roach mounted in a setting of reeds and grasses, in a gilt lined bowfronted case, labelled *'Roach, weight 1lb. 9¾ozs., taken by Mr Jno Roach at Shiplake, 4th March 1906'*, 19¼in. wide.
(Bonhams) $800

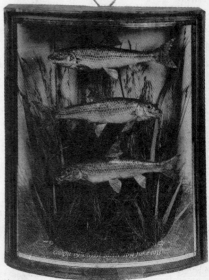

Three gudgeon, in a gilt lined bow fronted case, inscribed *Gudgeon, combined wgt 6oz. 11drms., Caught by L. Shipman 16th June 1933*, 10¼in. wide.
(Bonhams) $1,000

A pair of stuffed and mounted bream, displayed amongst reeds, bow fronted case, 15½ x 29in.
(Sotheby's) $740

A stuffed and mounted pike by J. Cooper & Sons, displayed amongst reeds, bow fronted case, inscribed *Pike. 28 lbs. Caught by James Hall, Lough Corrib, Ireland. 1929*, 19 x 53in.
(Sotheby's) $1,840

A Pike mounted in a flat-fronted case amongst a setting of reeds and rocks with a small fish in its mouth, no label, caught 1935 and circa 15lbs, 42in. wide.
(Christie's) $812

REELS

A brass trolling winch, ivory handle, crank winding arm, adapted foot, check 2¼in. diameter.
(Christie's) $217

A Meisselbach, "Takapart", bait casting reel, no. 480, with patents Dec '04 and March '07, turned ivory handle, counter-balanced arm, 2in. diameter.
(Christie's) $144

A Charles Farlow, 2¾in. brass reel, bone handle, crank-winding arm, engraved with 191 Strand address.
(Christie's) $397

A Hardy, "The Super Silex", 3¾in., extra wide reel, twin black handles, notched brass foot, ivorine brake handle and quadrant regulator.
(Christie's) $469

A pair of Farlow, 5in., brass reels, convex handles, Patent no. 3013, stamped with 10 Charles Street address.
(Christie's) $722

A Hardy, "The Fortuna", 9in. game reel, Andreas Patent, black handles, brass crossbar over a brass star drag adjuster, brass foot.
(Christie's) $831

A Hardy, "The Perfect", 4¼in., brass faced reel, ivorine nut, 1906 check engraved with initials.
(Christie's) $627

A Hardy, "The Perfect", 4¼in., alloy reel, ivorine handle, alloy foot, rim tension screw, central circular logo, Eunuch check.
(Christie's) $361

A Hardy, "The Silex Muliplier", 2¾in., alloy reel, black handle, rounded ivorine thumb bar and quadrant regulator.
(Christie's) $646

A Malloch 4in. brass sidecaster reel with a black horn handle and polished finish.
(Christie's) $253

A Victorian brass 2in. Gut Twister, crank winding arm, turned ivory handle, iron spike.
(Christie's) $794

An Illingworth no. 3 casting reel, brass with black handle, Series J.M.I., no. 4542.
(Christie's) $144

A Hardy, "The Super Silex", 3in. reel, twin ivorine handles, notched brass foot, ivorine brake handle and quadrant regulator, drum removal catch.
(Christie's) $469

A Hardy, "The Perfect", 2½in., brass reel, ivorine handle, foot with central pierced hole, dished drum with large and small perforations.
(Christie's) $2,076

A Hardy, "The Perfect", 4in., alloy reel, black handle, notched brass foot, tension screw, nickel line guard, Mark II double check.
(Christie's) $433

An Allcock, 6in. game reel, counter balanced winding arm, central drag adjuster, brake handle.
(Christie's) $181

A Hardy 'Perfect' alloy fly reel, 3³/₄in. diameter, ivorine handle, smooth brass foot, 'rod in hand' logo.
(Bonhams) $280

An Abu Ambassadeur 6000, baitcaster reel, red, white marbled handle, grooved rims, with applied crest.
(Christie's) $126

A Dutch ebonized reverse profile frame, 17th century, with various ripple and wave moldings, plain central ogee with eared corners, 9 x 7 x 4¼in.
(Christie's) $979

An Italian carved, gilded and painted frame, 17th century, the surround with pierced scrolling foliage in high relief, 6¾ x 4½ x 3¾in.
(Christie's) $7,130

A Florentine carved and gilded frame, 17th century, with pierced foliate surround and raised sight edge, 31½ x 24¾ x 8in.
(Christie's) $7,130

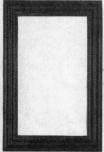  

A Dutch ebonized and tortoiseshell receding profile frame, in the 17th century style, the outer edge with various moldings, tortoiseshell ogee, cavetto, 20½ x 34¼ x 5in.
(Christie's) $3,208

A pair of Florentine 19th century carved, pierced and gilded oval frames, with leaves berries and flowers running from flowerhead bottom to top, each 8¼ x 6½ x 3in.
(Bonhams) $990

A Louis XIV carved and gilded frame, with stick-and-leaf outer edge, outer scotia, cabochon corners and anthemia centers flanked by c-scrolls, overall size: 32 x 27½in.
(Christie's) $6,417

A Spanish carved, gilded and painted reverse profile frame, 17th century, with acanthus leaf corners in high profile on black ground, 24 x 19 x 4¾in.
(Christie's) $3,921

A Dutch ebonized and tortoiseshell frame, 17th century, with ripple and wave moldings, the central plate with tortoiseshell, 5¼ x 5½ x 2½in.
(Christie's) $1,157

An Italian 16th/17th century carved and gilded 'Sansovino' frame, with volutes to the frieze, flanking female grotesques, 20½ x 14 x 4¼in.
(Bonhams) $1,096

An Italian carved and gilded frame, 16th century, the central plate with winged cherubs' head at center and stylized fleurs de lys at corners, 6 x 4¾ x 3⅛in. (Christie's) $3,208

A Dutch carved and gilded frame, late 17th century, the surround with putti holding garlands of fruit and flowers, 27¼ x 20 x 5½in. (Christie's) £7,130

An Italian early 19th century carved and gilded frame, with plain frieze, sanded wedge frieze with scrolling vine corners, 20¾ x 16½ x 6¼in. (Bonhams) $990

A Louis XIV carved and gilded frame, the pierced cresting centered with anthemion flanked by c-scrolls, scrolling foliage, flowers and berries, overall size: 39¼ x 26⅜in. (Christie's) $3,921

A pair of Dutch ebonized frames, 17th century, with moldings at outer and sight edges, the central plates with inlays, octagonal, 8¼ x 6¼ x 2in. (Christie's) $1,426

A carved, gilded and painted tabernacle frame, in the Italian 16th century style, the cresting with an urn at center flanked by scrolling foliage and lion heads in profile, 20¼ x 15in. (Christie's) $1,336

A Dutch, ebonized and tortoiseshell cassetta frame, late 17th century, the central plate with scrolling foliage inlaid with tortoiseshell, 6 x 8 x 2½in. (Christie's) $2,852

A rare Italian 15th century carved, gilded and painted tabernacle frame, with flanking foliage and urns sprouting leaves and flowers, 18½ x 14½ x 4¼in. (Bonhams) $1,675

An Alpine 18th century carved and ebonized ripple molding frame, of wide reverse profile, with extended corners, 13 x 10½ x 6¾in. (Bonhams) $548

BEDS & CRADLES

Portuguese rococo rosewood bedstead, 19th century, comprising a headboard, footboard, and rails.
(Skinner) $1,150

An Empire rosewood lit en bateau, by Alexandre Maigret, banded overall with brass lines, the head and foot-board with molded panels between detached paired fluted columns, 84½in. wide.
(Christie's) $13,455

A good dark green and red-painted maple and poplar lowpost bedstead, Pennsylvania, early 19th century, with ball finials on turned posts, 47½in.
(Sotheby's) $690

A late Victorian Arts and Crafts oak half-tester bed, the molded ebonized and gilt-embellished rounded rectangular canopy supported by square tapering columns, 68in. wide.
(Christie's) $2,180

A pair of oak single beds, designed by Sir Robert Lorimer, each with carved headboard carved with armorial crests, 34½in. wide.
(Christie's) $4,724

One of a pair of late Victorian mahogany four-poster single beds, of George III design, each with molded rectangular canopy, 37in. wide.
(Christie's)(Two) $7,631

A fine carved walnut bed, French, circa 1895, the headboard centered by a cherub mask and shell above carved panels, 98cm. wide.
(Sotheby's) $41,500

Painted and stencil decorated turned low post bed, New England, 1830–45, old red ground with black accents and gold stenciled decoration, 51in. wide.
(Skinner) $920

A 19th century French walnut and mahogany veneered Rococo Revival bed with floral carved decoration and hand-made Savoy Works white horsehair mattress, 60in. wide.
(David Lay) $1,310

BEDS & CRADLES

A cream and gray-painted day bed, the outswept paneled ends above squab cushions and a box spring, North European, early 19th century, 38in. wide. (Christie's) $1,218

A heart-decorated walnut cradle, Pennsylvania, circa 1800, the scrolled heart-pierced headboard and footboard flanked by canted reeded sides, 40in. long, (Sotheby's) $1,610

Classical carved mahogany and mahogany veneer bedstead, Mid Atlantic States, 1825–35, with reeded raked crest above spiral carved columns, 79in. wide. (Skinner) $1,265

A gray-painted bed, comprising: a padded head and footboard with overscrolled top-rails centered by a shell and foliate boss, French, late 19th century, 52¹/₂in. wide. (Christie's) $1,312

A Chinese hardwood six poster canopy bed with applied bone figural decoration and overall bat and peach-blossom motifs, 19th century, 51¹/₂in. wide. (Christie's) $2,084

A mahogany and checker lined four-poster bed, of George III design, the molded and dentiled cornice supported by slender turned baluster columns, 65in. wide. (Christie's) $4,175

A 19th century child's cot with canework canopy and sides, raised on turned mahogany supports, 41in. long. (Anderson & Garland) $673

A good Federal brown-painted birchwood and pine bedstead, North Coast New England, circa 1810, the octagonal headposts centering a pitched pine headboard, 4ft. 5in. wide. (Sotheby's) $11,500

A Chippendale cherrywood cradle, American, probably mid-Atlantic states, circa 1770, with two shaped flaring stiles mounted with brass carrying handles, 42in. long. (Sotheby's) $1,495

BOOKCASES

Victorian gilt metal mounted walnut and marquetry breakfront bookcase, late 19th century, 73in. wide.
(Skinner) $6,900

A mid-Victorian walnut and boxwood inlaid dwarf bookcase, the rounded rectangular top fitted with two pairs of glazed doors, 94in. wide.
(Christie's) $2,431

Renaissance Revival walnut and burl walnut bookcase, circa 1875–85, with wooden shelves, 55¼in. wide.
(Skinner) $1,955

A mahogany bookcase, the dentil-molded cornice above a pair of astragal glazed doors, glazed section 18th century, 50in. wide.
(Christie's) $1,910

An early Victorian mahogany breakfront bookcase with molded cornice over open adjustable shelves, 8ft. wide.
(Russell, Baldwin & Bright) $8,109

Guild of Handicraft Ltd, revolving bookcase, circa 1900, dark stained oak inlaid with white metal stylized flowers, 21¼in. wide.
(Sotheby's) $9,747

A late Victorian mahogany bookcase, the molded cornice fitted with a pair of geometrically-glazed doors enclosing shelves, 50in. wide.
(Christie's) $2,467

A late Georgian pale figured mahogany veneered breakfront bookcase, the upper section with four lancet and arched glazed doors, 90in. wide.
(David Lay) $12,899

A Victorian carved oak two stage bookcase, with molded arched cornice over four glazed doors with wrythen pilasters, 75in. wide.
(Andrew Hartley) $3,565

BOOKCASES

Classical mahogany veneer glazed bookcase, New England, circa 1840, the five-shelved upper case above recessed paneled doors, 48½in. wide. (Skinner) $2,990

An inlaid mahogany breakfront bookcase, four astragal glazed doors above four paneled doors carved with paterae, 96in. wide. (Christie's) $5,904

A late Victorian oak revolving bookcase, the molded rectangular top above two tiers of four open shelves, 18in. wide. (Christie's) $520

A mid-Victorian oak library bookcase, with flowerheads, acanthus and trefoils, above seventeen mesh-filled doors, with brass strapwork hinges, 163in. wide. (Christie's) $13,000

A Victorian mahogany breakfront bookcase with projecting molded cornice, over four arched glazed doors, 97in. wide. (Andrew Hartley) $11,130

A late 19th century mahogany breakfront bookcase, crossbanded with string inlay, molded and dentil cornice, 66in. wide. (Andrew Hartley) $4,620

A George III mahogany bookcase, the later molded and dentiled cornice with ebony and boxwood lined frieze, 52in. (Christie's) $2,362

An oak library bookcase with molded cornice and divided adjustable shelves flanked by fluted pilasters, late 19th century, 96in. wide. (Christie's) $2,815

Victorian walnut dwarf bookcase, the frieze inlaid with floral marquetry panels, feather banded glazed door below, mid 19th century, 29½in. (G. A. Key) $1,208

BUREAU BOOKCASES

South German baroque burl walnut secretary, 18th century, 39in. wide.
(Skinner) $25,300

A George III mahogany bureau bookcase, the line-inlaid sloping fall enclosing a fitted interior, 43in. (Christie's) $2,111

A late Victorian mahogany bureau cabinet, the molded and foliate-carved cornice fitted with a pair of glazed doors, 38in.
(Christie's) $3,270

An early 18th century later green japanned and chinoiserie decorated bureau cabinet, with all over figures in pagoda landscapes and birds, on bracket feet, 101cm. wide.
(Phillips) $9,600

A pair of Chinese Export black and gold-lacquer bureau-cabinets, late 18th century, decorated overall with foliate trails, foliage, latticework, birds and zig-zag stripes, 29¹/₂in.
(Christie's) $182,250

An Irish George II mahogany bureau-bookcase, the scrolled broken cornice above a pair of mirror-paneled doors enclosing three adjustable shelves, above a pair of short drawers, on shaped bracket feet, 40¹/₂in. wide.
(Christie's) $14,076

A walnut veneered slope front bureau bookcase, in early 18th century style, the glazed door incorporating fluted columns, one of which conceals the keyhole, 28¹/₂in. wide.
(David Lay) $6,710

A mahogany bureau bookcase, the dentil-molded cornice above an urn and swag-carved frieze and two astragal glazed doors, 50in. wide.
(Christie's) $1,910

A Georgian mahogany bureau cabinet having broken arched pediment, pair of solid paneled doors enclosing adjustable shelves.
(Russell, Baldwin & Bright)
                              $6,120

BUREAU BOOKCASES

A George III oak and mahogany
crossbanded bureau bookcase
with an arched dentil cornice
above a pair of paneled doors,
47in. wide.
(Anderson & Garland)

$3,660

South German baroque burl
walnut secretary/bookcase, first
half 18th century, 52¹/₂in. long.
(Skinner) $9,775

A Chinese Export mahogany
bureau-cabinet, late 18th
century, with hinged slope
enclosing a fitted interior with
six drawers and six pigeon-
holes, 39in. wide.
(Christie's) $4,398

A late Georgian mahogany
bureau bookcase, with dentil
cornice over pair of astragal
glazed doors enclosing
adjustable shelves, 4ft. wide.
(Russell, Baldwin & Bright)
                    $4,208

A large German burr-birch
bureau-cabinet, mid-18th
century, inlaid overall with
kingwood banding, the arched
broken and overhanging cornice
with central plinth, 56¹/₂in. wide.
(Christie's) $35,880

A Dutch East Indies (Sri Lanka)
kaliatur and calamander brass
mounted bureau cabinet, the
molded arched cornice above
two glazed doors, 18th century,
57in. wide.
(Christie's) $4,400

Chippendale mahogany carved
desk and bookcase, Boston area,
1770–1800, the scrolled
pediment with carved rosettes
above cyma curved paneled
doors, 40³/₈in. wide.
(Skinner) $14,950

An 18th century South German
mulberry, walnut crossbanded
and marquetry bureau cabinet
in three sections, with interlaced
strapwork cartouche inlay,
130cm. wide.
(Phillips) $9,300

A 19th century mahogany
bureau with bookcase over
inlaid fan quadrants and
stringing in satinwood.
(Russell, Baldwin & Bright)
                    $5,049

BUREAUX

Chippendale maple slant lid desk, New England, circa 1760, 36¼in. wide.
(Skinner) $3,105

Queen Anne walnut inlaid slant lid desk, Massachusetts, 1730–50, the hinged lid with two inlaid stellate devices, 38in. wide.
(Skinner) $5,463

Chippendale maple and tiger maple slant lid desk, probably Rhode Island, late 18th century, replaced brasses.
(Skinner) $4,888

Chippendale tiger maple slant lid desk, possibly New Jersey, last quarter 18th century, interior retains old black paint, 35¾in. wide.
(Skinner) $5,462

A Louis XV style walnut bombé bureau de dame, gilt-metal mounted and crossbanded in tulipwood, with three-quarter pierced gallery, 27in. wide.
(Christie's) $2,431

Chippendale mahogany oxbow serpentine fall-front desk, North Shore, Massachusetts, circa 1780, on ogee bracket feet, 43in. wide.
(Skinner) $5,462

Chippendale tiger maple slant lid desk, northern New England, late 18th century, the interior with small drawers and valanced compartments, 40in. wide.
(Skinner) $5,175

A mid 18th century walnut bureau, in two parts, the sloping flap enclosing a cupboard, drawers and pigeon holes, 39½in. wide.
(Bearne's) $3,981

William & Mary walnut inlaid and maple slant lid desk, Boston, early 18th century, slant lid and drawers inlaid with two panels of contrasting stringing, 34in. wide.
(Skinner) $4,888

BUREAUX

Chippendale maple slant-lid desk, New England, 18th century, with two-tier interior of valanced compartments and small drawers, 37¼in. wide. (Skinner) $3,105

A green-painted bombé bureau, decorated overall with floral bouquets and trellis borders, 49in. wide. (Christie's) $1,584

Chippendale cherry and tiger maple slant lid desk, possibly Massachusetts, last half 18th century, case of four thumb molded graduated drawers, 35⅝in. wide. (Skinner) $4,312

Dutch Colonial brass mounted red painted and part ebonized slant lid desk, 18th century, the backboards inscribed *SS MARTA GTB*, 38¼in. wide. (Skinner) $4,600

George I walnut block-fronted slant-lid desk, early 18th century, in two parts, 42½in. long. (Skinner) $3,105

Diminutive Italian neoclassical walnut and parquetry slant lid desk, late 18th/early 19th century, 30in. wide. (Skinner) $3,450

A Dutch oak bombé bureau, 19th century, the curved molded fall-flap opening to enclose a fitted interior, 56in. wide. (Christie's) $2,180

A line-inlaid and crossbanded walnut bureau, the sloping fall enclosing a fitted interior above four serpentine drawers, Italian, late 18th century, 47in. wide. (Christie's) $3,299

A Chippendale carved walnut slant-front desk, Philadelphia, 1769-80, the thumbmolded slant lid opening to a compartmented interior, 42in. wide. (Christie's) $29,900

BUREAUX

An Edwardian satinwood and tulipwood-banded cylinder bureau with overall ebonized line-inlay, 29½in. wide.
(Christie's) $2,605

A late 18th century Dutch walnut and floral marquetry bureau with well fitted interior with drawers, cupboard, well and pigeon holes, 3ft. 10in. wide.
(Russell, Baldwin & Bright) $5,049

An Edwardian inlaid mahogany cylinder bureau, the checker strung top with three-quarter pierced brass gallery, 32in. wide.
(Christie's) $2,431

A faded mahogany and marquetry bureau, with interior fittings, the top, the fall and two long drawers with lozenge shaped panels of seaweed marquetry, 45in wide.
(Dreweatt · Neate) $1,500

A George III mahogany tambour cylinder bureau, the fall enclosing a fitted interior with drawers and pigeonholes, on square tapered legs, brass cappings and castors, 108cm. wide.
(Phillips) $3,420

Federal mahogany and mahogany veneer inlaid slant lid desk, probably Massachusetts, circa 1800, the fall front above a case of four cockbeaded graduated drawers, 41½in. wide.
(Skinner) $3,105

An early 18th century oak bureau, the sloping flap enclosing a stepped interior, 37½in. wide.
(Bearne's) $3,185

A George III mahogany bureau, the rectangular top above a fall front opening to a fitted interior, on bracket feet, 36in. wide.
(Christie's) $2,261

An 18th century walnut, crossbanded and inlaid bureau, decorated with cartouche panels of lions and bordered with boxwood lines, 96cm. wide.
(Phillips) $4,200

CABINETS

Napoleon III gilt bronze mounted rosewood and marquetry side cabinet, third quarter 19th century, 57¹/₂in. wide.
(Skinner) $2,415

A Hille burr-walnut cocktail cabinet, with a pair of fluted cupboard doors, on u-shaped upright and plinth base, 55in. wide.
(Christie's) $2,411

An Aesthetic Movement amboyna and ebonized side cabinet, the rectangular top with mirrored and shelved superstructure, above two frieze drawers, 70in. wide.
(Christie's) $9,693

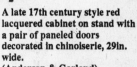

Flemish baroque style walnut, tortoiseshell, parquetry, and part-ebonized cabinet on stand, 19th century, 21¹/₂in. wide.
(Skinner) $1,495

A pair of giltmetal-mounted rosewood, simulated rosewood and parcel-gilt side cabinets, part early 19th century, each with pierced three-quarter galleried Gothic arcaded rectangular superstructure, 37¹/₂in. wide.
(Christie's) $8,446

A late 17th century style red lacquered cabinet on stand with a pair of paneled doors decorated in chinoiserie, 29in. wide.
(Anderson & Garland)
                             $793

A late Victorian mahogany music cabinet, the raised top on turned baluster supports above open compartments, 25¹/₂in. wide.
(Anderson & Garland)
                             $970

A Regency rosewood and burr-elm side cabinet, the overhanging molded rectangular top above a paneled frieze drawer with bead-and-reel molding, 48¼in. wide.
(Christie's) $9,149

A mid 19th century French style walnut pedestal cabinet, decorated with inlaid stringing and foliate motifs, 30in. wide.
(Anderson & Garland)
                             $1,033

CABINETS

A Regency rosewood veneered reverse breakfront side cabinet, at the center adjustable shelves behind glazed doors, 66in. wide. (David Lay) $8,660

An Art Deco sycamore cocktail cabinet, with a pair of carved cupboard doors, of stylized shell form, enclosing mirrored interior, 54in. wide. (Christie's) $3,152

A Victorian walnut and ebony inverted breakfront side cabinet, with string and marquetry inlay, three mirror backed central shelves, 67½in. wide. (Andrew Hartley) $6,975

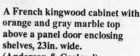

A Gordon Russell oak side cabinet, the rectangular top above fielded cupboard door, flanked by chamfered stiles, circa 1925, 20in. (Christie's) $834

Pair of Continental walnut side cabinets, the canted corners applied with ormolu, rosette and caryatid mounts, on plinth bases, 19th century, 35½in. wide. (G. A. Key) $9,500

A French kingwood cabinet with orange and gray marble top above a panel door enclosing shelves, 23in. wide. (Anderson & Garland) $1,830

An Art Deco macassar and satinwood-banded side cabinet, the rectangular marble top above a pair of panel doors enclosing shelves, Continental, 45½in. wide. (Christie's) $834

A Duncan Miller walnut and aluminium inlaid side cabinet, the rectangular top above a pair of cupboard doors with inset linear medallion, 63in. wide. (Christie's) $2,225

A parcel-gilt decorated and mirror-glass mounted cabinet, the stepped rectangular top above a pair of fielded cupboard doors, Continental, circa 1940, 32in. wide. (Christie's) $2,411

CANTERBURYS

A 19th century mahogany canterbury with turned finials on turned and block supports, dished slatted divisions, 18in. (Andrew Hartley) **$1,800**

A mid-Victorian walnut and burr-walnut three-division canterbury, with pierced scrolling fret dividers joined by turned stretchers, 24in. wide. (Christie's) **$2,991**

A George III mahogany four division canterbury, containing an ebony strung drawer on ring turned legs, 46cm. wide. (Phillips) **$1,875**

A mahogany gothic canterbury, the dished rectangular top with gothic arches, paneled pillar-angles, five divisions and a scrolled carrying handle, 19th century, 19$^{1}/_{2}$in. wide. (Christie's) **$3,000**

A Victorian burr-walnut canterbury whatnot, the foliate-carved three-quarter gallery above a serpentine top on spiral-turned uprights, on turned legs, 22in. wide. (Christie's) **$1,923**

An early Victorian rosewood three-division canterbury, on turned baluster supports with finials to the corners, 20$^{1}/_{4}$in. wide. (Christie's) **$1,477**

A Victorian walnut canterbury whatnot, the rectangular top with pierced raised back, on pierced end supports, 26in. wide. (Christie's) **$1,390**

An early Victorian mahogany four-division canterbury, with foliate and gadrooned scrolling decoration, 20in. wide. (Christie's) **$1,491**

A Victorian walnut canterbury whatnot, the rectangular top with three-quarter arcaded gallery, on turned uprights, 23$^{3}/_{4}$in. wide. (Christie's) **$1,215**

DINING CHAIRS

Two of a set of ten stained beech
dining chairs, each with arched
rectangular padded back above
square padded seat.
(Christie's)

(Ten) $1,739

One of a set of four mahogany
dining-chairs, of mid-Georgian
style, with paper-scrolled and
shell-carved toprails.
(Christie's)

(Four) $1,604

Two of a set of eleven Victorian
mahogany dining-chairs, the
oval molded backs with
molded horizontal splats.
(Christie's)

(Eleven) $4,862

Two of eleven dining chairs in
the manner of Charles Bevan,
circa 1860, oak, with openwork
backs, upholstered seats above
scalloped frieze, 35in.
(Sotheby's)

(Eleven) $5,998

One of a set of six Louis XVI
white-painted and parcel-gilt
chaises, by Jean-Baptiste,
Bernard Demay, on turned
tapering fluted legs headed by
stiff-leaves and paterae.
(Christie's)

(Six) $15,249

A pair of Spanish red and gilt-
japanned side chairs, first half
18th century, in the manner of
Giles Grendey, on cabriole legs
decorated with flowerheads and
joined by an H-shaped stretcher,
possibly English.
(Christie's) $15,249

Two of a set of eight William IV
mahogany dining chairs, each
with waisted back and scrolled
horizontal splat above a floral
needlework drop-in seat.
(Christie's)

(Eight) $7,866

One of a set of four mahogany
dining chairs, each with oval
top-rail above gilt-metal laurel
wreath splat, Scandinavian,
early 19th century.
(Christie's)

(Four) $1,351

Pair of fancy side chairs, New
York City, 1805–15, with
original faux tiger maple ground
accented with dark painted
striping and stenciled grape
clusters.
(Skinner) $1,725

DINING CHAIRS

Two of a set of twelve George III style mahogany framed dining chairs including two armchairs, each with arched back and bowed seat.
(Christie's)
(Twelve) $2,287

One of a set of six early Victorian mahogany balloon-back dining chairs, on ring-turned reeded tapering legs.
(Christie's)
(Six) $2,622

Two of a set of eight George III style mahogany dining chairs, including a pair of armchairs, each with shield-shaped back and pierced vase splat.
(Christie's)
(Eight) $2,605

Two of a set of eight mahogany dining chairs of early George III design, the yoked and foliate-carved toprails above pierced and interlaced vase-shaped splats.
(Christie's)
(Eight) $1,672

One of a set of nine George III mahogany dining-chairs, each with a tapering rectangular back, with foliate-scrolled cresting and pierced vase-shaped splat with C-scrolls.
(Christie's)
(Nine) $15,835

Two of a set of six Regency green-painted and parcel-gilt dining-chairs, the downswept paneled arms terminating in lion heads and on lion monopodia.
(Christie's)
(Six) $41,262

Two of a set of seven Victorian mahogany dining-chairs, including two armchairs, the curved toprails above molded horizontal splats.
(Christie's)
(Seven) $3,299

One of a set of eighteen Irish Regency mahogany dining-chairs, each with channeled scrolled uprights with spirally-reeded baluster toprail.
(Christie's)
(Eighteen) $52,026

Two of a set of eight mahogany dining-chairs of Regency design, the molded tablet toprails above trelliswork horizontal splats.
(Christie's)
(Eight) $1,410

DINING CHAIRS

One of a set of ten Victorian mahogany balloon back dining chairs with pierced vase shaped splat backs.
(Anderson & Garland)
(Ten) $4,226

Two of a set of six Victorian walnut dining chairs, each oval button-down padded back with foliate-carved top-rail above a serpentine padded seat.
(Christie's)
(Six) $1,563

One of a pair of Arts and Crafts oak side chairs, each with oval padded back and undulating pierced splat.
(Christie's)
(Two) $1,205

A pair of classical figured maple sidechairs, New England, 19th century, each with bowed, ring-turned crestrail above a pierced and scrolled splat.
(Christie's) $1,035

A Carlo Bugatti beechwood side chair, the rectangular close-nailed padded back with replacement vinyl, marked with paper label *Liberty & Co.*
(Christie's) $1,113

A pair of early 19th century Dutch mahogany floral marquetry and brass strung music chairs, with bar top rails and lyre shaped splats.
(Phillips) $1,190

One of a set of six oak side chairs designed by A.W.N. Pugin, on turned and chamfered legs joined by chamfered stretchers.
(Christie's) $2,400

A pair of carved mahogany armchairs in the Chippendale style, with serpentine arched top rails and pierced Gothic arched splats with foliate ornament.
(Phillips) $5,400

One of a set of six ebonized and parcel-gilt dining chairs, each arched top-rail centered by a blue plaque depicting a Grecian goddess, late 19th century .
(Christie's)
(Six) $2,257

One of a pair of early 19th century mahogany hall chairs with carved scrolling panel backs above solid seats, raised on turned tapering legs. (Anderson & Garland) (Two) $563

Two of a set of six Provincial elm dining-chairs, 19th century, the brass lined toprails above baluster-turned backs. (Christie's) (Six) $1,215

A walnut dining chair, the high-back with pierced solid splat, above a floral needlework drop-in seat, on cabriole legs, early 18th century. (Christie's) $245

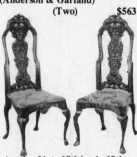

A pair of late 18th/early 19th century carved walnut side chairs, in the manner of Daniel Marot, the balloon shaped backs with vase cresting and pierced splats, on cabriole legs. (Phillips) $2,250

One of a set of fourteen George III mahogany dining-chairs, by Thomas Chippendale, each with waved, channeled, arched toprail above a pierced tapering splat centred by a channeled rosette and fluted patera. (Christie's) (Fourteen) $1,340,820

Two of a set of fourteen Victorian carved oak dining chairs including two elbow chairs, the padded back with arched crest and turned finials. (Andrew Hartley) (Fourteen) $4,770

One of six Gustav Stickley dining chairs, circa 1907, three horizontal slats, new seats in cream colored leather, 37½in. high. (Skinner) $2,900

Liberty & Co. after Richard Riemerschmid, two of a set of four chairs, circa 1900, oak, shaped rectangular back splat, notched front legs with similarly notched buttress supports. (Sotheby's) $5,249

One of a set of six mid-Victorian mahogany dining chairs, each with shaped balloon back, on cabriole legs. (Christie's) $2,200

DINING CHAIRS

Pair of Biedermeier fruitwood
and parcel-gilt side chairs, first
quarter 19th century.
(Skinner) $2,415

Cherry side chair, Connecticut,
1775–1800, with shaped crest
and block and ring turned legs.
(Skinner) $690

Pair of Spanish baroque walnut
side chairs, mid 18th century,
38in. high.
(Skinner) $575

Pair of George III style green
chinoiserie decorated side
chairs, 19th century, the
upholstered back and seat in a
chinoiserie decorated fabric,
34in. high.
(Skinner) $805

Queen Anne crooked-back
painted side chair,
Massachusetts, circa 1760, the
yoked carved crest rail above a
vasiform splat and raked
molded stiles.
(Skinner) $3,737

Two of a set of eight George III
style mahogany dining chairs,
late 19th/20th century,
comprising two armchairs and
six side chairs, 38in. high.
(Skinner)
    (Eight) $8,050

Pair of Empire ormolu mounted
mahogany and parcel-gilt
chaises, early 19th century,
31¼in. high.
(Skinner) $1,955

Worshipful Master's chair, New
Hampshire, 1850–70, painted
black with gold highlights, back
with pressed wood rosettes.
(Skinner) $633

Pair of Rococo Revival
laminated rosewood side chairs,
New York, John Henry Belter,
mid 19th century, 40in. high.
(Skinner) $5,463

DINING CHAIRS

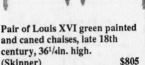

Pair of Louis XVI green painted and caned chaises, late 18th century, 36¼in. high. (Skinner) $805

Empire ormolu mounted mahogany side chair, early 19th century, 33¾in. high. (Skinner) $488

Pair of Queen Anne walnut side chairs, Boston area, 1730–60, with balloon seats. (Skinner) $13,800

Pair of classical side chairs, attributed to John and Hugh Finley, Baltimore, circa 1820, painted light yellow with gilt and black painted fruit filled compôtes. (Skinner) $747

One of a set of six Rococo Revival walnut dining chairs, mid 19th century, shaped back over button upholstered seat raised on cabriole legs. (Skinner) (Six) $1,150

Two of a set of eight Hepplewhite style mahogany dining chairs, two carvers with oval backs, pierced central splats, 20th century. (G. A. Key) (Eight) $4,408

Pair of mahogany Gothic Revival side chairs, New York City, 1850–60, with carved curving crest and stay rail above a serpentine front seat rail. (Skinner) $977

Transitional maple side chair, New England, 1760–80, with raked and molded crest terminals above a pierced splat. (Skinner) $748

Two of a set of six George II style mahogany dining chairs, late 19th century, comprising two armchairs and four side chairs. (Skinner) (Six) $3,450

EASY CHAIRS

A Louis XV style carved giltwood bergère with padded back and sides, shell cresting.
(Christie's) $793

Pair of Louis XV style oak and caned fauteuils, late 19th/20th century, with slip seats, 36¹/₂in. high.
(Skinner) $1,840

An early Victorian mahogany gentleman's armchair, the waisted buttoned back within a foliate scrolling frame, on cabriole legs.
(Christie's) $1,671

A Victorian walnut framed spoon back chair, with flower carved crest and button upholstered back.
(Andrew Hartley) $1,320

A Victorian walnut nursing chair, the waisted button-down padded back and serpentine padded seat on cabriole legs, with matching gents chair.
(Christie's) $1,400

A pair of early 19th century mahogany elbow chairs, the shield shaped back carved with ribbons and flower heads.
(Andrew Hartley) $509

A giltwood armchair of Louis XVI style, the rectangular padded back surmounted by a ribbon and foliate-carved cresting.
(Christie's) $1,496

A matched pair of early Victorian rosewood tub armchairs, each with a spoon-shaped padded back, on cabriole legs.
(Christie's) $2,463

A Regency mahogany bergère with rectangular cane-filled back, sides and padded armrests.
(Christie's) $7,631

272

EASY CHAIRS

Natural finish wicker side chair, late 19th century, 45in. high. (Skinner) **$403**

Two Renaissance Revival walnut, marquetry and part-ebonized slipper chairs, circa 1875–85, 36in. high. (Skinner) **$2,645**

Wakefield Rattan Co. natural finish wicker rocking chair, late 19th/20th century, bearing a paper label, 35in. high. (Skinner) **$633**

An early Victorian walnut lady's armchair, the waisted padded back within a foliate scrolling frame, on cabriole legs with scrolling feet. (Christie's) **$1,935**

A pair of walnut bergères of Louis XV style, with foliate-carved top-rail padded back and arms, French, early 19th century. (Christie's) **$2,952**

A mahogany cockfighting/reading chair, 19th century, on turned tapering baluster supports with later brass caps and castors. (Christie's) **$705**

Rococo Revival laminated rosewood side chair, probably John Henry Belter, New York, mid 19th century, with later rockers, 33in. high. (Skinner) **$633**

A pair of giltwood tub armchairs, each with a guilloché-carved frame and floral cresting, French, late 19th century. (Christie's) **$1,736**

An early Victorian rosewood easy armchair, upholstered with floral tapestry, on turned tapering legs, the castors stamped *I.W. Lewty's, Patent.* (Christie's) **$600**

EASY CHAIRS

Italian neoclassical blue painted and parcel-gilt armchair, late 18th/early 19th century. (Skinner) $1,610

Pair of diminutive Louis XVI style beechwood and upholstered bergères, late 19th/20th century, 35in. high. (Skinner) $1,610

Italian walnut swan-form grotto armchair, mid 19th century, 26in. high. (Skinner) $1,150

A good Louis XV-style child's walnut armchair, French, late 19th century, the square upholstered back framed by carved foliage and central scrolls. (Sotheby's) $1,272

Two turned wood children's chairs, French, late 19th century, each stained black, the larger with oval upholstered back carved with an acanthus leaf pediment. (Sotheby's) $2,726

American Aesthetic Movement rosewood, inlay and parcel-gilt slipper chair, attributed to Herter Brothers, New York City, circa 1880, 30¼in. high. (Skinner) $3,450

Federal mahogany lolling chair, probably Massachusetts, circa 1790, 45½in. high. (Skinner) $1,495

Pair of Victorian rosewood spoon back easy chairs, padded and scroll molded arm rests, on hoof front feet, circa 1860. (G. A. Key) $2,204

Louis XVI style giltwood fauteuil, late 19th century, with Beauvais tapestry upholstery, 37in. high. (Skinner) $2,185

EASY CHAIRS

William IV mahogany and red leather upholstered side chair, 34½in. high. (Skinner) **$920**

Pair of George II style walnut and parcel-gilt side chairs, 19th century, with needlework upholstery, 38in. high. (Skinner) **$3,335**

Empire mahogany bergère, circa 1825–30, with cut velvet upholstery, 37¼in. high. (Skinner) **$1,955**

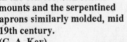

Austrian neoclassical mahogany, marquetry, part-ebonized and parcel-gilt desk armchair, signed *Joseph Weber, Wien*, early 19th century, 33in. high. (Skinner) **$1,725**

Two of a set of eight fine quality Victorian mahogany dining chairs, the spoon backs molded in the centers with foliate mounts and the serpentined aprons similarly molded, mid 19th century. (G. A. Key) (Eight) **$4,415**

Victorian mahogany elbow chair, the back crested with rosette and scrolled mount, raised on front baluster turned tapering fluted supports, circa 1870. (G. A. Key) **$491**

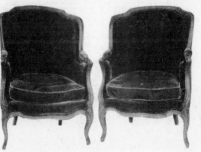

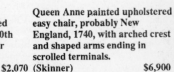

Federal mahogany upholstered easy chair, probably New England, circa 1800, upholstered in white damask. (Skinner) **$1,265**

Pair of Louis XV style beechwood and upholstered bergères, late 19th/early 20th century, pale green mohair upholstery, 37in. high. (Skinner) **$2,070**

Queen Anne painted upholstered easy chair, probably New England, 1740, with arched crest and shaped arms ending in scrolled terminals. (Skinner) **$6,900**

FURNITURE

EASY CHAIRS

 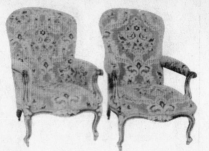 

A Federal carved mahogany easy chair, New York, 1790-1810, the arched back flanked by shaped wings continuing to outward scrolled arms.
(Christie's) $4,600

A buttoned gentleman's chair with upholstered arms, and a lady's chair with upholstered open arms.
(David Lay) $2,428

An early Victorian mahogany tub armchair, the padded back and downcurved padded arms with scroll terminals, on turned and gadrooned legs.
(Christie's) $669

 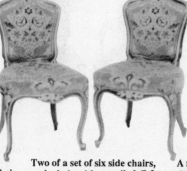

A George III close-studded leather-upholstered sedan chair, the domed hinged top above glazed sides, cut-velvet upholstered interior, 63in. high.
(Christie's) $2,605

Two of a set of six side chairs, each chair with stenciled *G.J. Morant* mark to the hessian and webbing beneath the seat.
(David Lay)   (Six) $3,794

A mahogany wing armchair in the George I style, the arched padded back flanked by out-curved arms above a squab seat, 19th century.
(Christie's) $1,667

A giltwood armchair of Rococo design, the foliate-carved top-rail above padded cartouche back and padded arms with downscrolled terminals, French, mid 19th century.
(Christie's) $1,129

Pair of Louis XV style beechwood fauteuils, late 19th century, upholstered in tapestry, 43¼in. high.
(Skinner) $2,185

Emile-Jacques Ruhlmann Maharadjah ref. 206 NR' swivel chair, 1929, upholstered in black leather, on circular chromium-plated metal base, 32⅜in.
(Sotheby's) $35,616

EASY CHAIRS

A mid-Victorian rosewood nursing-chair, the rectangular gros point needlework upholstered back flanked by spirally-turned columns. (Christie's) **$846**

One of a pair of Howard armchairs, each with a padded back, arms and seat, on turned tapering legs. (Christie's) (Two) **$2,631**

A green-painted and gilt-heightened bergère, the harebell-painted stepped top-rail above a solid splat. (Christie's) **$1,935**

A George III mahogany-framed wing armchair, the arched padded back and outscrolled arms above padded seat. (Christie's) **$1,216**

A pair of Victorian satin birch easy armchairs, by Howard & Son of London, with rectangular padded backs and upholstered seats. (Christie's) **$898**

A mahogany wing armchair of George III style, with a padded back flanked by outcurved arms. (Christie's) **$1,020**

Set of three Edwardian oak armchairs with upholstered backs and seats, scrolled arms with lattice panels. (Russell, Baldwin & Bright) **$4,743**

An antique French carved giltwood fauteuil in Louis XV style with giltwood frame carved in the rococo style, on slender supports, 3ft. 3in. wide. (Russell, Baldwin & Bright) **$3,213**

A walnut open armchair by Stanley W Davies, with sloping button upholstered back and similar seat cushion, and dated *1932.* (Andrew Hartley) **$1,526**

EASY CHAIRS

One of a pair of Louis XV style beechwood bergères, the acanthus and flowerhead carved top rails above padded backs.
(Phillips)(Two) $3,900

A Liberty & Co. oak adjustable armchair, with slatted back flanked by shaped slatted sides, on turned tapering legs.
(Christie's) $408

A Charles X mahogany bergère, the curved padded back, sides and drop-in seat with carved swan neck terminals.
(Phillips) $1,500

A pair of Thonet bentwood open armchairs, each with pierced and shaped padded back, on square tapering legs joined by arched stretchers.
(Christie's) $482

One of a pair of Gordon Russell oak lounge chairs, each with padded back and seat, flanked by paneled sides, on ebonized block feet.
(Christie's) $890

Fine carved cinnabar lacquer chair, 18/19th century, circular seat raised on four cabriole legs, framed by ruyi lappet apron.
(Butterfield & Butterfield)
$5,750

One of a set of six mid-Victorian Gothic Revival oak dining chairs, after a design by A.W.N. Pugin.
(Christie's)
(Six) $2,596

A North European mahogany rocking-chair, the arched channeled back and arms enclosing a padded back, sides and squab-cushion covered in close-nailed beige leather.
(Christie's) $13,455

A Charles II walnut open armchair, with stuffover rectangular back and seat with scroll arm supports, on Braganza scroll legs united by a scroll front stretcher.
(Phillips) $1,800

ELBOW CHAIRS

An early 19th century beech armchair with spindle back above the solid seat raised on turned legs.
(Anderson & Garland)
$1,800

A George III carved mahogany elbow chair, in the Hepplewhite taste, on square tapered legs united by stretchers.
(Phillips) $1,594

A pair of late-Victorian Gothic Revival pitch-pine open armchairs, each with open arcaded back, above rectangular panel seat.
(Christie's) $779

An Edwardian painted satinwood open armchair, the down and outswept arms above a red cotton-covered drop-in seat and serpentine seat-rail centred by a floral spray, on square tapering legs.
(Christie's) $1,759

An Arts and Crafts mahogany armchair, the slatted padded back with inswept finials, on turned tapering legs joined by stretchers.
(Christie's) $297

A 19th century Dutch walnut and floral marquetry open armchair, in the Louis XV style, the shaped back with a vase splat inlaid with birds and flowers.
(Phillips) $1,200

One of a set of six Regency simulated rosewood and brass inlaid dining chairs, including one open scroll armchair, with outswept legs.
(Phillips) (Six) $3,600

An Arts and Crafts oak armchair, by John Starkey, the rectangular chip-carved back above triangular panel seat, flanked by turned arms and turned uprights.
(Christie's) $742

A Regency ebonized and gilt decorated elbow chair, the back with turned top rail, on splayed legs.
(Phillips) $1,050

ELBOW CHAIRS

Chippendale cherry corner
chair, probably central
Massachusetts, circa 1780, 31in.
high.
(Skinner) $1,840

Sack-back Windsor chair,
Rhode Island or Massachusetts,
1770–90, old dark green paint,
36in. high.
(Skinner) $5,175

Painted roundabout writing
armchair, New England, mid
18th century, with black over
red paint.
(Skinner) $1,035

A 19th century ash and elm stick
back elbow chair with solid seat
on four splayed supports with
H-stretcher, having original
painted decoration.
(Russell, Baldwin & Bright)
        $2,907

Queen Anne walnut roundabout
chair, possibly Rhode Island,
last half 18th century, the
shaped crest projects above a
scrolled back rail ending in
circular handholds.
(Skinner) $4,312

Rare painted Windsor
highchair, possibly southeastern
Massachusetts, circa 1780, the
serpentine crest rail with
circular terminals above five
spindles and vase and ring
turned stiles.
(Skinner) $28,750

One of a set of three 19th
century mahogany elbow chairs
with caned seats and backs,
open trellis borders.
(Russell, Baldwin & Bright)
     (Three) $1,071

An early 19th century yew and
elm Windsor elbow chair with
pierced splat and stick back,
solid seat on turned supports.
(Russell, Baldwin & Bright)
        $1,071

A Regency beechwood elbow
chair, grained and painted with
classical putti to the trellis-
pierced bar back.
(Russell, Baldwin & Bright)
        $1,408

ELBOW CHAIRS

Red stained maple and ash roundabout chair, New England, 1780–1800, with traces of red paint.
(Skinner)   **$748**

Anglo-Indian camphorwood and caned child's armchair, mid 19th century, lacking bar-tray, 23in. high.
(Skinner)   **$863**

George II walnut corner armchair, mid 18th century, 31in. high.
(Skinner)   **$1,610**

An antique Welsh comb-back elbow chair in ash and elm with thick solid seat on four splayed supports with remains of original paint work.
(Russell, Baldwin & Bright)
                    $2,907

A 19th century yew and elm elbow chair, the bar back carved with a roundel, solid seat on turned supports with H-stretcher, stamped *C.S.*
(Russell, Baldwin & Bright)
                    $459

Georgian elmwood and yew wood Windsor armchair, mid 18th century, with shaped cresting and spindle inset back, ·39in. high.
(Skinner)   **$460**

Painted ladder-back armchair, Long Island or New Jersey, 1730–1800, old black paint with gold accents, old painted splint seat.
(Skinner)   **$1,610**

Grain painted and stencil decorated Windsor commode chair, Connecticut, early 19th century, the crest with floral stenciled decoration.
(Skinner)   **$1,725**

Queen Anne maple armchair, probably Massachusetts, mid 18th century, the shaped yoked crest rail above a chamfered vasiform splat.
(Skinner)   **$2,760**

ELBOW CHAIRS

A pair of pale green bergères, the elongated caned back within a molded frame flanked by outcurved arms, French. (Christie's) $702

Red stained maple roundabout chair, New England, early 19th century, old surface. (Skinner) $690

Painted Windsor rod-back highchair, New England, early 19th century, *TH* carved on underside of seat. (Skinner) $1,150

A late Victorian oak armchair, of 17th century style, the pierced crown and c-scroll carved toprail above two waved vertical splats. (Christie's) $400

Two pieces of natural finish wicker, late 19th/20th century, comprising a magazine stand, and a child's highchair. (Skinner) $288

A Regency mahogany metamorphic library armchair, in the manner of Morgan and Sanders, the reeded rectangular tablet toprail above a similar horizontal splat, 22in. wide. (Christie's) $8,722

One of a set of eight Continental straw-seat dining chairs, each with an asymmetrical top-rail and solid splat with a straw-seat. (Christie's)
(Eight) $2,280

Maple and ash turned armchair, coastal Massachusetts, mid 18th century, old mustard brown paint. (Skinner) $3,335

A 19th century Spanish walnut open armchair, with leaf carved finials, on square section uprights, with brass studs and enclosing two oblong marquetry panels. (Andrew Hartley) $620

ELBOW CHAIRS

One of a pair of walnut open
armchairs of Carolean style, the
arched top-rail above a padded
back and downscrolled arms,
late 19th/early 20th century.
(Christie's) (Two) $833

Joined carved oak great chair,
England or southern
Massachusetts, 17th century.
(Skinner) $1,150

A late Victorian oak armchair,
of 17th century style, the shaped
toprail centered by a crown
flanked by s-scrolls.
(Christie's) $509

One of a set of six mahogany
dining chairs in the Chippendale
style, including two armchairs,
each with foliate-carved
undulating top-rail.
(Christie's)
(Six) $2,463

Two of a set four elm corner
armchairs, the stepped toprails
above out-scrolled armrests.
(Christie's)
(Four) $6,360

A Queen Anne maple child's
armchair, American, 1740-60,
the yoked crestrail above a solid
vasiform splat, flanked by ring
and baluster turned stiles, 23in.
(Christie's) $1,150

One of a set of six walnut dining
chairs, including two armchairs,
each serpentine foliate-carved
top-rail above a pierced
scrolling vase splat.
(Christie's)
(Six) $1,929

Thonet, bentwood rocking chair,
circa 1880, stained beech,
serpentine frame with
curvilinear supports, 31½in.
(Sotheby's) $5,624

A William IV mahogany caned
open armchair, the curved
foliate-carved top-rail above a
caned back, on circular tapering
reeded legs.
(Christie's) $2,463

CHESTS OF DRAWERS

Italian neoclassical walnut and inlay bowfronted chest of drawers, early 19th century, 43in. wide.
(Skinner) $4,600

Federal cherry inlaid chest of drawers, probably Connecticut, circa 1790, the rectangular overhanging top with molded edge, 38³/₄in. wide.
(Skinner) $6,900

Diminutive George III mahogany serpentine-fronted chest of drawers, third quarter 18th century, 32³/₄in. wide.
(Skinner) $1,725

Federal mahogany and tiger maple bowfront bureau, probably Massachusetts, 1815–25, top with bowfront and ovolo corners and crossbanded edge, 40¹/₄in. wide.
(Skinner) $2,530

George III mahogany diminutive serpentine fronted chest of drawers, circa 1780, with four graduated drawers on shaped ogee bracket feet, 32in. wide.
(Skinner) $6,900

Federal cherry bird's-eye maple and mahogany chest of drawers, probably New Hampshire, 1820–30, the cockbeaded drawers outlined in stringing, 38⁵/₈in. wide.
(Skinner) $4,025

Joined oak and pine paneled chest of drawers, New England, 17th century, with pine thumb molded top above four drawers, 39in. wide.
(Skinner) $20,700

Maple, cherry and tiger maple veneer chest of drawers, inscribed *Made by Asa Loomis in the year 1816*, Shaftsbury, Vermont, 42¹/₂in. wide.
(Skinner) $6,325

Japanese tansu chest, late 19th century, rectangular form, three rows of double drawers above two larger single drawers, 29¹/₂in. wide.
(Skinner) $575

CHESTS OF DRAWERS

Painted pine tall chest of drawers, Connecticut River Valley, mid 18th century, replaced brasses, old red paint, 38¼in. wide.
(Skinner) $3,220

Painted pine blanket chest, probably Western Massachusetts, 1730–50, with original ball feet, half round moldings, 36in. wide.
(Skinner) $4,025

Jacobean oak chest of drawers, late 17th century, fitted with four drawers, each with raised panels, on later bun feet, 43in. wide.
(Skinner) $2,070

George III mahogany boxwood inlaid serpentine chest of drawers, late 18th century, serpentine top over three graduated drawers, raised on French feet, 37½in. long.
(Skinner) $1,955

Federal mahogany carved and mahogany veneer chest of drawers, probably Salem, Massachusetts, circa 1820, the rectangular top with ovolo corners and bead carved edge, 40¾in. wide.
(Skinner) $1,150

Federal cherry bureau, Massacusetts, circa 1800, rectangular top above a cockbeaded case of four graduated drawers, 37½in. wide.
(Skinner) $2,070

Rare Chippendale mahogany serpentine-front chest of drawers, Boston, 1760–80, four graduated drawers surrounded by cockbeading on a molded base, 33¼in. wide.
(Skinner) $178,500

Federal tiger maple tall chest of drawers, probably Pennsylvania, circa 1800, case of two cockbeaded short drawers above four graduated long drawers, 37½in. wide.
(Skinner) $4,025

Chippendale cherry chest of drawers, Massachusetts, late 18th century, with scratch beaded overhanging top above four thumb-molded drawers, 37in. wide.
(Skinner) $2,760

CHESTS ON CHESTS

An 18th century mahogany chest on chest, the upper section with Greek key cornice over a blind fret frieze, 44½in. wide.
(David Lay) $2,059

George III mahogany chest on chest, late 18th century, 43½in. wide.
(Skinner) $6,613

A George III mahogany tallboy with a flared cornice above three short and six graduated drawers, 45in. wide.
(Anderson & Garland)
          $7,043

An antique oak chest on chest with Greek key cornice over two short and six long drawers, raised on bracket feet, 3ft. 6in. wide.
(Russell, Baldwin & Bright)
          $2,219

A mahogany tallboy, the dentil-molded cornice above five graduated drawers, the lower section with two deep drawers, on ogee bracket feet, 18th century, 51½in. wide.
(Christie's) $1,320

A crossbanded walnut tallboy chest, the molded cornice above three short drawers and six further long drawers, on bracket feet, 41in. wide.
(Christie's) $2,778

An early George III mahogany chest on chest, the ogee molded dentil cornice above a blind fret carved frieze with two short and three long graduated drawers, 119cm. wide.
(Phillips) $9,300

A George II walnut tallboy, crossbanded and feather-banded overall, on later bracket feet, with numerical inscriptions to the underside of the top, 42½in. wide.
(Christie's) $30,498

A George II walnut and featherbanded chest on chest, the upper part with a molded broken triangular pediment and molded cornice, on bracket feet, 1m. wide.
(Phillips) $9,750

FURNITURE

Queen Anne walnut high chest of drawers, Boston or Salem, Massachusetts, circa 1750, on four cabriole legs ending in pad feet on platforms, 37³/₄in. wide. (Skinner) $29,900

William and Mary walnut and burl walnut highboy, 40in. wide. (Skinner) $1,380

Queen Anne carved walnut high chest, Hingham, Massachusetts area, 1740–60, with thumb molded drawers, one of which is fan carved, 39¹/₄in. wide. (Skinner) $34,500

An early 18th century walnut chest on stand, fitted ovolu frieze drawer over two short and three long drawers, 3ft. 8in. wide. (Russell, Baldwin & Bright) $3,672

A William and Mary brass-mounted coromandel lacquer cabinet-on-stand, decorated overall with trellis and floral borders, the rectangular doors with pierced brass hinges, 40in. wide. (Christie's) $26,910

A line-inlaid walnut chest-on-stand, the crossbanded molded rectangular top above two short and three long graduated drawers, the chest basically early 18th century, 41in. wide. (Christie's) $2,622

An early 18th century walnut-veneered chest on later stand, the crossbanded top above two short and three graduated long drawers, 39¹/₂in. wide. (Bearne's) $1,274

An ebonised line-inlaid walnut cabinet-on-stand, the molded cornice above a pair of geometrically inlaid doors, Dutch, 19th century, 66in. wide. (Christie's) $2,605

A feather-banded chest-on-stand, the molded cornice above three short and three long drawers, basically 18th century, 41¹/₂in. wide. (Christie's) $3,126

CHIFFONIERS

Victorian mahogany chiffonier, the pediment with scrolled back and the central shelf supported by scrolled mounts, mid to late 19th century, 36in. wide. (G. A. Key) $654

A George III mahogany bow front chiffonier, the top with two shelves and shaped supports, turned legs, 34in. wide. (David Lay) $2,352

A 19th century rosewood chiffonier, the arched mirrored back with shelf on scrolled supports, single carved frieze drawer, 44in. wide. (Andrew Hartley) $3,960

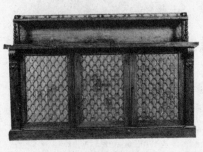

A Victorian burr walnut-veneered and inlaid chiffonier, the mirrored back with three graduated tiers, 30in. wide. (Bearne's) $1,624

A late Regency rosewood chiffonier, the rectangular top supporting a shelf with pierced three-quarter gallery supported by barley-twist columns, 78in. (Christie's) $3,634

An early Victorian rosewood chiffonier, the pierced mirrored back with foliate carving, on plinth base, 28^{1}/4in. wide. (Christie's) $1,400

A William IV rosewood chiffonier, the front of unusual concave shape with a drawer above two cupboard doors, 44in. wide. (Lawrence Fine Arts) $1,600

A Victorian mahogany chiffonier, the raised panel back with scrolled crest and shelf on turned and reeded supports, 34in. wide. (Andrew Hartley) $1,812

A Regency mahogany chiffonier, the arched shelved superstructure above two frieze drawers and a pair of paneled cupboard doors, on swept bracket feet, 35in. wide. (Christie's) $1,305

COMMODE CHESTS

A late **18th century Italian**
walnut and crossbanded
commode, inlaid with boxwood
lines, the rectangular molded
top with foliate inlaid oyster
veneers, 126cm. wide.
(Phillips)   **$5,100**

A Louis XV ormolu-mounted
tulipwood, harewood and
parquetry commode, attributed
to Charles Cressent, the later
waved brêche d'alep marble top
above two long drawers, 57¼in.
(Christie's)   **$173,940**

An 18th century Continental
commode in walnut, the bombé
serpentine front fitted with two
drawers on slender cabriole legs,
4ft. 1in.
(Russell, Baldwin & Bright)
                           $16,830

A George III mahogany
serpentine commode, the three
long drawers fitted with
molded brass handles and
raised on bracket feet, 43in.
wide.
(Anderson & Garland)
                            $1,251

Louis XV style gilt metal
mounted kingwood and
parquetry bombé commode, late
19th/early 20th century, antico
verde marble top, 30½in. long.
(Skinner)   **$2,185**

A George III satinwood and
marquetry bombé commode,
crossbanded overall in
rosewood, the serpentine-
fronted top and sides inlaid with
an urn issuing foliage scrolls,
45½in. wide.
(Christie's)   **$11,661**

A marquetry commode, the
rounded rectangular top inlaid
with two ovals with classical
figures, within a checker-
banded border, 47in. wide.
(Christie's)   **$2,463**

A Regencé ormolu-mounted
kingwood and parquetry
commode en tombeau, the later
serpentine-fronted rectangular
mottled-brown fossil marble top
above two walnut-lined short
drawers, 50¾in. wide.
(Christie's)   **$70,980**

A Louis XVI walnut rectangular
commode, with a fossilized gray
veined marble top, containing
three short and two long
drawers, 125cm. wide.
(Phillips)   **$2,550**

COMMODES & POT CUPBOARDS

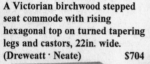

A Victorian birchwood stepped seat commode with rising hexagonal top on turned tapering legs and castors, 22in. wide. (Dreweatt · Neate)　$704

Pair of late Empire mahogany and marble top pot cupboards, mid 19th century, 14in. wide. (Skinner)　$1,093

A George III mahogany tray top chamber cupboard on reeded supports, the top with shaped front and pierced with lozenge motifs, 22in. wide. (Dreweatt Neate)　$811

L. & J.G. Stickley Handcraft cabinet, single drawer over door, arched base, interior intact, Handcraft decal, 29in. high. (Skinner)　$2,990

A pair of George III satinwood and marquetry bedside commodes, attributed to Mayhew and Ince, each inlaid with boxwood and ebonized lines, 23in. wide. (Christie's)　$40,089

A Victorian cylindrical pot cupboard, with one door, on plinth base, 30in. high. (Dreweatt Neate)　$717

One of a pair of gilt-metal mounted, kingwood and mahogany bedside cupboards, each with serpentine eared marble top, French, each 17¹/₂in. wide. (Christie's)　$3,519

A pair of walnut serpentine bedside cupboards, each with marble top and frieze drawer above a paneled cupboard door, French. (Christie's)　$956

A Regency mahogany bedside cupboard, the rectangular galleried top with pierced carrying handles, above a cupboard, 13³/₄in. wide. (Christie's)　$563

CORNER CUPBOARDS

A George III oak corner cupboard with molded cornice, two ogee paneled doors enclosing shaped shelving, 29in.
(Andrew Hartley) $1,275

A late Victorian mahogany standing corner cabinet with a pair of glazed panel doors enclosing lined shelves, 37¹/₂in. wide.
(Anderson & Garland)
$641

A George III oak standing corner cupboard with mahogany crossbanding, molded cornice two fielded panel doors, 53in.
(Andrew Hartley) $2,624

Pine glazed corner cupboard, probably New England, late 18th century, flat cove molded cornice above a glazed door, 45in. wide.
(Skinner) $2,415

Pair of Edwardian rosewood and inlay corner cabinets, circa 1900, 28¹/₂in. wide.
(Skinner) $1,495

Late 19th century mahogany standing corner cupboard in the manner of Voysey, the top with a shelf supported on slats with pierced heart decoration, 41in.
(Ewbank) $2,067

18th century oak bow-fronted corner cupboard, molded pediment and the doors below inlaid with boxwood stringing and enclosing fitted shelves, 33in.
(G. A. Key) $824

Oak and mahogany crossbanded corner cabinet, molded pediment, two paneled doors below enclosing a fitted interior, late 18th/early 19th century, 39in.
(G. A. Key) $462

A George III mahogany bow fronted corner cupboard, with satinwood banding and inlay, frieze with marquetry panel depicting Britannia, 29in. wide.
(Andrew Hartley) $1,630

CORNER CUPBOARDS

A George III mahogany standing corner cupboard, with molded cornice, canted sides, 43½in.
(Andrew Hartley) $2,945

Pine corner cupboard, probably New York State, 18th century, 57in. wide.
(Skinner) $3,680

Chippendale pine paneled corner cupboard, New England, 18th century, 45in. wide.
(Skinner) $4,600

An 18th century oak full height double door corner cupboard, having a dentil cornice, arched paneled double door and single cupboard door under, 48in. wide.
(H.C. Chapman) $2,028

A Federal paneled cherrywood corner cupboard, Lebanon County, Pennsylvania, circa 1830, in two parts, the cove molding above two glazed and mullioned doors, 4ft. 3¾in. wide.
(Sotheby's) $1,610

A rare paint-decorated pine corner cupboard, Pennsylvania, 1790-1820, in two parts, the molded and rope carved cornice above an arched glazed door, 4ft. ½in. wide.
(Sotheby's) $13,800

A 19th century mahogany standing corner cupboard, crossbanded with checker inlay, molded over two astragal glazed doors, 43½in. wide.
(Andrew Hartley) $3,339

A George III oak and mahogany crossbanded corner cabinet, the scrolled pediment above a molded cornice fitted with a pair of paneled cupboard doors, 42in. wide.
(Christie's) $2,952

A late 18th/early 19th century Dutch mahogany bowfronted standing corner cupboard, with architectural pediment, on square tapering feet, 43in. wide.
(Dreweatt Neate) $6,900

CREDENZAS

A Victorian ebonized and gilt metal mounted credenza with bowed ends, the whole inlaid with boxwood stringing, and with blue oval jasper-ware style plaque, 60in. wide.
(Canterbury) $1,600

A late Victorian ebonized and floral-marquetry dwarf side cabinet with gilt-metal mounts, 73in. wide.
(Christie's) $4,160

A fine Victorian burr walnut credenza decorated with inset Paris porcelain panels, a pair of convex glazed doors to each end, 71in. wide.
(Anderson & Garland) $9,150

American Renaissance Revival walnut, parquetry and part ebonized credenza, third quarter 19th century, the back stenciled *Manufactured by Edward Hixon & Co.*, 60 in. long
(Skinner) $4,025

A Napoleon III gilt-bronze boulle and ebonized meuble d'appui, Paris, circa 1860, with a black marble top, above a frieze and a pair of doors, 154cm. wide.
(Sotheby's) $7,873

A good 19th century English breakfront credenza in French taste in burr-walnut marquetry veneer, the central door flanked by curved doors, the whole chased with cast gilt brass mounts, 60in. wide.
(David Lay) $2,556

19th century walnut breakfront credenza with gilt mounts, the center section with a single paneled door inlaid with a vase of flowers, glazed door to each side, 68in. wide.
(Ewbank) $4,134

An Italian Renaissance parcel-gilt walnut credenza with dentiled top over two frieze drawers above cupboard doors, 67 in. long
(Sotheby's) $31,050

American Renaissance Revival gilt bronze mounted rosewood and marquetry credenza, probably New York, circa 1865–1875, with incised, ebonized and painted highlights, 74in. wide.
(Skinner) $11,500

CUPBOARDS

Painted pine paneled step-back cupboard, New England, early 19th century, the cornice molding above two raised panel doors, 36in. wide. (Skinner) **$2,415**

An oak court cupboard, the molded rectangular top above a foliate and scroll-carved frieze, with chevron inlay, partly 17th century, 75in. wide. (Christie's) **$11,810**

An oak dresser in early 16th century French style, 38in. wide. (David Lay) **$759**

Painted paneled and carved pine cupboard, New Jersey area, early 19th century, with molded overhanging top above a cupboard with applied moldings, 40½in. wide. (Skinner) **$3,450**

A Robert Thompson Mouseman oak cupboard, of rectangular two door construction with adze-finish, carved with a mouse, 108.5cm. wide. (Lawrence Fine Art) **$2,800**

An early 18th century Dutch walnut double-cupboard, the frieze with center panel carved with a cartouche, angelic masks and flowers, 60in. wide. (Anderson & Garland) **$3,756**

A red-painted poplar two-part pewter or 'Dutch' cupboard, Pennsylvania, circa 1840, the overhanging cornice above two glazed doors. (Sotheby's) **$16,100**

Cherry kas, Hudson River Valley, 18th century, the heavy cornice molding above paneled doors, 62in. wide. (Skinner) **$2,415**

A Victorian mahogany bow fronted cupboard on chest, with arched surmount on molded cornice, two paneled doors, 51½in. wide. (Andrew Hartley) **$1,193**

CUPBOARDS

A George III oak food cupboard with molded cornice, two pierced and paneled doors enclosing shelving, 41in. wide.
(Andrew Hartley) $4,134

An oak court cupboard, the projecting frieze with turned finials above a fielded panel front with two doors, 56in. wide, basically late 17th/early18th.
(Andrew Hartley) $1,780

Grained pine cupboard, Maine, mid-19th century, the molded top above a paneled door on four turned ball feet, 41½in. wide.
(Skinner) $2,300

An early 19th century Dutch oak and marquetry small bowfronted cupboard, decorated with urns of flowers, on square tapering feet, 27½in. wide.
(Dreweatt · Neate) $3,300

A Pine hanging cupboard enclosed by a pair of solid doors with stenciled decoration of trees, circa 1900.
(Dreweatt · Neate) $444

A walnut punched-tin-inset food safe, Pennsylvania, first half 19th century, the rectangular top above two short drawers and two cupboard doors, 41in. wide.
(Sotheby's) $2,587

An 18th century oak cupboard having two pairs of paneled doors enclosing shelves on bracket feet, 3ft. 8in. wide.
(Russell, Baldwin & Bright) $3,902

A Victorian teak and brass bound campaign cupboard, with solid doors and interior slides, a long and two short drawers under, 36in. wide.
(Dreweatt Neate) $1,565

A mahogany Estate's cabinet, with dentil-molded cornice and a pair of paneled cupboard doors enclosing a fitted interior, 42in. wide.
(Christie's) $1,910

A Victorian walnut davenport, fitted with a hinged pencil box, shaped molded leather-lined writing-slope, 21¼in. wide. (Christie's) $2,180

A Victorian walnut davenport the raised back with hinged lid having pierced grill, 21in. wide. (Andrew Hartley) $1,888

A Victorian walnut davenport with raised back, inset writing surface, fitted with four real and four dummy drawers, 1ft. 10in. wide. (Russell, Baldwin & Bright) $1,913

Early Victorian burr walnut davenport, the whole with satinwood stringing, the sloping cover with gilt tooled leather inset enclosing a fitted interior, circa 1840, 22in. wide. (G. A. Key) $2,393

A Regency rosewood davenport, the sliding top with tooled leather inset to the sloping flap and a hinged pen and ink side drawer, 19in. wide. (Bearne's) $4,301

Very fine Victorian burr walnut harlequin davenport, curved flap opening to reveal a slide out fitted writing surface and storage area, mid 19th century, 22in. wide. (G. A. Key) $3,985

A Victorian inlaid burr-walnut davenport, the hinged fitted superstructure above leather-lined sloping fall enclosing a bleached walnut interior, 21in. wide. (Christie's) $2,261

A Regency brass-inlaid calamander davenport, the rectangular top with three-quarter pierced brass gallery, 14½in. wide. (Christie's) $8,591

A Victorian walnut and boxwood lined davenport, the molded rectangular top fitted with a leather-lined hinged flap enclosing a partially-fitted interior, 21in. wide. (Christie's) $1,145

DAVENPORTS

A Victorian walnut davenport desk, raised ormolu gallery, interior with bird's eye maple fitted drawer, 1ft. 10in. wide.
(Russell, Baldwin & Bright)
$2,479

An early Victorian rosewood davenport, in the manner of Gillows of Lancaster, on squat bun feet, 23in. wide.
(Christie's) $2,731

A Victorian walnut davenport desk with scroll inlay and crossbanding, fitted gallery, 21in. wide.
(Russell, Baldwin & Bright)
$1,255

A Victorian walnut davenport, the hinged sloping leather lined writing surface fitted with a hinged domed pencil box above four drawers to one side, 21in. wide.
(Christie's) $1,392

A Victorian burr walnut davenport, the rising stationery compartment with pierced gallery and fitted with drawers and pigeon holes, 21½in. wide.
(Andrew Hartley) $5,775

Victorian walnut davenport, brass galleried back, the sloping cover with gilt tooled green leather inset enclosing fitted interior of six drawers, mid 19th century, 23in. wide.
(G. A. Key) $2,432

A Victorian burr walnut davenport with a pierced gallery above the hinged writing slope opening to reveal a fitted interior, 22½in. wide.
(Anderson & Garland)
$1,722

A Victorian walnut davenport, with three-quarter gallery above a leather-lined sloping fall enclosing two drawers, on turned column supports, 23in. wide.
(Christie's) $1,487

A Victorian walnut and boxwood lined davenport, with hinged domed pencil box and simulated leather-lined writing slope, 21in. wide.
(Christie's) $1,551

DESKS

Louis XV style parquetry bureau en pente, late 19th century.
(Skinner) $1,725

Italian neoclassical painted pine cylinder desk, circa 1800, 49in. wide.
(Skinner) $1,725

Dutch rococo style mahogany and floral marquetry lady's desk, late 19th/early 20th century, 27in. wide.
(Skinner) $1,495

A 19th century ebonized bureau de dame, the raised breakfront fitted with three doors with pietra dura panels, 3ft. 10in. wide.
(Russell, Baldwin & Bright) $2,830

Victorian bird's-eye maple faux bamboo lady's desk and chair, third quarter 19th century, 32in. wide.
(Skinner) $3,737

A German walnut, burrwood and parquetry writing cabinet, the superstructure fitted with a paneled cupboard door surrounded by two columns of five bowed drawers, 50in. wide.
(Christie's) $7,631

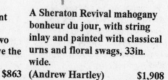

Stained pine carved fall front lady's desk, probably New England, circa 1900, with two exterior short drawers above the fall front, 24in. wide.
(Skinner) $863

A Sheraton Revival mahogany bonheur du jour, with string inlay and painted with classical urns and floral swags, 33in. wide.
(Andrew Hartley) $1,908

A Louis XV style rosewood and mahogany lady's writing desk, the superstructure with two cupboards with bookspine doors and three small drawers below, 27in. wide.
(Christie's) $1,736

DESKS

Empire mahogany small bonheur du jour, early 19th century, 27in. wide.
(Skinner) $1,092

An Edwardian mahogany bow fronted desk, crossbanded with string inlay, the arched back with two small drawers.
(Andrew Hartley) $2,557

Painted stand up desk, New England, with scrolled back splash above a hinged top, 26³/₈in. wide.
(Skinner) $862

A Victorian gilt-metal mounted rosewood crossbanded walnut and floral-marquetry bonheur du jour, the superstructure with a central mirror and short drawer, 35in. wide.
(Christie's) $3,473

A Victorian walnut bonheur du jour, with kingwood crossbanding and string inlaid, the raised upper section with central mirror over two drawers, 43½in. wide.
(Andrew Hartley) $5,425

A late George III satinwood-veneered and inlaid bonheur-du-jour, later painted with exotic birds, flowers and foliage, 29¹/₂in. wide.
(Bearne's) $4,618

Empire style ormolu mounted mahogany bonheur du jour, second half 19th century, 28¹/₄in. wide.
(Skinner) $1,840

A classic American school desk with chair, both height adjustable, circa 1920, desk 76 x 61 x 89 cm.
(Auction Team Köln) $171

Continental baroque style burl walnut and inlay desk on stand, 38¹/₄in. wide.
(Skinner) $3,738

DISPLAY CABINETS

George II walnut and parcel-gilt display cabinet, 47¼in. wide. (Skinner) **$5,750**

A brass-framed glazed shop display case of semi circular form, with quarter-veneered sliding doors and parquetry floor, 75in. wide. (Christie's) **$2,605**

An English mahogany two tier display cabinet in French taste with floral marquetry and two pairs of shaped glazed doors on cabriole legs, 42in. wide. (David Lay) **$2,428**

An Edwardian mahogany display cabinet, with crossbanding and string inlay, the stepped center with molded dentil cornice, 49½in. wide. (Andrew Hartley) **$2,250**

Art Nouveau period satin walnut side cabinet with molded edge over frieze drawer, flanked by two galleried open shelves, early 20th century, 47½in. (G. A. Key) **$610**

One of a pair of grained glazed cabinets, Massachusetts, mid-19th century, the glazed doors open to a four-shelf interior, 70¾in. wide, open. (Skinner) (Two) **$5,175**

An Edwardian mahogany display cabinet with central bowfront section, on square tapering legs with spade feet, 45in. wide. (Christie's) **$1,477**

A marquetry vitrine with overall floral marquetry, the undulating cornice above a pair of glazed doors, 80in. wide. (Christie's) **$4,223**

A late Victorian mahogany drawing room display cabinet, with arched mirrored and shelved superstructure, 54in. wide. (Christie's) **$1,215**

DISPLAY CABINETS

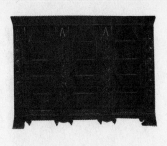

An Art Nouveau mahogany display cabinet, the shaped top above a beveled paneled glass cupboard flanked by square tapering columns, 47in. wide. (Christie's) $2,414

Display cabinet, 1920s, macassar ebony, of rectangular form with three doors with shaped arched glazed section, 104¼in. (Sotheby's) $3,749

Edwardian mahogany china display cabinet, inlaid with satinwood banding and boxwood and ebonized herringbone stringing, 36in. (G. A. Key) $1,144

An Edwardian painted mahogany display cabinet, crossbanded with string and parquetry inlay, 54in. wide. (Andrew Hartley) $1,238

Classical mahogany and mahogany veneer vitrine cabinet, Middle Atlantic States, 1815–25, the rectangular top with cockbeaded pedimented backboard, 28³/₄in. wide. (Skinner) $1,840

A satinwood mahogany and inlaid vitrine, the double-domed molded and checker-banded cornice above a harebell and ribbon-decorated frieze, late 19th century , 61in. wide. (Christie's) $3,695

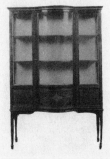

A mid-19th century side cabinet of Louis XV design in ebonized wood with ormolu mounts and porcelain plaques. (Russell, Baldwin & Bright) $1,102

An Edwardian display cabinet in mahogany with satinwood marquetry medallion and stringing, 3ft. 10in. wide. (Russell, Baldwin & Bright) $2,448

Victorian ebonized and ormolu mounted display cabinet with beaded and engraved edges to top, line inlay to side pilasters, mid 19th century, 30in. wide. (G. A. Key) $582

DISPLAY CABINETS

A French Louis XV style kingwood, marquetry and chased gilt bronze mounted vitrine with bombé base, 46in. wide.
(David Lay) $3,035

A late Victorian gilt-metal mounted and marquetry breakfront display cabinet, with three glazed doors, 60in. wide.
(Christie's) $2,639

A pair of late Victorian or Edwardian rosewood veneered and marquetry wall cabinets, each with swan neck pediments, two glazed doors, 23in. wide.
(David Lay) $1,598

An Edwardian mahogany display cabinet decorated with inlaid satinwood crossbanding and boxwood stringing, 44¹/₂in. wide.
(Anderson & Garland)
                     $2,516

An Edwardian mahogany display cabinet in the George II style, having molded cornice and blind fretwork frieze, 52in. wide.
(H.C. Chapman) $585

An Edwardian mahogany bowfront display cabinet, the raised back decorated with inlaid floral scrolls and ribbons, 42¹/₂in. wide.
(Anderson & Garland)
                     $1,127

A walnut display cabinet, the arched rectangular glazed door flanked by glazed angles and sides, on reeded ring-turned tapering legs.
(Christie's) $957

A Victorian walnut quarter veneered display cabinet, inlaid with ormolu mounts, the glazed door enclosing shelves, 36in. wide.
(Dreweatt Neate) $1,092

A French purple-heart and marquetry vitrine in the Louis XVI manner, applied throughout with finely cast gilt-brass moldings, 35¾in. wide.
(Bearne's) $3,981

302

DRESSERS

A George III oak pot board dresser, the delft rack with molded cornice and three molded edged shelves, 60in. (Andrew Hartley) $7,750

An 18th century oak dresser base, the three frieze drawers, two further lower drawers, arched center and with pot board base, 71in. wide. (Dreweatt · Neate) $7,650

Louis XV Provincial walnut buffet vaisselier, 18th century, in two parts, the upper section with open shelves, 55in. wide. (Skinner) $3,335

An 18th century oak dresser with mahogany crossbanding, the associated delft rack with molded cornice over pierced and scrolled frieze, 72in. wide. (Andrew Hartley) $4,495

An oak dresser, the open shelved plate-rack with four short drawers, flanked by fluted uprights above three foliate-carved drawers, 72in. wide. (Christie's) $1,923

A very fine and rare paint-decorated poplar paneled pewter cupboard, Pennsylvania, 1780-1800, in two parts, the upper section with molded projecting cornice, 5ft.½in. wide. (Sotheby's) $40,250

An 18th century oak dresser, the shelves with boarded back, the base fitted with three drawers, 5ft. 6in. wide. (Russell, Baldwin & Bright) $4,437

A late Georgian Anglesey dresser in oak, the enclosed base fitted with three frieze drawers and two cupboards, 5ft. 5in. wide. (Russell, Baldwin & Bright) $4,819

An early 19th century South Wales dresser in oak and elm, fitted with three frieze drawers and two spice drawers, 5ft. 5in. wide. (Russell, Baldwin & Bright) $6,120

KNEEHOLE DESKS

A 19th century French kneehole desk parquetry veneered in kingwood with satinwood stringing, having inset brown leather top, 4ft. 4in. wide. (Russell, Baldwin & Bright) $5,355

A 19th century Dutch burr walnut and floral marquetry kneehole desk, the undulating top with panels of flowers, vases and birds containing five drawers in the arched apron, the top overall 158cm. x 97cm., 75cm. high. (Phillips) $4,800

An early Victorian mahogany desk, the low superstructure with a single open shelf, topped by a high, chased bronze gallery, 60in. wide. (David Lay) $14,260

Queen Anne carved mahogany block front kneehole dressing table, Boston, circa 1750, the thumb-molded top with blocked front above a conforming case, 36in. wide. (Skinner) $20,700

An early 18th century burr elm kneehole desk, with walnut crossbanded quarter veneered top over two short frieze drawers and six drawers below, on later bracket feet. (Sotheby's) $9,208

A Georgian oak kneehole desk inlaid and crossbanded in mahogany, fitted with a long drawer and six small drawers, 2ft. 8in. wide. (Russell, Baldwin & Bright) $1,683

Satin walnut twin pedestal kneehole desk, tooled inset, three frieze drawers below, supported on two pedestals, each fitted with three drawers, 19th century, 42¹/₂in. wide. (G. A. Key) $770

A mahogany pedestal desk, the rectangular crossbanded and divided top with central hinged section revealing a ratcheted writing surface, 58¹/₂in. wide. (Christie's) $1,578

A walnut pedestal desk by Stanley W Davies with ebony inlay and carved edging, frieze drawer with block handles, 49¼in. wide. (Andrew Hartley) $7,314

KNEEHOLE DESKS

A 19th entury French Empire style mahogany kneehole desk, the rectangular top with canted corners and inset tooled leather surface, 55in. wide. (Anderson & Garland) $5,033

An early Victorian elm, walnut, oak parquetry and marquetry pedestal desk, banded overall in yewwood, the seaweed marquetry and oyster-veneers late 17th century and re-used, 62in. wide. (Christie's) $7,918

An Art Deco mahogany writing desk the curving rectangular top with inset leather writing surface, on tapering cabriole legs, Continental, 54in. wide. (Christie's) $1,298

A rare Chippendale figured mahogany kneehole desk, Philadelphia, circa 1775, the oblong molded top with notched corners above one long drawer, 39½in. wide. (Sotheby's) $9775

An early Victorian mahogany pedestal desk, with raised back containing pigeonholes and drawers, the two pedestals with six drawers, 60in. wide. (Dreweatt Neate) $2,184

An early Georgian kneehole desk in walnut with checkered banding and crossbanded top, on bracket feet, 2ft. 10in. wide. (Russell, Baldwin & Bright) $8,415

A George III architect's mahogany kneehole desk with hinged top opening to reveal a fitted interior, 35½in. wide. (Anderson & Garland) $2,191

An Edwardian satinwood and kingwood banded kidney desk, the top inset with green leather, having nine drawers about the kneehole, on square tapered legs with castors. (Tennants) $6,668

A mid 19th century French walnut partners' desk by Gueret Freres, Paris, the gilt-tooled leather insert within a carved border of trailing foliage, 71½in. wide. (Bearne's) $7,166

LINEN PRESSES

A Regency mahogany clothes-press, the arched molded cornice above a plain frieze centered by a satinwood tablet, above a pair of shaped-corner paneled doors, 55in. wide. (Christie's) **$3,695**

A George III linen press, the molded cornice above a pair of crossbanded paneled doors and two short and one long drawer, 50in. wide. (Christie's) **$1,563**

A fine late 18th century Dutch mahogany press with a breakfront dentil cornice above a pair of fielded panel doors, 68in. wide. (Anderson & Garland) **$4,575**

Chinese Export campaign camphorwood clothes press, second quarter 19th century, with one long fitted drawer above a pair of cupboard doors enclosing drawers, 38¼in. long. (Skinner) **$3,250**

A matched pair of Regency mahogany linen presses, each with molded cornice above two crossbanded and ebony lined paneled cupboard doors, 52in. (Christie's) **$8,722**

A Regency mahogany clothes press inlaid with ebony lines with shaped pediment flanked by akrotiri inlaid with anthemions above a molded cornice, on splayed bracket feet, 48in. wide. (Christie's) **$4,125**

A late Regency mahogany linen-press, the molded and dentiled cornice above a pair of paneled cupboard doors, 52in. wide. (Christie's) **$2,952**

A walnut press, the molded cornice fitted with two paneled crossbanded cupboard doors, basically 18th century, 68in. (Christie's) **$8,722**

A late George III mahogany and checker lined linen-press, the molded blind-fretwork carved cornice fitted with a pair of paneled cupboard doors, 48in. wide. (Christie's) **$1,823**

LOWBOYS

A mid 18th century mahogany lowboy with an arrangement of three small drawers over two larger drawers, 32¼in. wide.
(David Lay) $607

An 18th century mahogany lowboy, the molded top above two short and one long drawer, 2ft. 11in. wide.
(Russell, Baldwin & Bright)
                              $3,519

A mahogany lowboy, the rounded rectangular top above three drawers and shaped apron, on cabriole legs with pad feet, 30in. wide.
(Christie's) $1,129

A mahogany lowboy, with shaped apron and lappeted turned tapering legs with pad feet, mid 18th century, 30in. wide.
(Christie's) $2,609

A George I walnut lowboy, the top with quartered veneer within crossbanding and herringbone stringing, 32in. wide.
(David Lay) $7,194

A fine and rare Queen Anne carved cherrywood scalloped top lowboy, Connecticut, circa 1770, the oblong top with scalloped sides above a case with one long and three short drawers, 36in.
(Sotheby's) $387,500

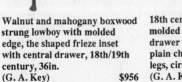

Walnut and mahogany boxwood strung lowboy with molded edge, the shaped frieze inset with central drawer, 18th/19th century, 36in.
(G. A. Key) $956

18th century oak lowboy, with molded edge, single frieze drawer over two short drawers, plain chamfered square front legs, circa 1780, 29in. wide.
(G. A. Key) $1,117

An oak lowboy with three drawers on square cabriole legs and pad feet, 29in. wide, partly 18th century but altered.
(Dreweatt · Neate) $704

FURNITURE

George III mahogany firescreen, third quarter 18th century, with a gros point and petit point panel, 51in. high.
(Skinner) $1,150

An 18th century French decorated four fold screen, painted on canvas with central giltwood foliate framed roundels, possibly Burgundian, each panel 1.8m. x 64cm.
(Phillips) $22,500

A William IV mahogany fire screen fitted with three sliding extensions each framing floral needlework panels, 22in. wide.
(Russell, Baldwin & Bright) $1,652

A 19th century gilt wood five fold draught screen, each fold with two beveled glazed panels in rococo style foliate surrounds, 70½in. high.
(Andrew Hartley) $2,945

A papier-peint six-fold screen, the front of the arched panels decorated with exotic birds among scrolling flowers and foliage on blue ground, 19th/20th century, each leaf 66¼ x 21½in.
(Christie's) $3,416

A Dutch gilt and polychrome-decorated four-leaf leather screen, late 18th/19th century, with a central river landscape scene with birds and butterflies, each leaf 89in. x 21½in.
(Christie's) $8,797

Dutch neoclassical style mahogany and marquetry four-panel floorscreen, late 19th/20th century, with inset fabric panels, each panel 84in. high, 25in. wide.
(Skinner) $4,313

A pair of Victorian giltwood screens, each with foliate cartouche glazed frame with foliate embroidered silk panel, 55¼in. high.
(Christie's) $3,978

A French giltwood and Aubusson tapestry screen in the Louis XV style, last quarter, 19th century, the three hinged panels each with an arched top, 61in. wide.
(Christie's) $6,329

SCREENS

Victorian mahogany screen, crested with acanthus leaf molded mount, decorated below with a swiveling Berlin woolwork panel, 19th century, 22in.
(G. A. Key) $605

A gilt-bronze fireguard, French, circa 1880, with a pierced, fan-shaped grill, on a lambrequin base, 72cm. high.
(Sotheby's) $5,998

A late 19th century Chinese two-fold screen mounted bas-relief design of birds amongst flowering branches, 5ft. 6in. wide.
(Russell, Baldwin & Bright)
$979

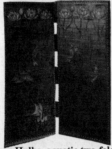

An Italian giltwood and leather three-leaf screen, late 19th century, each panel with a shaped beveled mirror plate within a foliate and rockwork shaped frame, 62in. wide.
(Christie's) $6,872

Georg Hulbe, aquatic two-fold screen, circa 1900, wood frame with tooled leather panels depicting a frieze of waterlilies above swimming fish and pond life, each panel, 20¼in.
(Sotheby's) $2,437

A Napoleon III giltwood and painted threefold screen, Paris, circa 1860, each fold with an arched cresting in Régence style, 197 x 61cm. each fold.
(Sotheby's) $15,933

A Chinese black and gold lacquer four-leaf screen, inlaid in ivory and colored soapstones, with figures in pagoda and floral gardens, 73 x 19in. each panel.
(Christie's) $2,400

A pair of pole screens, each with original circular floral needlework panel and tripod base.
(David Lay) $6,829

Dutch rococo painted and embossed leather six-panel floorscreen, 19th century, each panel 79in. high, 15½in. wide.
(Skinner) $2,645

SECRETAIRE BOOKCASES

Anglo-Indian faux grained secretary/bookcase, first half 19th century, 41³/₄in. wide. (Skinner) **$6,095**

Japanese Meiji fruitwood and elmwood parquetry secretary/bookcase, circa 1880–90, 44in. wide. (Skinner) **$2,300**

George III mahogany bookcase, 36¹/₂in. wide. (Skinner) **$2,300**

A George III mahogany, ebony and fruitwood secrétaire-bookcase, crossbanded overall in tulipwood and checker banded, the molded rectangular top, above a frieze of gothic arches hung with pendants, 43in. wide. (Christie's) **$26,392**

Federal mahogany and mahogany veneer desk bookcase, Massachusetts, circa 1820, top section with flat molded cornice above two glazed doors, 39in. wide. (Skinner) **$2,070**

A Victorian walnut secrétaire cabinet, two astragal glazed doors with stained glass Art Nouveau panels, the protruding base with profusely carved fall front, 58in. wide. (Andrew Hartley) **$2,090**

A late Victorian oak secrétaire side cabinet, stamped *GILLOWS, LANCASTER*, the two fall fronts each paneled enclosing fitted interiors, 56in. wide. (Christie's) **$1,910**

A Regency rosewood secrétaire-bookcase, banded overall in satinwood and with ebony lines, the arched crest with bowed angles above two shallow bands and two glazed doors with egg-and-dart molding, 42in. wide. (Christie's) **$8,446**

A Victorian mahogany secrétaire bookcase, the molded cornice above a pair of glazed doors with foliate carving, on serpentine plinth, 51in. wide. (Christie's) **$3,312**

SECRETAIRE BOOKCASES

A George III mahogany
secrétaire bookcase, crossbanded
with string inlay, molded
cornice over two astragal glazed
doors, 50in.
(Andrew Hartley) $3,816

Federal mahogany veneer
glazed desk and bookcase,
Massachusetts, circa 1820, the
pediment above glazed doors
with open to shelves and small
drawers, 36¼in. wide.
(Skinner) $1,610

A Regency mahogany secrétaire
bookcase, the adjustable shelves
enclosed by fifteen-pane doors,
on splay bracket feet, 3ft. 3in.
wide.
(Russell, Baldwin & Bright)
        $8,568

Federal mahogany inlaid glazed
desk bookcase, probably
Massachusetts, circa 1790,
shaped gallery with an inlaid
central panel above two
molded glazed doors, 40in.
wide.
(Skinner) $2,990

A federal flame birchwood-
veneered and figured mahogany
secretary bookcase, Massachusetts, circa 1800, the lower
section with hinged writing flap
and four crossbanded graduated
long drawers, 40½in. wide.
(Sotheby's) $4,600

A classical figured maple inlaid
and mahogany veneered
cherrywood secretary bookcase,
American, probably New York
or New England, circa 1830, in
three parts, on vase and ring-
turned feet, 46¼in. wide.
(Sotheby's) $8,050

A late George III inlaid
mahogany secrétaire bookcase,
with boxwood and stained wood
stringing throughout, 49¼in.
wide.
(Bearne's) $12,740

A George III mahogany
secrétaire bookcase, with
surface fret carved frieze and
glazed doors with arched glazing
bars, 3ft. 10in. wide.
(Russell, Baldwin & Bright)
        $10,098

A George IV mahogany
secrétaire bookcase,
crossbanded with purpleheart
and outlined with boxwood
stringing, 43¼in. wide.
(Bearne's) $3,822

SECRETAIRES & ESCRITOIRES

Miniature Dutch neoclassical style walnut bureau cabinet, 19th century, 21in. wide.
(Skinner) $1,725

Classical tiger maple bureau, probably New England, circa 1825, incised beaded drawers flanked by ring-turned columns, 47in. wide.
(Skinner) $2,415

George I chinoiserie decorated lacquer secretary/cabinet, early 18th century, 40½in. wide.
(Skinner) $6,900

A Charles X walnut secrétaire à abattant, the fall front opening to a leather-lined writing surface and fitted interior with three further drawers below, on bracket feet, 38in. wide.
(Christie's) $3,671

A Regency mahogany secrétaire chest, crossbanded overall in rosewood, with molded top and twin dummy drawer fall front, 46in. wide.
(Christie's) $3,820

An early 19th century Dutch walnut and floral marquetry secrétaire à abattant of small proportions, with shallow frieze drawer over fall down front, 2ft. 4in. wide.
(Russell, Baldwin & Bright)
                             $3,366

A 19th century German walnut escritoire, the raised top over a molded cornice and frieze drawer, 38in. wide.
(Andrew Hartley) $1,150

Federal cherry inlaid half sideboard/desk, Rutland, Vermont area, circa 1825, the rectangular top with ovolo corners and inlaid edge, 46⅛in. wide.
(Skinner) $4,025

An Iberian ebonized and verre eglomisé varguéno with a central architectural door flanked by a bank of ten further drawers, 19th century, 28½in. wide.
(Christie's) $2,952

SECRETAIRES & ESCRITOIRES

Biedermeier ormolu mounted mahogany secrétaire à abattant, first quarter 19th century, gray marble top, 39³/₄in. wide.
(Skinner) $3,910

A 19th century Continental walnut inverted breakfront secrétaire, part hinged with fall front drawer enclosing fitted interior, 77½in. wide.
(Andrew Hartley) $1,000

Biedermeier mahogany secrétaire à abattant, first quarter 19th century, 42in. wide.
(Skinner) $2,300

A fine Empire mahogany and ormolu mounted secrétaire attributable to Jacob Desmalter, surmounted by a white marble top, 98cm. wide.
(Phillips) $33,000

A Regency mahogany and inlaid secrétaire chest, with a fall front enclosing a fitted interior of drawers and pigeon-holes with lined writing surface, 47in. wide.
(Christie's) $2,349

A William and Mary seaweed-marquetry walnut escritoire, the rectangular molded cornice above a long cushion drawer and a paneled fall-front, 44½in. wide.
(Christie's) $7,918

A French secrétaire à abattant in boullework with simple fitted interior of rosewood, four drawers below, 2ft. 1in. wide.
(Russell, Baldwin & Bright)
                            $1,071

Empire style ormolu mounted mahogany secretaire à abattant, second half 19th century, 39in. wide.
(Skinner) $4,888

A fine Continental mahogany secrétaire in the Biedermeier style, surmounted by a pediment with applied acanthus scrolling brackets, 46in. wide.
(Anderson & Garland)
                            $4,617

SETTEES & COUCHES

Classical carved mahogany veneer sofa, North Shore, Massachusetts, 1830–50, upholstered in old stamped velvet, 77in. long.
(Skinner) $1,265

A sofa, the back with buttoned arched ends and central carving and gilding, stenciled mark to the hessian.
(David Lay) $2,276

George III period hoop back sofa, slightly splayed scrolled arms, with slightly bowed frieze and supported on tapering square legs, late 18th/ early 19th century, 86in.
(G. A. Key) $3,171

A good Federal mustard-painted and polychrome-decorated settee, Lehigh County, Pennsylvania, circa 1820, the shaped tripartite crest on turned supports, 6ft. 3in.
(Sotheby's) $1,092

George III period mahogany sofa with reeded back and arm rests, supported by similar spreading cylindrical columns, supported on four reeded tapering cylindrical front legs, early 19th century, 74in.
(G. A. Key) $1,525

Victorian rosewood double hoop back sofa, the splayed back joined in the center by circular back rest, crested with foliate molded motif and supported by splayed scroll molded uprights, cabriole legs, mid 19th century, 68in. wide.
(G. A. Key) $2,041

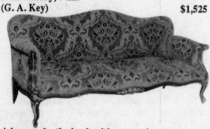

A large sofa, the back with serpentine top, stenciled mark to the hessian.
(David Lay) $3,794

Italian rococo walnut day bed, late 18th century, 84in. long.
(Skinner) $2,760

SETTEES & COUCHES

A mid-Victorian walnut chaise longue, with button-down arched back and scroll arm terminals carved with cabochons, 65in. long.
(Christie's) $1,563

Late Victorian rosewood chaise longue, the molded back rail terminating in a scroll, similarly molded apron, supported on turned bun feet, 79in. wide.
(G. A. Key) $1,413

An early Victorian rosewood settee, the curved top-rail with central floral and foliate cresting above a buttoned back, on cabriole legs with scroll feet, 66in. wide.
(Christie's) $1,496

Rococo Revival rosewood settee, circa 1850–60, 67in. long.
(Skinner) $2,070

A mahogany Howard style sofa, with a double-arched padded back flanked by padded arms above two squab cushions, 73in. wide.
(Christie's) $1,403

A Victorian rosewood settee with arched button upholstered back and serpentine upholstered seat between molded foliate-carved armrests, 78in. wide.
(Christie's) $2,544

A mid-Victorian simulated rosewood settee, the undulating button-down double chair-back with overscrolled arms, on cabriole legs with scroll feet, 69in. wide.
(Christie's) $968

Biedermeier fruitwood and part ebonized settee, 19th century, with black upholstery.
(Skinner) $1,725

SETTEES & COUCHES

A three-piece salon suite by Sinclair Melson Ltd., comprising: a Knole style three-seater settee, 76½in. wide; and two armchairs.
(Christie's) $4,020

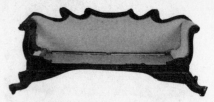

The Salisbury family classical carved mahogany sofa, Isaac Vose & Son, Boston, circa 1820, 88¾in. wide.
(Andrew Hartley) $25,300

A George IV giltwood sofa, the front of the arms with Grecian anthemions and lotus-leaves above reeded and ring-turned tapering legs headed by patera panels and lappeted bands, with channeled seatrails and scrolled back legs, 90½in. wide. (Christie's) $5,278

A Regency ormolu-mounted mahogany chaise-longue, the scrolled ends, seat cushion and bolster covered in deep buttoned red suede, the ends with gadrooned roundels and anthemion motifs, 76½in. wide.
(Christie's) $3,167

Louis XV Provincial walnut canapé, third quarter 18th century, with yellow silk damask upholstery, 66in. long.
(Skinner) $2,415

A nickel-plated metal and rattan chaise longue, designed by Rene Herbst, 1936, the wood framed seat with original interwoven rattan cover.
(Christie's) $1,205

A late Regency mahogany sofa, upholstered in a button-back green velour, with out-scrolled armrests, on foliate-carved turned baluster supports.
(Christie's) $1,057

A George III mahogany settee, the carved serpentine back and scrolling arm terminals decorated with paterae, raised on carved and molded square tapering legs, 80in. wide.
(Anderson & Garland) $7,199

SETTEES & COUCHES

Painted pine settle/bed, Scandinavia, early 19th century, the seat opens to pull out wood bed frame, original red paint, 73in. wide.
(Skinner) **$1,150**

George Nelson sling sofa, original cushions, 86in. wide, with metal frame.
(Skinner) **$1,610**

A Regency white-painted and parcel-gilt daybed, the channeled scrolling head and footboard and squab cushion with red and white striped silk on fluted turned tapering legs on brass castors, 81in. wide.
(Christie's) **$3,519**

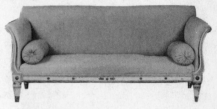

A Regency brass-mounted white-painted and parcel-gilt settee, the shaped arm-supports with spreading channels above a lacquered brass-mounted paneled frieze, on patera-headed stiff leaf-carved turned tapering legs, 82in. wide.
(Christie's) **$6,686**

A George IV mahogany and parcel-gilt daybed, possibly designed by Augustus Charles Pugin, inset overall with Gothic panels, on eight octagonal legs with foliate tops, 93in. long.
(Christie's) **$30,498**

A mid-Victorian walnut sofa, the button-down padded back with fluted cross splat supports and a central roundel, 49in. wide.
(Christie's) **$556**

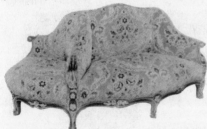

An oval section center sofa on eight legs, with four concealed weight bearing iron legs on castors.
(David Lay) **$7,284**

Arts and Crafts settle, with eleven vertical back slats, three slats under arms, 80in. wide.
(Skinner) **$863**

SIDEBOARDS

A Regency inlaid mahogany sideboard with boxwood and checkered lines throughout the reeded moldings, 86in. wide. (Bearne's) $4,300

George III style mahogany and inlay serpentine fronted sideboard, late 19th/20th century, 78¼in. long. (Skinner) $3,450

A George III mahogany bow front satinwood crossbanded sideboard fitted with a central drawer over an arch, 64½in. wide. (David Lay) $2,943

A late Victorian or Edwardian Georgian-style sideboard attributed to Edwards & Roberts, with a central bow front drawer over a shaped apron, 74in. wide. (David Lay) $3,994

A late Georgian mahogany small sideboard with three drawers over a central arch and two paneled doors, 49½in. wide. (David Lay) $759

A George III mahogany sideboard, crossbanded with ebony and satinwood stringing, the sepentine front with central napery drawer, 71in. wide. (Andrew Hartley) $4,185

A William IV mahogany sideboard table and pedestals with central breakfront, ebony banding and beaded frieze, 8ft. x 2ft. wide. (Russell, Baldwin & Bright) $19,890

A mahogany and burr-walnut sideboard, the rectangular crossbanded top above a cushion-molded central drawer flanked by two paneled doors, 54in. wide.(Christie's) $903

A George III mahogany bowfronted sideboard with checkered inlaid stringing having central slide, 4ft. 7in. (Russell, Baldwin & Bright) $4,360

A late Regency mahogany sideboard, the rectangular top with recessed center section and arched pediment, 62½in. wide. (Christie's) $1,477

SIDEBOARDS

Federal mahogany veneer sideboard, New England, 1790–1810, with stringing outlining drawers, cupboards and legs, cuff inlay, 71in. wide.
(Skinner) $4,888

A Regency mahogany breakfront sideboard with three-quarter gallery above three frieze drawers and a central cupboard, 90¹/₂in. wide.
(Christie's) $3,299

A mahogany and line-inlaid breakfront sideboard, each pedestal with a paneled line-inlaid door enclosing two deep drawers, one with cellaret.
(Christie's) $2,631

A late Victorian mahogany twin-pedestal sideboard, the pedestals of tapering rectangular form with rectangular gadrooned tops, 92in. wide.
(Christie's) $3,089

An early Victorian mahogany inverted breakfront sideboard, the shaped raised back with sliding door and arched surmount, 84in. wide.
(Andrew Hartley) $2,945

A George III mahogany and satinwood-banded sideboard with central frieze drawer and arched apron drawer (added later), 59in. wide.
(Christie's) $1,935

An Edwardian mahogany and marquetry pedestal sideboard, inlaid overall with scrolling foliage and ribbon-tied swags, on bracket feet, 58in. wide.
(Christie's) $2,815

R. Garnett & Sons, sideboard, circa 1865, oak, inlaid with geometric designs in ebonized wood, 81¼in. wide.
(Sotheby's) $6,748

Walnut inlaid sideboard, probably North or South Carolina, 1850–75, the top with central rectangular inlay, 44in. wide.
(Skinner) $3,738

A late Victorian serpentine-front sideboard in oak and walnut, heavily carved frieze of scrolled acanthus and rosettes, 9ft. 6in. wide.
(Russell, Baldwin & Bright) $12,393

A George III mahogany elliptical shaped sideboard, inlaid with boxwood and ebonized lines, the frieze with five drawers, 183cm. wide.
(Phillips) $7,500

Federal mahogany and maple veneer tiered sideboard, Massachusetts, early 19th century, the two-tiered shaped tops with beaded edges, 69⁵/₈in. wide.
(Skinner) $4,600

STANDS

A walnut floor-standing cache pot, the circular line-inlaid top with tin liner, above a waisted slatted side, 15in. diameter. (Christie's) **$666**

An early Victorian mahogany cased bidet, the rectangular lift-off top enclosing shaped ceramic bowl, 21in. wide. (Christie's) **$300**

A painted drinks cabinet in the form of a terrestrial globe, the hinged top enclosing a fitted painted interior, 29in. wide. (Christie's) **$868**

A Chippendale red-stained maple tilt-top candlestand, Pennsylvania, circa 1800, the circular top tilting and revolving above a birdcage support, 20½in. diameter. (Sotheby's) **$3,450**

A pair of Regency mahogany trunk-stands, in the manner of Gillows, each with a slatted rounded rectangular top with a plain frieze, on ring-turned and reeded tapering legs, 24in. wide. (Christie's) **$8,797**

Federal mahogany tilt top candlestand, Boston or North Shore, Massachusetts, circa 1790, the serpentine top with canted corners and molded edge, 19in. wide. (Skinner) **$4,025**

An Edwardian mahogany and line-inlaid magazine rack, with pierced back and three graduated compartments, on outswept bracket feet, 14½in. wide. (Christie's) **$129**

A set of Regency rosewood two-tread steps, the rectangular padded steps covered in close-nailed light green suede, on baluster legs, 18½in. wide. (Christie's) **$2,639**

Rococo Revival walnut etagère, mid 19th century, arched mirrored back with a grape cluster scroll carved crest, 50in. wide. (Skinner) **$1,840**

STANDS

A pair of walnut occasional tables/stands, each serpentine molded top with turbaned term supports, 15in. diameter.
(Christie's) $1,303

A Spanish walnut brazier stand, 19th century, the circular top carved with armorial panels, centered by a hammered brass brazier, 46in. diameter.
(Christie's) $2,650

A George II mahogany kettle stand, the pie-crust shaped top above a wreathed and ring turned shaft on cabriole legs with pad feet, 26cm. diameter.
(Phillips) $4,350

A George II mahogany basin stand, with open superstructure on columns and scrolls fitted with two triangular drawers, the top 29cm. diameter.
(Phillips) $1,500

A pair of gilt-metal mounted pedestals, each with octagonal marble top and tapered columns with classical mounts, 52in. high.
(Christie's) $1,407

Federal maple and birch candlestand, New England, circa 1800, molded top above vasiform post ending in curving legs, 15⅝in. diameter.
(Skinner) $1,495

A Louis XVI style oval jardinière with red tortoiseshell boulle frieze depicting birds, cherubs and scrolls, 2ft. 9in. wide.
(Russell, Baldwin & Bright) $2,601

Black Forest carved walnut figural hall tree/umbrella stand, late 19th century, 84in. high.
(Skinner) $4,600

STOOLS

Emile-Jacques Ruhlmann bench, circa 1930-31, rectangular upholstered seat above tapering, outwardly flared macassar ebony legs, 37in. wide.
(Sotheby's) $21,557

A George III mahogany window seat, the padded overscrolled ends above padded serpentine seat, 39in. wide.
(Christie's) $1,910

A Victorian walnut stool, the rectangular green-leather padded seat, on scrolling molded cabriole legs, 27½in. wide.
(Christie's) $1,042

Victorian mahogany adjustable metamorphic piano stool, the rexine upholstered seat supported on ring turned tapering supports, 19th century, 17in.
(G. A. Key) $228

Late 19th century stained beech adjustable piano stool with circular seat, supported by a central ring turned baluster column, the feet modeled as claws clutching glass balls, 14in. high.
(G. A. Key) $336

Classical mahogany footstool, Boston, 1830s, attributed to Hancock, Holden and Adams, overupholstered rectangular top above double C-scroll base, 16½in. wide.
(Skinner) $920

A mahogany stool, the rectangular padded back above scrolling apron, on cabriole legs, 19in. wide.
(Christie's) $1,368

A caned window seat in the Louis XV style, with overscrolled arms above foliate framed caned oval sides, French, 30½in. wide.
(Christie's) $615

William and Mary turned maple stool, possibly French Canada, 18th century, overupholstered rectangular top on four block turned legs, 15½in. wide.
(Skinner) $2,415

STOOLS

A Victorian rosewood centre stool, on cabriole supports and scrolled toes ending in brass caps and castors, 27in. wide. (Christie's) $2,362

Pair of Georgian style mahogany triangular footstools, 7in. high. (Skinner) $1,955

A walnut stool, the serpentine padded seat, on molded cabriole legs, 18$\frac{1}{2}$in. wide. (Christie's) $347

Classical rosewood piano stool, probably New England, first half 19th century, the circular adjustable molded top on a tapering column, approximately 18in. high. (Skinner) $460

Pair of George II style walnut and parcel-gilt stools, 19th century, 17in. high. (Skinner) $5,463

A William IV mahogany framed dressing stool with woolwork upholstered top on leafage carved X-frame, having turned stretcher. (Russell, Baldwin & Bright) $673

An early Victorian mahogany duet stool, the rectangular padded seat on roundel-decorated scrolling X-frame supports, 35$\frac{1}{2}$in. wide. (Christie's) $660

A pair of Victorian rosewood dressing stools, each with a square embroidered seat, above rocaille-capped cabriole legs, 15$\frac{1}{2}$in. wide. (Christie's) $845

A giltwood window seat, the rectangular padded seat flanked by outcurved sides with bobbin-turned handles, Baltic, early 19th century. (Christie's) $1,228

A late Victorian mahogany framed three-piece salon suite, comprising double chair-back settee and pair of chairs with leafage scroll inlaid splats, and shaped arms. (Russell, Baldwin & Bright) $826

A pair of mid-Victorian oak settees, the button upholstered downswept backs, above kidney-shaped upholstered seats, the molded chair-rails on fluted square supports with block toes, 50in. wide. (Christie's) $7,268

A Piedmontese walnut five-piece salon suite, comprising: a sofa, two open armchairs and two side chairs, each with padded back, the sofa and armchairs with downscrolled arms with foliate carving, late 19th century, the sofa 70in. wide. (Christie's) $3,299

FURNITURE

SUITES

Four-piece suite of Renaissance Revival rosewood, marquetry and gilt-incised seating furniture, third-quarter 19th century, comprising a settee, armchair and two side chairs, settee 64in. long.
(Skinner) $1,495

Victorian walnut cameo suite, the chaise longue with a hooped back molded with scrolls etc, with matching gents' and ladies' chairs and four dining chairs, with cabriole front legs.
(G. A. Key) $3,025

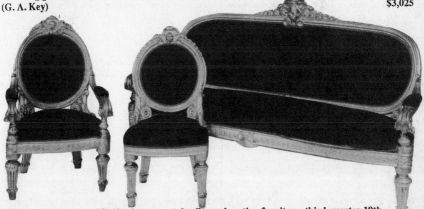

Thirteen piece suite of Italian baroque style giltwood seating furniture, third quarter 19th century, comprising two settees, four armchairs, and seven side chairs, with navy or burgundy mohair upholstery, settee 80in. long.
(Skinner) $6,900

BREAKFAST TABLES

A Regency mahogany breakfast table, the rounded oblong tip up top with reeded edge on ring turned stem, 53¼ x 35in.
(Andrew Hartley) $1,585

A mid-Victorian walnut breakfast table, the circular tilt-top with molded rim and plain frieze.
(Christie's) $2,287

A Regency amboyna breakfast table, the circular snap top on spreading canted angle concave column, 157cm. diameter.
(Phillips) $14,250

Federal mahogany veneer carved breakfast table, New England, 1810–20, rectangular leaves with rounded corners flank cockbeaded veneered sides, 19³/₄in. wide.
(Skinner) $1,092

An early Victorian burr-yew veneered breakfast table, on a faceted column and concave trefoil platform, with bun feet, 49³/₄in. wide.
(Christie's) $2,098

A Victorian walnut breakfast table, the burr walnut quarter veneered drop leaf oval with molded edge, 37in.
(Andrew Hartley) $2,416

A William IV rosewood circular breakfast table, with tip-up top and beaded frieze, on hexagonal column, 48in. diameter.
(Christie's) $3,126

An early Victorian rosewood and penwork breakfast table, on a fluted column and trefoil concave platform, with foliate-carved paw feet, 51¹/₂in. wide.
(Christie's) $2,098

A Regency mahogany breakfast table, the rectangular crossbanded snap top with a reeded edge on reeded quadruple scroll supports, 151cm. x 116cm.
(Phillips) $4,500

BREAKFAST TABLES

A William IV rosewood breakfast table, the tip up circular top with bead and reel edging, leaf carved turned stem, 49¾in. diameter.
(Andrew Hartley) $3,171

A Victorian burr-walnut breakfast table, the circular tilt-top on faceted support and splayed cabriole legs, 52in. wide.
(Christie's) $4,195

An early Victorian mahogany breakfast table, the circular tilt top on tripartite concave-sided column with scrolling corners, 60in. diameter.
(Christie's) $4,862

Federal cherry breakfast table, New England, circa 1800, serpentine shaped top above shaped skirts flanked by squared tapering molded legs, 17½in. wide.
(Skinner) $1,035

A Regency brass-inlaid and ormolu-mounted rosewood breakfast-table, the circular tilt-top with a foliate band, and guilloche edge above a ring-turned and spirally-reeded baluster column, 49in. diameter.
(Christie's) $5,278

Classical mahogany carved breakfast table, probably New York, circa 1825, the top with shaped drop leaves above a cockbeaded inlaid apron, 40in. wide.
(Skinner) $1,150

An Irish Regency yewwood breakfast-table, on a square sunk-paneled spreading support with four hipped downswept reeded legs, 48in. wide.
(Christie's) $17,043

A Victorian burr-walnut breakfast table, the oval tilt-top on floral ring-turned fluted supports with a central finial, 54in. wide.
(Christie's) $1,303

Victorian rosewood circular pedestal breakfast table with a ball and fillet molded surround, tripod base with scrolled feet, mid 19th century, 45in.
(G. A. Key) $2,128

327

CARD & TEA TABLES

A late Regency rosewood fold-top tea table of D-shape, the deep plain frieze with molded lower edge, 41in. wide.
(David Lay) $2,077

Federal mahogany inlaid card table, probably Massachusetts, circa 1815, 36in. wide.
(Skinner) $1,150

Charles X rosewood and inlay games table, circa 1830, toile lined gaming surface, 34³/₄in. wide.
(Skinner) $1,380

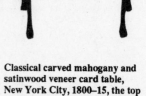

Classical mahogany carved and mahogany veneer card table, Massachusetts, circa 1820, the shaped top with beaded edge above a conforming skirt, 35¹/₂in. wide.
(Skinner) $1,725

Classical carved mahogany veneer and brass card table, probably New York or New Jersey, 1820s, with swivel top, veneered skirt and leaf carved lyre shaped pedestal, 35³/₄in. wide.
(Skinner) $2,300

Classical carved mahogany and satinwood veneer card table, New York City, 1800–15, the top with canted corners pivots above the satinwood skirt, 37¹/₂in. wide.
(Skinner) $6,900

Federal mahogany inlaid card table, Concord, New Hampshire, 1794–96, probably the work of Choate and Martin, 34¹/₈in. wide.
(Skinner) $2,070

A 19th century Continental rosewood veneered games table, the sliding reversible top plain on one side, a chess board on the other, 22in. wide.
(David Lay) $1,214

Federal mahogany veneer carved card table, North Shore, Massachusetts, with shaped top and ovolo corners above legs with leaf carving, 36in. wide.
(Skinner) $5,462

CARD & TEA TABLES

Napoleon III ormolu mounted
kingwood envelope table, third
quarter 19th century, 22³/₄in.
wide.
(Skinner) $2,990

Louis XVI style brass bound
mahogany handkerchief games
table, late 19th century, 21¹/₂in.
wide.
(Skinner) $805

Regency brass inlaid mahogany
games table, first quarter 19th
century, 36in. wide.
(Skinner) $575

William IV period mahogany
fold top tea table with rounded
corners, the frieze molded with
scrolls and foliage, the circular
base applied with four claw feet,
early 19th century, 36in. wide.
(G. A. Key) $1,945

Federal mahogany veneer
carved card table, North Shore
Massachusetts, 1815–25, the
bowed top with incised leading
edge flanked by ovolo corners
above legs with colonnettes,
36¹/₄in. wide.
(Skinner) $488

A Victorian bird's eye maple
card table with fold-over top,
molded front rail with scroll
and leafage carved ends, 3ft.
wide.
(Russell, Baldwin & Bright)
                              $1,530

Chippendale cherry inlaid card
table, Massachusetts, 1750–80,
rectangular top with fluted edge
above an undercut inner top,
31¹/₄in. wide.
(Skinner) $5,750

Late Victorian mahogany
envelope card table with single
drawer, supported on carved
cabriole legs and castors, 21in.
square.
(G. A. Key) $690

A George II mahogany card
table, the shaped rectangular
fold-over top with a bead-and-
cusp-carved edge, 32in. wide.
(Bearne's) $1,911

CARD & TEA TABLES

A George II mahogany tea-table with D-shaped twin-flap top enclosing a semi-circular well, with paneled frieze and gateleg action, on cabriole legs, 27¼in. wide. (Christie's) **$7,700**

An early Victorian rectangular mahogany tea table with a plain frieze and acanthus carved apron, 33½in. wide. (Anderson & Garland) **$976**

A George IV mahogany card table, on four turned column supports with lotus caps, and a beaded concave plinth, on scroll feet, 36in. wide. (Bonhams) **$1,337**

A fine French style kingwood envelope card table, the square shaped top decorated with crossbanding and inlaid floral scrolls, 23in. square. (Anderson & Garland) **$5,338**

A Louis XV tulipwood, marquetry and parquetry card-table, in the manner of Bernard II van Risen Burgh, BVRB II, on four tapering cabriole legs, the sliding back leg with a drawer, 43in. wide. (Christie's) **$28,704**

An Arts and Crafts inlaid oak card table, attributed to William Birch, the square top with four hinged triangular panels above arched aprons and plank legs, 74.6cm. high. (Christie's) **$1,360**

A late Victorian rosewood card-table of Louis XV style, the hinged serpentine quarter-veneered top inlaid with a central floral marquetry panel, 32in. wide. (Christie's) **$1,321**

A Regency mahogany card table with a rectangular hinged swivel top enclosing a red baize lining, 36in. wide. (Anderson & Garland) **$2,440**

A North Italian marquetry and parquetry card table, inlaid overall with flowerhead-filled trellis on an olive ground, crossbanded overall in tulipwood, on four square tapering legs, 35½in. wide. (Christie's) **$19,734**

CENTER TABLES

An early Victorian pollard oak and ebony molded pentagonal center table, in the Gothic taste with a molded edge and cavetto frieze, 136cm. diameter.
(Phillips) $5,700

A 17th century South German fruitwood, walnut and marquetry table top on later stand, possibly Augsburg, the top inlaid with a palace with walled parterre garden, the top 126cm. x 117cm.
(Phillips) $12,750

A giltwood center table, the inset serpentine yellow mottled marble top with a foliate-carved border, French, late 19th century, 42in. wide.
(Christie's) $1,660

An English bluejohn and giltwood center table, 19th century, the circular bluejohn-veneered top, above a Louis XIV style tripartite base, 29$\frac{1}{4}$in. diameter.
(Christie's) $26,910

A Regency pollard oak center table, the circular top with a gadrooned border edge and frieze, 123cm. diameter.
(Phillips) $4,500

One of a pair of ormolu-mounted mahogany gueridons, each with circular gray-veined white marble top with raised rim, on a domed socle mounted with stylized leaves and rounded six-pointed platform base, 38in.
(Christie's) $57,252

An Irish George II mahogany center table, the dished rectangular top with re-entrant corners above a plain frieze with shaped apron to the front, sides and reverse, 30in. wide.
(Christie's) $8,797

A Louis XVI style boullé work center table, with oval shaped serpentine top decorated with acanthus scrolls, cherubs and honeysuckle motifs, 36in. wide.
(Anderson & Garland) $1,601

A George I gilt gesso center table, decorated overall with strapwork and foliage on a pounced ground, the rounded rectangular top with re-entrant corners above a concave frieze and shaped apron, 33in. wide.
(Christie's) $35,880

CENTER TABLES

A Victorian pollard oak center table, on turned tapering end columns, carved and scrolled base and squat bun feet, 46in. (Andrew Hartley) $2,480

A Louis Philippe rosewood and brass-inlaid tripod table, the circular tilt top with central fruiting vine decoration, 25½in. diameter. (Christie's) $2,084

A walnut circular center table, stained spiral supports, joined by a wavy platform base centered with a large carved finial, on scroll feet, 49in. diameter. (Christie's) $1,650

Louis XV style porcelain mounted giltwood center table, late 19th/early 20th century, 30in. diameter. (Skinner) $10,925

An 18th century giltwood center table with rectangular top carved with scallops and leafage scrolls, on cabriole supports, 2ft. 3in. x 1ft. 8in. (Russell, Baldwin & Bright) $3,672

An oak center table, the circular top with shaped border and cruciform planked center, 42in. diameter. (Christie's) $25,438

Empire style ormolu mounted mahogany and marble top center table, second half 19th century, 27in. diameter. (Skinner) $8,625

Louis XVI style ormolu mounted giltwood and onyx center table, late 19th/early 20th century, 44in. wide. (Skinner) $6,900

A mahogany center table, the circular crossbanded top with cube marquetry, on a faceted tapering shaft, 19th century, 34in. diameter. (Christie's) $702

CENTER TABLES

Empire style ormolu mounted mahogany center table, late 19th century, 49in. diameter. (Skinner) $4,370

A rosewood center table, the rounded rectangular top above two frieze drawers, on hexagonal supports, early 19th century, 58in. wide. (Christie's) $2,778

A George IV mahogany center table, with crossbanded circular tip-up top, 64¼in. diameter. (Bearne's) $4,459

Napoleon III gilt bronze mounted kingwood, tulipwood, and porcelain inset center table, late 19th century, inset with seven handpainted floral decorated plaques, 31½in. diameter. (Skinner) $8,625

American Renaissance Revival gilt bronze mounted rosewood, marquetry and marble inset center table, third quarter 19th century, attributed to Pottier & Stymus, New York City, 51½in. wide. (Skinner) $19,550

A 19th century mahogany center table with applied gilt metal mounts, molded circular black table top, 32in. wide. (Andrew Hartley) $6,820

A French Restoration mahogany-veneered center table with circular veined black marble top, 41¾in. diameter. (Bearne's) $5,255

Rococo Revival walnut center table, mid 19th century, shaped cararra marble top on a base carved throughout with grape clusters and leaves, 39in. long. (Skinner) $2,530

A mid 19th century Italian cream-painted and giltwood center table, with oval red and green scagliola top, 56in. wide. (Bearne's) $3,026

CONSOLE TABLES

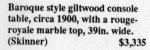

Baroque style giltwood console table, circa 1900, with a rouge-royale marble top, 39in. wide.
(Skinner) $3,335

Edgar Brandt, console, circa 1925, 'D' shaped marble top, on patinated wrought iron base with two scroll supports, 72½in. wide.
(Sotheby's) $28,118

A Louis XV giltwood console, the serpentine gray veined marble top above pierced scrolled and shell decorated apron and sides, 126cm. wide.
(Phillips) $2,250

A Louis XVI ormolu-mounted mahogany console desserte, in the manner of Bernard Molitor, on fluted turned-tapering legs with stiff-leaf capitals, 40½in.
(Christie's) $46,675

One of a pair of Louis Philippe style mahogany console tables, each with rectangular marble top and frieze drawer, 39in. wide.
(Christie's)
(Two) $1,739

Classical mahogany carved and mahogany veneer pier table, attributed to Williams and Everett, Boston, circa 1825, the marble top above a projecting frieze drawer, 45in. wide.
(Skinner) $5,463

A giltwood console table in the Louis XV style, the serpentine green marble top above a foliate and scroll-carved undulating frieze, 47in. wide.
(Christie's) $1,056

An early Louis XV giltwood console table, the serpentine-fronted rouge languedoc marble top above a partly-pierced waved apron centered by a cartouche of martial trophies, 49½in.
(Christie's) $50,232

A Régence gilded oak console table, the associated rounded rectangular verde antico marble top with molded brass edge, 54¾in. wide.
(Christie's) $21,000

CONSOLE TABLES

Portuguese rococo blue painted and parcel-gilt console table, 18th century, 33¼in. long. (Skinner) $1,610

Milanese ebony, ebonized and ivory inlaid console table, mid 19th century, 43in. wide. (Skinner) $8,000

Austrian neoclassical gilt-bronze mounted mahogany and parcel-gilt console table, with gray marble top, 49¼in. wide. (Skinner) $3,335

Regency style rosewood, brass inlaid and parcel-gilt pier table, 19th century, with a black marble top, 45in. long. (Skinner) $2,760

Classical mahogany veneer and gilt pier table, New York City, 1820-35, with stenciled veneered frieze and antique verte carved front feet, 42¼in. wide. (Skinner) $3,738

Classical carved mahogany veneer table, possibly mid-Atlantic States, 1830–40, the figured mahogany veneer splashboard supported by marble columns, 37½in. wide. (Skinner) $3,450

A Louis XV giltwood console table, the molded shaped liver fossil marble top above a pierced apron with C-scrolls and rockwork, 44in. wide. (Christie's) $14,318

Classical mahogany veneer pier table, Massachusetts, 1835–40, with old carrara marble top with thumb molded edge, 40in. wide. (Skinner) $2,415

19th century ornate gilt console table, of serpentine form, with marble top, the two foliate molded splayed legs with scrolled feet, 29in. (G. A. Key) $731

DINING TABLES

A mahogany oval breakfast table, with a reeded crossbanded top supported upon four ring turned columns, 190cm. wide. (Phillips) $3,600

A George III mahogany triple section D-end dining table, with plain molded frieze and square tapering legs, 83½in. extended. (Christie's) $3,519

A Regency mahogany breakfast table, the rounded rectangular tilt top on turned column and reeded splayed legs, 57in. wide. (Christie's) $1,650

A George III mahogany 'D' end dining table with plain frieze raised on a pair of turned columns, 52 x 69in. long. (Anderson & Garland) $5,338

An early Victorian mahogany dining table, the circular top with molded rim above an undulating frieze with scrolling border, 55in. diameter. (Christie's) $3,157

An early Victorian mahogany extending dining table, on turned and reeded tapering legs, including three extra leaves, 109in. extended. (Christie's) $6,436

A large Victorian extending mahogany dining table with 'D' shaped ends, 156in. long; complete with three spare leaves. (Anderson & Garland) $7,199

Classical mahogany and mahogany veneer banquet table, probably Massachusetts, circa 1825, the double hinged D-form top on a conforming beaded apron, 172¾in. long extended. (Skinner) $6,900

A mid-Victorian Gothic Revival oak center table, in the style of A.W.N. Pugin, the octagonal top with molded edge, on faceted uprights and square pedestal, 59½in. wide. (Christie's) $5,007

A large mahogany extending circular dining table, lacking extra leaves, with molded edge and wind out action, late 19th century, 162in. (Christie's) $3,820

A mahogany extending circular dining table with five extra leaves, on downswept legs joined by an undertier, 90in. fully extended. (Christie's) $2,431

An Edwardian mahogany extending dining table, circular when un-extended, with a reeded rim and plain frieze, 138½in. extended. (Christie's) $2,806

DINING TABLES

Arts and Crafts dining table, four octagonal column base, corbels, two leaves, original finish, 60in. diameter. (Skinner) **$3,335**

A Victorian mahogany concertina action extending dining table, including three extra leaves, 117in. extended. (Christie's) **$5,244**

A 19th century rosewood loo table with carved edged tip up top on carved wrythen turned and beaded stem, 59½ x 45in. (Andrew Hartley) **$1,485**

A Victorian walnut dining table, the quarter veneered molded edged oval top on four scrolled supports, 57½ x 44in. (Andrew Hartley) **$2,875**

A Victorian mahogany extending dining-table, the rounded rectangular molded top opening to enclose two extra leaves, 94in. long, extended. (Christie's) **$3,125**

A William IV mahogany dining table with 'D' shaped ends and molded frieze, raised on a pair of turned pedestals, 106in. (Anderson & Garland)

$10,955

An oak drawleaf dining-table, on spirally-turned and stop-fluted supports, joined by a massive molded doubly Y-shaped stretcher, 127in. long extended. (Christie's) **$57,986**

Mahogany extending single pedestal dining table with rounded corners and molded edge, early 19th century, extends to 79¹/₂in. including two loose leaves, 42¹/₂in. wide. (G. A. Key) **$4,160**

A late Victorian mahogany extending dining table, including five extra leaves, the rounded rectangular top on ring-turned reeded tapering legs, 155in. fully extended. (Christie's) **$3,126**

Victorian burr walnut tilt top pedestal loo table with ebonized rim, on a roundel molded balustered support, mid 19th century, 43in. (G. A. Key) **$1,096**

A Victorian mahogany extending dining table, including two extra leaves, the rounded rectangular top on turned tapering legs, 96in. extended. (Christie's) **$2,257**

A mid 19th century mahogany dining table with circular tip-up top and four molded square supports, 48in. diameter. (Bearne's) **$4,778**

DRESSING TABLES

A gilt-metal mounted, tulipwood and mahogany dressing table, of kidney-shape, with an arrangement of five drawers, 50in. wide.
(Christie's) $2,639

A large Edwardian satinwood bow-fronted dressing table with shield shape mirror, the square supports with fluted urn finials, 7ft. wide.
(Russell, Baldwin & Bright)
$1,913

A late Victorian mahogany and satinwood crossbanded dressing table, of George III style, the frieze fitted with three crossbanded and inlaid drawers, 48in. wide.
(Christie's) $2,083

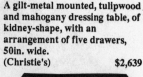

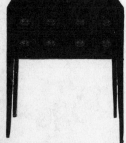

A Federal inlaid mahogany Beau Brummel, American or English, 1790-1800, the two-part hinged top opening to a compartmental interior fitted with a ratcheted mirror, 29¾in. wide.
(Christie's) $920

Queen Anne walnut veneer dressing table, Massachusetts, circa 1740, the overhanging top has thumbnail molding and four matched panels of crotch veneer, 29in. wide.
(Skinner) $11,500

Grain painted and stencil decorated dressing stand, Maine, circa 1820, old red and black graining with stenciled floral and fruit decoration, 29¼in. wide.
(Skinner) $460

A mid-Victorian pitch-pine and painted dressing table, the rectangular swing plate flanked by two pairs of drawers, 48in. wide.
(Christie's) $408

A George IV mahogany bow-fronted kneehole dressing table, with three drawers, on turned legs.
(Dreweatt Neate) $1,548

Classical mahogany and mahogany veneer carved dressing bureau, probably New York State, circa 1825, 38in. wide.
(Skinner) $805

FURNITURE

Federal painted and decorated dressing table, North Shore, Massachusetts, early 19th century, with early sage green paint, stenciled and freehand decoration, 34¼in. wide.
(Skinner) $920

Victorian mahogany Duchess dressing table, the central mirror supported by fluted and baluster turned columns, 53½in. wide.
(G. A. Key) $948

A George III mahogany side table of small proportions, inlaid with a boxwood band and with carved oval paterae to front and sides, 36in. wide.
(Dreweatt Neate) $7,009

The Bennett family Queen Anne mahogany dressing table, three thumbmolded drawers over a shaped skirt, Charleston, Carolina, circa 1750, 31in. wide.
(Christie's) $101,500

A George III satinwood dressing-table, the hinged rectangular top enclosing a fitted interior of lidded compartments around a central mirror, on a ratcheted support, 36in. wide.
(Christie's) $5,278

A Queen Anne carved mahogany dressing table, attributed to John Goddard, Newport, Rhode Island, 1750-1770, thumbmolded long drawer over two short drawers, 35½in. wide.
(Christie's) $310,500

Classical mahogany veneer dressing bureau, New England or New York, second quarter 19th century, polished black marble top above recessed paneled sides, 39in. wide.
(Skinner) $2,185

A Queen Anne walnut work or dressing table, with a molded rectangular top with re-entrant corners, on turned legs with club feet, 76cm. wide.
(Phillips) $3,300

Louis Majorelle, coiffeuse, circa 1900, the slim bow fronted drawer beneath table top inlaid in various fruitwoods, 28in. wide.
(Sotheby's) $6,748

DROP LEAF TABLES

Chippendale cherry drop leaf table, New England, 1750–80, 41¹/₂in. wide extended. (Skinner) $633

A late Georgian mahogany drop-leaf dining table decorated with inlaid crossbanding, raised on square tapering legs, 75in. long extended. (Anderson & Garland) $1,200

Queen Anne maple drop leaf dining table, New England, circa 1760, 44³/₈in. wide extended. (Skinner) $5,463

A mahogany drop-leaf table, the rounded rectangular twin-flap top above a frieze drawer, 18th century, 36in. wide. (Christie's) $695

Classical mahogany veneer breakfast table, probably Boston, circa 1815, the drop leaves over four curving beaded legs, 42in. wide. (Skinner) $1,120

George II mahogany drop-leaf table, mid 18th century, 28in. extended. (Skinner) $863

Queen Anne maple drop leaf dining table, New England, circa 1760, 46in. wide extended. (Skinner) $6,325

A George III mahogany spider leg table, the rectangular hinged top on turned legs joined by stretchers on pad feet, 73cm. wide extended. (Phillips) $1,500

Bird's-eye and tiger maple drop leaf table, New York or Ohio, circa 1840, rounded leaves on four ring-turned tapering legs, 20in. wide. (Skinner) $3,450

DROP LEAF TABLES

Queen Anne drop leaf table, York, Maine area, attributed to Samuel Sewall, late 18th century, 31¹/₈in. wide. (Skinner) **$9,200**

Queen Anne maple drop leaf table, New England, 18th century, with half-round ends on turned legs, 51¹/₄in. wide extended. (Skinner) **$1,955**

Chippendale walnut drop leaf dining table, possibly Pennsylvania, late 18th century, with shaped skirt and molded Marlborough legs, 15¹/₂in. wide. (Skinner) **$1,840**

Chippendale mahogany carved drop leaf table, probably Rhode Island, circa 1780, the rectangular drop leaf top on four square molded stop fluted legs, 47³/₄in. wide. (Skinner) **$1,725**

A good Queen Anne figured mahogany drop-leaf table, New England, probably Rhode Island, circa 1750, the oblong top with bowed ends flanked by D-shaped leaves, 4ft. 6in. (Sotheby's) **$2,300**

George III satinwood and rosewood crossbanded Pembroke table, last quarter 18th century, with a fitted work drawer and candleholder, 38¹/₂in. long. (Skinner) **$4,370**

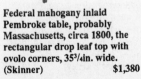

Federal mahogany inlaid Pembroke table, probably Massachusetts, circa 1800, the rectangular drop leaf top with ovolo corners, 35³/₄in. wide. (Skinner) **$1,380**

Classical mahogany veneer table, probably Baltimore, Maryland area, 1815–20, with reeded top, pedestal and four curving legs ending in brass paw feet, 42³/₄in. extended. (Skinner) **$978**

Chippendale mahogany Pembroke table, Connecticut River Valley, circa 1780, exotically grained drop leaf top on four square legs, 35in. wide. (Skinner) **$2,875**

DUMB WAITERS

George III period mahogany two tier circular dumb waiter, molded edge, ring turned cylindrical column, tripod base with hoof feet, 21in.
(G. A. Key) $854

A Regency brass-mounted mahogany revolving two-tiered dumb waiter, the circular top with pierced Greek key gallery, 22½in. diameter.
(Christie's) $17,181

An early George III mahogany two tier dumb waiter, with graduated revolving dished tops with egg and dart edges, 87cm. high.
(Phillips) $9,750

An Irish Regency brass-mounted mahogany dumb waiter by Gillingtons of Dublin, with two circular shelves, on turned baluster columns, 23½in. diameter.
(Christie's) $10,500

A William IV mahogany metamorphic tea-table and dumb-waiter, banded overall with beading, the serpentine rectangular hinged top enclosing a quarter-veneered interior, 31in. wide.
(Christie's) $4,398

A mahogany three-tier dumb waiter, of mid-Georgian style, the circular molded graduated tiers on a turned baluster stem, 46in. high.
(Christie's) $1,090

A George III mahogany dumb waiter, with three dished revolving tiers on gun barrel supports, on tripod cabriole base, 60cm. diameter.
(Tennants) $3,175

An early 19th century mahogany three tier metamorphic dumb waiter, the adjustable tiers on square section end supports, scrolled bracket feet, 48in. wide.
(Kidner) $1,560

A George III mahogany dumb waiter with three dished revolving tiers on baluster turned and gun barrel support, 45in. high.
(Andrew Hartley) $1,272

GATELEG TABLES

Irish mahogany oval drop-leaf double gate-leg table, 19th century, on square legs, 68in. long.
(Du Mouchelles) $2,250

A Georgian yewwood gate-leg table, the twin-flap oval top on turned baluster supports joined by cross stretchers on bobbin feet, two legs replaced, one end previously with a drawer, 64in. wide.
(Christie's) $4,398

Portuguese baroque oak gateleg drop leaf table, 17th/18th century, 56½in. wide.
(Skinner) $2,300

An oak gate-leg table, the demi-lune fold-over top on baluster column supports joined by stretchers, 37½in. wide.
(Christie's S. Ken) $2,900

A very fine and rare William and Mary turned and figured mahogany large gate-leg dining table, Philadelphia, 1710-40, 59½in. wide extended.
(Sotheby's) $18,400

An oak gate-leg table with oval hinged top on bobbin-turned supports joined by stretchers, 58in. wide.
(Christie's S. Ken) $3,300

An oak and elm oval gate leg table of 17th century origin with and end drawer on baluster turned legs and chamfered stretchers, 65½ x 72in.
(Dreweatt · Neate) $4,131

A Continental baroque style gate-leg drop-leaf table, the D shaped drop-leaves raised on turned legs joined by block stretchers, 29½ x 47 x 55½in. open.
(Sotheby's) $2,475

A Charles II oak gate-leg table, with oval top and on bobbin-turned legs with square stretchers, 50¾in. wide.
(Bearne's) $2,700

LARGE TABLES

George III mahogany three-pedestal dining table, with two leaves, 100½in. wide.
(Skinner) **$3,450**

Shaker cherry trestle table, probably Harvard, Massachusetts community, 72in. wide.
(Skinner) **$6,325**

Regency style brass inlaid rosewood double pedestal dining table, 20th century, 72in. long., with two leaves.
(Skinner) **$2,185**

George III style mahogany and satinwood crossbanded two-pedestal dining table, late 19th/20th century, 51in. long.
(Skinner) **$6,900**

Philip Webb, refectory table, 1880s, oak with traces of green staining, on five pairs of slightly angled barley twist legs, on stretcher, 126in. long.
(Sotheby's) **$81,337**

A late Regency mahogany extending dining table, including one extra leaf, the rectangular top with rounded corners, on ring-turned tapering legs, 77½in. wide fully extended.
(Christie's) **$2,605**

A Victorian carved oak extending dining table, with molded edged top, leaf carved and fluted frieze, on baluster turned and Ionic column supports, 89in. long.
(Andrew Hartley) **$1,590**

Anglo-Indian ivory inlaid hardwood banquet table, mid 19th century, D-shaped ends with frieze drawers, two rectangular center sections, 100in. long.
(Skinner) **$4,600**

LARGE TABLES

George III style mahogany and yewwood two-pedestal dining table, 19th century, 85in. wide.
(Skinner) $2,415

George III style mahogany drop leaf hunt table, 19th century, 83¹/₂in. wide.
(Skinner) $2,990

A mid-Georgian mahogany dining-table, the D-shaped end-sections, on cabriole supports and club feet, 104in. long, extended.
(Christie's) $3,299

A late George III mahogany three-pillar dining table with reeded edge, on three turned and reeded columns, with quadruped supports and brass claw castors, 90in. long overall.
(Dreweatt Neate) $21,190

French Provincial oak and walnut trestle table, 19th/20th century, rectangular slab top on trestle, support joined by a stretcher, 94¹/₂in. long.
(Skinner) $2,415

A Duncan Miller walnut and aluminium inlaid dining table, the rectangular top on square shaft with inset aluminium banding, 78in. wide; and a set of six matching dining chairs.
(Christie's) $2,596

A mahogany wake table, of mid-Georgian style, the oval gateleg twin-flap top, on cabriole supports and pad feet, 96in. long.
(Christie's) $2,544

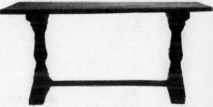

Italian baroque style walnut refectory table, comprising antique elements, 70in. wide.
(Skinner) $8,050

OCCASIONAL TABLES

An early 17th century oak joined chair/table with turned fluted supports, the seat rails carved with demi-florettes, 27½in. diameter.
(David Lay) $698

Emile Gallé, two tier table, circa 1900, shaped rectangular top inlaid in various fruitwoods with irises, 22in. wide.
(Sotheby's) $2,437

An antique elm cricket table with circular top and triangular undertray on three splayed supports, 2ft. 3½in. diameter.
(Russell, Baldwin & Bright)
                              $1,760

A 19th century specimen table of oblong form, with floral marquetry inlay and gilt metal mounts, 23½in. wide.
(Andrew Hartley) $2,067

A rare Queen Anne walnut tea table, Pennsylvania, 1730-80, the rectangular top above a shaped apron on cabriole legs, 35in.
(Sotheby's) $22,425

A mahogany and kingwood crossbanded occasional table of Louis XV style, the floral marquetry inlaid top fitted with four shaped hinged flaps, 40in. wide.
(Christie's) $1,145

A Victorian amboyna and ebonized occasional table, the molded edged octagonal top with incised banding, 30in. wide.
(Andrew Hartley) $1,471

Louis Majorelle, two-tier table, circa 1900, burr thuya wood and mahogany, the shaped top with carved surround, 28in. wide.
(Sotheby's) $63,407

A late Victorian ebonized, thuya-veneered and parcel-gilt occasional table by Marsh, Jones and Cribb, Leeds, 25in. diameter.
(Bearne's) $1,991

OCCASIONAL TABLES

A Terrazzo marble and painted wrought-iron occasional table, the circular top with brass banding, 22½in. diameter.
(Christie's) $439

A primitive Welsh cider table with thick sycamore circular top three turned ash supports and stretcher, 15in. diameter.
(Russell, Baldwin & Bright)
                                $1,255

A Victorian rosewood occasional table with string and marquetry inlay, on three turned and reeded supports, 27in. wide.
(Andrew Hartley) $994

A late Victorian rosewood and banded occasional table with string and marquetry inlay, the triform top with molded edged shaped flaps, 23¼in. wide.
(Andrew Hartley) $1,113

A classical gilt-stenciled mahogany architect's table, probably New York, 1820-30, on acanthus carved and reeded legs with rope-twist carved ankles, 37½in. wide.
(Christie's) $12,650

A 19th century green lacquered oblong silver table, pierced fret gallery on molded edged chinoiserie decorated top depicting a river scene with figures, 35¼in. high.
(Andrew Hartley) $3,021

An early Victorian burr-walnut occasional table, the circular top above a scallop frieze, on a column and circular base, 24in. diameter.
(Christie's) $956

An antique mahogany Chippendale style silver table with rectangular top over surface fret carved frieze, 27½ x 21½in.
(Russell, Baldwin & Bright)
                              $1,499

A 19th century Indian Bidderyware pillar table, finely inlaid silver in all-over designs of scrolled leafage and flowers, 28in. diameter.
(Russell, Baldwin & Bright)
                              $4,284

347

OCCASIONAL TABLES

Bermuda cedarwood tilt-top tripod table, circa 1760–90, 32³/₄in. diameter.
(Skinner) $1,725

An Art Deco burr-walnut and mahogany three-tier occasional table, on inswept uprights, on bracket feet, 23¹/₂in. wide.
(Christie's) $334

A Chippendale carved mahogany tilt-top tea table, on ring turned cylindrical pedestal, 31in. diameter.
(Christie's) $32,200

A George I burr-walnut octagonal tea-table, banded overall in two fruitwoods, the molded octagonal hinged top inlaid with octagonal segments, 30¹/₂in. wide.
(Christie's) $39,468

Two Sorrento poplar, fruitwood and parquetry tripod tables, the circular tops with differing stellar inlaid patterns, 60cm. and 61cm. diameter.
(Phillips) $2,250

A Queen Anne tavern table, Pennsylvania, 1730-50, the rectangular top with bread-board ends above an apron fitted with a thumbmolded drawer, 31³/₄in. wide.
(Christie's) $14,950

A 19th century Chinese lac burgauté octagonal occasional table, the snap top with an exotic bird perched on a branch of flowers and foliage, 81cm. diameter.
(Phillips) $1,800

An early George III mahogany draughtsman or architects table, the adjustable ratcheted hinged top with press out book rest and foliate and riband stipple molded edge, the top 91cm. x 60cm. (Phillips) $2,250

A mahogany silver table, the rectangular snap top with pierced scroll fret gallery, on a leaf carved baluster and fluted column, 61.5cm. wide.
(Phillips) $2,250

OCCASIONAL TABLES

A Betty Joel low occasional
table, on square tapering reeded
legs, 32in. wide.
(Christie's) $705

A William IV mahogany tripod
table, in the George II style, the
crossbanded pie-crust circular-
shaped hinged top on a fluted
and acanthus-wrapped baluster-
support, 44³/₄in. diameter.
(Christie's) $5,278

Renaissance style walnut,
marquetry and parcel-gilt
refectory table, late 19th/20th
century, 65¹/₂in. wide.
(Skinner) $7,475

A North Italian walnut
occasional table, the rectangular
top with canted angle, inlaid
with a panel of St. George and
the Dragon, between parquetry
bands, 24in. wide.
(Christie's) $557

Two pieces of Napoleon III paint
decorated furniture, third
quarter 19th century, an
occasional table and side chair.
(Skinner) $3,220

A Regency brass-inlaid
rosewood and parcel-gilt
occasional table, the rectangular
top inset with one hundred and
twenty squares of specimen
marbles, 20in. wide.
(Christie's) $67,548

A mahogany supper table, the
hinged round top with seven
circular shallow wells divided by
shells and foliage around a
larger central circular well,
29¹/₂in. diameter.
(Christie's) $3,167

An Art Deco bentwood serving
trolley, in the style of Alvar
Aalto, on shaped supports, disk
wheels with rubber tires,
28¹/₂in. wide.
(Christie's) $1,298

Chippendale walnut tilt-top
birdcage tea table, New
England, late 18th century,
circular top on a birdcage
platform, 33¹/₄in. diameter.
(Skinner) $2,300

PEMBROKE TABLES

Chippendale cherry Pembroke table, Portsmouth, New Hampshire, late 18th century, the rectangular drop leaf top overhangs a straight skirt, 35in. wide.
(Skinner) **$1,610**

Federal cherry inlaid Pembroke table, Massachusetts or Connecticut, circa 1800, the serpentine drop leaf top with frieze drawer and string inlay, 20in. wide.
(Skinner) **$2,645**

Federal mahogany and mahogany veneer Pembroke table, possibly New York, circa 1810, rectangular top with rounded leaves above a straight beaded skirt, 23in. wide.
(Skinner) **$863**

A Sheraton satinwood Pembroke table with crossbanded top having satinwood stringing, on square taper legs and casters, 2ft. 8in. x 3ft. 6in. open.
(Russell, Baldwin & Bright) **$5,045**

Mahogany Pembroke table, New England, late 18th century, serpentine drop leaf top above a base with beaded drawer and four molded Marlborough legs, 18in. wide.
(Skinner) **$1,380**

Federal mahogany inlaid Pembroke table, attributed to William Whitehead, New York, 1790–1810, the line inlaid oval top above bowed drawers at either end, 30³/₄in. wide.
(Skinner) **$8,050**

A George III mahogany and inlaid Pembroke table, the oval crossbanded hinged top containing a bowed frieze drawer on square tapered legs, the top 77cm. x 94cm.
(Phillips) **$2,700**

Dutch neoclassical satinwood and marquetry Pembroke table, late 18th/early 19th century, 30in. wide.
(Skinner) **$4,600**

A George III mahogany Pembroke table, satinwood banded and string inlaid, with rounded oblong top, 32in. wide.
(Andrew Hartley) **$1,908**

350

SIDE TABLES

An unusual George IV mahogany side table with a plain, outward curved three quarter gallery, 47in. wide. (David Lay) $1,519

Louis XIII oak side table, 18th century, 36in. wide. (Skinner) $1,955

Walnut side table with drawer, Lancaster County, Pennsylvania, mid 18th century, 38in. wide. (Skinner) $3,738

A 17th century Spanish walnut side table, the rectangular molded top containing two molded panel drawers in the frieze, 141cm. wide. (Phillips) $2,850

A George I gilt-gesso side table, the later rectangular Siena marble top above a concave frieze decorated with foliage, the shaped apron with conforming decoration on cabriole legs with pad feet, 30in. wide. (Christie's) $26,910

A George II mahogany side table, the associated shaped rectangular brêche violette marble top with re-entrant corners above a molded cornice, 60in. wide. (Christie's) $11,437

A Dutch oak side table, the molded rectangular planked top above a frieze with a long drawer, 18th century and later, 43in. wide. (Christie's) $1,999

A Dutch mahogany and inlaid side table, the top of serpentine outline with checker-banded frieze, 19th century, 34in. wide. (Christie's) $1,320

An oak side table, the D-shaped top on scrolled supports joined conforming stretchers, 48in. wide. (Christie's) $7,268

SOFA TABLES

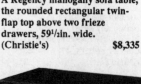

A Regency mahogany and ebony inlaid sofa table, the rectangular top above a frieze drawer and a simulated drawer, 137cm. wide.
(Phillips) $3,450

A Regency mahogany sofa table with kingwood crossbanding and ebony stringing, 56½in. wide.
(Bearne's) $3,981

A Regency mahogany sofa table, the rounded rectangular twin-flap top above two frieze drawers, 59½in. wide.
(Christie's) $8,335

A satinwood crossbanded rosewood sofa table, on lotus-lappeted turned column end standards, early 19th century, 58½in. wide.
(Christie's) $4,545

A Regency rosewood sofa table, the rounded rectangular twin-flap top above two frieze drawers with Greek key inlay, with claw feet, 40in. wide.
(Christie's) $3,871

A Regency ebony-inlaid satinwood sofa table, the canted rectangular top, above a mahogany-lined frieze drawer and a simulated drawer on either side, 59in. wide.
(Christie's) $7,038

A late Regency rosewood sofa table, banded in burr yew and crossbanded in tulipwood, on triple turned end supports, 56½in. long overall.
(Dreweatt Neate) $27,144

A Regency ormolu-mounted black and gilt-japanned sofa table, the rounded rectangular twin-flap Chinese lacquer top with paneled brass border, 57½in. wide.
(Christie's) $26,910

A mahogany and boxwood lined sofa table, of George III design, the reeded rounded rectangular twin-flap top above a frieze with two drawers, 55in. wide.
(Christie's) $2,362

SUTHERLAND TABLES

A late Victorian amboyna and ebonized Sutherland table, the rectangular twin-flap top with beaded rim.
(Christie's) $790

Edwardian rosewood Sutherland table with marquetry and bone inlay, on turned ring legs with baluster bottom stretcher, 24in. wide. (G.A. Key) $700

Victorian walnut Sutherland table, the two drop flaps with molded edges and rounded corners, 36in.
(G. A. Key) $1,561

Mahogany Sutherland table, supported at either end by pierced uprights, raised on ring turned tapering cylindrical supports, 19th century, 36in. wide.
(G. A. Key) $800

A Victorian rosewood Sutherland table, the rectangular top with hinged canted leaves, on ring-turned uprights and bracket feet, 36in. wide.
(Christie's) $680

A late Victorian mahogany and satinwood crossbanded Sutherland table, the rounded rectangular twin-flap top on square tapering supports, 32in. wide, open.
(Christie's) $920

Mahogany Sutherland table, molded edge, two drop flaps and rounded corners and raised on ring turned tulip baluster supports, 19th century, 30in. wide. (G. A. Key) $750

Victorian burr walnut Sutherland table, the two demi-lune drop flaps with molded edges, mid 19th century, 35½in.
(G. A. Key) $836

A Victorian walnut Sutherland table with oval top, on cheval base with carved and turned supports, turned stretcher.
(Russell, Baldwin & Bright) $1,408

WORKBOXES & TEAPOYS

A 19th century penwork decorated and gilt games table, the top painted for chess with guilloché border, 74cm. wide.
(Phillips) $12,300

George IV rosewood games table, with inlaid sliding checkerboard top with a well and backgammon 34in. wide.
(Dreweatt · Neate) $3,825

A mid 19th century mahogany work table with a hinged top and shaped frieze, raised on scrolling supports, 19¼in. wide.
(Anderson & Garland)
$1,127

A Regency brass-mounted rosewood and Vincennes porcelain work-table, the rectangular top with a Vincennes bleu celeste porcelain tray with central landscape scene.
(Christie's) $8,446

A Regency mahogany worktable, the rounded rectangular twin-flap top above a mahogany-lined frieze fitted drawer and a further drawer, above a workbasket slide, 40in. wide.
(Christie's) $3,870

A George III satinwood, tulipwood crossbanded and marquetry oval work table, the hinged top with sprays of rosehips heightened in harewood enclosing a well, the top 57cm. x 40cm.
(Phillips) $1,425

A late Regency pollard oak and maple drop flap work table with pouch drawer and false and opening drawers, 33in. wide.
(Dreweatt · Neate) $1,163

An Edwardian mahogany and satinwood banded work table with single frieze drawer and wool compartment, on square tapering legs, 24in.
(Dreweatt Neate) $1,027

A Regency mahogany and inlaid drop flap work table, the top with scroll and dart inlay containing four short drawers in the frieze, the top 90cm. x 46cm.
(Phillips) $3,000

WORKBOXES & TEAPOYS

A Regency mahogany and inlaid games table, the folding hinged top inlaid for chess, 91cm. x 45.5cm. overall extended top.
(Phillips) $4,500

A Regency rosewood writing/ work table, the rounded rectangular twin-flap top above a frieze drawer with writing surface, 34in. wide.
(Christie's) $2,447

William IV mahogany teapoy, the top section having a sarcophagus formed molded lid with concave sides, 18in.
(G. A. Key) $1,533

A Regency calamander tea-caddy on stand, crossbanded overall in partridgewood and boxwood, the tea-caddy with a hinged concave-stepped top enclosing a fitted interior, 13½in. wide.
(Christie's) $4,398

A Regency mahogany work-table, the rounded rectangular twin-flap top crossbanded in calamander, above a shallow drawer previously with divisions and a deep drawer simulated as two drawers, 28½in. wide.
(Christie's) $2,639

A Regency ormolu-mounted rosewood work-table, the concave stepped rectangular top crossbanded in tulipwood above a cedar-lined frieze drawer and work-box slide on lyre-end supports, 20in. wide.
(Christie's) $5,630

A Victorian round teapoy, the rising lid revealing the four original cylindrical lidded caddies, carved border, turned and carved column, 17¾in. diameter.
(Dreweatt Neate) $2,037

A Victorian rectangular mottled grey lacquered sewing table, the top decorated in low relief and gilded with a peacock and bird of paradise, 16½in. wide.
(Dreweatt Neate) $440

An early Victorian rosewood rectangular shaped work table, the hinged lid with canted corners enclosing a fitted interior, 17¼in. wide.
(Anderson & Garland) $1,434

WRITING TABLES

A mid-Victorian oak library table, with rectangular canted and leather-lined top above two end frieze drawers, 67in. wide. (Christie's) $3,167

A late Victorian ebonized and brass-mounted writing table, with rectangular leather-lined top, on fluted tapering legs, 45½in. wide. (Christie's) $1,583

A 19th century rosewood library table with rounded oblong top, shaped studded with two drawers, 48 x 28¾in. (Andrew Hartley) $2,945

A rare William and Mary walnut writing and games table of small size, the double baize lined folding top opening to reveal a leather lined and fitted interior with stationery compartments, 58cm. wide. (Phillips) $4,500

A George IV mahogany Carlton House desk, decorated overall with ripple molding, the demi-lune ended rectangular top with pierced foliate gallery, above three small part cedar-lined drawers, 56in. wide. (Christie's) $17,043

A fine Louis XVI style kingwood and ormolu writing desk, the raised back with mirrored panels and classical female figure supports, 55in. wide. (Anderson & Garland) $11,590

A South German walnut writing-table, 19th century, the molded kidney-shaped top with leather inset and shelved back, 43in. wide. (Christie's) $1,672

An Edwardian mahogany writing table with satinwood crossbanding and classical swag inlay, 42in. wide. (David Lay) $3,720

A late-Victorian Aesthetic Movement ebonized, inlaid and decorated writing table, raised superstructure, 42in. wide. (Christie's) $890

WRITING TABLES

A mahogany writing table, the rectangular leather-lined top above a paterae-applied frieze with three drawers and three dummy drawers.
(Christie's) $2,105

A late Victorian rosewood writing-table, the bowed rectangular boxwood inlaid and leather-lined top above a kneehole, 36in. wide.
(Christie's) $1,486

An Edwardian mahogany and rosewood-banded writing table, with inverted breakfront leather-lined top and central frieze drawer, 38in. wide.
(Christie's) $1,736

An Edwardian mahogany bonheur du jour in the Sheraton style with satinwood banding and floral inlay, 2ft. 6in. wide.
(Russell, Baldwin & Bright)
                    $1,499

Writing table and chair, late 1930s in the manner of Terrence Harold Robsjohn-Gibbings, blonde wood, the table with scroll-ended rectangular writing surface covered in vellum, 56¼in.
(Sotheby's) $16,871

A mid-Victorian burr-walnut and marquetry bonheur du jour, the superstructure with central arched mirror and drawer, the shaped aprons with cabriole legs, 32in. wide.
(Christie's) $3,479

A Louis XVI style walnut and marquetry writing table, with gilt-metal mounts, on cabriole legs trailing to sabots, 32in. wide.
(Christie's) $2,778

A Regency amboyna, rosewood and brass marquetry writing table, in the manner of Louis de Gaigneur, the top 75cm. x 66cm.
(Phillips) $12,000

A Regency pollard oak and gilt metal mounted writing table, after a design by Gillows, with a gray marble top with pierced brass gallery, 82 x 48.5cm.
(Phillips) $1,950

TRUNKS & COFFERS

A late 17th century oak coffer with paneled lid and sides, paneled fascia carved with flowers and leaves, 45½in. (Andrew Hartley) $1,860

Paint decorated dome top trunk, lined with southeastern Massachusetts newspaper dated *1814*, 21¾in. wide. (Skinner) $1,495

Oak and pine joined paneled six-board chest, probably Newbury, Massachusetts, circa 1700–10, 45in. wide. (Skinner) $518

A pine and turned poplar dough box, Pennsylvania, 19th century, the rectangular removeable top opening to a tapering well, 38in. (Sotheby's) $402

Painted and carved sea chest, New England, early 19th century, the rectangular lift top opens to reveal a polychrome portrait of the ship 'Molo', 34¾in. wide. (Skinner) $6,325

A Spanish stamped leather coffer, with hinged domed top, on a later carved oak and brass studded base, 28½in. wide. (Christie's) $521

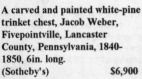

A carved and painted white-pine trinket chest, Jacob Weber, Fivepointville, Lancaster County, Pennsylvania, 1840-1850, 6in. long. (Sotheby's) $6,900

Renaissance style silvered metal and steel lock box, in the manner of Michael Mann, the exterior etched with elegant figures and foliage, 6in. wide. (Skinner) $1,610

Painted twig chest, Adirondack area, New York, early 20th century, the hinged top opens to a cavity, 33¾in. wide. (Skinner) $633

TRUNKS & COFFERS

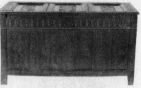

A giltwood cassone, the stepped hinged lid with foliate carved decoration above a painted paneled front depicting a courtly scene, Italian, 19th century, 75¹/₂in. wide.
(Christie's) $5,044

A George I oak blanket box, the three panel top carved with stylized foliage, fluted frieze, dated *1719*, stile feet, 137cm. long.
(Winterton's) $967

An unusual early 17th century paneled and painted oak coffer, the frieze and muntins lightly incised with geometric motifs, 32in. wide.
(Bearne's) $2,707

A 17th century oak box, the hinged planked cover above carved front, dated *1670*, 58.5cm. long.
(Winterton's) $702

A Victorian polychrome-painted and satinwood coffer-on-stand, decorated overall with hung ribbon-tied floral garlands, and crossbanded in tulipwood and inlaid with boxwood and ebony lines, 21³/₄in. wide.
(Christie's) $3,519

A blue-painted and polychrome-decorated pine blanket chest, Windsor Township, Northern Berks County, Pennsylvania, dated *1787*, 4ft. 2in. long.
(Sotheby's) $11,500

A 17th century oak ark coffer, the domed lid with molded edges, boarded fascia and sides on stile supports, 38in. wide, 23½in. high.
(Andrew Hartley) $1,085

Grain painted pine six-board chest, probably Connecticut, 1825–40, original mustard and burnt sienna paint to resemble mahogany, 35¹/₂in. wide.
(Skinner) $1,035

An early 18th century oak coffer, the triple fielded paneled front inlaid with symmetrical cross motifs, 35½in wide.
(Dreweatt · Neate) $1,346

WARDROBES & ARMOIRES

Louis XV Provincial oak armoire, 19th century, 51½in. wide.
(Skinner) $3,105

Dutch green chinoiserie decorated armoire, 18th century, 45in. wide.
(Skinner) $4,312

Louis XV Provincial oak armoire, late 18th/early 19th century, 56in. wide.
(Skinner) $3,738

A large Flemish 18th century armoire, the flared cornice above a pair of paneled doors with ornate pierced lock escutcheons, 63in. wide.
(Anderson & Garland) $1,906

A late Victorian mahogany and painted wardrobe, crossbanded in satinwood and inlaid with checker and boxwood lines, 82in. wide.
(Christie's) $2,180

Grain painted pine wardrobe, coastal Massachusetts, circa 1830, the molded cornice above a door with two raised panels opening to an interior of hooks with shelves to the right, 44in. wide.
(Skinner) $1,032

An 18th century walnut armoire with a molded cushion frieze cornice enclosed by a pair of panel doors with radiating fan cartouche panels, probably Savoie, 161cm. wide.
(Phillips) $6,000

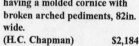

An Edwardian light oak break-front combination wardrobe, having a molded cornice with broken arched pediments, 82in. wide.
(H.C. Chapman) $2,184

A marquetry armoire with overall floral and foliate inlay, the top section with arched pediment above two shaped doors, 63in. wide.
(Christie's) $4,168

WARDROBES & ARMOIRES

A Victorian satinwood and parcel-gilt wardrobe, with a pair of shaped mirrored doors, on shaped plinth with foliate edging, 47in. wide.
(Christie's) $2,622

An early Victorian mahogany breakfront wardrobe, with molded cornice, two central paneled doors, 106¼in. wide.
(Bearne's) $3,185

A carved armoire with dentil-molded cornice and fielded paneled sides, French, 65in. wide.
(Christie's) $5,557

An early 19th century Tyrolean decorated armoire with canted angles, the molded cornice with peacock and flowers, 149cm. wide.
(Phillips) $4,050

An Arts and Crafts oak wardrobe and dressing table, the single wardrobe with canopy top on bracket supports, 54½in.
(Andrew Hartley) $1,625

A Normandy oak armoire, early 19th century, the molded cornice above a foliate-carved frieze, fitted with two similarly carved paneled cupboard doors, 60¼in. wide.
(Christie's) $4,543

An 18th century gentleman's wardrobe in oak with gouge carved cornice over pair of fielded paneled doors, 4ft. wide.
(Russell, Baldwin & Bright) $5,049

A fine quality Edwardian satinwood breakfront wardrobe, having dentil cornice over pair of central multi-paneled doors, 8ft. wide.
(Russell, Baldwin & Bright) $3,213

An 18th century French Provincial oak armoire with molded cornice, two arched paneled doors over two small drawers, 58½in. wide.
(Andrew Hartley) $1,352

WASHSTANDS

A late George III mahogany and brass bound military writing table and wash stand, the rising top with a mirror and compartments, 28in. wide.
(Dreweatt Neate) $1,560

A 19th century mahogany washstand having hinged top opening to reveal brass tap and blue and white wash bowl, 2ft. 11in. wide.
(Russell, Baldwin & Bright) $1,132

A George IV mahogany washstand, with rectangular lidded compartment and wells, false frieze drawer, 30in. wide.
(Dreweatt Neate) $811

A Chippendale mahogany washstand, American, circa 1780, the hinged two-part top opening to a pierced surface within a cyma-shaped moulding, 30in. wide (open).
(Sotheby's) $3,162

A George IV mahogany bow-fronted corner washstand with lift-up top, five dummy drawers, one drawer and central cupboard, 17in.
(Dreweatt Neate) $912

A late George IV mahogany bow-fronted corner washstand with raised back and three wells above an undertier with one drawer.
(Dreweatt Neate) $702

A mahogany washstand, of George III design, inlaid with boxwood and ebony lines, the rectangular hinged twin-flap top enclosing a plain interior.
(Christie's) $1,090

A Hepplewhite mahogany bowfront corner washstand, 23in. wide, with Staffordshire ewer and bowl.
(Russell, Baldwin & Bright) $1,010

A Georgian mahogany washstand, the folding tray top enclosing a later solid mahogany top over cupboard doors, 17¼in. wide.
(Dee, Atkinson & Harrison) $510

WHATNOTS

Federal mahogany stand, Middle Atlantic States, 1815–25, with four shelves and a single drawer on turned legs with original casters, 21½in. wide.
(Skinner) **$920**

An early Victorian mahogany three-tier buffet, the rectangular three-quarter galleried shelves supported by turned baluster columns, 60¼in. wide.
(Christie's) **$1,999**

A Regency mahogany whatnot, the four rectangular tiers above a drawer, 16¼in. wide.
(Christie's) **$1,578**

A Victorian figured walnut and ebony banded whatnot, the cut cornered top with gilt brass gallery raised on turned, tapered and fluted supports, 58cm. wide.
(Tennant's) **$906**

A pair of orange and gilt-lacquered two-tier étagères, each with a central peacock within a plain border and foliate-painted surround, 13½in. wide.
(Christie's) **$439**

A Victorian walnut canterbury whatnot, the upper tier with fretted gallery and inlaid in boxwood, fretted end supports, 24in. wide.
(Canterbury) **$1,280**

A George IV rosewood four-tier whatnot of small proportions, with slender turned uprights, the base fitted with one drawer, 16in. wide.
(Canterbury) **$3,500**

An early Victorian mahogany three-tier buffet, the centre shelf fitted with two drawers, 42in. wide.
(Christie's) **$1,649**

A Victorian mahogany rectangular three tier whatnot, on ring turned supports, 22in. wide.
(Dreweatt Neate) **$1,060**

WINE COOLERS

Georgian style brass-bound oak peat bucket on stand, 19th century, 25in. high.
(Skinner) $517

A Regency mahogany sarcophagus-shaped wine cooler, the domed hinged top with cavetto molded sides, 27in. wide.
(Christie's) $1,672

A George III mahogany octagonal wine cooler on stand, the brass-bound tapering body with side handles, 20¼in. wide.
(Bearne's) $2,309

A George III mahogany cellaret with satinwood stringing, the hinged top enclosing six divisions on molded square tapered legs and casters, 15in. wide.
(Russell, Baldwin & Bright) $1,714

Federal mahogany veneer cellaret, New York City, 1815–25, with cross-banded mahogany veneer outlining the octagonal shaped top, 24½in. wide.
(Skinner) $2,530

A George III mahogany and brass-bound wine cooler, the hinged octagonal lid enclosing a later two-handled tin liner, 18¾in. wide.
(Christie's) $3,089

A late 18th century Dutch cellaret, veneered in finely figured mahogany, the domed hinged top with a lignum vitae urn shaped finial, 11½in. wide.
(Dreweatt Neate) $3,000

A William IV mahogany sarcophagus cellaret, of tapering rectangular form, bold gadrooned borders, hairy paw lion feet, circa 1835, 71cm. wide.
(Winterton's) $2,340

A 19th century satinwood and banded cellaret, with hinged domed top and brass carrying handles, 46cm. wide.
(Phillips) $1,350

WINE COOLERS

A Georgian mahogany wine cooler/cellaret of octagonal form with bands and handles of brass, 18in.
(Russell, Baldwin & Bright) $3,672

A Regency mahogany wine cooler of sarcophagus shape with beaded friezes, on boldly carved paw feet, 3ft. x 4ft. 8¹/₂in.
(Russell, Baldwin & Bright) $5,814

A late George III mahogany and brass-bound octagonal wine cooler, the hinged top with molded rim enclosing a tin-lined interior, 20in. wide.
(Christie's) $2,287

A George III mahogany and brass-bound wine cooler, the hinged rectangular top with canted angles, enclosing a later divided interior, 25in. wide.
(Christie's) $3,600

A late George III mahogany hexagonal wine cooler, brass-bound, with hinged lid and small cupboard below, on bracket feet, 19in. wide.
(Christie's) $1,200

A George III brass-bound mahogany cellaret, the tapering body with ring-turned lion-mask handles on a molded plinth and on associated paw-feet, 21in. high.
(Christie's) $3,946

A George III mahogany and brass-bound wine cooler, the oval molded hinged lid enclosing a later divisioned interior, 21¼in. wide.
(Christie's) $2,727

A George III mahogany sarcophagus shaped cellaret, inlaid with ebony lines, the domed top with a cavetto border, 66cm. x 47cm.
(Phillips) $2,250

A George III mahogany oval shaped brass bound wine cooler with hinged lid and brass ring handles, raised on cabriole legs, 22¹/₂in. wide.
(Anderson & Garland) $1,251

A stone head of Buddha, 19¾in. high.
(Sotheby's) $1,955

A pair of painted terracotta covered pineapples, 23in. high.
(Sotheby's) $1,380

A marble bust of a bacchante, turned to dexter, 21in. high.
(Sotheby's) $2,587

One of a set of four painted composition chairs, the back and arms decorated as tufted upholstery within a scrolled frame.
(Sotheby's) (Four) $2,875

A pair of painted cast-iron urns, each with a shaped rim, the body centered by an elaborate cartouche on opposing sides, 23in. high.
(Sotheby's) $2,587

A gilt-bronze and brass bird cage, circa 1911, with a domed top, headed by a berried and feather finial, signed *FR. OT. ST. Wien 28-3 1911.* 43in. high.
(Sotheby's) $9,200

A painted cast-metal fountain, the octagonal basin above a circular standard cast with three addorsed storks, 39½in. high.
(Sotheby's) $1,495

A pair of patinated bronze side chairs, circa 1900 by Einbigler and Adler, New York, each back centered by a laurel wreath surmounted by a laurel garland.
(Sotheby's) $8,625

A marble urn, the gadrooned body of campana form with an outswept rim on a waisted circular foot, 34in. high.
(Sotheby's) $6,900

A painted cast-iron figure of a deer, 5ft. high.
(Sotheby's) $6,325

Two of a set of four stone sphinxes, 31in. high.
(Sotheby's) (Four) $2,587

A bronze figure of a swan, modern, 36in. high.
(Sotheby's) $2,587

An English porcelain garden seat, decorated overall with scrolls and flowers on a pink ground, 20½in. high.
(Sotheby's) $1,380

Two of a set of three limestone figural groups, each with a seated putto, two holding birds, the third seated upon a fish, tallest 29in. high.
(Sotheby's) (Three) $4,025

A glazed terracotta jardinière, the body decorated with alternating bands with cherub masks and rosettes, 31in. high.
(Sotheby's) $805

A marble bust of a woman, raised on a circular plinth, with an unrelated circular marble pedestal, 38½in. high.
(Sotheby's) $1,840

A set of six cast-iron armchairs, each with a lyre-form back, together with a cast-iron center table.
(Sotheby's) $5,462

A marble wall fountain, late 19th century, the rectangular backplate centered by a cherub mask, 4ft. 5in. high.
(Sotheby's) $10,925

An American painted cast-iron garden seat, 19th century, of fern pattern, stamped *James W. Carr Richmond VA.* 38in. high.
(Sotheby's) $3,737

A pair of stoneware 'rustic' garden seats, late 19th century, each as a tree stump, with branches as a back support, 44in. and 46in. high.
(Christie's) $2,815

A lead planter, late 19th century, of circular form, the sides raised with a continuous scene of playful putti and classical figures, 15in. high.
(Christie's) $2,815

An Italian white marble bust of a young woman, by F. Lupini, dated *1892*, wearing a 'jeweled' head-dress over her long hair, signed, 20in. high.
(Christie's) $1,091

A pair of white-painted cast-iron garden chairs, each with back and arms cast with fern leaves, with pierced seat, on shaped fern-cast legs.
(Christie's) $1,020

A white marble bust of Napoleon, second half 19th century, on a circular spreading socle, restoration to socle, 27in. high.
(Christie's) $2,639

One of a pair of Vicenza stone pedestals, each of square baluster form, the paneled sides carved with scrolling foliage, 33¹/₂in. high.
(Christie's)
                    (Two) $1,318

A rare and unusual pair of German rococo wrought-iron garden figures, 19th century, one modeled as a monkey, the other as a cat, 21in. high.
(Sotheby's) $17,250

One of a pair of composition armchairs, after the Antique, modern, each with a curved back, the top rail raised with foliage above a shield-shaped escutcheon and trophies.
(Christie's) $4,222

A stone satyr mask, 36in. high.
(Sotheby's) $2,875

A pair of marble lions, each roaring, full maned beast advancing on a rectangular plinth, 42in. long.
(Sotheby's) $8,050

A marble figure of the Capitoline Venus, losses, 26½in. high.
(Sotheby's) $2,875

A pair of George III stone urns, each with a circular overhanging rim carved with rosettes, above the waisted body carved with drapery swags, 32½in. high.
(Christie's) $7,038

A suite of marble garden furniture, comprising a settee, two armchairs and a table.
(Sotheby's) $20,700

A pair of Regency white-painted wrought and cast-iron jardinières on stands, supported on a central stem and three uprights joined by two bead-cast bands and each with scrolled ring top, 48in. high.
(Christie's) $7,389

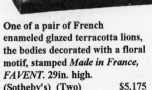

A terracotta jardinière, the tapering circular body with an egg and dart frieze, above a central panel with lion masks, 22½in. high.
(Sotheby's) $690

One of a pair of French enameled glazed terracotta lions, the bodies decorated with a floral motif, stamped *Made in France, FAVENT.* 29in. high.
(Sotheby's) (Two) $5,175

A pair of painted cast-iron garden benches, each back composed of interlacing circles surrounded by scrolls centering a mask, 44in. wide.
(Sotheby's) $4,025

Pair of white painted cast iron
figures of reclining whippets,
early 20th century, 39in. long.
(Skinner) $1,610

A pair of Renaissance style stone
figures of eagles, 44in. high.
(Sotheby's) $5,750

A stone eagle's head, 15½in.
high.
(Sotheby's) $977

A marble figural group, late
19th century, depicting putto
figures playing musical
instruments, on unrelated
marble pedestal, height of
sculpture 39in.
(Sotheby's) $5,175

A pair of Louis XVI style cast
iron urns, modern, with
opposing ram's head handles
joined by a fruiting grapevine,
23in. high.
(Sotheby's) $5,750

A pair of stone figural groups,
modern, each with a child beside
a figure of a dog or goat, topped
by a basket form urn, 4ft. 8in.
high.
(Sotheby's) $5,750

A gilt-metal figural fountain in
the form of a dolphin, the mouth
plumbed for water, 18in. high.
(Sotheby's) $2,587

A pair of cast-stone putto
figures, each reclining beside a
stylized dolphin figure, 15½in.
high.
(Sotheby's) $4,887

A marble bust of Dante
Alighieri, 19th century, signed
Prof. Carlo Rivalta, on circular
socle, 37in. high.
(Sotheby's) $4,312

Pair of cast stone pastoral figures, in the manner of John Cheere, 20th century, 45in. high. (Skinner) $805

A pair of pineapple finials, 15in. high. (Sotheby's) $3,737

A pair of cast stone figural groups of two putti, holding aloft an urn, 4ft. 11in. high. (Sotheby's) $4,887

A Byzantine style marble urn, the ovoid body carved all round with exotic animals and foliage. (Sotheby's) $2,300

A pair of Regency cast iron garden urns on stands, first quarter 19th century, each painted in two tones of green, on fluted circular plinths, 38 in. high. (Sotheby's) $5,750

A large Indian marble jardinière with a gadrooned mid section within tiers of scrolled leaf tips, 21in. high. (Sotheby's) $12,650

A bronze figural fountain, late 19th century, cast as a pelican with wings outstretched, stamped *Bruno Neri*, 28½in. high. (Sotheby's) $6,325

A pair of large patinated bronze lions by Antoine Durenne, Sommevoire, each seated on its hind legs, 19th century, 4ft. 4in. high. (Sotheby's) $63,000

A marble figure of a spaniel, late 19th century, wearing a collar inscribed *Jessie*, signed *M. Muldoon & Co. Lou L.N.*, 29in. high. (Sotheby's) $12,650

BEAKERS

A Bohemian transparent-enameled beaker, circa 1840, each side with a raised roundel enameled with chinoiserie figures, 5¹/₄in. high. (Christie's) $1,300

A Bohemian flared beaker, with a gilt leaf band, printed beneath with Venus and Cupid seated before a pedestal, 13.5cm. high. (Christie's) $349

A Bohemian engraved ruby-flash beaker, circa 1840, the central oval panel engraved in the manner of E. Hoffmann with an officer on horseback, 5⁴/₅in. (Christie's) $2,200

A Bohemian enameled and amber flash beaker, gilt to the rim above a band of flowering roses reserving a scene of a castle and cottage within landscape, 13cm. high, late 18th/19th century. (Christie's) $315

A Russian amethyst glass commemorative portrait beaker, transfer-printed en grisaille with a bust length portrait of the Tzar, probably Alexander II, and a blue beaker similarly printed with the Tzarina, mid 19th century. (Christie's) $725

A Bohemian transparent enameled beaker, cut with two bands of ovals, each painted in colors with a single fish and engraved stylized foliage, 12.5cm. high, late 19th century. (Christie's) $1,135

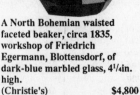

A South Bohemian lithyalin beaker, circa 1835, Buquoy's Glasshouse, of marbled blue translucent glass and shaped waisted faceted form, enameled and gilt, 4¹/₂in. high. (Christie's) $3,495

A North Bohemian waisted faceted beaker, circa 1835, workshop of Friedrich Egermann, Blottensdorf, of dark-blue marbled glass, 4¹/₄in. high. (Christie's) $4,800

A J. & L. Lobmyer enameled beaker in the Islamic taste, circa 1880, enameled and gilt with an Arabic inscription on a ground of stylized scrolling foliage, 4³/₈in. high. (Christie's) $3,565

BOWLS

Art glass encased centrebowl, with organic leafy mauve, amber and orange internal decoration, 5¹/₈in. high. (Skinner) $460

Bohemian pewter and art glass centerbowl, mounted with border of pressed blossom motif centering two glass 'jewel' medallions, 12in. wide. (Skinner) $431

Austrian art glass handled vase, Loetz-type colorless bowl raised on four applied feet with raised handles, 4¹/₂in. high. (Skinner) $575

Baroque Revival ormolu and etched glass punch bowl, circa 1880, etched with grapevines, with beast and foliate cast mounts, on boar's head feet, 17in. diameter. (Skinner) $1,725

A pair of mould blown oval bowls, each cut with a continuous band of diamond swags below flutes, 19cm. wide, 19th century. (Christie's) $245

Bohemian art glass centerbowl-compote, with transparent amber faceted bowl raised on deeply cupped pedestal foot, 11¹/₂in. diameter. (Skinner) $403

Bat coupe, circa 1905, attributed to Daum, clear glass bowl enameled in orange and black, with silvered metal mount cast with three bats, 5in. (Sotheby's) $2,812

Daum wild rosehip bowl and cover, circa 1913, internally mottled with pale pink, overlaid with green, brown, yellow and red, 5³/₄in. diameter maximum. (Sotheby's) $2,639

WMF Wurttemberg ikora bowl, flared rim on colorless body encasing brilliant ruby red, amber and white mottled and striated coloration, 9³/₈in. diameter. (Skinner) $230

CANDLESTICKS

An opaque-twist taper-stick, circa 1765, the cylindrical nozzle with everted rim, the stem enclosing an opaque gauze corkscrew twist with central thread, 6¼in. high.
(Christie's)   **$1,475**

Tiffany doré bronze and blue glass candlestick, with round candlecup of lustrous blue iridescent favrile glass, 8in. high.
(Skinner)   **$2,000**

A German faceted candlestick, circa 1750, the cylindrical nozzle above a faceted knopped stem and on a molded and cut domed foot, 7¾in. high.
(Christie's)   **$640**

A pair of Regency glass candlesticks with diamond-cut baluster stems, each hung with a double tier of prism drops, 25.5cm. high.
(Bearne's)   **$2,230**

Pair of A. Douglas Nash candlesticks, heavy walled ribbed holders with strong uneven golden luster, each inscribed *Nash 657*, 3¾in. high.
(Skinner)   **$575**

Pair of painted and gilded glass candlestick-form lamp bases, 20th century, painted with white foliage and with faceted prism drops, 12in. high.
(Skinner)   **$518**

Two Tiffany favrile glass candlelamps, with opal and green leaf design spring fittings and extended metal supports, 14in. high.
(Skinner)   **$3,220**

Tiffany bronze and favrile glass double candelabrum, brown patina on two-socket holder with green glass blown into pierced candlecups, 9in. high.
(Skinner)   **$3,565**

A pair of faceted candlesticks, circa 1790, the cylindrical nozzles cut with diamond facets, the similarly-cut stems with waist knops, 11⅛in. high.
(Christie's)   **$2,400**

DECANTERS

Pair of Bohemian white overlay cranberry glass decanters, late 19th century, painted with festoons of flowers, 9¼in. high.
(Skinner) **$288**

Green and white overlay decanter, bright emerald green color with engraved and stripped grapevine medial border, 7¼in. high.
(Skinner) **$173**

A pair of purple glass bottle decanters with matching faceted lozenge stoppers, inscribed in gold, *Rum* and *Brandy*, 25cm. high.
(Bearne's) **$510**

A pair of 'Bristol' blue glass decanters with matching lozenge stoppers, each decorated in gold, one inscribed *Hollands*, the other *Rum*, 23.5cm. high.
(Bearne's) **$573**

Dutch hallmarked silver and wheel cut glass decanter set, rococo style, pierced figural and floral frame, 11½in. high.
(Skinner) **$1,610**

A pair of magnum decanters and stoppers for ale, circa 1770, club shape and named for ALE within quatrefoil cartouches issuant with hops and barley, 13¼in. high.
(Christie's) **$3,680**

A mallet-shaped decanter and a stopper, circa 1780, named for *CYDER* within a shaped quatrefoil cartouche bordered by flowers and foliage, 14in. high.
(Christie's) **$3,500**

Matched pair of Bohemian ruby overlay cut and frosted glass decanters, 8¼in. high.
(Skinner) **$460**

Dutch hallmarked silver cased clear glass decanter, late 19th century, squared form with wheel-cut floral decoration, 7⅞in. high.
(Skinner) **$431**

DISHES

Regency period oval glass dish
with a dentil cut rim and star
cut center, on a cast metal stand
with scrolled feet, 19th century,
14in.
(G. A. Key) $76

A Continental gilt metal
mounted and cut centerpiece
the circular dish cut with an
outer ring of strawberry
diamonds and an inner ring of
graduating diamonds, 38.5cm.
diameter, 19th century.
(Christie's) $1,748

Sandwich canary pressed glass
princess feather medallion and
basket of flowers footed dish,
Boston and Sandwich Glass
Company, 1840–45, 6in. high.
(Skinner) $20,700

René Lalique coupe 'Sirene',
after 1920, opalescent glass,
molded on the underside with a
mermaid and set on three small
feet, 14³/₈in. diameter.
(Sotheby's) $5,630

A faceted double sweetmeat-
glass, circa 1760, the ogee bowl
cut with facets beneath a
beveled scalloped rim, 8½in.
high.
(Christie's) $1,475

Tiffany blue iridescent compote,
dark cobalt blue body with
extraordinary purple-gold-blue
iridescence stretched at flared
rim, 6¹/₂in. diameter.
(Skinner) $863

A Bohemian enameled and cut
bonbonnière, of faceted section
with petal cut rims, 15.5cm.
high, 19th century.
(Christie's) $559

François Décorchmont shallow
dish with female masks, circa
1920, streaked with shades of
blue and molded in high relief
with three female masks, 8¹/₂in.
diameter.
(Sotheby's) $6,686

A cut sweetmeat glass with
scalloped rim above faceted and
fluted slender ogee bowl,
16.5cm. high, circa 1790.
(Christie's) $300

DRINKING SETS

A Venetian amber glass pedestal punch bowl and cover with ten matching cups, each piece applied with prunts and brightly painted, 39.5cm.
(Bearne's) $1,117

Russian niello and gold washed silver vodka set, late 19th century, with unidentified maker's mark, tray with view of the Kremlin.
(Skinner) $6,900

Emile Gallé, Liqueur service comprising carafe and stopper, bowl and four small glasses, delicately enameled clear glass.
(Sotheby's) $3,374

Bohemian art glass covered punchbowl, on cupped pedestal foot, decorated by pink and yellow enameled blossoms, four matching punch glasses, 14in. high with cover.
(Skinner) $259

A Czechoslovakian cocktail set, comprising shaker, ice-bucket and four tumblers, each of clear glass decorated with stylized pink, blue, white and black flowers.
(Christie's) $297

Cranberry water set, comprising: jug with clear glass handle, decorated in the center with gilt key hole pattern; together with two matching beakers, 9in. and 5in.
(G. A. Key) $383

A Continental gilt decorated part liqueur set, painted with bands of flower sprays and laub und bandelwerk, 19th century.
(Christie's) $1,500

A Bohemian engraved lemonade set of faceted form, depicting deer within wooded landscapes, late 19th century.
(Christie's) $2,500

European cut overlay and enameled cordial set, decanter and six glasses of matching opal cut to emerald green, decanter 11in. high.
(Skinner) $431

GOBLETS

A baluster goblet with large slightly tapered bucket bowl above angular and tear knopped stem, 18cm. high, circa 1720.
(Christie's) $2,000

Steuben gold aurene goblet, lustrous iridescence on flared bell-form with ropetwist stem on disk foot, 6¼in. high.
(Skinner) $201

A Dutch engraved 'Friendship' goblet, circa 1760, engraved with Cupid and flaming hearts within a rococo-scroll cartouche, 7¼in. high.
(Christie's) $820

A facet-stemmed stipple-engraved goblet, circa 1770, attributed to 'Alius', the slightly flared funnel bowl with a scene emblematic of 'Friendship' of two boys shaking hands, 6³/₈in. high.
(Christie's) $12,000

A Bohemian engraved colour-twist goblet, circa 1750, the slender flared bowl with scrolling foliage, on a spiral-molded ball-knopped stem enclosing a blue thread, 6³/₈in. high.
(Christie's) $770

A Dutch-engraved royal armorial light-baluster goblet, circa 1760, the funnel bowl engraved and polished with the arms and supporters of Willem V of Orange and Nassau, 7¼in. high.
(Christie's) $1,300

A Dutch-engraved light-baluster goblet, circa 1750, the flared funnel bowl with three sailing-ships in full sail at sea beneath the inscription *S'LANTS WELVAREN*, 6½in. high.
(Christie's) $2,750

A Silesian engraved and dated goblet, the ogee bowl inscribed *Johann Friedrich Heufer 1766* within a rococo-scroll cartouche, 6in. high.
(Christie's) $2,200

A Dutch-engraved baluster goblet, circa 1720, the funnel bowl with Justice seated blindfolded, holding scales in one hand and a sword in the other, 8¼in. high.
(Christie's) $2,200

JUGS

Silver overlay glass decanter with stopper, America, late 19th century, floral and scrolled leaf design, 8¹/₂in. high.
(Skinner) $805

Bohemian art glass pitcher, attributed to Moser, of colorless crystal with extensive gold foliate decoration, 6¹/₄in. high.
(Skinner) $259

An early decanter-jug and cover, circa 1685, of straight-sided slightly flared shouldered form with plain applied trail to the footrim, 11¹/₂in. high.
(Christie's) $4,400

Pallme Konig art glass claret pitcher, with hot-applied red and white threading and integrated blossom bursts, 11in. high.
(Skinner) $431

Pair of Victorian glass and silver-gilt Regimental decanters, George Richards, Elkington, London, 1864, the spout pierced with the Prince of Wales's plumes, 9½in. high.
(Butterfield & Butterfield)
                          $3,450

An early 'crisselled' decanter-jug, circa 1674, probably Ravenscroft, the oviform body molded with 'nipt diamond' waies' and applied with vertical bands of pierced ornament, 8¹/₂in. high.
(Christie's) $7,000

Edwardian cut glass claret jug of tapering cylindrical design, having plain silver plated mounts and scrolled handle, 11in. high.
(G. A. Key) $152

An early decanter-jug, circa 1680, the oviform body with vertically gadrooned lower part below a band of applied chain ornament, 9¹/₄in. high.
(Christie's) $1,650

Moser art glass pitcher, of transparent topaz amber decorated with polychrome enameled blossoms and applied teal-blue angular handle, 7¹/₂in. high.
(Skinner) $374

MISCELLANEOUS

Persian blue and black glaze
Qajar bottle, circa 1800,
depicting flowerheads and
scrolling vines, 11in. high.
(Skinner) $575

French bronze and painted glass
tantalus, late 19th century, the
front painted with an eye-
shaped reserve of Cupid and
Psyche, 14in. wide.
(Skinner) $1,495

A Lalique frosted glass figure of a
cockerel *'Coq Nain'* , on round
base, 8¼in.
(Dreweatt · Neate) $660

René Lalique, mascot
'Libellule', after 1928, clear and
frosted glass, molded as a
dragonfly with raised wings,
8¹/₈in. high.
(Sotheby's) $3,167

Pair of Bohemian cobalt blue
overlay cut to clear glass lustres,
with slender faceted prisms,
12in. high.
(Skinner) $1,265

A Central European dated
Masonic flask, with a short
neck, enameled with Masonic
instruments in a basket, and
inscribed in white enamel to the
reverse *Das Ehr Bahre maurer
hand nerck 1791*, 4¹/₅in. high.
(Christie's) $1,560

Empire style leaded glass and
gilt bronze mounted domed box,
early 20th century, 9in. wide.
(Skinner) $1,840

Daum, Landscape bonbonnière
and cover, circa 1920, gray glass
internally streaked with lime
green, etched and enameled in
green, aubergine and yellow,
4¼in. (Sotheby's) $3,749

Walnut three bottle tantalus
with plated cover and mounts,
fitted with three heavily faceted
decanters, early 20th century,
16in.
(G. A. Key) $512

MISCELLANEOUS

Large lead crystal glass jardinière, with dentil cut rim, heavily faceted with diamond and arcaded panels, 10in.
(G. A. Key) $113

A glass posset pot, applied with loop handles and a high curved spout, 11cm. high.
(Bearne's) $1,812

Daum gentian flower box and cover, circa 1905, internally decorated with pale blue and orange, the cover with three violet marquetrie-sur-verre flowers, 5¼in. diameter.
(Sotheby's) $4,399

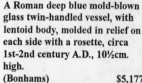

A Central European dated armorial amethyst flask, enameled in yellow, blue, white and red with the arms of Berne, the reverse with an inscription and the date 1736, 6½in. high.
(Christie's) $3,000

René Lalique Tete d'Aigle bookends, frosted colorless glass eagle head mounted on stepped colorless frosted glass base, 4¾in. high.
(Skinner) $863

A Roman deep blue mold-blown glass twin-handled vessel, with lentoid body, molded in relief on each side with a rosette, circa 1st-2nd century A.D., 10½cm. high.
(Bonhams) $5,177

Hawkes brilliant pueblo cut glass tray, with extremely fine hobstar cutting between bevelled circular interlocking devices, central 'Hawkes' trefoil mark, 11in. diameter.
(Skinner) $13,800

A 19th century French ebonized liqueur case, with brass string inlay and applied metal mounts centered by medallions, 12½in. wide.
(Andrew Hartley) $1,000

Almeric Walter pâte de verre crab tray, designed by Henri Berge in heart-shape with large crustacean at top, 6¼in. wide.
(Skinner) $5,463

PAPERWEIGHTS

Debbie Tarsitano bee-in-blossom paperweight, curved yellow centered pink blossom with full bumblebee inside, 3¼in. diameter.
(Skinner) $863

New England Glass Co. leaf nosegay, overlapping blue, pink, yellow and green leaves with millefiore cane at center, 2¾in. diameter.
(Skinner) $1,725

Rick Ayotte butterfly and blossoms paperweight, large green and yellow butterfly above a spray of yellow centered white flowers, 3½in. diameter.
(Skinner) $863

Yaffa Sikorsky-Todd scenic glass paperweight, colorless flattened sphere internally decorated front and back in landscape of green leafy trees, 5¾in. high.
(Skinner) $374

St. Louis double overlay bouquet paperweight, cluster of red, white and blue five-petal blossoms on leafy stems, star-cut base, 3in. diameter.
(Skinner) $489

Paul J. Stankard blueberries and butterfly paperweight, orange and brown butterfly above blueberry spray showing buds, with 'PS 95' cane, 3¼in. diameter.
(Skinner) $2,185

Bob Banford double overlay floral paperweight, yellow over white faceted to colorless with yellow centered purple blossoms, 'B' cane.
(Skinner) $690

Bob Banford basket of roses paperweight, double overlay red cut to white to colorless basket-form, 3in. diameter.
(Skinner) $1,150

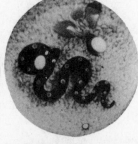

Bob Banford snake paperweight, red spotted black snake on yellow sand ground, blue flower at right, 'B' cane left, 2¾in. diameter.
(Skinner) $460

PAPERWEIGHTS

Paul J. Stankard trillium paperweight, cluster of three yellow and red centered white three-petal blossoms on green stem surrounds, $2^{3}/_{4}$in. diameter. (Skinner) $1,840

A Baccarat faceted garlanded sulphide weight mid 19th century, enclosing a half-bust portrait of Saint Nicholas named in blue enamel, $2^{5}/_{8}$in. diameter. (Christie's) $465

Clichy blue and white swirl paperweight, pinwheel centring four blue, four white, pink center canes, 3in. diameter. (Skinner) $1,035

Baccarat butterfly paperweight, red alternating white cane garland centering large butterfly with purple body, $3^{1}/_{8}$in. diameter. (Skinner) $3,738

Almeric Walter, Chameleon paper weight, 1920s, pâte-de-verre, realistically modeled in shades of mustard and mottled green/blue, 3in. (Sotheby's) $4,874

Kaziun silhouette portrait paperweight, black and white cameo reportedly of Louise Kaziun surrounded by four star and two red heart canes, 2in. diameter. (Skinner) $805

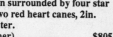

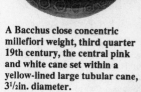

A Baccarat faceted garlanded sulphide weight, mid 19th century, Louis XIV facing to the right within a garland of green and white and pink and white canes, 3in. diameter. (Christie's) $775

St. Louis encased double overlay millefiore magnum paperweight, closepacked mushroom millefiore dated *SL 1978* within red cut to white, $4^{1}/_{2}$in. diameter. (Skinner) $1,380

A Bacchus close concentric millefiori weight, third quarter 19th century, the central pink and white cane set within a yellow-lined large tubular cane, $3^{1}/_{2}$in. diameter. (Christie's) $3,500

SCENT BOTTLES

Art Deco period faceted glass scent bottle with hallmarked silver collar and large faceted glass stopper, Birmingham 1919, 7in. high.
(G. A. Key) $146

A pair of Victorian silver-mounted cut-glass scent bottles, 15cm. high, maker's mark *C.M.*, Birmingham 1889.
(Bearne's) $430

Oval scent bottle with gilt metal cover and mount, painted with scene of figures in 18th century clothing, dancing in a garden, 19th century, 2in.
(G. A. Key) $259

A 19th century Dutch gold-mounted cut-glass scent bottle, the octagonal cover with filigree floral center, circa 1850, 9.6cm. long.
(Phillips) $426

Pair of Carder Steuben Flemish blue perfume jars, with swirled optic ribbing and threaded conforming stoppers, 3¾in. high.
(Skinner) $460

A William and Mary mounted glass scent bottle cum-vinaigrette with pomander fitted in ball finial, circa 1700, 9.5cm. long.
(Phillips) $988

A Victorian silver mounted globular scent bottle, the body and stopper engraved and painted with foliage and ribbons, London 1892.
(Bearne's) $503

Two metal mounted porcelain figural scent bottles, Germany, 19th century, modeled as male and female figures holding dogs, each with removable head, 3¼in. high.
(Skinner) $431

A Victorian silver-gilt mounted glass scent bottle with faceted body, the spring-action mount with engraved foliate scrolls, 1849.
(Phillips) $274

SCENT BOTTLES

'Maderas de Oriente', a clear
scent bottle and stopper for
Myrugia, of tapering cylindrical
form, applied paper label, 11cm.
high overall.
(Christie's) $203

Double overlay paperweight
cologne, crimson red over white
over colorless squat bottle with
five oval facet windows, 7in. high.
(Skinner) $460

'Au Soleil', a frosted scent bottle
and stopper, for Lubin, the
compressed base pulled into a
slender neck, 14cm. high.
(Christie's) $463

René Lalique Bouchon Mures
perfume flaçon, colorless
barrel shaped bottle with black
ribbing, molded flawless tiara
stopper of matte black, 5½in.
high.
(Skinner) $9,200

A pair of Victorian silver-
mounted cut-glass scent bottles
of oblong form, the glass with
star-cut decoration, 14.5cm.
high, William Crine, London
1893.
(Bearne's) $1,083

René Lalique Bouchon Fleurs de
Pommier perfume flaçon,
colorless barrel-shaped bottle
with green patine in scalloped
ridges, 5½in. high.
(Skinner) $10,062

A French opaque pale-turquoise
scent-bottle and stopper circa
1860, decorated with
irregularly-edged and plain gilt
bands, 6½in. high.
(Christie's) $927

European Art Deco cut glass
perfume bottle, angular squared
colorless vessel decorated with
overlaid black geometric designs
in the Josef Hoffman style, 8¼in.
(Skinner) $373

A Victorian mounted clear glass
scent bottle cum-vinaigrette
with a flat base and a bulbous
cover, unmarked, circa 1880,
7cm. long.
(Phillips) $334

SHADES

Leaded glass and silvered metal ceiling lamp, composed of opalescent white segments arranged in geometric progression with paneled apron drop, 20in. diameter.
(Skinner)   **$748**

Hanging parrot ceiling light, attributed to Pittsburgh, globe of crackled glass with two blue highly stylized exotic birds, 10in. diameter.
(Skinner)   **$431**

Leaded glass chandelier, umbrella-shaped dome shade in preponderantly pink, blue and green glass segments in floral motif, 27in. diameter.
(Skinner)   **$1,035**

Gallé cameo glass plafonnier, conical flaring shade of frosted shades of green and grey layered in maroon over green, 11½in. diameter.
(Skinner)   **$3,220**

Obverse painted hanging lantern, of crackled glass handpainted in stylized Persian scene with arched panels housing costumed figures and fountains, 13in. high.
(Skinner)   **$403**

Tiffany O'Brien lamp ceiling shade, hipped dome composed of leaded green glass segments arranged as brickwork, 22in. diameter.
(Skinner)   **$10,350**

TAZZAS

A baluster tazza, circa 1725, the stem with a triple annulated knop above a plain section enclosing an elongated tear and basal knop, 9½in. diameter.
(Christie's)   **$820**

A pair of French 'opale' ormolu-mounted opaline tazze, 19th century, with chased gilt-metal mounts to the rims and footrims, 6¾in. diameter.
(Christie's)   **$1,782**

A façon de Venise tazza bowl, the white latticino stripes alternately gauze and spiral, 18.5cm. diameter, late 17th century.
(Christie's)   **$962**

TUMBLERS

A Thuringian dated and engraved tumbler, engraved with the initials *GFS* on a coronet above the date *1739* and a heart, 4¹/₂in. high. (Christie's) **$2,000**

A Venetian latticinio cylindrical tumbler, late 17th/18th century, in vetro a reticello, 3⁵/₈in. high. (Christie's) **$1,560**

A Bohemian engraved cylindrical tumbler, circa 1810, with a continuous scene of equestrian figures, hounds and huntsmen in a landscape, 4in. high. (Christie's) **$2,200**

A lower Austrian Zwischengold dated armorial tumbler by Johann Joseph Mildner, 1792, Gutenbrunn, set with an oval double-walled medallion gilt on a ruby-ground with a coat-of-arms within a rope-twist, 4³/₈in. (Christie's) **$11,000**

A North Bohemian engraved cylindrical tumbler, circa 1830, engraved with a scene of a coach and four, the reverse with the monogram *AB* within a hunting-horn held in the talons of an eagle, 5⁵/₈in. high. (Christie's) **$5,150**

A German engraved tumbler, circa 1740, the four oval cartouches with figures at various pursuits representing the Seasons and inscribed *Frühling, Sommer, Herbst* and *Winter*, 5¹/₈in. high. (Christie's) **$1,560**

A north Bohemian dated cylindrical tumbler, engraved in the manner of Anton Simm, with the Virgin and Saint Anne above the inscription *S. Anna*, above the date *1841*, 5³/₈in. high. (Christie's) **$1,000**

A Baccarat cut cylindrical sulphide tumbler, cut and polished with a band of stylized leaves aside a central cabouchon, 10cm. high, mid 19th century. (Christie's) **$375**

A mammoth christening tumbler, circa 1800, inscribed *THE HIGH ROAD TO A CHRISTENING* on a banner above *H.C.A. SAVAGE/PRIORS HARDWICHE*, 7¹/₂in. high. (Christie's) **$640**

VASES

Loetz vase, circa 1905, cased orange with ripples of iridescent white and electric green, 6½in. (Sotheby's) $1,687

A pâte-de-verre glass vase, by Gabriel Argy-Rousseau, the ovoid body molded with scrolling foliage and tinted in pink and purple, 12.8cm. high. (Bearne's) $2,831

Daum, Bat vase, circa 1905, etched with airborne bats above a cityscape with steeple, 10in. (Sotheby's) $5,249

Gabriel Argy-Rousseau, Chameleon vase, 1929, pâte-de-verre, clear glass decorated in shades of purple, pink and lilac, 5½in. (Sotheby's) $5,624

Pair of Bohemian ruby overlay cut and frosted glass vases, late 19th century, each cut with deer in a forest landscape, 14½in. high. (Skinner) $1,035

A French amber and blue flattened oviform vase, each side applied with a frog below a seaweed rim, supported by four frog's leg feet, 24cm. high, late 19th century. (Christie's) $611

Loetz vase, circa 1905, cased purple glass with streaks of white and iridescent pale green, 3¼in. (Sotheby's) $2,812

Emile Gallé, Gentians vase, circa 1900, opaque cream glass, overlaid with turquoise and green and etched with flowers and foliage, 7in. (Sotheby's) $2,624

Emile Gallé, Prunus vase, circa 1900, gray glass internally decorated with orange/yellow, 10¾in. (Sotheby's) $5,624

VASES

René Lalique, vase 'Palestre', after 1928, frosted glass molded with a frieze of naked athletes, 16in.
(Sotheby's) $17,808

René Lalique, 'Archers' vase, after 1921, amber glass molded with archers beneath a flock of large birds, 10½in.
(Sotheby's) $6,748

Daum, Butterflies and Hortensia vase, circa 1905, clear glass internally decorated with pale yellow and pink, 19¾in.
(Sotheby's) $7,498

Daum, a rare and unusual floral vase, circa 1902-25, clear glass, internally decorated with mauve and mustard yellow trails and profuse internal bubbling, 5in.
(Sotheby's) $16,496

Pair of unusual Art Nouveau period pewter mounted glass vases of tapering cylindrical form, slightly flared rims, 1858, 13in. high.
(G. A. Key) $1,350

René Lalique, vase, 'Goblet Six Figurines', after 1912, smoked glass, molded with six vertical panels with draped female figures, 7½in.
(Sotheby's) $2,062

Emile Gallé, Landscape vase, circa 1900, gray glass decorated with ocher, etched with a wooded lake scene, 17in.
(Sotheby's) $5,249

Emile Gallé, Snake's head fritillary vase, circa 1900, gray glass internally decorated with yellow at the neck and base, 7½in.
(Sotheby's) $3,749

Daum, Bat vase, circa 1905, gray glass internally mottled with orange and yellow, overlaid with mauve, 9in.
(Sotheby's) $5,624

VASES

Czechoslovakian art glass vase, of transparent amber glass encasing broad brown gridwork decoration against bright orange interior, 9in. high.
(Skinner) **$201**

A Lalique Druides opalescent glass vase, with molded and polished berries, impressed *R Lalique* mark, 7in. high.
(Andrew Hartley) **$713**

Loetz dimpled vase, circa 1900, pale pink tinted iridescent glass washed with pale blue and green-gold iridescence, 7¼in. high.
(Sotheby's) **$1,935**

Important Orrefors Ariel underwater scenic portrait vase, decorated with purple-aubergine airtrap figures of two mermaids, Neptune and various marine life elements.
(Skinner) **$9,775**

Emile Gallé orchid vase, circa 1900, pink tinted glass internally mottled with cream, overlaid with warm brown and finely carved with orchid blossoms, 5½in. high.
(Sotheby's) **$7,038**

Rare Tiffany 'stone glass' vase, pinched to quatreform composed of mottled green-white-granite gray with deep green and iridescent gold pulled striations, 3⅜in. high.
(Skinner) **$3,565**

Early Orrefors Simon Gate Graal vase, of delicate smoky topaz crystal internally decorated with maroon colored leaf outlines, 7½in. high.
(Skinner) **$2,415**

René Lalique Chamilles vase, oversize frosted colorless glass sphere molded with overlapping leaves polished at high relief motif, 14in. high.
(Skinner) **$2,500**

Rare Tiffany reticulated gold iridescent vase, with eight pierced dimples at rim and interior flower arrangement webwork, 4in. high.
(Skinner) **$1,035**

VASES

An Orrefors glass vase, designed by Vicke Lindstrand, cut and etched with a naked female figure dancing with a scarf, 18.5cm. high.
(Christie's) $556

Durand crackle glass vase, extraordinary transparent ambergris with ten bright ruby red rib-stripes crackled and iridised overall, 6in. high.
(Skinner) $1,725

Schneider LeVerre cameo glass vase, angular bulbous vessel of mottled amber in colorless glass layered in orange and brown stripes, 12³/₄in. high.
(Skinner) $1,265

Gabriel Argy-Rousseau vase 'Le Jardin des Hesperides', 1926, with a frieze of Grecian maidens picking apples, the base with a band of Greek key design, 9⁵/₈in. high.
(Sotheby's) $28,152

Daum enameled cameo glass lilac vase, with olive green and white overlay cameo-etched front and back as lilac leafy branches and blossoms, 6³/₄in. high.
(Skinner) $3,450

Emile Gallé poppy vase, circa 1900, clear glass internally decorated with pale turquoise, overlaid with orange and etched with flowering sprays, 9³/₄in. high.
(Sotheby's) $1,232

Attributed to Steuben, decorated 'aurene' vase, circa 1900, pale green glass washed with pale blue, green and pinky gold iridescence, 8¹/₂in. high.
(Sotheby's) $1,935

Carder Steuben etched blue jade on alabaster vase, decorated by glossy medium Blue Jade etched in fine Sherwood stylized blossoms, 7in. high.
(Skinner) $978

Early Orrefors engraved art glass vase, decorated with a pair of graceful skaters engraved by Arthur Diessner in 1937, 9¹/₄in. high.
(Skinner) $748

Bohemian art glass vase, broad Loetz-type olive green rose bowl form raised on solid pedestal foot, 8in. high.
(Skinner)   **$275**

Tiffany 'favrile' 'Jack-in-the-Pulpit' vase, 1905, yellow glass washed with golden, amber and pink iridescence, 18¼in. high.
(Sotheby's)   **$7,918**

Loetz vase with undulating rim, circa 1910, emerald green glass striated with flame orange interspersed by spots, 7½in. high.
(Sotheby's)   **$1,760**

Emile Gallé trumpet flower vase, circa 1900, dichroic orange and green glass, overlaid with green and red and etched with sprays of trumpet flowers, 15³⁄₈in. high.
(Sotheby's)   **$13,196**

Baccarat pair of grasshopper vases, circa 1900, opalescent glass, molded with flowering stems, the bases molded as grasshoppers on blossoms, 8½in. high.
(Sotheby's)   **$2,639**

Emile Gallé cherry 'blow-out' vase, circa 1900, gray glass internally decorated with amber, overlaid with red and mold-blown in high relief, 11¼in. high.
(Sotheby's)   **$7,390**

Gabriel Argy-Rousseau coupe 'Etoiles', 1924, pâte-de-verre, clear glass internally streaked with sealing-wax red, purple and black, 3⁷⁄₈in. high.
(Sotheby's)   **$4,399**

Emile Gallé two-handled clematis vase, circa 1900, internally decorated with milky white, overlaid with purple and etched with flowering clematis, 10in. high.
(Sotheby's)   **$2,815**

Loetz silver overlaid art glass vase, decorated by iridised gold-amber horizontal chain elements and three applied trailing prunts, 6⁷⁄₈in. high.
(Skinner)   **$2,070**

GLASS

Loetz four-handled vase, circa 1910, pale green glass washed with purple, blue and green-gold iridescence, 9⁷/₈in. high.
(Sotheby's) $6,686

Bohemian art glass turtle vase, with applied transparent lavender icicle rim in the Harrach style, 5¹/₂in. high.
(Skinner) $345

Legras cameo glass vase, etched and tinted colorless oval body decorated in pink and maroon leafy branches overall, 10³/₄in. high.
(Skinner) $633

Legras cameo glass vase, flared colorless oval body tinted and etched overall with maroon and pink flowering branches, 12in. high.
(Skinner) $546

Pair of engraved overlaid british glass vases, attributed to Northwood school, of cobalt blue glass cased to opal white, 9in. high.
(Skinner) $1,725

Durand cobalt blue heart and vine vase, with broad silver-gold iridescent heart-leaf and vertical vine decoration, base signed in script, *Durand*, 9¹/₂in. high.
(Skinner) $1,380

Andre Delatte cameo glass vase, bulbous pink oval body layered in deep maroon cameo-etched as exotic blossoms, 8in. high.
(Skinner) $690

Daum, poppy vase, circa 1910, clear glass internally decorated with yellow and orange and etched and enameled with poppy stems, 4⁵/₈in. high.
(Sotheby's) $2,639

Tiffany 'favrile' lily pad vase, 1906, clear glass washed with golden iridescence, decorated with green leaves and stems, 8in. high.
(Sotheby's) $1,584

WINE GLASSES

A 'Beilby' wine glass, the ogee bowl enameled in white with a fruiting vine, 14.8cm. high. (Bearne's) $997

A goblet, the round funnel bowl set on a baluster stem containing a single tear, folded conical foot. (Bearne's) $695

A cordial glass, the small bucket bowl engraved with hatched panels and foliage, 17cm. high. (Bearne's) $1,238

A mercury-twist engraved cordial-glass, circa 1750, the bowl with fruiting-vine, the stem with a central core encircled by four spirals, 6⁷/₈in. high. (Christie's) $920

An engraved balustroid wine-glass, circa 1740, with a border of meandering fruiting-vine set on a cushion knop and double annular knop, 6¹/₂in. high. (Christie's) $880

An opaque-twist cordial-glass, circa 1765, with funnel bowl, the stem with a laminated corkscrew core encircled by two four-ply spirals, 6⁷/₈in. high. (Christie's) $700

A toasting glass, the drawn trumpet bowl set on a multi-ply stem in blue, red and white, 17.5cm. high. (Bearne's) $2,718

An emerald-green wine-glass, circa 1765, the cup-shaped bowl on an almost hollow plain stem and conical foot, 5¹/₄in. high. (Christie's) $440

A wine glass, the solid base round funnel bowl set on a baluster stem with annular knop, 14.2cm. high. (Bearne's) $1,787

WINE GLASSES

A wine glass, the bucket bowl set on a canary-yellow and opaque twist stem, 15cm. high.
(Bearne's) $1,359

A 'Privateer' wine glass, the small ovoid bowl, engraved with a ship and a dove, conical foot, 14.2cm. high.
(Bearne's) $3,020

A wine glass, the trumpet bowl engraved with a Jacobite rose with two buds, 16.4cm. high.
(Bearne's) $1,057

A goblet, the funnel bowl set on a four sided Salesian stem, containing a single tear, 18cm. high.
(Bearne's) $2,039

A pedestal-stemmed ale-flute, circa 1725, the slender funnel bowl set on a shouldered tapering octagonal stem with eight diamond-shaped molded bosses, $8^5/\sin$. high.
(Christie's) $825

An unusual wine glass, the round funnel bowl set on a thick 'Barrel' stem containing a single tear, 13.8cm. high.
(Bearne's) $2,114

A wine glass, the bell bowl set on knopped stem containing blue, red, green and white twists, 16.4cm. high.
(Bearne's) $4,077

A wine glass, the ogee bowl set on a knopped baluster stem containing a single tear, 16.6cm. high.
(Bearne's) $755

A cyder glass, the tall funnel bowl engraved with an apple spray and a moth, conical foot, 19.4cm. high.
(Bearne's) $1,268

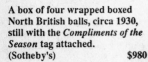

A box of four wrapped boxed North British balls, circa 1930, still with the *Compliments of the Season* tag attached.
(Sotheby's) $980

An 18th century tin box filled with member's voting papers for membership to the Thistle Golf Club, Leith, and documents relating to Committee meetings.
(Sotheby's) $80,755

An Art Deco jug, featuring a Louis Wain golfing cat, 6³/₄in. high.
(Sotheby's) $623

A silver two-handled golf trophy, inscribed *The Nairn Golf Club, Open Amateur Tournament Challenge Cup*, on stepped rectangular wooden base, 6¹/₄in. high.
(Christie's) $611

Golfing, The Great Indoor Golf Game, Invented by Sir Frederick Franklin Bt., Kompactum Edition, in original box, complete with folding board.
(Christie's) $331

The Vardon Trophy, 1952, won by Harry Weetman with a points average of 8.77, the trophy itself is an Elkington bronze figure of Harry Vardon, early 20th century, 8in. high.
(Sotheby's) $1,158

An Osmond automaton golf bag, circa 1910, in reasonable condition but with replacement handles.
(Sotheby's) $677

Three copies of the 1933 Ryder Cup souvenir program, 1933 together with a copy of the 1937 program.
(Sotheby's) $2,674

A Silver King golf ball advertising figure, circa 1930, in pressed cardboard, in good condition.
(Sotheby's) $2,406

A Royal Doulton advertising jug, for Colonel Bogey Whisky, 7¹/₂in. high.
(Christie's) **$1,224**

A pair of spelter bookends, circa 1930, being a golfer with his caddie, the golfer 10in. high.
(Sotheby's) **$713**

Interesting hallmarked small silver spirit flask, the front enameled with a golfer, 3 x 2¹/₂in., Chester 1933.
(G. A. Key) **$409**

The Rules of Thistle Golf Club, 1824, printed by James Ballantyne & Co. Edinburgh, in good condition with leather bindings.
(Sotheby's) **$13,369**

A white-metal figure, bearing a plaque inscribed *Presented to W.A. Wright of Wolverhampton Wanderers Football Club, by The Football League to mark the completion of 20 years loyal service as a player*, 8in. high.
(Christie's) **$1,780**

A Croham Hurst golf club course record '58', Harry Weetman, hallmarked silver frame, *Birmingham 1955*, card dated *29/1/56*.
(Sotheby's) **$801**

A silver and enamel match safe by Samson Morden, with a golfer at the top of his back swing, hallmarked *London 1899*.
(Sotheby's) **$2,317**

A set of three Bobby Jones Flicker Books, No. 1 Drive and Putt; Brassie and Iron Shots and Driver and Mashie Shots.
(Christie's) **$734**

A Dunlop golf ball man, circa 1935, together with a Penfold Man, circa 1935, in plaster of Paris.
(Sotheby's) **$1,158**

A Burleigh ware golfing jug, 1930s, yellow ground, handle a golfer having driven, 20cm. high.
(Sotheby's) $320

A silver mounted pocket watch stand of shaped rectangular form, worked with a humourous panel of a caddy, and fitted with a watch with white enamel dial, 6in. wide.
(Christie's) $845

A fine silver masonic golfing trophy, hallmarked *Sheffield 1927*, with good golfing figure to lid, and base bearing shields of winners, 21in.
(Sotheby's) $1,672

Royal Doulton Series Ware plate 'Fine feathers make fine birds', 'Old Saws speak the truth'.
(Lyle) $280

Royal Doulton rack plate 'The Nineteenth Hole', 10¾in. diam.
(Lyle) $280

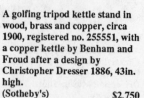

A glass vase of campana form painted with a panel of the Golfers at Blackheath after Abbot, 7½in. high.
(Christie's) $880

A golfing tripod kettle stand in wood, brass and copper, circa 1900, registered no. 255551, with a copper kettle by Benham and Froud after a design by Christopher Dresser 1886, 43in. high.
(Sotheby's) $2,750

Harry Vardon, an oak framed photographic print, published by the Swan Electric Engraving Company, 1905, signed by Vardon, 40 x 28cm.
(Sotheby's) $706

A late Victorian electro-plated metal inkstand, surmounted by a figure of a golfer at the top of his backswing, flanked on either side by a mesh-pattern golf ball ink-pot, 9in. wide.
(Christie's) $600

A ceramic tile, 20th century, reverse marked *C.S.A.* and signed in ink *VG*, cream ground painted with a golfing figure, 13 x 13cm.
(Sotheby's) $175

A Spalding Glory dozen golf ball box, circa 1920, containing eleven various golf balls.
(Sotheby's) $1,745

A cast iron parlour putter stand, the spreading column modeled with golf clubs, the arched tripod base cast with crossed golf clubs, 35in. high.
(Christie's) $500

A six box of Heavy Colonel Green Dot dimple golf balls.
(Phillips) $2,432

A Doulton Lambeth golfing mug, 1894, with silver rim hallmarked *Sheffield 1894*, 15cm. high.
(Sotheby's) $560

A huge purpose made unique leather golf bag, together with a Bogey putter made by Foster Bros. Ashbourne and 17 other woods, irons and putters.
(Sotheby's) $557

A Lenox silver mounted three handled cup, American, circa 1900, the body with three hand-painted scenes in green, with painter's name *Ignel*, 14cm. high.
(Sotheby's) $6,150

The Golf Courses of the British Isles, by Bernard Darwin, illustrated by Harry Rowntree, 1910, in good condition.
(Sotheby's) $749

A smooth gutta mold, circa 1855, together with a photocopy of a letter from David Stirk with regard to this mold.
(Sotheby's) $2,317

A fine Royal Doulton series ware biscuit barrel, circa 1925, inscribed *All fools are not Knaves but all Knaves are fools*.
(Sotheby's) $927

A Victorian silver salver, the center with presentation inscription *Dedicated to Henry Cotton MBE, on the Occasion of his Winning the Open Championship, 1948*, 18in. diameter.
(Christie's) $2,622

The Open Championship Medal for 1885, inscribed *1885 Won by Robert Martin, St. Andrews, 171 strokes*, with blue silk ribbon, in original box.
(Christie's) $41,952

The Thistle Golf Club, circa 1820, a finely bound hand written book with a list of members and their accounts, also the original manuscript for the Rules of the Thistle Golf Club.
(Sotheby's) $40,998

A framed and glazed photograph of old Tom Morris, in his traditional pose at St Andrews, photographed and copyrighted by J. Patrick.
(Sotheby's) $980

The Rules and Regulations of The Royal Perth Golfing Society, with a list of members printed for the Society, by R. Morrison, 1834.
(Christie's) $41,952

Viennese cold painted bronze figure of a golfer, early 20th century, painted in multicolors on a naturalistic base, 6$\frac{1}{2}$in. high.
(Skinner) $3,450

A Copeland late Spode jug, the
dark blue ground decorated in
white relief with golfing figures,
cracked, 6¾in. high.
(Christie's) $296

A pair of Irish Golf Union
medals, one hallmarked *15ct.
gold, Chester 1909* and one
hallmarked *Birmingham 1910.*
(Sotheby's) $1,569

British Golf Links, edited by
Horace Hutchinson, published
by J.S. Virtue & Co. Ltd 1897,
in good condition.
(Sotheby's) $801

Scotland, The Laws and Acts of
Parliament by various Scottish
Kings and Queens, collected by
Sir Thomas Murray of
Glendook, Edinburgh 1681,
including the Act of 1457.
(Phillips) $456

A North British golf ball
advertising wall clock, circa
1930, formerly belonging to A.J.
Miles who was a Canadian
Match Play Champion in 1925,
8in. diameter.
(Sotheby's) $499

A silver golfing trophy, on four
dimpled golf ball supports and
stepped wooden plinth,
inscribed *Kodogaya Country
Club, Presented by The HCC
Keiro-kai*, 1858, 5½in. high.
(Christie's) $664

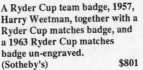

A fine silver enamel vesta case
by Samson Morden, hallmarked
London 1891, depicting a golfer
on his back swing, 57 x 31mm.
(Sotheby's) $2,762

A Ryder Cup team badge, 1957,
Harry Weetman, together with a
Ryder Cup matches badge, and
a 1963 Ryder Cup matches
badge un-engraved.
(Sotheby's) $801

Tulloch (W.W.), The Life of
Tom Morris, with glimpses of
St. Andrews and its golfing
celebrities, London 1908.
(Christie's) $839

BALLS

A feather ball of good color but well used.
(Phillips) $3,040

A wrapped Zoome.
(Phillips) $2,128

A feather-filled golf ball, circa 1840.
(Christie's) $4,195

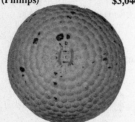

An Army & Navy No. 1 bramble (near mint).
(Phillips) $638

A smooth Gutty ball, circa 1850.
(Christie's) $3,165

A Pal early square dimple ball (mint).
(Phillips) $578

An Allan 28 feather ball, circa 1840, by Allan Robertson of St. Andrews, the *Allan* and *28* are reasonably legible.
(Sotheby's) $2,227

Ball No. 2 from the Woking golf club collection, a feather golf ball, circa 1840, in well-used condition, with identifying red spots to each pole.
(Sotheby's) $4,100

A good hand hammered gutty ball, circa 1855, by an unknown maker, in good, little used condition, 1.7in. diameter.
(Sotheby's) $3,387

A feather-filled golf ball, circa 1840, stamped *J. Ramsay* and *Dundas of Dundas*, twice.
(Christie's) $16,606

An unnamed feather golf ball, circa 1840, in good condition, approximately 1.58in. diameter.
(Sotheby's) $6,774

A hand hammered gutty ball, circa 1855, in used condition but still bearing the majority of its paint.
(Sotheby's) $1,693

BALLS

A red painted hand hammered gutty golf ball, circa 1855. (Sotheby's) $3,565

A wrapped Army & Navy No. 1 bramble. (Phillips) $760

A Henley with cross pattern (near mint). (Phillips) $7,600

The Corona early square dimple. (Phillips) $608

A feather-filled golf ball, circa 1840. (Christie's) $2,375

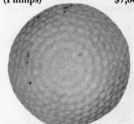

'The Club' bramble, (near mint). (Phillips) $426

A Tom Morris hand hammered gutta in the Forgan style, marked *T. Morris* and stamped *28*. (Phillips) $9,424

A smooth gutta percha golf ball, circa 1855, in very poor condition having been well chewed by a canine. (Sotheby's) $178

A feather ball marked *27*, circa 1840, with the last letter of the name showing ...*N*, probably being Allan Robertson. (Sotheby's) $4,278

A hand-cut gutta percha golf ball, circa 1850, badly damaged on one side. (Christie's) $489

Ball No. 1 from the Woking golf club collection, a good unnamed feather golf ball, circa 1830. (Sotheby's) $6,774

A mesh-pattern gutty by Robert Forgan & Son, St. Andrews, stamped *Forgan*, twice. (Christie's) $3,321

CLUBS

A Standard Golf Co. McPhee model long nosed putter. (Phillips) $290

A Marriott Patent croquet mallet chipper and putter, with hickory shaft. (Sotheby's) $1,283

A Standard Golf Co. 'Z' model putter. (Phillips) $200

A Brown's Patent major niblick, stamped *Montrose N.B.* (Phillips) $2,736

An unusual steel-shafted putter, the cylindrical brass-covered head enclosing a hardwood center core. (Christie's) $315

A Jonko putter by Gibson of Kinghorn, circa 1930, with snail-like profile and hickory shaft. (Sotheby's) $1,569

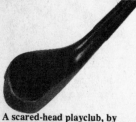

A scared-head playclub, by W.R. Reith, the head stamped *W.R. Reith*, with leather grip and listings. (Christie's) $385

A rare 'Coste' Jeu de Mail hardwood iron-bound club, French, mid 18th century, stamped on the head *COSTE*. (Sotheby's) $4,456

Club No. 1 from the Woking golf club collection, a James Wilson of St. Andrews putter, circa 1860, 38in. long. (Sotheby's) $7,487

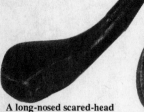

A long-nosed scared-head wooden niblick by Robert Forgan, with Prince of Wales feathers, the sole with brass plate, possibly re-shafted. (Christie's) $1,310

A Brown's Patent water mashie, with pierced face, possibly made by Wintons of Montrose, the shaft lacking grip. (Christie's) $734

A long-nosed scared-head playclub by Aitken, the sole with ram's horn inset, the bowed greenheart shaft, with leather grip and listing. (Christie's) $454

GOLFING MEMORABILIA

CLUBS

A Standard Golf Co. RL2½ duplex club.
(Phillips)　$1,225

Pope's Patent Blockhead putter (now illegal).
(Phillips)　$638

A McEwan short spoon in golden brown beech.
(Phillips)　$4,408

A cut-off nose iron clubhead, the shaft reduced, the hozel 5½in. long.
(Christie's)　$2,447

A very rare L.H. Vories Patent adjustable iron, patented December 28th 1916, with a strange three sided head.
(Sotheby's)　$2,139

A long-nosed scared-head playclub, by Tom Morris, the sole with ram's horn inset.
(Christie's)　$2,622

An Urquhart's Patent adjustable iron, No. 3157, now with later steel shaft and metal connector.
(Christie's)　$734

A fine Simplex Patent lofter, circa 1908, with brass inset leading edge to aluminium head with shaped hickory shaft.
(Sotheby's)　$2,674

A transitional scared-head driver, by Robert Forgan, the head stamped *R. Forgan*, the sole with ram's horn inset.
(Christie's)　$1,135

A Tom Morris long nosed putter, circa 1885, with beech head and hickory shaft, in reasonable condition.
(Sotheby's)　$1,783

A scared-head transitional playclub by Robert Forgan, with unusually wide face, with Prince of Wales feathers, with leather grip and listing, the head 2¼in. wide. (Christie's)　$1,485

A rare 'The Timperley' Schenectady type putter stamped *Mitchell & Co., Manchester, Patent No. 12743*.
(Phillips)　$274

405

An Edison Bell Handephon portable wooden gramophone, circa 1920.
(Auction Team Köln)

$195

A Swiss Mikiphone gramophone, round, plated case, and large collapsible black celluloid resonator, 1926.
(Auction Team Köln)

$935

An Odeon horn gramophone with ball-and-socket tonearm, double-spring motor and walnut case with egg-and-dart molding, 15in. diam.
(Christie's)

$968

A Tournaphone "A" horn gramophone, by Symphonion with Beltona-Tournaphone soundbox in oak case with Snell, Swansea retailer's label and shaded yellow and cream flower horn, 17in. diam., 1910.
(Christie's)

$879

A Mickey Mouse child's plastic gramophone by General Electric USA, in white plastic case, arm in the form of a Mickey Mouse arm, 1960s.
(Auction Team Köln)

$310

An EMG Mk. XB gramophone, No. 203 with Expert four-spring sound-box, replacement Garrard Super motor, oak case and papier-mache horn, 29½in. diameter.
(Christie's)

$4,750

An Edison disk phonograph Model B80, for Edison vertical disks, mahogany case, circa 1913.
(Auction Team Köln)

$583

A German Nirona tinplate toy gramophone, with spring drive and typical bell-shaped soundbox, 1915.
(Auction Team Köln)

$506

The Sonora gramophone, with original Sonora-Maestrophone reproducer, mahogany case, American, 1914.
(Auction Team Köln)

$350

His Master's Voice table gramophone, with built-in speaker and volume regulating front doors, mahogany case. (Auction Team Köln) **$365**

An HMV Model 5 (HEBM) mahogany horn gramophone, with Exhibition soundbox, single spring motor, 10-inch turntable and mahogany case, 18in. diam. (Christie's) **$1,231**

An HMV Model 460 table grand gramophone, with Lumière pleated diaphragm and gilt fittings, in quarter-veneered mahogany case, 1924-5. (Christie's) **$2,852**

A lacquer HMV cabinet gramophone, Model 160 but now with replacement motor-board, the cabinet with chinoiserie lacquer to the front, sides and lid, 40¾in. high, basically circa 1924. (Christie's) **$1,248**

The Tango Two, an English printed cardboard dancing couple, who dance on the gramophone edge in time to the music. (Auction Team Köln) **$375**

An HMV Model 163 mahogany cabinet gramophone with 5a soundbox and re-entrant tone-chamber enclosed by fret and paneled doors, 39½in. high. (Christie's) **$1,070**

A Pathéphone table-top gramophone for vertical discs, blue horn integrated into wooden case, circa 1910. (Auction Team Köln) **$1,790**

The Columbia Disc graphophone, a mahogany table-top machine with original chrome horn and amplifier, 1903. (Auction Team Köln) **$2,957**

An English standard Operaphone gramophone in the form of a mahogany grand piano, stores 40 disks vertically, circa 1920. (Auction Team Köln) **$1,712**

The Crucifixion with selected scenes from the Bible, Russia, early 19th century, traditionally painted, 42½ x 35in. (Christie's) $5,348

The Mother of God, 18th century, depicted half-length from a Deisis group, 45 x 40cm. (Christie's) $900

Christ Pantocrator, Russia, late 19th century, the oklad with maker's mark of A. Liubavin, St. Petersburg, circa 1895, 8¼ x 7in. (Christie's) $7,298

The Deisis and the Twelve Apostles, Balkans, possibly Serbia, 17th century, Christ enthroned flanked by the Mother of God and Saint John the Baptist in the central panel, 19¼ x 14½in. (Christie's) $3,457

Saints Policarp, Nikifor, Alexandra and Theodosia, Russia, Palekh style, 19th century, the oklad with maker's mark in cyrillic of E. Samokish, Moscow, 1899-1908, 11½ x 9½in. (Christie's) $2,317

Mother of God Enthroned, Greece, 17th century, the towered back of the throne surmounted by David and Solomon and Moses and Aaron, Avakum and Jeremiah, 35¾ x 23¼in. (Christie's) $6,145

The Annunciation, Greece, 17th century, traditionally painted in strong colors in an architectural background, 12 x 9½in. (Christie's) $16,324

Saint George with scenes from his life, North Russia, 17th century, the Saint astride a white charger spears the dragon protected by an angel, 39 x 38in. (Christie's) $28,807

The Mother of God of the Sign, Northern Russia, 18th century, the oklad with maker's mark in cyrillic of V. Akimov, Moscow, circa 1885, 11¼ x 9¼in. (Christie's) $1,961

Triptych of Christ Pantocrator and two Saints, Greece, possibly 14th century, Christ shown half length raises His right hand in blessing, the board 10½ x 14¾in.
(Christie's) $12,483

Mother of God enthroned, Greece, early 18th century, with Christ Child on her knee, with stippled haloes, 30¾ x 21in.
(Christie's) $5,761

Saint Alexander Nevskii, Russia, circa 1900, on copper, the Saint mounted on a white charger with members of his staff behind, 28½ x 28in.
(Christie's) $6,146

The Mandylion, Russia, late 19th century, the oklad marked *P. Ovchinnikov* with Imperial warrant, Moscow, 1886, realistically painted on gilt ground, 12¼ x 10½in.
(Christie's) $1,783

Saints Peter and Paul, Russia, Palekh style, late 19th century, the oklad with unrecorded maker's mark *H.I.T.*, Moscow, 1893, Christ the Saviour above, 12¼ x 10½in.
(Christie's) $1,693

Saint John the Baptist, the Forerunner, Greece, 17th century, shown three-quarter length, winged as the Messenger in a green himation over camel hair, 67 x 35½in.
(Christie's) $10,695

Saint George with scenes from his life, Greece, or possibly Asia Minor, early 18th century, painted in bright colors, 22½ x 17in.
(Christie's) $6,722

The Mother of God of Kazan, Russia, late 19th century, the oklad with maker's mark in cyrillic of Ivan Tarabrov, Moscow, 1899-1908, 12¼ x 10in.
(Christie's) $3,565

Mother of God of Kazan, Russia, circa 1900, the border inscribed with a prayer in Slavonic and corner pieces of seraphim, 28½ x 28in.
(Christie's) $5,761

Fine five case sheath-form landscape inro, 19th century, the interior rendered in near mirror image of pine trees, 3½in.
(Butterfield & Butterfield)
$2,875

Fine four case lacquer inro, 19th century, showing a portrait of a bijin holding a love letter, 2½in.
(Butterfield & Butterfield)
$3,163

A 19th century four-case black and gold lacquer inro, decorated with a night scene of boats beneath Mount Fuji, signed *Kajikawa*.
(Eldred's)
$1,100

Fine three case lacquer inro, 19th century, depicting a moored Genji in his boat, signed *Kansai saku*, 3in.
(Butterfield & Butterfield)
$4,312

Good four case inro of a karashishi, 19th century, signed *Kajikawa*, the temple lion bounding in a field of peony blossoms, 3¼in.
(Butterfield & Butterfield)
$6,900

Fine three case inlaid lacquer inro, 19th century, depicting a whimsical kappa seated on a river bank, 3in..
(Butterfield & Butterfield)
$10,925

Good four case lacquer inro, 19th century, signed *Kajikawa Hisataka*, with cloisonné enamel ojime and ivory netsuke, 3in.
(Butterfield & Butterfield)
$3,162

Fine two case inlaid lacquer inro of a birdcage, 19th century, fashioned as an exotic cage with silver cord runners, 4½in.
(Butterfield & Butterfield)
$5,750

Good two case gold inro, 19th century, the metal surface carved with a river landscape, with pleasure boat, 2½in.
(Butterfield & Butterfield)
$2,300

Fine lacquer tonkotsu, 19th century, depicting a recumbent ox seated by a torii gate, 2½in. (Butterfield & Butterfield)
$6,900

Early 19th century three-case black and gold lacquer inro with landscape design.
(Eldred's) $495

Good four case inro of courtesans, 19th century, rendered in iro-e togidashi, 3in. (Butterfield & Butterfield)
$3,450

Fine five case gold lacquer inro, 19th century, depciting Jo and Uba standing with a broom and rake under a pine tree, 3¾in. high.
(Butterfield & Butterfield)
$4,888

Koma School gilt lacquer miniature two-case inro, Meiji period, signed *Kansai,* in gold takamaki-e with oki-birame and aogai accents, 1⅜in. high.
(Butterfield & Butterfield)
$1,840

Fine four case metal inlaid inro, 19th century, signed *Kajikawa* and *Nobukatsu,* the front inlaid with two No figures reserved on a kinji ground, 3¼in.
(Butterfield & Butterfield)
$4,888

Rare five case inro of a snake, 19th century, signed *Kajikawa,* shown with mouth open and forked tongue extended, 3¾in.
(Butterfield & Butterfield)
$10,925

Fine four case lacquer inro, 19th century, exquisitely rendered with plum branches in full bloom, 3½in. high.
(Butterfield & Butterfield)
$24,150

Fine five case mixed metal inlaid inro, 19th century, depicting a mounted Hokei warrior and his attendant, 3¾in. high.
(Butterfield & Butterfiel)
$5,463

American 6in. celestial table globe, by Gilman Joslin, circa 1840, on a cherrywood stand.
(Skinner) $4,025

An English ebony and brass octant, in original box, circa 1850.
(Auction Team Köln)
$855

American 6in. terrestrial geographic educator globe, circa 1927, the laminated white metal sphere opening to reveal puzzle-form continents.
(Skinner) $575

A terrestrial library globe by Merzbach & Falk, Brussels, diameter 12in., overall height 35½in., made up of twelve lithographed and colored paper gores.
(Christie's) $6,577

Pair of Cary's 12in. terrestrial and celestial table globes, circa 1830, the terrestrial corrected to 1827, the celestial to 1800, 18in. high to top meridian.
(Skinner) $4,140

A good ship's binnacle and compass, the dial signed *Castle and Company, Hull*, the brass cover with oil lamp housing and flanked by Kelvin spheres, 57in. high overall.
(David Lay) $1,598

An ebony octant by Spencer Barrett & Co., London, 30cm. radius, in original wooden box, circa 1870.
(Auction Team Köln) $545

A Walker's Cherub Mark II brass ship's log, enamel dial calibrated to 100 miles, with subsidiary tenths, 10cm. diameter, English, circa 1935.
(Auction Team Köln) $210

A 19th century lacquered-brass compound monocular micro-scope, signed on the stand *Ross London*, with rack and pinion coarse focusing and fine adjustment, 12¼in. wide.
(Christie's) $873

An impressive letter and parcel balance by Sampson Mordan & Co., London, with three circular information tables, on oak plinth with eleven weights, base 19in. wide.
(David Lay) $392

A binnacle with petroleum burner, 21 cm. high.
(Auction Team Köln)
$467

Negretti & Zambra, London, an early 20th century barograph with mercury thermometer and seven-section chamber, in glazed oak case, 36cm. wide.
(Bearne's) $605

Celestial table globe, J. Wilson & Sons, Albany, New York, circa 1830, the papers corrected to 1826, on a four-legged stand, 18in. diameter.
(Skinner) $6,900

A brass 3in. telescope by F. Cox, London, with table tripod and other accessories in fitted box.
(David Lay) $768

An Admiralty-pattern sextant, the black-enameled frame of three-circle design, the arc signed *T.L. Ainsley Ltd, South Shields,* in teak case, 10¾in.
(Christie's) $489

An 18th century sundial in brass, the compass base engraved on steel, *T. Harris & Son, 52 Great Russell St, Blooms'y, London,* 3¹/₂in. diameter.
(Russell, Baldwin & Bright) $1,530

American 6in. terrestrial 'Franklin' globe, by Merriam, Moore & Co., Troy, New York, circa 1852, with scrolled wrought iron tripod base.
(Skinner) $2,415

A George III mahogany cased compass having silvered dial inscribed *Troughton, London,* dial 3¹/₂in. diameter.
(Russell, Baldwin & Bright) $260

An 18th century cube dial, signed *D. Beringer* on the base of the face inscribed *Nord*, the five faces with engraved, lightly colored, printed cards, 7¼in.
(Christie's) $1,745

A late 18th century brass horizontal garden sundial, the finely engraved horizontal dial with center wind rose and calendar scale, signed *Edward Hunter Fecit*, 15in. diameter.
(Christie's) $5,933

A wooden and brass tangent galvanometer by W. G. Pye & Co. Cambridge, circa 1900, 22cm. high.
(Auction Team Köln) $390

A late 18th century brass Butterfield-pattern dial, signed *Chapotot A Paris*, the underside engraved with the latitudes of twenty Continental cities and towns, in the original plush-lined fish-skin covered case, 3in.
(Christie's) £1,745

A late 19th century Powell & Lealand No. 1 compound binocular microscope, with rack and pinion coarse and micrometer fine focusing, in mahogany carrying case with two swing handles, 20½in high.
(Christie's) $13,088

A Russian star globe, with satin-chrome vertical half-circle and horizon ring, the stand inscribed *Freiberger Prazisionsmechanik made in DDR,* with instruction booklet, in wood carrying case, 10in. square.
(Christie's) $314

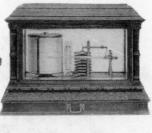

A lacquered-brass and enameled nephoscope, signed on the tripod stand *F. Barker & Son., Makers London*, with shaded glass surface plate, in mahogany case, 9in. wide.
(Christie's) $279

A late 19th century lacquered-brass barograph, unsigned, the recording drum with charts by Thomas Armstrong & Brothers Ltd., in carved and decorated glazed oak case, 15½in. high.
(Christie's) $698

A late 19th century brass heliochronometer, signed *Julio A Garcia,* on adjustable quadrant supports and stand, mounted on mahogany plinth base, overall height 14¾in.
(Christie's) $1,396

A black-enameled and lacquered-brass compound monocular microscope, by W. Watson & Sons Ltd., in mahogany case, 12¾in. high. (Christie's) $437

A 19th century black-enameled brass surveying theodolite, signed on the horizontal plate *Troughton & Simms LONDON,* 14½in. long. (Christie's) $524

An unusual 19th century lacquered-brass Continental Everest-pattern theodolite, unsigned, the telescope with rack and pinion focusing, 11in. (Christie's) $1,308

 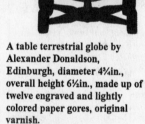 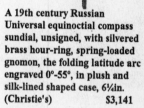

A rare 17th century brass gunner's level, unsigned, with vertical scale 0°-45°, with adjustable iron pin-hole sight, incorporating a quadrant with iron needle and scroll support, 3¼in. high. (Christie's) $2,792

A table terrestrial globe by Alexander Donaldson, Edinburgh, diameter 4¾in., overall height 6½in., made up of twelve engraved and lightly colored paper gores, original varnish. (Christie's) $4,154

A 19th century Russian Universal equinoctial compass sundial, unsigned, with silvered brass hour-ring, spring-loaded gnomon, the folding latitude arc engraved 0°-55°, in plush and silk-lined shaped case, 6¼in. (Christie's) $3,141

An 18th century French brass circumferenter, signed on the underside *Mavlevat a Paris,* the engraved circle with acanthus leaf decoration and fitted with four fixed sights, 9¾in. (Christie's) $3,141

A 19th century lacquered-brass compound binocular microscope, signed *R & J Beck, London & Philadelphia,* with rack and pinion coarse and fine focusing, contained in an oak carrying cabinet, 19¼in. wide. (Christie's) $3,839

A lacquered-brass and black-enamelled airship sextant, by Georg Butensohn, Hamburg with rack and pinion quadrant adjustment, in fitted fruitwood case, 10¼in. wide. (Christie's) $1,135

A previously unrecorded French simple microscope to the 1678 design of Christian Huygens, the inventor of the pendulum clock (1656), the microscope is made of brass and is contained in a simple case, 5in. long.
(Christie's) $8,726

A Japanese 'do'tchin' steelyard, the ebony and brass beam graduated with 'picqué' graduations, the pan stamped with various marks, 14in. long.
(Christie's) $419

A late 18th century lucernal microscope, signed on the stage *W & S Jones 30 Holborn, London*, the pyramid-shaped project on box supported by two pillars from the base, 30in. long.
(Christie's) $1,745

A rare mid 19th century[?] French set of brass nesting weights, circa 1850, the inner base of the master cups stamped with the sign of an eagle with outstretched wings, 7in. high.
(Christie's) $3,490

A pair of table globes by Gerard and Leonard Valk, Amsterdam, diameter 12in., overall height 19in., each globe comprising 12 hand-colored engraved gores, with polar calottes to the terrestrial.
(Christie's) $38,077

A rare late 19th century lacquered and marbled-finish brass goniometer, signed on the stand *Societé genevoise Instruments Physiques & Mécanique Genève*,15¼in. high.
(Christie's) $10,471

A late 16th century octagonal ivory diptych dial, unsigned, probably Nuremberg, stamped with geometric decoration and marked in red for 52°, 3½in.
(Christie's) $9,075

A large binocular microscope, with unusual brass tripod base, with lenses and complete mahogany equipment cupboard, British, circa 1880.
(Auction Team Köln) $3,424

A late 19th century lacquered-brass cased aneroid barometer, signed on the painted glass cover *Carl Sickler Karlsruhe Hofmecha-niker*, 8in. diameter.
(Christie's) $489

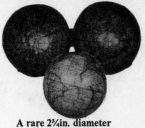

A Brewster-patent one-draw telescope kaleidoscope, with black lacquered outer barrel and brass inner tube, the viewing objective mount embossed *P. Carpenter Sole Maker.*
(Christie's) $1,431

A brass compass theodolite by Dennert & Pape, Altona, in original wooden box, circa 1928. (Auction Team Köln)
$373

A rare 2¾in. diameter terrestrial pocket globe by Leonard Cushee, London with twelve engraved gores, the continents colored in outline in red and green, with fish-skin covered pocket case.
(Christie's) $4,846

A German gilt-brass jointed rule, inscribed *Christophorvs Schissler faciebat avgvste anno 1565,* the compass joint allows the arms to be set in line providing a one-foot ruler.
(Christie's) $20,942

An early 19th century lacquered-brass Culpeper-type microscope, unsigned, with rack and pinion focusing, in pyramid-shaped mahogany case, 17in.
(Christie's) $3,490

A terrestrial library globe, diameter 18in., overall height 40in., made up of two sets of twelve engraved and colored gores by C. Smith and Son (fl. 1803-63), London.
(Christie's) $6,923

A lacquered-brass and vulcanite galvanometer, by Gambrell Bros. & Co. Ltd., London, with glazed front, Universal bubble-level and three adjustable feet, 9in. high.
(Christie's) $140

A Korean ivory diptych compass dial, with folding plate, the underside incised with place names and latitudes, the compass with needle, 5¼in. long.
(Christie's) $489

A 19th century lacquered-brass 2¾in. reflecting telescope, signed on the back-plate *Bate, London,* the 9in. long body-tube with starfinder fitted mahogany case, 11¼in. wide.
(Christie's) $1,571

170,462 - 1875, wood and metal Boot Tree, George W. Badger, Malden, MA, 6½ x 3½ x 1½ins. (Christie's) $288

234,303 - 1880, wooden Spring Bed, Caleb A. Libby Evansville, WI, 8 x 10 x 2ins. (Christie's) $92

42,138 - 1864, iron Bailed Hollow Ware, John B. Crowley, Cincinnati, OH, 8 x 8 x 8ins. (Christie's) $207

212,112 - 1879, wood, brass, metal and cat gut Mechanical Movement, George Raymond & Albert Raymond, Waupun, WI, 8 x 6 x 9ins. (Christie's) $863

48,791 - 1865, brass, iron and rubber Cooler for Beer and Other Liquids, Justus Chollar and Charles W. Cunningham, Washington, DC, 11 x 11 x 11ins. (Christie's) $115

209,22 - 1878, wood handled Saw Set made of iron with a sheet brass insert piece, Frank A. Buell, Brooklyn, NY, Wood Iron, 8½ x 3 x1½ins. (Christie's) $288

24,785 - 1859, Exhaust Mechanism for Locomotives, brass, Jacob Barney, Chicago, IL, 5 x 3 x 3ins. (Christie's) $460

135,738 - 1873, wood, brass and metal Swing, Edward A. Tuttle, Williamsburg, NY, 11 x 8 x 12ins. (Christie's) $690

219,773 - 1879, wood and brass Coal-Breaker, Philip Henry Sharp, Wilkesbarre, PA, 11 x 10 x 10ins. (Christie's) $748

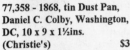

77,358 - 1868, tin Dust Pan, Daniel C. Colby, Washington, DC, 10 x 9 x 1½ins. (Christie's) $368

158,564 - 1875, glass Medicine Droppers, Joshua Barnes, Brooklyn, NY, 3½ x 1 x 1½ins. (Christie's) $138

217,853 - 1879, Improvements in Spurs, metal, Trangott Beck, Newark, NJ, 5 x 4 x 1½ins. (Christie's) $368

141,843 - 1873, Machine for Finishing Sole Edges on Boots/Shoes, Henry F. Wheeler, Boston, MA, wood brass and iron, 4 x 6 x 6ins. (Christie's) $207

152,595 - 1874, tin and brass Coalbox, beautifully decorated with sloping top, George S. Bruce, Cincinnati, OH, 7 x 7 x 12ins. (Christie's) $552

75,930 - 1868, Saddle and Harness, engraved name and decorative border, R.M. La Rue, Andersonville, IN, brass and steel, 2 x 2 x 2in., (Christie's) $17

191,900 - 1877, wood, brass and tin Coffee Roaster, George Tinsley and A. Hackman, Blakesburg, IA, 5 x 8 x 10ins. (Christie's) $230

124,775 - 1872, wood and iron Improvement in Dinner-Pots, Abraham F. Wolf, Beaver Falls, PA, 9 x 9 x 8ins. (Christie's) $184

66,038 - 1867, wood and brass Gymnastic Swing, Alonzo P. Payson, San Francisco, CA, 11 x 12 x 4½ins. (Christie's) $1,725

32,829 - 1861, tin Cooking Stove, Benjamin F. Gold, Reading, PA, 8 x 8 x 7ins.
(Christie's) $207

180,575 - 1876, Marine Safe, wood, Jean L. Gouley, New Orleans, LA, 6 x 6 x 11ins.
(Christie's) $978

178,243 - 1876, wood and brass Burglar Alarm, J.P. Kislingbury, Rochester, NY, 12 x 3½ x 12ins.
(Christie's) $690

207,232 - 1878, wood, brass and tin Washing Machine, Toliver A. Wilson, San Francisco, CA, 10 x 9 x 6ins.
(Christie's) $1,380

42,938 - 1864, wood and brass Submarine Port Hole, T. F. Gilliland, Chicago, IL, 6 x 6 x 6ins.
(Christie's) $460

214,893 - 1879, wood and brass Milk Receivers, Frank Donaldson, New York, NY, 8 x 3 x 11½ins.
(Christie's) $345

206,858 - 1878, Manufacture of Horse Shoes, George Bryden, Hartford, CT, wood, 4½ x 5 x 2½ins.
(Christie's) $207

30,207 - 1860, wood, brass and leather Riding Saddle (to hold gun etc.), John Commins, Charleston, SC, 11 x 7 x 6ins.
(Christie's) $483

169,997 - 1875, wood, iron and tin Extension Table, Ansel D. Jones and Samuel L. Jones, Kirksville, KY, 12 x 12 x 5ins.
(Christie's) $345

56,812 - 1866, brass and metal Coal Scuttle, George Smith, Brooklyn, NY, 8½ x 6½ x 6ins. (Christie's) $345

211,088 - 1879, wood and tin Oil Can Cabinets, James H. Clough, Quincy, MA, 7 x 7 x 12ins. (Christie's) $115

184,069 - 1876, brass, copper and tin Peanut Heater, Jean Esposito, New York, NY, 7½ x 5 x 9ins. (Christie's) $633

149,546 - 1874, wood and iron Sewing Machine Table and Cabinet, Harriet R. Tracy, New York, NY, 8½ x 6 x 10ins. (Christie's) $2,760

203,840 - 1878, brass and steel Machine for Trimming Last Blocks, John C. Kingston, Buffalo, NY, 8 x 4 x 6ins. (Christie's) $1,265

221,443 - 1879, wood, tin and metal Washing Machine, Tilmon A. H. Cameron, Slater, MO, 4 x 4 x 6ins. (Christie's) $115

185,706 - 1876, wood and iron Centring Device, William P. Tullock, Washington, DC, 9 x 6 x 2ins. (Christie's) $345

198,936 - 1878, wood Ore Crusher, Edward Gimson, Staleybridge, England, 12 x 6 x 9ins. (Christie's) $518

224,566 - 1880, Machine for Making Pills, brass, wood and iron, James A. Whitney, New York, NY, 10 x 6½ x 5ins. (Christie's) $7,475

A brass and steel dough scraper, Peter Derr, Pennsylvania, dated *1848*, with conical ring-turned brass handle, 4in. wide.
(Sotheby's) $920

Pair of life-size cast iron stag figures, made in Whitman Massachusetts foundry, mold cut by H. Mansbach, 1880–85, 54in. high.
(Skinner) $7,475

A red-painted sheet steel Coca Cola coolbox, double lids with aluminium handles, 1939, 80 x 87 x 70cm.
(Auction Team Köln)
                              $775

A group of painted cast-iron garden seat furniture, comprising a settee and two armchairs, the pierced arms and back composed of interlacing oak tree branches, length of settee 4ft. 3in. (Sotheby's) $5,175

A painted cast iron figural medallion, early 20th century, centered by a Medusa mask within a leaf tip border, 4ft. 8in. diameter.
(Sotheby's) $18,400

The Pioneer, a very decorative written till receipt register by the United Autographic Register Co., Chicago, 1883.
(Auction Team Köln)
                              $390

A J.M. Paillard French rotary pencil sharpener in attractive Art Nouveau case, circa 1920.
(Auction Team Köln)
                              $505

A cast iron urn shaped fire basket, with two serpent handles and swags and scrolls, and ash drawer.
(Dreweatt · Neate) $900

A massive Victorian metal figure of a swan, circa 1880, standing with wings aspread, 42in. high.
(Sotheby's) $11,500

An Egyptian metal foot iron, with Turkish height indicator, pre-1811.
(Auction Team Köln) $428

A porcelain electric iron, 220V, circa 1925.
(Auction Team Köln) $78

A small Robson chimney iron, circa 13 x 10.7 x 6.5cm.
(Auction Team Köln) $125

A Husqvarna charcoal chimney iron, Swedish, 30cm. long, with plate.
(Auction Team Köln)
                                    $155

A Swedish octagonal cast iron stove by Christianshavn Jernstebn, with contemporary irons, circa 1885.
(Auction Team Köln)
                                    $740

A Westinghouse electric sad iron, early model with detachable handle and original wooden box, 1911.
(Auction Team Köln)
                                    $170

An American Gas Machine Co. spirit iron original handle, and side tank, 1912.
(Auction Team Köln)
                                    $295

A Chinese pan-iron, with open charcoal pan and decorated, gold lacquered, wooden handle, circa 1900.
(Auction Team Köln)
                                    $195

A dragon's head chimney iron with original wooden handle, 16cm. long.
(Auction Team Köln)
                                    $194

IVORY

Prisoner of War bone multiple game box, 19th century, pierced carved box with geometric decoration, 5³/₄ x 6¹/₂in. (Skinner) **$690**

Pair of carved whale ivory door knobs, 7¹/₄in. long. (Skinner) **$978**

A 19th century ivory okimono depicting two fishermen entertaining two noblemen by fishing from their boat, 4¹/₂in. (Eldred's) **$880**

Large carved and reticulated ivory figure of Shoulao and attendants, the bearded immortal holding a fruiting peach branch, 11in. high. (Butterfield & Butterfield) **$1,725**

Three English carved ivory figures of Queens Josephine, Mary, and Elizabeth I, third quarter 19th century, each depicted in period dress and with hinged lower section revealing a scene, 9³/₄in. high. (Skinner) **$4,887**

A German silver and ivory thread holder, circa 1750, the ivory barrel form thread holder turned with bands, suspended from bracket and oval hook richly chased, 5in. high. (Sotheby's) **$2,760**

Whalebone hanging watch hutch, 19th century, the arched crest pierce carved with a star and crescent motifs, 7¹/₂in. high. (Skinner) **$8,625**

Pair of Continental carved ivory Renaissance style figures, third quarter 19th century, each signed *HV*, a mandolin player and a lady with a bird, 16in. high. (Skinner) **$33,350**

A Japanese carved ivory figure depicting a fisherman and his son, the man holding a net, signed, Meiji, 20cm. high. (Bearne's) **$1,115**

IVORY

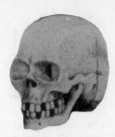  

Late 19th century marine ivory okimono by Mitsuchika in the form of a human with intricate detail carving, signed.
(Eldred's) $2,750

Carved ivory Emperor's barge on a carved wood supporting base, 10in.
(G. A. Key) $230

A late 19th century carved ivory brooch, depicting deer in a leafy glade.
(Bearne's) $236

Whalebone, ivory and wood three-tiered footed spool stand, 19th century, doughnut shaped ivory thimble holder above three graduated, scalloped tiers, 7¹/₈in. high.
(Skinner) $747

Pair of Japanese tusk vases profusely carved with warriors, dragons and fish amongst flowering shrubs, signed, on hardwood stands, 20in. high overall.
(Russell, Baldwin & Bright) $5,661

An Anglo-Indian vizagapatam ivory miniature bureau-cabinet, late 18th century, engraved overall with floral trails, the rectangular top with broken pediment with panels of birds on branches, 28in. wide.
(Christie's) $26,910

A 19th century French gilt metal and mother of pearl boudoir table stand, containing an oval miniature on ivory depicting a lady, 11½in. high.
(Andrew Hartley) $1,828

Pair of ivory quail form boxes, each carved as a quail nestled on millet stalks, the upper body forming the lid, 2½in. high.
(Butterfield & Butterfield) $1,725

Japanese carved ivory figure of a basket seller, late 19th/early 20th century, etched with geometric designs and foliage, 5½in. high.
(Skinner) $805

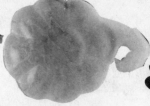

Carved nephrite Moghul style covered bowl, 19th/20th century, domical lid with reticulated leafy scrolls surrounding floral reserves, 7in. long.
(Butterfield & Butterfield)
$2,875

Mughal style celadon nephrite dish, a handle to one side in the form of a ram's head, 8½in. long.
(Butterfield & Butterfield)
$1,380

Fine carved nephrite horse, 18th/19th century, carved as a recumbent horse, with head turned back over its shoulder, 2in. long.
(Butterfield & Butterfield)
$1,380

A fine green jadeite archaistic tripod vessel and cover, late Qing dynasty, carved with two flaring leaf-shaped flanges with lingzhi handles suspending loose rings, 7in. high.
(Christie's) $10,500

Pair of spinach nephrite phoenix form vessels, each carved as a phoenix supporting an archaistic vase on its back, 7¼in. high.
(Butterfield & Butterfield)
$1,610

Fine gray nephrite libation cup, 19th century, fashioned as a deep cup with thin walls of ovoid section rising out of the open jaws of a dragon, 9in.
(Butterfield & Butterfield)
$4,600

Archaistic nephrite Bi disc, the thickly sectioned and opaque matrix varying in hue from light gray-green to cinnamon brown.
(Butterfield & Butterfield)
$316

A fine relief-carved celadon jade boulder, 18th century, the large pebble-shaped stone carved with the figure of Laozi with his water buffalo and attendant meeting a scholar and attendant beside pine trees, 8in. high.
(Christie's) $19,090

Celadon nephrite covered bowl, early 20th century, with neatly cut banded footring and upright rim grooved to fit the domical cover, 4in. diameter.
(Butterfield & Butterfield)
$690

JADE

A rare jadeite buddhistic-lion group, late Qing Dynasty, carved as a recumbent mythical beast with its right foreleg resting playfully on a small cub lying on its back, 6¼in. wide.
(Christie's) $17,181

Fine mottled jadeite mounted writing set with opener, comprising an inkwell formed from an overturned lotus bowl and lotus leaf tray, marked *Farmer New York Sterling* , 8in.
(Butterfield & Butterfield)
     $5,175

A very fine celadon jade recumbent mythical beast, 17th century, the stout animal carved crouching four-square with hooded downcast eyes, 4¾in. wide.
(Christie's) $24,817

Good celadon nephrite figural group of maiden and two children, 19th century, the maiden standing in flowing robes, 7¾in.
(Butterfield & Butterfield)
     $2,500

A pair of fine spinach jade circular landscape plaques, Kangxi, each carved in relief with a different scene depicting a gentleman and young atttendant standing on a steep and winding path, 9in. diam.
(Christie's) $28,635

A white and russet jade archaistic carved pendant, 18th century, of rounded rectangular shape, carved on one side with a small ribboned boy standing in the central aperture, 3½in. wide.
(Christie's) $6,109

  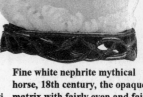

Ming style celadon nephrite model of two recumbent horses, well carved to depict a mare reclining beside a foal, 9¼in. long.
(Butterfield & Butterfield)
     $4,025

Celadon nephrite female immortal and attendant, the deity holding a flywhisk and ruyi scepter, 8in. high.
(Butterfield & Butterfield)
     $1,265

Fine white nephrite mythical horse, 18th century, the opaque matrix with fairly even and faint celadon cast, 4 ½in..
(Butterfield & Butterfield)
     $2,070

A seedpearl mounted circular pendant of flowerhead design, with safety chain.
(Bearne's) $453

An attractive 9ct. gold pink shell cameo brooch of a lady.
(G. A. Key) $450

A modern diamond, ruby, emerald and sapphire giardinetto brooch, designed as a basket of flowers.
(Bearne's) $1,027

A 19th century gold circular brooch, with the embossed head of an eagle, with ruby eye and diamond collet in its beak, 26mm.
(Tennant's) $423

A regimental brooch, with monogram within blue enamel garter and green leafage, surrounded by rose diamonds, in gold and platinum.
(Tennant's) $559

A Victorian gold and ceramic scarf pin, painted by William Bishop Ford, of circular form and depicting a mastiff, 1in. wide, signed on reverse.
(Andrew Hartley) $334

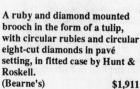

A Continental 19th century silver and enamel crucifix watch, inscribed *Etienne, Bordier*, cartouche of Adam and Eve below the VI, 19 x 55mm.
(Christie's) $3,187

A gold enamel and seed pearl verge pendant watch, unsigned, 1820s, the frosted gilt fusée movement with verge escapement and bridgecock, 30mm. diameter.
(Christie's) $1,898

A ruby and diamond mounted brooch in the form of a tulip, with circular rubies and circular eight-cut diamonds in pavé setting, in fitted case by Hunt & Roskell.
(Bearne's) $1,911

A late 19th century gold, silver and diamond mounted twelve-point star brooch pendant, with central circular cluster.
(Bearne's) $1,730

A pair of Middle Eastern gold-colored and enameled loop earrings with beadwork decoration.
(Bearne's) $319

A Bohemian garnet and gold star-shaped brooch.
(Bearne's) $255

A ruby and diamond mounted brooch in the form of raspberries, with circular cabochon rubies and old-mine brilliant-cut diamonds.
(Bearne's) $1,258

An enamelled shaped rectangular plaque brooch, the central oval panel depicting cherubs playing a harp within a foliate border.
(Bearne's) $924

A Victorian gold brooch of square lattice form, with five pearls and four rubies within bands of enamel, probably French, circa 1880, 40mm.
(Tennant's) $1,661

A pietra dura oval plaque brooch, depicting a white rose amongst flowers within a filigree gold frame.
(Bearne's) $468

A diamond mounted brooch, in the form of a dancer with circular brilliant and old-mine brilliant-cut diamonds.
(Bearne's) $1,447

An amethyst and seedpearl mounted circular brooch, the central circular amethyst within a surround of seedpearls.
(Bearne's) $701

429

Fine black and gilt lacquered wood Buddhist traveling shrine, Edo period, dated 1677, double folding doors with chased giltmetal mounts, 33¼in.
(Butterfield & Butterfield)
$16,100

A gold lacquer box and cover in the form of a fan and eboshi, 18th century, decorated in gold, silver and iroe hiramakie, kirigane and aogai, 14cm. wide.
(Christie's) $4,900

Large cinnabar lacquer square box with 'One Hundred Children' decoration, formed with cusped corners to the cover and base, 2¼ x 12in square.
(Butterfield & Butterfield)
$3,737

Pair of Japanese Export overlay decorated black lacquer bird and flower panels, early 20th century, each panel set in a carved rosewood dragon frame, 41 x 24 in.
(Butterfield & Butterfield)
$1,610

A roironuri ground suzuribako with Sasaki Takatsuna and Kajiwara Kagesue mounted and fording Uji river, late 19th century, 26.5 x 23cm.
(Christie's) $21,528

Fine Shibayama style silver and lacquer footed bowl, Meiji period, the four lobed body of compressed globular form supported on four feet of jui shape, 6in.
(Butterfield & Butterfield)
$3,450

Lacquered wood picnic box, the rectangular box fitted with smaller rectangular boxes and five trays, 8¾ x 9¼ x 5½in.
(Butterfield & Butterfield)
$978

Pair of fine carved cinnabar lacquer boxes and covers, 18th century, built with layers of black, dark green and cinnabar lacquer, 5½ x 9¾in.
(Butterfield & Butterfield)
$20,700

Carved cinnabar lacquer four tier stacking box, on skirted base raised on ruyi lappet corner feet, 8½ x 7 x 6¾in..
(Butterfield & Butterfield)
$2,875

Pairpoint reverse painted scenic lamp, domical textured glass shade in flared 'Copley' form with forest scene, 20in. high. (Skinner) $1,438

Unusual acetylene bicycle lamp, strong condenser lens, patented 1899.
(Auction Team Köln) $116

Pairpoint reverse painted table lamp, flared glass shade decorated in colorful tapestry motif with interior spatterwork, onyx platform base, 26in. high. (Skinner) $2,415

Handel scenic boudoir lamp, angular six-sided glass shade obverse painted with expansive colorful landscape, raised on bronzed metal tree trunk base, 14in. high. (Skinner) $3,680

Pair of blue and white pressed glass wedding lamps, D.C. Ripley and Co., patent dated *February 1, 1870*, and *September 20, 1870*, 13¼in. high. (Skinner) $2,645

A Loetz glass table lamp, the textured surface applied with circular prunts under golden iridescence, supported on an Osler gilt metal base, 42cm. high. (Christie's) $648

René Lalique, 'Ceylan' vase/lamp, after 1924, opalescent glass, molded with a frieze of four pairs of birds amongst branches, 9½in. (Sotheby's) $4,124

A Solar acetylene bicycle lamp by the Badger Brass Mfg. Co. USA., with handlebar fitting, 1896. (Auction Team Köln) $195

Victorian mantel lamp, round opal glass shade with handpainted stylized floral motif, mounted on gilt metal lamp base, 10in. high. (Skinner) $518

Persian blue turquoise glazed earthenware lamp base, decorated with rectangular panels of foliage, 11in. high. (Skinner) $575

Art Deco period table lamp, applied with a reclining bronze figure of a naked maiden clutching a serving bowl, circa 1920, 17in. (G. A. Key) $604

Blue opaline glass and clear glass oil lamp, late 19th century, dolphin-form stepped base and clear glass oil well, with frosted glass shade, 24in. high. (Skinner) $460

Emile-Jacques Ruhlmann, adjustable table lamp, circa 1925, deep burgundy painted bronze shade on gilt bronze base with three incurving tapered reeded supports, 27in. (Sotheby's) $20,620

Pair of patinated bronze double-arm argand lamps, H.N. Cooper and Co., Boston, mid 19th century, electrified, 17in. high. (Skinner) $1,610

A 1930s table lamp after an original by Max Le Verrier (1891–1973), cast with a naked woman holding the glass spherical shade on marble base, 18¹/₂in. high. (David Lay) $534

Daum, Geometric lamp, 1920s, gray glass, internally striated with amber/yellow and etched with geometric design, 17¾in. (Sotheby's) $8,998

Claire Jeanne Roberte Colinet, lamp dancer, 1920s, her outstretched arms holding two lanterns with frosted glass shades, 19¼in. (Sotheby's) $11,247

Good quality silver plated table lamp, boat shaped with scrolled side handles in rococo style, complete with gray silk shade, (G. A. Key) $190

Emile Gallé, small table lamp, circa 1900, gray glass internally decorated with yellow overlaid with red, 10½in.
(Sotheby's) $8,623

An Art Deco silvered spelter table lamp, cast in the form of an exotic dancer wearing beaded bodice and shorts, on a rectangular black striated onyx base, 32cm. high.
(Christie's) $519

Pâte-sur-pâte porcelain lamp base, France, circa 1875, brown ground with white classical relief, signed *F. Peyrat*, 15³⁄₄in. high to rim.
(Skinner) $1,092

Desny, adjustable table lamp. circa 1930s, nickel-plated metal with adjustable hemispherical shade with cream painted interior, 7in.
(Sotheby's) $3,187

Pair of French cobalt blue ground porcelain and gilt metal lamp bases, late 19th century, each with foliate spray, gilded surround, 16in. high.
(Skinner) $431

A Royal Doulton 'Sung' table lamp figure of a seated Buddha, covered in a warm multicolored flambé glaze, by Charles Noke and Fred Allen, 18.3cm. high, total height 51cm.
(Bearne's) $1,435

Lalique opalescent glass vase, 'Ceylan', molded in relief with four pairs of love birds perched amidst prunus blossom, 20in. high.
(G. A. Key) $2,791

Marcel Bouraine, 'Harlequin' lamp, 1920s, gilt and cold painted bronze and ivory, modeled as a female harlequin, 21³⁄₄in.
(Sotheby's) $33,741

Chinese sang de boeuf glazed porcelain lamp base, late 19th century, of bulbous form, with reticulated gilt metal neck and base, 14in. high.
(Skinner) $575

Duffner & Kimberly 'Greek No. 521' table lamp, conical shade in green-on-green leaded glass segments with bow ties around dropped apron, 24in. high. (Skinner) **$1,725**

Handel pond lily lamp, green and white leaded glass petals and bud on bronzed metal stems, 13½in. high. (Skinner) **$920**

Pairpoint ribbed scenic miniature lamp, rare closed-top 'Palm' glass shade reverse painted on blue background, 15in. high. (Skinner) **$5,175**

Tiffany bronze and dichroic glass Harvard lamp, of crimson red mottled olive-amber segments arranged around four multicolored Harvard University emblems, 24in. high. (Skinner) **$11,500**

Daum, pair of table lamps, 1920s, gray glass shades internally mottled with aubergine towards the top, and yellow and orange, 11¼in. (Sotheby's) **$3,749**

Tiffany bronze and favrile glass pansy lamp, domed shade with repeating clusters of conventionalized multicolored blossoms, buds and leaves, 19in. high. (Skinner) **$33,350**

Handel Art Deco lamp, half-round frosted shade decorated in etched yellow amber checkerboard squares, 12in. high. (Skinner) **$920**

Duffner & Kimberly French Renaissance table lamp, shade with gold leading on green and amber glass segments, 22in. high. (Skinner) **$2,875**

Daum, small table lamp, 1920s, opaque glass in horizontal bands alternating with bands of linear design against a textured ground, 12³/₈in. high. (Sotheby's) **$3,871**

Tiffany bronze and dichroic glass spider lamp, designed to depict the spider web within six panels of green-amber dichroic segments, 18in. high.
(Skinner) $18,400

Tiffany bronze seven-light lily lamp, conventionalized design of seven curving waterlily stems arising from lily pad cluster base, 21in. high.
(Skinner) $9,200

Pairpoint scenic boudoir lamp, flared sand finish miniature 'Copley' glass shade painted on exterior with stylized tree border, 14½in. high.
(Skinner) $690

Double panel slag glass table lamp, oversize eight-sided shade with reticulated foliate metal frame housing red-yellow over green slag glass flat glass panels, 27in. high.
(Skinner) $2,530

A pair of William IV gilt bronze colza oil lamps, in the manner of Thomas Messenger, each with fruiting finials, each 41cm. high.
(Phillips) $7,200

Emile Gallé mosque view lamp, circa 1900, gray glass internally decorated with orange, overlaid with orange and brown and etched with the silhouette of the Mosque at Istanbul, 7⅞in. high.
(Sotheby's) $3,800

Handel scenic lamp with bridge, domed glass shade reverse painted in naturalistic colors with trees and meadows, 23in. high.
(Skinner) $4,888

Pairpoint reverse painted harvest lamp, 'Exeter' glass shade decorated with team of horses pulling haywagon through cornfield, 21in. high.
(Skinner) $2,875

An American table lamp, in the style of Handel, the frosted yellow glass shade reverse polychrome painted with a rustic scene, 56.5cm. high.
(Christie's) $2,411

Cesare Lapini (Italian, b.1848), Girl with Parasol, carved white carrara marble, signed and dated *Firenze 1893*, 27¹/₂in. high.
(Skinner) $3,738

An Italian white marble group of Venus and Cupid, second half 19th century, the naked goddess reclining on a rectangular day-bed, the infant Cupid resting against her thighs, 53in. wide.
(Christie's) $10,557

A 19th century Italian statuary marble carving by Pietro Negro of a young girl signed and dated *Milan 1873*, 34¹/₂in. high.
(David Lay) $10,628

An Italian two-colored alabaster figure of a young child, by Pugi, late 19th/early 20th century, the child asleep on a chair, 20¾in. high.
(Christie's) $5,063

An Italian white marble allegorical bust of a young woman entitled *'Inverno'*, (Winter), third quarter 19th century, with long hair and wearing a bearskin over her head, 29¼in. high.
(Christie's) $8,138

A white marble group by Ferdinando Vichi, circa 1880, of two naked children with a cat, seated on a rocky base, signed and incised, 53cm. high.
(Sotheby's) $7,590

Italian carved Carrara marble bust of a maiden, by A. Bacherini (Italian, late 19th century), signed and dated *Florence, 1897*, 24in. high.
(Skinner) $1,725

Italian Carrara marble bust of Dante, by P. Bazzanti, signed and dated *Florence, 1923*, titled, 15in. high.
(Skinner) $517

Prof. A. Cambi (Italian, 19th century), Lost Love, carved white carrara marble, signed and dated *Firenze 1887*, on a circular socle, 25in. high.
(Skinner) $2,300

Italian carved Carrara marble bust of Augustus Caesar, 19th century, after the Antique, 22in. high.
(Skinner) $2,415

Francesco Pozzi (1779–1884), a white marble sculpture of a seated boy, one hand resting on a nest of turtles, signed and dated *1835*, 26¹/₂in. high.
(David Lay) $2,288

A white marble bust of a gentleman, on bowed square section base, 19th century, 28in. high.
(Christie's) $611

White marble bust of Theodore Roosevelt, attributed to Gutzon Borglum (American, 1871–1941), the chip carved base titled, 20in. high.
(Skinner) $5,750

A white marble group of Cupid and Psyche, after Antonio Canova, Italian, late 19th century, the mythological lovers shown in a passionate embrace, 112cm. high.
(Sotheby's) $18,055

An Italian white marble bust of a mother and child, by T. Carodossi, late 19th century, the infant clinging to its mother's neck, 23 in. high.
(Christie's) $6,872

An Italian white marble bust of Sappho, by Merlin?, late 19th/early 20th century, the young poetess with laurel to her hair, 28in. high.
(Christie's) $6,329

A Victorian white marble bust of a bearded gentleman, signed to the reverse *W. Theed. Fecit. Roma. 1845*, on spreading circular socle, 27¹/₄in. high.
(Christie's) $962

An Italian white marble figure of a shepherd boy by Cesare Lapini, Florence, dated *1884*, the boy resting his crook across his shoulders, 32¾in. high.
(Christie's) $13,563

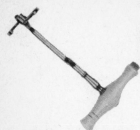

A late 18th century iron tooth key, with ivory handle, turned cranked shank and two claws, 5¾in. long.
(Christie's) $264

A lacquered-brass twelve-blade scarificator, unsigned, in linen-covered card case, 2⅜in. high.
(Christie's) $246

A 19th century pewter Gibson spoon with hinged flap and slit mouth, 6in. long.
(Christie's) $194

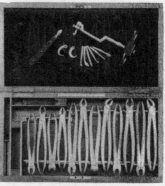

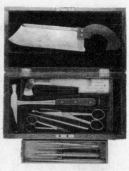

A 19th century embossed leather-covered apothecary's traveling case, the lid with prescription compartment and embossed in gilt *John Bell & Co.*, containing twelve (of thirteen) bottles, 10in. wide.
(Christie's) $281

A fine late 19th century nickel-plated iron set of twelve tooth extractors, by Evans & Co., with associated tooth key stamped *Savigny*, in plush-lined and fitted case, 15½in. wide.
(Christie's) $1,017

A late 19th century post mortem part-set, with ebony handled saw by Evans & Co., a chisel by Savigny & Co., a hammer, various knives, scissors, needles and other items, 12½in. wide.
(Christie's) $561

A superb German simple wood and ivory microscope to the fourth design (1678) of Christian Huygens, signed and dated *16.C.C.C. A.V.F. 92 (Cosmus Conrad Cuno Auguste Vindelicorum Fecit 1692).*
(Christie's) $38,393

An ivory anatomical model attributed to Stephen Zick, of a pregnant woman with articulated arms, the woman with removable torso revealing internal organs, 7½in. long. German, late 17th/early 18th century.
(Christie's) $8,769

A 19th century electro-medical machine, the dial inscribed *Mr W.H. Halse, Professor of Medical Galvanism, Warwick Lodge, No. 40, Addison Road, Kensington, London*, 7¼in. long.
(Christie's) $737

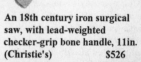

A 19th century leather and wood articulated leg, with nickel-plated iron supports, straps and buckles, 32in. long.
(Christie's) $229

An early 19th century mahogany domestic medicine chest, divided into two sections, hinged and opening to reveal two compartments of five bottles behind walnut slides, 11¼in.
(Christie's) $1,929

An 18th century iron surgical saw, with lead-weighted checker-grip bone handle, 11in.
(Christie's) $526

An optician's trial set, by Curry & Paxton Limited, the concave and convex lenses of cylindrical and spherical profile, with trial spectacle frame and ophthalmoscope, 20in. wide.
(Christie's) $421

A 19th century surgeon's kit, by S. Maw Son & Thompson, with bone-saw, two Heys saws, a finger-saw, four Liston knives, a lacquered-brass tourniquet, in mahogany case, 15½ wide.
(Christie's) $2,455

A fine optician's set of ceramic and glass artificial eyes, by Bruneau & Dr. Charpentier 28 rue Vignon Paris, comprising four trays of twenty artificial eyes, in fitted teak case, 16½in.
(Christie's) $3,280

A 19th century mahogany domestic medicine chest, the lid rising to reveal compartments for sixteen bottles and a pill slab, 10¼in. wide.
(Christie's) $965

A 19th century part-set of surgical instruments, the saw with ebony handle, with three Liston knives stamped *Durroch London*, in brass-bound mahogany case, 16½in wide.
(Christie's) $1,052

An unusual scarificator and cupping set, with thirty-five different cupping glasses and other items, in fitted leatherette-covered carrying case, 12½in.
(Christie's) $790

MINIATURE FURNITURE

An Empire-style miniature mahogany sofa, French, late 19th century, the arched back with scroll sides and feet, upholstered in striped silk, 18in. wide.
(Sotheby's) $545

Miniature Biedermeier elmwood part-ebonized cylinder desk, mid 19th century, fitted interior of three drawers, 11in. wide.
(Skinner) $403

A rare Arte Povera miniature chest, probably Venetian, mid 18th century, with serpentine front, three drawers with simple loop handles, 13in. long.
(Sotheby's) $5,851

A fine miniature parquetry bureau, German, circa 1780, veneered in walnut, the top, fall front and two drawers all inlaid with an oval of fruitwood cubes, 15in. wide.
(Sotheby's) $1,272

A Louis XVI doll's mahogany dressing table, French, early 19th century, stamped *E. Tuiller,* the top in three sections lifting to reveal a mirrored superstructure, 12½in. wide.
(Sotheby's) $1,180

A miniature marquetry chest of drawers, French, circa 1910, in mahogany with kingwood parquetry panels crossbanded in fruitwood, on splayed legs, 10½in. wide.
(Sotheby's) $581

Paint decorated child's chest of drawers, America, circa 1840, top surfaces painted with compôte of fruit, wreathed landscape reserves and floral sprays, 20in. wide.
(Skinner) $862

A miniature parquetry chest of drawers, German, circa 1780, the top inlaid with an ebony and fruitwood star centered by a mother-of-pearl flower, 15¾in.
(Sotheby's) $1,272

A mahogany armchair, French, mid 19th century, the back carved with a rose flanked by acanthus leaves, the arms with scroll ends, 11½in. high.
(Sotheby's) $1,362

A Waltershausen dolls house sofa, German, late 19th century, with scrolled curved ends and back, gilt scrollwork decoration, 6¼in. wide.
(Sotheby's) $537

Miniature engraved whalebone and baleen inlaid exotic wood stool, 19th century, with compass star and heart motif, 4³/₄in. high.
(Skinner) $1,150

Biedermeier walnut and part ebonized miniature chest of drawers, three drawers flanked by columnar supports on shaped feet, 17¹/₂in. wide.
(Skinner) $1,265

A miniature marquetry display cabinet, Dutch, circa 1825, the top and sides inlaid with fruitwood urns of flowers and with a striped frieze, on turned feet, 13in. wide.
(Sotheby's) $453

A set of miniature furniture, Continental, circa 1900, comprising a sofa and two armchairs each with simple rounded backs, on turned legs, the sofa 19 x 30in.
(Sotheby's) $999

A miniature mahogany dresser, Dutch or German, circa 1870, the broken arch pediment centered by a stained wood simulated coat of arms, 13in.
(Sotheby's) $545

A fine miniature roll-top desk, early 20th century in neo-classical style, opening to reveal seven drawers, some inlaid with satinwood obelisques and ebony fences, 25in. high.
(Sotheby's) $2,743

Dutch rococo style oak and elmwood miniature chest of drawers, 19th century, with serpentine top, the S-scrolled case fitted with three drawers, 20in. wide.
(Skinner) $1,840

A fine Waltershausen dressing cabinet and mirrored sideboard, German, late 19th century, the dressing chest with carved scrollwork, containing a mirror, 6½in. wide.
(Sotheby's) $768

Queen Anne walnut veneer
looking glass, England, 18th
century, 32in. high.
(Skinner)   **$1,840**

George III giltwood overmantel
mirror, third quarter 18th
century, 46in. wide.
(Skinner)   **$2,300**

A carved walnut mirror in early
18th century style, the shaped
crest with central shell.
(David Lay)   **$607**

A Chippendale style veneered
mahogany and parcel gilt
looking glass, the parcel gilt
swan's neck pediment above a
rectangular glass, 36½ x 28in.
(Christie's)   **$575**

A Regency dressing mirror with
chinoiserie penwork to the
satinwood veneer, the bowfront
base with three drawers, 21in.
wide.
(Russell, Baldwin & Bright)
                            $3,672

An églomisé polychrome-
decorated pine courting mirror,
probably Continental, 19th
century, molded frame with
projecting crest, 14¼in. high.
(Sotheby's)   **$345**

Mahogany dressing glass,
America or England, circa 1790,
the scrolled crest above a
molded frame and mirror plate
on tapering stiles, 13¼in. wide.
(Skinner)   **$518**

Giltwood girandole looking
glass, labeled *J.A. Butti ...
frame and looking glass manuf.
no. 1 Queen Street Edinburgh*,
39in. high.
(Skinner)   **$1,265**

An 18th century giltwood
framed wall mirror with floral
and leafage scroll carved
surround, 4ft. 2in. x 2ft. 10in.
(Russell, Baldwin & Bright)
                            $6,579

A Meissen porcelain oval mirror frame, applied with foliage and molded with petals, 58cm. high.
(Bearne's) $1,306

Mahogany inlaid dressing mirror, probably England, circa 1800, the rectangular mirror with arched top and shaped cresting, 21in. wide.
(Skinner) $920

Sterling mirror frame, maker J.R., rectangular form, high relief bird and floral design, 19⅝in. high, beveled mirror.
(Skinner) $1,150

Federal carved giltwood and eglomisé looking glass, Baltimore, circa 1801, the molded cornice with gilt spherules above white reverse painted on glass panels, 42½in. high.
(Skinner) $18,400

Pair of 19th century French carved giltwood framed oval wall mirrors with ribbon surmounts, laurel wreath surround, 25in. high.
(Russell, Baldwin & Bright)
                             $2,372

A Federal eglomisé and figured maple looking glass, New England, 19th century, the rectangular frame with outset squared corners above an eglomisé panel, 33¾ x 19in.
(Christie's) $1,840

Victorian mahogany cheval mirror, the adjustable mirror back supported on two scroll molded uprights, on splayed feet, 32in.
(G. A. Key) $638

Edwardian painted satinwood dressing mirror, circa 1895, with oval beveled plate and bowfronted base fitted with three drawers.
(Skinner) $373

A large 19th century wall mirror, the gold-painted frame molded with classical details, with floral swag and leafage scroll surmount, 5ft. wide.
(Russell, Baldwin & Bright)
                             $1,316

A George III giltwood mirror, the shaped rectangular plate in a pierced rockwork and C-scroll border, 52 x 30in.
(Christie's) $5,345

Federal gilt gesso looking glass, cornice with spheres above the reverse painted tablet of two children dancing, 13½in. wide.
(Skinner) $1,150

A William IV mahogany cheval mirror with oblong plate on molded square tapering supports with scrolled ends, 64½in. high.
(Andrew Hartley) $1,550

A very rare red-japanned pine small wall mirror, England or Boston, Massachusetts, circa 1735, the shaped crest centering an exotic bird, 17½in. high.
(Sotheby's) $10,350

A George III gilt carved wood screen on scroll and leaf supports, the frame carved in the rococo taste, the central panel of figured mustard silk, 35in. wide.
(Dreweatt Neate) $1,435

A Regencé giltwood mirror, the central arched divided plate in a mirrored border with pierced scrolls and acanthus, the arched cresting centered by a rockwork cartouche, Paris, 1725, 77in. x 45½in.
(Christie's) $22,425

A 19th century French Dieppe dome top mirror, the wood frame entirely covered with carved bone decoration, circa 1850, 54in. high.
(Dreweatt Neate) $7,176

Federal gilt gesso looking glass, possibly Massachusetts, circa 1810, cornice with applied spiral molding and foliate banding, 45in. high.
(Skinner) $2,415

A 19th century gilt wood framed mirror of oblong form carved en rocaille with scrolls, rockwork and trailing garland, 49½in. high.
(Andrew Hartley) $2,146

A late Victorian mahogany and satinwood crossbanded toilet mirror, the shield-shaped plate supported by scrolled columns, 23in. wide.
(Christie's)   **$486**

A Regency period giltwood circular convex hanging mirror, having ebonized reeded surround, molded gilt ball frame, 25in. diameter.
(H.C. Chapman)   **$936**

A Victorian mahogany cheval mirror, on acanthus-carved arched bar feet ending in scrolled toes, 27½in. wide.
(Christie's)   **$781**

A red-painted pine wall mirror, American, 18th century, the arched and peaked crest above a rectangular mirror plate, 15in. high.
(Sotheby's)   **$4,887**

A pair of giltwood frames, late 17th/early 18th century, each with later oval mirror plate, one framed by a chain of office issuing from a Royal crown supported by a pair of lions, Austrian, 75in. x 57in.
(Christie's)   **$64,116**

A Victorian walnut and parcel-gilt toilet miror, the oval plate within a reeded frame decorated with flower garlands, 29¼in. wide.
(Christie's)   **$15,272**

A mahogany cheval mirror of large size, the rectangular plate within a cushion-molded border surmounted by a cabochon, German, 19th century, 87in. high.
(Christie's)   **$1,403**

An Anglo-Indian ivory inlaid ebony toilet mirror, late 18th century, inlaid overall with scrolling exotic flowers and foliage, 33in. high.
(Christie's)   **$4,200**

A George I giltwood pier mirror, attributed to John Belchier, the later rectangular plate with a shaped arched top in a concave frame, 69¼ x 32¾in.
(Christie's)   **$38,180**

Schooner sailing model, late 19th/early 20th
century, with top mast, 45in. long on deck.
(Skinner) $316

A Bing 66CM painted tinplate submarine,
German, circa 1906, with clockwork motor,
finished in gray with red lining, 26in. long.
(Sotheby's) $1,632

Shadowbox ship model, America, 19th century,
depicting a three-masted ship under full sail,
23 x 43in.
(Skinner) $1,840

Shadowbox ship model, America, 19th century,
depicting the cutter 'Sevo' under full sail, 21$^{1}/_{4}$ x
28$^{1}/_{4}$in.
(Skinner) $2,185

A Falk tinplate three funnel ocean liner,
German, circa 1905, hand painted in red and
cream with the deck finished in orange, having
two masts, 16in. long.
(Sotheby's) $4,225

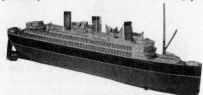

A Bing 83cm. clockwork three-funnel liner,
painted in dark blue, ivory and red, with four
original card funnel inserts and cork, circa
1924.
(Christie's) $5,261

Prisoner of War bone ship model, 19th century,
in period mirrored case, 18$^{1}/_{4}$in. wide.
(Skinner) $4,313

Cased Prisoner of War bone ship model, 19th
century, sixty-six gun ship of the line with full
slanting rigging, in mahogany case, 24in. long.
(Skinner) $5,463

A Bing Gauge O clockwork 'Windcutter'
Atlantic 4-4-2 locomotive and tender, German,
circa 1925, finished in black with red lining, and
eight wheeled bogie tender.
(Sotheby's) $671

A 3½in. Gauge model GWR 4-4-0 County Class
locomotive 'County Carlow' & 3000 gallon
tender, built by F.H. Price 1971-78 from D.
Young design plans, 44in. long.
(Sotheby's) $1,536

A Hornby series clockwork no. 2 special LNER
locomotive, 'The Bramham Moor', English,
circa 1935, numbered *201*, finished in light
green LNER livery with matching six wheeled
tender in maker's box. (Sotheby's) $768

FV (Emile Favre), circa 1865 floor train
consisting of clockwork locomotive and tender
No.15, two Paris-Madrid coaches and a goods
wagon, original box with a full color label.
(Christie's) $1,575

A Bing tinplate Continental station, German,
circa 1912, transfer painted with two storey
design with railings and one arched canopy to
the side, 14¼in. wide.
(Sotheby's) $1,824

A rare Carette Gauge I Metropolitan Railway
Company Westinghouse Electric locomotive,
German, circa 1908, the lithographed tinplate
body with company crest and 'No. 5'.
(Sotheby's) $4,801

A model of a 3½in. Gauge LMSR no. 6160 Royal
Scot Class locomotive 'Queen Victoria's
Rifleman,' built by A.A. Tilley from 1950-1970,
made entirely from polished stainless steel
except for the wheels and frame, 49½in. long.
(Sotheby's) $2,113

Aster for Fulgurex K. Bay. STS.B GT2X4/4
Class Mallet type tank locomotive, Japanese,
circa 1980, the electric model made for 45mm
gauge, built to scale 1:32in. and finished in
Bavarian state livery.
(Sotheby's) $2,881

447

A rare J. & E. Stevens 'I always did 'spise a mule' or 'kicking mule' cast iron money bank, American, circa 1879, 10in. long. (Sotheby's) $1,920

A good J. & E. Stevens William Tell cast iron money bank, American, bearing 1896 patent date, the elaborately robed marksman fires a coin into a slot in the castle, 10¼in. long, (Sotheby's) $639

A rare J. & E. Stevens 'I always did 'spise a mule' or 'kicking mule' cast iron money bank, American, circa 1879, 10in. long. (Sotheby's) $1,463

A Porky Piggy Bank papier-mâché, hand-painted money bank, American, 1950s, 16cm. high. (Auction Team Köln) $95

A rare tinplate Mickey Mouse mechanical bank, German, probably by Sehulmer & Strauss, early 1930s, 7in. high. (Bonhams) $9,353

A Little Joe Bank cast-iron, red-brown painted mechanical money bank, when handle is pulled the coin laid on hand is transferred to mouth and swallowed. (Auction Team Köln) $116

A Jolly Nigger mechanical money bank, possibly by Starkies, England, eyes roll and ears twitch. (Auction Team Köln) $78

A Kyser Rex & Co. mechanical lion & monkey money bank, American, late 19th century, 9½in. high, (Sotheby's) $1,097

A fine Mickey Mouse mechanical bank, German, early 1930's, possibly made by Sehulmer and Strauss, 7in. high. (Sotheby's) $18,285

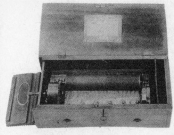  

A musical box by Nicole Freres, No.27016, playing four airs, with key-wind, tune-sheet and end-flap in fruitwood case with stringing to front and lid, 14¼in.
(Christie's) $1,783

Swiss 13in. cylinder music box on stand, circa 1900, with three additional cylinders, on a burl walnut and ebonized stand, 43in. wide.
(Skinner) $6,612

A full-organ musical box, playing six airs with 32-key movement in grained case, 22in. wide.
(Christie's) $3,565

A drum and bells musical box, No. 31204, playing ten popular ballads with six engraved bells, amboyna-crossbanded rosewood front and lid with inlay, 52cm wide.
(Christie's) $1,158

A musical box playing eight airs with six optional bells with bird strikers in veneered and cross-banded case with brass carrying handles, 23in. wide.
(Christie's) $2,991

A musical box with nine bells, No. 18643, playing ten Scottish airs, George Bendon style tune sheet and crossbanded figured walnut case, 26in. wide.
(Christie's) $4,927

A mandoline musical box by Nicole Freres, No. 51558, playing six airs with double-spring nickel-plated motor, speed-control, tune-sheet and grained case, 21½in. wide.
(Christie's) $3,922

A late 19th century French rosewood and ebonized musical box, the 13¹/₂in. cylinder playing twelve airs on two combs by Nicole Freres, 2ft. 6in. overall.
(Russell, Baldwin & Bright) $2,371

A musical box by Mermod Frères, No. 15514, playing twelve airs, with crank-wind motor, and Jacot safety check, in stained case with tune sheet, 20in. wide.
(Christie's) $1,407

A good violin by
Alexander Smillie,
bearing label and date
1899, l.o.b. 14in.
(Phillips)

$3,473

An Italian violoncello,
School of Jorio, Naples,
circa 1840, labeled
Lorenzo Ventapane,
l.o.b. 29¼in.
(Phillips)

$45,300

A flat-backed mandolin
by Ibanez, with eight
strings, in a case.
(Christie's)

$760

A handsome English
violoncello by Thomas
Kennedy, London 1833,
l.o.b. 29in.
(Phillips)

$21,140

A good violoncello by
Arthur Edward Smith,
the one-piece back cut on
the slab, the ribs similar,
the length of back
29⁷/₈in.
(Christie's)

$18,596

An interesting
violoncello, possibly
Neapolitan, labeled
Gagliano, the two-piece
back of plain wood, the
length of back 29³/₁₆in.
(Christie's)

$26,565

An Italian violin by
Tomaso Eberle, the two-
piece back of small
irregular curl, the scroll
similar, the length of
back 14in.
(Christie's)

$28,336

An Italian violin by
Giovanni Battista
Gabrielli the two-piece
back of faint small curl,
the ribs and scroll
similar, the length of
back 13¹⁵/₁₆in.
(Christie's)

$30,107

A fine violoncello by Charles J.B. Collin-Mezin, Paris, bearing maker's original 1896 dated label, l.o.b. 30in. (Phillips)

$18,120

A flat-backed mandolin labeled *M. Vanden/December1980*, with eight strings, in a case. (Christie's)

$475

A fine violin by Nicolas François Vuillaume, dated on back *1863*, l.o.b. 14in. (Phillips)

$18,120

A Neapolitan mandolin labeled ... *Raffaele Calace & Figlio...1969*, with rosewood banding and inlay. (Christie's)

$1,700

A fine violin by William E. Hill & Sons, London 1889, the one-piece back cut on the slab, the ribs and scroll similar, the length of back 14¹/₈in. (Christie's)

$8,501

An Italian violin by Giovanni Grancino, *Corona 1662*, the two-piece back of plain wood, the ribs and scroll similar, the length of back 13¹⁵/₁₆in. (Christie's)

$73,458

A good French violin by Gand & Bernardel, the two-piece back of handsome medium curl, the ribs and scroll similar, the length of back 14¹/₈in. (Christie's)

$8,501

An interesting violin, probably Neapolitan, labeled *Lorenzo Ventapane*, the one-piece back of medium to small curl, the length of back 14¹/₁₆in. (Christie's)

$12,397

Early 19th century, ivory netsuke by Tomochika depicting a wolf resting a paw on a human skull, signed.
(Eldred's) $935

Ivory netsuke by Minko, depicting a karako who has crawled into a fencer's helmet, Meiji Period, signed.
(Eldred's) $330

Ivory netsuke by Masaharu depicting a man examining a carbuncle on his leg, Meiji Period, signed.
(Eldred's) $660

A 19th century ivory netsuke by Yoshiyama depicting a man making huge boots for Shoki while other parts of Shoki's costume lie about him, signed.
(Eldred's) $825

Ivory study of three karako, 18th century, the children playing around a large water jar, 2in. high.
(Butterfield & Butterfield) $690

A 20th century ivory netsuke in the manner of Kaigyokusai depicting a monkey and young eating peaches, signed *Masatsugu.*
(Eldred's) $495

Good inlaid boxwood study of a lotus pod, 19th century, signed *Minko*, the realistically carved pod containing loose seeds, 1in. high.
(Butterfield & Butterfield) $1,150

Ivory study of a sleeping sage, 20th century, signed *Meigyokusai*, the elder depicted resting on a dragon decorated platform, 2in. long.
(Butterfield & Butterfield) $1,265

Ivory study of a seated Hotei, late 18th century, the happy corpulent immortal shown seated and leaning on his bag of worldly goods, 2in. high.
(Butterfield & Butterfield)
                                     $2,587

Ivory study of a Dutchman, late 19th/early 20th century, the standing figure wearing long coat and tasseled hat, 2¾in.
(Butterfield & Butterfield)
                                     $1,092

An ivory netsuke with silver mounts, with signature *Tomotada*, 18th century, of a reclining ox with young, with silver inlaid details, 6.5cm wide.
(Christie's) $10,400

Boxwood and ivory study of a dancer, the kneeling performer wearing an Okame mask, signed *Yumin*, 19th century, 2in. high.
(Butterfield & Butterfield)
                                       $517

Boxwood study of a dragon coiled around a pearl, 19th century, 1½in. high. (Butterfield & Butterfield) $575

Boxwood study of a snail on a lotus leaf, 19th century, 2¼in. long. (Butterfield & Butterfield) $748

Ivory netsuke by Mitsuhiro, in the form of a loosely carved chicken in an egg, signed and seal marked, Meiji Period. (Eldred's) $248

Good ivory mask study, Meiji period, signed *Gyokuhide*, elegantly rendered as a snarling oni, 2in. (Butterfield & Butterfield) $1,150

Unusual carved ivory study of monkeys, frogs and a fish, Meiji period, details stained in sepia wash, 2¾in. (Butterfield & Butterfield) $748

A 20th century ivory netsuke, a karako sits at a low table painting on a scroll while a cat crouches in front of the table, signed. (Eldred's) $308

Humorous ivory study of Hotei with a young attendant, 20th century, signed *Otoman*, the deity carrying new year's beans, 1½in. (Butterfield & Butterfield) $5,462

Ivory tiger group, 19th century, signed *Hakuryu*, depicting a menacing tigress with one paw on her sleeping cub, another cub on her back, 1in. high. (Butterfield & Butterfield) $690

Polychromed ivory study of a man with a lantern, early 20th century, signed *Yasutaka*, the vendor carrying his wares in a basket, 2½in. high. (Butterfield & Butterfield) $518

Ivory netsuke by Ryomin depicting a lohan holding a beggar's bowl from which emerges a dragon, Meiji Period, signed. (Eldred's) $963

A 19th century ivory figure of a Daikoku standing with his treasure sack on his back and a karako climbing about his shoulders, 2¾in. high. (Eldred's) $248

Early 20th century polychrome ivory netsuke by Yamaji, depicting Okame waving goodbye while holding a folded fan, signed. (Eldred's) $248

Magic lantern Maison de la Bonne Presse, Paris, pierced-metal lamphouse, lacquered-brass lens mount and lens, and wood slide carrier.
(Christie's) $159

Achromatic stereoscope no. 2292 R. & J. Beck, London, walnut body in maker's fitted leather box, eleven stereo cards including French harbor scenes.
(Christie's) $454

Achromatic stereoscope no. 1397, Smith, Beck & Beck, London, mahogany body, lacquered-brass fittings and mahogany cover.
(Christie's) $531

A Luxus Stereo viewer, for fifteen 9 x 18cm. stereo cards, burr walnut case, with fold-out lighting mirror, French, circa 1880.
(Auction Team Köln)
                               $595

Stereoscope and stereographs comprising a wood-body table-top stereoscope, two stereograph inserts, each with fifty 10 x 15cm. wire and wood stereo-positive holders, dated circa 1916-1920s.
(Christie's) $874

Anonymous, table-top stereoscope, walnut body with rack and pinion focusing viewing lenses, and a quantity of glass stereo slides of English and French scenes.
(Christie's) $759

Projector no. 258630, Ernemann-Werke A.G., Dresden, with black-enameled lamphouse, an Ernemann 25cm. lens, chimney and electric illuminant.
(Christie's) $97

Stereo-graphoscope, Roswells patent, mahogany-body, with magnifying lens, a pair of stereo viewing lenses and photograph holder.
(Christie's) $352

The Matagraph cinematograph Levi, Jones & Co. Ltd, London 35mm., the mahogany-body stamped 11, hand-crank, brass bound lens, lacquered-brass beater movement.
(Christie's) $3,146

Automatic table stereoscope no. 279, wood-body, with four J. Richard 6 x 13cm. stereo magazines and eleven glass slides showing Fontainebleau.
(Christie's) $673

A hand-cranked Kinora viewer with three reels comprising no. 288 (couple dancing), no. 130 (man tying bow-tie), no. 135 (dancing girl in white dress).
(Christie's) $1,484

Zoetrope, 12in. diameter drum, on a turned wood base, with five double sided picture strips, in a wood box.
(Christie's) $489

Lapierre, France, a bright nickel-plated upright cylinder lantern with lens, electric illuminant and chimney, in maker's wood box, a quantity of strip slides.
(Christie's) $612

Pedestal stereoscope, French, polished wood-body, hinged top, rack and pinion focusing eyepieces and two stereograph holder inserts, each stamped *P.F. Marque Déposée*.
(Christie's) $564

Taxiphoto stereo viewer, J. Richard, France, 45 x 107mm. wood-body internal slide changing mechanism and a quantity of 45 x 107mm. stereo positives in base storage drawer.
(Christie's) $881

A Multiplast table stereoscope in oak case, on adjustable base, for 25 45 x 107 stereo slides, by ICA, Dresden, 1910.
(Auction Team Köln)
                               $870

Biunial lantern, brass and mahogany, with chimney, in fitted wood box, a pair of lenses, a pair of 14in. lenses, two pairs of extension tubes, pressure gauge and accessories.
(Christie's) $3,496

Zograscope, the wood stand with inlaid decoration, the mirror set into a decorative panel, with 5½in. diameter lens and turned wood base.
(Christie's) $531

1915 Bank of Japan 5 yen in gold.
(Phillips) $260

Provincial Bank of Ireland £1, 1 January
1874, black on white uniface proof on paper
with portrait of Queen Victoria upper left.
(Phillips) $208

1877 Imperial Japanese National Bank 1 yen,
sailors at right.
(Phillips) $375

1885 Bank of Japan 1 yen, blue with Daikoku
sitting on rice bales at right.
(Phillips) $625

South Africa, 1871 London & South African
Bank £5, issued at Port Elizabeth, black and
white on purple underprint.
(Phillips) $750

Bank of England £20, 1933-95 pair of error
notes which have been miscut, leaving large
border at bottom.
(Phillips) $400

Ireland, Clonmell Bank (Rials) 30/- 1816, split
and rejoined.
(Phillips) $547

Romford Agricultural Bank £1, 1824, pale
blue *one* overlay at center, slightly trimmed
but not affecting design. (Phillips) $300

1899-1910 Bank of Japan 5 yen in gold, portrait of Takeuchi Sukune at center (Phillips) $800

Canada, 1865 Bank of British North America $5, uniface black and white proof on paper for Toronto. (Phillips) $330

1873 Imperial Currency 1 yen, warrior with bow and arrows at left. (Phillips) $2,000

1965 Bank of Ghana 1,000 cedis. (Phillips) $441

Commercial Bank £1, 1826, black on white *Payable to J.S. Cunningham* and engraved by Perkins, Bacon & Petch. (Phillips) $1,825

Great Britain, C.P. Mahon £5, 3 August 1927, issued at Hull. (Phillips) $450

Australia, 1918 Commonwealth of Australia £1, signed *Cerutty-Collins.* (Phillips) $243

1937 Japanese Imperial Government 10 yen, military issue for China, black on green with cockerels above dragons in vertical format. (Phillips) $2,415

Russia, Vladikavkaz Railroad Company
10,000 roubles.
(Phillips) $274

Monmouthshire & Glamorganshire Bank, £10
issued at Newport on March 26 1846,
overstamped at center in red *Barclay &
Company Ltd.* (Phillips) $699

1873 Imperial Japanese Currency 5 yen, field
workers at left and right, printed by
Continental Banknote Co., New York.
(Phillips) $9,725

Isle of Man, 10/- dated 18 September 1941
plus handwritten *Not Negotiable* on back of an
issued Onchan Internment Camp 10/-.
(Phillips) $456

New Zealand, 1905 Union Bank of Australia
Limited £1, issued at Wellington, attractive
design with portrait of Queen Victoria.
(Phillips) $625

Russia, Vladikavkaz Railroad Company 5,000
roubles.
(Phillips) $319

Great Britain, L.K. O'Brien, £5 (2) 1957,
errors both with prefix and serial number D57
386217. (Phillips) $304

Venezuela, 1862 Banco de Venezuela 8 and 10
reales, large uniface note.
(Phillips) $330

Bank of Scotland £1, 22 July 1867, with *one* overprint in red at center. (Phillips) $699

1906 Chinese Revolutionary Government $100, payable 1 year after the establishment of said Government in China, attractive red design. (Phillips) $578

1873 Imperial Japanese Currency 2 yen, warriors at left and right, printed by Continental Banknote Co., New York. (Phillips) $6,950

1878 Military issue by The Combined Services for 5 yen, printed in black with red and blue stamps on starched linen. (Phillips) $470

Great Britain, G. Kentfield, £50 1994, error mis-cut with extra flap of paper left side. (Phillips) $289

Monmouthshire, 5 guineas 1791, pinholes, two small holes in body and worn at top right corner. (Phillips) $441

1878 Imperial Japanese National Bank 5 yen, black on green with blacksmiths at right. (Phillips) $2,860

Hong Kong 1941 Chartered Bank $5. (Phillips) $350

Waterman's, an 0552 Gothic with no. 2 nib, American, 1920's, barrel engraved. (Bonhams) $148

Le Boeuf, a gray marble Holywater sprinkler, American, 1920's. (Bonhams) $528

Parker, a gold plated 65 Cirrus, with broad italic nib, English, 1970's. (Bonhams) $165

Conklin, a 'Halloween' lever-filler, with Toledo nib, American, 1930's. (Bonhams) $363

S. & N., a black Balance piston-filler decorated with an iridescent finish and with warranted nib, Japanese 1950's. (Bonhams) $107

Mont Blanc, a red 214 pen and 15 pencil, with no. 4 nib, Danish, 1950's. (Bonhams) $313

Waterman's, a cardinal-red 414 filigree eyedropper, marked *sterling* with no. 4 nib, American, circa 1910. (Bonhams) $1,485

Mont Blanc, a limited edition Hemingway no. NE3305/04, with two-color 4810 nib, German, 1992, mint and boxed. (Bonhams) $990

Michael L. Fultz, a limited edition Spider pen no. 0285/500, with two-color Duofold nib, American, 1990's. (Bonhams) $693

Pelikan, a yellow metal 100, marked *14k*, German, 1930's.
(Bonhams) $1,815

Wahl Eversharp, a pearl and black Gold Seal Deco Band, with Skyline nib, American, circa
1930. (Bonhams) $214

Mont Blanc, a red 204, with no. 4 nib, Danish, 1950's.
(Bonhams) $198

Mabie Todd, a [/50] Jade Swan self-filler, with black cap bands and no. 2 Swan nib, American,
circa 1927. (Bonhams) $165

Parker, a golden Pearl Major Vacumatic with flexible arrow nib, American, circa 1939.
(Bonhams) $148

Mont Blanc, a green striped 144 pen and 172 pencil, with two-color 4810 nib, German, 1950's.
(Bonhams) $528

Sheaffer, a limited edition W. A. Sheaffer Commemorative lever-filling fountain pen no.
0799/6000, American, 1996. (Bonhams) $528

Mont Blanc, a 9ct. gold 149 overlay, by S.J. Rose with two-color 4810 nib, London 1971.
(Bonhams) $1,567

Parker, a red Lucky Curve Duofold Special with Duofold pen nib, American, circa 1928.
(Bonhams) $148

Anon, a gold plated filigree eyedropper, with no. 2 warranted nib, American, circa 1910.
(Bonhams)
$115

Conway Stewart, a green herringbone 58 with broad 58 Duro nib, English, 1950's.
(Bonhams)
$115

Conklin, a chased black hard rubber M51 crescent-filler, with twin gold plated barrel bands
and Toledo no.4 nib, American, circa 1901. (Bonhams)
$363

Parker, a gold plated 61 Cumulus, English, 1960's, mint and boxed.
(Bonhams)
$165

Pelikan, a limited edition Wall Street pen and ballpen no. 1714/4500, with two-color broad nib,
German 1995. (Bonhams)
$627

Pelikan, a tortoiseshell-brown M400 with 14ct. nib, German, modern, mint.
(Bonhams)
$148

Parker, a red Lucky Curve Duofold Senior, with Duofold nib, America, circa 1926.
(Bonhams)
$165

Mont Blanc, a limited edition Louis XIV no. 2493/4810, with vermeil overlay, German, 1994.
(Bonhams)
$2,227

Mont Blanc, a white metal Meisterstuck ballpen, marked *925,* German, modern.
(Bonhams)
$198

Pilot, a Maki-E lacquer pen, decorated with a dragon, executed in Iroe-Hira Maki-E on a roironuri ground, with Pilot nib, Japanese 1986, inscribed *In Commemoration of Pilot Prize, 1986,*
boxed. (Bonhams)
$165

Wyvern, a silver safety eyedropper, with warranted nib and Wyvern Pen Co. hallmark, London 1910. (Bonhams) $132

Parker, a gray geometric Duofold, with Parker nib, Danish, 1930's. (Bonhams) $99

Waterman's, an ivory pearl nurse's pen, with red cap top and Ideal nib, American, 1940's. (Bonhams) $36

Conway Stewart, a cracked ice no. 33 propeling pencil, English, 1950's. (Bonhams) $132

Parker, a limited edition R.M.S. Queen Elizabeth 75, no. 1242/5000, American, circa 1974. (Bonhams) $1,033

Mont Blanc, a limited edition Imperial Dragon no. 436/888, with 18k. gold dragon clip, German, 1994. (Bonhams) $4,620

Mont Blanc, a limited edition Lorenzo De Medici no. 1726/4810, with octagonal silver overlay, German, 1992, sealed in factory bag. (Bonhams) $4,950

Waterman's, a black 14, clip and twin-barrel bands, marked *14* with no. 4 nib, American, circa 1910. (Bonhams) $206

St. Dupont, a blue agate lacque de Chine with 18ct., Dupont nib, French, modern. boxed. (Bonhams) $80

Waterman's, a 412½ P.O.C. 'Oriental', marked *sterling* with no. 2 nib, American, circa 1908-15. (Bonhams) $1,650

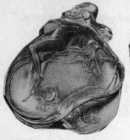

A W.M.F. silvered pewter card tray, cast in low relief with a naked female fairy to one side amongst scrolling and whiplash foliage, 25.5cm. diameter.
(Christie's) $630

An Oriental silver-colored metal rectangular cigarette box, decorated in relief with a dragon, 15cm. long.
(Bearne's) $283

A W.M.F. silvered pewter card tray, cast in relief with the reclining figure of an Art Nouveau maiden amongst whiplash foliage, 25.5cm. diameter.
(Christie's) $1,298

Hugo Leven for Kayserzinn, five branch candelabrum, circa 1900, pewter, the four arms and central column terminating in candleholders and drip pans, 19in. high.
(Sotheby's) $2,991

F. Nicoud Aesthetic teapot, circa 1880, silvered colored metal, the body with engraved decoration in the Japanese taste incorporating two herons, bamboo and aquatic plants, 4$\frac{1}{2}$in. high.
(Sotheby's) $2,463

Albert Reimann mounted vase, circa 1900, earthenware with deep blue-green glaze, with openwork pewter mounts, 11^{7}/$_{8}$in. high.
(Sotheby's) $1,319

A W.M.F. silvered metal toilet mirror, the hinged circular glass supported on two scrolling arms leading to the head of a panther, 76cm. high.
(Christie's) $1,669

A W.M.F. silvered pewter liqueur set, with organic scrolling and six clear glass tumblers, with central Art Nouveau figure, 37cm. high.
(Christie's) $1,150

An Osiris pewter table clock, the gilded metal circular dial set within shaped face cast in low relief, 35.5cm. high.
(Christie's) $2,782

Tiffany and Co. finger bowl in the Japanese taste, circa 1885, silver colored metal, gilt silver colored metal interior, everted petaled rim, 4⅛in. diameter.
(Sotheby's) $1,760

A W.M.F. silvered pewter double photograph frame, pierced and cast with rows of squares between oval, dot and linear motifs, 24cm. high.
(Christie's) $593

A W.M.F. silvered pewter card tray, cast in low relief with Diana and attendants hunting, 40cm. diameter.
(Christie's) $408

An Art Deco white metal cocktail shaker, in the form of a coffee pot, stamped marks *Asahi Shoten, Sterling 950*, 22.5cm. high.
(Christie's) $648

Gorham Co., retailed by Shreve, Crump & Low Co., pair 'Martele' beakers in the Japanese style, 1902, silver colored metal, cast and decorated with stylized fish and tendrils, 3¼in. high.
(Sotheby's) $2,463

A W.M.F. silvered pewter picture frame, pierced and cast in low relief with scrolling foliage and berries and stylized linear motifs, 30cm. high.
(Christie's) $779

A W.M.F. silvered pewter card tray, cast in low relief with the figure of a scantily clad Art Nouveau maiden leaning to one side against a lyre, 22cm. diameter.
(Christie's) $352

A Tiffany & Co. white metal bowl, the spot hammered surface incised with stylized chinoiserie foliage and applied with four copper tortoises in low relief, 21.4cm. diameter.
(Christie's) $2,782

A rare pewter porringer, Chester County, Pennsylvania, dated *1807*, of circular form with projecting rim and pierced tab handle, 7¼in. diameter.
(Sotheby's) $1,840

A Le Coquet phonograph by
Pathé, France, with aluminium
horn, 1903.
(Auction Team Köln)

$583

An Excelsior phonograph with
brass horn, German.
(Auction Team Köln)

$660

La Sirène phonograph, the base
in the form of a mermaid
painted in green and gold,
original horn, 1904.
(Auction Team Köln)

$933

An Angelica cylinder disk
phonograph by the Excelsior
Works, Cologne, with black and
gold decorated tin horn.
(Auction Team Köln)

$465

An early Edison suitcase
Standard phonograph, No. S184
with Automatic reproducer,
shaving device and Edison-Bell
licence plate No. 5151 in oak
case with side-mounted suitcase
clips, circa 1898-9.
(Christie's)

$792

A green Pathé Le Menestrel
phonograph, on a green and gold
Louis XV-style cast base and
similar cover, aluminium horn,
circa 1905.
(Auction Team Köln)

$2,646

A Carette Puck phonograph,
with black and gold cast lyre
base, and plated tin horn,
separate brake and speed
regulator.
(Auction Team Köln)

$622

An Edison-Bell New Duplex
phonograph, No. C10717 with D
reproducer and slip-on Concert
mandrel, in New Style oak case
with 31-inch William Still brass
horn.
(Christie's)

$3,695

A Carette Mignon phonograph,
with red/yellow horn and
polychrome base painted with
birds and flowers, 1904.
(Auction Team Köln)

$700

PHOTOGRAPHS

Paul Caponigro, 'Stonehenge, Wiltshire, England', 1970/later, gelatin silver print, signed and editioned *28/75* in pencil on the mount, 9½ x 13¼ins.
(Butterfield & Butterfield)
$1,092

Duke Ellington, early signed sepia 8x10 photograph, head and shoulders.
(Vennett Smith) $135

Lee Friedlander, New York City, 1962/later, gelatin silver print, signed, titled and dated in pencil, 8¼ x 12¼ins.
(Butterfield & Butterfield)
$1,150

A signed publicity photograph of Marilyn Monroe, 1950s, black and white, showing her in a scarcely seen pose, signed and dedicated to *Bill* in red ink, 6¼ x 12¼in.
(Sotheby's) $5,382

Henri Cartier-Bresson, Selected Works, 1947-71/1991, two gelatin silver prints: A Preacher and His Family, San Antonio and July 4, Aspen, Colorado, each 9½x14¼in.
(Butterfield & Butterfield)
$3,162

Ed Pfizenmaier, Cecil Beaton and Marilyn Monroe, 1956/later, four gelatin silver prints, signed and dated in pencil, each 9x6½in. approx.
(Butterfield & Butterfield)
$805

Kolb Brothers, Portrait of a Navaho, circa 1900, gelatin silver print, with the photographers' blindstamp on image, 13½x10¼in.
(Butterfield & Butterfield)
$747

Arnold Newman, Portrait of Milton Avery, 1960/later, gelatin silver print, signed, titled and dated, 7½in.x9¾in.
(Butterfield & Butterfield)
$920

Doris Ulmann, Lillian Gish, 1930s, waxed platinum print, signed in pencil on the mount, 8x6in.
(Butterfield & Butterfield)
$575

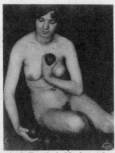

Jan Saudek, 'Hey Joe, Prague', 1986, hand colored gelatin silver print, signed in ink on image, 14x11¼in.
(Butterfield & Butterfield)
$1,380

Henri Cartier-Bresson, Sunday on the Banks of the Marne, 1938/later, gelatin silver print, signed in ink, 9¼x14¼in.
(Butterfield & Butterfield)
$2,875

Frantisek Drtikol, Nude with Fruit, 1920s, bromagraph, with the photographer's stamp in the negative, 11¼x9in.
(Butterfield & Butterfield)
$747

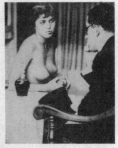

Josef Breitenbach, Dr. Riegler and J. Greno, 1933/89, photogravure printed on a larger sheet with embossed border, 11¾x9½in.
(Butterfield & Butterfield)
$488

Alfred Eisenstaedt, Selected Works, 1929/later, two gelatin silver prints titled *Truempy Dance School, Berlin*, each 10x13in. approx.
(Butterfield & Butterfield)
$1,840

Annie Leibovitz, Mikhail Baryshnikov, New York, 1989, Cibachrome print, signed, titled, and dated on margin, 14¼x11½in.
(Butterfield & Butterfield)
$1,725

Herb Ritts, Djimon with Octopus, 1989, gelatin silver print, photographer's copyright blindstamp in margin, 17x15in.
(Butterfield & Butterfield)
$5,175

Ralph Steiner, American Rural Baroque, 1929/1979, gelatin silver print, signed and dated in pencil on verso, 7½x9¾in.
(Butterfield & Butterfield)
$2,185

Lotte Jacobi, Portrait of Albert Einstein, 1938/later, gelatin silver print, signed in pencil on image, 9¼x 6¾in.
(Butterfield & Butterfield)
$1,092

PHOTOGRAPHS

Laure Albin-Guillot, Lillian Gish as Romola, 1910, gelatin silver print, signed *Albin* twice in image, 19¼x15¼in.
(Butterfield & Butterfield)
$862

Zeke Berman, Table Study, Clay, 1983, gelatin silver print, signed, titled and dated on verso, 14¾x18¾in.
(Butterfield & Butterfield)
$920

Joyce Tenneson, Suzanne, 1986/1993, Cibachrome print, signed and editioned in ink on verso, 34½x29½in.
(Butterfield & Butterfield)
$2,185

Herman Leonard, Billie Holliday, 1949/later, gelatin silver print, signed, titled and dated in ink on margin, 16¾ x 14in.
(Butterfield & Butterfield)
$1,840

Thomas Annan, Main Street, Gorba!s, Looking South, 1868/78, carbon print mounted to board, number and title printed on mount, 8½x12¼in.
(Butterfield & Butterfield)
$1,092

Herman Leonard, Dizzy Gillespie, Royal Roost, NYC, 1948/later, gelatin silver print, signed, titled and dated, 17¾x14½in.
(Butterfield & Butterfield)
$2,587

William Klein, Smoke and Veil, Paris, 1958/later, gelatin silver print, signed, titled and dated on verso, 13½x10in.
(Butterfield & Butterfield)
$1,495

Henri Cartier-Bresson, Valencia, Spain, 1933/later, gelatin silver print, signed in ink, 9½x14¼in.
(Butterfield & Butterfield)
$1,840

Frantisek Drtikol, Portrait of Drtikol's Wife, 1920s, gelatin silver print, signed in pencil in mount, 11½x9in.
(Butterfield & Butterfield)
$1,382

Anonymous, portrait of a carpenter with his tools, 1850's, sixth-plate daguerreotype, gilt-metal mount, in folding case.
(Christie's) $1,898

Richard Avedon, The Duke and Duchess of Windsor, New York City, 1957, gelatin silver print, image size 16¼ x 13¾in.
(Christie's) $569

Lotte Jacobi, 'Alfred Stieglitz at An American Place', circa 1940, gelatin silver print, 10 x 7¼in., signed in pencil on recto.
(Christie's) $607

Edward S. Curtis, 'Chief of the Desert, Navaho', 1904, toned gelatin silver print adhered to a heavy brown paper mount, signed in ink on the image, framed, 7¾ x 5⅝ins.
(Butterfield & Butterfield) $3,450

Ansel Adams, 'Moonrise, Hernandez, N.M.' 1942/later, gelatin silver print, signed in pencil on the mount, 15½ x 19½ins.
(Butterfield & Butterfield) $9,200

Lewis Hine, selected works: Young Workers, circa 1910, two gelatin silver prints: Young Workers and Young Boy Outside Mill, each approx. 4¾ x 3¾ins.
(Butterfield & Butterfield) $517

Herbert Ponting, 'Cavern in an iceberg', 1910-1912, gray/green carbon print, image size 18 x 12½in., mounted on card.
(Christie's) $3,795

Ida Kar, Georges Braque, 1960, gelatin silver print, 9¼ x 9¼in., signed in white ink on recto.
(Christie's) $607

Bill Brandt, London, 1956, printed circa 1980, gelatin silver print, 13½ x 11½in., matted and framed.
(Christie's) $949

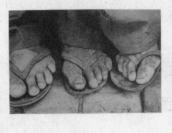

Vincenzo Galdi, Female nude, late 19th century, albumen print, 7½ x 5½in.
(Christie's) $114

Sebastiao Salgado, 'Brasil, 1983', gelatin silver print, image size 6¾ x 10¼in., signed, titled and dated in pencil on verso.
(Christie's) $1,422

Dorothy Wilding, Yul Bryner, 1951, gelatin silver print, 9¾ x 9¼in., black linear border, mounted on tissue.
(Christie's) $949

Clarence John Laughlin, 'The Three Distances, Near Salt Lake City, Utah', 1955, gelatin silver print, signed, titled and dated, 7½ x 9½ins.
(Butterfield & Butterfield) $1,495

Alfred Eisenstaedt, Dr. Joseph Goebbels, Geneva 1933/1979, gelatin silver print, signed and numbered 7/50 in ink in the margin, 9 x 6ins.
(Butterfield & Butterfield) $1,150

O. Winston Link, 'Rural Retreat', 1950s/1986, gelatin silver print, signed, dated and numbered in pencil, 15¼ x 19¼ins.
(Butterfield & Butterfield) $1,150

Baron Wilhelm von Gloeden, Water carriers, Sicily, circa 1900, albumen print, 8¾ x 6½in., photographer's ink credit stamp.
(Christie's) $721

Weegee, Jazz singers, Harlem, 1940's, gloss gelatin silver print, image size 10¾ x 10¾in.
(Christie's) $1,898

Angus McBean, Self-portrait, 1989, gelatin silver print, image size 13¼ x 10¼in., signed and dated.
(Christie's) $663

PHOTOGRAPHS

Walker Evans, 'Barker with Top Hat and Tails, 1940s, gelatin silver print, signed and titled in pencil on verso, 9¼ x 5½ins.
(Butterfield & Butterfield)
$1,840

Larry Clark, Tulsa, 1971, four gelatin silver prints each signed in pencil on verso, each 8¼ x 12½ins.
(Butterfield & Butterfield)
$1,725

George Rodger, Wrestlers of the Korongo Nuba tribe of Kordofan, Sudan, 1949, printed 1993, gelatin silver print, image size 13 x 9in.
(Christie's)
$1,802

Horst P. Horst, 'Army Leaves, Fort Belvoir, Virginia', 1944, printed later, gelatin silver print, image size 16½ x 14¾in., signed *Horst* in pencil.
(Christie's)
$1,708

Brassaï, 'Market Porter', 1939/later, gelatin silver print, signed and editioned *4/30* in ink, 11½ x 9ins.
(Butterfield & Butterfield)
$690

Tessa Traeger, 'Onion Hands, Devon', 1995, warm-toned gelatin silver print, image size 20¾ x 16in., signed and dated *July 1996.*
(Christie's)
$1,139

Dorothy Norman, portrait of Alfred Stieglitz, 1933, gelatin silver print, signed in ink, titled and dated in pencil, 3¾ x 2¾ins.
(Butterfield & Butterfield)
$920

Ansel Adams, 'Aspens, Northern New Mexico', 1958/later, gelatin silver print, signed in pencil on the mount, 15¼ x 19¾ins.
(Butterfield & Butterfield)
$10,350

Ruth Bernhard, 'In Box - Vertical', c. 1962, gelatin silver print, signed in pencil on the mount, 13¾ x 8ins.
(Butterfield & Butterfield)
$2,185

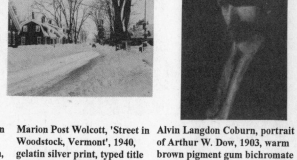

Edward Steichen, Mary Steichen Martin, 1920's, gelatin silver print, titled in ink in the margin, 5¼ x 4ins.
(Butterfield & Butterfield)
$1,150

Marion Post Wolcott, 'Street in Woodstock, Vermont', 1940, gelatin silver print, typed title and date, 7¼ x 9½ins.
(Butterfield & Butterfield)
$1,092

Alvin Langdon Coburn, portrait of Arthur W. Dow, 1903, warm brown pigment gum bichromate over platinum print, 9¼ x 7¼in., signed and inscribed.
(Christie's)
$15,180

Julia Margaret Cameron, 'The Kiss of Peace', 1869, printed by J.B. Obernetter circa 1886, photogravure (Lichtkupferdruck) image size 10¾ x 8½in.,
(Christie's)
$2,087

Bill Brandt, Nude, circa 1950/later, gelatin silver print, signed in ink in the margin, 13½ x 11½ins.
(Butterfield & Butterfield)
$1,035

Julia Margaret Cameron, Profile of an elderly gentleman, 1867, albumen print, 11¼ x 9¼in., mounted on card, dated and inscribed *From Life July 1867*.
(Christie's)
$1,422

Arnold Genthe, Greta Garbo, circa 1925, gelatin silver print, Garbo indentified in ink on verso, 9½ x 7¾ins.
(Butterfield & Butterfield)
$1,725

Frith's Series and others, oak screen mounted with travel photographs, mainly British, late 19th century, each panel 77 x 27in.
(Christie's)
$1,422

Basil Shackleton, portrait of Kyra Nijinsky, circa 1930, gelatin silver print, image size 9¼ x 7in., autographed in ink on recto.
(Christie's)
$228

PHOTOGRAPHS

Ruth Bernhard, Classic Torso, 1952/later, gelatin silver print, signed in pencil on the mount, 13½x10½in.
(Butterfield & Butterfield)
$2,070

Sally Mann, Gorjus, 1989, gelatin silver print, titled signed and dated on verso, 18¾x23¼in.
(Butterfield & Butterfield)
$5,175

Edward S. Curtis, Chief of the Desert, 1904, orotone, signed in the negative, 13½x10½in.
(Butterfield & Butterfield)
$11,500

Horace Bristol, Invasion of North Africa, Loading Dive Bomber on Carrier, 1942, gelatin silver print, signed in pencil on verso, 10½x10½in.
(Butterfield & Butterfield)
$575

Mickey Pallas, Buicks and Their Owners; Buick Convertible and Suburban Man, 1959/later, gelatin print, signed and dated, 14¼x14½in.
(Butterfield & Butterfield)
$575

Diane Arbus/Neil Selkirk, A Family One Evening in a Nudist Camp PA, 1965/later, gelatin silver print signed by Doon Arbus, 14¼x14½in.
(Butterfield & Butterfield)
$1,092

Edward Weston, Clarence and Grace Chandler, 1910, platinum print tipped to a layered mount, 8x6in.
(Butterfield & Butterfield)
$2,300

Eugene Smith, Man Walking Down a Tunnel, 1953, gelatin silver print, mounted to board, 10½x13½in.
(Butterfield & Butterfield)
$1,955

Brassaï, Boulevard Aarago, 1932/later, gelatin silver print, signed in ink on margin, 11 x 8 in.
(Butterfield & Butterfield)
$2,185

PHOTOGRAPHS

Ed Pfizenmaier, Salvador Dali, 1959/later, gelatin silver print, signed, titled and dated in pencil on verso, 10¼x8in.
(Butterfield & Butterfield)
$575

Josef Sudek, Misty Forest, circa 1950, gelatin silver print, signed by Anna Forova, 4½x6¼in.
(Butterfield & Butterfield)
$1,150

Edward S. Curtis, Mosquito Hawk - Assiniboin, 1908, photogravure printed on tissue, tipped to paper mount, 15 x10½in.
(Butterfield & Butterfield)
$2,070

Herbert George Ponting, The Terra Nova Icebound in the Pack, 1910-12, carbon print, with photographer's blindstamp on image 28¾x 21¾in.
(Butterfield & Butterfield)
$6,325

Ansel Adams, Half Dome, Merced River, Winter, Yosemite, circa 1938, gelatin silver print, mounted to a layered board, 40½in. x 61in,
(Butterfield & Butterfield)
$9,200

Jock Sturges, Standing on Water, 1984-90/1991, portfolio of 10 photographs, each signed, titled and dated, each approx. 22x17¾in.
(Butterfield & Butterfield)
$6,900

Mario Cravo Neto, Ode 1989/1992, gelatin silver print, signed and editioned in margin, 18x18in.
(Butterfield & Butterfield)
$1,725

Edward Weston, Out of My Window, San Francisco, 1925, gelatin silver print, signed, dated and editioned on the mount, 7x9½in.
(Butterfield & Butterfield)
$2,300

Diane Arbus/Neil Selkirk, Untitled (6), 1970-1/later, gelatin silver print signed by Doon Arbus, 15x 14½in.
(Butterfield & Butterfield)
$1,092

A Stella 17¼in. disk musical box with double comb movement, in mahogany case with carved front panel, 25¼in. high.
(Christie's) $2,639

A 14¾in. Symphonion disk musical box with two combs and walnut case with astragal panels, and thirteen disks.
(Christie's) $4,635

A 13¼in. Symphonion disk musical box, with single comb, 'dimple-drive' movement in walnut case with sixteen disks.
(Christie's) $2,674

A small Symphonion Simplex record player for 14.5cm. disks, with 41-tone comb, with three disks.
(Auction Team Köln) $390

A Kalliope upright disk musical box with two combs, coin mechanism and typical walnut case with arched glazed door, 39½in. high.
(Christie's) $4,575

An 8¼in. Orphenion disk musical box with single comb movement in walnut case with color print in lid, with seven zinc disks
(Christie's) $801

The Polyphon No. 104 gramophone for 50cm. tinplate disks, 120 tone double comb, with ten disks, 1890.
(Auction Team Köln) $6,616

A 15½in. disk musical box by Chevob & Co., Geneva, with two combs with zither attachments and 43 disks.
(Christie's) $4,635

A 24½in. Polyphon disk musical box with twin comb movement, coin-mechanism and drawer, 45½in. high, with nine disks.
(Christie's) $9,804

Louis-André Fabre (1750-1814), a fine portrait miniature of a gentleman, seated three-quarter length with crossed legs, 3in. (Christie's) $23,104

George Engleheart (1750-1829), a young lady, full face in white dress, oval, 1¾in. high. (Christie's) $3,199

Louis Sené (1747-1804), a young lady called Marquise de Fontenay, later Madame Tallien, 3¼in. diameter. (Christie's) $7,997

Joseph Pellizza (fl. c.1797-1815), a young poet, seated at a green covered table, signed and dated *1801*, 2½in. diameter. (Christie's) $3,554

Nicholas Hilliard (1547-1619), King James I (1566-1625), facing right in black and gold embroidered white goblet with high ruff on vellum oval, ½in. (Christie's) $66,916

François Dumont (1751-1831), Citizen Audoÿ, nearly full-face, in double-breasted blue coat, signed, 3in. diam. (Christie's) $13,329

English School, circa 1800, a young officer, facing left in blue uniform, oval, 3¼in. high. (Christie's) $2,488

French School, circa 1800, two young girls embracing, 2½in. diam., silver frame with rope-twist border. (Christie's) $4,976

Diana Hill, née Dietz (d. 1844), a young officer, facing right in blue uniform, oval, 2¾in. high. (Christie's) $1,777

John Wood Dodge (1807-1893), Theodore Broadway, facing right in blue coat with gold buttons, signed on the backing card, oval, 2in. high. (Christie's) $2,133

Charles Fraser (1782-1860), Adam Tunno, facing right in black coat and waistcoat and frilled cravat, signed on the obverse, rectangular, 4 x 3¼in. (Christie's) $3,910

Rosalba Carriera (1675-1757), a highly important portrait miniature of Marco Ricci, full face in embroidered gold coat, oval, 3in. high. (Christie's) $49,762

Ozias Humphrey, R.A. (1742-1810), an important portrait miniature of The Sahibzada, full face in orange and white robe, signed and dated on reverse, oval, 3½in. high. (Christie's) $104,315

Attributed to Frans Pourbus (1569-1622) Archduke Albert VII of Habsburg, facing right in armor with eleborate gilt decorations, oil on card, oval, 3in. high. (Christie's) $10,663

John Smart (1742/43-1811), an important portrait miniature of a young lady, facing left in brown dress with blue collar, signed and dated 'JS/1787/I', oval, 2½in. high. (Christie's) $35,544

American School, 19th century, miniature portrait of Jeremiah Evarts, Boston, 1837, at the age of 32, watercolor on ivory, 2½ x 1⅞in., framed. (Skinner) $863

Thomas Seir Cummings (American, 1804–1894), miniature portrait of a New York lady, identified on back, watercolor on ivory, 3 x 2⅜in. (Skinner) $2,185

German School oval miniature portrait, 19th century, of Ludwig van Beethoven, by Schozzer, in a gilt metal frame, 3⅜in. high. (Skinner) $575

Edward Samuel Dodge (1816-1857), a young lady, facing left in black dress, signed and dated on the backing card '*1842*', oval, 2½in. high.
(Christie's) $2,133

Jean-François-Marie Huet-Villiers, (1772-1813), a young officer, facing left in gold-braided white uniform, signed and dated, 2¾ x 2½in.
(Christie's) $1,955

John Bogle (1746-1803), a lady, facing right in lace-bordered turquoise colored dress, signed with initials and dated '*IB/177⁸/⁹*', oval, 1¾in. high.
(Christie's) $1,422

School of Jean-Baptiste-Jacques Augustin, circa 1815, John Braham, full face in brown coat with blue collar, with signature and date '*Saint. 1816*', oval, 4¼in. high.
(Christie's) $2,488

J. Lecourt (fl. c.1804-1838), a young lady, full face in black dress with frilled white underslip, signed and dated in gold '*Lecourt 1838 Janvier*', rectangular, 2 x 1¾in.
(Christie's) $1,688

Moritz Michael Daffinger (1790-1849), after Sir Thomas Lawrence (1769-1830), Princess Clementina Metternich as Hebe, full face in loose white dress, signed, oval, 3in. high.
(Christie's) $16,884

French School portrait miniature, 19th century, of Madame Recamier, after Francois Gerard, unsigned, 2⁵/₈in. high.
(Skinner) $288

Marie-Nicolas Ponce-Camus (1778-1839), a young lady seated on a chair, signed and dated on the chair *1800*, rectangular, 2½ x 2¼in.
(Christie's) $2,310

James Peale (1749-1831), a young gentleman, facing right in blue jacket with black collar, signed with initials and dated '*IP/1800*', oval, 2¾in. high.
(Christie's) $1,777

John Wood Dodge (1807-1893), Miss Major, full face in dark blue dress, signed, oval, 2½in. high.
(Christie's) $2,310

Natale Schiavoni (1777-1858), Marcia Arbuthnot and her four children, signed and dated *1805,* oval, 4¼in. wide.
(Christie's) $2,300

Archibald Robertson (1765-1835), Clarina Louise Underhill, full face in white dress with brown bodice, oval, 3in. high.
(Christie's) $1,599

James Peale (1749-1831), a young lady called A. Sisters, facing right in frill-bordered black dress, signed with initials and dated *'IP/1797'*, oval, 2½in. high.
(Christie's) $3,732

Pierre Rouvier (b.after 1742), a young gentleman called Baron de Fingerlin, seated half-length at a pianoforte, signed *'Rouvier. 1784',* 2¼in. diameter.
(Christie's) $1,688

Continental School, circa 1770, Princess Eulalie of Saxony, Abbess of Remiremont, facing left in black lace dress with jeweled buttons and bodice, on parchment, oval, 2¾in. high.
(Christie's) $1,244

Henry Colton Shumway (1807-1884), a young gentleman, facing right in black coat and white waistcoat, signed and dated, *1832,* oval, 2¾in. high.
(Christie's) $1,154

Jeremiah Meyer (1735-1789), a young lady, in white dress with frilled border and surcoat, oval, 2¾in. wide.
(Christie's) $3,554

Samuel Shelley (1750/56-1808), a young boy, facing right in blue uniform with red facings, signed and dated *1785,* navette shaped, 1¾in. high.
(Christie's) $9,775

Fanny d'Ivrey (fl. c.1831-1842), a young officer of the Bodyguard of the King of France, signed, oval, 4in. high.
(Christie's) $977

Elie Dignat (fl.1808-1824), a self-portrait of the artist in his studio painting a miniature of a seated gentleman, 3in. diam.
(Christie's) $9,775

Andrew Plimer (1763-1837), a young gentleman, facing left in blue coat with black collar, oval, 3in. high.
(Christie's) $1,688

D.M. (fl. c. 1659-1676), a portrait miniature believed to be a self-portrait of the artist, facing left in black robes signed with monogram and dated 'DM. Nö/the 19/1664', on vellum oval, 2¼in. high.
(Christie's) $5,687

Samuel Shelley (1750/56-1808), James George, 3rd Earl of Courtown, and his brothers as children, signed with monogram and dated 'SS/1774', oval 2¾in.
(Christie's) $7,109

Horace Hone (1754-1825), Mrs Elizabeth Prentice, in profile to the left, in décolleté white dress, signed with monogram and dated 1807, enamel on copper, oval, 4¼in high.
(Christie's) $12,440

Rosalba Carriera (1675-1757), an important portrait miniature of Sebastiano Ricci, facing right in gold-bordered mole-colored coat, oval, 2¾in. high.
(Christie's) $33,767

Samuel Shelley (1750/56-1808), a mother and her two children all holding hands, signed with initials and dated 'SS/ 1774', oval, 3½in. wide.
(Christie's) $4,621

French School, circa 1640, a young gentleman, facing right in open shirt with lawn collar and tassels, on vellum, oval, 1¾in. high.
(Christie's) $7,997

Siamese Twins: Daisy and Violet Hilton, circa 1930, tears, some with retouch, water staining, 40¹/₂ x 28in.
(Skinner) $575

Lawson Wood, Ringling Bros. Barnum & Bailey, 1943, tears, creases and minor margin patching, 28¹/₂ x 42in.
(Skinner) $373

Ambrosa Select Parfum, circa 1895, time toning, minor scattered foxing, 51³/₄ x 39¹/₄in., linen backed.
(Skinner) $690

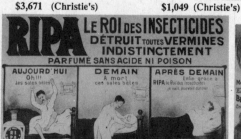

Nover, Absinthe Vichet, lithograph in colors, circa 1900, printed by L. Revon & Cie., Paris, generally in excellent condition, backed on linen, 54 x 38in.
(Christie's) $3,671

Anonymous, Montana Frank Shows, lithograph in colors circa 1910, printed by American Show Print, Milwaukee, faint vertical and horizontal fold marks, backed on Japan, 28 x 42in.
(Christie's) $1,049

Hans Neumann, Benger Ribana, lithograph in colors, circa 1950, vertical and horizontal fold marks with corresponding defects, other minor defects, 46¹/₂ x 33in.
(Christie's) $1,710

Manner, No Wet, No Cold, lithograph in colors, 1929 vertical and horizontal fold marks, slight skimming, framed, 39¹/₂ x 24in.
(Christie's) $1,748

Ripa Le Roi des Insecticides, minor toning, 28 x 40¹/₂in., linen backed.
(Skinner) $230

A. Gallice, Les Hannkinski Patineurs de l'Hippodrome de Paris, small tears, small areas of restoration, 39 x 46in., linen backed.
(Skinner) $402

POSTERS

Kunsthaus Maskenfest, 1926, creases, time toning, patch lower margin, minor water stain, 50¹/₂ x 35³/₄in., linen backed. (Skinner) **$977**

Deval, Fap'Anis, circa 1930, creases, minor foxing, 54¹/₄ x 41¹/₂in., framed. (Skinner) **$460**

Hermann Blaser, Burger-Kehl & Co. PKZ, 1926, minor tears, tape shadows, toning, 50 x 34¹/₂in. (Skinner) **$2,185**

Bury, Ovaltine, for Health & Vitality, lithographs in colors circa 1950, printed by A. Wander Ltd., London, on six sheets, generally in excellent condition, 121 x 80in. (Christie's) **$375**

Jacques Faria, Jupiter Trio, lithograph in colors, circa 1900, printed by Formstecher, Paris, vertical and horizontal fold marks, 36¹/₂ x 50in. (Christie's) **$734**

Paolo Henri, Parfumerie Manon, lithograph in colors circa 1895, printed by Mr. Poncet, Lyon, generally in excellent condition, backed on japan, 32 x 24in. (Christie's) **$350**

Theophile Alexandre Steinlen, Prochainement, Chat Noir, lithograph in colors, 1896, printed by Charles Verneau, Paris, faint vertical and horizontal fold marks, 24 x 16in. (Christie's) **$6,498**

John Gilroy (1898–?), Guinness for Strength, lithograph in colors, circa 1947, printed by Sanders, Phillips & Co. Ltd., London, 29¹/₂ x 39¹/₂in. (Christie's) **$649**

Jules Alexandre Grun (1868–1934), Scala, c'est d'un Raid, lithograph in colors, 1902, printed by Bourgerie & Cie., Paris, minor creases and fold marks, 49 x 35in. (Christie's) **$1,748**

J. Mille, Qu'en Pensez-Vous?, 1929, minor toning along edges, 47 x 31¹/₈in., linen backed. (Skinner) $287

Ringling Bros. and Barnum & Bailey Circus, signed *G.H.* in matrix, creases, tape. (Skinner) $115

Les Sables d'Olonne, circa 1910, minor tears, 42¹/₄ x 30¹/₂in., linen backed. (Skinner) $287

Anonymous, Opening Time is Guinness Time, lithograph in colors, circa 1938, printed by John Waddington Ltd., Leeds, vertical and horizontal fold marks, other minor defects, backed on linen, 58¹/₂ x 40in. (Christie's) $874

Anonymous, Au Grand Chic, lithograph in colors, circa 1920, printed by Foulon Freres & M. Peuchet, Paris, faint vertical and horizontal fold marks, backed on linen, 47 x 31in. (Christie's) $524

Anonymous, See the Guinness Animals at Edinburgh Zoo, lithograph in colors, circa 1938, printed by Wickham Displays Ltd., London, small tears and creases, backed on linen, 30 x 20in. (Christie's) $610

Anonymous, Kina-Lillet, lithograph in colors, circa 1900, printed by Reunies De Levallois, minor defects, backed on linen, 53¹/₂ x 27¹/₂in. (Christie's) $786

Anonymous, Parker Duofold, lithograph in colors, circa 1925, foxing, faint vertical and horizontal fold marks, backed on linen, 21 x 12¹/₂in. (Christie's) $261

Anonymous, Kina, Chateau d'If, lithograph in colors, circa 1900, printed by Courbe-Rouzet, Dole, Pellegrin Ag., Marseille, 50 x 35in. (Christie's) $427

Patzenhofer German Lager, circa 1940, creasing, 18³/₄ x 13¹/₄in., framed. (Skinner) $143

Bernard Villemot, Parly, creasing, scuffing, 62 x 46¹/₂in., linen backed. (Skinner) $546

Louis Rhead, Prang's Easter Publications, 1896, restoration, 23³/₄ x 17¹/₄in., linen backed. (Skinner) $575

Camels, circa 1940, printed on linen by Crinnell Litho. Co. creases, 28³/₄ x 59¹/₂in., framed. (Skinner) $230

L. Damare (?–1927), Parisiana, lithograph in colors, circa 1900, printed by L. Galice, Paris, minor tears and creases mainly at the edges, 49 x 35in. (Christie's) $1,135

Clear, 1910, signed on stone *V. Hibberd. Bkline*, minor scattered foxing, water staining lower margin, 27¹/₂ x 21¹/₂in., framed. (Skinner) $287

Anonymous, La Florestine des Alpes, lithograph in colors, circa 1900, printed by Moullot, Marseille, some foxing, 56¹/₂ x 44in. (Christie's) $597

AERONAUTICAL

Georges Villa, *Grande Semaine d'Aviation Rouen 1910*, printed by Rolf, on linen, 122 x 84cm. (Onslow's) $1,675

S. Horfespringer, Venez En Suisse Par Avion, printed by Fretz Zurich, framed, 1937. (Onslow's) $456

Frank Newbould, Use The Air Mail The Fastest Mail, published by GPO, 51 x 38cm. (Onslow's) $365

Albert Solan, Les Grandes Express Aeriens.Lignes Farman, 1930, creases, very minor tears in margin, 38¼ x 24¼in., linen backed, framed. (Skinner) $575

Ernest Gabard (1879–1957), Pau -Aviation, lithograph in colors, circa 1912, printed by Garet & Haristoy, Pau, slight staining, backed on linen, 31 x 46½in. (Christie's) $1,049

Anonymous, TWA Over The Atlantic and Across The USA You Can Depend On TWA World Proved Constellations, framed. (Onslow's) $395

Albert Brenet, Imperial Airways 28 New Empire Flying Boats 200mph Europe Africa India The Far East Australia, published by Imperial Airways, April 1937. (Onslow's) $1,078

Lovis, Pastilles au Miel, lithograph in colors, circa 1900, printed by Imp. Generale, Clermont-Ferrand, on two sheets, generally in excellent condition, backed on linen, 50 x 38½in. (Christie's) $315

E. Rouny, René Paulhan, lithograph in colors, circa 1935, printed by Jean Ruckert, Paris, vertical and horizontal fold marks with corresponding defects, 47 x 31in. (Christie's) $616

AERONAUTICAL

Guy Arnoux, Air France North America, printed by Baille, French text, on linen, 1946. (Onslow's) $760

Bourgoin, Aerodrome des Landes de Bussac Sponsored by Aero-Shell, printed by Reine, on linen, 113 x 78cm. (Onslow's) $304

Anonymous, Jersey Airways, lithograph in colors, circa 1950, faint vertical and horizontal fold marks, 40 x 24^{1}/$_{2}$in. (Christie's) $3,420

Roy Nockolds, BEA, lithograph in colors, circa 1949, creases and small tears, sellotape stains, 39^{1}/$_{2}$ x 24^{1}/$_{2}$in. (Christie's) $471

Aeroplanes Bleriot G Borel & Cie 25 Rue Brunel Paris, printed by Affiche Louis Galice Paris, 76 x 100cm. (Onslow's) $924

Hot, Pilote D'Avion, lithograph in colors, circa 1930, print by Imp. Nationale, restored tears and losses, backed on linen, 46^{1}/$_{2}$ x 31in. (Christie's) $532

Bouchamp, Vol a Voile, lithograph in colors, 1945, printed by Henri Francoise, Paris, minor defects, generally in excellent condition, 31 x 23^{1}/$_{2}$in. (Christie's) $629

Anonymous, MISR Airlines, Cairo, lithograph in colors, circa 1935, printed by Gale & Polden Ltd., London, vertical and horizontal fold marks, some restored losses, backed on linen, 40 x 25in.(Christie's) $1,573

Anonymous, Paris-Madrid, Le Petit Parisien, lithograph in colors, circa 1913, new right hand margin, otherwise generally in excellent condition, backed on linen, 17 x 12in. (Christie's) $1,049

Francisco Tamango, Cycles Wonder, lithograph in colors, circa 1915, printed by La Lithography Parisienne, Paris, backed on linen, 21 x 14in.
(Christie's) $274

Geo Weiss, Société la Française, lithograph in colors, circa 1895, printed by P. Dupont, Paris, minor defects, generally in excellent condition, 63 x 45in.
(Christie's) $489

Anonymous, Griffon, lithograph in colors, circa 1910, printed by L. Arnault, Neuilly-sur-Seine, faint vertical and horizontal fold marks, 47 x 31in.
(Christie's) $342

Anonymous, Velocipèdes, lithograph in colors, circa 1915, vertical and horizontal fold marks with corresponding defects, backed on linen, 57^1/$_2$ x 38in.
(Christie's) $342

Henri Thiriet, Dayton Cycles, Tentation Supreme, time toning, tape shadows, splits and minor losses, 64 x 94in., linen backed.
(Skinner) $2,070

Dion Raoul, Bicyclettes, La Francaise Diamant, lithograph in colors, circa 1910, printed by Gaillard, Paris, faint vertical and horizontal fold marks, 45^1/$_2$ x 31in.
(Christie's) $427

H. L. Roowy, Michelin, lithograph in colors, 1920 printed by Chaix, Paris, new bottom margin, other minor defects, backed on linen, 41 x 31in.
(Christie's) $874

Anonymous, Armor, lithograph in colors, circa 1910, faint vertical and horizontal fold marks, minor staining, backed on linen, 28 x 22in.
(Christie's) $245

Francisco Tamango (1851–?), Terrot & Cie, Dijon, lithograph in colors, circa 1910, printed by La Lithographie Parisienne, Paris, vertical and horizontal fold marks, 54 x 39in.
(Christie's) $939

CYCLING

Cycles Ouragan, 1894, signed on stone *L.B.G.*, tears, time toning, minor scattered, foxing to margin, 50³/₄ x 37¹/₄in., linen backed.
(Skinner) $632

Raleigh, circa 1935, creases, retouch and patching lower edge, 28¹/₄ x 38in., linen backed.
(Skinner) $460

Misti, (Ferdinand Mifliez), Le Vélo, 1897, corner patches, time toning, repaired tears, minor scattered foxing, 49 x 35in., linen backed.
(Skinner) $488

C.R., Cycles Horer, lithograph in colors, circa 1900, printed by La Lithographie Parisienne, Paris, faint vertical and horizontal fold marks, backed on linen, 53 x 38in.
(Christie's) $512

Marcello Dudovich, Convegno Turistico Ciclismo e Automobilismo, lithograph in colors, 1899, printed by E. Chappuis, Bologna, on two sheets, some tears and small losses, 52 x 35in.
(Christie's) $3,420

Anonymous, Jacquelin sur sa Bicyclette la Française, lithograph in colors, circa 1900, printed by P. Dupont, Paris, some tears and staining, 59 x 43in.
(Christie's) $611

Anonymous, Excelsior, lithograph in colors, circa 1900, minor defects, generally in excellent condition, backed on linen, 31 x 20¹/₂in.
(Christie's) $489

Paolo Henri, Cycles Gladiator, lithograph in colors, circa 1900, printed by Kossuth & Cie., Paris, minor tears and defects, backed on linen, 14¹/₂ x 26¹/₂in.
(Christie's) $274

Emile Lequeux, Manufacture Gle. de Caoutchouc, lithograph in colors, circa 1910, printed by R. Carvin, minor tears, backed on linen, 27 x 18in.
(Christie's) $699

POSTERS

MOTORING

Les Fautes ..., repaired tears, creases, very minor scuffing, 28 x 21³/⁴in., linen backed. (Skinner) $258

J. Pelling, MG Series T.F.: Safety Fast, 1953, repaired tears, 25¹/⁴ x 35in., linen backed. (Skinner) $632

A. J. Foyt Wins Indianapolis 500, a rare original achievements poster for Esso racing fuel, framed and glazed, 20 x 13in. (Christie's) $633

O'Galop (Marius Rossillon 1867–1946), Nunc est Bibendum, lithograph in colors, 1896, printed by Ch. Verneau, Paris, vertical and horizontal fold marks, staining, backed on linen, 61 x 45¹/₂in. (Christie's) $5,244

Anonymous, Permis de Conduire, lithograph in colors, circa 1930, printed by Marchand-Thoissey, Ain, vertical and horizontal fold marks, backed on linen, 33 x 47¹/₂in. (Christie's) $1,049

After E. Montaut, En Reconnaissance, Clement Bayard, a rare early poster depicting airship, aeroplane and four-seater tourer, full color lithograph, linen backed, 62 x 45in. (Christie's) $2,185

After E, Montaut, Michelin - Le Pneu Michelin a Vaincu le Rail, very rare original poster, full color lithograph, linen backed, 61 x 43cm. (Christie's) $3,450

Francisco Tamango, La Mouche, lithograph in colors circa 1900, printed by Romanet, Paris, backed on linen, 36 x 53¹/₂in. (Christie's) $1,880

After Georges Ham, Montlhéry - Grand Prix de Paris de 24 Heures de Paris, 1955, a good original poster, full color lithograph, framed and glazed, 23½ x 15in. (Christie's) $690

490

MOTORING

Zandvoort - Dutch Grand Prix 1948, a scarce early post-war poster, full color lithograph, framed and glazed, 27 x 14in. (Christie's) $518

Renault - Billancourt Seine, a good poster for the marque, showing various coach styles on the 40CV chassis, 46 x 63in. (Christie's) $1,150

Roger Perot (1908–1976), Delahaye, lithograph in colors, 1932, printed by Les Ateliers A.B.C., Paris, minor defects, backed on linen, 62 x 46in. (Christie's) $5,244

After Cappiello, Peugeot, original poster, full color lithograph, linen backed depicting torpedo-style tourer, French circa 1925, 60 x 46in. (Christie's) $978

After Bombled, Clément Cycles and Automobiles, a good early poster for military machines, full color lithograph, linen-backed, 37 x 50in. (Christie's) $978

Porto - Portuguese Grand Prix 1960, an original poster depicting Stirling Moss Cooper, full color lithograph, framed and glazed, 39 x 26in. (Christie's) $633

Reinhold, Dunlop, offset lithograph in colors, 1964, restored losses, other repaired tears and creases, backed on linen, framed, 38 x 25in. (Christie's) $315

Eric de Coulon, Renault, lithograph in colors, 1928, printed by Draeger, Paris, some foxing and mold, vertical and horizontal fold marks, backed on linen, 46½ x 62in. (Christie's) $1,660

Charles Kuhn (1903–?), 77.77, lithograph in colors, 1930, printed by Wolfsberg, Zürich, faint horizontal fold marks, minor creases, 50 x 35½in. (Christie's) $2,622

OCEAN LINER

Anonymous, Ellerman's City Line, lithograph in colors, circa 1930, printed by McCorquodale & Co. Ltd., London, backed on linen, 40 x 25in.
(Christie's) $717

Hans Bohrde?, Norddeutscher Lloyd-Brema, chromo-lithograph, circa 1900, vertical and horizontal fold marks with corresponding defects, 34 x 45in.
(Christie's) $1,026

Odin Rosenvinge, Canadian Pacific, lithograph in colors circa 1920, vertical and horizontal fold marks, surface dirt, 39½ x 24in.
(Christie's) $717

Korn, United States Lines, No Finer Way to USA, lithograph in colors, circa 1950, printed by L. Jeanrot, Paris, generally in excellent condition, backed on linen, 39 x 24in.
(Christie's) $489

Sandy Hook, Les Messageries Maritimes Font le Tour du Monde, lithograph in colors, circa 1935, printed by Les Imp. Frses Reunies, Paris, 33 x 24in.
(Christie's) $821

Henri Hudaux, Messageries Maritimes, Anvers Extreme-Orient, lithograph in colors, 1908, printed by E. Dauvissat, Paris, foxing, small tears, creases and losses, 42 x 30in.
(Christie's) $629

Henri Cassiers (1858–1944), Red Star Line, Antwerpen, New York, lithograph in colors 1898, printed by O. De Rycker & Mendel, Bruxelles, 32½ x 20½in.
(Christie's) $961

Albert Sebille (1874–1953), Compagnie Generale Transatlantique, Havre, New York, lithograph in colors circa 1910, printed by Ste. Gle. d'Impression, Paris, 31½ x 46in.
(Christie's) $2,906

Paul Emile Colin, Cie.Gle. Transatlantique Le Havre-Southampton-New York French Line, cockled, needs to be rebacked, 39 x 24½in., linen backed, framed.
(Skinner) $747

OCEAN LINER

Turbinia of the Canada-Jamaica Steamship Co., toning, minor repair, wear along creases, 29³/₄ x 19¹/₂in.
(Skinner) $373

Louis Lessieux, Cie. Gle. Transatlantique, lithograph in colors, circa 1910, printed in C.H. Verneau, Paris, minor defects, generally in excellent condition, 30 x 39¹/₂in.
(Christie's) $2,906

Odin Rosenvinge, Canadian Pacific To Canada & United States (girl with steamer in background).
(Onslow's) $339

S. Patrone, North American Express, Italia Cosulich, lithograph in colors, 1934, printed by Barabino & Graeve, Genova, minor staining, 39 x 25in.
(Christie's) $769

Anonymous, Cunard Line New York-Liverpool RMS Mauretania, shaped printed tin sign depicting port bow view of the ship, 71 x 98cm.
(Onslow's) $1,155

Ciganer?, Last Time, French Line, reproduction in colors, 1982, printed by Dorgeval, France, backed on linen, 35 x 21in.
(Christie's) $342

F. Le Quesne, Cie. Gle. Transatlantique, Havre-New-York, lithograph in colors, circa 1900, printed by Ch. Verneau, Paris, minor defects, backed on linen, 39¹/₂ x 27¹/₂in.
(Christie's) $1,623

W. G. Hurrie, La Ruta del Ferry, lithograph in colors 1930, printed by Kraft Ltda., faint vertical and horizontal fold marks, backed on linen, 27 x 39in.
(Christie's) $854

Kenneth Denton Shoesmith (1890–1939), Canadian Pacific & Great Southern Railways, lithograph in colors, circa 1930, printed by The Baynard Press, London, 40 x 25in.
(Christie's) $2,736

OLYMPICS

1972 Munich Olympics:
Fencing, not examined out of
frame, 32³/₄ x 23in., framed.
(Skinner) $300

Herz, Olympic Games London
1948, printed by McCorquodale.
(Onslow's) $654

Anonymous, La Grande
Olimpiade, offset lithograph in
colors, 1960, generally in
excellent condition, 28¹/₂ x 20in.
(Christie's) $1,135

Jean Brian (1915–), X.
Olympische Winterspiele,
Grenoble 1968, lithograph in
colors, 1968, printed by
Imprimerie Generale, Grenoble,
creasing and minor tears, 37¹/₂ x
25in.
(Christie's) $649

Jean Droit, (1884–1961), VIIIe
Olympiade, Paris 1924,
lithograph in colors, 1924,
printed by Hachard & Cie.,
Paris, faint vertical and
horizontal fold marks, 45¹/₂ x
30in.
(Christie's) $5,130

Ludwig Hohlwein, Germany
1936 IVth Olympic Winter
Games Garmisch-
Partenkarchen 6th–16th
February 1936, published by
Reichsbahnzentrale Berlin.
(Onslow's) $2,156

Anonymous, Tokyo Olympiad,
offset lithograph in colors,
1965, printed by Toho Co. Ltd.,
generally in excellent condition,
28¹/₂ x 20in.
(Christie's) $839

Ilmari Sysimetsä (1912–1955),
XVth Olympic Games, Helsinki,
Pan American World Airways,
lithograph in colors, 1952
printed by Oy. Tilgmann, 39¹/₂ x
24¹/₂in.
(Christie's) $1,196

Olle Hjortzberg (1872–1959),
Olympische Spiele, Stockholm
1912, lithograph in colors
1912, printed by A. Börtzells Tr.
A. B. Stockholm, 41 x 29in.
(Christie's) $2,797

PSYCHEDELIC

Ricky Tick/The Yardbirds, appearing at the Craw Daddy Club.
(Bonhams) $455

Osiris Vision, 'Soft Machine Turns on', Oaioi U.F.O. gig poster, silver black and red.
(Bonhams) $580

Oz/Martin Sharp, 'Oz Is A New Magazine' poster, 20 x 30in. clip frame.
(Bonhams) $455

Ricky Tick/The Jimi Hendrix Experience, at the Ricky Tick, Hounslow, Friday 3rd February 1967, rare silkscreened poster in pink and black with Hendrix graphics.
(Bonhams) $5,775

Virgin/Roger Dean, Big O poster, GA25, depicting twins with entwinned lizard design, 33 x 24in.
(Bonhams) $85

Original limited edition mystical Jimi Hendrix poster by Paper Tiger, top left hand corner missing and has a 10in. rip which has been sellotaped on back.
(Bonhams) $152

The Rolling Stones, David Byrd concert poster for the December concerts at the Saville and Lyceum Theatre.
(Bonhams) $215

Silkscreened poster for Pink Floyd at the U.F.O. Club, circa 1967 by Hapshash And The Coloured Coat, framed and glazed, 24 x 34in.
(Bonhams) $730

Rick Griffin, a Berkeley Bonaparte poster titled 'Psychedelic Dream', by Rick Griffin, 1967, 23 x 35in.
(Bonhams) $152

WINTER SPORTS

Paul Ordner, Mont.Revard, circa 1935, creases, retouch lower margin, 38¼ x 24in. (Skinner) $460

Sascha Maurer, Stowe Vermont, circa 1930, tears and restoration especially on right edge, 28½ x 22½in., linen backed. (Skinner) $920

Jo Roux, Les Lainages Bisanne, circa 1930, creases, minor tears, 45¾ x 30⅞in., linen backed. (Skinner) $460

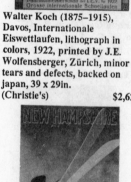

Roger Broders, Winter Sports in the French Alps, lithograph in colors, circa 1929, printed by L. Serre & Cie., Paris, generally in excellent condition, 40 x 25in. (Christie's) $1,923

Walter Koch (1875–1915), Davos, Internationale Eiswettlaufen, lithograph in colors, 1922, printed by J.E. Wolfensberger, Zürich, minor tears and defects, backed on japan, 39 x 29in. (Christie's) $2,622

Sascha Maurer, Winter Sports/ The New Haven R.R., circa 1940, minor scuffing, small tear, minor toning, 22 x 14in., linen backed. (Skinner) $546

R. & Avril, A. Onichaud, Chatel, lithograph in colors circa 1950, printed by L'Imp., Générale, Grenoble, vertical and horizontal fold marks, 39 x 24in. (Christie's) $821

Hechenbergen, New Hampshire, 1941, creasing, scuffing, patches upper edge, 36 x 25in., linen backed. (Skinner) $805

Greif, Alpes & Jura, PLM, lithograph in colors, circa 1930, printed by Hachard & Cie., Paris, vertical and horizontal fold marks, 39 x 24in. (Christie's) $1,880

WINTER SPORTS

E.J. Kealey, Winter Sports. American Express, fold creases, minor tears and staining, 39³/₄ x 25in., linen backed, framed. (Skinner) **$862**

Greif, Partez PLM, lithograph in colors, circa 1935, printed by Fortin, Paris, vertical and horizontal fold marks, 39 x 24in. (Christie's) **$2,736**

M. Hectepoba, Downhill Racer, lithograph in colors, circa 1950, fold marks, tears and small losses, 39 x 24in. (Christie's) **$597**

Alex Walter Diggelmann (1902–1987), Sils, lithograph in colors, circa 1940, printed by Fretz A.G., Zurich, generally in excellent condition, backed on japan, 39 x 25in. (Christie's) **$839**

Carl Moos (1878–1959), Attenhofer, Alpina Bindung, lithograph in colors, circa 1935, printed by Eidenbenz-Seitz & Co., St. Gallen, small losses and creases along the edges, 50 x 35¹/₂in. (Christie's) **$874**

Roger Broders (1883–1953), Saint-Gervais-les-Bains, PLM, lithograph in colors, circa 1930, printed by S.I.P.E., Paris, vertical and horizontal fold marks, 39 x 25in. (Christie's) **$1,538**

Roger Broders, Chamonix Mt. Blanc. Tous les Sports d'Hiver, 1930, tears, creases, retouch to fold lines, 39¹/₂ x 24³/₄in., linen backed. (Skinner) **$1,150**

Jupp Wiertz (1881–1939), Allemagne, lithograph in colors, circa 1930, repaired creasing and tears, backed on linen, 38 x 24¹/₂in. (Christie's) **$1,196**

Hans-Wilh Plessen, Winter in Germany, lithograph in colors, circa 1940, printed by R.D.V., Berli, tears and small losses, 40 x 25in. (Christie's) **$444**

Glazed chintz quilt, America, early 19th century, 100 x 98in.
(Skinner) $1,380

An appliqué quilt with a central star surrounded by hearts, circa 1860, 96 x 84in.
(Christie's) $699

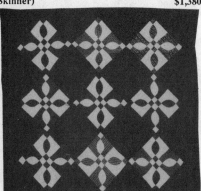

A Mennonite pieced cotton calico 'Orange Slices' quilt, Pennsylvania, 19th century, composed of brown, white and blue printed calico and solid patches, on a blue and white calico ground, approx. 80in. x 80in.
(Sotheby's) $287

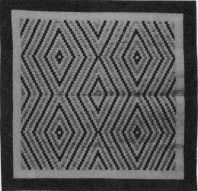

A pieced cotton calico 'Philadelphia Pavements' quilt, Pennsylvania, late 19th/early 20th century, composed of blue, red, orange and white square printed and solid patches, approx. 84in. x 80in.
(Sotheby's) $805

A silk appliqué quilt signed *Anna G. Todd, Dec. 1833,* with a central velvet Theorem Painting of fruit, probably American, 64 x 72in.
(Christie's) $611

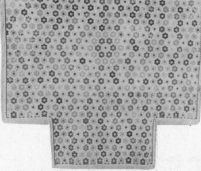

A Grandmother's Flower Garden shaped quilt of printed cottons, the middle flowers of turkey red and pale blue, with white cotton fringe, circa 1820, 94 x 96in.
(Christie's) $1,224

A Mennonite pieced cotton calico 'Flower Garden' quilt, Pennsylvania, 19th century, 90in. x 74in. (Sotheby's) $1,035

A fine Quaker pieced cotton calico Friendship quilt, Middleton, Bucks County, Pennsylvania, dated *1845-1849*. (Sotheby's) $3,450

A Mennonite pieced cotton calico 'Spider Web' quilt, Pennsylvania, late 19th century, composed of pink, red, blue, purple, green, peach and brown printed calico patches, approx. 82in. x 80in.
(Sotheby's) $805

A pieced cotton calico 'Chinese Lanterns' quilt, Pennsylvania, late 19th/early 20th century, composed of green, red, blue, yellow and white printed calico pattern and solid patches, approx. 82in. x 84in.
(Sotheby's) $1,495

A patchwork and appliqué quilt of printed and embroidered cottons, the centre with an appliqué flower head within a star frame, signed *Mary Pickrene 1801* (?), 88 x 92in.
(Christie's) $839

A pieced cotton calico 'Tulips in Square' quilt, Pennsylvania, 19th century, composed of red, green and yellow printed calico patches, approx. 94in. x 91in.
(Sotheby's) $920

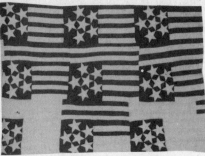

A pieced and appliqued cotton quilted coverlet, African-American, circa 1920, worked in red, white and blue cottons 54½in. x 76in.(Christie's) $2,760

A pieced cotton coverlet, American, circa 1920, worked in red, white and blue cottons, centring an American flag,, 50½ x 67½in. (Christie's) $1,150

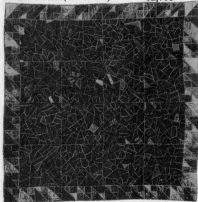

A pieced velvet crazy quilt, late 19th century, composed of black, burgundy, purple, red, gold, green, gray and brown solid and printed shaped velvet patches, approx. 72in x 74in. (Sotheby's) $805

A Star of Bethlehem quilt, the star of turkey red and lime green printed cotton, framed with a border and zigzag of brown printed cotton, mid 19th century, 96in. square. (Christie's) $786

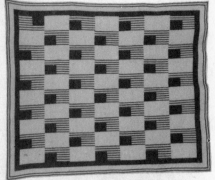

A pieced cotton quilted coverlet, American, 1885-1895, worked in red, white and blue cottons in stepped diagonal alternating rows of white and American flag blocks, 82 x 69in. (Christie's) $4,600

A pieced and appliqued cotton quilted coverlet, American, 1885-1895, worked in red, white and blue cottons, centering forty-eight white stars within a blue field, 67 x 71½in. (Christie's) $1,265

A pieced cotton quilted coverlet, American, 1940, worked in red, white and blue in the form of an American flag, 89½ x 62¾in. (Christie's) $4,025

A pieced and appliqued cotton quilted crib coverlet, American, circa 1940, centring the profile of an eagle head, 38 x 27in. (Christie's) $2,300

A brown and white pieced cotton 'Delectable Mountain' quilt, Pennsylvania, 19th century, composed of brown and white printed calico triangular patches, approx. 92in. x 92in. (Sotheby's) $2,070

A pieced, appliqued and trapunto cotton quilted coverlet, Pennsylvania, circa 1885, worked in white, red, green and mustard calicos centering a rose and wreath, 81¼ x 82 in. (Christie's) $1,495

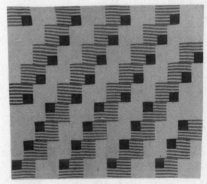

A pieced and appliqued cotton quilted coverlet, American, 1890-1910, worked in white, blue and salmon cottons centering an American flag, 88½ x 79½in. (Christie's) $2,530

A pieced and appliqued cotton quilted coverlet, American, 1920-30, worked in red, white and blue cottons in stepped diagonal alternating rows of white and American flag blocks, 85 x 99in. (Christie's) $2,990

Boxed table tennis set, complete with bats, balls, laws and well-preserved label, circa 1900.
(The Gurney Collection)
$160

'The Game of Ping-Pong or Gossima', by John Jacques and Son, circa 1900, with battledores,
original balls and net in solid mahogany box with brass plate.
(The Gurney Collection)
$1,200

Fine label for one of the earliest French table tennis sets, circa 1900, 18 x 10in.
(The Gurney Collection)
$160

Silver-plated vesta case with
table tennis scene, circa 1900.
(The Gurney Collection) $65

Rare fret-work table tennis bats,
circa 1900, all cut from jelutong.
(The Gurney Collection)
$40 each

Keiller's Cream Toffee tin, circa
1930, with lawn tennis scene.
(The Gurney Collection) $48

Lawn tennis postcards from the
turn of the century.
(The Gurney Collection)
$25 each

1920s lawn tennis blazer for the
R.D. Hardcourt Lawn Tennis
Club, with finely embroidered
arms.
(The Gurney Collection) $120

The Ladies Home Journal,
October 1902, showing an
unusual end-on view of domestic
table tennis in the USA.
(The Gurney Collection) $48

Sheet music for Ping-Pong Polka
for the Pianoforte by James B.
Smart.
(The Gurney Collection) $32

The Lawn Tennis Magazine,
Number 1, June 1885, one of the
earliest lawn tennis magazines in
any language, with photograph
of Ernest Renshaw.
(The Gurney Collection) $480

The Lawn Tennis
Championship Meeting 1931
(fifth day).
(The Gurney Collection) $32

RACKET & BAT GAMES

Silver-mounted table tennis mirror for a lady's chatelaine, circa 1900.
(The Gurney Collection) $48

Table Tennis, The Latest Indoor Game, with fine illustration of domestic play. $240

Rare lawn tennis fan, circa 1910, hand-painted on cloth.
(The Gurney Collection) $160

A rare example of a Victorian battledore bag.
(The Gurney Collection) $80

Slazenger & Sons catalogue of 1906, with eight chromolithographic plates including 'The Demon' racket.
(The Gurney Collection) $640

Large shuttlecock made of cork, chicken feathers, kid leather and velvet trim, India, circa 1850.
(The Gurney Collection) $160

Box of Gardiner's Conquero lawn tennis balls, unused, circa 1920. $120

Feltham and Co.'s Game of Tennis, a pine games trunk bearing two labels and mounted with two handles (lacks contents).
(Bonhams) $560

The only known example of a Lazy Susan, decorated with transfer prints of lawn tennis items, probably Crescent China by Stoke and Sons, circa 1880, 18in. diameter. $2,400

The only known surviving example of Pouch Ball, an American variant of table tennis, circa 1900. $400

'Gossima', The New Table Game', by John Jacques and Son, 1891, the first version of table tennis, in wooden box with battledores, ball and 12 inch net.
(The Gurney Collection) $1,600

Ping-Pong, The Great Tennis Game for the Table, sole makers Parker Brothers, Salem, Massachusetts, circa 1900. $400

BADMINTON

Hazell's 'Streamline' badminton racket from the 1930s.
(The Gurney Collection) $120

Fine 'Varsity' badminton racket by G. G. Bussey, with unusual bound grip, circa 1910.
(The Gurney Collection) $80

A 1930's 'Vitiv' badminton racket with decorations characteristic of the period. $48

Badminton racket made in India, circa 1885. $160

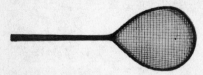

Early badminton racket, made in Sialkote, India, in the late 19th century.
(The Gurney Collection) $80

Very rare badminton racket with steel frame (strung with piano wire) and made by the Dayton Company, Ohio, USA, in the 1920's.
(The Gurney Collection) $320

BATTLEDORE

Table tennis battledore with single vellum sheet in bamboo frame, circa 1900, made by J. R. Mally. $80

Unusual table tennis battledore by F. H. Ayres, circa 1900, with single sheet of vellum.
(The Gurney Collection) $48

Late 19th century vellum battledore for the game of battledore and shuttlecock. $65

Table Tennis racket, circa 1900, modeled on a lawn tennis racket and made by Gray & Sons.
(The Gurney Collection) $48

Large vellum battledore, 22 inches, and shuttlecock, about 5inches, designed for the game of battledore and shuttlecock, both circa 1850. (The Gurney Collection) $240

Vellum battledore for the game of battledore and shuttlecock, finely decorated by the lady of the house, circa 1890, 16 1/2in. long.
(The Gurney Collection) $40

TENNIS

Fine 'fish-tail' lawn tennis racket, circa 1920.
$160

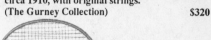

Fine Slazenger's 'La Belle' lawn tennis racket, circa 1910, with original strings.
(The Gurney Collection) $320

Very rare lawn tennis racket with steel frame (strung with piano wire) and made by the Dayton Company, Ohio, USA, in the 1920's.
(The Gurney Collection) $320

A 1920s steel racket, 'Thors', manufactured by Slazenger, with double center main piano wire strings and two double strings each side.
(Bonhams) $190

An 1880s racket with flat-top head, convex wedge and octagonal scored handle (some strings defective).
(Bonhams) $640

A 1920s steel racket manufactured by Dayton, piano wire strings and wooden octagonal handle with rubber sleeve.
(Bonhams) $112

A 'Real' tennis racket manufactured by Cassiobury, circa 1900, with tilted head, convex wedge and square handle. (Bonhams) $1,920

'Central Racket Press' by F. H. Ayres, in solid mahogany, circa 1900.
(The Gurney Collection) $65

Early lawn tennis racket by Feltham of London, with hand-carved, barley-sugar turning of the grip and registration date for 1884.
(The Gurney Collection) $800

An early example of a laminated lawn tennis racket, with unusual metal re-inforcement at the throat, made by Williams, Paris, circa 1910.
(The Gurney Collection) $3.0

A flat-top, asymmetrical lawn tennis racket by the famous maker Thomas Tate, probably made in the 1880s.
(The Gurney Collection) $1,600

Hazell's 'Streamline' lawn tennis racket designed by 'Bunny' Austin and used personally by him in the 1930s, his initials engraved in the shaft.
(The Gurney Collection) $800

A Philips two-circuit straight receiver Type 830A, 1931. (Auction Team Köln)

$435

A Seibt EA 530 five-tube, triple circuit Neutrodyne radio, circa 1926. (Auction Team Köln)

$6,225

A Seibt 326 W two-circuit straight receiver, circa 1935. (Auction Team Köln)

$780

An Atwater Kent Model 206 'cathedral' radio with wooden knobs,6-tube superhet receiver, 1934. (Auction Team Köln)

$186

Radiosonanz Type DR12 two tube Audion receiver with RTV stamp of 8.4.25. (Auction Team Köln)

$4,280

A Telefunken Bayreuth radio, wave band scale altered after the war, apparently by the manufacturer, circa 1933. (Auction Team Köln)

$935

The Kennedy Type 220 early single tube receiver, with variometer tuning, 1921. (Auction Team Köln)

$1,400

An Atwater Kent Mod. 33 American five-tube, three circuit receiver, 1926. (Auction Team Köln)

$295

A Körting Transmare 40, the most expensive German prewar radio, with twenty tuning buttons, circa 1939. (Auction Team Köln)

$1,865

A Zenith Golden Triangle radio alarm, rotates on its base. (Auction Team Köln)
$171

A Loewe OE 333 local receiver, circa 1926. (Auction Team Köln)
$2,950

An Ekco AD 76 receiver in circular brown bakelite case. (Christie's)
$792

A Carlton S.G.4 radio, unusual wooden case, circa 1931. (Auction Team Köln)
$170

A blue-green ceramic Jumbo radio in the form of an elephant before a palm tree, with integral detector radio. (Auction Team Köln)
$450

A Gecophone Model 3032R three-valve battery receiver in mahogany case, circa 1929. (Christie's)
$623

A Lumophon WD-310 single circuit straight receiver, typical steam radio, circa 1933. (Auction Team Köln)
$428

An Apex crystal set with detector on ebonite panel above variometer with dial, on ebonite base with aeriel, 6in. high. (Christie's)
$457

A Telefunken 337 WP superhet receiver with A-tube hard facing, 1936/7. (Auction Team Köln)
$171

Bob Marley, a color photograph of the musician together with a cut signature Love and Peace Bob Marley, 19$^{1}/_{2}$ x 15$^{1}/_{2}$in.
(Christie's) $1,093

Kiss, a pair of stage boots worn by band member Paul Stanley, 1973–1974, the black and white checkered leather boots with four inch heel.
(Christie's) $1,495

A black and white machine-print photograph of The Rolling Stones on the banks of the river Thames, circa 1963, signed in black biro by all five, 9$^{1}/_{2}$ x 7in.
(Christie's) $880

A rare concert poster for the Jimi Hendrix Experience at the Plaza, Newbury, 10th February 1967, printed in black and brown on yellow, 20 x 30in.
(Sotheby's) $1,615

The Rolling Stones, a black and white machine-print photograph circa 1964, signed in three different colored inks by all five, 9$^{1}/_{4}$ x 13$^{1}/_{2}$in.
(Christie's) $528

Mick Jagger, a black and white half-length portrait photograph by Terry O'Neil, signed in the margin by photographer in black felt pen, 19$^{1}/_{4}$ x 15in.
(Christie's) $493

Eric Clapton, a rare concert poster *Eric Clapton presents his new group Derek And The Dominos...*, Marquay Club, Torquay Town Hall, Friday, 21st August, 1970, 30 x 20in.
(Christie's) $528

Roger Daltrey, a long-sleeved tunic of beige suede decorated throughout with copious fringing, with press cutting of Roger Daltrey wearing a similar tunic in the early 1970s.
(Christie's) $2,097

Jim Morrison, a piece of paper signed in blue biro by subject in common mount with a black and white machine-print photograph, 17$^{1}/_{2}$ x 15$^{1}/_{4}$in. overall.
(Christie's) $613

A UK Tour poster for Buddy
Holly and the Crickets, 1958,
red and blue lettering, for the
Liverpool Philharmonic Hall,
20th March, 16½ x 24½in.
(Sotheby's) $1,328

A pair of Elton John white
Roller Derby boots with *EJ 76*
transfers on the ankles, together
with an Adidas football shirt
with *ELTON* and *1* on the back.
(Bonhams) $158

Sid Vicious, a Virgin
promotional poster, featuring a
portrait of Sid Vicious holding a
beer bottle and listing song
titles, 28 x 39in.
(Bonhams) $237

Sid Vicious, a gold and blue
lamé jacket owned and worn by
Sid Vicious and also worn on
stage by Johnny Rotten at the
Lyceum gig on 10th July 1976.
(Bonhams) $3,950

The Who, a 10 x 8in. black and
white early photograph from the
60s, signed across each image by
the respective band members,
14 x 12½in.
(Bonhams) $411

Cher, a black wet-look jumpsuit
with zipped fastening and cuffs
and flared trousers, signed on
the collar in silver felt pen *love
Cher*, circa early 1970s.
(Christie's) $704

The Who, a color machine
print photograph of the group
taken from Jackie magazine
circa mid 1960s, signed in blue
biro by all four members, 13 x
9½in.
(Christie's) $528

Billy Fury, a V-necked sweater
of tweed-colored wools, with
color xerox of the E.P. cover
Forget Him featuring Fury
wearing the sweater.
(Christie's) $493

Bill Haley and his Comets, a
Brunswick Recording Artist
publicity card featuring the
band and signed by Bill Haley
and other members of the
group.
(Christie's) $1,380

A rare concert poster for Janis Joplin in Amsterdam, 11th April 1969, black and white, 32 x 44in. (Sotheby's) $1,612

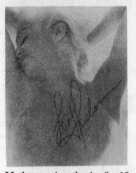

Madonna, signed color 8 x 10, half-length naked, in green. (T. Vennett-Smith) $130

Cream, a Cibachrome color portrait photograph of the group, circa 1966, 24 x 24in. (Christie's) $176

A piece of paper signed and inscribed in blue biro to *Wendy love forever stay sweet Jimi Hendrix* and annotated with a heart motif, in common mount with a black and white publicity photograph, 17¼ x 11¼in. (Christie's) $1,584

Bruce Springsteen and the E Street Band, an album cover The River, 1980, Columbia Records, signed by Bruce Springsteen, Roy Bittan, Clarence Clemons, Max Weinberg, Danny Federici and Little Steven. (Christie's) $349

An original drawing by John Lennon in black felt pen on white paper, the caricature faces of John and Yoko, the sun, the moon, and the earth are titled *One World*, signed *John Lennon '69*, 2ft. 10in. x 2ft. 1in., framed. (Christie's) $18,400

Brian Jones, an autograph letter, signed, circa mid 1960s, to a fan called Jill, thanking her for her letter. (Christie's) $612

Marc Bolan, a Regency Radio Car Company receipt signed *Love Marc Bolan* in black biro, mounted, framed and glazed, 25 x 18in. (Bonhams) $174

Queen, a black and white publicity photograph, circa 1975, signed in different inks by all four, 10 x 8in. (Christie's) $387

Queen, 'Radio Ga Ga' 12in. signed by all band members. (Bonhams) $269

Madonna, signed color 8 x 10, head and shoulders. (T. Vennett-Smith) $153

Freddie Mercury, signed record sleeve, from Barcelona, 5 x 5. (T. Vennett-Smith) $122

Stevie Nicks/Fleetwood Mac, a black velvet stage jacket, signed on the lining Stevie Nicks, worn by Nicks during Fleetwood Mac's Tango In The Night Tour, 1987, and a black wool beret, worn by Nicks. (Christie's) $664

John Lennon and Yoko Ono, an album Unfinished Music Number 1: Two Virgins, 1968, Apple Records, signed and inscribed on the front cover in black biro *John Lennon '79* and annotated with a self-portrait caricature. (Christie's) $704

Jimi Hendrix's guitar strap, circa 1970, black leather with animal fur, stamped in gold, *Bobby Lee No-Mishap Guitar Strap*, sold with a color poster, showing the item in use, the strap 46in. long. (Sotheby's) $17,940

A poster for Led Zeppelin at the Baths Hall, Ipswich, 16th November 1970, printed in blue and red, 20 x 30in. (Sotheby's) $2,087

Bob Dylan, an album The Times They Are A-Changin', 1964, CBS Records, signed on the front cover in blue felt pen by subject. (Christie's) $457

An 8 x 10in. black and white early photograph of The Moody Blues, signed across each image by each member of the group. (Bonhams) $142

A rare acetate recording of 'Hey Joe'/'Stone Free', 1966, a double-sided, 7in. disc Emidisc, labels with typewritten details and band's name in blue ballpoint.
(Sotheby's) $3,588

A silver and turquoise Navajo Indian finger ring owned and worn by Jimi Hendrix.
(Bonhams) $948

A promotional album slick for Something To Remember, 1995, Warner Bros. Records, signed and inscribed in blue felt pen *love Madonna*, 12¼ x 12¼in.
(Christie's) $263

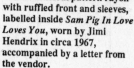

A glass Evian mineral water bottle, the label signed in black felt pen *Madonna*, the neck with traces of pink lipstick, 12¾in. high.
(Christie's) $962

A signed copy of the album 'Axis Bold as Love', 1967, inside cover signed in black ink by all three members and with dedications *To Claire*.
(Sotheby's) $3,036

A shirt of floral pattern rayon with ruffled front and sleeves, labelled inside *Sam Pig In Love Loves You*, worn by Jimi Hendrix in circa 1967, accompanied by a letter from the vendor.
(Christie's) $4,864

Bob Dylan, signed and inscribed 8 x 10.
(T. Vennett-Smith) $275

Sonny and Cher, two vinyl portrait dolls modeled as Sonny and Cher in original clothes, made by Mega Corp, 1976, both in original boxes, both 12in. high. (Christie's) $282

Buddy Holly, signed album page, 5 x 4, also signed by Joe Mauldin (Crickets).
(T. Vennett-Smith) $428

A Jimi Hendrix ring, late 60s, in gold-colored metal set with an opal, as given to Mitch Mitchell's mother by Jimi as a keepsake.
(Sotheby's) $1,708

Pete Townshend's Gibson 'Les Paul' guitar, serial No. 00129875, 1970s, dark cherry finish, body applied back and front with number 5 in white adhesive plastic.
(Sotheby's) $23,322

Bono's 'Fly' sunglasses, worn by him as McPhisto on the U2 'Zooropa' tour, one-piece wraparound style in dark green plastic, with documents of provenance.
(Sotheby's) $1,435

Jimi Hendrix, a piece of card attached to a page from an autograph book signed and inscribed in blue biro *Love & Happiness Jimi Hendrix*, 3^1/$_2$ x 4in.
(Christie's) $962

A door from Tittenhurst Park, John Lennon and Yoko Ono's home from 1969–1971.
(Bonhams) $3,799

A black and white photograph by Bruce Fleming of Jimi Hendrix performing on stage at the Monterey Rock Festival, 1967, 11^1/$_2$ x 15^1/$_4$in.
(Christie's) $263

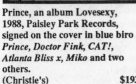

Prince, an album Lovesexy, 1988, Paisley Park Records, signed on the cover in blue biro *Prince, Doctor Fink, CAT!, Atlanta Bliss x, Miko* and two others.
(Christie's) $193

A pair of knee-length snakeskin boots worn by Brian Jones in the late 1960s, with a photograph of Jones wearing the boots.
(Christie's) $3,146

A piece of paper signed and inscribed in black biro Jimi Hendrix, *Be Sweet for me*, in common mount with a black and white machine-print photograph of subject, 14^3/$_4$ x 13^3/$_4$in.
(Christie's) $1,232

George Michael's 'Rockers Revenge' black leather jacket, as featured in the video 'Faith' and subsequently in 'Freedom', with a copy of a letter of authenticity.
(Sotheby's) $3,036

Sid Vicious, an eight-lined lyric, handwritten in blue ink by Sid Vicious on line notepaper and titled *Pronucreant*.
(Bonhams) $664

Jimi Hendrix, a Ludwig professional tambourine owned by Jimi and used both for live and studio recordings.
(Bonhams) $1,580

An unpublished photograph of Jimi Hendrix, June 1967, the color 8 x 10 print showing Jimi walking down Carnaby Street, London, with negative and sold with copyright.
(Sotheby's) $3,947

Queen, one of two Cibachrome color portrait photographs of the group, circa mid 1970s (printed later), 16 x 20in. and 20 x 16in.
(Christie's) (Two) $352

Jimi Hendrix's 'Afghan' jacket, circa 1968, trimmed and lined with different wools, the left sleeve signed and inscribed by Jimi Hendrix, *To Jools Stay free.*
(Sotheby's) $17,581

A colour reproduction of a photograph of Madonna wearing a topless dress, signed by the subject in black felt pen, 15 1/2 x 11in.
(Christie's) $528

Eric Clapton's stage-worn shirt, 1960s, together with a VHS showing the guitarist wearing the shirt onstage with Cream, circa 1968.
(Sotheby's) $1,898

A signed copy of Buddy Holly and the Crickets U.K. tour program, 1958, the back cover portrait signed in different ballpoints.
(Sotheby's) $1,220

An early black and white photograph 8 x 10in. of Madonna, signed in black pen *Love Madonna*.
(Bonhams) $284

A pair of Madonna's gloves, black with matching beaded decoration, mounted for display with a machine-print photograph.
(Sotheby's) $759

Michael Jackson, signed color 15 x 22 poster, from Heal The World, three quarter length in black jacket.
(T. Vennett-Smith) $107

A Coral Records publicity postcard, 1958, signed on the front in black or blue biro by Buddy Holly, Jerry Allison and Joe Mauldin, 5³/₄ x 3¹/₂in. framed.
(Christie's) $1,232

The Monkees, an 8 x 10in. color photograph signed by each, with a concert pass for their Japan gig and an album cover for 'The Monkees Live 1967'.
(Bonhams) $142

Little Eva, a scarce poster for Little Eva, 1964, for her appearance at the Pill Social Centre, Milford Haven, Wales, 9th October, red and black on white, 20 x 30in.
(Sotheby's) $448

A black and white publicity photograph of Madonna dressed in her underwear, signed by subject in blue felt pen, 10 x 8in.
(Christie's) $612

The Jam, a cotton t-shirt printed with a Union Jack pattern signed on the front in black felt pen by all three members of the group.
(Christie's) $279

An autograph of Buddy Holly, mounted with an 8 x 10in. black and white photograph of the star.
(Bonhams) $569

Queen, a Gatefold album sleeve for Queen II, signed on the inside by the four band members.
(Bonhams) $340

The Animals, signed postcard by all five.
(T. Vennett-Smith) $148

An autographed copy of the album 'The Works' by Queen, the front cover signed by all four, with a concert ticket for 12th July, 1986 taped to inner sleeve.
(Sotheby's) $607

Frank Zappa, a 5 x 6in. black and white photograph signed in gold felt pen matted with an album sleeve, framed and glazed, 18 x 27in.
(Bonhams) $640

Jim Morrison, original artwork for Berkeley Community Theatre, San Francisco by artist Salasky, signed also by Jim Morrison in silver pen, mounted and glazed.
(Bonhams) $1,520

Bono/U2, a 9 x 7in. black and white photograph of Bono signed in black felt pen across the image, framed with three backstage passes, 18 x 25in.
(Bonhams) $152

Buddy Holly, a roneo biology test from Lubbock High School, no.22, on digestion, dated 3rd February 1953, signed by Holly 'Holley' to top, with a certificate of authenticity.
(T. Vennett-Smith) $643

The Sex Pistols, a Virgin publicity photograph of The Sex Pistols, outside the 100 Club, signed by the four present members of the original punk band.
(Bonhams) $200

The Rolling Stones, 1973 European tour poster designed by John Pasche and photographed by David Thorpe, approx. 23 x 33in.
(Bonhams) $245

BEATLES

George Harrison, signed 8x10 photograph, playing guitar from 'Help'.
(Vennett Smith)   **$288**

Paul McCartney, a Bank of England one pound note, signed in blue pen *To Carla and Trevor – Best Wishes Paul McCartney*.
(Bonhams)   **$150**

Paul McCartney, signed color 5.5 x 8, full length with guitar.
(T. Vennett-Smith)   **$280**

Paul McCartney's Birth Certificate, 1942, No. DC004399, the original certificate for entry of birth number 240 in Walton Park sub-district of Liverpool, 14 x 6¼in.
(Bonhams)   **$71,215**

The only guitar autographed by all four Beatles, 1964, the Rickenbacker guitar signed on the body in gold leaf by all four Beatles in 1964, (and in 1985 on the back by Julian Lennon).
(Bonhams)   **$118,691**

The Beatles, an early publicity postcard, circa 1962, signed on the reverse in black biro by John Lennon, George Harrison and Ringo Starr, and in green biro by Paul McCartney, 5½ x 3½in. (Christie's)   **$1,760**

Lennon and Starr, signed album page, 6.5 x 5, by John Lennon and Ringo Starr, with attached photos and an unsigned postcard of The Beatles.
(T. Vennett-Smith)   **$553**

Ringo Starr, signed postcard, head and shoulders holding up another photo of himself.
(T. Vennett-Smith)   **$69**

A signed photograph of the Beatles, 1963, black and white, signed in blue ballpoint, 10 x 8in.
(Sotheby's)   **$2,780**

BEATLES

An exceptional signed Beatles'
concert poster, Swedish, July
1964, signed by the band in blue
ballpoint pen, 27¹/₂ x 39¹/₄in.
(Sotheby's) $26,013

A pair of white leather and beige
suede brogues, made by Foot
Loose and once owned by Ringo
Starr, with a letter of
authenticity.
(Bonhams) $474

A rare Cavern handbill, 1963,
buff-colored paper, listing acts
appearing at the club in March-
April, 9 x 11¹/₂in.
(Sotheby's) $2,846

A rare 'Beatles Invade America'
news-stand poster, English,
1964, printed in red and black
letterpress on white paper for
the 'Swindon Echo' newspaper,
30 x 20in.
(Bonhams) $285

An autographed Royal Variety
Performance program,
English, 1963, a program for
The 1963 Royal Variety
Performance, signed by all four
Beatles, 11¹/₂ x 8¹/₄in.
(Bonhams) $5,934

John Lennon's tax check, 1971,
a Lennon Productions Ltd
check dated 6th July 1971,
signed by *John Lennon*,
mounted with a photograph of
Lennon.
(Bonhams) $2,374

A Beatles-style jacket
autographed by Paul
McCartney, 1994, signed in blue
felt pen on the breast of a fawn
linen, 40in. chest.
(Bonhams) $1,898

John Lennon's black velvet
cape-coat, circa 1964–65, with
tab and single button for the
high soft collar, batwing sleeves,
lined in black satin.
(Bonhams) $26,904

A Williams 'The Bootles' Beat
Time pinball machine,
American circa 1964, size 48in.
approx.
(Bonhams) $1,582

BEATLES

A signed cover for The Beatles Book No. 5, December 1963, signed by the group in blue ballpoint and pencil.
(Sotheby's) $1,435

John Lennon's hiking boots, circa 1964–66, the pair of brown leather hiking boots, labeled *Original Chippewa Shoe Company, USA*, size 6¹/₂ approx.
(Bonhams) $2,611

An unpublished photograph of the Quarry Men at St. Peter's Church Fête, 6th July 1957, black and white, 2¹/₄ x 3¹/₄in.
(Sotheby's) $853

A rare poster: 'Follow the Fab Four – Wear Your Safety Gear', British, mid 1960s, blue, orange, black and white, issued on behalf of the British Safety Council, 23 x 32in.
(Sotheby's) $986

The Beatles, a portrait photograph by Astrid Kirchherr of The Beatles on a freight train, Hamburg, October, 1960, 7 x 9¹/₂in., framed.
(Christie's) $1,398

An exceptionally rare signed Beatles publicity photograph, 1963, the black and white Starpics card signed by the Beatles and Brian Epstein, 3¹/₂ x 5¹/₂in.
(Sotheby's) $4,175

A 1990 stage worn vest from Paul McCartney's World Tour, signed across the front in black ink *All The Best Paul McCartney 1990–91*.
(Christie's) $1,840

A set of four glass tumblers, each with a gold rim and an individual colour portrait of each Beatle, manufactured by Joseph Long Company Ltd., in its original box.
(Bonhams) $1,027

A two-tone blue and gray silk tailored jacket made for John Lennon for the film production of 'Help', but was rejected for use in the film.
(Bonhams) $2,686

BEATLES

A signed copy of 'The Beatles Book' monthly, No. 3, October 1963, the front cover signed in blue ballpoint by all four Beatles.
(Sotheby's) $2,870

An unusually large signed photograph of the Beatles, 1963, taken at one of the group's appearances on Juke Box Jury, 18¼ x 15¼in.
(Sotheby's) $3,409

A signed B.O.A.C. 'Beatles Bahamas Special' menu card, 1965, signed by the group, Eleanor Bron, Roy Kinnear and Victor Spinetti, 4½ x 7in.
(Sotheby's) $3,757

A letter from Paul McCartney written in Hamburg, 1962, on one side of blue airmail paper, with original airmail envelope, postmarked November 1962, letter 11½ x 8¼in.
(Bonhams) $8,071

The Beatles, a rare set of four blown glass Christmas tree decorations, modeled as the Beatles with handpainted faces, shirts, ties, hands and feet, 6¼in. high, in original box stamped *Made in Italy*, circa 1960s.
(Christie's) $1,486

An unusually large signed photograph of the Beatles, 1963, signed in black ballpoint with dedication by George, *To Joy love from the Beatles*, 12¼ x 15in.
(Sotheby's) $3,767

A scarce Swedish poster: 'Europas Popband Nummer Ett', 1963, black and white on red, 27 x 31¼in.
(Sotheby's) $1,422

The birthplace of Ringo Starr, a freehold terrace building, to be offered with Full Vacant Possession, 9 Madryn Street, Liverpool, L8.
(Bonhams) $20,670

A poster for the Beatles at the 'St. Patrick's Night Rock Gala', Knotty Ash Hall, 17th March 1962, printed in green and black, 19¾ x 28in.
(Sotheby's) $2,512

BEATLES

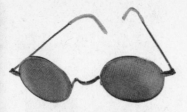

The Beatles, one of four black and white photographs by Jurgen Vollmer, circa 1962 (printed later), each 23 x 18½in. framed.
(Christie's) $439

A pair of sunglasses believed to have been worn by John Lennon on a U.S. tour, 1960s, metal frames with circular, non-prescription mirrored lenses and plastic earpieces, with a copy of a statement of provenance.
(Sotheby's) $3,947

George Harrison and Ringo Starr autographs on an album page mounted with an archival black and white print of them both in the studio, 29 x 20in.
(Bonhams) $316

An unusual signed Beatles' publicity photograph, 1962/3, the black and white Peter Kaye portrait signed in blue ballpoint, 10 x 8in.
(Sotheby's) $3,605

Ringo Starr, a pair of P.R. Percussion drum sticks, both signed in blue ink *Ringo **, both 16in. long.
(Christie's) $489

A signed Beatles' fan club photograph, signed in blue ballpoints, together with a copy of a photograph of them with a support group on tour in Sweden.
(Sotheby's) $2,691

A signed Beatles' postcard, 1963, the black and white Valex portrait signed in blue ballpoint and black ink, also signed on the front in blue ballpoint by John.
(Sotheby's) $1,974

The Beatles, a purple bomber style tour jacket, with press-stud fastening on the front, with *Beatles, 1965 American Tour* printed in yellow on the back.
(Bonhams) $948

A publicity photograph of The Beatles on board a ferry, circa 1963, signed and inscribed by all four, and inscribed in Harrison's hand, 10 x 7¾in.
(Christie's) $3,846

ELVIS

Elvis Presley, a white gaberdine suit with high collar jacket with flared suit cuffs, worn between 1971–72 primarily at the Las Vegas Hilton.
(Bonhams) **$6,636**

Elvis Presley, a copy of 'Elvis For Everyone', signed in black ink *'Elvis Presley'*.
(Bonhams) **$395**

Elvis Presley, a rare page of autograph lyrics, signed, circa 1959, for an unreleased song Mississippi River.
(Christie's) **$29,716**

A black and white photograph of Elvis Presley and Sammy Davis Jr. backstage, circa late 1960s (printed later), 20 x 16in., laminated on card.
(Christie's) **$211**

Elvis Presley, a page from an autograph book signed and inscribed *To Joe, Best Wishes Elvis Presley*, a songsheet for Are You Lonesome Tonight; a Photoplay magazine, and a Mirabelle, circa 1960.
(Bonhams) **$524**

Elvis Presley, a black army fatigues webbing belt with gold plated buckle worn by Elvis whilst in the service.
(Bonhams) **$822**

Elvis Presley, a Siechen-Bier beermat signed in blue biro *Elvis Presley*, 4¼in. diam., the autograph obtained in Bad-Nauheim, Germany in 1959.
(Bonhams) **$297**

Elvis Presley, a red velvet comforter which was used on Elvis Presley's bed in the early 1970s, a letter of authenticity accompanies the lot, 9ft. 5in. x 8ft. 3in.
(Christie's) **$1,150**

Two scarce acetate recordings of Elvis Presley, British, 1950s, each a 78rpm 10in., comprising 'Heartbreak Hotel' and 'I Don't Care If The Sun Don't Shine'.
(Sotheby's) **$569**

ELVIS

A Copy of the H.M.V. album 'The Best of Elvis', 1957, 10in., DLP 1159.
(Sotheby's) $380

King Creole, 1958, Paramount, US, unfolded, 60x40in.
(Christie's) $2,097

Elvis Presley, a copy of the L.P. 'Legendary Performer', signed *Elvis Presley* in blue ink.
(Bonhams) $474

Elvis Presley, a piece of card signed and inscribed *To Betty yours Elvis Presley*, a membership card for the Elvis Presley Fan Club, 1955, with a single sleeve All Shook Up.
(Bonhams) $962

Elvis Presley, an autograph and unpublished photograph of Elvis Presley in Germany, 1959, signed by *C. Ballance Lt* and Elvis Presley in blue ballpoints and stamped *2 Medium Battery Royal Artillery*, 4 x 5³/₄in.
(Sotheby's) $1,708

A piece of card signed in blue biro *Elvis Presley*; and a piece of Elvis Presley Enterprises headed notepaper, in common mount with a black and white machine-print photograph of Presley, 12 x 9in.
(Christie's) $880

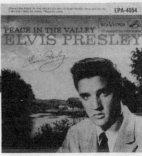

Elvis Presley, a copy of 'Elvis' Gold Records', signed *Elvis Presley*.
(Bonhams) $442

A circa late 1960s pair of black leather boots worn by Elvis Presley during his 'comeback' engagement and press conference at the International Hotel in Las Vegas, Nevada.
(Christie's) $6,325

Elvis Presley, 'Peace In The Valley' E.P., signed *Elvis Presley* on the front sleeve.
(Bonhams) $425

Shirvan Kelim, East Caucasus, last quarter 19th century, (three small holes), 10ft. 6in. by 6ft. 2in.
(Skinner) $1,725

Yomud Asmalyk, West Turkestan, late 19th century, hexagonal lattice with midnight blue, ivory, and brown ashik guls, 3ft. 10in. by 2ft. 8in.
(Skinner) $1,495

Northwest Persian rug, early 20th century, quatrefoil floral group with four birds in slate and sky blue, 4ft. 8in. by 3ft. 6in.
(Skinner) $862

Joshighan rug, Central Persia, mid 20th century, diamond medallion and diamond-shaped floral groups in midnight and royal blue, red, violet, gold and green, 5ft. 4in. x 3ft. 8in.
(Skinner) $374

A Napoleon III Aubusson tapestry rug, the pistacchio and pale jade green field decorated with a central bouquet of summer flowers, 7ft. 7in. x 6ft. 8in.
(Phillips) $3,600

Shirvan rug, East Caucasus, last quarter 19th century, three stepped hexagonal medallions and geometric motifs in red, sky blue, gold and tan, 5ft. by 3ft. 2in.
(Skinner) $403

Verneh, Southwest Caucasus, late 19th century, grid of large squares surrounded by small squares, 8ft. 8in. by 7ft.
(Skinner) $3,738

Daghestan prayer rug, Northwest Caucasus, last quarter 19th century, (good condition), 5ft. 6in. by 3ft. 10in.
(Skinner) $4,312

Kashan carpet, West Central Persia, late 19th century, square grid with cartouches inset with vines, 13ft. 6in. by 10ft. 6in.
(Skinner) $21,850

Shirvan rug, East Caucasus, early 20th century, pictorial mosque and minarets above three mihrabs, 5ft. 5in. by 4ft. (Skinner) $1,380

Velvet Ikat Chapan, Central Asia, 19th century, circular medallions, hooked motifs, and palmettes. (Skinner) $4,888

Shirvan rug, East Caucasus, last quarter 19th century, six squares, each set with a hooked diamond, 5ft. by 4ft. 2in. (Skinner) $2,645

Bidjar sampler, Northwest Persia, late 19th century, partial stepped medallion inset with rosettes in dark brown, navy blue, rose, and red-brown, 5ft. 6in. by 3ft. 10in. (Skinner) $2,070

Shirvan rug, East Caucasus, late 19th century, two diamond medallion and small animal motifs on the royal blue field, ivory 'wine glass' border, 5ft. x 3ft. 9in. (Skinner) $862

Kazak rug, Southwest Caucasus, last quarter 19th century, staggered rows of palmette motifs in red, sky blue, bright gold, and blue-green, 6ft. 10in. by 4ft. (Skinner) $3,335

Qashqai rug, Southwest Persia, second half 19th century, narrow vertical stripes with palmettes, 10ft. 2in. by 5ft. 6in. (Skinner) $7,475

Khamehs bagface, Southwest Persia, early 20th century, small square medallion surrounded by bird motifs, 2ft. 3in. by 1ft. 7in. (Skinner) $863

Chi-Chi rug, Northeast Caucasus, late 19th century, alternating rows of octagons and hooked polygons, 6ft. by 4ft. 2in. (Skinner) $2,300

Shirvan rug, East Caucasus, last quarter 19th century, elongated 'keyhole' medallion in sky blue, gold, tan, and blue-green, 5ft. by 3ft. 7in.
(Skinner) $1,955

Kurd bagface, Northwest Persia, early 20th century, four squares inset with cruciform 'arrowhead' motifs, 1ft. 10in. by 1ft. 7in.
(Skinner) $403

South Caucasus prayer rug, dated *1876*, square medallion, large palmette, and numerous small geometric motifs, 5ft. by 3ft. 2in.
(Skinner) $1,380

Marasali prayer rug, East Caucasus, last quarter 19th century, diamond lattice with blossoming plants, 4ft. 10in. by 3ft. 8in.
(Skinner) $2,070

Chinese mat, second half 19th century, circular medallion and four floral motifs in navy and royal blue, gold, and ivory, 2ft. 2in. by 2ft. 2in.
(Skinner) $460

Kirghiz prayer rug, Central Asia, late 19th century, ivory column and small flowerheads in navy and sky blue, gold, apricot and green, 4ft. 4in. by 3ft.
(Skinner) $690

Baluch prayer rug, Northeast Persia, last quarter 19th century, 'tree of life' design in midnight blue, red, and aubergine, 4ft. 6in. by 3ft.
(Skinner) $2,070

Baluch Ru-Korsi, Northeast Persia, early 20th century, five small midnight blue, red and light aubergine geometric motifs, 4ft. 7in. by 4ft. 5in.
(Skinner) $805

Kerman pictorial mat, Southeast Persia, early 20th century, nobleman stabbing a winged lion within an architectural setting, 2ft. 5in. by 1ft. 10in.
(Skinner) $460

Shirvan rug, East Caucasus, last quarter 19th century, (small areas of minor wear, slight moth damage, small crease) 6ft. by 4ft. 3in.
(Skinner) $5,175

Pair of Veramin bagfaces, North Persia, early 20th century, stepped polygon surrounded by serrated leaves, each 2ft. 4in. by 2ft.
(Skinner) $403

Kelim bag, Northwest Persia, early 20th century, stepped navy blue and red hexagonal medallion on the dark brown field, 1ft. 8in. by 1ft. 6in.
(Skinner) $403

Kazak rug, Southwest Caucasus, last quarter 19th century, three hooked diamond medallions in navy blue, gold, ivory and blue green, 7ft. 6in. by 5ft.
(Skinner) $1,840

Baluch bagface, Northeast Persia, last quarter 19th century, large, red, rust, and ivory octagon, 2ft. 5in. by 2ft. 3in.
(Skinner) $288

Erzurum prayer Kelim, Northeast Anatolia, last quarter 19th century, ivory and blue flowering plants on the rust field, 6ft. 6in. by 3ft. 10in.
(Skinner) $575

Qashqai rug, Southwest Persia, second quarter 20th century, staggered hexagons in red, royal blue, gold and ivory, 8ft. by 5ft. 4in.
(Skinner) $2,415

Uzbek velvet Ikat and embroidered tent hanging, Central Asia, 19th century, central plant stem with four boteh, 2ft. by 2ft.
(Skinner) $345

Hamadan rug, Northwest Persia, early 20th century, concentric diamond medallion in rust, navy blue and light blue-green, 5ft. 3in. by 3ft. 5in.
(Skinner) $863

Needlework sampler, *Huldah Louisa Baldwin's sampler wrought in the twelfth year of her age Watertown Aug 27 1836 M. Buell*, 16 x 17¹/₂in., framed. (Skinner) **$1,093**

Needlework sampler, *Barbara Johnson Her sampler Worked in the Fourteenth Year of her Age 1770*, 10 x 7in., framed. (Skinner) **$1,725**

Needlework family register, *Laura H. Clark Middlesex Vermont*, register above townscape surrounded by grape vine border, 16³/₄ x 21¹/₂in. (Skinner) **$2,415**

Needlework sampler, *Mary Tinsley's Sampler made in the year of our Lord 1827*, Pennsylvania, pious verses surrounding basket of flowers, 16¹/₄ x 17in. (Skinner) **$1,380**

Oval petit point sampler silk stitched on gauze, alphabet in capitals, verse and inscribed at the foot *Elizabeth Cooper, Wrought This In The 8th Year of Her Age, 1795.* (G. A. Key) **$724**

Needlework family register, *Sarah Ramsdel born May 15th 1802*, dated *1837*, Rhode Island, family register and pious verses, 17¹/₄ x 16in. (Skinner) **$2,645**

Sampler, silk stitched on gauze, central verse and inscribed below *Ann Woods, her work in the year of her age, November 1842*, 12 x 13in. (G. A. Key) **$330**

Needlework sampler, *Wrought by Mary Ann C. Alley aged 12 years and seven months*, possibly Lynn, Massachusetts, or Portland, Maine, 16¹/₄ x 12in. (Skinner) **$3,737**

Needlework sampler/Silver family register, wrought by Hannah Silver aged 11 years 1801, Salem, Massachusetts, 22 x 21in. (Skinner) **$25,300**

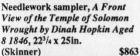

Needlework sampler, *A Front View of the Temple of Solomon Wrought by Dinah Hopkin Aged 8 1846*, 22³/₄ x 25in.
(Skinner) $863

Needlework sampler, *Theodate Newhall is my Name and with my needle I workt the Same in the Year 1785*, 15¹/₂ x 9³/₄in.
(Skinner) $2,415

Needlework family register, *Sally L. Ingells aged 12 years 1828*, probably Massachusetts, 15³/₄ x 16¹/₄in.
(Skinner) $1,380

Needlework sampler, wrought by Charlotte Daggett, 1808, possibly Balch School, Providence, Rhode Island, rows of alphabets above with variant of Boton & Coe verse 152, 21 x 18in.
(Skinner) $3,105

Needlework sampler, Essex County, Massachusetts, *Lucy Lambert Aged 9 years August 1829*, rows of alphabets on green linsey-woolsey ground, 17¹/₂ x 13in., framed.
(Skinner) $978

Sampler, silk stitched on gauze, alphabet in capitals and italics, central verse and inscribed below, *Hannah James, Aged Nine Years, February, 1825*, 16 x 17in.
(G. A. Key) $495

Needlework sampler, *1822 Wrought by Harriet Brown AE XIV*, Federal house with flowering trees above pious verses, 17 x 16¹/₂in.
(Skinner) $1,610

Needlework sampler, *Ana Newell is my name English is my nation Holden is my dwelling place in Christ is my salvation 1794*, framed, 14¹/₄ x 8¹/₈in.
(Skinner) $690

Sampler, silk stitched on gauze, verse, geometric decoration and inscribed at foot, *Elizabeth Cooke, Aged 12 Years, 1832*, 12 x 13¹/₂in.
(G. A. Key) $480

A sampler by Susannah Turner, 1844 with verse, 'Remember now thy Creator' and cross stitch dog in centre, 16 x 19in.
(Christie's) $489

A sampler by Eliza Grindly, worked with verse and alphabets in stylized floral border, early 19th century, 18in. square.
(Christie's) $456

A sampler by Sarah Appleton, 1799, with verse bordered by two birds in stylized floral border, 15½ x 18½in.
(Christie's) $1,310

A fine needlework sampler, signed *Hannah Nimblett*, Marblehead, Massachusetts, circa 1795, with bands of alphabets above figures of a lady and gentleman in top hats, 10½ x 7¼in.
(Sotheby's) $28,750

A needlework sampler, signed *Martha Newbold*, Wilmington Boarding School, Delaware, dated *1818*, executed in dark brown silk with bands of alphabets over a verse, 11½ x 13½in.
(Sotheby's) $8,050

A needlework family record sampler signed *Alice Clark*, Waltham, Massachusetts, circa 1807, with a large tree bearing fruit inscribed with family details of the Clark family, 15¾ x 12½in.
(Sotheby's) $25,300

A fine needlework sampler, signed *Anna Huntington*, Franklin, Connecticut, dated 1803, with exotic and American scenes surrounding a central diamond, 16 x 15¾in.
(Sotheby's) $34,500

An important needlework sampler, signed *Hannah Goddard*, Brookline, Massachusetts, dated *1773*, alphabets and numbers above a verse, 18 x 13¾in.
(Sotheby's) $31,050

An important needlework sampler, signed *Anna Braddock*, Burlington County, New Jersey, dated *1826*, executed in blue, green, yellow, brown and white silk, 22 x 26in.
(Sotheby's) $145,500

A fine sampler by Jessy Dun, 181?, worked with Adam and Eve and a verse, within stylized floral border, 13¾ x 14¼in. (Christie's) $1,583

A sampler by Anna Mercer, circa 1811, worked with a verse, a house and other spot motifs, 14 x 18½in. (Christie's) $699

Needlework sampler, Ireland, *Eleanor OBeirne October the 14th 1823*, flowering vase flanked by crowns, butterflies and pine trees, 17³/₈ x 17in. (Skinner) $1,265

A needlework sampler, signed *Kezia Ridgway*, Salem County, New Jersey, or possibly Philadelphia, Pennsylvania, dated *1800*, with alphabets over two birds perched on a vase of flowers, 16¼ x 12½in. (Sotheby's) $4,600

A fine needlework sampler, signed *S. Richardson*, Groton, Massachusetts, date *1831*, with bands of alphabets and a pious verse above a landscape scene, 16¼ x 17in. (Sotheby's) $63,000

A needlework sampler, signed *Anna Gould*, probably Massachusetts, dated *1748*, executed in various stitches on a linen ground with bands of alphabets in a zigzag border, 11½ x 8¼in. (Sotheby's) $5,750

A rare needlework sampler, signed *Eliza McMannus, Female Association School, New York*, dated *1813*, executed in cross stitches with baskets of fruit and rose sprigs, 7½ x 8¾in. (Sotheby's) $16,100

A needlework family record sampler, signed *Nancy Batten*, Salem, Massachusetts, dated *1809,* with names and dates of members of the Batten-Thorp family, 26 x 19¾in. (Sotheby's) $33,350

A needlework sampler, signed *Sarah J. Hildreth*, Dracut, Massachusetts, circa 1828, with alphabets under a floral border above a scene with a house, 14¼ x 18in. (Sotheby's) $19,550

A Becker SA Brussels precision balance, in fine wooden case, 40 x 50x30 cm.
(Auction Team Köln)

$295

Swedish kitchen scales by C.M. Engstrom, gold bronze cast body with painted tin dial, circa 1890.
(Auction Team Köln)

$155

German jeweler's scales in glass case with drawer under, circa 1880.
(Auction Team Köln)

$2,180

AEG letter scales in the form of a contemporary electric meter, plated metal body with black painted base, circa 16cm. high, 1910.
(Auction Team Köln)

$350

A 17th century German steel balance, the beam with 'trumpet' ends, with triangular and dished pans contained in a fruitwood case, 9¾in. wide.
(Christie's) $2,443

A mid 18th century German coin balance, with brass pans, the pillar with 'lion-lift' mechanism, with label *poids des monnaies*, 11in. wide.
(Christie's) $2,269

Duplex kitchen scales, green cast body with gold decoration, German, for the Swedish market, enamel dial.
(Auction Team Köln)

$280

18th century English coin scales by Henry Mudge of Truro, in original mahogany case, with steel beam and brass scales, two weights missing.
(Auction Team Köln)

$855

German Orig. Columbus Bilateral desk scales, with two stage calibration (100 and 500g.) and two red pointers, circa 1910.
(Auction Team Köln)

$155

German Cito household scales, white painted cast metal body, circa 34cm. high.
(Auction Team Köln) $70

British brass shop scales by R. Simpson of Edinburgh, circa 1890, 40cm. high..
(Auction Team Köln)
$660

Krups cast iron Art Nouveau household scales, with enamel dial up to 10kg.
(Auction Team Köln) $140

A mid 18th century balance de changeur, by Jacques François Neusts, the oak plinth base with drawer containing twenty-four weights, matching the trade label dated *1749*, 9in. wide.
(Christie's) $1,571

A rare 17th century steel coin balance, with triangular and concave pans, by G.D. with a comprehensive collection of money and gold weights by PH, 1648, Pierre Herck of Antwerp, of various currencies, 6¾in.
(Christie's) $1,308

A late 18th century English steel beam balance, engraved *James Schooling*, the date obscured by a proof punch mark, with wrought iron stand on mahogany base, 46in. high.
(Christie's) $873

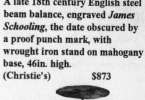

A postal balance, with quadrant, balance weight, square pan, on gilded stand modeled in the form of three swans, 7½in. high.
(Christie's) $524

An early 18th century German iron spice balance, with shaped brass pan and bowl, the shears decorated with the double-headed eagle, the beam, 8½in.
(Christie's) $785

A rare Continental postal balance, the silver-plated copper pan chased and etched with the figure of a young woman learning to play the lute, 6½in.
(Christie's) $1,012

An American Improved Little Comfort chain stitch machine by Smith & Egge, circa 1905.
(Auction Team Köln) $132

A rare American Clark's Foliage chain stitch machine, lacking needle, circa 1859.
(Auction Team Köln)

$4,675

A Little Wanzer-type Canadian bow shuttle machine, on unusual cast base, with shuttle.
(Auction Team Köln)

$545

American Peerless Automatic child's chain stitch machine, circa 1900.
(Auction Team Köln)
$155

The Müller No. 1 German chain stitch child's sewing machine in original box, circa 1910.
(Auction Team Köln)
$272

Rare German bow shuttle domestic sewing machine, called Machine de Plaisir, on decorative tripod base, circa 1875.
(Auction Team Köln)
$1,945

An undocumented New England-type sewing machine, circa 1870.
(Auction Team Köln)
$186

Grover & Baker portable American twin thread chain stitch machine with typical gripper, circa 1858.
(Auction Team Köln)
$1,560

American Wheeler & Wilson No.1 frame sewing machine, without spool, circa 1880.
(Auction Team Köln)
$342

A Jacob L. Frey original US patent machine, wooden, with brass mechanism, 1865. (Auction Team Köln)
$4,500

A Raymond American chain-stitch machine, circa 1870. (Auction Team Köln)
$295

A Nussey & Pilling improved Little Stranger lockstitch sewing machine, with circular stitchplate, on cast-iron foot. (Christie's)
$1,361

A Canadian Little Wanzer swing shuttle manual sewing machine, complete with shuttle, circa 1890. (Auction Team Köln)
$195

A rare 'Mary' German chain stitch machine by Müller, circa 1890. (Auction Team Köln)
$1,560

A French Peugeot No.1 frame swing-shuttle machine, with shuttle, circa 1880. (Auction Team Köln)
$1,557

An early Grant Brothers model of the American New England-type chain stitch machine, lacks needle, circa 1870. (Auction Team Köln)
$220

Shaw & Clark Monitor(?) American chain stitch machine, with floral hand painted and gilt decoration, circa 1865. (Auction Team Köln)
$622

A Taylor bow shuttle sewing machine, with shuttle but lacking spool, English, circa 1875. (Auction Team Köln)
$700

BASKETS

A George II silver cake basket, Elizabeth Godfrey, London, 1753, in the form of a raffia basket, with ropetwist overhead swing handle, 12½in. long, 35oz. (Christie's) $13,800

A large Dutch two-handled basket in the 18th century taste, the tapering oval body pierced with trelliswork and rosettes, bearing import marks for London 1896, 15¾in. overall, 38.25oz. (Christie's) $2,707

A George II silver cake basket, Frederick Kandler, London, 1759, applied with female masks, with leaf- and bust-clad swing handle, 16in. long, 62oz. (Christie's) $16,100

A silver cake basket, Whiting Mfg. Co., circa 1875, realistically chased as a tropical leaf with overhead wire-form handle, 11¾in. high, 29oz. (Christie's) $3,220

A set of four George III silver sweetmeat baskets, Thomas Pitts, London, 1768, each on four shell, scroll and flower feet, 5¾in. long, 24oz. (Christie's) $6,641

A Russian mid 19th century swing-handled cake basket of tapering oval form and on a rising foot, St. Petersburg 1859, 10½in., 23oz. (Christie's) $395

A Russian 19th century gilt-lined swing-handled cake basket, the part-fluted tapering oblong body with die-rolled floral border, Moscow 1830, 8¼in., 14.5oz. (Christie's) $1,167

A pair of George III silver-gilt baskets, Wakelin & Tayler, London, 1786, each pierced shaped oval, the rim with scroll and rocaille, 9½in. long, 34oz. (Christie's) $18,400

A George III swing-handled cake basket of shaped oval form, applied with rope-twist borders and decorated with spiral-fluting, William Plummer, London 1772, 13½in., 22.25oz. (Christie's) $1,748

538

BEAKERS

A Russian mid 18th century beaker, the sides with three oval cartouches, chased with a lion, a unicorn, and Cupid, 1746, 3¼in. (Christie's) $682

A French 18th century beaker, one side engraved with a crest within an elaborate draped ermine cartouche, a crown above, Paris circa 1770, 2¼in. (Christie's) $506

A Russian 18th century beaker of tapering circular form and with molded rim, Moscow, 3¼in. (Christie's) $613

An 18th century Russian beaker, embossed with classical figures, a man flying a bird of prey on a rope, by Grigoriy Lakomkin, Moscow, 1745, 10.5cm. high, 4oz. (Phillips) $906

A pair of Salzburg Empire covered beakers, gilt lined, the edge with palmette frieze, high, angular twin handles, circa 1810, 13cm. high, 505gr. (Dorotheum) $2,828

A 17th century German parcel-gilt beaker on ball feet, sides chased and embossed with three scroll-edged oval panels, probably by Johann Jacob Wolrab, Nuremberg, circa 1685, 7.8cm. high, 3oz. (Phillips) $1,359

An Augsburg bell-form beaker, gadrooned lower body, by Tobias Drescher, mid 18th century, 5.5cm. high, 55gr. (Dorotheum) $300

A German silver beaker, Biberach, 17th century, on circular domed base, rising to a tapering lower body, 4in. high, 3oz. 10dwt. (Christie's) $3,220

A 19th century Russian beaker, the sides with pierced frieze of classical warriors, Moscow, 1842, 8.7cm. high, 4.25oz. (Phillips) $486

BOWLS

A Viennese silver bowl, the sides richly chased with hunting scenes, the base with portrait of Marie Antoinette, Peter Breithut, 12cm. high, 905gr. (Dorotheum) $1,885

A Russian vodka bowl with six vodka cups and a ladle with kovsh-shaped bowl, upon a circular stand, by Peter Pavlovitch Milyukov, circa 1896, bowl 12.75cm. diameter. (Phillips) $2,340

Tiffany sterling punch bowl, circa 1913, round form with wide chased flower and scroll border at rim, ribbed body, 12in. diameter, approximately 60 troy oz. (Skinner) $4,600

Victorian silver punch bowl, London, circa 1889, makers Hunt & Roskell, round form with chased leaf and acanthus leaf bands, 10in. diameter, approximately 30 troy oz. (Skinner) $977

George III silver open sugar bowl, London, 1809–10, possibly Peter Podie, scalloped canoe shape with swing handle, 6⅞in. high with handle, approximately 8 troy oz. (Skinner) $633

A late Victorian reproduction of a William III monteith with part-fluted sides, the shaped rim with beaded masks, by Robert Dicker, 1896, 28cm. diameter, 64.5oz. (Phillips) $2,584

A George III silver christening bowl, cover and stand, Henry Green, London, 1788, engraved with foliage and panels with wrigglework borders, the stand 8¼in. diameter, 23oz. (Christie's) $7,210

Reed & Barton sterling bowl, Francis I pattern, shaped edge lobed form, chased design, 11¼in. diameter, approximately 23 troy oz. (Skinner) $1,093

An Edward VII two-handled circular rose bowl in early 18th century monteith-style, 22cm. diameter, Hancocks & Co., London 1908, 29oz. (Bearne's) $987

BOWLS

A silver bowl, Charles Clement Pilling, Sheffield, 1910, the spreading circular foot applied with four standing soldiers, 10¹/₂in. high, 72oz.
(Christie's) $1,898

Gorham sterling hammer textured presentation bowl, 1882, low round form, applied three-dimensional pond lilies and leaves on one side, 6⁵/₈in. diameter, approximately 10 troy oz.
(Skinner) $2,185

An Edward VII rose bowl with chased floral decoration, 29cm. diameter, George Nathan & Ridley Hayes, Chester 1906, 28.9oz.
(Bearne's) $733

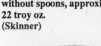

Tiffany silver covered bowl/spoon holder, 1854–70, baluster form, raised and chased grape leaf decoration, 6in. high without spoons, approximately 22 troy oz.
(Skinner) $2,530

Pair of Victorian silver reticulated bowls, Birmingham, 1895–96, E & Cold maker, shaped edge oval form, stylized floral and scroll decoration, 8⁷/₈in. long, approximately 16 troy oz.
(Skinner) $978

European hallmarked silver reticulated fruit bowl, chased with shell, scroll, floral and Bacchanalian children, 8³/₄in. diameter, approximately 30 troy oz.
(Skinner) $863

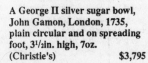

A George II silver sugar bowl, John Gamon, London, 1735, plain circular and on spreading foot, 3¹/₂in. high, 7oz.
(Christie's) $3,795

J.E. Caldwell & Co. wastebowl, Philadelphia, mid 19th century, overall chased chinoiserie design, 4⁵/₈in. high, approximately 14 troy oz.
(Skinner) $517

A George II covered sugar bowl of hemispherical form, engraved with armorials on cover and side, 1737, 10cm. high, 9oz.
(Phillips) $5,016

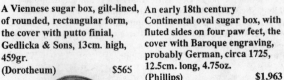

A Regency Irish silver Freedom box, Carden Terry & Jane Williams, Cork, 1820, the hinged cover with bright-cut engraved foliage, thistles, harps and crowns, 3in. long.
(Christie's) $3,450

A Viennese sugar box, gilt-lined, of rounded, rectangular form, the cover with putto finial, Gedlicka & Sons, 13cm. high, 459gr.
(Dorotheum) $565

An early 18th century Continental oval sugar box, with fluted sides on four paw feet, the cover with Baroque engraving, probably German, circa 1725, 12.5cm. long, 4.75oz.
(Phillips) $1,963

A Continental gilt-lined sugar box, of fluted bombé-shaped oval form and on bun feet, probably Austro-Hungarian or German, late 19th century, 5³/₄in., 12oz.
(Christie's) $489

A George III gold portrait box, Gabriel Wirgman, London, 1795, the hinged cover set with a portrait miniature and with glazed hair panel above, 3³/₈in. long.
(Christie's) $16,100

An Austro-Hungarian 19th century gilt-lined sugar box, of oblong bombé shape and on foliate-capped stylized paw feet, maker's initials J.G., Vienna 1861, 6in., 14.5oz.
(Christie's) $1,129

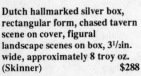

Dutch hallmarked silver box, rectangular form, chased tavern scene on cover, figural landscape scenes on box, 3¹/₂in. wide, approximately 8 troy oz.
(Skinner) $288

A Russian 19th century gilt-lined sugar box or soap box of spherical form and on a rising foot, St. Petersburg, the date indistinct, 5in., 8oz.
(Christie's) $538

A Russian 19th century gilt-lined box modeled as a domed-top trunk on bracket feet and with a hasp fastener, Moscow 1877, 4¹/₂in., 12.75oz.
(Christie's) $961

BOXES

An Edward VII silver and tortoiseshell shaped rectangular dressing table box, 12.5cm. long, H. Matthews, Birmingham 1909. (Bearne's) $362

A girl and mistletoe box attributed to Koloman Moser for George Anton Scheidt, Vienna, circa 1900, 2 x 3in. (Sotheby's) $6,373

An Arts & Crafts rectangular cigarette box with stud-work decoration, 11cm. long, Chester 1903. (Bearne's) $207

Guild of Handicraft Ltd., Peacock box and cover, 1903, silver, the cover and central circular panel enameled in shades of leaf green and deep blue, 2½in. (Sotheby's) $2,437

Liberty & Co., 'Cymric' tripod box, 1902, set around the shoulders with three triangular panels enameled in shades of forest green and deep blue, 5¼in. (Sotheby's) $4,311

A George III Irish silver Freedom box, William Reynolds, Cork, circa 1760, the removable cover repoussé with a coat of arms, 3¼in. diameter, 4oz. (Christie's) $6,325

Guild of Handicraft Ltd., Butterfly box and cover, 1900, silver, the cover with central circular panel enameled with a stylized butterfly, 2¼in. (Sotheby's) $3,187

A box of silver colored metal, the hinged cover richly enameled with the head and shoulders of a young girl in a red scarf, 4in. diameter. (Sotheby's) $4,499

A Piet Regenspurg box and cover, after 1922, the domed cover cast with swirling wave motifs with three highly stylized fish, 4in. (Sotheby's) $937

CADDY SPOONS

A parcel gilt sea life motif spoon with serpentine handle, Victorian hallmark concealed. (David Lay) $336

A George III E. Morley acorn spoon, London, 1809. (David Lay) $336

A modern caddy spoon by H.G. Murphy, with a hammered finish, drop shaped bowl, 1929. (Phillips) $258

A Victorian caddy spoon with scalloped bowl and waterlily handle by Hilliard & Thomason, Birmingham, 1857. (Phillips) $608

A George III jockey cap caddy spoon, reeled in oak pendent foliage, by Joseph Taylor, Birmingham, 1800. (Phillips) $578

A George III Provincial caddy spoon with a fluted shell bowl, by J. Langlands & J. Robelson, Newcastle, circa 1790. (Phillips) $517

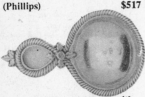

A Victorian Provincial caddy spoon with feather-edge stem engraved with foliate spray, the plain circular parcel-gilt bowl, Chester, 1856. (Phillips) $517

A modern caddy spoon by Liberty & Co., with a round bowl and a shaped lug handle decorated in red, blue and green enamel, Birmingham, 1928. (Phillips) $486

Edwardian caddy spoon by The Keswick School of Industrial Art, with a dished oval bowl and a lug handle chased with a stylized rose, Birmingham, 1901. (Phillips) $182

A George III caddy spoon with circular bowl, the stamped ropework border continuing upwards to form a loop handle, by Samuel Pemberton, Birmingham, 1800. (Phillips) $547

A Victorian caddy spoon with parcel-gilt scalloped bowl stamped with rose, thistles and shamrocks, possibly by Henry Wilkinson & Co., Sheffield, 1856. (Phillips) $258

A stylish Arts and Crafts caddy spoon with hammered heart-shaped bowl, the handle with simulated snakeskin panel, by Florence Maud Rimmington, 1905. (Phillips) $258

A Victorian cast caddy spoon with clam shell bowl and waterlily handle, unmarked but in the manner of Francis Higgins, circa 1850. (Phillips) $942

A modern drop shaped caddy spoon by Omar Ramsden, with a hammered finish, the stem formed by symmetrical coiled tendrils, 1923. (Phillips) $882

A George III scallop bowl caddy spoon, stem bright engraved with monogram in oval cartouche, stem engraved with chevrons. (Phillips) $395

CADDY SPOONS

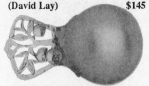

A Hester Bateman George III shell bowl and bright-cut spoon, London, 1789.
(David Lay) $145

A George III caddy spoon, the stem with two projecting points, engraved with leafage below a vacant cartouche, by Cocks & Bethridge, Birmingham, 1810.
(Phillips) $730

A George III Joseph Wilmore vine-cast spoon with wire ring handle, Birmingham, 1810.
(David Lay) $168

A modern caddy spoon by Bernard Instone, with a round bowl and a lug handle, Birmingham, 1929.
(Phillips) $334

Rare George III natural shell caddy spoon with silver mounts and fiddle pattern handle, circa 1810, by Matthew Linwood.
(G. A. Key) $560

A metalware plique-à-jour enameled caddy spoon with a circular polychrome scene in the center of the bowl.
(Phillips) $669

A Victorian die-stamped caddy spoon, bowl decorated with convolvulus leaves and flowers, by Ashforth & Harthorn, Sheffield, 1847.
(Phillips) $365

A George III caddy spoon with pastern hoof bowl, engraved with crescent panel of leafage, by Cocks & Bethridge, Birmingham, 1816.
(Phillips) $395

A George III tea leaf caddy spoon embossed with bunch of grapes and tendrils, tendril ringhandle, by Joseph Wilhouse, Birmingham, 1814.
(Phillips) $456

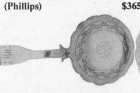

A George III fiddle pattern caddy spoon, monogrammed, large shaped circular bowl, engraved with circlet of foliage around central rosette, by Thomas James, 1814.
(Phillips) $395

A George III right-hand caddy spoon, the flat fan shaped handle with wavy rim and bright-engraved decoration, by Josiah Snatt, 1806.
(Phillips) $699

A Victorian caddy spoon with scalloped bowl stamped with flowers and grapes, the loop handle applied with vine leaves, by George Unite, Birmingham, 1868.
(Phillips) $258

A late 19th century Russian parcel gilt caddy spoon with a tapering stem, border engraving and a sunburst cartouche by Ivan Chlebrikow, Moscow, 1882.
(Phillips) $228

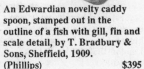

An Edwardian novelty caddy spoon, stamped out in the outline of a fish with gill, fin and scale detail, by T. Bradbury & Sons, Sheffield, 1909.
(Phillips) $395

A George III spade caddy spoon, the bowl bright engraved with a wavy line interrupted by scrolls on a frosted ground, by Cocks & Bethridge, Birmingham, 1809.
(Phillips) $547

CANDELABRA

A pair of electroplated four-light candelabra, the faceted stem, drip pans and detachable nozzles, 54cm. high.
(Bearne's) $1,083

A pair of Continental plated six-light candelabrum, unmarked, late 19th century, each on shaped-circular base with four foliate scroll feet, 19in. high.
(Christie's) $3,226

A fine pair of electroplated five-light candelabra, with leaf capped branches, 60cm. high.
(Bearne's) $2,946

A Victorian silver plated table center, comprising fluted glass bowl on baluster stem, with six scrolling foliate branches, 23in. high.
(Andrew Hartley) $2,480

A pair of American silver nine-light candelabra, Tiffany & Co., New York, 1884, chased and cast, one stem with mermaids riding dolphins, the other with mermen leading seahorses, 240oz., 16in. high.
(Sotheby's) $123,500

An Art Deco candelabrum, the central fluted column headed by a ball issuing four spiral arms, maker's mark EJ, 23cm. high, 722gr.
(Dorotheum) $942

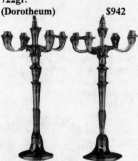

A pair of Victorian silver four-light candelabra, by J Crichton, Edinburgh, 1880, each on a circular base with foliate border, 24½in. high, 190oz.
(Christie's) $9,373

A Victorian table centerpiece with an openwork tapering stem decorated with fruit and foliage, the center with a pierced bowl holder, Messrs. Barnard, London 1850, 23¾in., 138oz.
(Christie's) $4,894

A pair of French silver four-light candelabra, Jean-Baptiste-Claude Odiot, Paris, 1795, the leaf-clad scroll branches with flaring sockets, 20in. high, 145oz. 10dwt.
(Christie's) $20,700

CANDELABRA

A pair of George III silver two-light candelabra, Matthew Boulton, Birmingham, 1805, the branches 1810, 18³/₄in. high. (Christie's) $9,200

A pair of Austro-Hungarian Rococo Revival two-light candelabra on domed circular bases with openwork shell and foliate feet, 9in. (Christie's) $1,615

A Victorian silver three-light centerpiece candelabrum, Thomas Bradbury, Sheffield, 1878, 25¹/₂in. high, 146oz. (Christie's) $4,600

A pair of late victorian silver three-light candelabra, by Walker & Hall, Sheffield, 1896, on square base with beaded, patera and garland border, 18¹/₂in. high. (Christie's) $5,061

Large Victorian silver plated table centerpiece on domed shaped square four footed base, the vase shaped center with scrolled and shell applied flanged top, 17in. high, circa 1860. (G. A. Key) $1,276

A pair of German silver two-light candelabra, Balthasar Friedrich Behrens, Hanover, circa 1750, each on shaped incurved square base, rising to a knopped stem, 15³/₄in. high, 106oz. (Christie's) $43,700

Carl Stock for P. Bruckmann & Söhne, four light candelabrum, circa 1900, silver-colored metal, central knopped stem rising from domed base, 17in. (Sotheby's) $2,812

Two German silver two-light candelabra, the first maker's mark of Mueller Bros, Berlin, circa 1770, the second apparently Kronstadt, 9³/₄in. high, 37oz. (Christie's) $4,600

M.H. Wilkens & Söhne, Art Nouveau candelabrum, circa 1900, silver-colored metal, formed as a waterlily, leaf form base, 11in. (Sotheby's) $2,437

CANDLESTICKS

A pair of 18th century German cast candlesticks of spirally fluted form, by Johann (II) Pepfenhauser, Augsburg, 1731/33, 18.5cm. high, 16oz. (Phillips) $4,553

A pair of Elkington electroplated Corinthian column table candlesticks, the square bases decorated with rams masks, 31cm. high. (Bearne's) $472

Two Continental candlesticks, the fluted cylindrical stems applied with laurel swags, one by J.R. Haller, Augsburg circa 1830, the other Dutch, 8in. (Christie's) $1,076

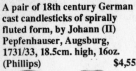

A pair of late 18th century Dutch Neo-Classical cast candlesticks, on fluted square bases with square, tapering, fluted columns, by Jan Smit, Amsterdam, 1785, 28.5cm. high, 50oz. (Phillips) $9,362

A pair of late Victorian candlesticks, each with a fluted column, Corinthian capital and gadrooned shaped square detachable nozzle, Walker & Hall, Birmingham 1899, 5in. (Christie's) $787

A pair of Victorian cast figural candlesticks, one surmounted by the figure of a young lady in 18th century dress stooping to pour water from a watering can, by Charles Thomas & George Fox, 1853, 20.5cm. high, 28oz. (Phillips) $9,880

A pair of Dutch silver candlesticks, Matthijs Crayenschot, Amsterdam, 1778, each on circular base with spiraling rocaille, 10¾in. high, 32oz. (Christie's) $8,050

Pair of Danish silver candlesticks, 19th century, baluster form with twisted neck, raised on three scroll form feet, 13in. high, approximately 55 troy oz. (Skinner) $2,185

A pair of George III silver candlesticks, Thomas Heming, London, 1768, stem in the form of a classical maiden supporting a foliate wax-pan, 14¼in. high, 88oz. (Christie's) $10,925

548

CANDLESTICKS

Pair of Continental neoclassical style silver plated candlesticks, late 19th century, applied foliage fruit and theatrical masks, 11³/₈in. high.
(Skinner) $1,495

Pair of silver dressing table candlesticks, the loaded square bases with beaded decoration, 4¹/₂in. high, London 1904 by the Goldsmiths and Silversmiths Co.
(G. A. Key) $318

A pair of George V table candlesticks of tapering circular form, Edward Barnard & Sons Ltd., 24cm. high, London 1926, loaded.
(Bearne's) $315

Pair of hallmarked silver encased bedroom candlesticks on shaped square bases, embossed with anthemia and fluted designs, with reeded column and detachable sconces, 5in. high, Birmingham 1901.
(G. A. Key) $536

A pair of American silver and other metals 'Japanese style' large table candlesticks, Tiffany & Co., New York, circa 1879–80, chased with copper-tinged dripping wax on a ground of graduating spot-hammering, 39oz. gross, 11¹/₄in. high.
(Sotheby's) $44,850

F.B., Czechoslovakian, pair of Modernist candlesticks, circa 1930, silver-colored metal, each with columnar support terminating in hemispherical knop above three circular bands.
(Sotheby's) $5,624

Good pair of late Victorian telescopic plated candlesticks on loaded circular bases with gadrooned detail on bases, 9in. high.
(G. A. Key) $216

A pair of William IV silver candlesticks, Paul Storr, London, 1836, each on shaped circular base with band of ovolo and paterae with shells at intervals, 9¹/₂in. high, 46oz.
(Christie's) $23,000

A pair of Queen Anne silver candlesticks, Simon Pantin, London, 1709, each on octagonal molded base, rising to a baluster stem, 6¹/₄in. high, 25oz.
(Christie's) $8,625

CENTERPIECES

Tiffany sterling Renaissance Revival centerpiece, 1860s, 12in. diameter, approximately 45 troy oz.
(Skinner)   **$1,495**

An Old Sheffield plate table centerpiece with a central knopped stem with openwork holder fitted with a tapering cut glass bowl, 19³/₄in. overall.
(Christie's)   **$1,748**

Silver plate and clear glass centerpiece with figural base, 19th century, *J.D. & S. Co.*, rock formation and oak tree base with giraffe and deer, 9¹/₈in. diameter. (Skinner)   **$374**

Fine pair of Victorian silver plated table centerpieces in the form of palm trees with paneled rococo styled bases, 11in. high, mid 19th century.
(G. A. Key)   **$540**

A Victorian silver-gilt centerpiece, Benjamin Preston, London, 1844, cylindrical plinth, surmounted by three frolicking putti, 17³/₄in. high, 80oz. 10dwt. (Christie's)   **$9,775**

A pair of Victorian parcel-gilt centerpieces modeled as vines, each on a fluted circular base with scrolling foliate feet, Stephen Smith, London 1865, 7in., 41.25oz.
(Christie's)   **$1,615**

A Victorian silver-gilt centerpiece, George Angell, London, 1877, shell-form, surmounting entwined dolphin stem with two sea putti, 13in. high, 90oz. 10dwt.
(Christie's)   **$20,700**

A Victorian Scottish parcel-gilt centerpiece, Edinburgh, 1875, maker's mark *MC & Co.*, on quatrefoil base and with four openwork scroll supports, 9³/₄in. high, 195oz.
(Christie's)   **$3,605**

Elaborate silver centerpiece, Europe, 20th century, gold washed chased floral decoration, bowl supported by three angels, 20in. high, approximately 756 troy oz.
(Skinner)   **$12,650**

CHAMBERSTICKS

A William III silver chamberstick, John Smith, London, 1698, circular, with cylindrical socket pierced for wax removal, 4¼in. diameter, 4oz.
(Christie's) $7,130

A pair of electroplated chamber candlesticks, the detachable nozzles and bases with shell and gadroon edging.
(Bearne's) $157

Sheffield plated chamber candlestick, octagonal shaped with shell and gadrooned rim, foliate scrolled handle, complete with sconce and snuffer.
(G. A. Key) $80

A pair of Regency silver chambersticks, William Stroud, London, 1813, each shaped circular, on three tab feet, the rim applied with rocaille and scrolls, 6¾in. long over handle, 32oz.
(Christie's) $5,175

A late Biedermeier chamberstick on fluted hexagonal base, with waved guilloche ornament, F. Dominik, Vienna, 1860, 11cm., high, 154gr.
(Dorotheum) $707

A pair of Warsaw classical chambersticks on triangular bases with central leaves and bud, the handles with thumb rests, Pavel Siennicki, circa 1790, 13cm. high, 326gr.
(Dorotheum) $2,074

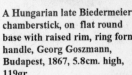

A William IV chamber candlestick on a shaped circular base decorated with alternating plain and textured leaves, Robert Gainsford, Sheffield 1831, the snuffer 1832, 4¾in., 9.75oz.
(Christie's) $699

A pair of Biedermeier chambersticks, on octagonal bases, the ring form handle with thumb rest, Benedikt Ranninger, Vienna, 9cm. high, 293gr.
(Dorotheum) $1,500

A Hungarian late Biedermeier chamberstick, on flat round base with raised rim, ring form handle, Georg Goszmann, Budapest, 1867, 5.8cm. high, 119gr.
(Dorotheum) $565

CHAMBERSTICKS

Fine George III silver chamber stick, circular shaped with gadrooned rim and detachable sconce, marked for London 1808 by William Bateman, 13oz. (G. A. Key) $610

A Viennese chamberstick on domed, rectangular, fluted base, Adolf Kohl, 1863, 10cm. high, 143gr. (Dorotheum) $282

George III small silver chamber stick and snuffer, oblong shaped with rounded corners, gadrooned edges, looped handle, London 1808, by T. Jones. (G. A. Key) $536

CHOCOLATE POTS

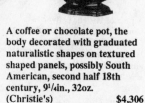

Repoussé sterling chocolate pot, late 19th century, tapered cylindrical form, chased overall floral decoration, ivory side handle, 8in. high, approximately 17 troy oz. (Skinner) $546

Viennese Art Nouveau coffee and chocolate pots, of tapering cylindrical form, with floral relief decoration, 18cm. high, 765gr. total gross weight. (Dorotheum) $1,131

A coffee or chocolate pot, the body decorated with graduated naturalistic shapes on textured shaped panels, possibly South American, second half 18th century, 9¼in., 32oz. (Christie's) $4,306

A Dresden spiral fluted chocolate pot, ebonized handle and finial, Austrian import marks for 1902-22, 14cm. high, 236gr. gross weight. (Dorotheum) $375

A good George III chocolate pot of baluster form embossed and chased with wrythen fluting, floral sprays and a rocaille cartouche, by Francis Crump, 1764, 30.5cm. high, 37oz. (Phillips) $4,560

A Louis XV pear-shaped covered chocolate pot, with domed cover and ball finial, François Delapierre, 18th century, 11.5cm. high, 236gr. (Dorotheum) $1,885

CIGARETTE CASES

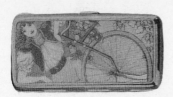

After *Alphonse Mucha* for Louis Kuppenheim, Pforzheim, girl with a bicycle cigarette case, circa 1900, 3¼ x 1½in. (Sotheby's) $4,124

Louis Kuppenheim, Pforzheim, cat cigarette case, 1920s, silver-colored metal, cast front and back with a stylized cat with green hardstone eyes, 4¼ x 2½in. (Sotheby's) $1,125

Oriental nude cigarette case, circa 1900, the hinged cover enameled with a bejeweled female nude, maker's mongram *H.G.?*, 3 x 4in. (Sotheby's) $1,875

Cigarette case designed by Patriz Huber, manufactured by Martin Mayer, Mainz, circa 1900, the hinged cover and base with repoussé abstract design, 3½ x 2¼in. (Sotheby's) $2,800

In the style of Koloman Moser for Georg Anton Scheidt, Vienna, berries cigarette case, circa 1900, the hinged cover with a curvilinear design of highly stylized berries, 3½ x 3¼in. (Sotheby's) $1,405

A Continental silver and enamel cigarette case, import marks *Birmingham, 1902*, cover inset with an oblong enamel plaque depicting a half-length voluptuous female figure in a state of artful undress, 3½in. (Christie's) $1,544

A jeweled silver cigarette case, marked *Fabergé*, Moscow, 1908–1917, with ribbon design and sapphire thumbpiece, 3⁵/₈in. wide. (Christie's) $2,990

A Continental cigarette case, concealed cover enameled with three nude girls reclining in rowing boat with lake behind, import for Birmingham, 1905. (Phillips) $1,280

A tennis players cigarette case by Bruno Paul for Louis Kuppenheim, Pforzheim, the hinged cover enameled with two girls in voluminous dresses, 3¼ x 2½in. (Sotheby's) $1,875

Good quality cut glass claret jug, the silver plated mount and handle with overlaid grapevine detail, 10in. high, circa 1880. (G. A. Key) $464

A Victorian silver mounted glass claret jug, decorated with Bacchus masks, 27cm. high, London 1838. (Bearne's) $393

A Viennese claret jug, silver mounted clear glass, on spreading glass foot, 29cm. high. (Dorotheum) $1,130

A late 19th century French mounted cut glass claret jug with pierced rococo style mounts, circa 1890, 28cm. high. (Phillips) $1,600

A silver-mounted glass claret jug, designed by Paulding Farnham, Tiffany & Co., New York, Renaissance pattern, fluted vase shape, 1905-7, 11¼in. high. (Christie's) $6,900

An Edwardian silver-mounted clear cut glass claret jug, with ovoid body, plain mount, bracket handle and flat hinged cover, J. Grinsell & Sons, Birmingham 1907, 7¾in. (Christie's) $590

A Victorian mounted cut glass claret jug with pierced fruiting vines, bunch of grapes finial and vine handle, by Cartwright & Woodward, Birmingham, 1859, 30.5cm. high. (Phillips) $1,520

Attractive cranberry glass claret jug of inverted baluster design, having an angular hallmarked silver handle and plain mount, 7in. high, Birmingham 1893. (G. A. Key) $566

Fine Victorian glass claret jug, wheel engraved with grapevine detail and having engraved silver plated mounts, 11in. high, circa 1875. (G. A. Key) $366

CLARET JUGS

Indian Export silver claret jug,
19th century, elaborate chased
design, 19¼in. high,
approximately 63 troy oz.
(Skinner) $1,380

A pair of German silver-
mounted claret jugs, the hinged
covers with ball thumb-pieces,
maker's mark *AP*, late 19th
century, 28cm. high.
(Dorotheum) $1,414

W.M.F., claret jug no. 144, circa
1900, electroplated metal, with
domed hinged cover and flaring
body, 15in.
(Sotheby's) $3,374

W.M.F. claret jug no 138D,
circa 1900, silver-plated
Britannia metal, the body
decorated in low relief with
flowers and leaves, 14¾in.
(Sotheby's) $1,875

Pair of etched glass claret jugs
with EPBM mounts and leaf
capped scrolled handles, 9in.
high, circa 1875.
(G. A. Key) $382

A Viennese claret jug, the
swollen oval body of clear glass,
the silver hinged cover and spout
richly decorated in relief ,
Vincent Carl Dub, 40.5cm. high.
(Dorotheum) $4,242

A Victorian gilt-lined claret jug,
the body chased with a broad
frieze of classical figures on a
textured ground, Stephen Smith,
London 1881, 12in., 27.5oz.
(Christie's) $2,257

A pair of German silver
mounted cut-glass claret jugs,
Johann Friedrich Brahmfeld
and Johann Georg Gutruf,
Hamburg, circa 1860, each on
octafoil foot, 13in. high.
(Christie's) $4,175

A Victorian mounted glass
claret jug, the finial modeled as
a rampant lion supporting a
shield inscribed *GH*, by William
Edwards, 1876, 28cm. high.
(Phillips) $1,375

COASTERS

Sterling wine coaster, chased boar hunt scenes around body, 6in. diameter, approximately 9 troy oz.
(Skinner) $373

A pair of electroplated circular coasters with turned wood bases and scalloped edge, 15cm. diameter.
(Bearne's) $267

A pair of George III wine coasters of circular form and with reeded rims and turned wood bases, John Emes, London 1800, 5in.
(Christie's) $1,923

A set of four George III wine coasters of circular form and with beaded borders and turned wood bases, Robert Hennell, London 1792, 4³/₄in.
(Christie's) $4,927

A set of four Regency silver wine coasters, Benjamin Smith II and III, London, 1817, with pierced grapevine gallery and gadrooned rim, 6in. diameter.
(Christie's) $48,300

A set of four Regency silver wine coasters, William Elliot, London, 1813, each fluted circular with gadrooned rim, 6¹/₈in.
(Christie's) $4,600

Two pairs of George III silver wine coasters, Michael Plummer, London, one pair 1792, the other 1793, circular and with molded waved rim, 5¹/₄in. diameter.
(Christie's) $13,283

A pair of George III silver wine coasters, Hester Bateman, London, 1779, the pierced sides bright-cut engraved with entwined decoration, 4³/₄in. diameter.
(Christie's) $3,036

Pair of Georgian silver decanter coasters, treen bases, gadrooned decoration to edges, London 1808 by R. & S. Hennell, 6¹/₂in. diameter.
(G. A. Key) $1,225

COFFEE POTS

A German 18th century coffee pot of fluted oval baluster form and on a rising shaped oval foot, 7¼in., 12oz. gross.
(Christie's) $1,615

A Dutch silver coffee urn, Amsterdam, 1742, pear-shaped, on three scroll feet with ebony disks, 11in., 24oz. 10dwt. gross.
(Christie's) $10,350

A Swiss silver coffee pot, Mise-Gabriel Ducre, Geneva, 1791–93, pear shaped, on three hoof feet, 8¾in. high, 15oz. 10dwt.
(Christie's) $3,220

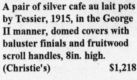

A George III coffee jug on stand with burner, the former of tapering circular form and enhanced with molded body bands and an egg and dart frieze, Paul Storr, London 1805, 12in. overall, 55.25oz.
(Christie's) $7,866

A pair of silver cafe au lait pots by Tessier, 1915, in the George II manner, domed covers with baluster finials and fruitwood scroll handles, 8in. high.
(Christie's) $1,218

A silver-mounted patinated copper coffee pot, Gorham Mfg. Co., Providence, circa 1880, in the Turkish taste, with spot-hammered patinated copper surface, 13in. high.
(Christie's) $1,495

A George III silver coffee pot, Peter and Anne Bateman, London, 1792, pear-shaped and on spreading circular foot, 12in. 28oz. gross.
(Christie's) $2,277

An 18th century French Provincial cafetière of baluster form on three hoof feet, by Jean-François (II) Jouet, Bordeaux, 1787, 22.5cm. high, 21oz.
(Phillips) $1,745

A George III silver coffee pot, Hester Bateman, London, 1787, with beaded bands, with beaded scroll spout, 13¼in. high, 28oz. gross.
(Christie's) $4,600

COFFEE POTS

A late 18th century French Provincial vase shaped coffee pot, on three leaf mask supports with paw feet, circa 1800, 28.5cm. high, 23.5oz.
(Phillips) $2,265

A coffee pot and hot milk jug en suite by Georg Jensen, of hammered ovoid form with ebonized wood side handles, coffee pot 19.5cm. high.
(Phillips) $1,244

A George II silver coffee jug, Thomas Whipham, London, 1742, with hinged domed cover and pineapple finial, 9$^1/_2$in. high, 27oz.
(Christie's) $3,036

A George III baluster coffee pot with bat's wing fluting and engraved crest of stag's head with acorn sprig in mouth, by Francis Crump, 1763, 29.5cm. high, 33.5oz.
(Phillips) $2,204

An 18th century German coffee pot and hot water or hot milk jug en suite of spirally fluted baluster shape, the fluting of rococo form, by Johann Georg Kloss, Augsburg, 1749/51, 29cm. high and 22cm. high, 34oz.
(Phillips) $5,463

An Edward VII pear-shaped coffee pot on domed foot, ebonized wood handle, maker's mark *W.W.H. & Co Sheffield*, 1907-8, 25cm. high, 436gr. gross weight.
(Dorotheum) $470

George II silver coffee pot of circular baluster design to a stepped circular foot and having a curved treen handle, 8$^1/_2$in. high, London 1742, 24oz. all in.
(G. A. Key) $722

A pair of George V coffee and milk pots, of plain circular tapering form, 22.5cm. high, Jay, Richard Attenborough & Co. Ltd., Chester 1933, 38.4oz.
(Bearne's) $906

A George II Irish silver coffee pot, Alexander Brown, Dublin, 1739, with leaf-capped partly-fluted curved spout, 8$^3/_4$in. high, 30oz. gross.
(Christie's) $9,867

A George III silver coffee pot, George Smith, London, 1789, vase-shaped and on spreading circular foot, 12¼in. high, 27oz. gross.
(Christie's) $3,226

Coin silver coffeepot, Robert and William Wilson, Philadelphia, 1825–46, acorn finial above bulbous form, 10½in. high, 31 troy oz.
(Skinner) $690

Re-hallmarked small silver coffee pot in George II style with leaf mounted spout, treen handle, 8in. high, London Assay, 16oz. all in.
(G. A. Key) $256

A George II Irish silver coffee pot, stand and lamp, Alexander Brown, Dublin, 1737, the stand on three leaf-capped shell and scroll feet and with circular lamp, 13¾in. high overall, 64oz. gross.
(Christie's) $36,052

A modern coffee pot and matching hot milk jug, of plain tapering cylindrical form, 26cm. high, makers J.C.L., London 1973, the hot milk jug, Garrard & Co. Ltd., London 1972, 49.2oz. all in.
(Bearne's) $660

George II style silver coffee pot of circular baluster design with gadrooned foot and rim, acanthus mounted spout, domed lid with turned treen finial, scrolled treen handle, London 1960, 30oz.
(G. A. Key) $429

Ball, Black & Company silver medallion coffeepot, mid 19th century, engraved decoration, 10¼in. high, approximately 29 troy oz.
(Skinner) $1,150

Fine Victorian silver plated coffee pot of compressed circular design, well engraved with arabesque and scrolled patterns, grayhound finial to lid, 8½in. high, circa 1850.
(G. A. Key) $169

A George II coffee pot of tapering conical form, foliate spout and hinged domed cover, Peter Archambo II and Peter Meure, 23cm. high, 718gr.
(Dorotheum) $3,000

CREAM JUGS

A Victorian Continental cow creamer, the hinged cover with insect finial, import mark: Chester 1898, 7¹/₂in. (Russell, Baldwin & Bright)
$765

A matched pair of George II/ George III silver-gilt cast cream jugs, of inverted pear shape with waisted neck, the bodies chased in relief, 12.8cm. high, 23.75oz. (Phillips)
$2,128

An Irish Provincial silver cream jug, Cork, circa 1770, plain helmet shaped on three mask and scroll supports, 3½in. high, 4oz.
(Christie's)
$1,272

Coin silver cream pot, Joseph Richardson, Philadelphia, 1711– 84, pear-shaped body with serrated rim and long, wide pouring spout, 4in. high, 4 troy oz.
(Skinner)
$1,495

A silver sugar bowl and creamer jug, Shiebler & Co., New York, circa 1890, each formed as a large leaf with a crumpled rim, bowl 6¾in. long over handles, 14oz.
(Christie's)
$3,220

A George II baluster cream jug with leaf-capped scroll handle, the wavy rim with unusual small 'horns', by William Justis, 1757, 10.5cm. high, 3.5oz.
(Phillips)
$638

A George II baluster cream jug with gadroon rim on shell feet, with leaf-capped, diagonally ribbed handle, possibly by William Plummer, 1754, 11cm. high.
(Phillips)
$759

Pair of German hallmarked silver creamer and sugar bowls, 19th century, scroll handles, lion head and paw feet, creamer 4¹/₄in. high, approximately 8 troy oz.
(Skinner)
$259

A Victorian silver cream jug, Martin & Hall, 1878, Britannia standard, in the Irish mid 18th century style, 4½in., 6oz.
(Christie's)
$400

CREAM JUGS

A George III plain oval cream jug with thread edging, angular handle and ball feet, 13.5cm. long, Joseph Hicks, Exeter circa 1800.
(Bearne's) $204

Large Newcastle silver cream jug of slightly compressed oval design, gilt interior, reeded angular handle, circa 1820 by Robertson and Walton.
(G. A. Key) $400

An American silver and other metals Japanese style creamer, Dominick & Haff, New York, 1879, in the form of a coal scuttle, 8oz., 6³/₈in. high.
(Sotheby's) $5,175

Victorian silver cream jug, tapering body to a turned edge, sparrow beak spout, chased decoration in Celtic/Art & Crafts style, London 1874, 6¹/₂oz.
(G. A. Key) $257

Italian hallmarked silver creamer and sugar, early 20th century, baluster-form, chased Italian Renaissance decoration, pitcher 5in. high, approximately 11 troy oz.
(Skinner) $287

A George II baluster cream jug on a circular spreading foot with a shaped rim and a double scroll handle, by William Shaw I, 1733, 8.75cm. high, 3.75oz.
(Phillips) $942

Edwardian silver cream pail, the trellis work sides overlaid with floral and leafy garlands, blue glass liner, London 1906 by William Comyns.
(G. A. Key) $349

A Victorian cream jug modeled as an ancient Greek Ascos or drinking vessel on a rising oval foot, James Barclay Hennell, London 1877, 3¹/₂in., 6.25oz.
(Christie's) $809

A George III cream jug of exceptionally large size, embossed with trailing flowers and scrolls, 1767, 21.3cm. high, 14oz.
(Phillips) $1,246

CRUETS

William Gale and Son silver condiment stand, New York, 1858–60, baluster column, five revolving bowls with rope rims, 12in. high, 27 troy oz. (Skinner) $690

A William IV eight-division shaped oval cruet stand, the octafoil base with reeded edging, Joseph and John Angel, London 1831, 37.5oz. (Bearne's) $1,415

George III silver cruet of oval form, hallmarked for London 1803, with seven contemporary bottles, flute cut with silver tops. (G. A. Key) $1,068

A George I silver oil and vinegar-stand, Paul Crespin, London, 1723, shaped-oblong and on four leaf-capped scroll and pad feet, 6½in. wide, the stand 19oz. (Christie's) $50,232

A Viennese Biedermeier drinking glass stand, the central column with loop handle, on six ball feet, Wenzel John, circa 1840, with six later glasses, 25cm. high, 648gr. (Dorotheum) $565

A French 19th century oil and vinegar cruet, the two openwork tapering circular bottle holders with quiver and arrow supports, Paris 1819–1838, cruet 12¾in. high, 19oz. free. (Christie's) $1,973

A George II silver Warwick cruet, William Beilby, Newcastle, 1743, the baluster central standard with rocaille ring handle, 9½in. high, 55oz. (Christie's) $8,625

A George IV eight bottle cruet frame, reeded borders, shell and scroll posted loop handle, maker's mark J.K. & Co., Sheffield 1828, 17cm. long, 24oz. (Winterton's) $1,279

A George III eight-bottle cruet of oval form and on claw and ball feet, the beaded sides pierced with slats, foliage and Vitruvian scrolls, Thomas Daniell, London 1783, 10¾in. (Christie's) $2,111

CRUETS

A George III silver Warwick cruet, Jabez Daniell & James Mince, London, 1770, cinquefoil, on four pierced feet rising to scroll feet, 11¹/₂in. high, 69oz. (Christie's) $8,625

An unusual novelty cut glass cruet modeled as the Spirit of St. Louis, London 1927, 6³/₄in. (Christie's) $395

English brass standish, mid 19th century, complete with pair of candleholders, covered canisters and powder jars, 8in. high, 7in. long. (Skinner) $373

George III silver cruet stand, rectangular shaped with rounded corners and supported on four feet, the superstructure with reeded decoration, London 1808, probably by Thomas James. (G. A. Key) $570

A George II cruet, George Methuen, London, 1752, fitted with three inverted pear-shaped casters, six plain cylindrical spice boxes, and with three cut-glass bottles, the stand 10³/₄in. high, 110oz. (Christie's) $156,750

A George III silver cruet, Hester Bateman, London, 1786, the gallery pierced and bright-cut engraved with foliage, 9¹/₂in. high. (Christie's) $4,025

A George III silver cruet stand, Paul Storr, London, 1800, on four fluted feet, the molded supports with fluted and angular central standard, 16in. long, 37oz. 10dwt. (Christie's) $5,750

A Victorian egg cruet of molded oval form, decorated with simulated basketwork and with rope-twist borders and handle, probably Francis Higgins, London, the cruet and the egg cups 1860, the spoons 1862, 36oz. (Christie's) $2,432

A Viennese cruet of gondola form, applied swan at each end, the central column with child figure supporting a pierced basket, 34cm. high, 1038gr. (Dorotheum) $3,582

A late 18th/early 19th century silver-mounted coconut cup, on a spreading circular foot and with a bright-cut rim mount, circa 1800, 5¹/₂in.
(Christie's) $347

Gorham sterling loving cup, 1896, baluster-form lobed at base, chased leaf and flower detail, scrolled handles, 6³/₄in. high, approximately 41 troy oz.
(Skinner) $978

A George II silver two-handled cup and cover, Paul de Lamerie, London, 1748, the body chased overall with rocaille and foliage, 13³/₄in. high, 77oz.
(Christie's) $13,800

A George III silver cup and cover, Richard Sibley, London, 1813, partly-fluted spreading foot chased with a band of acanthus leaves, 16¹/₂in. high, 131oz.
(Christie's) $8,349

Pair of Russian silver wager cups, in the form of crinoline women supporting bowls with floral and scroll design, gilt interiors, 8in. high.
(Russell, Baldwin & Bright)
                              $2,295

A George III silver two-handled cup and cover, William Holmes, London, 1800, the lower body with stiff leaves and band of grapevine and military trophies under rim, 19¹/₂in. high, 114oz. 10dwt.
(Christie's) $7,475

An American silver love cup, Tiffany & Co., New York, circa 1903, of pear form, etched with Art Nouveau flowers, fish and bugs, 54oz. 10¹/₂in. high.
(Sotheby's) $3,450

A Commonwealth silver wine cup, maker's mark of *ET*, circa 1655, the bowl punched with stylized rosettes, 6in. high, 11oz.
(Christie's) $5,313

An early Charles II ox-eye or college cup of baluster form with flared top and 'ox-eye' handles, 13.2cm. high, 14.25oz.
(Phillips) $6,980

CUPS

A late 18th century Channel Islands christening cup with beaded S-scroll handles, IH crowned, unascribed, Guernsey, circa 1770, 6.75cm. high, 2.5oz. (Phillips) $850

A silver vodka cup, marked *Fabergé*, Moscow, 1908–1917, the handle set with a silver ten kopeck coin dated *1799*, 2¼in. high, 2oz. 10dwt. (Christie's) $4,140

A Charles II silver caudle cup, London, 1667, maker's mark *CM* three pellets above and below, baluster, with scroll handles headed by busts, 7in. long over handles, 9oz. (Christie's) $3,680

A George III large silver-gilt two-handled cup and cover, Rebecca Emes and Edward Barnard, London, 1818, with foliate scroll handles terminating in a satyr's mask, 19in. high, 190oz. (Christie's) $21,528

Two pairs of Swedish silver cups and saucers, circa 1913, footed baluster form with bas relief rib and floral swag decoration, cup 4¼in. high, approximately 23 troy oz. (Skinner) $230

A George III silver-gilt racing trophy, Benjamin Smith, London, 1819, the finial by John S. Hunt, London, circa 1848, campana shaped and with spreading circular foot, 16in. high, 112oz. (Christie's) $9,108

An important two-handled silver cup and cover, Nathaniel Hurd, Boston, circa 1755, the lower body repoussé and chased with twisted flutes, 13¼in. high, 71oz. (Christie's) $56,350

A William III silver two-handled cup and cover, Hugh Roberts, London, 1700, the lower body with swirling flutes, 7½in. high, 29oz. (Christie's) $12,650

Mauser sterling loving cup presentation trophy, 1900, baluster form, deer horn handles, chased body decoration, 7¼in. high, approximately 14 troy oz. (Skinner) $460

DISHES

A George V oval dish, pierced and decorated with scrolling foliage, 21cm. long, maker's mark *D & A*, Birmingham 1892, 10.8oz.
(Bearne's) $315

A George III entrée dish, cover and handle of shaped oblong form, Paul Storr, London 1809, on an Old Sheffield plate two-handled warming stand, 14in. overall, 66.25oz. free.
(Christie's) $3,846

Evald Nielsen, dish and cover, 1930s silver-colored metal, the domed cover with openwork foliate finial, 7in.
(Sotheby's) $4,686

A George I Irish strawberry dish of typical shaped circular form, John Cuthbert, Dublin 1715, 4¹/₂in., 3.25oz.
(Christie's) $1,615

Eight William IV silver-gilt dishes, six Sheffield, 1830, one 1828, Robert Gainsford, one Martin & Hall, London, 1891, 9in. long, 95oz.
(Christie's) $32,200

Two Charles I silver sweetmeat dishes, William Maddox, London, 1630, chased with stylized foliage, with two shell form tab handles, 7¹/₄in. long over handles, 5oz. 10dwt.
(Christie's) $3,220

A Commonwealth silver sweetmeat dish, London, 1649, maker's mark *ES* in a dotted oval, circular, chased with stylized Tudor rose, 10in. long over handles, 7oz.
(Christie's) $3,450

Pair of Tiffany & Co. sterling compôtes, 1875–91, chased floral rim and base, 10in. diameter, approximately 50 troy oz.
(Skinner) $3,450

A German late 17th/early 18th century gilt-lined and parcel-gilt sweet meat dish or wine taster of tapering octafoil form and with applied scrolling foliate handles, circa 1700, 5¹/₄in. overall.
(Christie's) $987

EWERS

Sheffield silver mounted cut glass ewer, England, circa 1877, design of fish and underwater vegetation, 8³/₄in. high. (Skinner) $2,645

A good Victorian ewer of ovoid form with classical mask under spout, by Frederick Elkington, 1881, 38.6cm. high, 29oz. (Phillips) $1,490

A George III Scottish wine ewer, the body decorated with a frieze of scrolling foliage incorporating two vacant C-scroll cartouches, J. McKay, Edinburgh 1808, 12¹/₂in., 22oz. gross. (Christie's) $1,487

An Italian silver-gilt ewer, unmarked, 17th century, vase-shaped and on spreading circular foot, the body chased with vertical spiral flutes and with scroll handle, 12in. high, 65oz. (Christie's) $122,460

Pair of French hallmarked vermeil Sacrament ewers, circa 1819, chased figural and floral decoration, one featuring cattails, the other grapes, 6⁷/₈in. high, approximately 10 troy oz. (Skinner) $862

A Belgian Biedermeier ewer, gilt-lined, with chased foliate band, broad spout and high-drawn handle, Antwerp, mid 19th century, 20.5cm. high, 351gr. (Dorotheum) $518

A Victorian 'Cellini' pattern ewer with caryatid handle, the mounted cork finial modeled as a Roman warrior, by George Fox, 1873, 33.5cm. high, weighable silver 27oz. (Phillips) $1,093

A large Victorian ewer of cylindrical form and on a spreading foot decorated with lobing and foliage, Messrs. Barnard, London 1892, 12¹/₄in., 48.25oz. (Christie's) $3,588

George III silver covered ewer, circa 1783, Abraham Peterson & Peter Podie makers, baluster form, carved ivory handle, 12³/₈in. high, approximately 23 troy oz. (Skinner) $1,092

FLATWARE

A Victorian cheese scoop with ivory handle, 25cm., Sheffield 1899, in fitted case.
(Bearne's) $299

A Victorian medicine spoon with one large and one small bowl by Messrs. Lias, 1863, initialed, 14cm. long.
(Phillips) $197

A rare William III sucket spoon and fork with a teaspoon sized bowl and a chamfered stem, by Benjamin Watts, 1699, 14.5cm. long.
(Phillips) $1,824

Whiting sterling soup ladle, 1901, King Edward pattern, monogram, 12³/₄in. long, approximately 8 troy oz.
(Skinner) $373

A 18th century Friesland spoon with putto finial and inscribed around back of bend, *Aantje Aanes Post is Geboren den 28 November 1754*, by Richaeus Elgersma (II), Leeuwarden, circa 1765.
(Phillips) $377

Irish Provincial, George III basting spoon with a strainer dividing the bowl and a pointed terminal, by John Nicholson of Cork, circa 1790, 3.5oz.
(Phillips) $669

A Portuguese soup ladle with shell-fluted bowl, the reeded handle decorated at the end with a stylized rococo leaf, Oporto, mid to late 18th century, 6.75oz.
(Christie's) $449

A George III meat skewer, 30.5cm. long, Wm. Eley & Wm. Fearn, London 1803.
(Bearne's) $173

A William IV cast preserve spoon with a shell bowl, a rocaille terminal and a fruiting foliate stem, by Charles Fox (II), 1831, 2oz.
(Phillips) $228

A George III Old English pattern serving spoon with bright-cut decoration, initialed, Hester Bateman, London 1787, 3.4oz.
(Bearne's) $220

Pair of Whiting sterling salad servers, 1800, Heraldic pattern, engraved Old English *C*, approximately 9 troy oz.
(Skinner) $316

A pair of Victorian silver gilt shovel spoons, each with a pierced and embossed fruiting vine stem, 24.2cm. long, Francis Higgins, London 1877, 10.2oz.
(Bearne's) $876

A George III feather edge basting spoon with a half covered 'strainer' bowl, the detachable strainer pierced with C-scrolls, 1777, initialed, 3oz.
(Phillips) $608

An American silver letter opener, Tiffany & Co., New York, circa 1880, the handle cast in the form of a monkey with arched back and outstretched paws, 6oz., 12¹/₄in. long.
(Sotheby's) $6,325

FLATWARE

A bright-cut Old English pattern tablespoon, Francis Parsons, Exeter.
(Bearne's) $48

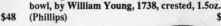

A George II marrow-scoop with a single drop bowl, by William Young, 1738, crested, 1.5oz.
(Phillips) $198

Tiffany & Co. sterling serving fork, 1875–91, raised grapevine design, 9in. long, approximately 3 troy oz.
(Skinner) $287

A good Queen Anne wavy end tablespoon with contemporary engraved monograms and rat-tail, oval bowl, by Lawrence Jones, 1704.
(Phillips) $486

A good late 17th century Dutch (Friesland) lion sejant spoon, the stem decorated with overlapping scales, Leeuwarden, 1691.
(Phillips) $1,087

A George III fish slice with pierced and engraved decoration, 32cm. long, William Sutton, London 1778.
(Bearne's) $398

Pair of Tiffany sterling berry spoons, 1880, chrysanthemum pattern, engraved monogram, approximately 6 troy oz.
(Skinner) $690

Durgin sterling partial flatware service, 1918, Victorian pattern, seventy pieces, script monogram, approximately 71 troy oz.
(Skinner) $690

A pair of unusual Victorian Irish sugar nips, the arms terminating to form an eagle's head, the central part of scallop form, by John Smyth, Dublin, 1844.
(Phillips) $819

A pair of Victorian fish servers with pierced and bright-cut blade and tines and carved ivory handles with beaded edging, Josiah Williams and Co., Exeter 1877.
(Bearne's) $462

A George III Irish marrow scoop of good gauge, the pointed oval bowl engraved with crest, possibly by John Power, Dublin, 1798, 20.5cm. long.
(Phillips) $456

A pair of George III Irish asparagus tongs of bowed form, with bright-engraved zig-zag borders and crested navette-shaped cartouche, by Benjamin Tait, Dublin, circa 1785, 4.25oz.
(Phillips) $637

An American silver Japanese style shoe horn, Gorham Mfg. Co., Providence, RI, 1884, with twisted handle, decorated with ovals, 4oz., 10in. long.
(Sotheby's) $1,035

A pair of American silver 'Japanese style' grape scissors, Tiffany & Co., New York, circa 1880, of serpentine form, the handles pierced with cloud-like forms, 5oz. 10dwt., 8in. long.
(Sotheby's) $2,645

GOBLETS

An 18th century German goblet
with spiral fluting and domed
circular foot, by Horst
Leschhorn, Frankfurt-am-Main,
circa 1765, 12.5cm. high, 3.5oz.
(Phillips) $1,359

A Regency goblet of plain form,
on a rising circular foot and
with a molded rim, William
Bateman, London 1818, 5¼in.,
5oz. (Christie's) $528

A Victorian goblet decorated in
high relief with a goat and kids
in farmyard setting, by Robert
Hennell, 1860, 11.5cm. high,
5.25oz.
(Phillips) $1,034

A Regency gilt-lined goblet, the
part-fluted campana-shaped
bowl decorated in relief with a
broad frieze of flowers, fruit and
foliage, London 1820, 6in.,
6.75oz.
(Christie's) $387

Two 17th century silver-gilt
goblets, of tapering shape with
filigree scroll handles, the upper
part with filigree cagework
sleeve enameled with stylized
leaves, probably Hungarian or
East European, 15cm. high.
(Phillips) $2,400

An 18th century German beaker
of tapering shape chased with
rococo decoration, on tucked-in
trumpet foot, probably East
German/Silesian(?), circa 1760,
8.9cm. high, 1.75oz.
(Phillips) $304

INKWELLS

A George V silver-mounted
glass inkwell with cut-glass base,
12cm. high, London 1911.
(Bearne's) $191

An E.P. inkwell in the form of
an eagle, the hinged head
opening to reveal an inkwell,
20cm. high.
(Bearne's) $350

A late Victorian silver-mounted
clear glass inkwell of circular
form and with star-cut base,
William Comyns, London 1901,
4in.
(Christie's) $352

INKSTANDS

A Regency silver inkstand, Paul Storr, London, 1817, oblong, on four acanthus feet, 13¼in. long over handles, 34oz.
(Christie's)   **$6,325**

A George V two-division ink stand in the form of a cleat on a wooden base, 19cm. long, London 1903.
(Bearne's)   **$145**

A George II silver inkstand, William Kidney, London, 1745, the molded rim with shells at intervals, with ink and pounce pots, 9in. long, 17oz. 10dwt.
(Christie's)   **$5,750**

A George III silver inkstand, Henry Nutting, London, 1806, oblong, on four claw and ball feet, with gadrooned rim, 11¼in. long, 35oz. 10dwt.
(Christie's)   **$1,840**

Victorian Sheffield plated ink stand in rococo style of waisted rectagular form, having an applied foliate and shell edge, and holding two glass bottles, 14 x 10in., circa 1840.
(G. A. Key)   **$300**

Victorian silver double inkstand, London 1878–84, footed oval tray with polished cut bottles, acanthus leaf and Greek key decoration, 3⅞in. high, with bottle approximately 21 troy oz.
(Skinner)   **$748**

An Edwardian piqué d'argent inkstand, standing on four bun feet, the outer border and hexagonal well, both decorated with flowers and scrolls, London, 1906.
(David Lay)   **$1,275**

A Victorian silver inkstand, Henry Wilkinson & Co., Sheffield, 1853-56, with scroll shaped border pierced with further scrolls, 9¾in. long.
(Christie's)   **$817**

A Victorian inkstand of scallop-shell form with mermaid figure handle, shell finial and rocky base, 5in. wide, London 1848.
(Russell, Baldwin & Bright)
                    $2,020

A fine George III silver-gilt inkstand, Digby Scott & Benjamin Smith, London, 1804, the three pots each vase-form with acanthus on a matted ground, 13½in. long over handles, 65oz.
(Christie's)   **$123,500**

A late Victorian two-bottle inkstand of shaped rounded oblong form, on stylized hoof feet and with a gadroon, shell and foliate border, William Hutton & Sons Ltd., Sheffield 1899, 9¾in., 20oz. free.
(Christie's)   **$1,042**

A presentation oblong ink stand with canted corners and molded rim, central stamp box flanked by two square cut glass ink bottles, 11in. wide, London 1913, 13oz.
(Andrew Hartley)   **$1,023**

JUGS

An 18th century German jug of paneled form on shaped circular foot, by Franz Anton Renner, Hannover, circa 1740. (Phillips) $1,442

A gilt-lined Russian milk jug, with swollen fluted body and broad spout, St. Petersburg, 11cm. high, 173gr. (Dorotheum) $470

European silver jug with figural details, 20th century, applied Apollo head and leaping horses opposite handle, 5¹/₈in. high. (Skinner) $173

A Russian oval milk jug, the swollen fluted body with rocaille decorated lip, bone handle, Moscow, 1847, 13cm. high, 224gr. (Dorotheum) $518

A George III silver argyle, possibly Walter Brind, 1773, wicker covered handle and detachable stepped domed cover, 6in., 10ozs. (Christie's) $1,454

Victorian silver milk jug of circular baluster style, the body embossed with flowers and foliage and standing on a shaped shell mounted foot, London 1840. (G. A. Key) $209

A late Victorian hot water jug, with a foliate-decorated spout, ebonized wood scroll handle and part-fluted domed hinged cover, William Hutton & Sons Ltd., London 1895, 7³/₄in., 13oz. gross. (Christie's) $395

Late George II small oval silver cream boat with card cut rim, leaf capped flying scrolled handle and standing on three shell and hoof feet, later embossed with foliate design, London 1758. (G. A. Key) $164

Gorham sterling strapwork ice bucket, 1911, swing handle, engraved monogram on top of spout, 5³/₈in. high without handle, approximately 6 troy oz. (Skinner) $920

JUGS

A George III hot water jug, of plain baluster circular form, 27cm. high, Charles Wright, London 1770, 21oz. (Bearne's) **$598**

Attractive Regency styled large silver milk jug of slightly compressed circular design on cast four shell base, Birmingham 1901, 8oz. (G. A. Key) **$175**

A George IV hot water pot, with leaf capped double scroll ebony handle, 26cm. high, London 1824, 36oz. (Bearne's) **$1,415**

An attractive Victorian Aesthetic Movement jug, parcel-gilt and decorated in the Japanese style, by Frederick Elkington, Birmingham, 1879, 22cm. high, 30oz. (Phillips) **$4,256**

Emmy Roth, milk and sugar set, circa 1930, comprising milk jug, sugar basin, and holder, each piece with martelé surface, the holder with central columnar support. (Sotheby's) **$4,499**

A William IV Scottish hot water jug of baluster form profusely chased with vines and floral scrolls, by Marshall & Sons, Edinburgh, 1831, initialed 22.5cm. high, 30.5oz. (Phillips) **$1,138**

A George III hot water jug with hexagonal vase-shaped body, reeded borders and a reeded loop handle, by Daniel Smith & Robert Sharp, 1788, 30.5cm. high, 29oz. (Phillips) **$2,432**

A George III milk jug, the swollen body with band of gadrooning, C-form foliate handle, William Fountain, 1820s, 10cm. high, 203gr. (Dorotheum) **$425**

A Victorian baluster hot water jug decorated with thread edging and ribbon tied drapes, 18.5cm. high, Hamilton & Inches, Edinburgh 1898, 8.4oz. (Bearne's) **$303**

SILVER

Dunhill, a black leather covered 'Standard' silver plated table lighter, English, late 1940's.
(Bonhams) $79

A Ronson 'Touch-Tip' petrol-fuelled table lighter, shaped as a bar with a negro barman, partially chromium-plated and enamel painted, circa 1935, 15.3cm. long
(Christie's) $1,100

Dunhill, an 18ct. rose gold 'Aldunil Petit Modele', lighter, with engine turned decoration, French 1960's.
(Bonhams) $886

Cartier, an 18 carat gold, enamel and diamond set petrol burning lighter, 1910s, the top and bottom edges of the case surmounted by rose-cut diamonds, 30 x 10mm.
(Christie's) $5,313

German smoker's companion, 1930s, nickel plated metal in the form of an aeroplane, the body forming the cigar compartments, the cockpit doubling as matchholder and striker, $9^{1}/_{2}$in. long.
(Sotheby's) $2,815

A French table lighter with Swiss twin barrel eight day watch, nickeled three quarter plate keyless movement with two going barrels, signed *Lancel Automatique*, circa 1930, 92 x 85mm.
(Pieces of Time) $1,014

Dunhill-Namiki, a Maki-E lacquer 'Tallboy' lighter with Iroe-hira maki-e Mura Nishiji and Oki-Birami decoration, English, circa 1934 for the Spanish market.
(Bonhams) $1,424

Dunhill, an 'Aquarium' table lighter with chrome plated metal parts, English 1960's.
(Bonhams) $538

A chrome pocket cigarette case combined with a lighter and watch, Swiss rectangular wrist watch movement, signed *Evans*, circa 1950, 115 x 62mm.
(Pieces of Time) $335

LIGHTERS

Dunhill, a silver 'Sports' lighter, with engine turned decoration, English 1947.
(Bonhams) $190

Chromium cigarette lighter, modeled as a jet aircraft, on adjustable pedestal, circa 1960, 9in. wide.
(G. A. Key) $28

Dunhill, an 18ct. gold 'Unique' pocket lighter, French, circa 1926-29.
(Bonhams) $1,583

Dunhill, a silver plated 'Giant' table lighter, English, circa 1975 together with a gold plated 'Handy' (1960s) and a gold plated Unique (circa 1990).
(Bonhams) $665

A nine carat gold compact by Dunhill, opening to reveal an ivory aide memoire, cigarette lighter, timepiece and pencil.
(Phillips) $2,900

Dunhill, an 18ct. white gold, diamond and emerald-set petrol burning lighter with watch inset to the hinged front cover, 43 x 38mm.
(Christie's) $4,500

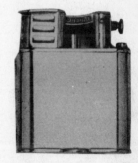

Dunhill, a silver 'Standard' lighter, English, 1948.
(Bonhams) $301

Dunhill, a silver 'Ball' lighter, English, 1929.
(Bonhams) $506

Dunhill, a silver plated 'Sports' lighter, English, 1930's-40's.
(Bonhams) $142

MISCELLANEOUS

Sterling overlay glass flask, America, late 19th/early 20th century, floral and scrolled leaf design, 6½in. high. (Skinner) $373

Sheffield domed lid, England, early 19th century, engraved with armorial whippet, 22in. high. (Skinner) $575

An electroplated swing handle biscuitière, of oval form with strapwork decoration, 22cm. (Bearne's) $440

  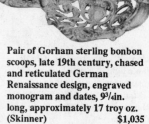

Pair of Shiebler sterling cordial bottles, circa 1900, baluster form, bas relief chrysanthemum and leaf pattern on finial and shoulder, 7in. high, approximately 11 troy oz. (Skinner) $1,035

Harald Nielsen for Georg Jensen, tazza, manufactured post 1945, the deep bowl on openwork stem of stylized furled leaves and bunches of grapes, 5½in. (Sotheby's) $2,062

Pair of Gorham sterling bonbon scoops, late 19th century, chased and reticulated German Renaissance design, engraved monogram and dates, 9¾in. long, approximately 17 troy oz. (Skinner) $1,035

An electroplated cylindrical biscuitière with beaded edging and lightly engraved decoration, 18.5cm. high. (Bearne's) $252

Good quality hallmarked silver desk postage stamp damper with glass rolling cylinder to top, fluted capstan shaped base, London 1896. (G. A. Key) $182

Hallmarked German silver nef, late 19th century, in the form of a three masted man-o-war under full sail, 23in. high, approximately 81 troy oz. (Skinner) $5,750

MISCELLANEOUS

A silver bust of Napoleon, maker's mark *RC*, circa 1870, 14cm. high, 286gr.
(Dorotheum) $660

A George III brandy warming saucepan and cover of baluster circular form, 15cm. high, Henry Chawner and John Emes, London 1796, 10.5oz.
(Bearne's) $944

Hallmarked silver model of an owl with gilt work detail, 6½in. high, 20oz.
(G. A. Key) $365

An Edward VII Art Nouveau shaped rectangular photograph frame of slightly hammered finish on an oak frame, 27cm. high, Birmingham 1904.
(Bearne's) $828

Pair of silver fighting cocks, Europe, cast and chased figures, 5½in. high, approximately 22 troy oz.
(Skinner) $863

A late Victorian silver mounted heart shape mirror frame, pierced and embossed with cherubs and masks, 44cm. high, William Comyns, London 1899.
(Bearne's) $566

Georgian styled silver sugar basin of circular tapering form with trellis pierced sides, with Bristol blue glass liner plus sifting spoon, London 1930.
(G. A. Key) $213

Charles Edwards, Art Nouveau épergne, 1909, silver, three shaped shallow bowls supported on shaped stem applied with flowing drapes, 12in.
(Sotheby's) $4,686

Victorian silver plated egg warmer, ovium shaped with three beaded scrolled supports, the engraved lid with swan finial, with spirit burner base.
(G. A. Key) $114

MISCELLANEOUS

A Dutch 18th century silver-gilt two-handled sugar basin of tapering boat shape, with reeded and beaded borders, 6in., 6oz. free.
(Christie's) $1,137

A pair of George IV silver flasks, William Elliott, London, 1823, the spool-form threaded cap with trefoil finial and linked chain, 17in. high, 258oz.
(Christie's) $151,000

A George III silver honey skep, Paul Storr, London, 1799, of typical form realistically chased, on circular stand, 4in. high, 14oz.
(Christie's) $19,924

An American silver and other metals Japanese style scent flask, Gorham Mfg. Co., Providence, RI, 1879, applied with a bird, branch and a pipe player, 1oz. 15dwt., 3in. high.
(Sotheby's) $460

A pair of Irish dish rings, pierced and embossed in the antique manner with cows, buildings, birds, seated shepherdess, by S.D. Neill (of Belfast), Dublin, 1913, 17.5cm. diameter, 27oz.
(Phillips) $2,732

A Victorian four-piece christening set, comprising: a pedestal mug, knife, fork and spoon with vacant cartouches, Martin Hall & Co., London and Sheffield, 6.25oz. excluding knife.
(Christie's) $897

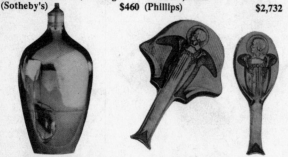

A rare George III Scottish silver flask, Edinburgh, 1804, maker's mark possibly that of James Dempster, oval, with molded threaded cap, with removable oval cup, 9in. high, 22oz.
(Christie's) $2,760

An unusual Art Nouveau handmirror shaped as a manta ray and chased with a bonneted female head in profile, brush en suite by William Hutton & Sons Ltd., Birmingham, 1907.
(Phillips) $759

A George III swing-handled pedestal sugar basin of tapering molded oval form and with reeded borders, Peter, Ann & William Bateman, London 1799, 5½in., 5.5oz.
(Christie's) $613

SILVER

A silver-plated roast beef wagon, on oak trolley support with fluted columns and hinged plate rest, 41in. high, 33¹/₂in. wide.

(Christie's) $11,500

A pair of Continental models of fighting cockerels, each in typical aggressive stance and with realistically-cast and chased plumage, 11in. and smaller.

(Christie's) $845

A George III ovoid nutmeg grater crisply chased with fluting and flowers on a frosted ground, by Samuel Meriton (II), circa 1775.

(Phillips) $531

An American silver and enamel 'Japanese style' flask, Tiffany & Co., New York, circa 1880, of oval form, applied with a seated frog with partially black enameled body and one enameled eye, 5oz., 5in. high.

(Sotheby's) $2,300

An Art Nouveau biscuit barrel with matching smaller preserve jar, each pierced with naturalistic forms and with scroll handles, Birmingham 1907 and 1909, 7³/₄in. and smaller, weight of silver 35.75oz.

(Christie's) $2,447

A large presentation silver-gilt wood-mounted photograph frame, marked *Fabergé*, containing an original photograph by Boissonnas and Eggler signed by the Imperial children, 17in. high.

(Christie's) $43,700

Lucien Gaillard, set of four buttons in original fitted case, circa 1900, each with a pierced design of a foliate flower, 1in. diameter.

(Sotheby's) $2,062

A pair of German statuettes modeled as knights in armor, their helmets with winged visors revealing ivory faces, probably circa 1910, 23.1cm. and 24.2cm. high, 31.5oz.

(Phillips) $2,114

A French silver dressing glass, Debain, Paris, circa 1880, cartouche shaped, the frame and feet formed of scrolls and rocaille, 23¹/₂in. high.

(Christie's) $3,450

MUGS

A George III mug of baluster form, later-chased with spiral fluting, flowers, foliage and fruits, Peter & William Bateman, London 1806, 5¼in., 10oz.
(Christie's) $563

A William IV mug of baluster form, on spreading shaped circular base, 12cm. high, Samuel Hayne & Dudley Cater, London 1836, 51oz.
(Bearne's) $239

A George III mug of baluster form with leaf capped double-scroll handle, 13cm. high, David Crawford, Newcastle 1774, 11.3oz.
(Bearne's) $557

A 19th century Chinese Export mug, of tapering shape with fruiting in the handle, Canton circa 1835, 9cm. high, 7oz.
(Phillips) $483

A pair of George III Irish silver mugs, Dublin, 1807, maker's mark *IS*, each cylindrical, applied with bands of grapevine near base and rim, 5¼in. high, 47oz.
(Christie's) $19,550

A late George II large mug of plain baluster form and on a spreading circular foot, with a molded rim, William Shaw & William Priest, London 1756, 6in., 18.25oz.
(Christie's) $1,487

A George II mug, later-chased with spiral fluting, flowers, foliage and fruit and with a molded rim, maker's initials I.T., London 1735, 4in., 6.5oz.
(Christie's) $528

A George III mug, the body later-chased with game birds within landscapes, Thomas & Richard Payne, London 1768, 6½in., 19oz.
(Christie's) $1,256

A George IV pint mug of barrel shape and with a molded rim and scroll handle, possibly William Bateman, London 1823, 5in., 15.25oz.
(Christie's) $1,135

MUGS

A George II mug of baluster circular form, later decorated with birds, 10cm. high, maker's mark probably that of Samuel Whitiford, London 1763, 5.8oz. (Bearne's) $303

A Queen Anne mug of tapering cylindrical form, 11cm. high, possibly John Sutton, possibly 1708, 9.9oz. (Bearne's) $573

A George III baluster mug with leaf-capped double scroll handle, embossed foliage, 10cm. high, London 1762, 8.8oz. (Bearne's) $605

A Victorian mug, with a molded rim and elaborate beaded and foliate-decorated scroll handle, probably Alexander Macrae, London 1869, 5in., 9.75oz. (Christie's) $431

An American silver and other metals Japanese style mug, Whiting Mfg. Co., Providence, RI, 1893, applied with a spray of cherries and a basket of flowers in copper and brass, 7oz., 3¼in. high. (Sotheby's) $2,185

A George I beer mug, the slightly swollen body with volute handle and raised lip, by William Darker, 18th century, 9.3cm. high, 204gr. (Dorotheum) $660

A George III mug of tapering cylindrical form, chased with scrolls and foliage, 13cm. high, Peter, Ann & William Bateman, London 1799, 10.5oz. (Bearne's) $409

A George III tapering cylindrical mug, incribed within reeded bands, 14.5cm., William Burwash & Richard Sibley I, London 1811. (Bearne's) $414

A George III mug, later-chased with rococo flowers and foliage and also later gilt-lined, maker's mark indistinct, London 1775, 4in., 7.75oz. (Christie's) $317

MUSTARDS

Fine George III silver mustard with ¾ lobed sides, gadrooned rim and leaf capped reeded handle, with blue glass liner, London 1817, by Rebecca Emes and Edward Barnard.
(G. A. Key) $253

Fine pair of Edwardian silver mustard pots of cylindrical form with gadrooned bases and rims, pierced sides, with blue glass liners and spoons, Sheffield 1902.
(G. A. Key) $368

Attractive Edwardian Art Nouveau styled silver mustard, the body pierced with scrolled designs, plus blue glass liner and spoon, Birmingham 1908.
(G. A. Key) $170

An 18th century Dutch mustard pot of spirally fluted baluster form, by J.A.G. L'Herminotte, Maastricht, 1758–60, 16.7cm. high, 7.75oz.
(Phillips) $7,852

A pair of Edward VII mustard pots in the form of miniature tankards, 7.5cm. high, Elkington & Co. Ltd., London 1908, 7.8oz.
(Bearne's) $526

An 18th century German mustard pot of baluster caster form with domed cover capped by a fruiting vine finial, by Johann Christoph Berns, Magdeburg, circa 1765, 19cm. high, 8oz. (Phillips) $2,883

A Victorian parcel-gilt novelty three piece chinoiserie condiment set, mustard pot and two pepperettes modeled as monkeys, by E.C. Brown, 1867, the larger monkey 10.5cm. high, 8oz.
(Phillips) $15,960

Victorian silver mustard of circular baluster style to a circular flanged foot, leaf embossed lid, plus blue glass liner, London 1901.
(G. A. Key) $197

A pair of American silver and other metals Japanese style salts and a mustard pot and spoon, Dominick & Haff, New York, 1881 and 1880, the salts applied with copper branches, 8oz., mustard pot 2⅝in. high.
(Sotheby's) $2,185

PEPPERS

A pair of Viennese Biedermeier baluster form pepperettes, with rocaille and rose frieze, circa 1838, 10.3cm. high, 125 gr. (Dorotheum) $1,037

A small Queen Anne pepper caster with a baluster body, molded girdle and a domed hole pierced cover, circa 1705, 9cm. high, 1.5oz. (Phillips) $228

Two Victorian novelty owl peppers with colored glass eyes, by Charles Thomas Fox and George Fox, 1860, 8cm. high, 3.25ozs. (Phillips) $960

Pair of sterling salt and pepper shakers, sold by Marshal Field & Co., baluster form, chased floral and figural decoration, 6^{1}/$_{2}$in. high, approximately 11 troy oz. (Skinner) $259

A Viennese sugar caster and pepperette, of pear shape, engraved with a medallion, 13 and 10cm.. high, 163gr. total weight. (Dorotheum) $265

A pair of late 18th century pepper casters, with vase shaped bodies and low circular pedestal bases, probably American/ Canadian Eastern Seaboard region, circa 1785, 17.5cm. high, 11oz. (Phillips) $604

A Viennese Biedermeier pepperette, the baluster form body decorated with rocaille and foliate ornament, Josef Karl, 1840s, 10.5cm. high, 46gr. (Dorotheum) $235

Pair of George II silver pepper casters, London, 1742–43, Samuel Wood, baluster form, engraved crest, 5^{5}/$_{8}$in. high, approximately 10 troy oz. (Skinner) $748

A Viennese Biedermeier pepperette of pear shape with pierced foliate cover, Martin Lutz, 1829, 9cm. high, 57gr. (Dorotheum) $424

PITCHERS

Ball, Black & Co. coin pitcher, mid 19th century, New York, marked *W.F.*, handle with bearded face, 11in. high, approximately 32 troy oz. (Skinner) $1,092

Kirk repoussé sterling water pitcher, 1880–90, chased floral and leaf decoration, engraved monogram on base, 7³/₈in. high, approximately 20 troy oz. (Skinner) $1,093

Tiffany sterling mounted cut glass lemonade pitcher, early 20th century, silver spout with Art Nouveau border, 13¹/₂in. high. (Skinner) $1,495

Graff, Washburne & Dunn sterling water pitcher, 1909, paneled baluster form with chased Colonial and Renaissance Revival design, 11¹/₈in. high, approximately 50 troy oz. (Skinner) $2,300

Pair of Renaissance Revival sterling and clear glass covered pitchers, circa 1900, maker F.M.T., vintage decoration with children and cupids, 11in. high. (Skinner) $1,725

An American silver and other metals 'Japanese style' hot water jug, Tiffany & Co., New York, circa 1880, of gourd form, applied with a mokume butterfly, 12oz. gross, 7¹/₄in. high. (Sotheby's) $13,800

Reed & Barton silver plated ice water pitcher on stand, Renaissance Revival design, stand, pitcher, drip tray and goblet, porcelain liner, 19in. high. (Skinner) $288

An American parcel-gilt 'Japanese style' water pitcher, Tiffany & Co., New York, circa 1877–78, boldly engraved with a dragonfly on a spreading lotus plant, 28oz., 7¹/₂in. high. (Sotheby's) $4,025

American silver overlay cranberry glass pitcher, Alvin Silversmiths, circa 1900, design of Bacchus mask and grape bunches, 10³/₄in. high. (Skinner) $690

PITCHERS

American silver mounted cranberry glass pitcher, circa 1900, the silver collar with band of foliage and seraphim, 10in. high.
(Skinner) $1,725

A silver pitcher, Tiffany & Co., New York, 1896-1902, Richelieu pattern, baluster, on domed spreading circular base, 9¾in. high, 38oz.
(Christie's) $3,450

Sterling overlay cranberry glass pitcher, America, 19th century, scrolled leaf and berry design, monogrammed, 9¼in. high.
(Skinner) $2,645

A silver and mixed-metal pitcher, Whiting Mfg. Co., circa 1881, the spot-hammered surface engraved with foliage and with copper inlay, 8½in. high, 32oz. gross weight.
(Christie's) $13,800

Pair of Art Nouveau sterling and clear glass covered pitchers, maker F.M.T., circa 1900, iris decoration, 10¾in. high.
(Skinner) $1,725

An American silver 'Japanese style' pitcher, Tiffany & Co., New York, circa 1879, applied with two lobsters and two crabs on a ground of graduated spot-hammering, 11oz. 10dwt., 6in. high.
(Sotheby's) $9,775

An American silver 'Japanese style' covered pitcher, Tiffany & Co., New York, 1887, applied with a school of exotic fish swimming around the body, 22oz. 15dwt., 8¹⁄₈in. high.
(Sotheby's) $10,350

An important silver and mixed-metal pitcher, Tiffany & Co., New York, circa 1878, the base spreading to imitate water, spot-hammered sides and handle, 9in. high. gross weight 36oz.
(Christie's) $66,300

A silver pitcher, Tiffany & Co., New York, 1878-91, baluster, the body and neck with chased braided band, with scroll handle, 7¾in. high, 25oz. 10dwt.
(Christie's) $2,185

PLATES

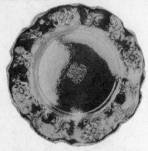

Black, Starr & Frost sterling cake plate, circa 1900, chased poppy border, engraved monogram, 11¹/₁₆in. diameter, approximately 30 troy oz. (Skinner) **$632**

German hallmarked silver Art Nouveau plate, circa 1900, raised and chased leaf form, three-dimensional pond lily, 10in. diameter, approximately 13 troy oz. (Skinner) **$978**

A Regency second course plate, the border applied with fluting, flowers, foliage and tied ears of corn, William & John Frisbee, London 1811, 9³/₄in., 19.75oz. (Christie's) **$524**

Suite of three graduated American Arts & Crafts platters, Gorham, Providence, Rhode Island, 1915(2) and 1916. (Butterfield & Butterfield) **$2,185**

A set of twelve George II silver dinner-plates, John Le Sage, London, 1743, shaped-circular and with gadrooned borders, 183oz. (Christie's) **$28,704**

Pair of mid 19th century Sheffield plated serving dishes, circular shaped with shell and scrolled rims, dished centers, 12in. diameter. (G. A. Key) **$305**

A set of six George III silver dinner plates, Paul Storr, London, 1808, shaped-circular and with gadrooned border, each engraved with a coat-of-arms, 10¹/₄in. diameter, 131oz. (Christie's) **$10,436**

A set of twelve silver dinner plates, Gorham Mfg. Co., Providence, circa 1920, shaped circular, with reeded rim, engraved with script monogram, 10½in., 177oz. (Christie's) **$3,450**

Set of six William IV gold washed silver plates, London 1836, maker R. Garrard, gadroon and shell rim, engraved crest on rim, 10³/₁₆in. diameter, approximately 137 troy oz. (Skinner) **$4,312**

PORRINGERS

Georgian silver two handled porringer with gadrooned base and band, punched detail either side of the middle section, London 1728.
(G. A. Key) $458

A rare silver porringer by Paul Revere, Boston, 1725–54, unusually large circular bowl with convex sides and a slightly raised center, 6in. diameter, 9 troy oz.
(Skinner) $10,350

George II silver porringer with two swept handles, half fluted body, punched banded decoration, London 1730, 3½in. high.
(G. A. Key) $334

A silver porringer, John Tanner, Newport, circa 1765, with pierced keyhole handle, engraved with later monogram, 7¾in. long over handle, 7oz. 10dwt.
(Christie's) $1,725

Three sterling children's tablewares, 1920s, Kerr breakfast set, porringer and cup, paneled cylindrical-form McChesney plate, all have acid-etched nursery rhymes decoration, approximately 13 troy oz.
(Skinner) $690

An American silver porringer, Moody Russell, Barnstaple, Mass., circa 1720-30, of typical form, 5in. diam., 6oz.
(Sotheby's) $2,070

POTS

A pot and cover by William Comyns, 1902, the slightly domed cover centered by a highly stylized flower form motif rising on four stems, 4¼in.
(Sotheby's) $1,405

Liberty & Co., 'Cymric' pot and cover, 1901, raised circular cover above broad flat rim, the rim with four panels of entrelac decoration, 4in.
(Sotheby's) $2,624

Liberty & Co., jam pot, cover and spoon, 1906, clear glass bowl with silver collar and handle set with lapis lazuli cabochon, 5⅜in.
(Sotheby's) $4,499

SALTS

A pair of Victorian cast shell salts, on three mollusc feet by Elkington & Co., 1847, 12.3cm. long.
(Phillips) $393

A set of four unusual William IV silver salt cellars, Benjamin Smith III, London, 1831, each realistically formed as a shell, 5in. long, 46oz. 10dwt.
(Christie's) $23,000

A pair of William IV salt cellars of circular form, and a pair of Victorian King's pattern salt spoons.
(Christie's) $400

A pair of William IV/Victorian cast nautilus shell salts on floral rockwork bases with gilded interiors, by Joseph & Albert Savory, 1835/40, 9.5cm. wide, 12oz. (Phillips) $1,368

A set of four George V silver-gilt figural salt cellars, Crichton Bros., London, 1912, the base formed of water and with dolphin stem, 4^1/2in. long, 49oz.
(Christie's) $8,625

Set of four silver circular salts with embossed decoration and gadrooned top border, raised on three bovine feet with shell shoulders, hallmarked for London 1853, maker William Kerr Read. (G. A. Key)

$351

A pair of George IV cast circular salts with gilt interiors, scroll and gadrooned rims, by William Barrett (II), 1824, 9.5cm. diam., 6.1cm. high.
(Phillips) $960

A set of four George IV gilt-lined salt cellars, the fluted tapering bodies with ivy leaf and berry borders, Charles Fox, London, 1828, 4¼in., 15oz.
(Christie's) $1,150

Crichton Brothers, a pair of Britannia standard trencher salt cellars, 3^1/2in. diam., London, 1909, 10oz.
(Bonhams) $498

SALTS

A pair of early Victorian salts in the form of scallop shells resting on three cast whelk feet, by Paul Storr, 1837, 9cm. wide, 5oz. (Phillips) $1,442

An American parcel-gilt 'Japanese style' pedestal salt, Tiffany & Co., New York, circa 1882, applied with a song bird on a pine branch, 7oz. 4in. high. (Sotheby's) $1,495

A pair of George III oval salts with reeded rims, claw and ball feet, blue glass liners with star-cut bases, 1786. (Phillips) $486

A pair of George III cast salt cellars of cauldron form, each on lion's mask and paw feet, Robert & David Hennell, London 1765, 3$\frac{1}{2}$in., 20.75oz. (Christie's) $1,487

A pair of German salt cellars, the bowls on wheeled dolphin supports with a child with sword and shield, late 19th century, 6cm. high, 200 gr. total weight. (Dorotheum) $330

A German late 17th/early 18th century trencher salt cellar of octagonal form, the spreading base chased with shells, Gisbertus Geilmburg, Cologne circa 1700, 4in., 2.75oz. (Christie's) $1,615

A pair of George III salt cellars each on shell and hoof feet and with a gadrooned rim, Robert & David Hennell, London, 1767, 5.75oz. (Christie's) $240

A set of six George III pedestal salt cellars of tapering oval form and with beaded borders with scroll handles, London 1790, 5$\frac{1}{2}$in. overall, 22oz. (Christie's) $2,111

A pair of George III oval salts with bead borders, ball and claw feet, Tudor & Leader, Sheffield, 1782, 7.9cm. long, 4.25oz. (Phillips) $607

SAUCEBOATS

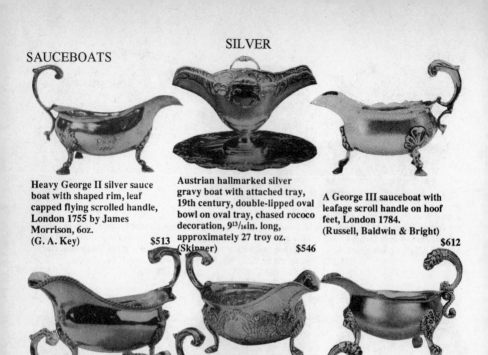

Heavy George II silver sauce boat with shaped rim, leaf capped flying scrolled handle, London 1755 by James Morrison, 6oz.
(G. A. Key) $513

Austrian hallmarked silver gravy boat with attached tray, 19th century, double-lipped oval bowl on oval tray, chased rococo decoration, 9¹³/₁₆in. long, approximately 27 troy oz.
(Skinner) $546

A George III sauceboat with leafage scroll handle on hoof feet, London 1784.
(Russell, Baldwin & Bright)
                               $612

A pair of George III silver sauceboats, John Emes, London, 1802, boat-shaped, on three ball and claw feet, 8¹/₂in. long over handle, 35oz. 10dwt.
(Christie's) $4,025

A pair of silver sauceboats, John & Peter Targee, New York, 1809-14, the sides chased with rocaille, scrolls and foliage, 8in. long over handle, 24oz. 10dwt.
(Christie's) $3,450

A pair of large Regency sauce boats on lion's mask and claw and ball feet, maker's mark indistinct, London 1811, 7¹/₂in. overall, 40oz.
(Christie's) $2,447

Kirk repoussé sterling gravy boat, S. Kirk & Son, Co., circa 1900, chased landscape and floral decoration, 7³/₄in. long, approximately 10 troy oz.
(Skinner) $633

A pair of Belgian two-handled double-lipped sauceboats, Mons, 1774, maker's mark a paschal lamb, shaped-oval and on four scroll feet, chased with spiral flutes and with fluted lips, 7³/₄in. long, 20oz.
(Christie's) $26,910

Tiffany & Co., a 19th century American sauceboat of oval form, the angular bifurcated handle with ram's head mask, circa 1870, 26cm. long, 15.5oz.
(Phillips) $1,138

SNUFF BOXES

An 18th century French cartouche-shaped parcel-gilt snuff box, cover with reclining female classical figure pointing out to a putto, Paris, 1731, 6.1cm. long.(Phillips) $730

An 18th century German snuff box of horseshoe shape, chased with flowers and scrolls, Ivo Gaukes Swartte(?), Norden, circa 1765, 7.5cm. (Phillips) $836

A decorative William IV silver-gilt snuff box, the frosted cover applied with six freshwater pearls around a pearl-set gold wreath, by Nathaniel Mills, Birmingham, 1834, 7.5cm. long. (Phillips) $1,186

A William IV snuff box, the cover set with a fine micromosaic panel, depicting four dogs savaging a wild boar beside a lake, by Edward Smith, Birmingham, 1830, 8cm. long. (Phillips) $3,600

An interesting George II mounted tortoiseshell snuff mull, the cover inlaid with scrolling foliage around an oval plaque, circa 1740, 4.5cm. high, 6.5cm. long. (Phillips) $760

An early 18th century ivory snuff box, the cover with piqué decoration of a peacock, foliage and butterflies, Continental, circa 1735, 8.4cm. long. (Phillips) $1,280

A George III Irish silver-mounted cowrie shell snuff box, the plain hinged cover with thread edging, 7cm. long, Aneas Ryan, Dublin circa 1805. (Bearne's) $362

A good George IV snuff box, the cover decorated in relief with 'Man with Hambone' after Gerrit van Honthurst, by John Linnit, 1824, 8cm. long, 5.25oz. (Phillips) $10,336

Dagobert Peche for the Wiener Werkstätte, Tabatière, before 1918, the hinged cover with openwork design incorporating a stylized female head, 4¼in. (Sotheby's) $19,682

591

A Charles II silver tankard, London, 1677, cylindrical, on molded rim base, chased with a band of acanthus, 7in. high, 23oz. 10dwt.
(Christie's) $8,050

A Charles II silver tankard, *EG*, London, 1683, with scroll handle, corkscrew thumbpiece and hinged slightly domed cover, 7³/₄in. high, 33oz.
(Christie's) $13,662

A Scandinavian parcel-gilt tankard, circa 1720, maker's mark indistinct, chased with panels of scrolls and foliage, 6in. high, 15oz.
(Christie's) $3,415

A William III silver tankard, Robert Cooper, London, 1697, the lower part of the body applied with molded rib and with scroll handle, 6¹/₂in. high, 22oz.
(Christie's) $8,729

A late 17th century German parcel-gilt tankard, the cylindrical body embossed with classical portrait busts in profile, by Friedrich Bisterveldt, Hamburg, circa 1680, 18cm. high, 19.5oz.
(Phillips) $7,284

A Charles II lidded tankard on a flaring foot and with a scroll handle and rising hinged cover with scroll thumbpiece, maker's initials T.C., London 1683, 6¹/₄in., 22oz.
(Christie's) $2,622

A George II silver Provincial tankard, Exeter, 1736, maker's mark *R.F.*, plain tapering cylindrical and on molded rim base, 7in. high, 24oz.
(Christie's) $4,554

Late Georgian silver half pint tankard of slightly tapering circular design, banded reeded decoration, London 1817, 5oz.
(G. A. Key) $159

A William III silver tankard, Seth Lofthouse, London, 1698, the flat hinged cover with scroll thumbpiece, 7¹/₂in. high, 30oz. 10dwt.
(Christie's) $8,050

SILVER

A Scandinavian silver tankard, unmarked, circa 1690, on three winged cherubim and pomegranate feet, 6¼in. high, 17oz.
(Christie's) $5,693

A Commonwealth silver-mounted serpentine tankard, London, 1653, the base mounted with pierced silver band, 26½in. high.
(Christie's) $7,475

A German silver tankard, Carl Schuch, Augsburg, 1705, the body engraved with scrolling foliage and birds, 8½in. high, 39oz.
(Christie's) $9,775

A German parcel-gilt silver tankard, Israel Thelott, Augsburg, 1680–1685, with chased cagework sleeve with frolicking putti and foliage, 6¼in. high, 22oz.
(Christie's) $10,235

A George II silver tankard, George Wickes, London, 1728, tapering cylindrical, the hinged domed cover with wirework thumbpiece, 7½in. high, 35oz. 10dwt.
(Christie's) $17,250

A George III barrel-shaped tankard, the slightly domed hinged cover with openwork thumbpiece, 18.5cm. high, mark possibly that of John Troby, London 1795.
(Bearne's) $1,115

A George III silver tankard, Charles Wright, London, 1773, the hinged domed cover with open shell thumbpiece, 8½in. high, 40oz. 10dwt.
(Christie's) $5,980

A Continental parcel-gilt silver tankard, second half 17th century, body applied with Greek gods and goddesses with names inscribed above, 6in. high, 26oz.
(Christie's) $17,250

Rare silver tankard, marked J. Turner, Boston, 1746, engraved with the Derby coat of arms and marked *R*(Richard) *M*(Mary) Derby, 8⅞in. high, 28 troy oz.
(Skinner) $113,600

TEA & COFFEE SETS

A Victorian three-piece tea service, each piece of compressed circular form, Joseph Savory & Albert Savory, London 1843, 42.2oz. (Bearne's) $906

A Danish four piece coffee set by Georg Jensen, of squat circular form, with a plain oval coffee tray ensuite, coffee pot 17.5cm. high, tray 42.1cm. long. (Phillips) $4,097

A five piece tea service comprising: kettle on stand with burner, hot water jug, teapot, milk jug, sugar bowl and matching two handled tray, by Charles Stuart Harris & Sons, 1919, the tray 291.5oz. (Phillips) $6,342

A Victorian four-piece tea and coffee service of tapering oval form, each decorated with lines of spiraling beading interspersed with finely-engraved flowers and foliage, Robert Hennell, London 1871, coffee pot 9^{1}/₂in. high, 58oz. (Christie's) $3,947

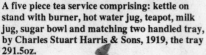

A fine Victorian three piece Aesthetic Movement bachelor's teaset, engraved in the Japanese style with ducks and cranes amidst overhanging foliage, by Elkington & Co., 1878, together with a pair of silver sugar tongs en suite, by Frederick Elkington, Birmingham, 1878. (Phillips) $1,087

A Victorian three-piece afternoon tea service of tapering molded circular form, each decorated with foliage on textured shaped panels and with vacant shaped cartouches, John Tucker & Robert Edwards, London 1870 and 1872, teapot 4^{1}/₄in. high, 13.5oz. (Christie's) $734

An Edwardian three piece teaset, the teapot of bombé oblong form, ivory finial on domed lid, flared rim, double scroll handle, 9in. wide, Birmingham 1906, 25ozs. 6dwts. (Andrew Hartley) $1,320

A Victorian style three-piece tea service of compressed molded circular form and engraved with crests, the teapot with paneled rising curved spout, Sebastian Garrard, London 1911 and 1913, teapot 6^{1}/₄in. high, 45oz. gross. (Christie's) $1,398

TEA & COFFEE SETS

An early 19th century Irish three-piece tea service of lobed compressed circular form, E. Crofton, Dublin 1828/30, 56.5oz. (Bearne's) $1,147

A George III three-piece tea service of boat shape with floral and leafage engraving on ball feet, London 1814, makers *SH & IT*. (Russell, Baldwin & Bright) $1,255

Delheide, five piece tea service, circa 1930, comprising teapot, hot water jug, sugar basin and cover, milk jug and tray, silver-colored metal, the bulbous bodies with undulating contours, tray 7in. wide. (Sotheby's) $8,623

A Victorian three piece teaset, the teapot oval bombé form, with ebony finial and loop handle, the fluted body with embossed scrolling foliate banding, 7¼in. wide, Birmingham 1893, 12ozs. 16dwts. (Andrew Hartley) $710

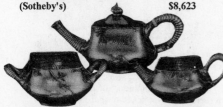

An American silver and other metals Japanese style three-piece breakfast set, Dominick & Haff, New York, 1879, retailed by Howard & Co., comprising: teapot, sugar bowl and creamer, applied with various Japanese motifs, 26oz., teapot 3¾in. high. (Sotheby's) $4,600

A Victorian Scottish three-piece tea service of tapering shaped circular form and on C-scroll and foliate bases, with conforming rims and elaborate openwork C-scroll handles, possibly J. Murray or J. Mitchell, Glasgow 1856, teapot 7½in. high, 51.25oz. (Christie's) $1,496

A Norwegian three piece gilt coffee set, with cloisonné enamel geometric and floral decoration in various colors with dragon handles, by David Andersen, circa 1900. (Phillips) $3,171

A Victorian four-piece tea and coffee service, each piece of rectangular form with canted corners, Elkington & Co. Ltd., Birmingham 1890/91 and Frederick Elkington, Birmingham 1889, 66.1oz. (Bearne's) $755

TEA CADDIES

A Continental shaped oval tea canister with lid, decorated with figures in landscapes, 9cm. high, import marks for Berthold Muller, London 1911, 170gm. (Bearne's) $440

A fine George III silver tea caddy, William Pitts & Joseph Preedy, London, 1790, urn-form, on four columnar supports with reeded lower band, 8in. long, 26oz. (Christie's) $25,300

A silver-colored metal and cloisonné tea canister, decorated with birds, flowers and foliage, 9cm. high, 350gm., stamped *Shanghai.* (Bearne's) $660

A Victorian tea caddy in the Chinese Chippendale style, embossed and chased with pagodas, flowers and scrolls, London 1893. (Russell, Baldwin & Bright) $1,255

A pair of George II silver tea caddies, Samuel Taylor, London, 1748, chased with foliate garlands and cartouches, the domed cap with rocaille finial, 5¼in. high, 19oz. (Christie's) $8,050

An American silver and other metals 'Japanese style' tea caddy, Tiffany & Co., New York, circa 1878, decorated with mokume butterfly and copper cricket on spot-hammered ground, 8oz., 4⅝in. high. (Sotheby's) $5,750

A George III silver tea caddy, Robert Hennell, London, 1788, plain oval and with hinged domed cover and part-wood finial, 5¼in. high, 11oz. gross. (Christie's) $3,226

Ramsden & Carr, caddy and cover with spoon, 1911, the caddy with domed cover and repoussé decoration, six arched supports holding a deep red cabochon, caddy 4¼in. (Sotheby's) $4,311

Italian hallmarked silver tea caddy, baluster form, chased landscape with putti decoration, 6⅜in. high, approximately 11 troy oz. (Skinner) $488

TEA CADDIES

A German late 19th century tea caddy in the 17th century taste, the body chased in relief with flowers, birds and foliage, 5¹/₂in., 9oz.
(Christie's) $323

A pair of George III silver tea and sugar vases, John Carter, London, 1774, chased with calyx of acanthus, laurel garland and guilloché band, 6in. high, 23oz.
(Christie's) $4,025

A George III oval tea caddy decorated with bands of foliage, 15cm. high, Henry Chawner & John Emes, London 1796, 10.7oz.
(Bearne's) $1,179

A George III silver-gilt tea caddy, the front and back applied with oval vignettes of putti gathering fruit and playing music, Andrew Fogelberg & Stephen Gilbert, London 1784, 5¹/₄in., 14.75oz.
(Christie's) $2,272

An early Victorian silver-gilt Rococo Revival tea caddy of oblong form, chased with Oriental figures, Joseph & John Angell, London 1837, 4¹/₄in., 15.75oz.
(Christie's) $2,098

A George III silver tea caddy, Hester Bateman, London, 1783, oval, on beaded rim base, bright-cut engraved with floral garlands and borders, 5¹/₄in. high, 10oz. 10dwt.
(Christie's) $6,325

Attractive late Victorian silver tea caddy, well embossed with foliate and floral designs, the hinged lid with treen finial, gilt interior, 4¹/₂in. wide, 3¹/₂in. high, Birmingham 1896.
(G. A. Key) $300

A pair of George I upright oblong caddies with canted corners, sliding bases and octagonal paneled and domed pull-off covers, by John Farrell, 1717, 12.6cm. high, 14.5oz.
(Phillips) $5,320

An important George II silver tea caddy, Paul de Lamerie, London, 1744, chased on each side with chinoiserie harvest landscapes and figures, 5¹/₄in. high, 14oz. 10dwt.
(Christie's) $107,000

TEA KETTLES

Late Victorian silver plated spirit kettle, burner and stand with naturalistic twig formed handle and spout, similar stand, 12in. high.
(G. A. Key) $139

Silver plated spirit kettle, stand and burner in early 18th century style, the teapot bullet shaped, leaf capped spout, swing handle, circa 1875.
(G. A. Key) $227

Fine quality pierced shaped embossed plated spirit kettle with stand, raised on four cast feet in the manner of Elkington & Co., 18in. high.
(G. A. Key) $534

A George II silver tea kettle, stand and lamp, by Edward Feline, 1749, the stand on three shell and scroll feet, and with garland and scrolled cartouche chased lamp and cover, 12¼in. 4oz.(Christie's) $1,875

A Japanese tea kettle and stand, embossed in high relief with an iris swamp on a simulated shagreen ground, with stand and spirit lamp, by Kuhn & Komor, circa 1910.
(Phillips) $1,280

An Art Nouveau tea kettle and burner, the round, swollen body chased in relief with floral decoration, mark *EBS Ld*, 1911-12, 31cm. high, 1343gr. total weight.
(Dorotheum) $1,414

A plated tea kettle, stand and lamp, by Crichton Bros., the pear-shaped tea kettle with curved and faceted spout, 14in. high with handle raised.
(Christie's) $344

An Edward VII oblong tea kettle with reeded lower body, on stand, 31.5cm. high overall, Goldsmiths & Silversmiths Co. Ltd., London 1909, 40.9oz.
(Bearne's) $468

A George II inverted pear-shaped tea kettle, stand and lamp, by John Jacobs, 1754, 15¼in. high, gross 76oz.
(Christie's) $5,360

TEA KETTLES

English silver plated kettle on
stand, late 19th century, melon-
form kettle on shell and scroll
base, with burners, 14¹/₂in. high.
(Skinner) $460

Victorian circular spirit kettle
and stand, of plain spherical
design with naturalistic twig
formed handle, circa 1870.
(G. A. Key) $183

A George V circular tea kettle
on stand with burner, 28cm.
high, maker's mark *W.S.*,
London 1930, 39.4oz.
(Bearne's) $733

Attractive Edwardian E.P.B.M.
spirit kettle, burner and stand,
the kettle of compressed circular
baluster form, well engraved
with foliate designs, 17in. high,
mid 19th century.
(G. A. Key) $300

An unmarked 18th century
Continental kettle and stand, the
latter with replacement plated
spirit lamp, probably Dutch,
mid 18th century, 33.5cm. high,
47.25oz.
(Phillips) $1,812

A George II silver kettle on
stand, Benjamin Gignac,
London, 1752, the circular
teapot chased with foliage and
rocaille, 10¹/₄in. high, 40oz.
gross.
(Christie's) $5,520

A Victorian tea kettle on stand
of compressed circular form
with swing handle, flower finial,
London 1839, maker *I.E.T.*
(Russell, Baldwin & Bright)
                           $1,530

A 19th century tea kettle of
melon-fluted compressed
inverted pear shape and with an
ivory swing handle, 15½in.
overall.
(Christie's) $560

Victorian silver plated hot water
kettle on stand, 19th century,
swing handle, ribbed melon
form, alcohol burner, 15³/₄in.
high in total.
(Skinner) $805

TEAPOTS

A George III shaped oblong teapot and stand, the teapot with thread edging, 16.5cm. high, probably William Simons, London 1791, teapot 20oz, stand 4.8oz. (Bearne's) **$2,150**

A George IV teapot of compressed melon form, the shoulder applied with acanthus and rose blossoms, 1829-30, 11 cm. high, 517gr. (Dorotheum) **$1,320**

A George I silver teapot, London, circa 1720, possibly John Penfold, the body engraved with a coat-of-arms 4¼in. high, 15oz. gross. (Christie's) **$3,415**

A George II teapot of inverted baluster form, embossed and chased with two vacant cartouches flanked by shells, by Gabriel Sleath, 1751, 14oz. (Phillips) **$1,094**

A George I silver teapot, Thomas Tearle, London, 1726, octagonal, on octagonal molded base, with straight spout, 7¾in. long over handle, 13oz. gross. (Christie's) **$11,500**

A Viennese pear-shaped, fluted teapot, on round, fluted base, the domed lid with foliate finial, Ferdinand Vogel, 21cm. high, 798gr. (Dorotheum) **$942**

A George III silver teapot and stand, John Emes, London, 1799, the oval teapot with curved spout and hinged domed cover, the teapot 6½in. high, 20oz. gross. (Christie's) **$3,226**

An 18th century German teapot of squat baluster form with domed cover and faceted spout, by Lewin Dedeke, Celle, circa 1730, 13.5oz. (Phillips) **$6,840**

William IV silver teapot of circular baluster style, well chased and embossed with flowers and foliate designs, London 1834 by the Barnards, 28oz. (G. A. Key) **$787**

Edwardian bachelor's teapot in George III style, oval shaped with bright cut trailing foliate decoration, angular spout, treen finial and handle, Birmingham 1904, 9oz. all in. (G. A. Key) **$559**

A George III oval teapot with engraved floral cartouche, London 1801, makers: Peter, Anne and William Bateman, 15oz. all in. (Russell, Baldwin & Bright) **$551**

A George III Provincial teapot and stand, shaped oval with engraved decoration and initialled cartouche, by Thomas Watson & Co., Sheffield, 1798, 22oz. (Phillips) **$1,292**

TEAPOTS

A Victorian teapot of circular form with leaf capped double scroll handle, 8cm. high, Savory & Sons, London 1880, 24oz.
(Bearne's) $566

A George III teapot of circular form with reeded edging, Hannah Northcote, London 1806, 17.7oz.
(Bearne's) $336

Victorian silver teapot, melon shaped with foliate engraved panels, scrolled handle, London 1847, 25 1/2oz.
(G. A. Key) $759

A Viennese Art Nouveau oval teapot, with agate handle and finial, by Alexander Sturm, 11.5cm. high, 465gr. gross weight.
(Dorotheum) $1,508

A St Petersburg Imperial teapot, of melon form with part gadrooned body, the domed hinged lid with wooden finial, circa 1820, 13.5cm. high, 482gr.
(Dorotheum) $1,700

A George IV circular teapot, engraved with armorials amongst scrolls, 14.5cm. high, William Bateman, London 1823, 21.8oz.
(Bearne's) $660

George III hallmarked silver teapot on stand, London, 1788–89, by Charles Hougham and Edward Jay, Federal paneled ovoid form, 6 5/8in. high with stand, approximately 18 troy oz.
(Skinner) $1,265

A French silver teapot, Martin Guillaume Biennais, Paris, 1798–1809, the hinged flat cover with oval ebony finial, 9 1/2in. long over handle, 18oz. 10dwt. gross
(Christie's) $2,760

Fine George III silver teapot of slightly compressed oblong design, reeded body band with engraved band of flowers, foliage and crest above, London 1812, 20oz.
(G. A. Key) $597

Victorian silver teapot, London, 1857–58, *WS* maker, squat melon form, melon and leaf finial, 5 3/4in. high, approximately 23 troy oz.
(Skinner) $748

George IV silver teapot of compressed circular design with half fluted decoration, leaf capped scrolled handle, London 1827, 20oz. all in.
(G. A. Key) $523

A St. Petersburg Biedermeier teapot of compressed melon form, the rim with foliate frieze, gilt lined, 1843, 16cm. high, 800gr.(Dorotheum) $1,130

TEAPOTS

A George III teapot of oval form, with tapering angular spout, polished wood scroll handle, William Vincent, London 1778, 4³/₄in., 14oz. gross.
(Christie's) $1,320

Victorian silver teapot of circular baluster form, the body engraved with foliate and floral designs, London 1852, 22¹/₂oz.
(G. A. Key) $378

A George III silver teapot and stand, Henry Chawner, London, 1792, the stand 1793, each octagonal, with bright-cut engraved scroll border, 21oz. gross.
(Christie's) $2,070

An American silver and other metals 'Japanese style' large teapot, Tiffany & Co., New York, circa 1877, applied with trailing silver vines hung with one mokume gourd and copper gourds, 25oz. gross, 7¹/₄in. high.
(Sotheby's) $11,500

A George III silver teapot and sugar basket, Hester Bateman, London, the teapot 1784, the basket 1788, the teapot oval, with beaded base and bright-cut engraved bands, 20oz. gross.
(Christie's) $8,050

A Victorian Scottish silver teapot, Marshall & Sons, Edinburgh, 1837, engraved about the shoulders, cover, handle and spout with tied sprays of flowering foliage, 47oz..
(Christie's) $763

A George III silver teapot, George Smith II and Thomas Hayter, scroll handle, bright-cut engraved with roundels and single swags, 7in.
(Christie's) $999

Attractive Victorian silver plated teapot of tapering circular design, arabesque engraved, bud finial to lid, circa 1875.
(G. A. Key) $109

A George I silver teapot, David Tanqueray, London, 1718, with part-faceted scroll spout and wood scroll handle, 6in. high, 17oz. 10dwt. gross.
(Christie's) $34,500

TOASTERS

Late Victorian silver toast rack on oval base with seven hooped bars and central carrying handle, London 1900, 8¹/₂oz. (G. A. Key) $166

Christopher Dresser for Hukin & Heath, toast rack, 1878, electroplated metal, rectangular base with upright prongs and 'T' shaped handle, 5½in. (Sotheby's) $3,749

Good Victorian silver toast rack of seven oval hooped bars to a rectangular base, all supported on four cast acanthus feet, 6 x 3in., London 1846, by the Barnards, 10¹/₂oz. (G. A. Key) $390

TOILET BOXES

An early Victorian tortoiseshell necessaire, modeled as a book, opening to velvet lined interior with silver plated fittings, 5¹/₂in. high. (Christie's) $1,218

A Victorian ebony dressing table box, with brass bound angles and brass decorative inlay to the borders, 13in. wide. (Christie's) $557

An Edward VII silver-backed dressing table set, Edmund Bennett, London 1901 & 1902, in fitted red leather case. (Bearne's) $398

A Victorian silver-gilt lady's traveling toilet service, Frederick Purnell, London, 1880, all in gilt brass-bound coromandel wood case with key, weighable silver 13oz. (Christie's) $3,795

A French gold-mounted tortoiseshell gentleman's traveling case, Pentueau, Paris, circa 1920, in fitted leather case. (Christie's) $9,108

A Victorian parcel-gilt lady's traveling toilet service, Abraham Brownett and John Rose, London, 1859, in fitted brass-bound coromandel wood case, weighable silver 8oz. (Christie's) $2,657

TRAYS & SALVERS

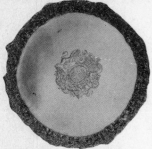

A George II silver salver, John Robinson, London, 1758, shaped-circular and on four pierced vine and scroll feet, 14³/₄in. diameter, 54oz. (Christie's) $3,226

A George III silver salver, William Eaton, London, 1816, the openwork cast border pierced and chased with shells, 11³/₄in. diameter, 44oz. (Christie's) $4,175

Mid 20th century silver salver in early 18th century style with shell and gadrooned rim, 11in. diameter, Birmingham 1952, 24oz. (G. A. Key) $480

Good quality silver plated two handled tea tray in rococo style, rectangular shaped with heavy shell and scrolled edge, 25 x 16in., late 19th/early 20th century. (G. A. Key) $360

A pair of George III waiters, the grounds engraved with armorials surrounded by bows and floral and foliate swags, maker's initials R.R., London 1771, 7in., 18oz. (Christie's) $834

A French silver-gilt presentation tray, Odiot, Paris, circa 1865, with ovolo and foliate rim and two panels of frolicking putti, 33¹/₄in. long over handles, 284oz. 10dwt. (Christie's) $14,950

A George II waiter of shaped square form, the ground engraved with an armorial within a scalework and scroll cartouche, Humphrey Payne, London 1730, 6¹/₄in., 8.75oz. (Christie's) $1,398

A George V shaped-square salver with stepped rim, on four hoof feet, 45cm. diameter, Birmingham 1928, 65.9oz. (Bearne's) $944

A George IV silver salver, Joseph Craddock & William Reid, London, 1823, with cast openwork border with masks and animals, 23³/₄in. diameter, 184oz. (Christie's) $9,775

604

A George VI circular salver with central presentation inscription, 30.5cm. diameter, Goldsmiths and Silversmiths Co. Ltd., London 1944, 31.8oz. (Bearne's) $723

A pair of George II silver salvers, George Hindmarsh, London, 1732, chased with a band of shells, scrolls, latticework and four crests, 10in. square, 44oz. (Christie's) $9,867

A George III Irish silver salver, James le Bass, Dublin, 1810, shaped-circular and on four shell and scroll feet, 17³/₄in. diameter, 94oz. (Christie's) $4,175

A Victorian shaped circular salver, with scalloped edge decorated with flowers and foliage, on three scroll feet, crested, 27cm. diameter, London 1867, 21.5oz. (Bearne's) $440

A silver tray, Tiffany & Co., New York, 1865-1870, on four openwork feet, the border with woven band, 12in. long, 27oz. 10dwt. (Christie's) $3,450

A George I shaped circular salver with scalloped edge and engraved foliage decoration, 19.5cm. diameter, possibly John Eckfourd Jr., London 1726, 11.1oz. (Bearne's) $582

A George III Irish Provincial salver, circular with reeded rim, crested center and raised on three narrow bracket feet, by John Toleken, Cork, circa 1800, 18.5cm. diameter, 6oz. (Phillips) $835

A pair of George III silver-gilt salvers, Benjamin Smith, London, 1818, shaped-circular and on three lion's paw, shell and foliate scroll feet, 18¹/₂in. diameter, 206oz. (Christie's) $23,322

An early 19th century Maltese oval salver, with reeded rim and hatchet feet, probably by Gioacchino Lerun, Ball period 1800–09, 35.7cm. long, 36oz. (Phillips) $3,926

TUREENS

A pair of George III plain oval boat-shaped sauce tureens and covers, domed covers with urn finials, by Richard Cooke, 1801, 24cm. long, 47.5oz. (Phillips) $3,490

A pair of George III silver sauce tureens and covers, Hester Bateman, Londo, 1790, each oval, on spreading oval reeded base, 9⅝in. long over handles, 31oz. 10dwt. (Christie's) $8,050

A pair of George III sauce tureens and covers, the bodies engraved with armorials, Napthali Hunt, London 1800, 8¾in. overall, 37.5oz. (Christie's) $4,575

A silver covered soup tureen, Theodore B. Starr, New York, circa 1890, chased overall with scrolling foliage, 11¾in. long over handles, 53oz. 10dwt. (Christie's) $2,990

A pair of George III silver sauce tureens and covers, Henry Greenway, London, 1782, the bodies each with two reeded leaf-capped loop handles, 8¾in. long, 32oz. (Christie's) $4,934

A George III silver soup tureen and cover, William Frisbee, London, 1804, with leaf-capped reeded loop handles, domed cover, 15½in. wide, 96oz. (Christie's) $12,334

A pair of George III sauce tureens and covers of tapering molded oblong form and on lion's paw feet, William Frisbee, London 1808, 8in. overall, 40oz. (Christie's) $2,797

A George III silver soup tureen and cover and later liner and stand, tureen Edward Wakelin, London, 1751, the liner George Clements, London, 1825, the stand William Frisbee, London, 1803, 203oz. (Christie's) $20,872

A pair of George III silver sauce tureens and covers, London, 1802, maker's mark indistinct, each with two reeded leaf-capped loop handles, 9¾in. long, 54oz. (Christie's) $3,796

SILVER

Victorian silver plated hot water urn, mid 19th century, bulbous urn form, chrysanthemum finial, 16in. high.
(Skinner) $748

A George IV silver tea urn, Paul Storr, London, 1823, the waisted circular body with acanthus below, 16in. high, 185oz. gross.
(Christie's) $14,950

A 19th century silver plated two-handled tea urn of lobed form with square base on four feet.
(Bearne's) $717

A George III silver tea-urn, John Edwards, London, 1810, the partly-fluted circular body with reeded spigot and hinged foliate scroll and anthemion tap, 14¹/₂in. high, 132oz.
(Christie's) $14,352

Unusual late 19th century silver plated wine urn, the urn attached to a revolving plated gallery edged tray with polished oak center.
(G. A. Key) $159

An 18th century Sheffield plated Daniel Holy Wilkinson & Co. tea urn in Adams style, the vase shaped urn with twin handles and engraved shoulder, 18¹/₂in. high.
(David Lay) $558

Durgin sterling covered urn, circa 1900, baluster form scroll handles, heraldic crest on either side of body, 18¹/₂in. high, approximately 58 troy oz.
(Skinner) $1,150

A Dutch silver coffee urn, Matthijs Crayenschot, Amsterdam, 1760, the base with openwork scroll apron, 16³/₄in. high, 107oz. gross.
(Christie's) $21,275

A George III silver coffee urn, Hester Bateman, London, 1784, the spout with ivory spigot, with two scroll handles, 14¹/₄in. high, 33oz. 10dwt. gross.
(Christie's) $6,325

607

A George III two-handled pedestal sugar vase on a gadrooned and pierced foot and with a beaded rim, London 1774, 7½in., 7oz. free. (Christie's) $718

Coin silver covered sugar, Whartenby and Bumm, Philadelphia, 1816–18, monogrammed, 9in. high, approximately 25 troy oz. (Skinner) $431

Liberty & Co., Cymric vase, 1903, set with three lapis lazuli cabochons at the neck, 5¾in. (Sotheby's) $2,812

A Viennese Empire sugar vase, chased with floral decoration, pierced, galleried rim, slightly domed cover with bud finial, Carl Blasius, 18.5cm., 431gr. (Dorotheum) $2,828

Fine decorative pair of Dutch import hallmarked silver flower vases on pierced foliate bases, the bodies well chased with classical figures, 6in. high., 15oz. total. (G. A. Key) $531

A Hungarian shooting trophy, the body carved in relief with floral ornament and cartouche with portrait of Franz Josef I, Budapest, 1896, 20cm. high, 199gr. (Dorotheum) $330

An American silver and other metals 'Japanese style' vase, Tiffany & Co., New York, circa 1880, of sake bottle shape, 5oz.10dwt., 6½in. high. (Sotheby's) $3,162

An American silver 'Japanese style' vase, Tiffany & Co., New York, circa 1880, spot-hammered in a graduated concentric pattern and with dragonfly handles, 14oz. 15dwt., 6¾in. high. (Sotheby's) $8,050

Jones, Ball & Poor coin silver vase, Boston, 1846, raised baluster form, chased vintage pattern, 7⅛in. high, approximately 9 troy oz. (Skinner) $978

VASES

Ball, Black and Company medallion sterling footed vase, chased and engraved decoration, 10½in. high, approximately 20 troy oz.
(Skinner) $805

A pair of George II silver condiment vases, Paul de Lamerie, London, 1745, the body and cover with fluted stylized shells and leaves, 7in. high, 25oz.
(Christie's) $51,570

Tiffany sterling vase, 1938–1947, flared baluster-form, applied relief shell and scroll band around base, 10⁹⁄₁₆in. high, approximately 21 troy oz.
(Skinner) $633

A Viennese Empire sugar vase, the circular foot with chased acanthus decoration, pierced rim, circa 1816, 17cm. high, 395gr.
(Dorotheum) $1,225

A late Victorian copy of the Warwick Vase with entwined reeded vine handles on square pedestal foot, Sheffield, 1900, on ebonized wooden plinth, 26cm. high, 107oz.
(Phillips) $4,553

A French 19th century sucrier and cover on a foliate-pierced square base with leaf-capped lion's paw feet, J.P. Biberon, Paris 1819–1838, 10¼in., 14.25oz. free.
(Christie's) $987

An American silver Indian style vase, Gorham Mfg. Co., Providence, 1880, chased with circles of exotic flowers, 16oz., 8½in. high.
(Sotheby's) $1,840

A pair of Turkish vases on cast and chased domed shaped square bases decorated with foliage and trelliswork, 7½in.
(Christie's) $1,526

Wood & Hughes sterling vase, 1870–90s, baluster form, exotic bird handles, chased and engraved decoration, 9½in. high, approximately 14 troy oz.
(Skinner) $518

An Edwardian oblong vesta case enameled in polychrome with a lyrebird, Birmingham, 1909, 4.5 x 3cm.
(Phillips) $228

A jeweled two-color gold match case, by Fabergé, 1908–1917, with spring-hinged cover, cabochon sapphire pushpiece and suspension loop, 1¾in. high.
(Christie's) $4,025

An Edwardian rectangular vesta case, the front enameled with a two-horse carriage in a rural landscape, Birmingham 1901.
(Christie's S. Ken) $320

A late Victorian vesta case, with petal and flower overall design, maker Nathan and Hayes, Chester 1897.
(Woolley & Wallis) $160

A late Victorian rectangular vesta case chased on the cover in relief with a horse-racing scene, Chester, 1895, apparently no maker's mark.
(Phillips) $523

An Edwardian silver vesta case, the fascia repoussé with a golfer about to strike the ball, London 1903, by H. Matthews, 32 grms.
(Phillips) $290

A Victorian silver and enamel novelty vesta case, H. & A., Birmingham, 1886, decorated with a pipe in brown, black and white enamel, 2¼in.
(Christie's) $545

A late Victorian vesta case, presumably commemorating the relief of Mafeking, cover applied with a portrait of Baden-Powell, maker's mark R·B^s., Birmingham, 1899.
(Phillips) $683

An Edwardian vesta case by The Goldsmiths & Silversmiths Co. Ltd., 1905, chased with characters from Shakespeare's A Midsummer Night's Dream.
(Phillips) $228

A Victorian vesta case by William Summers, 1877, oblong with rounded ends engraved with diagonal bands of decorative diaperwork, 5.7 cm long.
(Phillips) $167

An Edwardian novelty vesta case in the form of a football of flattened circular form by W.H. Sparrow, Birmingham, 1905, 4.5cm. diameter.
(Phillips) $669

A late Victorian novelty oblong vesta case, enameled on the cover in monochrome to resemble a calling card, by William Neal & Son, Sheffield, 5.5 x 3cm. (Phillips) $440

A vinaigrette, engraved with a view, probably by Edward Smith, Birmingham, 1848, 38mm.
(Tennants) $635

A George III curved oblong vinaigrette engraved with vertical wrigglework bands over horizontal bars on stippled ground, by Samuel Pemberton, Birmingham, 1803.
(Phillips) $182

Regency silver-gilt and agate vinaigrette, maker unmarked, (London), 1815, the hinged lid set with an amber colored translucent agate.
(Butterfield & Butterfield) $575

A 19th century gold and enamel vinaigrette of slender vase shape, small oval cover concealing the quille, probably Swiss, circa 1840, 5.8cm. high.
(Phillips) $2,128

A George III silver-gilt watchcase vinaigrette engraved with flowers on stippled ground, by Wardell & Kempson, Birmingham, 1814.
(Phillips) $212

Fine William IV silver gilt vinaigrette, book shaped with engine turned decoration to all sides, foliate pierced grill, London 1832.
(G. A. Key) $362

A silver rectangular vinaigrette, modeled as Newstead Abbey, with chased borders and engine turned sides and base, by Taylor & Perry, Birmingham, 1836, 45mm.
(Tennants) $794

A rare silver gilt vinaigrette, of rectangular shape, the grill filigree by Matthew Linwood, Birmingham, 1811, 30mm.
(Tennants) $1,191

An early Victorian shaped oblong vinaigrette, base engraved with a view of the Liverpool and Manchester Railway viaduct, by Nathaniel Mills, Birmingham, 1839, 3.9cm. long.
(Phillips) $790

French pink agate and gold vinaigrette, maker *CP* with horizontal bar between, with small guarantee mark for Paris, post 1819.
(Butterfield & Butterfield) $2,300

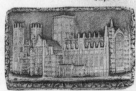

A silver vinaigrette with St. Pauls Cathedral from the south west, makers probably Wheeler & Cronin, Birmingham, 1843, 48mm.
(Tennants) $1,905

A silver rectangular vinaigrette, the cover with a view of York Minster from the south east, by Nathaniel Mills, Birmingham, 1841, 47mm. long.
(Tennants) $2,540

SILVER

WINE COOLERS

A pair of Regency silver-gilt wine coolers, Robert Garrard, London, 1816, barrel form, with gadrooned rim and base, 8in. high, 205oz. 10dwt.
(Christie's) **$167,500**

A Regency silver wine cooler, Paul Storr, London, 1818, on four scroll feet applied with oak leaves, 9in. high, 144oz.
(Christie's) **$17,250**

A pair of George III silver-gilt Warwick vase wine coolers, Paul Storr, London, 1810, the body cast and applied with bacchic masks, lion's pelts, foliage and trailing vines, 9¹/₂in. high, 416oz.
(Christie's) **$71,445**

A French silver wine cooler and a matching silver-plated example, one with maker's mark of Jean-Baptiste-Claude Odiot, Paris, 1819–1838, 11³/₄in. high, 82oz. 10dwt.
(Christie's) **$10,350**

A silver wine cooler, John Wakelin and William Taylor, London, 1795, the body with two lion's mask and drop-ring handles, 8in. high, 47oz.
(Christie's) **$5,313**

A pair of French silver wine coolers with plated liners, Bointaburet, Paris, circa 1900, the plain bodies with incurved angles, foliate scroll bracket handles, 9¹/₄in. high, 192oz.
(Christie's) **$10,436**

Victorian campana formed silver plated ice bucket with reeded side handles, fluted decoration to body and detachable top rim.
(G. A. Key) **$411**

A pair of George II silver-gilt wine coolers, Paul Crespin, London, 1728 and 1729, the lower part of the body applied with strapwork on a matted ground, 8in. high, 173oz.
(Christie's) **$148,200**

A Victorian silver wine cooler, Benjamin Smith, 1849, the circular fluted foot with a berried border, 12in. high.
(Christie's) **$11,810**

SILVER

WINE FUNNELS

George III two part silver wine funnel of usual form with gadrooned edge and plain clip, London 1771.
(G. A. Key) $514

An Irish Provincial wine funnel stand, maker's mark of John Nicolson, Cork, circa 1790, and a George III Irish silver wine funnel, circa 1780, 4½in. high.
(Christie's) $909

A George IV wine funnel, crested, the everted rim with acanthus edging and shell clip, 14cm. long, Charles Fox, London 1828, 3.8oz.
(Bearne's) $1,147

WINE LABELS

A pair of George III wine labels of lion mask, shell, scroll and fruiting vine design, engraved with pierced titles *'Hock'* and *'Claret'*, by Daniel Hockley, 1816.
(Phillips) $510

A pair of Regency silver wine labels, Paul Storr, London, 1816, engraved *SHERRY* on one and *WHISKEY* on another, 2³/₈in. long, 2oz.
(Christie's) $1,035

A pair of George III rectangular wine labels with incurved, canted corners and reeded borders, incised *SERCIAL* and *HOCK* by Phipps, Robinson & Phipps, 1813.
(Phillips) $182

WINE TASTERS

A French 18th century wine taster with serpent handle, the tapering circular bowl decorated with fluting and lobing, circa 1765, 3³/₄in. overall.
(Christie's) $574

A 19th century French wine taster, plain with serpent ring handle, maker's mark *GB* with orb between, circa 1870, 4.5oz.
(Phillips) $982

A French 19th century wine taster, the tapering circular bowl decorated with fluting and lobing, 4¹/₄in.
(Christie's) $502

A 19th century cameo agate snuff bottle in ovoid form with a finely carved white horse on a grey body, 2in. high.
(Eldred's) $523

Polychrome figural ivory snuff bottle, depicting a woman riding on a kylin, head forms stopper, 3in. high.
(Eldred's) $275

Good shadow agate snuff bottle, 1800-80, with carved depiction of two sages playing weiqi.
(Butterfield & Butterfield)
                              $1,035

Export polychromed ivory snuff bottle, late 19th century, for the Japanese market, decorated with a continuous scene of phoenixes in landscapes.
(Butterfield & Butterfield)
                              $805

A famille rose 'European subject' snuff bottle, iron-red Daoguang seal mark and of the period, enameled on one side with Queen Victoria seated upon a throne holding a scepter.
(Christie's) $4,963

Inside painted snuff bottle, signed *Ye Zhongsan the Younger*, depicting the poet Du Fu astride a mule in a snowy landscape.
(Butterfield & Butterfield)
                              $1,200

Good nephrite snuff bottle, Qianlong period, matrix of even yellow-green color, carved with a sage and crane under a pine.
(Butterfield & Butterfield)
                              $1,035

Carved shadow agate snuff bottle, 1800-50, semi-translucent pale gray matrix showing russet and dark brown inclusions.
(Butterfield & Butterfield)
                              $1,150

Hornbill snuff bottle, circa 1900 or later, depicting dragons carved in low relief to each face, phoenixes to each shoulder.
(Butterfield & Butterfield)
                              $920

SNUFF BOTTLES

Fine Suzhou agate snuff bottle, 1800-80, carved with a scene from the story of Xiyou ji. (Butterfield & Butterfield)
$4,888

Red and white porcelain snuff bottle, 18th century, one side with figures and a water buffalo in a landscape, 2½in. high. (Skinner) $201

Fine white nephrite snuff bottle, 1750-1850, expertly fashioned as persimmon wrapped in further fruiting branches. (Butterfield & Butterfield)
$2,875

Embellished white nephrite snuff bottle, decorated to one side with a bird among flowering plants, in coral, mother of pearl and hardstone. (Butterfield & Butterfield)
$2,875

Silver inlaid bronze snuff bottle, 19th century, the thinly cast bottle embellished with inlaid silver wire decoration of a sage and phoenix. (Butterfield & Butterfield)
$1,495

Rare, later-embellished jadeite snuff bottle, bottle 1750-1825, overlaid with a depiction of Emperor Ming Huang and his favourite consort. (Butterfield & Butterfield)
$8,050

A moss agate snuff bottle, 19th century, carved in low relief with figures and a mule beside a bridge and trees in a river landscape. (Christie's) $2,864

Yi Hsing pottery snuff bottle in hexagonal form with mask handles and a tan landscape design on a dark brown body, circa 1900, 2½in. high. (Eldred's) $330

Rare rhinoceros horn snuff bottle in temple jar form with dragon medallions and mask and mock ring handles, conforming stopper, 2⅜in. high. (Eldred's) $743

Yangzhou School Peking glass snuff bottle, 1750-1825, the milky white body overlaid in red glass and carved as bats and a crane.
(Butterfield & Butterfield)
$2,875

White nephrite double peach form snuff bottle, converted from an 18th century finely carved toggle.
(Butterfield & Butterfield)
$748

Unusual reticulated porcelain snuff bottle, the exterior molded and pierced with winged mythical animals on a network of branches, 83mm.
(Butterfield & Butterfield)
$460

Cloisonné snuff bottle, Qianlong four character mark on base, auspicious symbols amid clouds on a yellow ground lappet border along base, 3in. high.
(Skinner)
$172

Pair of unusual polychromed ivory snuff bottles, late 19th century, each carved as a well ripened ear of corn covered by its husk, the stoppers as corn stalks.(Butterfield & Butterfield)
$1,380

Ruby red glass snuff bottle, 19th century, flattened ovoid form, side with chilongs carved in relief.
(Skinner)
$115

An ivory and Lac Burgaute snuff bottle, iron-red Qianlong seal mark, one side painted with a lady reclining on a bed.
(Christie's)
$2,460

Good double agate snuff bottle, 1800-1880, well hollowed and highly polished to accentuate the semi-translucent matrix.
(Butterfield & Butterfield)
$2,000

Early 20th century opal snuff bottle in temple jar form with relief carving of lobster and lotus, 2½in. high.
(Eldred's)
$468

Soapstone figure of a seated official, 18th century, the rotund figure shown grasping his belt in one hand, 5½in.
(Butterfield & Butterfield)
$1,725

Large soapstone seal carved with qilin and cloud design, the irregularly formed top carved with two swirling dragons emerging from clouds, 3¾in. high. (Butterfield & Butterfield)
$575

Soapstone figure of Shoulao on a deer, the bearded immortal shown holding a staff, 7¼in. high.
(Butterfield & Butterfield)
$460

Soapstone group of two lovers on a carved steatite cliff, their elaborate costumes gilt and highlighted in polychrome pigments, 9¼in.
(Butterfield & Butterfield)
$4,600

Two large soapstone figures of a man and woman, the old man holding a bamboo flute, the woman with a basket, 11¼ and 11½in.
(Butterfield & Butterfield)
$3,450

Soapstone figural group, depicting three immortals in ceremonial robes on crescent shaped base, 4¾in.
(Butterfield & Butterfield)
$460

Large carved soapstone seal, of natural boulder form and carved to the top with dragon spewing smoke, 4½in. high.
(Butterfield & Butterfield)
$460

Carved soapstone libation cup, 19th century, the opaque butterscotch colored matrix displaying whitish veins, 3in. high.
(Butterfield & Butterfield)
$800

Soapstone carving of a lohan and a boy, the smiling sage seated holding a child on his knee, 3in. high.
(Butterfield & Butterfield)
$1,035

Gentleman's black woolen trunks from the late 1930s. (The Gurney Collection) $30

A 1930s toffee tin with beach scene. (The Gurney Collection) $23

Crested china beach chair with seated swimmer, early 1920s. (The Gurney Collection) $30

Crested china bathing machine recording the Rumour of John Constable's early morning swim in the River Stour, pre 1920. (The Gurney Collection) $38

1934 cotton 'hire' trunks from the Nottingham Baths, often intended to be worn under a more concealing costume for added modesty. (The Gurney Collection) $15

One of a series of French plates depicting the history of sea bathing, 1880s. (The Gurney Collection) $38

Late 1940s rubber swimming helmet with dolphin ears. (The Gurney Collection) $8

Inflatable rubber waist ring by Lilo, circa 1965. (The Gurney Collection) $8

A silver plated swimming trophy, Rossall, 1883. (The Gurney Collection) $38

Chrome and enamel Art Deco brooch. (The Gurney Collection) $23

A 1920s/30s toffee tin with various sporting scenes, including a beach scene. (The Gurney Collection) $45

A Crested china ashtray with a reclining swimmer, 1930s. (The Gurney Collection) $30

'The Badminton Library – Swimming', 1893 (First Edition). (The Gurney Collection) $60

Royal Doulton figure 'Sunshine Girl' HN 1344, designed by L Harradine, 5in. high, issued 1929-1938. $1,800

Lady's chrome cigarette case with bathing belles illustration on the lid, 1920s. (The Gurney Collection) $30

Late 1930s rubber swimming helmet. (The Gurney Collection) $8

Ayvad's inflatable cotton water wings in pristine condition, made in the U.S.A., circa 1910. (The Gurney Collection) $30

A fine Art Deco scent bottle, glazed on the back and with a bisque bathing panel on the front. (The Gurney Collection) $60

COSTUMES

Early 1920s gentleman's pure woolen one-piece with 'modesty' skirt.
(The Gurney Collection) $30

Lady's hand knitted woolen one-piece from the austere years of the early 40s.
(The Gurney Collection) $30

Gentleman's one-piece bathing costume with striped top, early 1920s.
(The Gurney Collection) $30

Early 1920s gentleman's one-piece bathing costume by Nunsuch, with canvas belt.
(The Gurney Collection) $30

Young woman's bathing dress in extremely fine woolen weave, still bearing a sale label by Monito, circa 1900.
(The Gurney Collection) $60

Gentleman's one-piece bathing costume with fake belt, early 1920s.
(The Gurney Collection) $30

COSTUMES

Lady's grey flannel Victorian bathing dress with detachable skirt.
(The Gurney Collection)
$230

Child's woolen costume with 'Diving Champion' logo, 20in. long, late 1930s.
(The Gurney Collection) $60

Lady's late Victorian red flannel bathing dress with detachable skirt.
(The Gurney Collection) $200

A pair of lady's beach pyjamas which first made their appearance on the French Riviera in the 1920s.
(The Gurney Collection) $50

Lady's one piece interlock cotton bathing suit with built-in skirt by Meridian, 1908.
(The Gurney Collection) $90

Late 1920s man's woolen one-piece bathing suit with the top plain fawn and the bottom half dark brown.
(The Gurney Collection) $30

COSTUMES

Lady's woolen one-piece by
Bukta, 1930s.
(The Gurney Collection) $30

Late 1940s lady's elasticated
linen one-piece bathing costume.
(The Gurney Collection) $30

Gentleman's woolen one-piece
by Jantzen, 1930s.
(The Gurney Collection) $30

A very rare gentleman's Victorian interchangeable three-piece set in matching cotton jersey,
marked *A.S.A. regulation costume.*
(The Gurney Collection) $300

COSTUMES

One of the first two-piece lady's costumes in elasticated linen from the late 40s, early 50s. (The Gurney Collection) $30

1930s gentleman's ribbed woolen one-piece with 'modesty' skirt by Jaeger. (The Gurney Collection) $30

1960s lady's cotton two piece by Slix. (The Gurney Collection) $25

Lady's 'artificial' silk costume, 1910. (The Gurney Collection) $40

Late 1940s lady's linen beach play-suit. (The Gurney Collection) $30

Child's one-piece woolen costume, 18in. long, late 1930s. (The Gurney Collection) $55

A dual plush covered teddy bear with brown and black glass eyes, pronounced snout, black stitched nose, 27in. tall, 1930s.
(Christie's) $1,083

A Chiltern Hygienic Toys long blonde fur musical teddy bear, with musical movement playing Brahms lullaby, 16in. high.
(Phillips) $224

A Steiff teddy bear with golden mohair, black shoe button eyes, swivel head, jointed shaped limbs, 12in. tall, circa 1910.
(Christie's) $1,264

A good large Steiff center seam gold teddy bear, German, circa 1908, with black stitched center seamed snout, boot button eyes, wide apart rounded ears, 29in.
(Sotheby's) $13,444

A rare Steiff rod-bear, German, circa 1904, bearing rare elephant button to ear, of yellow plush, with early sharp-featured head, 15½in., together with two X-rays.
(Sotheby's) $8,228

A white plush Steiff teddy bear, German, circa 1920, with button in ear, brown stitched snout, brown and black glass eyes, 19½in. high.
(Sotheby's) $2,015

A Steiff teddy bear with dark brown mohair, brown and black glass eyes, black stitched nose, mouth and claws, 16in. tall, 1920s.
(Christie's) $1,444

A white Steiff teddy bear with brown and black eyes, pronounced snout, brown stitched nose, 13in. tall, circa 1925.
(Christie's) $2,708

A German teddy bear with pale golden mohair, clear and black glass eyes painted on reverse, hump and growler, 18in. tall, 1920s.
(Christie's) $361

A Chad Valley teddy bear with golden curly mohair, deep amber and black glass eyes, 12in. tall, 1950s.
(Christie's) $325

A Bing teddy bear with golden mohair, black shoe button eyes, pronounced clipped snout, 9in. tall, circa 1910.
(Christie's) $578

A Steiff teddy bear with golden mohair, black boot button eyes, pronounced clipped snout, felt pads, 13in. tall, circa 1910.
(Christie's) $1,535

A gold mohair Alpha Farnel bear, English, circa 1910, with black boot button eyes, small ears, fully jointed, felt pads, kapok and excelsior filled, 10in.
(Bonhams) $227

A pair of Steiff rod jointed blonde plush teddy bears, German, circa 1904, with sealing wax noses and boot button eyes, swivel and metal rod jointed with excelsior stuffing, 17¾in. and 18½in.
(Sotheby's) $20,165

A Steiff gold plush teddy bear, German, circa 1925, with button in ear and remains of yellow label, black stitched snout, brown glass eyes, 17in.
(Sotheby's) $3,265

A golden plush covered teddy bear with brown and black glass eyes, pronounced snout, black stitched nose, mouth and claws, 30in. tall, 1930s.
(Christie's) $325

A Merrythought teddy bear with golden mohair, pronounced clipped snout, swivel head, jointed limbs and brown felt pads, 23in. tall, 1930s.
(Christie's) $722

A tan mohair Steiff bear, German, circa 1909, with black boot button eyes, kapok and straw filled, felt pads, four claws, 9½in.
(Bonhams) $785

A Bing teddy bear with rich golden mohair, brown and black glass eyes, felt pads and growler, 15in. high, 1920s.
(Christie's) $1,296

An early German teddy bear with pale blond mohair, black boot button eyes, 18in. high, possibly Bing, circa 1910.
(Christie's) $1,487

A rare Steiff 'Zooby' bear with pale brown mohair, brown and black plastic eyes, airbrush features, 11in. high, circa 1960.
(Christie's) $1,110

A rare Merrythought Woppit teddy bear with brown plush body, black stitched nose and smiling mouth, 9in. high, circa 1956.
(Christie's) $3,518

A Steiff teddy bear with golden curly mohair, large, spoon shaped paws and feet, felt pads and hump, 25in. high, circa 1905.
(Christie's) $9,257

A Steiff apricot wool plush teddy baby, German, circa 1935, with button in ear, open felt-lined mouth, brown stitched snout and brown glass eyes, 13in.
(Sotheby's) $5,377

A rare Anker Zotty teddy bear with cream tipped beige mohair, deep amber and black glass eyes, cut muzzle, 22in. high, 1950s.
(Christie's) $518

A Farnell teddy bear with white mohair, deep amber and black glass eyes, pronounced square snout, pink stitched nose, mouth and claws, 28in. tall, 1930s.
(Christie's) $903

A Chad Valley teddy bear with golden mohair, center seam large deep amber and black glass eyes, black stitched button nose, 30in. high, 1950s.
(Christie's) $704

'Charlie', a Steiff teddy bear with golden curly mohair, operative growler and button in ear, 24in. high, circa 1910. (Christie's) $5,925

A Farnell teddy bear with bright golden mohair, pronounced snout, jointed shaped limbs and rexine pads, 18in. high, 1930s. (Christie's) $1,018

A brown Steiff teddy bear with large black boot button eyes, stitched nose, mouth and claws, 28in. high, circa 1910. (Christie's) $11,109

A Steiff center seam teddy bear with dark golden mohair, black boot button eyes, pronounced clipped snout, 15in. high, circa 1908. (Christie's) $4,814

A rare Steiff 'Teddy-Clown' bear with beige tipped cream mohair, original felt clown hat with blue pom-poms, cream and blue ruff, 19in. high, circa 1926. (Christie's) $11,111

An Eduard Crämer teddy bear with short blond mohair, pronounced snout, brown and black glass eyes, 14in. high, circa 1920. (Christie's) $2,962

A white Steiff teddy bear with black boot button eyes, pronounced clipped snout, beige stitched nose, 16in. high, circa 1910. (Christie's) $3,333

A rare blue Schuco 'Yes/No' teddy bear with dark blue short mohair, black boot button eyes, pronounced clipped snout, 14in. high, circa 1926. (Christie's) $18,515

A fine Steiff teddy bear with rich golden curly mohair, cream felt pads, large spoon shaped paws and feet, 30in. high, circa 1920. (Christie's) $27,773

A Steiff Teddy Baby with cream mohair, brown and black glass eyes, US Zone label stitched to right arm, 11in. high, circa 1950.
(Christie's) $1,388

A Chiltern teddy bear with golden mohair, large clear and black glass eyes painted on reverse, 26in. high, 1930s.
(Christie's) $1,110

'Paul', a Chiltern teddy bear with golden mohair, clear and black glass eyes painted on reverse, 21in. high, circa 1927.
(Christie's) $891

An unusual white, long plush teddy bear, probably German, circa 1920s, the blonde stitched snout shaped to indicate nostrils, pricked ears, jointed and with press growler, 18in.
(Sotheby's) $1,536

'Sneezy' a miniature Chad Valley teddy bear with pale golden mohair, 5in. high, with two photographs of original owner.
(Christie's) $926

A Dean's 'Tru-to Life' bear with blonde mohair, brown and black glass eyes cut into internal rubber face mask with rubber eye sockets, 20in. high, circa 1950.
(Christie's) $1,290

A blonde mohair teddy bear, English, circa 1910, with black boot button eyes, vertically stitched nose, straw and hair filled, 15in. tall.
(Bonhams) $226

A clockwork Bing teddy bear with cinnamon mohair, operative to and fro dancing movement and keyhole to tummy, 9in. high, circa 1910.
(Christie's) $1,481

A Chad Valley teddy bear with golden curly mohair, deep amber and black glass eyes, jointed shaped limbs and brown felt pads, 21in. high, 1950s.
(Christie's) $704

A Steiff teddy bear with blonde curly mohair, brown and black glass eyes, black stitched nose, mouth and claws, 24in. tall, 1920s.
(Christie's) $5,416

An Invicta teddy bear with long golden mohair, clear and black glass eyes painted on reverse, 16in. high, 1950s.
(Christie's) $351

A Chiltern teddy bear with pale golden mohair, large deep amber and black glass eyes, cardboard lined feet, 25in. tall, 1930s.
(Christie's) $397

A Steiff teddy bear with pale blonde mohair, black boot button eyes, felt pads, hump and button in ear, 13in. tall, circa 1910.
(Christie's) $4,694

'Tommy' a Steiff teddy bear with golden mohair, dressed in contemporary 1st World War uniform, 12in. high. circa 1910.
(Christie's) $3,148

A Schuco Tricky musical 'Yes/No' teddy bear, tail operating Yes/No head movement, fixed key-wind musical movement to back, 20in. high, 1950s.
(Christie's) $3,333

A Merrythought Bingie bear cub with pale brown mohair, cream plush inner ears, deep amber and black glass eyes, 9in. high, 1930s.
(Christie's) $407

A Gebrüder Sussenguth 'Peter' bear with cream tipped back mohair, black and white glass googlie eyes, 13in. high, circa 1925.
(Christie's) $3,333

A rare and large golden mohair Chiltern Huggmee bear, English, 1940s, with brown glass eyes, black embroidered nose and mouth and large ears, 37in.
(Bonhams) $755

An L. M. Ericsson wall telephone, with two bells, magneto, handset and desk. (Auction Team Köln)

$467

A ZB SA 25 'cow hoof' desk telephone by the Merck Telefonbau, Munich, circa 1930. (Auction Team Köln)

$622

A Stevens Autophone, the first candlestick telephone with spring dialing, by S.H. Couch Co., Boston. (Auction Team Köln)

$404

A Fuld & Co. internal desk telephone, with three extensions and bell, circa 1905. (Auction Team Köln)

$272

An English battery-powered diver's telephone by Siebe Gorman & Co, with earphones and separate mouthpiece for surface operator. (Auction Team Köln)

$202

A Scandinavian telephone exchange in a wood and metal housing with key sender and dial on front. (Auction Team Köln)

$155

An Ericsson Swedish skeleton desk telephone with magneto, earth key, circa 1910. (Auction Team Köln)

$1,012

An L.M. Ericsson pointer-dial desk telephone. (Auction Team Köln)

$1,089

A KTAS desk telephone, with call button, dial and bell, circa 1945. (Auction Team Köln)

$155

An early L.M. Ericsson wall telephone.
(Auction Team Köln)
$622

A W25 telephone switchboard with box by Mix & Genest, Berlin, circa 1942.
(Auction Team Köln)
$235

A telephone doll with brocade dress and china head and arms, 50cm. high, circa 1900.
(Auction Team Köln)
$978

An early German M 1900 wall extension with adjustable mouthpiece and original spoon receiver.
(Auction Team Köln)
£1,285

A DeTeWe field telephone, the receiver with speech button, circa 1943.
(Auction Team Köln)
$171

A very rare Gower telephone, by Frederick Gower, an American inventor who in 1877 improved upon Bell's original model.
(Auction Team Köln)
$3,390

An L.M. Ericsson wooden desktop pointer-dial telephone, with call button and horn mouthpiece.
(Auction Team Köln)
$1,054

A Siemens & Halske pointer dialing telephone in bakelite case, circa 1940.
(Auction Team Köln)
$218

A Siemens & Halske Art Nouveau style wall telephone 1920s.
(Auction Team Köln)
$2,568

TELEVISIONS

Pilot Radio Model TV-37, small 3in. tube TV set, the first US television at under $100, 1947. (Auction Team Köln)
$390

A Cossor Model 1210 television radio receiver in upright walnut case with radio tuning dial on top, fourteen-inch screen, 47½in. (Christie's)
$1,320

RCA Victor Model 8-T-241 TV set, with 9in. tubes, in mahogany case. (Auction Team Köln)
$311

A Marconi 705 early prewar mirror television, lacking picture tubes and other parts, 1937. (Auction Team Köln)
$940

A Saba Telerama television projector Schauinsland P1026H, with original projection screen, circa 1955. (Auction Team Köln)
$1,010

An HMV Model 904 television with radio, in walnut table cabinet with crossbanding, 23in. wide, 1938-9. (Christie's)
$4,278

Ekcovision Model TMB 272 early postwar portable television, for mains and car battery-power. (Auction Team Köln) $132

General Electric Model 800 bakelite television with 9 in. tubes, circa 1948. (Auction Team Köln)
$365

An early postwar English Bush Type TV62 television, with 36 tubes, circa 1953. (Auction Team Köln)
$295

A crewelwork pocket, monogrammed *MW*, (Mary Whiting), New England, 18th century, executed in green, red, blue, yellow, pink, ocher and brown wool stitches, 15 x 10½in. (Sotheby's) $1,495

A fine canvaswork pocketbook, signed *Charles Samson*, probably Maine, dated *1773*, executed in blue, pink, red, green, ocher, yellow, lavender, black and white wool Irish stitches, 5½ x 9in. (Sotheby's) $4,312

A baby's bonnet of fine white cotton worked with a drawn threadwork and needlefilling rosette at the crown, Ayrshire, early 19th century. (Christie's) $606

A fine silk embroidered picture depicting Cymbelene, signed *Mehitable Neal at Mrs Saunders and Mrs Beach's Academy*, Dorchester, Massachusetts, circa 1807, 17 x 22½in. (Sotheby's) $23,000

A knitted silk pinball, signed *Sarah Hockey*, Pennsylvania, dated *1796*, the oval ball executed in red, yellow, and white silk knitted stitches with a crown and hearts, 2in. long. (Sotheby's) $690

A needlework mourning picture, signed *Eliza I. Blanchard*, Mrs Buchanan's School, Marietta, Pennsylvania, dated *1825*, with ladies and girls flanking a plinth beneath a willow tree, 16 x 16¼in. (Sotheby's) $11,500

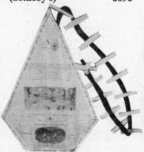

A silk embroidered picture depicting an Emblem of America, a memorial to George Washington, circa 1809, oval, 18 x 16¼in. (Sotheby's) $16,100

'A.J. Whitcomb's Indestructible Pocket Kite', patented 1876 Utica, New York, yellow glazed cotton with engraved decoration and directions, 26½in. high. (Skinner) $1,035

A printed handkerchief, late 19th century, printed in black with school scenes surrounding a central panel with alphabets and numbers, 11¼ x 11in. (Sotheby's) $517

A General Electric D-12 ceramic toaster, American, circa 1910. (Auction Team Köln) $342

A Toastrite blue-gray ceramic toaster. (Auction Team Köln) $1,167

A Universal E 7712 A toaster with pressed glass handles and electric flex. (Auction Team Köln) $125

A rare Epeha two sided folding toaster with radiant plates, wooden base and original flex, circa 1930. (Auction Team Köln) $155

A Toastove-style horizontal toaster, with heating coil, unused. (Auction Team Köln) $78

A Universal D-12 ceramic toaster, with floral decoration and warming tray. (Auction Team Köln) $583

A Universal E 9410 heart-shaped push button toaster, circa 1929. (Auction Team Köln) $855

A Saluta No. 584 four-slice toaster with turning handle, red feet and handle. (Auction Team Köln) $100

A General Electric D-12 toaster on ceramic base, American, circa 1910. (Auction Team Köln) $195

Smoke decorated tin house bank, America, 19th century, 7½in. high.
(Skinner) $510

Regency tole ware two handled covered urn, applied with a foliate decorated pine cone finial, the sides applied with lion mask mounts, early 19th century, 7in.
(G. A. Key) $556

Ebonised toleware purdonium with original scoop, the top applied with a looped acorn and foliate molded handle, 19th century, 13in.
(G. A. Key) $152

A tinned sheet metal candlemold, Pennsylvania, 19th century, the rectangular dished top centering ten tapering cylindrical moulds, 10¾in. high.
(Sotheby's) $431

A rare punchwork-decorated toleware coffee pot, signed *M. Uebele*, Berks or Montgomery County, Pennsylvania, circa 1840, of conical form with domed lid, brass finial, 11¼in. high. (Sotheby's) $2,300

A tinned sheet metal fat lamp, Lebanon County, Pennsylvania, 19th century, the kettle of squared ovoid form centering a wick above a cylindrical shaft, 6¾in. high.
(Sotheby's) $287

A fine and rare wriggle-work decorated toleware coffee pot, Pennsylvania, circa 1810, of tapered body with hinged dome lid, 9½in. high.
(Sotheby's) $13,800

A green painted pine and tin thirty-six cavity candlemold, American, 19th century, of rectangular form, 16in. wide.
(Sotheby's) $1,150

A rare punchwork-decorated tôleware coffee pot, Pennsylvania, circa 1820, each side decorated with a compote filled with flowers, 11¼in.
(Sotheby's) $1,265

AXES & EDGED TOOLS

A well proportioned European goose-wing axe, with Smith's stamp.
(Tony Murland) $135

A Wheelwrights' bearded axe by Sorby, original handle with some worm.
(Tony Murland) $85

A Woodman's axe from the Dordoyne, used to tap the resin from pine trees.
(Tony Murland) $210

A 14in. froe with its original cudgel or maul.
(Tony Murland) $120

A pair of French shears stamped A. Noyers.
(Tony Murland) $135

A French vineyard cutting tool by Foures.
(Tony Murland) $85

A very rare large left hand side axe with 11in. blade stamped three times, *Parigot Sol a la Chapelle'*.
(Tony Murland) $151

A late 16th/early 17th century, 30½in. trimming axe, with two Smith's marks.
(Tony Murland) $660

A rare right hand French Coopers' side axe with 9in. curved blade by Auguste Cros a Bezier.
(Tony Murland) $130

A fine and large billhook by English Tools Ltd., Wigan & Leeds.
(Tony Murland) $38

A Shipwrights' mast axe with ash handle, 17in. long blade, 5in. cutting edge, pitted.
(Tony Murland) $120

A 10½in. broad axe by Beatty & Co., Chester, original cranked handle.
(Tony Murland) $105

(Tool Shop Auctions)

AXES & EDGED TOOLS

A stylish 18th century French Coachmakers' side axe, hand forged out of one piece of metal. (Tony Murland) $250

A fine example of the elusive double socketed French beheading axe, unhandled. (Tony Murland) $450

An elegant 18th century meat cleaver with deep Smith's stamp II. (Tony Murland) $180

A magnificent sugar cleaver, mid 19th century. (Tony Murland) $135

An impressive French Coopers' doloire with original handle. (Tony Murland) $225

A stylish French axe with makers' stamp *FB*. (Tony Murland) $100

An elegant Coachmakers' side axe from the Charente with original handle, blade marked *'Vieu a Cruecy'*. (Tony Murland) $120

A No. 2 Shipwrights adze by Gilpin with attractive brass bound lignum handle. (Tony Murland) $75

An extremely rare curved billhook by Elwell, the blade thickening across its width and length. (Tony Murland) $75

A 21in. European fighting axe with delightful tail to the bottom of the blade. (Tony Murland) $240

A Wheelwrights' side axe by I. Sorby with ash handle and 7¾ cutting edge, pitted. (Tony Murland) $100

(Tool Shop Auctions)

A beheading axe with a simple elegance which belies its sinister purpose, early replaced handle. (Tony Murland) $210

EEL & FISH SPEARS

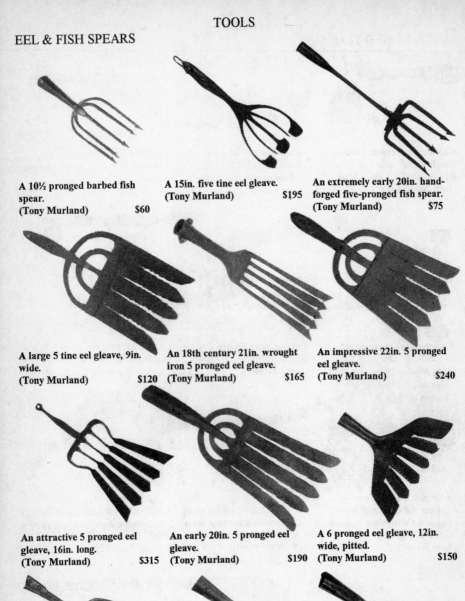

A 10½ pronged barbed fish spear.
(Tony Murland) $60

A 15in. five tine eel gleave.
(Tony Murland) $195

An extremely early 20in. hand-forged five-pronged fish spear.
(Tony Murland) $75

A large 5 tine eel gleave, 9in. wide.
(Tony Murland) $120

An 18th century 21in. wrought iron 5 pronged eel gleave.
(Tony Murland) $165

An impressive 22in. 5 pronged eel gleave.
(Tony Murland) $240

An attractive 5 pronged eel gleave, 16in. long.
(Tony Murland) $315

An early 20in. 5 pronged eel gleave.
(Tony Murland) $190

A 6 pronged eel gleave, 12in. wide, pitted.
(Tony Murland) $150

An impressive 20in. early five pronged eel gleave.
(Tony Murland) $235

An unusual 14½in. 5 pronged fish spear.
(Tony Murland) $180

A 5 pronged eel gleave, 18in. long, pitted.
(Tony Murland) $160

(Tool Shop Auctions)

TOOLS

HAMMERS

A Coopers' hammer by
Mathieson.
(Tony Murland) $70

A Panelbeaters' hammer.
(Tony Murland) $55

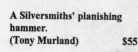

A Silversmiths' planishing
hammer.
(Tony Murland) $55

An unusual Patternmakers'
hammer.
(Tony Murland) $55

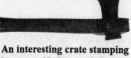

An interesting crate stamping
hammer, *'J. Barnes & Sons
1917'*.
(Tony Murland) $45

A very rare Shipwrights'
coppering hammer.
(Tony Murland) $45

A Plumb claw hammer with the
stamped autograph *'Fayette R.
Plumb'* on the handle.
(Tony Murland) $45

An unusual combination
hammer and pincers operated
by a rod through the handle.
(Tony Murland) $115

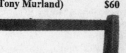

A rare veneering hammer, often
found in wood but seldom in
steel.
(Tony Murland) $60

A good Slaters' hammer by
Brades.
(Tony Murland) $30

A scarce Filemakers' hammer
and 3 file chisels.
(Tony Murland) $300

A Filemakers' hammer with 2
chisels.
(Tony Murland) $225

MORTICE & MARKING GAUGES

An ebony mortise gauge with
solid brass head.
(Tony Murland) $75

A rare Parker Thompson
mortise gauge.
(Tony Murland) $165

A brass stemmed mortise gauge
with solid brass head.
(Tony Murland) $45

A combination marking and
mortise gauge in ebony with
solid brass head and scale on the
slide.
(Tony Murland) $75

An early cabinetmakers'
marking gauge in Cuban
mahogany.
(Tony Murland) $90

A rare ebony and brass mortise
gauge by Fenton & Marsden,
'redg. Feb 19, 1847', adjustable
through screws each end.
(Tony Murland) $280

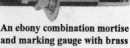

An ebony combination mortise
and marking gauge with brass
graduated rule to 8in. and solid
brass head.
(Tony Murland) $165

An early 18th century hornbeam
and boxwood marking gauge
with early hand stamped scale
on stem.
(Tony Murland) $85

An unusual ebony and brass
faced slitting gauge, the stock
and cutter deliberately set 2° off
square by W. Marples.
(Tony Murland) $90

(Tool Shop Auctions)

PLANES

A Stanley No. 340 furring plane.
(Tony Murland) $960

An early trap plane in elm, with brass lined throat.
(Tony Murland) $70

A fenced handrail plane by Edwards, Manchester.
(Tony Murland) $315

An excellent quality manufactured spill plane by T. Turner.
(Tony Murland) $130

A dovetailed steel parallel sided smoothing plane by Spiers.
(Tony Murland) $420

An extemely significant 10¾in. long No. 1 hollow plane by Thomas Granford.
(Tony Murland) $1,380

A good example of the rare Silcock plough plane, complete with brass plaque.
(Tony Murland) $1,530

A Mathieson 9b handled plough plane, the white beech crisp and unfinished and the boxwood arms with a slight polished appearance.
(Tony Murland) $465

A 4¼ x 15in. handled twin-iron cornice plane by A. Mathieson, Glasgow.
(Tony Murland) $540

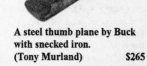

An elegant D router with brass fittings.
(Tony Murland) $63

A Spiers 20½in. dovetailed jointing plane with rosewood infill.
(Tony Murland) $555

A steel thumb plane by Buck with snecked iron.
(Tony Murland) $265

(Tool Shop Auctions)

PLANES

A gun metal chariot plane, 3¼ x 1½.
(Tony Murland) $70

A 22in. Norris A72 beech try plane with Patent adjustment.
(Tony Murland) $300

A rare Stanley 212 scraper plane.
(Tony Murland) $840

A Stanley 164, plane with the remains of the trade label on the handle.
(Tony Murland) $4,275

A Millers Patent No. 41 plough plane complete with 2 fences, fillister bed and blade.
(Tony Murland) $1,230

A Stanley No. 1 in original conditional, most of the lacquer is still on the handle.
(Tony Murland) $1,230

A 2¼in. round both ways Cellomakers' plane by Preston, the largest and rarest size in this range of planes.
(Tony Murland) $720

A unique 16 x 2⅝in. steel soled gun metal Norris No. 54G panel plane, over 2in. of original iron remaining.
(Tony Murland) $6,300

A truly stylish Scottish brass bullnose plane with rosewood wedge and Cupid's Bow decoration to the top.
(Tony Murland) $210

A pretty gun metal chariot plane with a steel sole and an ebony wedge.
(Tony Murland) $150

An all brass bodied plow plane stamped *William Cowell, Newcastle.*
(Tony Murland) $930

A solid boxwood smoothing plane with ebony handle and beech wedge.
(Tony Murland) $75

(Tool Shop Auctions)

PLUMB BOBS

A brass and steel 'Ridgeley Patent Jan-12-09, paperhangers' plumb bob.
(Tony Murland) $240

A No. 344, 18oz. plumb bob with removeable tip and black painted cap.
(Tony Murland) $23

An early 5in. steel pointed plumb bob with well balanced turned top.
(Tony Murland) $85

An enormous original mid 19th century, 9½in. 'Cathedral Builders' plumb bob, brass with a steel point.
(Tony Murland) $480

A No. 317, 32oz. Griffin lighted plumb bob, with two AAAA batteries and a bulb which is activated by the weight of the bob on the line.
(Tony Murland) $375

An unusual 16oz. gunmetal plumb bob, the steel point can be unscrewed and used either end or plugged.
(Tony Murland) $120

An extremely unusual early 18th century stone plumb bob stamped *'A. Tyler'*, hewn from a piece of rock.
(Tony Murland) $115

A true Prince amongst plumb bobs, 4½in., solid brass with a steel point, mid 19th century.
(Tony Murland) $465

A tidy 3in. aluminium and steel! Paperhangers bob, a small steel pointer slides neatly behind the integral wheel.
(Tony Murland) $75

SAWS

A 10in. brass back saw by Mathieson.
(Tony Murland) $55

An attractive brass back dovetail saw with beech handle.
(Tony Murland) $75

An early 12in. table saw by Blith, London.
(Tony Murland) $70

An 18th century surgeons' bone saw with file cut decoration to the extremities, pitted.
(Tony Murland) $200

A most unusual boxwood handled saw with deeply cast decorative floral plate.
(Tony Murland) $225

A rare 17th century saw with molded decoration at the front, 2ft. long.
(Tony Murland) $450

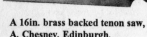

A 16in. brass backed tenon saw, A. Chesney, Edinburgh.
(Tony Murland) $60

A unique Bowmakers' nock saw for cutting the notches at the tip of the bow for holding the string.
(Tony Murland) $160

A charming small fretsaw, 9in. overall with a rosewood handle.
(Tony Murland) $195

(Tool Shop Auctions)

SCREWDRIVERS

A 5¾in. boxwood handled screwdriver by Mathieson. (Tony Murland) $55

A massive 28½in. turnscrew by William Clay with a beech handle. (Tony Murland) $90

A quality 17in. London pattern beech handled cabinetmakers' screwdriver. (Tony Murland) $30

A handsome 26in. ash handled turnscrew with heavy brass ferrule. (Tony Murland) $33

An ebony handled, late 18th century turnscrew from the workshop of a group of Church carpenters used on the enormous screws found in church pews. (Tony Murland) $180

A rare example of an 18th century turnscrew with the additional rare feature of a hole to take a bar for extra torque. (Tony Murland) $75

A very flamboyant early 19th century turnscrew with a rosewood handle. (Tony Murland) $145

An elaborate 22½in. turnscrew with a rosewood handle, early 19th century. (Tony Murland) $150

A heavy 21in. 19th century turnscrew by S. Arnold, with ash handle. (Tony Murland) $60

WRENCHES

William Baxter double-ended nut wrench, patent (granted February 2nd 1856) J. Charlton of Newark, New Jersey. (Tony Murland) $150

An early carriage wrench, patented March 28th 1882, which incorporates into its cast iron frame an opening to accommodate an oil can. (Tony Murland) $280

A 5in. mid-19th century English adjustable wrench and combined hammer stamped *'warranted wrought'*. (Tony Murland) $21

A rare, easy action, spring loaded pipe wrench by The Goodell Pratt Co., 6¾in. overall. (Tony Murland) $340

A rare 'William Fuller's Patented & Warranted' iron 4-way bed wrench, dated 1874. (Tony Murland) $45

An adjustable wrench with a pliers action by Starrett, Patent Jan 3rd 1911. (Tony Murland) $38

A crafty adjustable wrench marked D. R. Patent, the bottom jaw rides over a cam thus adjusting the aperture. (Tony Murland) $45

An extremely rare and early patented combination tool (Pat. November 4th 1902), features include a hammer, pipe wrench, nut wrench, nail puller, wire cutter and screwdriver. $90

A bicycle wrench, marked the *'Dodge Cycle Tool'*, from the early days of cycling incorporating an air pump. (Tony Murland) $255

(Tool Shop Auctions)

A Nomura battery operated 'Radar Robot', pale metallic grayish-green painted and lithographed tinplate in original box.
(Christie's) $1,403

A Lehmann 'Zirka' tinplate toy, German, circa 1920, with green lithographed driver and striped zebra, 7¼in.
(Sotheby's) $731

An Asakusa battery operated 'Thunder Robot', Japanese, 1960-65, the tin body finished in brown with red feet, 11¾in.
(Sotheby's) $2,467

A Masudaya Space Man, red battery operated astronaut with extending antenna and electric headlamp, in original box, late 1950's, 8in.
(Christie's) $1,929

A child's galloper-drawn carriage, English, circa 1877, the two cream painted carved wooden horses with black rivet eyes, 58in.
(Sotheby's) $1,828

An Alps for VIA Distributors 'Happy Santa', remote control battery operated fabric covered drumming figure, in original box, late 1950's, 11in. high.
(Christie's) $229

A Lehmann 'Halloh' tinplate motorcyclist, German, circa 1920, with blue lithographed motorcycle, black garbed rider with white trousers, 8½in. long.
(Sotheby's) $2,743

A fine suite of doll's house furniture, English, circa 1910-20, of softwood stained to resemble mahogany, the sideboard 6¼in. long,
(Sotheby's) $804

A Gebrüder Bing clockwork teddy bear having brown mohair plush, with two small metal wheel to feet, playing with large painted metal ball with rotating action.
(Phillips) $4,500

Jouet de Paris clockwork Hotchkiss Avion Voisin saloon car lithographed in brown/black with orange lining and has electric fog lamp.
(Phillips) $975

A Horikawa battery operated 'Dino Robot', Japanese, 1960's, as he walks forward, his robot head opens to reveal the plastic dinosaur head, 12¼in. high.
(Sotheby's) $1,097

Miniature walnut spool bed, America, 19th century, complete with bedding and miniature brass and wood bed warmer, 13¼in. wide.
(Skinner) $143

A rare 'Hong Kong Airways' Schuco Elektro Radiant 5600 Airliner, white, blue and silver lithographed tinplate battery operated Vickers Viscount, circa 1960, 17in. long.
(Christie's) $2,105

A Fernand Martin 'Le Petit Marchand d'Oranges' mechanical tinplate toy, French, circa 1901, the orange seller with hand enameled head and material clothed body, 7¼in.
(Sotheby's) $731

An unusual parcel-gilt doll's tester bed, probably Spanish, partly 17th century, each end elaborately carved with a shell and scrollwork above a balustrade, 39in. wide.
(Sotheby's) $6,178

A Roullet & Decamps walking elephant automaton, French, circa 1880, the chamois leather covered beast with keywind to one side.
(Sotheby's) $6,034

Set 61 silver RAF Aeroplanes, comprising pair Fairey Battle Bombers, pair Gloster Gladiators and Singapore Flying Boat, lid dated *1.39*.
(Christie's) $386

A Lehmann 'Tap-Tap' tinplate toy, German, circa 1920, with blue uniformed gardener pushing a yellow lithographed wheelbarrow, 6in. long.
(Sotheby's) $1,097

Tidy Tim, an American tinplate wind-up street sweeper toy by Louis Marx, 1933. (Auction Team Köln) $350

A USA-NASA Gemini battery-powered, tinplate toy by Modern Toys, Japan, in original box, 1960s. (Auction Team Köln) $200

A Lehmann hand-painted wind-up Cheeky Boy tinplate toy, 1904-35. (Auction Team Köln) $430

A clockwork three-wheeled lady, probably by Theroude, French, circa 1860, platform containing the keywind mechanism causing her to turn her head and raise a bouquet, 12in. (Sotheby's) $909

A Chad Valley Snow White and the seven dwarfs, English, circa 1930s, Snow White in a dress with velvet top, each dwarf wearing brightly colored clothes and hat, Snow White 17in., dwarfs 10in. (Bonhams) $1,854

A battery-powered tinplate Wise Monkey 'Hy Que' toy by Nomura Toys, Japan, vinyl hands and face, 42cm. high. (Auction Team Köln) $310

A rare Lehmann EPL 495 'Naughty Boy', German for American market 1904-1914, two seated figures of a boy in blue sailor suit and the driver in brown suit with hat. (Bonhams) $725

Cragstan's battery-powered and remote controled, tinplate Gun Sheriff by Yonezawa, Japan, vinyl head, lacking revolver, 27cm. high. (Auction Team Köln) $95

A Steiff cow on wheels with brown and white mohair, standing on four metal spoked wheels joined by four metal rods, 20in. long, circa 1910. (Christie's) $813

A Bing tinplate tender with two-part turntable ladder, lacking bell and lamps, circa 1930. (Auction Team Köln) $375

A Distler Electro Magic Porsche 7.500 FS, battery-powered, with optional remote control, 1955. (Auction Team Köln) $1,089

An American wind-up tinplate model Dodgem car, , with lithographed figures, circa 23 cm. long. (Auction Team Köln) $155

A pull-along of two bisque headed clowns, German, circa 1890, the Schoenau and Hoffmeister heads impressed *SstarPBH*, on platform 13½in. long. (Sotheby's) $1,907

Steiff rabbit skittles, velvet covered with black shoe button eyes standing on turned wooden base, incomplete set, 8in. tall each, circa 1900. (Christie's) $3,069

A battery-powered tinplate Blushing Frankenstein toy by Nomura, Japan, he drops his trousers and blushes, with original box, 1960s, 32cm. high. (Auction Team Köln) $180

Schuco Curvo 1000 tinplate wind-up motorcyclist, detachable front wheel, red, 1950-54, with original box. (Auction Team Köln) $770

American Airlines DC7 tinplate, battery-powered toy aeroplane, by Linemar, Japan, 1950s, 45cm. long. (Auction Team Köln) $117

A rare Strunz elephant, burlap covered with black boot button eyes, white felt tusks, rod and metal button jointing, circa 1903, 14in. long. (Christie's) $686

A Louis Vuitton trunk, covered in beige and brown striped canvas, bound in leather and brass, circa 1880, 29½ x 12 x 16½in.
(Christie's) $1,748

A Louis Vuitton trunk covered in beige and brown striped canvas, bound in leather and brass with wooden banding, 27½ x 16 x 12½in., circa 1880.
(Christie's) $1,075

A brown, stamped calf leather, brass mounted doctor's bag, brown linen lining.
(Auction Team Köln) $31

A Goyard desk trunk covered in black canvas, bound in brass with painted wooden banding, labeled *Malles Goyard, Paris,* 22 x 19 x 32in.
(Christie's) $2,000

A Louis Vuitton hatbox covered in checkered canvas and bound with leather and brass, labeled, circa 1889, 18 x 15½ x 17in.
(Christie's) $1,363

A Louis Vuitton shoe secrétaire, covered in LV fabric and bound in leather and brass, the interior fitted with thirty drawers for pairs of shoes, 16 x 25 x 45in.
(Christie's) $9,000

A writing case of brown crocodile leather, with foul weather case, stamped *Finnegans New Bond Street,* 14 x 9½ x 4in.
(Christie's) $611

A small, nickel mounted leather case, with wine red cloth lining, 54 x 34 x 18cm.
(Auction Team Köln)
                     $155

A lady's crocodile skin traveling case, the top tray converting into smaller traveling case.
(Bearne's) $573

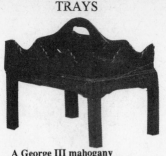

A Victorian floral-painted black papier-mâché tray, on later ebonized stand with simulated bamboo legs, 30in. wide. (Christie's) **$1,137**

A George III mahogany decanter-tray-on-stand, the rectangular tray with arched carrying-handle and six divisions with waved borders on a rectangular stand with square legs, 20in. wide. (Christie's) **$1,495**

A Regency papier mâché rectangular tray with gilt floral friezes on a scarlet ground, 30 x 22in. (Russell, Baldwin & Bright) **$2,754**

A pair of Neapolitan gold-inlaid tortoiseshell pique trays, mid-18th century, centred by a landscape of Roman buildings and various figures, 12in. wide. (Christie's) **$13,455**

A butler's George III mahogany folding oval tray with four flush panels and flush brass hinges, folding stand. (David Lay) **$1,032**

A rare George III mahogany oval tray top tea or occasional table, with a gallery and crossbanded top and molded frieze, top 76cm. x 50cm. overall. (Phillips) **$8,250**

A set of three graduated papier mâché trays, with foliate gilt decoration on a black ground and stamped to the reverse *JENNENS & BETTRIDGE*, early 19th century, the largest 27in. wide. (Christie's) **$962**

A Regency polychrome-decorated papier-mâché tray-on-stand, the rounded rectangular galleried tray with two handles and a central scene of a spaniel chasing a rabbit, 31in. wide. (Christie's) **$5,454**

A Victorian black and gilt-embellished papier mâché tray, by Jennens & Bettridge, London, the shaped rectangular border enclosing blue and gilt-painted spandrels, 31in. (Christie's) **$1,126**

Xochipala figure, circa 900–600 B.C., standing on sandaled feet, youthful torso with punctate navel, 12¹/₂in. high. (Butterfield & Butterfield)
$1,725

Eskimo wood mask, probably from Saint Michaels, the central part of face and hinged lower jaw a natural brown wood color, 7¼in. high. (without feathers). (Butterfield & Butterfield)
$6,325

Chinesco seated figure, circa 100 B.C.–250 A.D., seated with hands and elbow resting on bent knee, 6¹/₂in. high. (Butterfield & Butterfield)
$1,150

Olmec porphyry mask, circa 1150–550 B.C., carved following contours of the deep blue-green mottled stone, 5¹/₄in. high. (Butterfield & Butterfield)
$1,150

Cocle pedestal plate, circa 800–1500 A.D., the interior painted in plum, orange, and black on beige ground, 6¹/₄in. high. (Butterfield & Butterfield)
$805

Eskimo wood human effigy, the half-figure with arms raised, head outstretched on long neck, 4¹/₂in. long. (Butterfield & Butterfield)
$546

Sepik River ancestral board, May River area, the slightly undulating round-edged rectangle carved in low relief on front, 63in. high. (Butterfield & Butterfield)
$1,150

Pende helmet mask, Giphogo, light wood with red, white and dark brown, pigments, fiber cord beneath nose, slit eyes, 10¹/₂in. high. (Butterfield & Butterfield)
$690

Prehistoric Eskimo ivory root pick, the beveled and tapering curved ivory head with incised linear and circle-dot decoration, 8¹/₂in. long. (Butterfield & Butterfield)
$316

Bembe mask, of egg-shape form with almond-shape eyeholes and mouth, applied brown stain covering surface, 11¹/₂in. high. (Butterfield & Butterfield)

$805

Aboriginal ceremonial object, Tjuringa, reportedly Aranda tribe at Aroaka Kanta, Central Australia, flat oval stone covered with reddish brown pigment, 7¹/₂in. long. (Butterfield & Butterfield)

$3,450

Makonde body mask, pregnant female torso with voluptuous distended belly and full breasts, 23¹/₄in. high. (Butterfield & Butterfield)

$2,300

Costa Rican painted pottery figure, circa 1100–1300 A.D., Guanacaste-Nicoya zone, seated female with arms akimbo, 8in. high. (Butterfield & Butterfield)

$862

Kuba helmet mask, Bwoom, copper strips on mouth, cheeks, nostrils, and brow, numerous circle and dot marks, 12in. high. (Butterfield & Butterfield)

$575

Teotihuacan incensario, circa 250–650 A.D., Escuintla region, Pacific Coast, in two parts, the circular waisted bottom containing basin in upper half, 21¹/₂in. high. (Butterfield & Butterfield)

$5,750

Maori whalebone club, Kotiate paraoa, of characteristic broad spatula form with notched sides and butt end of handle, 13¹/₄in. long. (Butterfield & Butterfield)

$4,887

Moche owl vessel, circa 400–700 A.D., painted reddish brown and cream with dark brown eyes, beak and feathers, 10in. high. (Butterfield & Butterfield)

$1,092

Maori bailer, Tata or tiheru, the scoop with edges slightly waisted and divided laterally by slightly raised ridge near center, 21in. long. (Butterfield & Butterfield)

$8,050

A Klein Adler, three-row keyboard German typewriter with wooden case, Cyrillic font, circa 1913.
(Auction Team Köln)

$430

A Picht Braille typewriter by Bruno Herde and Friedrich Wendt, Berlin, with original instructions.
(Auction Team Köln)

$272

A white export model Mignon Mod. 4 German pointer typewriter for the French market, 1923.
(Auction Team Köln)

$740

A small German Stoewer Elite type bar machine with three-row keyboard and elegant suspended ribbon rollers, with SS-Rune key, 1912.
(Auction Team Köln)

$467

An Orga- Privat type bar machine designed by Bing, an attempt to launch an inexpensive standard office typewriter onto the market, 1923.
(Auction Team Köln)

$235

The Ideal A German swing carriage office typewriter, circa 1900.
(Auction Team Köln)

$325

A German Bing No. 2 type bar machine with tin cover, lacking ribbon, 1925.
(Auction Team Köln)

$310

The Sun Index, one of the first pointer typewriters, with cast iron base, 1885.
(Auction Team Köln)

$3,890

An English Salter Visible type bar machine with transverse type basket, 1913.
(Auction Team Köln)

$1,790

The American Typewriter, a pointer machine, with half-round scale and index, 1893. (Auction Team Köln)
$428

A very rare McCool No. 2 type bar machine with removable hammer row for reversed strike, three-row keyboard, with original wooden case, 1904. (Auction Team Köln)
$5,058

A Lambert decorative American typewriter, by the New York inventor Frank Lambert, 1896. (Auction Team Köln)
$1,400

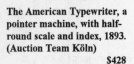

The Odell No. 1b, the first mass produced example of this American pointer typewriter, Indian motifs on the base plate, 1888. (Auction Team Köln)
$1,633

A Hammond No. 12 American type shuttle machine with Ideal keyboard and reverse hammer action, with original table and swivel chair, 1893. (Auction Team Köln)
$1,089

The Crandall typewriter, 1879, with mother of pearl inlay and gold decoration. (Auction Team Köln)
$5,450

An amusing Babycyl French tinplate toy pointer typewriter with 2-row keyboard, circa 1920. (Auction Team Köln)
$311

An early Berlin Graphic pointer typewriter, with original rubber platen, in original wooden case, 1895. (Auction Team Köln)
$6,225

An attractive English Royal Bar Lock type bar machine with full keyboard, 1902. (Auction Team Köln)
$310

A carved dogwood walking stick, Pennsylvania, circa 1900, carved in relief with soldiers on horseback, 36½in.
(Sotheby's) $1,380

A carved dogwood walking stick, 'Bally Carver' (R. Heinz), Bally, Berks County, Pennsylvania, circa 1900, 37in. long.
(Sotheby's) $575

A carved dogwood walking stick, Pennsylvania, circa 1900, the curved handle finely carved with the head of a duck, 35in. long.
(Sotheby's) $690

An unusual carved and stained dogwood walking stick, Pennsylvania, circa 1900, the curved handle carved in high relief with a reclining sheep, 36in. long.
(Sotheby's) $575

A humorous carved ivory cane handle, French, mid 19th century, carved in the form of a bald headed smiling face, on ebonized wood stick, the handle 1¾in. high.
(Sotheby's) $453

A porcelain cane handle, German mid 19th century, painted in Meissen style with shaped handle terminating at one end with a mask of a veiled lady, 5in. long.
(Sotheby's) $1,180

A carved ivory cane handle, Japanese mid 19th century, signed *Yoshitoshi*, carved as a cluster of grimacing faces, on ebonized wood stick with horn tip, the handle 1½in. high.
(Sotheby's) $271

A Meissen gold-mounted yellow-ground cane-handle, circa 1740, in the form of a parrot's head with an iron-red beak and blue and green head, the handle 2³/₄in. high.
(Christie's) $11,661

A spherical bluejohn cane handle, mid 19th century, on gilt brass mount above cane with horn tip, the handle 1½in diameter.
(Sotheby's) $162

A carved dogwood walking stick, 'Schtockschnitzler' Simmons, Pennsylvania, circa 1900, 35in. long.
(Sotheby's) $575

A carved wood pug dog cane handle seated on a cushion with shield at the front and tassels at the side, 5in.
(Sotheby's) $1,053

Whalebone and ivory pointer, 19th century, with carved eagle's head handle and exotic wood spacers, 24¼in. long.
(Skinner) $977

A carved and painted dogwood walking stick, Pennsylvania, circa 1900, the curved handle carved with a figure of a horse, 36¾in. long.
(Sotheby's) $805

A rare ivory monkey head automaton cane handle, Japanese, mid 19th century, signed *Yoshikuni Kyoto,* lever operates eyes to roll, mouth to open and tongue to stick out, bamboo stick, 2in. high.
(Sotheby's) $3,634

A carved ivory mermaid cane handle, French mid 19th century, mermaid with garlanded hair and a curled tail, on bamboo stem, handle 5in.
(Sotheby's) $654

A carved wood bull mastiff cane handle, probably French, circa 1880, with glass eyes, bone ring and tip on mahogany stick, the handle 8in..
(Sotheby's) $218

A carved dogwood walking stick, signed *AK.,* Pennsylvania, circa 1900, the handle carved in high relief with the figure of a reclining dog, 32¼in.
(Sotheby's) $345

A 19th century ivory cane handle in the form of a phrenology head, the cranium divided into 35 named sentiments and attributes, 3½in. high.
(Phillips) $3,020

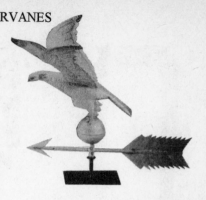

A carved and painted pine and sheet metal horse and Civil War soldier weathervane, American, 20th century, the Confederate soldier wielding a saber, 52in. long. (Sotheby's) $13,800

Eagle gilt zinc weathervane, early 20th century, 15¹/₂in. high. (Skinner) $748

Rooster cast and sheet iron weather vane, America, second half 19th century, 32in. high. (Skinner) $4,888

Griffin copper banner weathervane, America, 19th century, fine verdigris surface, 33¹/₂in. high. (Skinner) $2,300

A very large painted sheet metal cow weathervane, American, early 20th century, the silhouetted figure of a cow standing on an arrow directional, 138in. long. (Sothebys) $5,000

A large molded copper squirrel weathervane, American, early 20th century, with swell-bodied figures of two squirrels, one holding an acorn, the other lunging for an acorn between them, 94½in. long. (Sothebys) $6,900

Running horse gilt copper weathervane, America, late 19th century, with traces of verdigris, 25¹/₂in. long. (Skinner) $1,495

A gilded cast-zinc hunter weathervane, American, late 19th century, the flattened figure holding a rifle on an arrow directional, 28in. long. (Sothebys) $2,500

Copper horse and rider weather vane, attributed to A.L. Jewell & Co., Waltham, Massachusetts, third quarter 19th century, surface with traces of gilt, 27in. high. (Skinner) $7,475

Leaping stag gilt copper weathervane, attributed to Harris & Co., Boston, last quarter 19th century, gilt bole surface, 25in. long. (Skinner) $13,800

Prancing horse gilt copper weathervane, America, late 19th century, attributed to W.A. Snow, Boston, 25¹/₂in. high. (Skinner) $2,415

Running horse copper weathervane, America, late 19th century, fine verdigris surface, 25in. long. (Skinner) $1,380

Stewart's Cream of The Barley, circa 1924, blended by Alexander Stewart & Son, Dundee, Scotland.
(Christie's) $693

King George IV Liqueur Whisky, early 20th century, The Distillers Company Ltd., Edinburgh.
(Christie's) $539

Glenfiddich, circa 1930, pure Malt, Special Whisky bottled at The Distillery and guaranteed by William Grant & Sons Ltd.
(Christie's) $924

Strathisla, circa 1940, finest Highland Malt Whisky, William Longmore & Co. Ltd., Milton Distillery, Keith, Banffshire, The Oldest Highland Malt Distillery in Scotland.
(Christie's) $2,926

Special Purest and Oldest Whiskey, 1890, has been ageing all these years expressly for Family Use Guaranteed under the Pure Food and Drug Act, June 30th 1906 N. Glen Williams' Estate, Williams, N.C.
(Christie's) $539

Sandeman Scotch Whisky, Geo G. Sandeman Sons & Co. Ltd., Edinburgh, brown colored glass bottle, stopper cork, lead capsule embossed on top and around neck.
(Christie's) $339

Toby, blended and bottled by The Old Blairmhor Whisky Co. Ltd., Glasgow, brown colored glass bottle, stopper cork, lead capsule.
(Christie's) $647

Drambuie, believed 1945, prepared by The Drambuie Liqueur Co. Ltd., York Place, Edinburgh, driven cork, printed paper seal.
(Christie's) $400

Old Grans Special Scotch, 10 years old, Charles Wright & Son Ltd., Wirksworth, Leith & London, stopper cork, remains of lead capsule around neck.
(Christie's) $400

WHISKEY

The McNee Blend, 12 years old, early 20th century, sole proprietor John McNee, Eglinton Toll, Glasgow, hand blown bottle.
(Christie's) $400

John Begg Gold Cap, circa 1940, stopper cork, lead capsule embossed *"Take a peg of John Begg"* on top.
(Christie's) $616

Glen Grant, 10 year old, bottled by Moray Bonding Co., (London) Ltd., brown colored glass bottle, stopper cork embossed.
(Christie's) $370

Stodart's Special Scotch Whisky, early 20th century, H. Stodart & Co., Whisky Merchants and Blenders, 20 Suffolk Street, Pall Mall, S.W. London & Glasgow.
(Christie's) $431

A three piece molded whisky flask engraved *Dewars Perth Whisky, John Dewar & Sons, Distillers*, of globular form lacking contents, 19th century.
(Christie's) $462

White Horse, early 20th century, unlabeled, green colored two piece molded bottle embossed *"White Horse Whisky"*, white metal locking capsule with three keys.
(Christie's) $1,540

Grant's Liqueur Scotch Whisky, circa 1940, bottled and guaranteed by Wm. Grant & Sons Ltd., green colored glass bottle, stopper cork.
(Christie's) $585

Highland Park, circa 1940, James Grant & Company (Highland Park Distillery) Ltd, stopper cork, lead capsule embossed *"Scotch Whisky"*.
(Christie's) $616

Fine Old Glenstrath Liqueur Scotch Whisky, proprietors Wallace, Robertson & Co., Edinburgh, driven cork, lead capsule.
(Christie's) $524

WOOD

An important carved and painted pine and gesso American eagle, Wilhelm Schimmel, Cumberland Valley, Pennsylvania, circa 1870, 10¼in. high.
(Sotheby's) $37,950

A pair of Spanish gilt and painted wood figures of angels, 17th century, each carved with curly hair and set with glass eyes, clad in short skirts, 20 and 18¼in. high.
(Sotheby's) $5,750

A fine carved and painted pine and gesso carousel rooster, probably English, 19th century, carved in the full round, 48in. high overall.
(Sotheby's) $8,050

One of a pair of French of Flemish oak panels, 16th century, originally from a panel, one centered by a profile portrait of a gentleman, the other with putti and armorials, 20 x 14¼in.
(Sotheby's) (Two) $1,035

A fine pair of carved, gilded and paint-decorated eagle wall brackets, possibly American, circa 1820, each with bowed shelf.
(Sotheby's) $2,530

Painted and gilt 'Independence' tavern sign, New England, circa 1800, the black painted frame of turned flanking posts enclosing molded panels, 41¼in. high.
(Skinner) $17,250

Two fine carved wood butter presses, Pennsylvania, 19th century, the first of carved maple with rounded handle, the second with stellar motifs and hearts, 8in. and 11¼in.
(Sotheby's) $1,955

A pair of carved mahogany eagles, mid 19th century, each carved in relief, on a plinth base, 76cm. high.
(Sotheby's) $3,562

A rare red-stained butternut folding book stand, New England, 1750-85, with cyma shaped crest, painted red, with early German Bible, 11¼in. wide.
(Sotheby's) $6,900

An amusing carved and painted wood figure of Abraham Lincoln with wings, David Lawhead, Pennsylvania, circa 1955, the figure seated on a rocking chair, 19in. high.
(Sotheby's) $13,800

Carved and painted eagle, America, early 19th century, 19½in. wide.
(Skinner) $2,990

An unusual chip-carved double-sided 'Lollipop' butter print, Pennsylvania, 19th century, of circular form with paddle handle, 3¾in.
(Sotheby's) $517

A Netherlandish painted wood figure of a female saint, early 16th century, her head slightly bowed and with soft cap and her hair in plaits, 16in. high.
(Sotheby's) $5,750

A pair of carved giltwood wall brackets, with shaped molded tops and foliate bearded grotesque masks, 26cm. high.
(Phillips) $12,750

A carved ivory and wood group of a man and a girl dancing, each wearing 18th century dress, he holding a lute, on chamfered stepped base, figures 6½in. high.
(Christie's) $6,872

A carved and painted pine carousel rooster, attributed to Frederick Savage, late 19th/early 20th century, carved as a stander, 32¾in. high.
(Christie's) $4,600

A large brown-stained carved pine eagle, 19th/20th century, the fierce, fully modeled glass-eyed body with wings spread and gazing left, perched on a rocky crag, 25in. high.
(Sotheby's) $2,875

An American carved and painted wood carousel figure of a middle row jumper, Armitage Herschell, New York, circa 1895, 46in. high.
(Sotheby's) $4,600

Large carved wood figure of a seated oni, of joined block construction, the bare chested demon shown seated, with layered skirt, 31½in. (Butterfield & Butterfield) $2,875

A pair of 18th century Italian giltwood and ebonized blackamoor figures, in the forms of boys wearing turbans holding oval platters, 112cm. high. (Phillips) $21,000

Hagenauer, antelope head, 1930s, polished wood, carved as the stylized head of an antelope, with black patinated iron horns, 13½in. (Sotheby's) $3,749

A parcel-gilt and painted pine door and surround, in the Italian Renaissance style, 19th century, the surround with rectangular pediment with dentil edge, the surround: 69in. wide; 107in. high. (Christie's) $9,149

Painted wood checkerboard, America, 19th century, the reverse decorated with a caricature of Zachary Taylor, painted in mustard and dark brown, 14¼in. square. (Skinner) $2,185

Painted wood tavern sign, New England, late 18th century, with pewter gray paint and black, lettering on the two-sided sign, 67in. high, 42in. long. (Skinner) $4,312

Continental carved walnut panel of Madonna and Child, probably 17th century, Italian, traces of polychrome decoration 20 x 14½in. (Skinner) $2,415

Pair of German carved whimsical ivory and wood dancing groups, 18th century, with ivory face and hands, all in peasant garb, 12in. high. (Skinner) $4,600

Paint decorated wood and wire birdcage, America, 19th century, decorated with stars and a flowering tree, 17in. high. (Skinner) $920

INDEX

Tracy, Harriet R. 421
Tracy, Spencer 243
Traeger, Tessa 472
Tranter 30, 31, 32
Travel Luggage 648
Travolta, John 227, 228, 241
Trays & Salvers, Silver 604, 605
Trays 649
Tribal Art 650, 651
Trico 213
Troughton & Simms 415
Troughton 413
Trulock & Son 31
Trunks & Coffers 358, 359
Tsubas 66, 67
Tuiller, E. 440
Tullock, William P. 421
Tumblers 387
Tureens, Silver 606
Turner, Lana 224
Tuttle, Edward A. 418
Twain, Mark 81
Typewriters 652, 653

Ulmann, Doris 467
Underwood 48
Uniforms 68–71
Union Bank of Austrialia 458
United Autographic Register 422
United States Centennial
    International Exhibition 95
Universal 184, 185, 204, 634
Urns, Silver 607
Vacheron & Constantin 184, 186, 187
Valentino, Rudolph 240
Valk, Gerard and Leonard 416
Vanden, M. 451
Vardon Trophy, The 396
Vardon, Harry 398
Vases 388–393
Vases, Silver 608
Ventapane, Lorenzo 451
Verneuil & Nicol 175
Vernon Kilns 118
Vernon, Thomas 164
Vesta Cases, Silver 610
Vichi, Ferdinando 436
Vichy, Gustave 82, 83, 85
Vichy/Triboulet 82, 85
Vielmetter, Phillip 84
Vinaigrettes, Silver 611
Vladikavkaz Railroad Company 458

Volcanic Repeating Arms Co., The 54
Vose, Isaac & Son 316
Vuillaume, François 451
Vuitton, Louis 648
Vulliamy 152

Waffen Loesche Berlin 48
Wahl 461
Wain, Louis 396
Wakefield Rattan Co. 273
Wakelin & Taylor 538
Wales and McCullock 155
Walker & Hall 547
Walking Sticks 654, 655
Wall Clocks 176, 177
Walley 149
Wallis, Richard 164
Walter, Almeric 381, 383
Ward, Robert 182
Ward, Steve and Lem 114
Wardrobes & Armoires 360, 361
Washstands 362
Watches 178–182
Waterman's 460, 463
Waters, A.H. & Co. 54
Watson, W. & Sons 415
Wayne, John 238, 242
Weapons 72, 73
Weathervanes 656, 657
Webb, Philip 344
Weber, Jacob 358
Weber, Joseph 275
Webster 175
Wedgwood 149
Weegee 471
Weetman, Harry 396, 397, 401
Wegelin Fils 170
Welch, Raquel 231
Welles, Orson 231, 239
Wells Fargo & Co. 50
Wemyss 149
West, Mae 227, 238
Weston, Edward 474, 475
Weyersberg, Paul 37, 62
Whatnots 363
Wheeler, Henry F. 419
Whipham, Thomas 558
Whiskey 658, 659
White, Edward 159
Whiting Mfg. Co. 538
Whiting, Riley 162, 163
Whitney, James A. 421
Who, The 511

Widenham 170
Wilding, Dorothy 471
Wilkens, M.H. 547
Wilkinson 29
Willard, Aaron 177
Williamson 180
Willis, Bruce 224, 230
Willmore 41
Wilson, J. & Sons 413
Wilson, Toliver A. 420
Wimshurst 205
Windmills, Joseph 153
Windsor, Duke and Duchess 79
Wine Coolers 364, 365
Wine Coolers, Silver 612
Wine Funnels, Silver 613
Wine Glasses 394, 395
Wine Labels, Silver 613
Wine Tasters, Silver 613
Winter Sports, Posters 496, 497
Wirgman, Gabriel 542
WMF 464, 465, 555
WMF Wurttemberg 373
Wolcott, Marion Post 473
Wolf, Abraham F. 419
Wolrab, Johann Jacob 539
Wood 180, 660
Wood, Gilbert 14
Wood, Natalie 229
Wood, Robert 152, 153
Wood, Syroco 193
Woolf, Virginia 77
Worcester 150, 151
Workboxes & Teapoys 354, 355
Wray, Fay 226
Wrenches 643
Wright, Tho. 192
Wrist Watches 183–187
Writing Tables 356, 357
WWH & Co. 558
Wyatt, Joseph 105
Wyvern 463

Yamaji 453
Yasutaka 453
York Safe & Lock Co. 203
Yoshiyama 452
Yumin 452

Zach, Bruno 97
Zappa, Frank 518
Zenith 509
Zick, Stephen 438
Ziegfeld, Florenz 74